THE
CHERNAGOR
PIRATES

THE
CHERNAGOR
PIRATES

BOOK TWO OF THE SCEPTER OF MERCY

DAN CHERNENKO

A ROC BOOK

8 -ot 1995 *pub*

ROC
Published by New American Library, a division of
Penguin Group (USA) Inc., 375 Hudson Street,
New York, New York 10014, U.S.A.
Penguin Books Ltd, 80 Strand,
London WC2R 0RL, England
Penguin Books Australia Ltd, 250 Camberwell Road,
Camberwell, Victoria 3124, Australia
Penguin Books Canada Ltd, 10 Alcorn Avenue,
Toronto, Ontario, Canada M4V 3B2
Penguin Books (N.Z.) Ltd, Cnr Rosedale and Airborne Roads,
Albany, Auckland 1310, New Zealand

Penguin Books Ltd, Registered Offices: 80 Strand, London WC2R 0RL, England

First published by Roc, an imprint of New American Library,
a division of Penguin Group (USA) Inc.

First Printing, April 2004
10   9   8   7   6   5   4   3   2   1

LIBRARY OF CONGRESS CATALOGING-IN-PUBLICATION DATA:
Chernenko, Dan.
The chernagor pirates / Dan Chernenko.
p. cm.—(The scepter of mercy ; bk. 2)
ISBN 0-451-45956-3
I. Title.   II. Series: Chernenko, Dan. Scepter of mercy ; bk. 2.
PS3603.H48C48 2004
813'.6—dc22

Printed in the United States of America
Set in Adobe Garamond
Designed by Ginger Legato

THE
CHERNAGOR
PIRATES

CHAPTER ONE

Not for the first time—not for the hundredth, either—King Lanius wondered what it would be like to rule Avornis. His ancestors for a dozen generations had been kings. They'd ruled. He, on the other hand . . .

He, on the other hand, sighed and went on poking through the royal archives. Avornis was a proud and ancient kingdom. That meant it had been accumulating scrolls and codices and sheets of parchment and the occasional (often broken) potsherd for centuries. Lanius, fascinated by history, dug through them as eagerly as a miner went after a rich vein of gold.

The King—well, one of the Kings—of Avornis looked more like a scholar than a ruler. He was a tall, thin, weedy man in his midtwenties, with dark brown hair that needed combing and a beard with a chunk of dust in it down low on his right cheek where he couldn't see it and flick it away. Instead of royal robes, he wore an ordinary—in fact, rather grubby—linen tunic and baggy wool trousers. The servants had complained that he always came back from the archives covered in dust and dirt, and that robes so smirched were impossible to clean. Lanius didn't like to cause people trouble when he didn't have to.

Dispirited sunbeams came through the dusty skylights set into the ceiling. Motes of dust Lanius had kicked up danced in the light. Somewhere off in the distance, far beyond the heavy doors that shut the archives away from the rest of the palace, a couple of serving women shrilly squabbled over something or other. Lanius smiled—he couldn't make out a word they were saying.

He bent for a closer look at the latest parchment he'd unearthed. It talked about Yozgat—the great southern city where the barbarous Menteshe held the Scepter of Mercy for their master, the Banished One—back in the lost and distant days when Yozgat was not Yozgat but rather Prusa, an Avornan town.

Lanius sighed. "Why do I bother?" he muttered under his breath. Prusa had been made into Yozgat more than five hundred years before, when the wild Menteshe horsemen rode out of the hills and took the southern part of the kingdom away from an Avornis wracked by civil war. It had housed the Scepter of Mercy, once the great talisman of the Kings of Avornis, for four centuries. All efforts to reclaim the Scepter had failed, most of them horribly.

Maybe some clue in Prusa-that-was would yield a key to Yozgat. So Lanius hoped. In that hope, he kept going through the manuscripts in the archives one after another. If he didn't look, he would assuredly find nothing.

"And if I do look, I'll probably find nothing," he said, and sighed again. Odds were, all his efforts were futile. The Banished One might have been cast down from the heavens to earth below, but he remained much, much more than a mere mortal man. He'd spent the intervening years fortifying Yozgat against assault. Even if an Avornan army fought its way to the place, what could it do then? Lanius hoped he would find something, anything, to tell him.

Not on this parchment, which was a tax register and said very little about Prusa's geography. The next one . . . The next one talked about a border squabble between Avornis and the Chernagor city-states at the opposite end of the kingdom. No one could be sure how, or if, the archives were organized.

One of these days, I'll have to do something about that. Lanius laughed at himself. He'd had the same thought ever since he started coming into the archives as a youth. It hadn't happened yet. He didn't intend to hold his breath waiting for it to happen. He put down the parchment that didn't interest him, got up from the chair where he'd been sitting for a long time, and stretched. Something in his back popped. With a glance over his shoulder, as though to say he'd be back, he left the archives.

Servants bowed. "Your Majesty," they murmured. Their respect might have shown that Lanius was the ruler of Avornis. It might have, but it didn't. All it showed was that he was the descendant of a long line of kings.

As though to underscore his lack of power, one of the servants said, "Oh, Your Majesty, King Grus wants to see you."

Not, *King Grus wants to see you at your convenience,* or anything of the sort. No one worried about Lanius' convenience—Grus certainly didn't. "Where is Grus?" Lanius asked. He seldom used the other king's royal title—as seldom as he could get away with, in fact.

"He's at the entranceway to the palace, Your Majesty, enjoying the fine spring day," the servant replied.

Lanius couldn't quarrel with Grus about that. Spring had come late to the city of Avornis this year. Now that it was finally here, it was worth savoring. "I'll meet him there, then," Lanius said.

If he hadn't gone, Grus wouldn't have done anything to him. His fellow sovereign wasn't a cruel or vindictive man. Lanius would have had an easier time disliking him if he were. The rightful King of Avornis—so he thought of himself—still managed it, but it was sometimes hard work.

Serving women smiled at him as he went past. Sleeping with even a powerless king might let them escape a life of drudgery. Lanius passed the chambers where he kept his white-mustached monkeys and his moncats. He didn't have time for the menagerie now, either.

Unfiltered by dusty, dirty glass, the sunlight streaming through the open doors of the palace made Lanius first blink and then smile. Birdsong came in with the sunshine. Warblers and flycatchers and other birds were finally coming back from the south. Lanius hadn't realized how much he'd missed their music until he started hearing it again.

Storks were coming back from the south, too, building great ramshackle nests in trees and on rooftops. They didn't sing—their voices were raucous croaks—but most people took them for good luck.

Grus stood in the sunshine, not so much basking in it as seeming to cause it. He had a knack for attaching to himself anything good that happened. His royal robes, encrusted with jewels and pearls and shot through with golden threads, gleamed and glittered as though they had come down from the heavens to illuminate the dull, gross, all-too-material earth. Their splendor made Lanius in his plain, dirty clothes seem all the shabbier by contrast.

Turning at the sound of Lanius' footfalls, Grus smiled and said, "Hello, Your Majesty. Meaning no offense, but you look like a teamster."

"I was in the archives," Lanius said shortly.

"Oh. I'm sorry." In spite of the apology, Grus' smile got wider. "That means you want to clout me in the head for dragging you out."

Lanius didn't care to think what would happen to him if he tried to clout Grus in the head. The other king was about twice his age and several inches shorter than he. But Grus, despite a grizzled beard, was solidly made and trained as a fighting man. Not much in the way of muscle had ever clung to Lanius' long bones, while he knew far less of fighting than of ancient dialects of Avornan. And so, while he might think wistfully of clouting the usurper, he knew better than to have a go at it.

"It's all right," he said now. "I'd come out anyhow. What can I do for you?"

Before Grus could answer, a priest whose yellow robe displayed his high rank walked in through the entrance. He bowed to Grus, murmuring, "Your Majesty." He started to go on by Lanius, whose attire was anything but royal, but then stopped and stared and at last bowed again. "Your Majesties," he corrected himself, and walked on.

A real teamster with a couple of barrels of ale in a handcart came in right after the priest. Intent on his work, he noticed neither king. "Let's find some quiet place where we can talk," Grus said.

"Lead on," Lanius said. *You will anyhow,* he thought glumly.

King Grus sat down on a stool in one of the several small dining rooms in the palace. Servants ate here; royalty didn't. Grus watched with some amusement as Lanius perched on another stool a few feet away. *Perched* was the right word—with his long limbs and awkward gait, Lanius put Grus in mind of a crane or a stork or some other large bird.

"This seems quiet enough," Lanius remarked. A stout door—oak barred with iron—muffled the noise from the hallway outside, and would keep people from eavesdropping on what the two kings said.

"It will do." Grus watched the younger man fidget. He wondered if Lanius had any idea he was doing it. Probably not, Grus judged.

"What is it, then?" Lanius sounded hostile and more than a little nervous. Grus knew his son-in-law didn't love him. He wouldn't have loved a man who'd taken the power rightfully his, either. As for the nerves . . . Grus thought he understood those, too.

"Tell me what you know about the Chernagors," he said.

Lanius started. *He thought I was going to ask him something else.* Grus clicked his tongue between his teeth. He expected they would get around to that, too. Lanius said, "You'll know a lot already. Hard to be King of Avornis"—he made a sour face at that—"and not know a good deal about the Chernagors."

"I'm not interested in all the trading they do out on the Northern Sea," Grus said. "They'll do that come what may. I'm interested in the rivalries between their city-states."

"All right." Lanius thought for a moment. "Some of them, you know, go back a long way, back even before the days when their pirate ancestors took the northern coastline away from us."

"That's fine," Grus said agreeably. "If knowing why they hated each other before helps me know how they hate each other now, I'll listen. If it doesn't"—he shrugged—"it can wait for some other time."

Grus was a relentlessly practical man. One of his complaints about Lanius was that his son-in-law was anything but. Of course, had Lanius been more like him, he would also have been more likely to try to overthrow him—and much more likely to succeed.

"What's this all about?" Lanius asked now, a practical enough question. "The Chernagors haven't troubled us much lately—certainly no sea raids on our coast like the ones in my great-grandfather's day, and not more than the usual nuisance raids across the land frontier. Thervingia's been a lot bigger problem."

"Not since Prince Berto became King Berto," Grus said. Avornis' western neighbor was quiet under a king who would rather build cathedrals than fight. Grus approved of a pious sovereign for a neighbor. Berto's father, King Dagipert, had almost made Thervingia the master of Avornis and himself Lanius' father-in-law instead of Grus. He'd also come unpleasantly close to killing Grus on the battlefield. The news that Dagipert had finally died was some of the best Grus had ever gotten.

"You know what I mean." Lanius let his impatience show. He had scant patience for comments he found foolish.

"All right." Grus spread his hands, trying to placate the younger king. "I'm concerned because the Banished One may be trying to get a foothold in some of the Chernagor city-states. With Berto on the throne in Thervingia, he won't have any luck there, and he could use a lever against us besides the Menteshe."

"I wonder if the Banished One and Dagipert connived together,"

Lanius said. Grus only shrugged once more. He'd wondered the same thing. Avornans had never proved it. Dagipert had always denied it. Doubt lingered even so.

"Any which way, our spies have seen Menteshe—which is to say, they've surely seen the Banished One's—agents in several Chernagor towns," Grus said.

"*Milvago.*" Lanius' lips shaped the name without a sound.

"Don't say it." Grus shook his head in warning. "Don't even come as close as you did. That's nobody's business but ours—and I wouldn't be sorry if we didn't know, either."

"Yes." Despite the warm spring weather, Lanius shivered. Grus didn't blame him a bit. Everyone knew King Olor and Queen Quelea and the rest of the gods had joined together to cast the Banished One out of the heavens and down to earth more than a thousand years before.

Everyone knew that, yes. What no one knew, these days, was that the Banished One—Milvago, as he'd been known when he still dwelt in the heavens—hadn't been any minor deity. Lanius had found that truth in the ecclesiastical archives, far below the great cathedral in the capital.

No, Milvago hadn't been any ordinary god, a god of weather or anger or earthquakes or other such well-defined function. From what the ancient archives said, Milvago had fathered Olor and Quelea and the rest. Until they cast him forth, he'd been Lord of All.

He remained, or seemed to remain, immortal, though he wasn't all-powerful anymore—wasn't, in fact, a god at all anymore. He wanted dominion on earth, not only for its own sake but also, somehow, as a stepping-stone back to the heavens. Avornis had always resisted him. Grus wondered how long his kingdom could go on resisting a power greater than it held.

"Do you know what I think?" Lanius said.

Grus shook his head. "I haven't the faintest idea, Your Majesty." He stayed polite to Lanius. The other king seldom used his royal title. Lanius resented reigning rather than ruling. Grus didn't worry about that, as long as the resentment stayed no more than resentment. Polite still, Grus added, "Tell me, please."

"I think the Banished One is stirring up trouble among the Chernagors to keep us too busy even to try to go after the Scepter of Mercy down in the south," Lanius said.

That hadn't occurred to Grus. He realized it should have. The Banished One saw the world as a whole. He had to try to do the same himself. "You may very well be right," he said slowly. "But even if you are, what can we do about it?"

"I don't know," Lanius admitted. "I was hoping you might think of something."

"Thanks—I think," Grus said.

"If we get in trouble in the north, what can we do but try to calm it down before it gets worse?" Lanius asked. "Nothing I can see. We can't very well pretend it isn't there, can we?"

"I don't see how. I wish I did." Grus' laugh was sour as green apples. "Well, Your Majesty, the Scepter of Mercy has been out of our hands for a long time now. I don't suppose a little longer will make that much difference."

Lanius' answering nod was unhappy. Four hundred years ago, the then–King of Avornis had brought the great talisman down from the capital to the south to help resist the inroads of the Menteshe. But the hard-riding nomads had fallen on the Scepter's escort, galloped off with it to Yozgat, and held it there ever since. After several disastrously unsuccessful efforts to retake it, the Avornans hadn't tried for a couple of centuries. And yet . . .

Lanius said, "As long as we go without it, the Banished One has the advantage. All we can do is respond to his moves. Playing the game that way, we lose sooner or later. With it, maybe we can call the tune."

"I know." Now Grus sounded unhappy, too. Sending Avornan soldiers south of the Stura River was asking either to lose them or to see them made into thralls—half-mindless men bound to the Menteshe and to the Banished One. And Yozgat, these days the chief town of the Menteshe Prince Ulash, lay a long way south of the Stura. "If only our magic could stand up against what the Banished One can aim at us."

"Wish for the moon while you're at it." But King Lanius caught himself. "No. Wish for the Scepter of Mercy."

"If I need to have it already before I can hope to get it—" Grus stopped. Even if he went around that twenty-two times, he'd still get caught.

"We have to try. Sooner or later, we have to try," Lanius said. But Lanius was no soldier. How much of the bitter consequences of failure did he grasp?

On the other hand, *not* trying to take back the Scepter of Mercy would also be a failure, a failure most bitter. Grus understood that, too.

He'd never wished more to disagree than when he made his head go up and down and said, "You're right."

Lanius dreamed. He knew he dreamed. But dreams in which the Banished One appeared were not of the ordinary sort. That supremely cold, supremely beautiful face seemed more real than most of the things he saw while wide awake. The Banished One said, "And so you know my name. You know who I was, who I am, who I shall be again."

His voice was as beautiful—and as cold—as his features. Lanius heard in these dreams with the same spectral clarity as he saw. *Milvago.* The name, and the knowledge of what it meant, echoed and reechoed in his mind.

He didn't speak the name—however one spoke in dreams—but the Banished One sensed it. "Yes, I am Milvago, shaper of this miserable world," he declared. "How dare you presume to stand against me?"

"You want to conquer my kingdom," Lanius replied. He could answer honestly; the Banished One, he'd seen, might commandeer his dreams, but couldn't harm him in them. "You want to make my people into thralls. If I can keep you from doing that, I will."

"No mere mortal may hinder me," the Banished One said.

"Not so." Lanius shook his head, or it felt as though he shook his head, there in this dream that was all too real. "You were cast down from the heavens long ago. If no man could hinder you, you would have ruled the world long since."

"Rule it I shall." The Banished One tossed his head in more than mortal scorn. "What is time? Time means nothing to me, not when I created time. Think you I am trapped in it, to gutter out one day like a lamp running dry? You had best think again, you mayfly, you brief pimple on the buttock of the world."

Lanius knew he would die. He didn't know the Banished One wouldn't, but Milvago had shown no sign of aging in all the long years since coming down from the heavens. He couldn't assume the Banished One was lying. Still, that didn't matter. The king's tutors had trained him well. However intimidating the Banished One was, Lanius saw he was trying to distract him here. Whether he would die wasn't the essence of the argument. Whether he remained omnipotent—if, indeed, he'd ever been omnipotent—was.

"If you were all you say you are, you would have ruled the world since you came into it," Lanius said. "That you don't proves you can be beaten. I will do everything I know how to do to stop you."

"Everything you know how to do." The Banished One's laughter flayed like whips of ice. "What do you know? What *can* you know, who live but for a season and then go back to the nothingness from which you sprang?"

"I know it is better to live free than as one of your thralls," Lanius answered. "Did the gods who sprang from you decide the same thing?"

Normally, the Banished One's perfect countenance showed no emotion. Rage rippled over it now, though. "After yours, their turn shall come," he snarled. "You need not doubt that. Oh, no, do not doubt it. *Their turn shall come.*"

He *reached* for Lanius, the nails on his fingers sharpening into talons as his hands drew near. As one will in dreams, Lanius turned to flee. As one will in dreams, he knew he fled too slow. He looked back to see how much danger he was in. The Banished One, apparently, could make his arms as long as he chose. His hand closed on the shoulder of the King of Avornis.

Lanius shrieked himself awake.

"Are you all right?" The hand on his shoulder belonged to his wife. Even in the dim light of the royal bedchamber, Sosia looked alarmed. "I haven't heard you make a noise like that in . . ." Grus' daughter shook her head. "I don't know if I've ever heard you make a noise like that."

"Bad dream," Lanius said.

He would have left it there. He didn't want to worry Sosia. Grus had arranged the marriage—forced it on both of them, in other words. The new king wanted to tie himself to Avornis' ancient dynasty as closely as he could. In their seven years of marriage, though, Lanius and Sosia had come to care for each other as much as a married couple could reasonably be expected to do—which was, perhaps, more than anything else, a triumph of good manners and patience on both sides.

Sosia shook her head. Her dark, wavy hair, down for the night, brushed across his face. "That wasn't any ordinary dream," she said. "You don't have dreams like that—nightmares, I should say. Did you see . . . him?"

She didn't even want to call him the Banished One. She didn't know the name Milvago, or what the Banished One had been before his ouster from the heavens. So far as Lanius knew, only he and Grus knew that. Grus had told him not to tell anyone—not his wife, who was Grus' daughter, and not the Arch-Hallow of Avornis, who was Grus' bastard son. Lanius hadn't argued. He too could see that the fewer people who knew about exactly what sort of enemy Avornis faced, the better.

After his scream, he couldn't very well lie to Sosia. "Yes, I saw him," he said with a reluctant nod.

"Why doesn't he leave you alone?" She sounded indignant, as though, could she have been alone with the Banished One, she would have given him a piece of her mind. She probably would have, too.

"He sends me dreams. He sends your father dreams. He doesn't bother other people—General Hirundo never gets them, for instance," Lanius said. The Banished One didn't trouble Sosia, either, but Lanius forbore to mention that.

His wife sounded more irate than ever. "He should bother other people, and leave you alone."

But Lanius shook his head. "In an odd way, I think it's a compliment," he said. "He knows your father and I are dangerous to him, so we're the ones he visits in dreams. That's what we think, anyhow."

Maybe we're giving ourselves too much credit, he thought. *Could* he and Grus—could any mortals—seriously discommode the Banished One? On days when Lanius felt gloomy, he had his doubts. But why had thralls under the Banished One's will tried to murder the two Kings of Avornis the winter before, if those kings didn't represent some kind of danger?

Sosia said, "What I think is, you ought to go back to sleep, and hope no more bad dreams come. And if they don't, you can worry about all these things in the morning, when you feel better."

Lanius leaned over and kissed her. "That's good advice," he said. In fact, he could think of no better advice for the wee small hours of the morning. He took it, and the Banished One left him alone . . . then.

King Grus and the man he hoped to make his new wizard eyed each other. The wizard, whose name was Pterocles, said, "I'll do everything I can for you, Your Majesty." He was young and earnest and very bright. Grus was sure he would be diligent. Whether he would be versatile enough, or discreet enough, to make a royal wizard . . . Grus wished he weren't *quite* so young.

And what was Pterocles thinking about as he sat studying Grus? The king couldn't read his face. That was, if anything, a point in the wizard's favor. After dealing with so many petitioners and courtiers over the years, Grus knew how transparent most men were. Not this one.

"One of the things a king's wizard needs to do," Grus said, "is keep his mouth shut. I think you can manage that."

"I hope so," Pterocles replied. "I don't want to cause you scandal."

"Good," Grus said, a little more heartily than he should have.

"And I do have a certain advantage along those lines," the wizard went on.

"Oh? What's that?" Grus asked.

"I'm a man," Pterocles answered, and stroked his silky brown beard as though to emphasize the point.

Grus' glower would have made most men hoping for royal favor cringe, or more likely despair. Pterocles sat impassive. Grudgingly, Grus said, "You've got nerve."

"I hope so, Your Majesty. I wouldn't be much good to you if I didn't," Pterocles replied. "And would you want me if I were so stupid—no, so ignorant—that I didn't know why you need a new wizard?"

"Mph." Grus pursed his lips and blew a hissing stream of air out through them. Everyone in the palace, and probably everyone in the city of Avornis, knew why he needed a new wizard. Alca the witch had been as skilled at sorcery as anyone in the capital. She'd saved Grus' life from murder by magic before he became king. Grus had admired her, used her talents . . . had an affair with her. Her husband found out. So did Estrilda, Grus' wife. The king made himself bring his attention back to Pterocles. "Are you too frank for your own good?" he wondered aloud.

"If you decide I am, you'll pick someone else," the wizard said. "But if I can't speak openly to you, what good am I?"

"A point. Yes, definitely a point." Grus drummed his fingers on the marble-topped table in front of him. The stone was cool under his fingertips. "Tell me," he said, "has the Banished One ever appeared to you in dreams?"

That cracked Pterocles' shell of calm. He jerked as though bitten by a horsefly. His eyes opened very wide. "Once, Your Majesty. Only once, King Olor and Queen Quelea be praised," he said. "But how could you know about that?"

"Wizards aren't the only ones who know strange things," Grus answered. "I wouldn't want you as my wizard if the Banished One took no interest in you."

"Why ever not?" the wizard asked. "*I* would be much happier if I had never seen that perfect, perfectly sneering face, if I had never been reminded I was to him no more than some crawling insect is to me."

The way he spoke convinced Grus he told the truth. Nobody who had not had the Banished One invade at least one of his nights could have imagined the boundless contempt with which the castaway from the heavens viewed the human race. The king said, "If you're going to be a bug, how would you like to be a bug with a sting?"

He'd surprised Pterocles again; he saw as much. "If I thought I could sting the Banished One, I would," the wizard said. "But how?"

"What do you know of the Scepter of Mercy?" Grus asked.

"Why, Your Majesty, I know as much as any Avornan living," Pterocles exclaimed, springing to his feet and bowing. Grus' hopes suddenly soared. Had good luck—or the hands of the gods, disguised as good luck—led him to a man who could truly help him against the Banished One? But then, with another bow, the wizard added, "Which is to say, not very much," and perched himself on his stool once more.

"I see." Grus did his best to sound severe, but the corners of his mouth couldn't help twitching up. Pterocles' grin made him look very young indeed. Grus said, "How would you like to learn?"

Before answering, Pterocles pulled an amulet on a silver chain out from under his linen tunic—a fine opal, shimmering in blue and red, half covered by a laurel leaf. He murmured a low-voiced charm, then explained, "My amulet and my magic will make me invisible to those who would do me evil. That being so, Your Majesty, I will tell you I would give all I have to learn those secrets."

"Good. You may, and at just the price you offer," Grus said. If he could frighten Pterocles away, he wanted to find out now. But the wizard only nodded, his eyes glowing with excitement. Grus went on, "And I'll tell you something else, too. Amulets like that are fine for warding yourself against an ordinary wizard. All they do against the Banished One is draw his notice. You might as well be saying, *I'm talking about something I don't want the Banished One to hear.* Going about your business in the most ordinary way is more likely to confuse him. Do you understand me?"

"Yes, and I wish I didn't." Pterocles had put the amulet away. Now he drew it out again and looked it over. "This is as strong a spell as any man can hope to cast."

"I believe you," Grus said. "Do you really think you can hope to beat the Banished One by being stronger than he is?"

Had Pterocles said yes to that, Grus would have dismissed him. The wizard started to—he had a young man's confidence in his own strength and power. But he also had some sense, for he checked himself. "Mm . . . maybe not."

"Good," Grus said. "In that case, you just may do."

Lanius' crown lay heavy on his head. His neck would ache tonight from bearing up under the weight of the gold. He wore it as seldom as he could. But an embassy from one of the Chernagor city-states was a formal occasion.

He entered the throne room a quarter of an hour before a servant would escort the Chernagors into his presence. Courtiers bowed low as he walked past them. They had to be polite, but he knew they were there more to see the Chernagors than to see him. He went through the palace all the time. The Chernagors, on the other hand, came to the city of Avornis but seldom.

The royal throne rose several feet above the floor, to let the king look down on the envoys who came before him. Two stalwart bodyguards stood in front of it, one to the left, the other to the right. They both wore gilded mailshirts and gilded helms with crests of crimson-dyed horsehair. As Lanius ascended to the throne, the guards thumped the butts of their spears against the floor in salute.

He settled himself on the throne as best he could. It was made to look imposing, not to be comfortable. In his younger days, his mother and Marshal Lepturus, the commander of the royal guards, would have taken those places in front of the throne. No more. Grus had exiled both of them to the Maze, the boggy, swampy country east and south of the capital. Queen Certhia had tried to kill Grus by sorcery. Lepturus' crime was more recent. He'd refused to let his granddaughter marry Grus' son. Lanius sympathized. He wouldn't have wanted anyone connected to him marrying Ortalis, either.

A stir in the throne room swept such thoughts from his mind. Here came the Chernagors, advancing up the central aisle toward the throne.

They were big, blocky men with bushy beards and dark hair fixed in neat buns at the napes of their necks. They wore linen shirts bright with fancy embroidery and knee-length kilts that left hairy calves on display.

Their leader, whose hair and beard were frosted with gray, bowed low before Lanius. "Your Majesty," he said in fluent, gutturally accented Avornan. "I am Lyut, Your Majesty. I bring you greetings from Prince Vsevolod of Nishevatz, and from all the other Princes of the Chernagors."

That last was polite nonsense; most of the other princes of the Chernagors were Vsevolod's rivals, not his allies. "I am pleased to greet Prince Vsevolod in return," Lanius replied, and then, deviating from the usual formalities, "Do you know the ambassador Yaropolk, who has represented your city-state here in times past?"

"I do, Your Majesty," Lyut replied. "In fact, I have the honor to be second cousin to his junior wife."

"He is an able man," Lanius said, which seemed a safe enough compliment. "I have gifts for you and your men." At his nod, a courtier brought leather sacks of coins for Lyut and his followers. The ambassador's sack was larger and heavier than any of the others. Ancient custom dictated just how much went into each sack.

Lyut bowed. "Many thanks, Your Majesty. Your generosity knows no bounds. We have gifts for you as well."

King Lanius leaned forward. So did the other Avornans in the throne room. The Chernagors were wide-faring sailors and traders. Equally ancient custom said their gifts to Kings of Avornis might be anything at all, as long as they were interesting. Lyut gestured to the men behind him.

"Here, Your Majesty," Lyut said as the other Chernagors took skins out of leather sacks and unrolled them. The skins were from great cats, lion-sized, with orange hair striped with black. "These come from lands far away."

"I'm sure they must," Lanius said politely. "You must tell me more later." He tried to sound enthusiastic. The skins *were* interesting, but the Chernagors had done better. The mustachioed monkeys and the strange moncats Lanius raised were, to his way of thinking, cases in point.

With another bow, Lyut said, "That would be my pleasure, Your Majesty. In the meantime, though, I hope you will hear my petition."

"You have come from far away to make it," Lanius said. "Speak, then. Tell me what is in your mind."

"Thank you, Your Majesty. You are as gracious as you are wise." Lyut paused, then went on, "Let me be blunt, Your Majesty. There are men in Nishevatz who would let my city-state fall under the shadow of the Banished One. More—there are men in my city-state who would *help* Nishevatz fall under the shadow of the Banished One. Prince Vsevolod resists them, but he is not a young man. And who knows in which direction his son, Prince Vasilko, will turn? We need your help, Your Majesty. We need Avornis' help."

King Lanius wanted to laugh. He also wanted to cry. By himself, he didn't have the power to help a Chernagor city-state. That lay in Grus' hands. Lanius said, "What I can do, I will do." Lyut bowed again. Maybe he took that as a promise of aid. Or maybe he knew how weak Lanius truly was, and took it for a promise of nothing at all.

CHAPTER TWO

Grus hated riding horseback. He wished he could reach the Chernagor city-states by river galley. He'd been a sailor—a galley captain, a commodore—for years. Aboard ship, he knew what he was doing. On a horse, he felt like a buffoon. Very often, the horse he was riding thought he was a buffoon, too.

Unfortunately, if he wanted to bring an army into the lands of the Chernagors, he had to go by horseback. Rivers in Avornis came out of the Bantian Mountains in the west, and flowed east and south to the sea. A low spur of the Bantians ran west from their northern extremity. Thanks to that watershed, no one could travel from Avornis to the Chernagor country by river.

And so, muttering under his breath, Grus turned to General Hirundo and said, "There has to be another way to do this."

Hirundo was a cavalry officer. Grus tried not to hold it against him. Grinning, he said, "Oh, there is, Your Majesty."

"By Olor's beard, what is it?" Grus was ready to grasp at any straw.

"Instead of riding, you could walk like a pikeman," Hirundo said.

"Thanks so much. I'm glad I asked *you* for advice," Grus said. Hirundo laughed out loud.

The army moved north, horses' hooves and the feet of marching men kicking up a cloud of dust that clung to everything and left eyes and mouths feeling as though they'd been dipped in grit. Out in the fields, farmers plowed the rich black soil. Down in the south, where

Grus and Hirundo had spent their younger days, crops went into the ground with the fall rains and were harvested in the spring. Things were different here.

Some things were different, anyhow. Most of the farmers, though, fled as soon as they saw soldiers. Grus had seen that countless times before, in the south and here, not far from the capital. Some farmers took Avornan soldiers for the enemy. Some simply weren't inclined to take chances. Avornans were also known to pillage, to rob, and to kill for the sport of it.

Grus said, "We aren't running things as smoothly as we ought to. Our farmers shouldn't think they have to run away from our soldiers. If it weren't for the soldiers, the farmers would have plenty of worse things to worry about."

"Well, yes," Hirundo said. "My best guess is, they already know that. But they know our boys can turn on 'em, too. I wish it didn't happen as much as you do. You know what wishes are worth, though. Give men swords and spears and bows and pay 'em to fight, and you'll find they'll go into business for themselves along with fighting for you."

"'Go into business for themselves,'" Grus echoed. "That's the politest way to say 'turn brigand' I've ever heard."

"Oh, I'm polite, Your Majesty," Hirundo said. "In fact, I'm about the politest son of a whore you're ever likely to meet."

Laughing, Grus said, "So I see."

Wagons full of grain and a shambling herd of cattle accompanied the army on the march. This early in the year, the only way the men could have lived off the countryside was by stealing every cow and sheep and pig for miles around. That wouldn't have endeared them to the peasants they were supposed to protect.

When they camped for the night, some of them slept on bare ground under the stars, others in little tents of canvas or leather. Grus and Hirundo had fancy, airy pavilions of silk, the king's larger than the general's. Grus ate the same porridge and beef as his soldiers, though. Eating with them was the best way to make sure they got food worth eating.

After supper, Hirundo poked his nose into Grus' tent and said, "Ask you a couple of things, Your Majesty?"

"Of course. Come in." Grus picked up a folding chair and unfolded it. He pointed to a jug of wine with a couple of cups beside it. "Have something to drink." The wine was better than what his soldiers drank.

"Don't mind if I do." After looking a question at Grus, Hirundo poured the king a cup, too. "What do you think we can do when we get up to Nishevatz?" the general asked after they'd both sipped.

"I *hope* we can knock down whatever faction the Banished One's backers have put together there," Grus answered.

"That would be good," Hirundo agreed. "But how likely is it? The Banished One has a long reach. We've seen as much."

"Haven't we just?" Grus agreed. "But the Chernagor country is right at the end of it. We'll be on the spot. That will make a difference. I hope it will, anyhow."

"It had better," Hirundo said. "If it doesn't, we're in a lot of trouble, you know."

Grus took a long pull at his wine. He wanted to ease the situation with a joke, as Hirundo so often did. He wanted to, but couldn't come up with one for the life of him. "We *are* in a lot of trouble," he said at last. "The Banished One hasn't tried interfering in affairs so openly in a long time—maybe not ever. Lanius says he never tried to kill Kings of Avornis before when they weren't in the field against him."

Hirundo smiled. "Lanius ought to know."

"Oh, yes. He knows all sorts of things." Grus let it go at that. The one thing Lanius didn't know, as far as Grus could see, was what was important and what wasn't. Grus went on, "You said you wanted to ask me a couple of things. What's the other one?"

The general's mobile features squeezed into a frown. After a moment, he brightened and said, "All right, now I remember. Once we settle this mess in Nishevatz, do you think we'll be able to turn around and march home again? Or are we going to spend the next five or ten years putting out fires in the Chernagor country?"

"I *hope* we'll be able to do this quickly and neatly and then go home again," Grus said. "I don't *know* whether that will happen, though. It's not just up to me, you know. The Banished One will have something to do with it. So will the Chernagors. They *like* squabbling among themselves—and they don't always like outsiders sticking their noses in on one side or the other."

"Might as well be a family," Hirundo said.

That startled a laugh out of Grus. He said, "You're right. But it's also what worries me most."

As the army pushed north, the mountains climbed ever higher on the horizon. They were neither as tall nor as jagged as the Bantians proper. Snow was already melting from their peaks. In the range to the west, it would cling to the mountaintops all summer long.

Several passes gave entry to the Chernagor country on the far side of the mountains. Naturally, Grus led his men to the one closest to Nishevatz. He ordered scouts out well ahead of the main body of the army. If the Banished One's backers (who might include Prince Vasilko) wanted to ambush them before they got to Nishevatz, the pass was the best place to try it. Grus remembered Count Corvus coming to grief against the Thervings because he didn't watch out for an ambush. Had Corvus found it instead of the other way around, he likely would have made himself King of Avornis. As things were, he was a monk in the Maze these days, and would never come out.

No ambush waited in the pass. But one of the scouts said, "Your Majesty, we rode up to the watershed and then down a ways. When we looked to the north, we saw the whole country was full of smoke." Several other riders nodded.

Grus and Hirundo exchanged glances. They both knew what was most likely to cause that. A company of cavalry around him, Grus rode out ahead of the army to see for himself. Sure enough, when he got to the top of the pass and peered north, it was just as the scout had said. Grus caught Hirundo's eye again. "They've gone and started their war without us," he said. "I'll bet I can tell you which side Vasilko's on, too."

"Not ours," Hirundo said. Grus nodded.

King Lanius hated being disturbed when he was with his moncats. Servants in the palace generally knew better than to bother him there. When someone knocked on the door to the moncats' room, Lanius muttered in annoyance—he had Bronze on his lap. "Who is it?" he called. "What do you want?"

He sat on the floor with Bronze. The reddish female was one of the first pair Yaropolk of Nishevatz had given him several years before. She was about the size of an ordinary house cat, and of a temperament not far removed from that of an ordinary cat. But moncats' paws were not those of ordinary cats. They had hands with real thumbs and feet with big toes that worked the same way. Even their tails could grip. They were made for life in the trees on their native islands somewhere out in the Northern Sea—just where, Yaropolk hadn't said.

"It's me," came the answer from the other side of the door.

"And who are you?" Lanius knew he sounded irritated. He *was* irritated. He did his best not to show it to Bronze, stroking the moncat's back and scratching at the corner of its jaw to try to coax a purr out of it.

The door to the room opened. That made Lanius spring to his feet in fury, spilling Bronze out of his lap. The moncat yowled at such cavalier treatment. Lanius whirled to see who besides Grus had the nerve to disturb him in here. Moncats were smarter than ordinary cats. They realized at once that an open door meant a chance to get away. With gripping hands and feet, they could go places ordinary cats couldn't, too. A couple of escapes had proved that. One of the few rules Lanius had been able to enforce as though he really ruled was that servants were banned from his animals' chambers.

But this wasn't a servant. Prince Ortalis stood in the doorway. "Olor's beard, shut that before they all get loose!" Lanius exclaimed.

For a wonder, Ortalis did. Grus' legitimate son was a couple of years older than Lanius. He was taller, handsomer—and, most of the time, fouler-tempered. He looked around now with considerable curiosity; as far as Lanius knew, he'd never been in the moncats' chamber before. "What peculiar beasts," he said. "Are they good for anything?"

"No more—and no less—than any other cat is," Lanius answered. "Did you come here to ask me that?"

Ortalis made a horrible face. The question must have reminded him of why he *had* come. "You've got to help me, Lanius," he said.

Lanius' heart sank. If Ortalis was in trouble, he feared he knew what sort. Hoping he was wrong, he asked, "Why? What did you do?"

"It wasn't the way she says it was," his brother-in-law answered, which proved he was right. Ortalis went on, "By the gods, she liked it as much as I did, up until. . . ." He shook his head. "It's all kind of fuzzy now. We both drank a lot of wine."

"What happened?" Lanius wondered if he really wanted to know. He decided he needed to, whether he wanted to or not. "What did you do?"

"She . . . got hurt a little." Quickly, Ortalis went on, "It's not as bad as she says it is, though—I swear it's not. And she wanted more while it was going on. I wouldn't lie to you, Lanius. She did. She really did."

"Your father won't be very happy with you when he finds out," Lanius said.

"That's what I'm saying!" Ortalis howled. "You've got to help me make sure he doesn't. If he does . . ." He tapped the back of his neck with a forefinger, as though the headsman's ax were falling.

"What can I do?" Lanius asked. "I haven't got the power to do *anything* to speak of. You ought to know that." Even if he could have done something, he would have only for Sosia's sake. Her brother repelled, revolted, and frightened him.

Ortalis said, "Money. She wants money."

"Who doesn't?" Lanius pointed to one of the moncats. "You know, I've been painting pictures of these beasts and selling them because the treasury minister doesn't give me as much as I need."

"Oh," Ortalis said, as though Lanius had betrayed him when he needed help most. Maybe Lanius had. Grus' son went on, "I was hoping you could talk to Petrosus and get whatever I need—whatever you need, I mean."

"Not likely," Lanius said, thinking, *You meant what you said the first time. You're the only one you ever cared about.*

"But what am I going to do?" Ortalis sounded desperate. "What am I going to *do*? If she doesn't get paid, she *will* blab. And then who knows what my father will do? He's yelled at me before."

Yes, and that's because you've done nasty things to your women before— one more thing Lanius saw no point in saying. Ortalis never paid attention to anyone but himself, and turned nasty—nastier—when he was crossed. As much to get his brother-in-law out of his hair as for any other reason, the king said, "Maybe you ought to talk to Arch-Hallow Anser, instead. He heads the temples, so he can get his hands on money that doesn't come through Petrosus."

"Already tried him. He turned me down. My own flesh and blood, and he turned me down. Flat." Anser was also Grus' son, but a bastard. Despite his irregular past, Lanius—and everybody else—found him much more agreeable than Ortalis. The king wasn't sure how bright Anser was. He was sure Grus' bastard, unlike his legitimate son, had his heart in the right place.

More than ever, he wanted Ortalis gone. Spreading his hands, he said, "I'm sorry, but I don't know what else to tell you now."

"She's got to disappear," Ortalis muttered. "One way or another, she's got to disappear."

"By the gods, don't make it worse than it is already!" Lanius exclaimed in alarm.

"It can't get any worse than it is already," his brother-in-law replied. "Just *you* remember, Lanius—you haven't heard a thing."

"I remember," Lanius said. "If you think I want to walk into the middle of a quarrel between your father and you, you'd better think again." He'd made promises to keep quiet about certain things before, made them and kept them. He didn't promise now, and hoped Ortalis wouldn't notice.

Full of other worries, Ortalis didn't. "She's got to disappear," he said once more, and then rushed out of the chamber.

The king hurried after him. As Lanius had feared, Ortalis didn't bother closing the door behind himself. Lanius did it before any of the moncats could get out. They did harm to their prey, too, but innocently and without malice. He wished he could say the same about Ortalis.

Whenever Grus breathed in, he tasted smoke. When he spat, he spat black. He turned to Hirundo and said, "It's so nice that we're welcome in the land of the Chernagors."

"Oh, yes. Oh, yes, indeed." The general spat black, too. Hirundo swigged from a cup of ale, swallowed, and said, "I'm also glad the men of Nishevatz invited us to their city-state. Just think what kind of a greeting they would have given us if they hadn't."

"If it's all the same to you, I'd rather not," Grus said wearily. The Avornan army had yet to see the city of Nishevatz itself. It was still busy reducing forts south of the town. Had it left them behind, the garrisons in them would have fallen on Grus' men as soon as they'd gone by, or else on his supply wagons later.

Varazdin, the latest of them, wasn't much different from any of the rest. The local limestone was golden, which made the walls and the keep inside look deceptively cheerful. As Grus had already seen with three other fortresses, Varazdin's looks were indeed deceiving. His men ringed the fortress, just out of range of the archers and catapults on the walls. Whenever they came close enough, the Chernagors inside started shooting and flinging things at them.

A handful of Chernagors of Prince Vsevolod's party made their way toward Grus. Several more Avornan bodyguards accompanied them. The Chernagors *said* they were of Vsevolod's faction. Up until now, they'd acted as though they were of his faction. But if Grus' men trusted them on account of that, and if one of them really favored the rebels and Prince Vasilko, favored the Banished One who backed the rebels and the young prince . . . If that happened, Avornis would suddenly have Lanius on the throne, and then things would look very different.

Grus didn't intend that things should look different. The Chernagors, fortunately, didn't seem offended at guardsmen shadowing them wherever they went. They too played political games with knife and poison and dark wizardry. Their leader, Duke Radim, bowed to Grus. In gutturally accented Avornan, he said, "I have found out who commands in Varazdin, Your Majesty."

"Have you? Good." King Grus took a big swig from his mug of ale. He drank as much to wash the smoke out of his mouth as because he was thirsty. "Who is he?"

"He is Baron Lev, Your Majesty," Radim answered. He was an old man, his beard white, his shoulders stooped. He put Grus in mind of a fortress much more ancient and weathered than Varazdin. What remained showed how mighty he must have been in his younger days. He added, "He is, or should be, loyal to Vsevolod."

"He has an odd way of showing it," Hirundo exclaimed.

Radim nodded gravely. "He was not reckoned an important man. No one told him Vsevolod would seek aid from Avornis. He thought your coming was a real invasion."

"Doesn't he know better now?" Grus asked.

"Oh, yes." Radim nodded again. "But his honor is touched. How can he yield you passage when his sovereign insulted him?"

"We're trying to help his sovereign," Grus pointed out.

"He knows that. But the insult comes first."

"Do you mean he's gone over to Vasilko?" Hirundo asked.

Now Radim shook his head. The Chernagors with him seemed shocked. "Oh, no," he said. "Nothing like that. Still, how can a man who has been treated as though he were of no account cooperate in any way with those who so abused him? Should a woman who is taken by force cooperate with her ravisher and lie with him as though they truly loved each other?"

King Grus' head started to ache. He was a practical man. He'd always thought the Chernagors were practical men, too. Of course, most of the Chernagors who came to the city of Avornis were merchants. By the nature of things, merchants needed to be practical men. He wished the same held true for nobles. But it didn't. He'd already seen that in Avornis.

"Well," he said, "if we have to take the most honorable Baron Lev by force, that's what we have to do."

And, three days later, he did. He thinned his line around the fortress of Varazdin, using the men thus freed to form two storming parties. Just as dawn was breaking, the men of the first one rushed at the north wall, shouting Grus' name—and, for good measure, Vsevolod's, too. Archers rushed forward with them, shooting as fast as they could to make the Chernagors inside the fort keep their heads down.

Up went ladders against those golden walls. Up swarmed Avornans, and Chernagors who were not only loyal to the rightful Prince of Nishevatz but willing to admit it. Lev's men inside Varazdin rushed to defend the fort. They pushed over some of the scaling ladders. They poured boiling water and hot oil on the men ascending others. They were as loyal to their commander, and as brave, as any soldiers Grus had ever seen.

When the battle in the north was well and truly joined, when the besieged Chernagors were fully engaged—or so Grus hoped—he ordered the second assault party forward, against Varazdin's southern wall. This time, his men approached the wall without shouting anything. They couldn't sneak across a quarter of a mile of open ground, but they did their best not to draw undue notice.

And it worked. Even though the handful of defenders who hadn't run to the north wall cried out in alarm, nobody else inside the fortress paid much attention to them. Maybe, with the din and excitement of the fight on the far wall, none of the other Chernagors even heard them.

They were brave. Instead of running away or yielding, they did everything they could to throw back Grus' storming party. Using more long, forked poles, they did manage to tip over some of the scaling ladders that went up against the wall. Avornans shrieked as they fell. The clank of chainmail-clad soldiers striking the ground made Grus flinch.

But more Avornans, and Chernagors with them, gained a foothold on the south wall. They began dropping down into the courtyard. Some of them rushed to seize the keep, so that Lev's men would have no chance to make a last stand there. Seeing that, the defenders of Varazdin threw down their weapons, threw up their hands, and yielded.

Avornan soldiers brought Baron Lev, none too gently, before King Grus. The Chernagor noble had a red-soaked bandage tied around his forehead to stanch a cut. He also bled from a wounded hand. He glared at the king. Grus glared back. "Your Excellency, you are an idiot," he growled.

"I would not expect an Avornan to know anything of honor," Lev growled in return.

"Do you favor Vsevolod or Vasilko?" King Grus pronounced the Chernagor names with care; the hums and hisses were alien to Avornan, and he did not want to confuse the man he backed and the one he opposed.

"Vsevolod, of course," Lev replied, as though to a half-wit.

"All right, then. I thought as much, but I was not sure. Did you know—do you know—I have come to aid him if I can?" Grus asked. He waited until Lev grudged him a nod. Then he threw his hands in the air and demanded, "In that case, why did you keep trying to murder my men?"

"I told you an Avornan would not understand honor. My countrymen do." Lev spoke with somber pride.

"Honor? I have my own notions about that. I understand stupidity when I see it. I understand stupidity very plainly," Grus said. "We should fight on the same side, against Vasilko. Instead, you delayed me, cost me men, cost yourself men, and helped the man you say you oppose. The Banished One understands that sort of honor. You are right when you tell me I do not."

"We could have put down Vasilko without your interference," Lev said sullenly.

"That's not what Vsevolod thought. He was the one who asked Avornis for help."

"He made a mistake. He made another mistake in slighting me," Baron Lev said.

"I see." Grus nodded. "And so you had to make a mistake in turn, to pay Vsevolod back."

"Yes," Lev said, and then, "No! It was not a mistake. I did what I had to do."

Grus turned to Duke Radim, who was listening off to one side. Radim seemed not at all surprised at the way the conversation was going. Indeed, he'd seemed to understand why Lev hadn't yielded Varazdin even before the fortress fell. If not for that, Grus would have wondered whether the Banished One was somehow clouding Lev's thoughts, such as those were.

"Let me ask another question," Grus said. "Now that we've peeled you out of your shell here"—he pointed to Varazdin, which dominated the horizon from where they stood—"will you and your men fight for Vsevolod?"

"Of course." Now the baron sounded surprised. Grus glanced Radim's way once more. Radim nodded. He believed Lev. Grus was not at all sure *he* did. Still, he'd just proved he didn't understand how Chernagor nobles' minds worked. If Radim was willing to rely on Lev, he supposed he would, too . . . up to a point.

He also looked toward General Hirundo. His own countryman seemed about ready to jump out of his shoes at the idea of trusting Lev. Grus saw that, but he'd known Hirundo for many years. He doubted the Chernagors would realize just how upset Hirundo was.

"Very well. I accept your service," Grus said to Lev, and then, "Excuse me for a moment." He took Hirundo aside and spoke in a low voice. "We'll break up his men into small bands and put them among Avornans. If they turn their coats, we'll slaughter them. Does that suit you?"

"Yes, Your Majesty," Hirundo said at once. "I was afraid you'd lost your mind, too."

"Oh, no," Grus said. "Not me."

King Lanius wished he ruled Avornis instead of just reigning over it. When a courier came rushing into the palace and was brought before Lanius, he felt for a heady moment as though he *did* rule. The man looked weary unto death. Sweat streaked his dirty face. He stank of more sweat, and of horse.

"I hope my mount lives, Your Majesty," he said around an enormous yawn. "It's not the first beast I almost killed, coming up from the south with the news."

"It must be important, then," Lanius said gravely. The courier nodded. The king went on, "Suppose you tell me what it is."

The courier looked flabbergasted. "King Olor's beard," he muttered. "I haven't said, have I?"

"No," Lanius said. "You haven't."

"I'd better, then. Here it is, Your Majesty—on the way up from the south behind me is an ambassador from Prince Ulash, the Menteshe lord."

"Oh." Lanius had to force the word out through lips suddenly numb. Ulash was far and away the most important of the princes ruling the southern nomads who bowed down to the Banished One—the Fallen Star, they called him. That wasn't because he had the widest realm, though he did. It wasn't because his capital, Yozgat, housed the Scepter of Mercy, though it did. It was because he'd held his place for almost forty years. He was a sly old fox who got what he wanted as much through guile as through the arrows and scimitars of his hard-riding horsemen.

"Yes, Your Majesty," the courier said. "I knew you and King Grus had to know as soon as you could." He paused, seeming to realize for the first time that he was speaking with the ceremonial king, not the real one. "Where *is* King Grus?"

If he'd just ridden up from the south, he wouldn't have heard. "He's in the land of the Chernagors," Lanius answered. "There's civil war among them; we're seeing what we can gain from it."

Now the courier said, "Oh," in a dispirited way. Lanius understood what that meant—he would have to deal with Ulash's envoy himself. He wouldn't have been disappointed then to have Grus back in the capital to take care of that for him.

It could be worse, he told himself, and then immediately asked, *How?* But that had an answer. Once, the Banished One himself had sent an ambassador to the city of Avornis—the first time he'd done so in more than a hundred years. The kingdom had gotten through that; Lanius supposed it would get through this, too.

He asked, "When will the Menteshe get here?"

"Not for a while, Your Majesty," the courier replied. "Nobody down south'll hurry him along. We know you need to get ready."

"Good," Lanius said.

"Will King Grus be able to get back in time to deal with him?" the courier asked hopefully.

"No." That was the only answer Lanius could give. The courier looked disappointed. The king affected not to notice. This fellow had done all he could to help. *What would Grus do for a man like that? He'd reward him, that's what.* Lanius said, "You'll have gold for your hard ride."

He was annoyed at himself. He should have thought of that without needing to think of Grus. The courier didn't seem upset—of course, he couldn't know what was in Lanius' mind. He only knew he was getting a gift. Bowing low, he said, "Thank you very much, Your Majesty!"

"You're welcome. You've earned it." Lanius snapped his fingers.

"One thing more. Does Ulash's ambassador have a wizard with him, or is he by any chance a wizard himself?"

"He had several servants with him when he crossed over the Stura, but I didn't see one who looked like a wizard," the rider said. "Of course, that doesn't mean there isn't one dressed up like an ordinary servant. And I have no idea whether he's a wizard himself. I'm sorry, Your Majesty."

"It's all right. You've told me what you know, and you haven't tried to make up stories to pad that out." Lanius gestured in dismissal. The courier bowed again and left his presence. *To stay on the safe side, I'll have to have a wizard with me when the envoy gets here,* Lanius thought.

He wished Alca the witch were still in the city of Avornis. She remained the best sorceress he'd known. He also wished Grus hadn't taken Pterocles with him when he went north to the land of the Chernagors. Now he would have to find someone else, someone whose power and reliability he wouldn't know nearly so well.

No help for it, though, not unless he wanted to face Ulash's man without any wizard at his side. And he didn't. Ulash was a powerful prince in his own right. That made him dangerous. But he was also a glove manipulated by the hand of the Banished One. That made him dangerous, too, but in a different way. "A wizard," Lanius muttered. "I must see about a wizard." The wizard he needed to see was Pterocles . . . and Pterocles, unfortunately, was far, far away.

Grus' army advanced through fog. Men muttered about the uncanny weather. As they came down into the seaside lowlands of the Chernagor country, they met these ghostly mists almost every morning. "Do they know what they're talking about?" Grus asked his wizard. "Is there anything unnatural about these fogs?"

"Not that I can find, Your Majesty," Pterocles answered. "We're down by the Northern Sea, after all. It's only to be expected that we have fog in the morning. Men who come from the plains and the uplands haven't seen anything like it, and so they get upset. Foolishness, if you ask me. You don't see the Chernagors jumping up and down and flapping their arms, do you?"

"Well, no," Grus admitted. "As a matter of fact, I'd like to see the Chernagors jumping up and down and flapping their arms. That would be more interesting than anything that's happened since we came down from Varazdin."

Pterocles gave him a reproachful look. The wizard was a serious man. He wanted everyone else to be serious, too. Grus wasn't, not often enough to suit him. The king missed Alca. She'd had a sense of whimsy. That was one of the things that had made her attractive to him—and one of the reasons he'd had to send her away.

He sighed. His breath made more fog, a little billow amidst the great cottony swirls of the stuff. It tasted like water and salt on his lips. *Kisses and tears,* he thought, and shook his head. *Stop that.*

The mist seemed to swallow most of his soldiers. He looked around. By what his senses told him, he had men close by him, wavering specters a little farther away, and creatures that made noise but could not be seen beyond those ghosts. He hoped his senses were wrong. He also hoped his outriders would note other creatures that made noise before they could be seen.

Pterocles was muttering to himself. He would drop the reins, make a few passes, and then grab for what he'd just dropped; he wasn't much of a horseman. Alca had never had any trouble casting a spell and staying on her horse at the same time. Grus did a little muttering of his own. Law allowed a King of Avornis six wives. Estrilda, whom Grus had married long before he dreamt of becoming King of Avornis, had strong opinions on the subject—opinions that had nothing to do with what the law allowed.

When Pterocles went on muttering and mumbling, Grus pushed Alca out of his mind—a relief and a pain at the same time—and asked, "Something?"

"I don't know," the wizard answered, which was not at all what Grus wanted to hear. Pterocles went on, "If I had to guess, I'd say it was another wizard, feeling for me the same way as I'm feeling for him."

"I . . . see." Grus drummed the fingers of his right hand against his thigh. "You're not supposed to guess, not on something like this. You're supposed to *know.*"

"I work magic, Your Majesty. I don't work miracles," Pterocles said tartly. "If I had to guess" —he took an obvious sour pleasure in repeating the phrase— "that other groping wizard out there is as confused as I am."

No, you don't work miracles, Grus thought. *But the Banished One is liable to.* He didn't say that to Pterocles. His wizard had to know it already. Harping on it would hurt the man's confidence, which wouldn't help his magic.

From out of the mist ahead came a shout. "Who goes there?" Grus needed a moment to realize the call was in Avornan, which meant it had to have come from the throat of one of his own scouts. His hand dropped to the hilt of his sword. He hated fighting from horseback. Whether he hated it or not, though, it was enormously preferable to getting killed out of hand.

An answering shout came back. Grus did some muttering and mumbling of his own. The fog played tricks with sound as well as with sight. Not only did he fail to make out any words in that answer, he couldn't even tell in what language it had been. Logically, those had to be Chernagors out there . . . didn't they? *What do you expect?* he asked himself. *Menteshe to spring out of nowhere, here, hundreds of miles from their land?*

He wished he hadn't just thought that the Banished One might work miracles.

But it wasn't the Banished One. A couple of minutes later, the scout came back to the main body of the Avornan army. "Your Majesty! Your Majesty! We've met Prince Vsevolod and his men!"

For a moment, Grus took that for good news. Then, realizing what it was likely to mean, he cursed furiously. "Why isn't Vsevolod in Nishevatz, by the gods?" he demanded.

The answer was what he'd feared. The scout said, "Because Prince Vasilko's cast him out." Grus cursed again. He'd come too late. The man the Banished One backed had seized the city.

CHAPTER THREE

The more Lanius thought about it, the more he wondered why on earth he'd ever wanted to rule Avornis. Too much was happening too fast, and not enough of it was good. Prince Ulash's ambassador now waited in a hostel only a couple of blocks from the royal palace. Lanius didn't want to have anything to do with the fellow, whose name was Farrukh-Zad. The king had sent quiet orders to delay the envoy's arrival as much as possible. He'd hoped Grus would get back and deal with the fellow. But Grus had troubles of his own in the north.

His father-in-law couldn't do much about the Menteshe while he was campaigning up in the Chernagor country. And the news Grus sent back from the north wasn't good. About half the Chernagors seemed to welcome Avornan soldiers with open arms. The other half seemed just as ready to fight them to the death. Maybe that showed the hand of the Banished One. Maybe it just showed that the Chernagors didn't welcome invaders of any sort.

And the palace still buzzed with whatever had happened or might have happened or someone imagined had happened between Prince Ortalis and a serving girl (or two or three serving girls, depending on who was telling the story and sometimes on who was listening). Lanius hadn't yet sent Grus that delightful news. His father-in-law was already worrying about enough other things.

Sighing because things had fallen into *his* lap, Lanius decked himself in his most splendid robes. The sunlight pouring through an open window gleamed and sparkled off pearls and jewels and gold thread running through the scarlet silk. Admiring him, Sosia said, "You look magnificent."

"I don't feel any too magnificent." Lanius picked up the heavy crown and set it on his head. "And I'll have a stiff neck tomorrow, on account of this miserable thing."

"Would you rather you didn't wear it?" his wife asked sharply.

"No," he admitted. His laugh was rueful. Up until now, he'd chafed at being king in name without being king in fact. Now, with Grus away, what he said did matter, and he felt that weight of responsibility much more than he'd expected to. He went on, "And I have to keep the Menteshe from noticing anything is bothering me. That should be . . . interesting all by itself."

But sitting on the Diamond Throne and looking down the length of the throne room helped steady him. He *was* king. Farrukh-Zad was only an ambassador. Whatever happened, he would soon go back to the south. Lanius laughed again, there on the throne. *No matter what kind of a mess I make of this meeting, Grus is the one who'll have to pay the price.*

Courtiers stared at him. But then the guardsmen in front of the throne stiffened to alertness, and Lanius pulled his face straight. Prince Ulash's ambassador advanced up the long central aisle of the throne room. He strode with a conqueror's arrogance. That clumping march would have seemed even more impressive had he not been badly bow-legged. He was swarthy and hook-nosed, with a black mustache and a hawk's glittering black eyes in a forward-thrusting face sharp as the blade of an ax. He wore a fur cap, a fur jacket, and trousers of sueded leather. A saffron cloak streamed out behind him.

Three other Menteshe followed in his wake, but Lanius hardly noticed them. Farrukh-Zad was the man who counted. *And doesn't he know it?* Lanius thought. Just seeing the Menteshe was plenty to make Lanius' bodyguards take half a step out from the throne toward him. Farrukh-Zad noticed as much, too, and smiled as though they'd paid him a compliment. To his way of thinking, they probably had.

When Prince Ulash's envoy reached the throne, he bowed so low, he made a mockery of the ceremony. "Greetings, Your Majesty," he said in excellent Avornan. "May peace lie between us."

"Yes. May there be peace indeed," Lanius replied. Even polite ritual had its place. It was no more than polite ritual. He and Farrukh-Zad surely both knew as much. Ulash's Menteshe and Avornis might not fight every year, but there was no peace between them, any more than there was peace between the gods and the Banished One.

Farrukh-Zad bowed again, even more sardonically than before. "I bring greetings, Your Majesty, from my sovereign, Prince Ulash, and from his sovereign. . . ." He did not name the Banished One, but he came close enough to make an angry murmur run through the throne room. Then he went on, "They send their warmest regards to you, King Lanius, and to your sovereign. . . ." He did not name King Grus, either, but the salutation was no less insulting on account of that.

He is trying to provoke me, Lanius thought, and then, *He is doing a good job.* "I *am* King of Avornis," he remarked.

"Of course, Your Majesty," Farrukh-Zad said, in a tone that could only mean, *Of course* not, *Your Majesty.*

"For example," Lanius continued, affecting to ignore that tone, "if I were to order you seized and your head struck off for insolence, I would have no trouble getting my guards to obey me."

Farrukh-Zad jerked, as though something had bitten him. So did one of his retainers. *That may be the wizard,* Lanius thought. His own stood in courtier's clothing close by the throne. The Menteshe ambassador said, "If you did, that would mean war between Avornis and my folk."

"True," Lanius agreed. "But I have two things to say there. First is, you would not see the war, no matter how it turned out. And second, when Prince Evren's Menteshe invaded Avornis last year, they hurt themselves more than they hurt us."

"Prince Ulash is not Prince Evren," Farrukh-Zad said. "Where his riders range, no crops ever grow again."

"That must make life difficult in Ulash's realm," King Lanius said. "Perhaps if his riders bathed more often, they would not have the problem."

Avornan courtiers tittered. Farrukh-Zad was not swarthy enough to keep an angry flush of his own from showing on his cheeks. He gave Lanius a thin smile. "Your Majesty is pleased to make a joke."

"As you were earlier," Lanius replied. "Shall we both settle down to business now, and speak of what Prince Ulash wants of me, and of Avornis?"

Before answering, Farrukh-Zad gave him a long, measuring stare. "Things are not quite as I was led to believe." He sounded accusing.

"Life is full of surprises," Lanius said. "I ask once more, shall we go on?"

"Maybe we had better." Farrukh-Zad turned and spoke in a low voice with one of the other Menteshe—the one who had started when Lanius warned him. *They expected me to be less than I am,* Lanius thought. *That must be why the embassy came when Grus was away. I've surprised them.* That was a compliment—of sorts. The ambassador gave his attention back to the king. "In the name of my sovereign, Prince Ulash, I ask you what Avornis intends to do with the thralls who have left his lands and come to those you rule."

"Do you also ask that in the name of Prince Ulash's sovereign?" Lanius inquired, partly to jab Farrukh-Zad again, partly because he did want to know. Thralls—the descendants of the Avornan farmers who'd worked the southern lands before the Menteshe conquered them— were less than full men, only a little more than barnyard animals, thanks to spells from the Banished One. Every so often, thralls escaped those dark spells and fled. Every so often, too, the Banished One and the Menteshe used thralls who feigned escaping those spells as spies and assassins.

Again Farrukh-Zad conferred with his henchman before answering. "I am Ulash's ambassador," he said, but his hesitation gave the words the lie. "These thralls are Ulash's people."

"When they wake up, they have a different opinion," Lanius said dryly. He wished Avornan wizards had had better luck with spells that could liberate a thrall from his bondage. The Banished One's sorceries, though, were stronger than those of any mere mortals. If all of Avornis fell to the Menteshe, would everyone in the kingdom fall into thrall- dom? The thought made Lanius shudder.

Farrukh-Zad said, "You have in your hands—you have in this very palace—many who fled without awakening. What do you say of them?"

"Yes, we do," Lanius agreed. "One of them tried to kill me this past winter, while another tried to kill King Grus. We hold your sovereign's sovereign to blame for that."

"You are unjust," the Menteshe envoy said.

"I doubt it," Lanius said. "Thralls who stay thralls usually stay on the land. Why would these men have crossed the Stura River into Avor- nis, if not through the will of the Banished One?" *There,* he thought. *Let Farrukh-Zad know I'm not—much—afraid to speak his master's name.*

Now the ambassador's companion leaned forward to speak to him.

Nodding, Farrukh-Zad said, "If you admit that these men belong to the Fallen Star, then you must also admit you should return them to him."

Lanius would sooner have been pawing through the archives than playing verbal cut-and-thrust with a tool of a tool of the Banished One. No help for it, though. He said, "I did not admit that. I said the Banished One had compelled them to cross the river. Compulsion is not the same as ownership, and certainly not the same as right."

"You refuse to give them back, then?" Farrukh-Zad's voice was silky with danger.

Avornan wizards still studied the thralls, learning what they could from them. Maybe the Banished One wanted them back because he was afraid the wizards would find out something important. Maybe. Lanius didn't know what the odds were, but he could only hope. "I do," he said. "As long as they have done no wrong in Avornis, they may stay here."

"I shall take your words back to Prince Ulash," the envoy said. "Do not believe you have heard the last of this. You have not." His last bow held enough polite irony to satisfy even the most exacting Avornan courtier. Having given it, he didn't wait for any response, or even dismissal, from King Lanius, but simply turned and strode out of the throne room, the other Menteshe in his wake.

Lanius stared after him. He'd always thought about the power that went with being king in fact as well as in name. As he began to use it, he saw that worry went with the job, too.

Riding as usual at the head of his army, Grus got his first good look at Nishevatz. Seeing the town did not delight him. If anything, it horrified him. "Olor's beard, Hirundo, how are we supposed to take that place?" he yelped.

"Good question, Your Majesty," his general replied. "Maybe the defenders inside will laugh themselves to death when they see we're crazy enough to try to winkle them out."

It wasn't quite as bad as that, but it wasn't good. Nishevatz had originally been a small island a quarter of a mile or so off the coast of the mainland. Before the Chernagors took the northern coast away from Avornis, the townsfolk had built a causeway from the shore to the island. The slow wheel of centuries since had seen silt widen the causeway from a road to a real neck of land. Even so, the approach remained formidable.

King Grus tried to make the best of things, saying, "Well, if it were easy, Vsevolod wouldn't have needed to ask us for help."

"Huzzah," Hirundo said sourly. "He was still in charge of things when he did ask us here, remember. He's not anymore."

"I know. We'll have to see what we can do about that." He called to Vsevolod, who rode in the middle of a small party of Chernagor noblemen not far away. "Your Highness!"

"What you want, Your Majesty?" Vsevolod spoke Avornan with a thick, guttural accent. He was about sixty, with thinning white hair, bushy eyebrows, and an enormous hooked nose.

"Do you know any secret ways into your city?" Grus asked. "We could use one about now, you know."

"I know some, yes. I use one to get away," Vsevolod replied. "Vasilko know most of these, too, though. I show him, so he get away if he ever have trouble when he ruling prince. I not show him this one, in case *I* have trouble." He jabbed a large, callused thumb—more the thumb of a fisherman or metalworker than that of a ruling prince—at his own broad chest.

"Can an army use it, or just one man?" Grus asked.

The ousted ruler ran a hand through his long, curly beard. A couple of white hairs clung to his fingers. He brushed his hand against his kilt to dislodge them. "Would not be easy for army," he said at last. "Passage is narrow. Few men could hold it against host."

"Does Vasilko know *how* you got out? Or does he just know *that* you did?"

"He did not know of this way ahead of time. I am sure of that," Vsevolod replied. "He would have blocked. If he knows now . . . This I cannot say. I am sorry."

Hirundo said, "Maybe our wizard could tell us."

"Maybe." Grus frowned. "Maybe he'd give it away trying to find out, too." He frowned again, hating indecision yet trapped into it. "We'd better see what he thinks, eh?"

Pterocles seemed determined to think as little as possible, or at least to admit to as little thought as possible. "I really could not say, Your Majesty. I know little of the blocking magics the Chernagors use these days, and how they match against ours. We haven't warred with them in their own lands for a long time, so we haven't had much need to learn such things. Maybe I can sneak past whatever wizardly wards he has without his being the wiser, or maybe I would put his wind up at once."

"Helpful," Grus said, meaning anything but. "Duke Radim is bound to have a wizard or two with him, eh? Talk to them, why don't you? You can see what sorts of things the Chernagors do. Maybe that will tell you what you need to know."

"Maybe." Pterocles seemed glum, not convinced. Grus longed for Alca. He longed for her a couple of ways, in fact, even if he had made up with Estrilda.

He would have pushed Pterocles when the army camped that night, but a courier galloped into the encampment with a long letter from Lanius. Reading about the visit from Farrukh-Zad, Grus wished he were back in the city of Avornis. By what was in the letter, Lanius had done as well as anyone could have hoped to do. Grus wondered how closely the letter reflected truth; Lanius was, after all, telling his own story. Even if Lanius had gotten everything straight, was that all good news? Would he decide he liked this taste of real kingship and crave more?

Grus summarized the letter in a few sentences for the courier, then asked, "Is that how it happened?"

"Yes, Your Majesty, as far as I know," the man replied. "I wasn't in the throne room, you understand, but that pretty much matches what I've heard."

Ah, gossip, Grus thought with a smile. "What all *have* you heard?" he asked, hoping to pick up some more news about the embassy, or at least to get more of a feel for what had gone on.

That wasn't what he got. The courier hesitated, then shrugged and said, "Well, you'll have heard about that other business by now, won't you?"

"I don't know," Grus answered. "What other business?"

"About your son."

"No, I hadn't heard about that. What about him?" Grus tried to keep his tone as light and casual as he could. If he'd asked the question the way he wanted to, he would have frightened the courier out of saying another word.

He evidently succeeded, for the fellow just asked, "You haven't heard about him and the girl?"

"No," Grus said, again in as mild a voice as he could muster. "What happened? Is some serving girl going to have his bastard?" Next to a lot of the things Ortalis might have done, that would be good news. The only real trouble with royal bastards was finding a fitting place for them once they grew up.

But the courier said, "Uh, no, Your Majesty, no bastards. Not that I know about, anyhow."

That *Uh, no* worried Grus. Carefully, he asked, "Well, what *do* you know about?" Staying casual wasn't easy, not anymore.

"About how he—" The courier stopped. He suddenly seemed to remember he wasn't passing time with somebody in a tavern. "It wasn't so good," he finished.

"Tell me everything you know," Grus said. "About how he *what? What* wasn't so good?" The courier stood mute. Grus snapped his fingers. "Come on. You know more than you're letting on. Out with it."

"Your Majesty, I don't really *know* anything." The man seemed very unhappy. "I've just heard things people are talking about."

"Tell me those, then," Grus said. "I swear by the gods I'll remember they don't come from you. I don't even know your name."

"No, but you know my face," the courier muttered. King Grus folded his arms and waited. Trapped, the man gave him what was bound to be as cleaned-up a version of the gossip he'd heard as he could manage on the spur of the moment. It boiled down to the same sort of story as Grus had already heard about Ortalis too many times. At last, the man stumbled to a stop, saying, "And that's everything I heard."

Grus doubted it was. Such tales were usually much more lurid. But he thought he would need a torturer to pull anything else from the fellow. "All right, you can go," he said, and the courier fled. "I'll deal with this . . . whenever I get a chance." Only he heard that.

He looked ahead to Nishevatz. The Chernagor city-state would take up all of his time for who could guess how long. He sighed. Whatever Ortalis had done was done. With a little luck, he wouldn't do anything worse until Grus got back to the capital. Grus looked up at the heavens, wondering if that could be too much to ask of the gods.

Every once in a while, Lanius liked getting out of the royal palace. He especially liked going over to the great cathedral not far away, partly because some of the ecclesiastical archives went back even further than those in the palace and partly because he liked Arch-Hallow Anser.

He didn't know anyone who didn't like Grus' bastard son. Even Queen Estrilda liked Anser, and she'd borne Grus' two legitimate children. Prince Ortalis liked Anser, too, even though they had quarreled now and again, and Ortalis rarely liked anybody.

That didn't mean Lanius thought Anser made a perfect arch-hallow. He'd been a layman when Grus first named him to the post, and had worn the black, green, and yellow robes of the ascending grades of the priesthood on successive days before donning the arch-hallow's scarlet garb. He still knew—and cared—little about the gods or the structure of the ecclesiastical hierarchy. His chief passion, almost his only passion, was hunting.

But he was loyal to Grus. To the man who held the real power in Avornis, that counted for much more than anything else. Lanius might prove a problem for Grus. Ortalis might, too. Anser? No. Anser never would.

He bowed to the king when Lanius stepped into his chamber in a back part of the cathedral where ordinary worshipers never went. "Good to see you, Your Majesty!" he exclaimed with a smile, and he sounded as though he meant it.

"Good to see you, too, most holy sir." Lanius also meant it. You couldn't help being glad to see Anser. He wasn't far from Lanius' own age, and looked a lot like Grus—more like him than either Ortalis or Sosia. They favored their mother, which probably made them better-looking.

"What can I do for you today?" Anser asked. "Did you come to visit me, or shall I just send for Ixoreus and wave while you wander down to the archives?" He grinned at Lanius.

Ixoreus, one of his secretaries, knew more about the ecclesiastical archives than any man living. But Lanius smiled back and, not without a certain regret, shook his head. "No, thanks, though it is tempting," he said. "I wanted to ask you a question."

"Well, here I am. Go right ahead," Anser replied. "If I know, I'll tell you."

And he would, too. Lanius had no doubt of it. He thought back to the days of Arch-Hallow Bucco, Anser's predecessor. Bucco had been a formidable scholar, administrator, and diplomat. He'd been regent during part of Lanius' childhood; he'd even sent Lanius' mother into exile. *He* wouldn't have told anyone his own name unless he saw some profit or advantage in it. All things considered, Lanius preferred Anser.

He said, "What I want to know is, did you write to King Grus about . . . any troubles Ortalis has had lately with women?"

"Not me," the arch-hallow said at once. "I've heard a few things, but I wouldn't send gossip to . . . the other king." The hesitation was so small, Lanius barely noticed it. Anser really did work hard at being polite to everybody.

"It's not just gossip. I wish it were," Lanius said. "But I've heard about it from Ortalis himself. He didn't want Grus to find out. Now Grus has. By the letter I have from him, he's not very happy about it, either."

"I can see how he wouldn't be. Ortalis . . . I *like* my half brother, most ways," Anser said. He saw the good in people—maybe that was why everybody liked him. He proved as much now, for he went on, "He's a clever fellow, and I enjoyed hunting with him, at least until he. . . ." His voice trailed away again.

"Yes. Until he." Lanius didn't finish the sentence, either. Ortalis would sooner have hunted men, or rather women, than beasts. And what he would have done when he caught them . . . was one more thing Lanius didn't care to contemplate. "*Somebody* told Grus about this latest news."

"It wasn't me," Anser said again. He looked up at the ceiling, as though hoping to find answers there. "I wish we hadn't had that . . . trouble with the hunting. It did seem to help, for a while."

"Yes, for a while," Lanius agreed. For several years, Ortalis had held his demons at bay by killing beasts instead of doing anything with or to people. But that hadn't satisfied him, not for good. And so . . . *And so I'm hashing this out with Anser,* Lanius thought unhappily.

"I wish I knew what to tell you, Your Majesty. I wish I knew what to tell Ortalis, too," the arch-hallow said.

"No one has ever been able to tell Ortalis anything. That's a big part of the problem," Lanius said.

Anser nodded. "So it is." Suddenly, he grinned again. "Now don't you wish you'd gone down under the cathedral with Ixoreus?"

"Now that you mention it, yes," Lanius said. They both laughed. Then Lanius had another thought. He asked, "You grew up down in the south, didn't you?"

"Yes, that's right—in Drepanum, right along the Stura River," Anser said, and Lanius remembered that Grus had captained a river galley that patrolled the Stura. Anser went on, "Why do you want to know?"

"I just wondered if you knew anything special about Sanjar and Korkut—you know, things you might hear because you're right across the border but would never come all the way up to the city of Avornis."

"About Ulash's sons?" The arch-hallow frowned and shook his head. "The only thing I ever heard is that they don't like each other very well—but you can say that about half the brothers in the world, especially when they're princes."

"I suppose so." Lanius had no brothers. When King Mergus, his father, at last had a son by his concubine Certhia, he'd married her although that made her his seventh wife. All the ecclesiastics in Avornis had screamed at the top of their lungs, since even King Olor up in the heavens had only six. A lot of them had reckoned—some still did reckon—Lanius a bastard because of Mergus' irregularities. Thanks to his own past, he had a certain amount of sympathy for Anser. He wondered if that sympathy ran the other way, too. Anser had never said a word along those lines—but then, Lanius was known to be touchy about his ancestry.

Anser didn't say anything about ancestors now, either. He said, "Sorry I can't tell you more about them."

"Who knows when it might matter?" Lanius replied with a shrug. "Who knows if it will matter at all?"

Slowly—too slowly to suit King Grus—twilight deepened toward darkness. The tall, frowning walls of Nishevatz seemed to melt into the northern sky. Only the torches Chernagor sentries carried as they paced along their stretches of walkway told where the top of the wall was.

Grus turned to Calcarius and Malk, the Avornan and Chernagor officers who would lead a mixed assault party back through the secret tunnel Prince Vsevolod had used to flee the city. "You know what you're going to do?" he said, and felt foolish a moment later—if they didn't know by now, why were they trying it?

"Yes, Your Majesty," they chorused. Grus had to fight down a laugh. They were both big, gruff fighting men, but they sounded like a couple of youths impatient with an overly fussy mother.

The men they would lead waited behind them—Avornans in pants and kilted Chernagors, their chainmail shirts clanking now and again as they shifted from foot to foot. They were all big, gruff fighting men, too, and all volunteers. "Gods go with you, then," Grus said. "When you seize the gate near the other end of the tunnel, we'll come in and take the city. You don't need to hold it long. We'll be there to help as soon as it opens."

"Yes, Your Majesty." Calcarius and Malk spoke at the same time once more. They smiled at each other. They acted like a couple of impatient youths, too—youths eager to be off on a lark. Calcarius looked around and asked, "Is it dark enough yet? Can we start?"

"Another half hour," Grus said after looking around. Color had faded out of the air, but shape remained. Not only the officers in charge of the storming party but all the men who would go on it pouted and fumed. Grus wagged a finger at them. "You hush, every one of you, or I'll send you to bed without supper."

They jeered at him. Some of the Chernagors translated what he'd said into their language for those who didn't speak Avornan. Some of the burly men in kilts said things that didn't sound as though they would do with being translated back into Avornan.

Time crawled past. It might have gone on hands and knees. The stars came out. They grew brighter as twilight ebbed. They too crawled—across the sky. Grus used them to judge both the time and the darkness. At last, he slapped Calcarius on his mailed shoulder and said, "Now."

Even in the darkness, the Avornan officer's face lit up. "See you soon, Your Majesty."

The tunnel by which Prince Vsevolod had emerged from Nishevatz opened from behind a boulder, which let an escapee leave it without drawing attention from the walls of the city. He'd covered the trapdoor with dirt once more after coming out. By all the signs his spies and Grus' could gather, and by everything Pterocles' wizardry and that of the Chernagors showed, Prince Vasilko and his henchmen in the city still didn't know how Vsevolod had gotten away. Grus hoped the spies and the wizards knew what they were talking about. If they didn't . . . Grus shook his head. He'd made up his mind that they did. He would—he had to—believe that until and unless it turned out not to be so.

Two soldiers with spades uncovered the doorway Vsevolod had buried. When it was mostly clear of dirt, one of them stooped and seized the heavy bronze ring mounted on the tarred timbers. Iron might have rusted to uselessness; not so, bronze. Grunting, the soldier—he was a Chernagor, and immensely broad through the shoulders—pulled up the trap door. A deeper darkness appeared, a hole in the night. Calcarius vanished into it first—vanished as though he had never been. Malk followed. Starlight glittered for an instant on the honed edge of his sword. Then the black swallowed him, too.

One by one—now an Avornan, now a Chernagor, now a clump of one folk, now of the other—the warriors in the storming party disappeared into the tunnel. After what seemed a very short time, the last man was gone.

Grus found Hirundo and asked, "We *are* ready to move when the signal comes and the gate opens?"

"Oh, yes, Your Majesty," the general answered. "And once we get inside Nishevatz, it's ours. I don't care what Vasilko has in there. If his men can't use the walls to save themselves, we'll whip them."

"Good. That's what I wanted you to tell me." Grus cocked his head toward the gate the attackers aimed to seize. "We ought to hear the fight start pretty soon, eh?"

Hirundo nodded in the darkness. "I'd certainly think so, unless all the Chernagors in there are sleeping and there *is* no fight. That'd be nice, wouldn't it?"

"I wouldn't mind," Grus said. "I wouldn't mind a bit."

Whether he minded or not, he didn't believe that would happen. Prince Vasilko wasn't—Grus hoped Vasilko wasn't—expecting attack through the secret passage. But the new master of Nishevatz did know the Avornan army was out there. The men who followed him needed to stay alert.

"How long do you think our men will need to get through the tunnel?" Grus asked Hirundo.

"Well, I don't exactly know, Your Majesty, but I don't suppose it will take very long," Hirundo replied. "It can't stretch for more than a quarter of a mile."

"No, I wouldn't think so," Grus agreed. He called to a servant. The man hurried off and returned with a cup of wine for him. He sipped and waited. His fingers drummed on his thigh. A quarter of a mile—even a quarter of a mile in darkness absolute, through a tunnel shored up with planks with dirt sifting down between the planks and falling on the back of a soldier's neck when he least expected it . . . that was surely a matter of minutes, and only a few of them.

He waited. He would know—the whole army would know—when

the fighting inside the city started. Things might go wrong. If they did, the marauders might not carry the gate. But no one would be in any doubt about when things began.

Hirundo said, "Won't be long now." Grus nodded. The general had thought along with him. That Hirundo often thought along with him was one reason they worked well together.

More time passed. Now Grus was the one who said, "*Can't* be long now," and Hirundo the one who nodded. Grus got up and started to pace. It should have started already. He knew as much. He tried to convince himself he didn't.

"Something's not right." Hirundo spoke in a low voice, as though he wanted to be able to pretend he'd never said any such thing in case he happened to be mistaken.

King Grus nodded. He stopped pacing, stopped pretending. "Pterocles!" he called, pitching his voice to carry.

"Yes, Your Majesty?" The wizard hurried up to him. "What do you need?"

"What can you tell me about the men in the tunnel?" Grus tried to hide his exasperation. Alca would have known what he wanted without asking. If the men went into the tunnel and didn't come out when they were supposed to, what was he likely to need but some notion of what had happened to them?

"I'll do my best, Your Majesty." Pterocles was willing enough. Grus only wished he were more aggressive.

The wizard got to work. He peered through crystals and lit braziers fueled with leaves and twigs that produced odd-scented smokes, some spicy, others nasty. He cast powders onto the flames, which flared up blue or crimson or green. His hands twisted in intricate passes. He chanted in Avornan, and in other languages the king neither knew nor recognized.

Grus kept hoping the fighting would break out while Pterocles was in the middle of a conjuration. That might make the wizard seem foolish, but it would show all the worry had been over nothing. No matter what Grus hoped, it didn't happen. The spells went on and on. So did the peaceful, hateful silence inside Nishevatz.

At last, unwillingly, the wizard shook his head. "I can establish no mystical bond with the men, Your Majesty."

"What does that mean?" Grus asked harshly.

"It may mean they are not there—" Pterocles began.

"What? What are you talking about? You saw them go. Where else would they be, could they be, but in Nishevatz?"

"I do not know, Your Majesty," Pterocles said. "The other possibility is that they are dead." He winced. Maybe he hadn't intended to say that. Whether he had or not, it seemed hideously probable.

"What could have happened? What could have gone wrong?" Grus demanded.

"I don't know that, either," Pterocles said miserably.

"Can you find out?" What Grus wanted to say was, *What good are you?* He didn't, but holding back wasn't easy. It got harder when Prince Vsevolod, who'd also had men go into the tunnel, came over and glowered at Pterocles. Vsevolod had a face made for glowering; in the firelight, he looked like an ancient, wattled vulture with glittering eyes.

Looking more flustered by having two sovereigns watch him than he had with only one, Pterocles got to work again. He was in the middle of a spell when he suddenly stiffened, gasped out, "Oh, no!"—and toppled to the ground, unconscious or worse. At Grus' shout, healers tried to rouse him. But, whatever had befallen him, whatever he had seen, he was far past rousing.

And when morning came the next day, not a sound had been heard from Nishevatz.

CHAPTER FOUR

"**Y**our Majesty! Your Majesty!" A servant chased Lanius down the corridors of the royal palace.

"What is it, Bubulcus?" Lanius asked apprehensively. When any servant called in that tone of voice, something had gone wrong somewhere. When Bubulcus called in that tone of voice, something dreadful had gone horribly wrong, and he'd had something to do with it.

And, sure enough, now that he had Lanius' attention, he didn't seem to want it anymore. Looking down at the mosaic flooring, he mumbled, "Well, Your Majesty, a couple of those moncats have gotten loose."

He made it sound as though the animals had done it all by themselves. That probably wasn't impossible, but it certainly wasn't likely. If they had done it all by themselves, Bubulcus wouldn't have seemed so nervous, either. "And how did the moncats get loose?" Lanius inquired with what he hoped was ominous calm.

Bubulcus flinched, which surprised the king not at all. The palace servant said, "Well, it was when I went into one of their rooms for a minute, and—"

"Are you supposed to do that?" Lanius asked gently. None of the servants was supposed to do that. Even when powerless over the rest of Avornis, Lanius had ruled the rooms where his animals dwelt. He'd laid down that law after the last time one of Bubulcus' visits let a moncat escape.

Angrily defensive, Bubulcus said, "Which I wouldn't have done if I hadn't thought you were in there." He made his lapse sound as though it were Lanius' fault.

"You're not supposed to go into one of those rooms whether you think I'm there or not," Lanius snapped. Bubulcus only glared at him. Nothing would convince the servant that what he'd done was his fault. Still angry, Lanius demanded, "Which moncats got away?"

Bubulcus threw his hands in the air. "How am I supposed to know? You never let anybody but you into those miserable rooms, so who but you can tell one of those miserable creatures from the next? All I know is, there were two of 'em. They scooted out fast as an arrow from a bow. If I hadn't slammed the door, more would've gotten loose." Instead of being embarrassed at letting any of the animals escape, he seemed proud it hadn't been worse.

"If you hadn't slammed the door, Bubulcus, you'd be on your way to the Maze right now," Lanius said.

Where nothing else had, that got through to Bubulcus. Kings of Avornis had exiled people who dissatisfied them to the swamps and marshes east of the capital for years uncounted. The servant's smile tried to seem ingratiating, but came out frightened. "Your Majesty is joking," he said, sounding as though he hoped to convince himself.

"My Majesty is doing no such thing," Lanius replied. "Do you want to see if I'm joking?" Bubulcus shook his head, looking more frightened than ever. *This is the power Grus knows all the time,* Lanius thought. *Am I jealous?* He didn't need to wonder long. *Yes, I'm jealous.* But that too would have to wait. "Where did the moncats go?"

"Out of that room—that's all I can tell you," Bubulcus answered, as self-righteous as ever. "Nobody could keep track of those . . . things once they get moving. They aren't natural, you ask me."

Lanius wished he knew which moncats had gotten out. Maybe his special calls would have helped lure them back. Or maybe not; moncats could be as willful and perverse as ordinary felines. As things were, elegant solutions would have to fly straight out the window. "Go to the kitchens," he told Bubulcus.

"To the kitchens?" the servant echoed. "Why should I do that?"

"To get some raw flesh for me to use to catch the moncats." Lanius suddenly looked as fierce as he knew how. "Or would you rather have me carve some raw flesh from your carcass?"

Bubulcus fled.

When he got back, he had some lovely beef that would probably have gone on the royal table tonight. And he proved to be capable of thought on his own, for he also carried a couple of dead mice by the tail. "Good," Lanius murmured. "Maybe I won't have to carve you after all."

He walked through palace hallways near the moncats' room, clucking as though it were general feeding time and holding up the meat and the mice. Only when servants' eyes went big did he stop to reflect that this was a curious thing for a King of Avornis to do. Having reflected, he then quit letting it bother him. He'd done all sorts of curious things. What was one more?

As he walked, he eyed wall niches and candelabra hanging from the ceiling. Unlike ordinary cats, moncats climbed at any excuse or none; they lived their lives in the trees. That made them especially delightful to catch when they got loose. It was also the reason Lanius had told his servants not to come into the animals' rooms—not that Bubulcus bothered remembering anything so trivial as a royal order.

A woman saw the meat in Lanius' hand and waved to him. "Your Majesty, one of those funny animals of yours is around that corner over there. It hissed at me, the nasty thing."

"Thank you, Parula. You'll have a reward," Lanius said. He glowered at Bubulcus. "What *you'll* have . . ."

"*I* didn't do anything, Your Majesty." Bubulcus sounded affronted. The next time he did do something wrong would be the first, as far as he was concerned.

Lanius hurried around the corner at which Parula had pointed. Sure enough, the moncat was there. It was trying to get out a window. Since the royal palace was also a citadel, the windows were narrow and set with iron bars. The moncat couldn't get out that way, though it might have dashed out a door.

"Rusty!" Lanius called.

"How can you tell one of the miserable creatures from another?" asked Bubulcus, who'd trailed along behind him.

"How?" Lanius shrugged. "I can, that's all." From then on, he ignored Bubulcus. Dangling one of the dead mice by the tail, he called the moncat's name again.

Rusty turned large green eyes his way. Moncats were smarter than ordinary cats; they did come to learn the names Lanius called them. And the offer of a mouse would have tempted any feline small enough to care about such a morsel. Rusty dropped down from the window and hurried over to the king.

He gave the moncat the mouse. Rusty held the treat in its hind feet—whose first toes did duty as thumbs—and used the claws of its front feet and sharp teeth to butcher it. The moncat ate the mouse in chunks. It didn't scratch or bite when Lanius picked it up and carried it off to the room from which it had escaped.

"There. That's all taken care of," Bubulcus said happily, as though he'd caught the moncat instead of letting it escape.

"No." Lanius shook his head. "This is one moncat. Two got away, you said. If the other one isn't caught soon, you will be very, very sorry. Do you understand me?" He sounded like a king who ruled as well as reigned. Bubulcus looked unhappy enough to make Lanius feel like that kind of king, too.

King Grus stared up at the frowning walls of Nishevatz. He still had no sure notion of what had happened to the Avornans and Chernagors he'd tried to sneak into the city. Prince Vasilko hadn't gloated about them from the wall or shot their heads out of catapults or anything of the sort. He gave no sign of knowing they'd tried to enter Nishevatz. In a way, that silence was more intimidating than anything blatant he might have done. What *had* his men done to them? Or, worse, what were they *doing* to them?

Not knowing gnawed at Grus. Still, he had to go on. With one effort a failure, he tried another. An interpreter, a squad of guards, and Prince Vsevolod at his side, he approached the Chernagor fortress.

"Here is your rightful prince!" he called, and pointed to Vsevolod. The interpreter turned his words into those of the throaty Chernagor tongue.

Faces, pale dots in the distance, peered down at Grus from the top of the frowning wall. Here and there, the sun sparkled off an iron helmet, or perhaps a sword blade. No one on the wall said a word. The wind blew cold and salty off the gray sea beyond the city-state.

"Here is your rightful prince!" Grus said again. "Cast down the ungrateful, unnatural son who has stolen your throne. Do you want the servants of the Banished One loose in your land? That is what Vasilko will give you."

Vsevolod strode forward. Despite his years, he still stood very straight, very erect. He looked every inch a prince. He shouted up at the warriors on the wall. He surely knew a lot of them as men, not merely as Chernagors.

"What does he say?" Grus asked the interpreter.

"He says he will not punish them if they yield up Vasilko to him," the Chernagor answered. "He says he knows they were fooled. He says he will not even kill Vasilko. He says he will send him into exile in Avornis, where he can learn the error of his ways."

"Hmm." Grus wondered how Vsevolod had meant that. He didn't much want Vasilko in his kingdom, not even in the Maze. But he supposed Vsevolod was doing the best he could. If the old man had promised to torture his son to death the minute he got his throne back, which of them was really likely to have fallen under the influence of the Banished One?

That thought brought on another. *How do I know Vasilko really is the man the Banished One backs?* Grus wondered. He sent Vsevolod a sudden hard stare. He'd always believed the old lord of Nishevatz. Why would Vsevolod have summoned him up to the Chernagor country, if not to fight the forces of the Banished One? Why? *What if the answer is, to lure me into a danger I can't hope to escape?*

"He is calling on them to open the gates," the interpreter said. Grus knew he'd missed a couple of sentences. That jolt of suspicion had driven everything else out of his mind for a moment. The older he got, the more complicated life looked. He eyed Vsevolod again. By the time he got *that* old, how would things seem? Would he be able to find any straight paths at all, or would every choice twist back on itself like a snake with indigestion? The interpreter added, "He says he will not harm any of them, if they return to his side now. He also says you Avornans will go home then."

"Yes, that's true." Grus saw no point to putting a permanent garrison in Nishevatz. That would just embroil him in a war against all the other Chernagor city-states. Unless he aimed to conquer this whole stretch of coast, seizing a little of it would be more trouble than it was worth.

Vsevolod called to the men on the wall one more time. The interpreter said, "He asks them, what is their answer?"

They did not keep him waiting long. Almost as one man, they drew their bows and started shooting at him and Grus and their companions. The guardsmen threw up their shields.

Thock! Thock! Thock! Arrows thudded into metal-faced wood. A softer splat was an arrow striking flesh rather than a shield. A guard gasped, trying to hold in the pain. Then, failing, he howled.

Guards and the royalty they guarded got out of range as fast as they could. Avornan archers rushed forward to shoot back at the Chernagors on the walls. Grus doubted they hit many, but maybe they did make the Chernagors keep their heads down. That would at least spoil the foe's aim.

After what seemed like forever but couldn't have been more than half a minute, the arrows the Chernagors kept shooting thudded into the ground behind Grus, and not into shields or flesh. He wasn't ashamed to let out a sigh of relief. He turned to Vsevolod and asked, "Are you all right?"

Panting, the deposed lord of Nishevatz nodded. "Only—winded. I am not—as swift—as I used to be." He paused to catch his breath. "What will you do now?"

"Well, we've tried being sneaky, and that doesn't work," Grus said. "We've tried being reasonable, and that didn't work, either. We can't very well starve them out, can we, not when they can bring in food by sea?"

"What does that leave?" Vsevolod asked morosely.

"Assaulting the walls," Grus answered. He stared toward those walls again. The Chernagors were still trading arrows with his archers. They were getting the better of it, too; they had the advantage of height. Grus sighed. "Assaulting the walls," he repeated, and sighed again. "And I hate to think about it, let alone try."

Whenever Bubulcus saw King Lanius coming, he did his best to disappear. With one moncat still on the loose, that was wise of him. It wasn't wise enough, though. The longer Pouncer stayed missing, the angrier Lanius got. Had Bubulcus been truly wise, he would have fled the palace and not just ducked into another room or around the corner when the king drew near.

"One of these days," Lanius told Sosia, "I am going to lose all of my temper, and I really will send that simpering simpleton to the Maze."

"Go ahead," his wife answered. "If you're going to act like a king, act like a *king*."

The only trouble here was, acting like a king meant acting like an ogre. No matter how angry at Bubulcus Lanius got, at heart he remained a mild-mannered man better suited to scholarship than to ruling. He could too easily imagine what a disaster exiling Bubulcus would be to the servant's family. And so he muttered curses under his breath, and told himself he would condemn Bubulcus tomorrow, and then put it off for another day.

He left meat in places to which he hoped the moncat might come. A couple of times, the moncat did come to one of those places . . . and stole the meat and disappeared again before anybody could catch it. Bubulcus came very close to exile the first time that happened, very close indeed.

Lanius did his best to live his life as though nothing were wrong. He went into the archives, trying to find out as much as he could about Nishevatz and the Chernagors for Grus. He doubted his father-in-law would be grateful, but, grateful or not, Grus still might find the information worth having.

Of course, Lanius would have enjoyed going to the archives regardless of whether he found anything useful to Grus. He liked nothing better than poking around through old sheets of parchment. Whenever he did, he learned something. He had to keep reminding himself he was trying to find out about the Chernagors. Otherwise, he might have happily wandered down any of half a dozen sidetracks.

He also liked going into the archives for the same reason he liked caring for his animals—while he was doing it, people were unlikely to bother him. Palace servants weren't forbidden to come into the archives after him. Old tax records and ambassadors' reports, unlike moncats and monkeys, couldn't escape and cause trouble. But no one in the royal palace except Lanius seemed to want to venture into the dark, dusty chambers that held the records of Avornis' past.

When the Chernagors first descended on the north coast, Avornans had reacted with horror. Lanius already knew that. The Chernagors hadn't been merchant adventurers in those distant days. They'd been sea-raiders and corsairs. Lanius suspected—he was, in fact, as near sure as made no difference—they were still sea-raiders and corsairs whenever and wherever they could get away with it.

He'd just come across an interesting series of letters from an Avornan envoy who'd visited Nishevatz in the days of Prince Vsevolod's great-grandfather when a flash of motion caught from the corner of his eye made him look up. His first thought was that a servant had come into the archives after all. He saw no one, though.

"Who's there?" he called.

Only silence answered.

He suddenly realized his seclusion in the archives had disadvantages as well as advantages. If anything happened to him here, who would know? Who would come to his rescue? If an assassin came after him, with what could he fight back? The most lethal weapon he had was a bronze letter opener.

And if the Banished One had somehow learned he spent a lot of time alone in the archives . . . Unease turned to fear. A thrall under the spell of the Banished One had already tried to murder him while he was caring for his animals. Flinging a treaty in an assassin's face wouldn't work nearly as well as throwing a moncat had.

"Who's there?" This time, Lanius couldn't keep a wobble of alarm from his voice.

That alarm got worse when, again, no answer came back.

Slowly, fighting his fear, Lanius rose from the stool where he'd perched. He clutched the letter opener in his right hand. He was no warrior. He would never be a warrior. But he intended to put up as much of a fight as he could.

Another flash of motion, this one from behind a cabinet untidily full of officers' reports from a long-ago war against the Thervings. "Who's there?" Lanius demanded for a third time. "Come out. I see you." *And oh, how I wish I didn't.*

More motion—and, at last, a sound to go with it. "Mrowr?"

Lanius' joints felt all springy with relief. "Olor's beard!" he said, and then, "Come out of there, you stupid moncat!"

The moncat, of course, didn't. All Lanius could see of it now was the twitching tip of its tail. He hurried over to the oak cabinet. Any moment now, the moncat was only too likely to start scrambling up the wall, to somewhere too high for him to reach it.

He was, in fact, a little surprised it hadn't fled already. With his fear gone and his wits returning, he clucked as he did when he was about to feed the moncats. "Mrowr?" this one said again, now on a questioning note. He hoped it was hungry. Though mice skittered here and there through the royal palace, hunting them would surely be harder work than coming up to a dish and getting meat and offal. Wouldn't it?

"It's all right," Lanius said soothingly, stepping around the cabinet. "It's not your fault. I'm not angry at you. I wouldn't mind booting that bungling Bubulcus into the middle of next month—no, I wouldn't mind that at all—but I'm not angry at you."

There sat the moncat, staring up at him out of greenish-yellow eyes. It seemed to think it was in trouble no matter how soothingly he spoke, for it sat on its haunches clutching in its little clawed hands and feet an enormous wooden serving spoon it must have stolen from the kitchens. The spoon was at least as tall as the moncat, and that included the animal's tail.

"Why, you little thief!" Lanius burst out laughing. "If you went sneaking through the kitchens, maybe you're not so hungry after all." He stooped to pick up the moncat.

It started to run away, but couldn't make itself let go of the prize it had stolen. It was much less agile trying to run with one hand and one foot still holding the spoon. Lanius scooped it up.

Still hanging on to the spoon, the moncat twisted and snapped. He smacked it on the nose. "Don't you bite me!" he said loudly. It subsided. Most of the moncats knew what that meant, because most of them had tried biting him at one time or another.

Feeling like a soldier who'd just finished a triumphant campaign, Lanius carried the moncat—and the spoon, which it refused to drop—back to its room. Once he'd returned it to its fellows, he sent a couple of servants after Bubulcus.

"Yes, Your Majesty?" Bubulcus asked apprehensively. Even servants rarely sounded apprehensive around Lanius. He savored Bubulcus' fear—and, savoring it, began to understand how an ordinary man could turn into a tyrant. Bubulcus went on, "Is it . . . is it the Maze for me?"

"No, not that you don't deserve it," Lanius said. "I caught the missing moncat myself, so it isn't missing anymore. Next time, though, by the gods . . . There had better not be a next time for this, that's all. Do you understand me?"

"Yes, Your Majesty! Thank you, Your Majesty! Gods bless you, Your Majesty!" Blubbering, Bubulcus fell to his knees. Lanius turned away. Yes, he understood how a man could turn into a tyrant, all right.

The Chernagor stared at Grus. Words poured out of him, a great, guttural flood. They were in his own language, so Grus understood not a one of them. Turning to the interpreter, he asked, "What is he saying? Why did he sneak out of Nishevatz and come here?"

"He says he cannot stand it in there anymore." The interpreter's words were calm, dispassionate, while passion filled the escapee's voice. Grus could understand that much, even if he followed not a word of what the man was saying. "He says Vasilko is worse than Vsevolod ever dreamed of being."

Grus glanced over toward Vsevolod, who stood only a few feet away. Vsevolod, of course, didn't need the translation to understand what the other Chernagor was saying. His forward-thrusting features and beaky nose made him look like an angry bird of prey—not that Grus had ever seen a bird of prey with a big, bushy white beard.

More excited speech burst from the Chernagor who'd just gotten out of Nishevatz. He pointed back toward the city he'd just left. "What's he going on about now?" Grus asked.

"He says a man does not even have to do anything to oppose Vasilko." Again, the interpreter's flat, unemotional voice contrasted oddly with the tones of the man whose words he was translating. "He says, half the time a man only has to realize Vasilko is a galloping horse turd"—the Chernagor obscenity sounded bizarre when rendered literally into Avornan—"and then he disappears. He never has a chance to do anything against Vasilko."

"You see?" Vsevolod said. "Is how I told you. Banished One works through my son." Now grief washed over his face.

"I see." Grus left it at that, for he still had doubts that worried him, even if he kept quiet about them. Some of those doubts had to do with Vsevolod. Others he could voice without offending the refugee Chernagor. He told the interpreter, "Ask this fellow how he managed to escape from Nishevatz once he decided Vasilko was . . . not a good man." He didn't try to imitate that picturesque curse.

The interpreter spoke in throaty gutturals. The man who'd gotten out of Nishevatz gave back more of them. The interpreter asked him something else. His voice showed more life while speaking the Chernagor tongue than when he used Avornan. He turned back to Grus. "He says he did not linger. He says he ran away before Vasilko could send anyone after him. He says—"

Before the interpreter could finish, the other Chernagor gasped. He flung his arms wide. "No!" he shouted—that was one word of the Chernagor speech Grus understood. He staggered and began to crumple, as though an arrow had hit him in the chest. "No!" he shouted again, this time blurrily. Blood ran from his mouth—and from his nose and from the corners of his eyes and from his ears, as well. After a moment, it began to drip from under his fingernails, too. He slumped to the ground, twitched two or three times, and lay still.

Grimly, Vsevolod said, "Now you see, Your Majesty. This is what my son, flesh of my life, now does to people." He covered his face with his gnarled hands.

"Apparently, Your Majesty, this man did not escape Vasilko's vengeance after all." The interpreter's dispassionate way of speaking clashed with Vsevolod's anguish.

"Apparently. Yes." Grus took a gingerly step away from the Chernagor's corpse, which still leaked blood from every orifice. He took a deep breath and tried to force his stunned wits into action. "Fetch me Pterocles," he told a young officer standing close by. He had to repeat himself. The officer was staring at the body in horrified fascination. Once Grus got his attention, he nodded jerkily and hurried away.

The wizard came quickly, but not quickly enough to suit Grus. Pterocles took one look at the dead Chernagor, then recoiled in dread and dismay. "Oh, by the gods!" he said harshly. "By the gods!"

Grus thought of Milvago, who was now the Banished One. He wished he hadn't. It only made Pterocles righter than he knew. "Do you recognize the spell that did this?" the king asked.

"Recognize it? No, Your Majesty." Pterocles shook his head. "But if I ever saw the man who used it, I'd wash my eyes before I looked at anything else. Can't you feel how filthy it is?"

"I can see how filthy it is. Feel it? No. I'm blind that particular way."

"Most of the time, I pity ordinary men because they can't see what I take for granted." Pterocles looked at the Chernagor's corpse again, then recoiled. "Every once in a while, though, you're lucky. This, I fear, is one of *those* times."

Bowing nervously before King Lanius, the peasant said, "If my baron ever finds out I've come before you, I'm in a lot of trouble, Your Majesty."

"If the King of Avornis can't protect you, who can?" Lanius asked.

"You're here. I live a long ways off from the capital. Wasn't that I had a cousin move here more than twenty years ago, give me a place to stay, I never would've come. But Baron Clamator, he's right there where I'm at."

That probably—no, certainly—reflected reality. Lanius wished it didn't, but recognized that it did. "Well, go on . . ." he said.

Knowing the pause for what it was, the peasant said, "My name's Flammeus, Your Majesty."

"Flammeus. Yes, of course." Lanius was annoyed with himself. A steward had whispered it to him, and he'd gone and forgotten it. He didn't like forgetting anything. "Go on, then, Flammeus." If he said it a few times, it *would* stick in his memory. "What's Baron Clamator doing?" He had a pretty good idea. Farmers usually brought one complaint in particular against their local nobility.

Sure enough, Flammeus said, "He's taking land he's got no right to. He's buying some and using his retainers to take more. We're free men down there, and he's doing his best to turn us into thralls like the Menteshe have."

He didn't know much about the thralls, or about the magic that robbed them of their essential humanity. He was just a farmer who, even after cleaning up and putting on his best clothes, still smelled of sweat and onions. He wanted to stay his own master. Lanius, who longed to be fully his own master, had trouble blaming him for that.

Grus had issued laws making it much harder for nobles to acquire land from ordinary farmers. He hadn't done it for the farmers' sake. He'd done it to make sure they went on paying taxes to Kings of Avornis and didn't become men who looked first to barons and counts and dukes and not to the crown. Lanius had seen how that helped him keep unruly nobles in line.

And what helped Grus could help any King of Avornis. "Baron Clamator will hear from me, Flammeus," Lanius promised.

"He doesn't listen any too well," the farmer warned.

"He'll listen to soldiers," Lanius said.

"Ahh," Flammeus said. "I figured King Grus would do that. I didn't know about you." Courtiers stirred and murmured. Flammeus realized he had gone too far, and quickly added, "Meaning no disrespect, of course."

"Of course," Lanius said dryly. Some Kings of Avornis would have slit the farmer's tongue for a slip like that. Lanius' own father, King Mergus, probably would have. Even Grus might have. Lanius, though, had no taste for blood—Bubulcus, luckily for him, was living proof of that. "I *will* send soldiers," the king told Flammeus.

The farmer bowed and made his escape from the throne room. He would have quite a tale to tell the cousin he was staying with. Lanius found new worries of his own. He'd never given orders to any soldiers except the royal bodyguards. Would the men obey him? Would they refer his orders to Grus, to make sure they were real orders after all? Or would they simply ignore him? Grus was the king with the power in Avornis, and everybody knew it.

Should I write to Grus myself? That might get rid of trouble before it starts, Lanius thought. But it would also delay things at least two weeks. Lanius wanted to punish Clamator as quickly as he could, before the baron got word he was going to be punished. *I'll write Grus, telling him what I'm doing and why.* That pleased Lanius. It would work fine . . . unless the soldiers refused to obey him at all.

His heart pounded against his ribs when he summoned an officer from the barracks. He had to work hard to hold his voice steady as he said, "Captain Icterus, I am sending you and your troop of riders to the south to deal with Baron Clamator. He is laying hold of peasant land in a way King Grus' laws forbid." He hoped that would help.

Maybe it did. Or maybe he'd worried over trifles. Captain Icterus didn't argue. He didn't say a word about referring the question to King Grus. He just bowed low, said, "Yes, Your Majesty," and went off to do what Lanius had told him to do. His squadron rode out of the city of Avornis that very afternoon.

Yes, this is what it's like to be a real *King,* Lanius thought happily. His sphere was no longer limited to the royal chambers, the archives, and the rooms where his moncats and monkeys lived. With Grus away from the capital, his reach stretched over the whole kingdom.

It did, at least, until he wrote to the other king to justify what he'd done. Writing the letter made him want to go wash afterwards. It wasn't merely the most abject thing he'd ever written. It was, far and away, the most abject thing he'd ever imagined. It had to be. He knew that. Grus would not take kindly to his behaving like a real king. But reading the words on parchment once he'd set them down . . . He couldn't stomach it. He sealed the letter without going through it a second time.

Sosia said, "I'm proud of you. You did what needed doing."

"I think so," Lanius said. "I'm glad you do, too. But what will your father think?"

"He can't stand nobles who take peasants under their own wing and away from Avornis," his wife answered. "He won't complain about whatever you do to stop them. You're not about to overthrow him."

"No, of course not," Lanius said quickly. He would have denied it even if—especially if—it were true. But it wasn't. He didn't want to try to oust Grus. For one thing, his father-in-law was much too likely to win if they measured themselves against each other. And, for another, this little taste of ruling Lanius was getting convinced him that Grus was welcome to most of it. When it came to animals or to ancient manuscripts, Lanius was patience personified; the smallest details fascinated him. When it came to the day-to-day work of governing, he had to fight back yawns. He also knew he would never make a great, or even a good, general. Grus was welcome to all of that.

Sosia said, "I wish things were going better up in the Chernagor country. Then Father could come home."

"I wish things were going better up in the Chernagor country, too," Lanius said. "The only reason they aren't going so well is that the Banished One must be stronger up there than we thought."

"That's not good," Sosia said.

"No, it isn't." Lanius said no more than that.

Sosia asked, "Can we do anything here to make things easier for Father up there? Would it be worth our while to start trouble with the Menteshe, to make the Banished One have to pay attention to two places at once?"

Lanius looked at her with admiration. She thought as though she were King of Avornis. He answered, "The only trouble I can see with that is, we'd have to pay attention to two places at once, too. Would it work a bigger hardship on the Banished One or on us? I don't know, not offhand. One more thing to go into a letter to your father."

"One *more* thing?" Sosia cocked her head to one side. "What's Ortalis gone and done now?"

"I don't know that he's done anything since the last time," Lanius said. They both made sour faces. Saying he didn't know that Ortalis had done anything new and dreadful wasn't the same as saying Sosia's brother hadn't done any such thing. How much had Ortalis done that nobody but he knew about?

Lanius shook his head. Whenever Ortalis did such things, *somebody* else knew about it. But how many of those *somebodies* weren't around anymore to tell their stories? Only Ortalis knew that.

"He should start hunting again," Sosia said. Something must have changed on Lanius' face. Quickly, his wife added, "Hunting bear and boar and birds and deer and rabbits—things like that."

"I suppose so." Lanius wished he could sound more cheerful. For a while, Ortalis had seemed . . . almost civilized. Hunting and killing animals had let him satiate his lust for blood and hurt in a way no one much minded. If only it hadn't lost the power to satisfy him.

Sosia said, "I wish things were simpler."

"Wish for the moon while you're at it," Lanius said. "The older I get, the more complicated everything looks." He was married to the daughter of the man who'd exiled his mother to the Maze. Not only that, he loved her. If that wasn't complicated enough for any ordinary use, what could be?

CHAPTER FIVE

King Grus looked from Hirundo to Pterocles to Vsevolod, then back again. They nodded, one after another. Grus' eyes went to the walls of Nishevatz. They frowned down at him, as they had ever since the Avornan army came before them. "We are agreed?" Grus said. "This is the only thing we have left to do?"

The general, the wizard, and the deposed Prince of Nishevatz all nodded again. Hirundo said, "If we didn't come to fight, why did we come?"

"I haven't got an answer for that," Grus said. *But oh, how I wish I did!* Since he didn't, he also nodded, brusquely. "All right, then. We'll see what happens. Go to your places. I know you'll all do everything you can."

Hirundo and Pterocles hurried away. Vsevolod's place was by Grus. "I thank you for this," he said in his ponderous Avornan. "I will do, my folk will do, all things possible to do to help."

"I know." Grus turned away. He thought Vsevolod meant well, but still had other things on his mind. A trumpeter stood by, face tense and alert. Grus pointed to him. "Signal the attack."

"Yes, Your Majesty." The trumpeter raised the horn to his lips. Martial music rang out. Only for a moment did it come from one trumpet alone. Then every horn player in the Avornan army blared forth the identical call.

Cheering Avornan soldiers swarmed forward. Grus wouldn't have cheered, not attacking a place like Nishevatz. Maybe the common soldiers didn't realize what they were up against. Some of them came within arrow range of that formidable wall and started shooting at the defenders on top of it, trying to make them keep their heads down. Others carried scaling ladders that they leaned up against the gray stone blocks. More Avornans—and some Chernagors, too—raced up the ladders toward the top of the wall.

"Come on!" Grus muttered, watching them through the clouds of dust the assault kicked up. "Come on, you mad bastards! You can do it! You *can*!"

He blinked. Beside him, King Vsevolod exclaimed in his own guttural language. Vsevolod grabbed Grus' arm, hard enough to hurt. The old man still had strength. "What is that?" he said. "I see ladders. Then I see no ladders."

Pterocles was doing his job. "I hope Prince Vasilko's men don't see them, either," Grus said. "If the men can get to the top of the wall, get down into Nishevatz . . ."

"Yes," Vsevolod said. "Then to my son I have some things to say." His big, gnarled hands opened and closed, opened and closed. Grus hadn't cared to be caught in that grip, and didn't think Vasilko would, either.

Even from so far away, the din was tremendous, deafening. Men shouted and screamed. Armor clattered. Dart-throwing engines bucked and snapped. Stones crashed down on soldiers storming up—the wizard's magic wasn't perfect. Ladders went over or broke, spilling soldiers off them.

And, much closer than the walls of Nishevatz, Pterocles suddenly howled like a wounded wolf. "Noooo!" he cried, his voice getting higher and shriller every instant. All at once, every siege ladder became fully visible again. The ladders started toppling one after another when that happened. Pterocles also toppled, still wailing.

Vsevolod said something in his own language that sounded incandescent. Grus said the foulest things he knew how to say in Avornan. None of their curses did any good. It quickly grew plain the assault on the wall wouldn't do any good, either.

Grus hauled Pterocles to his feet. The wizard's face was a mask of pain. Grus shook him. "Do something!" he shouted. "Don't just sound like a wheel that needs grease. *Do* something!"

"I can't." Pterocles didn't just sound like an ungreased wheel. He sounded like a man who might be about to die, and who knew it. "I can't, Your Majesty. He's too strong. What happened to me before, this is ten times worse—a hundred times. Whoever's in there, he's too strong for me." Tears ran down his cheeks. Grus didn't think he knew he shed them.

The king shook the wizard again. "You have to try. By the gods, Pterocles, the soldiers are depending on you. The kingdom is depending on you."

"I can't," Pterocles whispered, but from somewhere he found strength. He straightened. Grus let go of him. He still swayed, but he stayed on his feet. "I'll try," he said, even more quietly than before. "I don't know what will happen to me, but I'll try."

Before Grus could even praise him, he exploded into motion. He had a long, angular frame, and every separate part of him seemed to be moving in a different direction. Grus had never seen a wizard incant so furiously. It was as though Pterocles were taking pieces of his pain and flinging them back into Nishevatz. His magic didn't seemed aimed at the Chernagor soldiers on the walls anymore. Whatever he was doing, he was doing against—doing to—the wizard who'd come so close to killing him moments before.

"Take that!" he shouted again and again. "Take *that,* and see how you like it!"

Vsevolod nudged Grus. "He is mad," the old Chernagor said, and tapped the side of his head with a forefinger.

"Sometimes, with a wizard, it helps," Grus said. But he wondered exactly whom Pterocles was fighting. Was it some Chernagor wizard who, like Vasilko, had abandoned the gods and turned to the Banished One, or was it the being the Menteshe called the Fallen Star himself, in his own person? If it was the Banished One himself, could any merely mortal wizard stand against him?

Before Grus got even a hint of an answer, Hirundo distracted him. The general was bleeding from a cut over one eye. His gilded helmet had a dent in it, and was jammed down over one ear, which also bled. He seemed unaware of the small wounds. "Your Majesty, we can't get over the wall," he said without preamble. "You're just throwing more men away if you keep trying."

"No hope?" Grus asked.

"None. Not a bit. No chance." Hirundo sounded absolutely certain.

"All right. Pull them back," Grus said. The general bowed and hurried away. Vsevolod made a wordless noise full of fury and pain. He turned his back on Grus. Grus started to tell him he was sorry, but checked himself. If Vsevolod couldn't figure that out without being told, too bad.

"Take that!" Pterocles shouted again, and laughed a wild, crazy laugh. "Ha! See how you like it this time!"

He thought he was getting home against whoever or whatever his foe was. And the more confident he grew, the harder and quicker came the spells he cast. Maybe—probably—it was madness, but it was inspired madness.

And then, like a man who'd been hit square in the jaw, Pterocles toppled, right in the middle of an incantation. All his bones might have turned to water. When Grus stooped beside him, he was sure the wizard was dead. But, to his surprise, Pterocles went on breathing and still had a pulse. Grus slapped him in the face, none too gently, to try to bring him around. He stirred and muttered, but would not wake.

"Will he have any mind when he rouses?" Vsevolod asked.

Grus could only shrug. "We'll have to see, that's all. I just hope he *does* wake up. Something bigger than he was hit him there."

"It is mark of Banished One," the Prince of Nishevatz declared. Grus found himself nodding. He didn't see what else it could be, either.

Hirundo, meanwhile, pulled the Avornans back from the walls of the city-state where Vsevolod had ruled for so long. Many of them limped and bled. More than a few helped wounded comrades escape the rain of stones and arrows from the battlements.

"What now?" Vsevolod asked.

The last time Grus had faced that question, he'd decided to try to storm Nishevatz. Now he'd not only tried that, he'd also seen how thoroughly it didn't work. He gave the man who'd asked for his help the only answer he could—a shrug. "Your Highness, right now I just don't know what to tell you."

He waited for Vsevolod to get angry. Instead, the Chernagor nodded in dour approval. "At least you do not give me opium in honey sauce. This is something. You make no fog of pretty, sweet-smelling promises to lull me to sleep and make me not notice you say nothing."

"No. I come right out and say nothing," Grus replied.

"Is better." Prince Vsevolod sounded certain. Grus had his doubts.

King Lanius read the letter aloud to Queen Sosia, Queen Estrilda, Prince Ortalis, and Arch-Hallow Anser—Grus' daughter, wife, legitimate son, and bastard. "'And so we were repulsed from the walls of Nishevatz,' Grus writes," he said. "'I should never have tried to storm them, but looking back is always easier than looking forward.'"

"What will he do now?" The question, which should have come from Ortalis' lips if he had the least bit of interest in ruling Avornis, instead came from Estrilda's.

"I'm just getting to that," Lanius answered. "He writes, 'I do not know what I'll do next. I think I will stay in front of the city and see what happens next inside of it. Maybe Vasilko will make himself hated enough to spark an uprising against him. I can hope, anyhow.'"

He would have written a much more formal, much more detailed account of the campaign than Grus had. But Grus' letter had an interest, an appeal, of its own. *If it were three hundred years old and I'd found it in the archives, I'd be delighted,* Lanius thought. *It makes me feel I'm there.*

Anser asked, "What happened to the wizard?"

"To Pterocles? That's farther down. Here, this is what he says. 'Pterocles started coming back to himself the morning after he lost the magical fight with the wizard in Nishevatz—or with the wizard's Master. He knows who he is, and where, but he is not yet strong enough to try sorcery. This gives me one more reason to wait and see what happens here.'"

"He's probably doing the smart thing by not charging ahead with the war," Sosia said.

"Yes, probably," Lanius agreed. "But if we can't take Nishevatz with our soldiers or with our magic, what are we doing there?"

His wife had no answer for that. Lanius had none, either. He wondered if Grus did. He also wondered whether to write to the other King of Avornis and ask him. But he didn't need long to decide not to. Grus would be suspicious because Lanius had ordered soldiers to the south. If he also wrote a letter questioning what Grus was doing up in the Chernagor country, the other king might suspect him of ambitions he didn't have. Even more dangerous, Grus might suspect him of ambitions he *did* have.

Sosia said, "You're right—if we aren't doing anything worthwhile up there, our men ought to come back to Avornis."

"If Grus decides he needs to do that, I expect he will," Lanius answered, and wondered if Grus would have the sense to cut his losses. The other king was usually a man who saw what needed doing and did it.

Less than a week later, Captain Icterus rode back into the city of Avornis and reported to Lanius. The grin on the officer's face told the king most of what he needed to know before Icterus started talking. When he did speak, he got his message into one sentence. "You don't need to worry about Baron Clamator anymore, Your Majesty."

"That's good news, Captain," Lanius said. "And how did it happen that I don't?"

Icterus' grin got wider. "We happened to ride past him as he was on his way to drink with the baron who lives the next castle to the west. We scooped him up smooth as you please, and he was on his way to the Maze before his people even knew he was missing."

"Well done, Colonel!" Lanius said, and Icterus' smile got bigger and brighter still. Lanius hadn't thought it could.

The good news kept the king happy the rest of the morning. But he went back to worrying about the north as he examined tax records from the provinces later in the day. Almost in spite of himself, he was learning how the kingdom was administered. The numbers were all they should have been—better than Lanius had expected, in fact. But that let him worry more about the land of the Chernagors. Had Pterocles met a powerful wizard who inclined toward the Banished One? Or had the Banished One himself reached out from the far south to smite the Avornan wizard? Maybe it didn't matter. With the Banished One, though—with Milvago that was—how could any man say for certain?

And then Lanius got distracted again, this time much more pleasantly. A serving woman stuck her head into the chamber where he was working and said, "I beg pardon, Your Majesty, but may I speak to you for a moment?"

"Yes, of course," Lanius answered. "What do you want—uh—?" He couldn't come up with her name.

"I'm Cristata, Your Majesty," she said. She was a few years younger than Lanius—say, about twenty—with light brown hair, green eyes, a pert nose, and everything else a girl of about twenty should have. But she looked so nervous and fearful, the king almost didn't notice how pretty she was.

"Say whatever you want, Cristata," he told her now. "Whatever it is, I promise it won't land you in trouble."

That visibly lifted her spirits; the smile she gave him was dazzling enough to lift his, too. "Thank you, Your Majesty," she breathed, but then looked worried again. She asked, "Even if it's about . . . someone in the royal family?"

Lanius grimaced. He had a fear of his own now—that he knew what sort of thing Cristata was going to talk about. He had to answer quickly, to make her see he had no second thoughts. "Even then." He made his voice as firm as he could.

"Will you swear by the gods?" He hadn't satisfied her.

"By the gods," he declared. "By all the gods in the heavens." That left Milvago—the Banished One—out.

"All right, then," Cristata said. "This has to do with Prince Ortalis, Your Majesty. Remember, you swore."

"I remember." Lanius started to tell her he'd heard stories about Ortalis before. But the words never passed his lips. That wasn't fair to Grus' legitimate son. What he'd heard before could have been lies. He didn't think so, but it could have been. And, for that matter, what Cristata was about to tell him might be a lie, too. Lying about a prince to a king was a risky business for a servant, yet who could say for certain? Ortalis might—no, Ortalis was bound to—have enemies who could use her as a tool. With a sigh, Lanius said, "Go ahead."

Cristata did. The way she told her story made Lanius think it was likely true. Ortalis' good looks and his status had both drawn her. That seemed plausible—and even had Ortalis been wizened and homely, a serving girl would have taken a chance if she said no when he beckoned. That wasn't fair. It probably wasn't right. But it was the way life worked. Lanius had taken advantage of it himself, back in the days before he was married.

Everything between Ortalis and Cristata seemed to have started well. He'd been sweet. He'd given her presents. She didn't try to hide that she'd said yes for reasons partly mercenary, which again made Lanius more inclined to believe her.

Little by little, things had gone wrong. Cristata had trouble saying exactly when. Some of what later seemed dreadful had been exciting at the time . . . at first, anyhow. But when she did begin to get alarmed, she found herself in too deep to get away easily. Her voice became bitter. "By then, I was just a piece of meat for him, a piece of meat that had the right kind of holes. Before long, he even stopped caring about those."

She paused. Lanius didn't know what to say. Not knowing, he made a questioning noise.

It must have meant something to Cristata. Nodding as though he'd just made a clever comment, she said, "I can show you some of it. I can show you all of it if you like, but some will do." Her linen tunic fit loosely. As she turned her back on Lanius, she slipped it down off one shoulder, baring what should have been soft, smooth skin.

"Oh," he said, and involuntarily closed his eyes. He didn't think anyone with a grudge against Ortalis could have persuaded her to go through with . . . that for money.

She quickly set her tunic to rights again. "At least it did heal," she said matter-of-factly. "And he gave me . . . something for it afterwards. I thought about just taking that and keeping quiet. But is it right, Your Majesty, when somebody can just take somebody else and use her for a toy? What would he have done if he'd killed me? He could have, easy enough. Some of the girls who've left the court . . . Did they really leave, or did they disappear a different way?"

Lanius had wondered the same thing. But no one had ever found anything connecting Ortalis to those disappearances—except for the couple of maidservants who'd gone back to the provinces well rewarded for keeping their mouths shut afterwards. Cristata, evidently, didn't want to go that way. Lanius asked her, "What do you think I should do?"

"Punish him," she said at once. "You're the king, aren't you?"

The real answer to that question was, *yes and no.* He reigned, but he hardly ruled. Explaining his own troubles, though, would do Cristata no good. He said, "King Grus would be a better one to do that than I am."

Cristata sent him a look he was more used to feeling on his own face than to seeing on someone else's. The look said, *My, you're not as smart as I thought you were, are you?* Cristata herself said, carefully, "Prince Ortalis is His Majesty's son." Sure enough, she might have been speaking to an idiot child.

"Yes, I know," Lanius answered. "But King Grus, please believe me, doesn't like him doing these things." Cristata looked eloquently unconvinced. Sighing, Lanius added, "And King Grus, please believe me, is also the one who has the power to punish him when he does these things. I am not, and I do not."

"Oh," she said in a dull voice. "I should have realized that, shouldn't I? I'm sorry I bothered you, Your Majesty."

"It wasn't a bother. I wish I could do more. You're—" Lanius stopped. He'd been about to say something like, *You're too pretty for it to have been a bother.* If he did say something like that, it would be the first step toward complicating his life with Sosia. And, all too likely, Cristata would have heard the same sort of thing from Ortalis. She'd believed it from him, and been sorry afterwards. What did she think Lanius might do to her if she were rash enough to believe again?

Even though he'd stopped, her eyes showed she understood what he'd meant. Now she was the one who sighed. Perhaps as much to herself as to him, she said, "I used to think being pretty was nice. If you'd told me it was dangerous . . ." She shrugged—prettily. "I'm sorry I took up your time, Your Majesty." Before Lanius could find anything to say, she swept out of the little chamber.

The king spent the next few minutes cursing his brother-in-law, not so much for exactly what Ortalis had done as for making Lanius himself embarrassed to be a man.

No one knew the river galleys that prowled Avornan waters better than King Grus. The deep-bellied, tall-masted ships that went into and out of Nishevatz were a different breed of vessel altogether, even more different than cart horses from jumpers. Sailing on the Northern Sea was not the same business as going up and down the Nine Rivers that cut the Avornan plain.

"We need ships of our own," Grus said to Hirundo. "Without them, we'll never pry Vasilko out of that city."

"Yes, Your Majesty," the general answered. "We do need ships. But where will we get 'em? Build 'em ourselves? We haven't got the woodworkers to build 'em or sailors to man 'em. We haven't got the time, either. We might hire 'em from the Chernagors, except the next Chernagor city-state that wants to let us use any'll be the first."

"I know," Grus said. "They think if we have ships, we'll use 'em against them next."

Hirundo didn't reply. Many years before, the Chernagor city-states had belonged to Avornis. A strong king might want to take them back again. Grus liked to think of himself as a strong king. That the Chernagors evidently thought of him the same way was a compliment of sorts. It was, at the moment, a compliment he could have done without.

His chief wizard walked by. "How are you, Pterocles?" Grus called.

"How am I?" Pterocles echoed, his voice and expression both vague. "I've . . . been better."

He hadn't been the same since the sorcerer inside Nishevatz laid him low. Grus still marveled that he'd survived. So did all the other Avornan wizards who'd since helped him try to recover. Maybe the same thing would have happened to Alca—exiled from the capital, if not from Grus' heart—had the same spell struck her. Maybe.

Did the power that had smashed Pterocles mean the magic came from the Banished One himself, and not from one of his mortal minions? Like Vsevolod, the Avornan wizards seemed to think so. They didn't want to commit themselves—one more reason Grus wished he had straight-talking Alca at his side—but that was the impression he got.

"Can you work magic at need?" Grus asked.

"I suppose so." But Pterocles didn't sound as though he fully believed it.

Grus didn't fully believe it, either. Pterocles still looked and acted like a man who'd been hit over the head with a large, pointy rock. Sometimes he seemed better, sometimes worse, but even *better* didn't mean the same as *good*.

Under his own tunic, Grus wore an old protective amulet, one he'd had since before becoming King of Avornis. It had helped save his life once, when Queen Certhia, Lanius' mother, tried to slay him by sorcery. Would it protect him if the Banished One tried to do the same thing? Grus had his doubts. He knew he didn't want to find out the hard way.

Pterocles said, "Half of me makes more of a wizard than a lot of these odds and sods, Your Majesty—or half of me would, if I didn't feel so . . . empty inside." He tapped the side of his head with his fist. It didn't sound like a jar from which all the wine was gone, but Grus—and maybe Pterocles, too—thought it should have.

"You'll be all right." Grus hoped he was telling the truth. When he added, "You *are* getting better," he felt on safer ground. On the other hand, how much of a compliment was that? If Pterocles hadn't gotten any better, the sorcerous stroke he'd taken would have laid him on his pyre.

A messenger came up to Grus. He stood there waiting to be noticed. When Grus nodded to him, he said, "Your Majesty, a sack of letters from Avornis is here."

"Oh, good," Grus said. "I do want to keep track of what's going on back home." He'd already stayed out of the kingdom longer than he'd intended. Back in the capital, Lanius behaved more like a real king every day. If he wanted to try ousting Grus, he might have a chance now. From what Grus had seen, though, Lanius didn't like actually governing. Grus chuckled, not that he really felt amused. That was a small, flimsy platform on which to rest his own rule.

He turned to walk back to his tent and look at those letters. He hadn't gone far, though, before another messenger ran up to him. This one didn't wait to be noticed. He shouted, "Your Majesty, they're coming!"

"Who's coming?" Grus asked.

"Chernagors! A whole army of Chernagors, from out of the east!" the messenger answered. "They aren't on their way to ask us to dance, either."

"No?" Grus slid gracefully from heel to toe and back again. The messenger stared at him. He sighed. "Well, probably not. Tell me more."

"We sent men to them to find out if they were coming to help us and Prince Vsevolod," the messenger said. "They shot at our men."

"Then they probably aren't." Grus' eyes involuntarily went back to the walls of Nishevatz. "If they aren't coming to help Vsevolod, Vasilko will be glad to see them. Nice to think someone is, eh?"

"Er—yes." The messenger didn't seem to think that was good news. Grus didn't think it was good news, either. Unlike the messenger, he knew just how bad it was liable to be.

He ordered his own army into line of battle facing east. Things could have been worse. He supposed they could have been worse, anyhow. The army could have gone on about the business of besieging Nishevatz without sending scouts out to the east and west. That would have been worse, sure enough. The Chernagors from the east might have crashed into his force unsuspected. Instead of a mere disaster, he would have had a catastrophe on his hands then.

Avornan soldiers were still taking their places when Grus saw a cloud of dust on the coastal road that came out of the east. He'd had some practice judging the clouds of dust advancing armies kicked up. He turned to Hirundo, who'd had considerably more. "Looks like a lot of Chernagors," he said.

"Does, doesn't it?" Hirundo agreed. "Of course, they may be playing games with us. Send some horses along in front of an army with saplings fastened on behind them and they'll stir up enough dust to make you think every soldier in the world is heading your way."

"Do you think that's likely here?" Grus inquired.

Hirundo pursed his lips. "I'd like to," he answered. But that wasn't what the king had asked. Reluctantly, the general shook his head. "No, I don't think so. The scouts saw Chernagors, lots of Chernagors. . . . I'm going to pull some men back out of the line, if that's all right with you."

"Why?"

"Because I'd like to have a reserve handy, in case Vasilko decides to sally from Nishevatz while we're busy with these other bastards." Hirundo gave an airy wave of the hand. "Nothing puts a hole in your day like getting attacked from two directions at once, if you know what I mean."

"I wish I didn't, but I do," Grus said heavily. "That's a good idea. See to it." Hirundo sketched a salute and hurried off.

Prince Vsevolod came up to Grus. He tugged on the sleeve of the king's tunic. "Your Majesty, I am sorry I put you in this place," he said. "I fight hard for you." His age-spotted hand fell to the hilt of his sword.

"Thank you, your Highness. We'll all do some fighting before long," Grus replied. For him, that would mean donning a mailshirt and mounting a horse. He hated fighting from horseback, as anyone who'd spent more time on a river galley would have. A tilting deck was one thing, a rearing mount something else again. He clapped Vsevolod on the back. "You didn't put me in this place. Vasilko and the Banished One did. I know who my enemies are."

"I thank you, Your Majesty. You are all King of Avornis should be," Vsevolod said. "I fight hard. You see."

"Good." Grus raised his voice and called, "Let's move out against them," to Hirundo. He went on, "We don't want them thinking we're afraid to face them."

"Afraid to face a bunch of Chernagors? We'd better not be!" Hirundo sounded light and cheerful, for the benefit of his men, and probably for Grus' benefit, too. But the general knew—and King Grus also knew—the traders who lived by the Northern Sea made formidable warriors when they took it into their heads to fight.

Avornan trumpets blared. Shouting Grus' name and Prince Vsevolod's (many of them making a mess of it), the soldiers rode and marched forward. Soon, through the dust ahead, Grus made out sun-sparkles off spearheads and swords, helmets and coats of mail. The Chernagors rode big, ponderous horses, not fast but heavy and strong enough to be formidable in the charge.

Hirundo shouted orders. Like a painter working on a fresco inside a temple, he saw how he wanted everything to go long before the scene was done. Avornan mounted archers galloped out to the wings and started peppering the Chernagors with arrows. Some of the big, stocky men from the north slid out of their saddles and crashed to the ground. Some of the big, stocky horses they rode crashed down, too. Unwounded beasts tripped over them and also fell.

But most of the Chernagors ignored the arrows and kept coming. They had archers of their own, more of them afoot than on horseback, and started shooting at Grus' men as soon as they got into range. Arrows thudded into shields. They clattered off helms and armor. Now and then, they smacked home against flesh. Every cry of pain made Grus flinch.

An arrow hissed past his head, sounding malevolent as a wasp. A few inches to one side and he would have been screaming, too. Or maybe he wouldn't. Not far away, an Avornan took an arrow in the face and fell from his horse without a sound. He never knew what hit him. That was an easy way to go, easier than most men got on the battlefield or off it.

Grus had hoped Hirundo's mounted archers would make the Chernagors think twice about closing with his army. But no. Shouting fierce-sounding incomprehensibilities in their own throaty language, the bushy-bearded warriors slammed into their Avornan foes.

"Come on, men! Let's show them what we can do now that we've got them in the open!" Grus shouted. "Up until now, they've hidden in forts, afraid to meet us face-to-face." Had he commanded the Chernagors, he would have done the same thing, which had nothing to do with anything when he was trying to hearten his men. "Let 'em see they knew what they were doing when they wouldn't come out against us."

A few heartbeats later, he was trading sword strokes with a large Chernagor who had a large wart by the side of his nose. After almost cutting off his own horse's ear, Grus managed to wound the enemy warrior. The fellow howled pain-filled curses at him. The fighting swept them apart. As so often happened, Grus never found out what happened to the foe.

Shouts from the north drew the king's attention. As Hirundo had feared, Prince Vasilko's men were swarming out of Nishevatz and into the fight. Grus wondered whether the general had pulled enough soldiers to hold them off before they took the main part of the Avornan army in the flank and rolled it up. One way or the other, he would find out.

His army didn't come to pieces, which proved Hirundo had a good notion of what he was doing after all. But the Avornans didn't win— they didn't come close to winning—the sort of victory Grus would have wanted. All he could do was fight hard and send men now here, now there, to shore up weak spots in his line. He had the feeling the Chernagor generals were doing the same thing; it certainly seemed to be a battle with no subtlety, no surprises.

Late in the afternoon, Vasilko's sortie collapsed. The men from Nishevatz still on their feet streamed back into the city. Had things been going better in the fight against the rest of the Chernagors, Grus' men might have chased them harder and gotten into Nishevatz with them. But things weren't, and the Avornans didn't. Having only one foe to worry about struck Grus as being good enough for the time being.

At last, sullenly, the rest of the Chernagors withdrew from the field. It was a victory, of sorts. Grus thought about ordering a pursuit. He thought about it, looked at how exhausted and battered his own men were, and changed his mind. Hirundo rode up to him and dismounted. The general looked as weary as Grus felt. "Well, Your Majesty, we threw 'em back," he said. "Threw 'em back twice, as a matter of fact."

Grus nodded. The motion made some bones in his neck pop like cracking knuckles. "Yes, we did," he said, and yawned enormously. "King Olor's beard, but I'm worn."

"Me, too," Hirundo said. "We did everything we could do there, though."

"Yes," Grus said again. He wished he weren't agreeing. They'd done everything they could, and they were no closer to ousting Vasilko from Nishevatz or restoring Vsevolod. Grus looked around for the rightful Prince of Nishevatz, but didn't see him.

"Now the next interesting question," Hirundo said, "is whether the Chernagors will come back at us tomorrow, or whether they've had enough."

"Interesting," Grus repeated. "Well, that's one way to put it. What do you think?"

"Hard to say," Hirundo answered. "I wouldn't care to send this army forward to attack them tomorrow, and we had the better of it today. But you never can tell. Some generals are like goats—they just keep butting."

"Would one more Chernagor attack be likelier to ruin them or us?" Grus asked.

"Another good question," his general replied. "I think it's likelier to ruin them, but you don't *know* until the fight starts. For that matter, another fight where everybody's torn up could ruin both sides."

"You're full of cheery notions, aren't you?"

Hirundo bowed. Something in his back creaked, too. "I'm supposed to think about these things. I wouldn't be doing my job if I didn't."

"I know." Grus looked around for Vsevolod again. When he didn't see him, he yelled for a messenger. "Find out if the prince is hale," he told the young man. "If he is, tell him I'd like to see him when he gets the chance."

Nodding, the youngster hurried off. A few minutes later, Prince Vsevolod joined Grus. The ousted lord of Nishevatz wasn't perfectly hale. He had a bloody bandage wrapped around his head. Even so, he waved aside Grus' worried questions. "You should see man who did this to me," he said. "Somewhere now, ravens pick out his eyes."

"Good," Grus said. "I have a question for you."

"Ask," Vsevolod said.

"How likely is it that we'll see more Chernagor armies that don't want us in this country anymore?"

Vsevolod frowned. Even before donning the bandage, he'd had a face made for frowning. With it, he looked like a man contemplating his own doom and not liking what he saw. "It could be," he said at last. "Yes, it could be."

"How likely do you think it is?" Grus persisted.

Now Prince Vsevolod looked as though he hated him. "If I were prince in another city-state, I would lead forth my warriors," he said.

"I was afraid of that," Grus said. "We don't have the men here to fight off every Chernagor breathing, you know."

"What will you do, then?" Vsevolod asked in turn. "Will you say you are beaten? Will you run back to Avornis with tail between your legs?"

He's trying to make me ashamed, Grus realized. *He's trying to embarrass me into staying up here and going on with the war.* Grus understood why the Prince of Nishevatz was doing that. Had he worn Vsevolod's boots, he wouldn't have wanted his ally to give up the fight, either. Being who and what he was, though, he didn't want to risk throwing away his whole army. And so, regretfully, he said, "Yes."

CHAPTER SIX

"Coming back here to the capital?" Lanius asked Grus' messenger. "Are you sure?"

"Yes, Your Majesty." The young man sounded offended Lanius should doubt him. "Didn't he tell me with his own mouth? Didn't he give me the letter you're holding?"

Lanius hadn't read the letter yet. He'd enjoyed being King of Avornis in something more than name for a little while—he'd discovered he *could* run the kingdom, something he'd never been sure of before. Now he would go back to being nothing in fancy robes and crown. Grasping at straws, he asked, "How soon will he return?"

"It's in the letter, Your Majesty. Everything is in the letter," the messenger replied. When Lanius gave no sign he wanted to open the letter, the fellow sighed and went on, "They should be back inside of a month—less than that if they don't have to fight their way out."

"Oh." Lanius didn't much want to read the letter—seeing Grus' hand reminded him how much more power the other king held. Talking to the courier made *him* the stronger one. "How has the fighting gone?"

"We're better than they are. One of us is worth more than one of them," the messenger said. "But there are more of them than there are of us, and so . . ." He shrugged. "What can you do?" He didn't seem downcast at pulling back from the land of the Chernagors. Did that mean Grus wasn't, or did it only mean he'd done a good job of persuading his men he wasn't? Lanius couldn't tell.

Even after dismissing the messenger and reading his father-in-law's letter, he still wasn't sure. Grus presented the withdrawal as the only thing he could do, and as one step in what looked like a long struggle. *The Banished One will not do with the Chernagors as he has done in the south,* he wrote. *Whatever we have to do to stop him, we will.*

He wasn't wrong about how important keeping the Banished One from dominating the land of the Chernagors was. Lanius saw that, too. But, when he read Grus' letter, he wondered if his father-in-law was saying everything he had in mind. Was he leaving the north country to make sure Lanius didn't decide he could rule Avornis all by himself? Again, Lanius couldn't tell.

Would I throw Grus out of the palace if I had the chance? As usual, Lanius found himself torn. Part of him insisted that, as scion of a dynasty going back a dozen generations, he ought to rule as well as reign. That was his pride talking. But, now that he'd had a taste of running the kingdom day by day, he found he would sooner spend time with his animals and in the archives. If Grus wanted to handle things as they came up, wasn't he welcome to the job?

All things considered, Lanius was inclined to answer *yes* to that. Another question also sprang to mind. *If I try to get rid of Grus and fail, the way I likely would, won't he kill me to make sure I don't try it again?* Lanius was inclined to answer *yes* to that, too. Maybe—probably—the present arrangement was best after all.

No sooner had he decided, yet again, to let things go on as they were going than another messenger came before him. This one thrust a letter at him, murmured, "I'm very sorry, Your Majesty," and withdrew before Lanius could even ask him why he was sorry.

The king stared at the letter. It gave no obvious clues; he didn't even recognize the seal that helped hold it closed or the hand that addressed it to him. Shrugging, he broke the seal, slid off the ribbon around the letter, unrolled it, and began to read.

It was, he discovered, from the abbess of a convent dedicated to preserving the memory of a holy woman who'd died several hundred years before. For a moment—for more than a moment—the convent's name meant nothing to him. He couldn't have said where in Avornis it lay, whether in the capital or over in the west near the border with Thervingia or in the middle of the fertile southern plains. Then, abrupt as stubbing a toe, he remembered. The convent stood in the middle of the swamps and bogs of the Maze, not far from the city of Avornis as the crow flies but a million miles away in terms of everything that mattered. It had held his mother ever since she'd tried and failed to slay Grus by sorcery.

No more. Queen Certhia was dead. That was what the letter said. The messenger must have known. That had to be why he'd said he was sorry. It had to be why he'd slipped away, too—he didn't want Lanius blaming him for the news.

"I wouldn't do that," Lanius said aloud. But a messenger from out of the Maze, a messenger who didn't know him, wouldn't know about that, either.

He made himself finish the letter. The abbess said his mother's passing had been easy. Of course, she likely would say that whether it was true or not. She added praise for Certhia's piety. *Never,* she wrote, *was your mother heard to complain of her fate.*

Lanius' mouth twisted when he read that. Anger? Grief? Laughter? He couldn't tell. Some of all of them, he supposed. Maybe his mother hadn't complained because she was grateful Grus hadn't done to her what she'd tried to do to him. Lanius sighed. That might be noble, but it struck him as unlikely. From all he remembered, gratitude had never been a large part of Queen Certhia's makeup. Odds were she hadn't complained simply because she'd known it would do no good.

Her pyre was set ablaze this morning, the abbess wrote. *What is your desire for her ashes? Shall they remain here, or would you rather bring them back to the city of Avornis for interment in the cathedral?*

The king called for parchment and pen. *Let her remains be returned to the capital,* he wrote. *She served Avornis as well as the gods, acting as Queen Regnant in the days of my youth. She will be remembered with all due ceremony.*

"And if Grus doesn't like it, too bad," Lanius muttered. He hadn't seen his mother for years. He'd known he was unlikely ever to see her again. He'd also known ambition burned more brightly in her than love ever had. Even so, as he stared down at the words he'd written, they suddenly seemed to run and smear before his eyes. He blinked. The tears that had blurred his sight ran down his face. He buried his head in his hands and wept as though his heart would break.

Even now that he was well back inside Avornis, King Grus kept looking back over his shoulder to make sure the Chernagors weren't pursuing his army anymore. Beside him, General Hirundo whistled cheerfully.

"Can't win 'em all, Your Majesty," the general said. "We'll have another go at those bushy-bearded bastards next spring, I expect."

"Yes, I suppose so," Grus agreed. He took the defeat harder than Hirundo did. He knew more about the nature of the true foe they faced than did his general. Part of him wished Lanius had never told him who and what Milvago had been—part of him, indeed, wished Lanius had never found out. Fighting a god cast out of the heavens was bad enough. Fighting the onetime lord of the gods cast down from the heavens . . . No, he didn't want his men knowing that was what they had to do.

Not far away, Prince Vsevolod rode along with slumped shoulders and lowered head. He'd doubtless hoped for better than he'd gotten when he called on the Avornans to help him hold on to his throne. But his ungrateful son, Prince Vasilko, still held Nishevatz. And Vasilko would go right on holding it at least until next spring.

Hirundo looked ahead, not behind. "We'll be back to the city of Avornis in a couple of days," he said.

Vsevolod muttered something his beard muffled. He wasn't delighted about riding into exile, even if he was heading toward the greatest city in the world. Grus said, "Coming home is always good." Vsevolod muttered again. He wasn't coming home. He was going away from his, and had to fear he would never see it again.

With a grin, Hirundo said, "You'll get a chance to see what the other king's been up to, Your Majesty."

"So I will." Grus knew he sounded less gleeful at the prospect than Hirundo did. Lanius had done very well while he was gone—perhaps too well for comfort. If the other king was becoming a *king* . . . well, what could Grus do about it? Stay home and watch him all the time? He knew he couldn't. The two of them could either clash or find a way of working together. Grus saw no other choices.

He looked around for Pterocles. There was the wizard, as hollow-eyed as he'd been since the sorcerer in Nishevatz struck him down for the second time. Grus waved to him. Pterocles nodded back and said, "Still here, Your Majesty—I think."

"Good. I know you're getting better." Grus knew no such thing. Pterocles had shown less improvement than the king would have liked. Saying so, though, wouldn't have made things any better. Grus wondered if he ought to have other wizards look Pterocles over when they got back to the city of Avornis. Then he wondered if that would help.

Pterocles was the best he had. Could some lesser wizard judge whether something was really wrong with him?

Too many things to worry about at the same time, Grus thought. *All we'd need would be an invasion from the Menteshe to make everything perfect.*

He glanced up to the heavens and muttered a quick prayer. He didn't want the gods taking him seriously. The only question he had was whether they would pay any attention to him at all. "You'd better," he murmured. If things went wrong down here on earth, the gods in the heavens might yet have to face their outraged sire. Grus wondered if they knew that. He also wondered how much help they could deliver even if they did.

Those were no thoughts to be having about gods he'd worshiped all his life. All the same, he would have been happier if he'd seen more in the way of real benefits from them. *King Olor, if you happen to be listening, I could use a few blessings that aren't in disguise.* Grus laughed when that prayer crossed his mind. How many mortals couldn't use a few blessings like that?

The men who followed the Banished One—the Menteshe, and presumably Prince Vasilko and his followers as well—knew what sort of rewards they got. Those who opposed him weren't so sure. What they got wasn't so obvious in this world. In the next, yes—provided the Banished One lost the struggle with his children and stayed banished. If he didn't . . . Grus preferred not to think about that.

He had a lot of things he didn't want to think about. By the time the army got back to the city of Avornis, those seemed to outnumber the things that were worth contemplating.

He'd sent messengers ahead. Lanius knew to the hour when he and the army would arrive. One more thing he'd wondered was whether he ought to do that. If Lanius had anything . . . unpleasant in mind, Grus was letting his fellow king know things that could be very useful to him. Grus didn't think Lanius was plotting anything like that. His own spies back in the capital hadn't warned him his son-in-law was hatching plots. Was Lanius clever enough to do some hatching without drawing their notice? Grus would have worried less if he hadn't known how clever Lanius really was.

But no soldiers held the gates and walls of the city of Avornis against him. Lanius came out through the North Gate to greet him along with

Sosia; with Prince Crex and Princess Pitta, their children; with Ortalis; with Estrilda; and with Arch-Hallow Anser. "Welcome home!" Lanius said.

"Thank you, Your Majesty," Grus replied, hoping his relief didn't show. He would have worried more if Lanius had used his royal title in greeting him. He knew his fellow monarch didn't think him a legitimate king. Had Lanius been plotting something, he might have tried buttering him up. This way, things were as they should be.

"Grandpa!" Crex and Pitta squealed. They ran toward Grus' horse. He dismounted—something he was always glad to do—stooped, and squeezed them. That they were glad to see him made him feel he'd done something right with his life. Unlike adults, children gave you just what they thought you deserved.

A groom came forward to take charge of the horse. It was a docile beast, but Grus was still happy to see someone else dealing with it. Sosia and Anser greeted Grus only a couple of steps behind his grandchildren. "Good to have you home," they said, almost in chorus, and both started to laugh. So did Grus. Neither his daughter nor his bastard boy seemed to have any reason to regret his return. And Sosia's anger at his affair with Alca seemed to have faded, which was also good news.

"I wish things had gone better up in the Chernagor country," Grus said. Lanius, hanging back, raised an eyebrow at that. Grus needed a moment to figure out why. A lot of Kings of Avornis, he supposed, would have proclaimed victories whether they'd won them or not. He saw no point to that. He knew what the truth was. So did the whole army. It would get out even if he did proclaim victory. If he did, the truth would make him look like a liar or a fool. This way, he would look like an honest man who'd lost a battle. He hoped that would serve him better.

Grus understood why Lanius hung back. His son-in-law had solid reasons not to care for him, and was a reserved—even a shy—young man. Ortalis hung back, too. Grus also understood that. His legitimate son had done plenty to displease him. He and Ortalis traded looks filled with venom.

And Estrilda also hung back. That hurt. Was his wife still steaming over Alca? He'd thought they'd patched that up. In fact, they had—but then he'd gone off to war. Maybe the patch had torn loose. Maybe she wasn't angry about Alca, but suspected a Chernagor girl had warmed his bed while he was in the north. That hadn't happened, not least because, again, he'd worried about the truth getting back to her. But, of course, she didn't know it hadn't happened.

King Grus sighed. *Half my family likes me, the other half wishes I were still off fighting the Chernagors. It could be worse. But, by Olor and Quelea, it could be better, too.*

He turned to Hirundo. Whether his family liked him or not, the kingdom's business had to go on. "Send the men to the barracks," he said. "Give them leave a brigade at a time. That way, they shouldn't tear the city to pieces."

"Here's hoping," Hirundo said. "If it looks like the ones who haven't gotten leave are turning sour and nasty, I may speed things up."

Grus nodded. "Do whatever you think best. The point of the exercise is to keep things as orderly as you can. They won't be perfect. I don't expect them to be. But I don't want riots and looting, either."

"I understand." Hirundo called out orders to his officers.

"What of me, Your Majesty?" Prince Vsevolod asked. "You send me to barracks, too?"

"As soon as I can, I aim to send you back to Nishevatz, Your Highness." Grus pretended not to hear the Chernagor's bitterness. "In the meantime, you'll stay in the palace as my guest."

"And mine," Lanius added. "I have many questions to ask you about the land of the Chernagors and about your customs."

Grus had all he could do not to laugh out loud. By the look on Sosia's face, so did she. Lanius had pet moncats. He had pet monkeys, too. (The Chernagors, Grus remembered, had brought those beasts here to the capital.) And now, at last, Lanius had his very own pet Chernagor.

"Your Majesty, what I know, I tell you." Vsevolod sounded flattered that Lanius should be interested. Grus had to turn away so neither the prince nor his fellow king would see him smile. If Vsevolod made a promise like that, it only proved he didn't know what he was getting into.

Prince Vsevolod looked discontented. King Lanius had never seen anyone whose face, all harsh planes and vertical lines and with that formidable prow of a nose, was better suited to looking discontented. "Questions, questions, questions!" he said, throwing his hands in the air. "Am I prisoner, you should ask so many questions?"

"You told me you would tell me what you knew," Lanius said.

"By gods, not all at once!" Vsevolod exploded.

"Oh." By the way Lanius sounded, the Prince of Nishevatz might have just thrown a rock at his favorite moncat. "I *am* sorry, Your Highness. I want you to be happy here."

Vsevolod nodded heavily. Lanius let out a small sigh of relief—he'd been right about that, anyhow. The exiled prince said, "How can I, cooped up in palace all time?"

"I am," Lanius said in honest surprise. "What would you like to do?"

"Hunt," Vsevolod said at once. "Hunt anything. Hunt boar, goose, even rabbit. You are hunter, Your Majesty?"

"Well . . . no," Lanius replied. Vsevolod's lip curled. Lanius said, "Arch-Hallow Anser is a keen hunter." After another, longer, hesitation, he added, "Prince Ortalis also sometimes hunts."

"Ah. Is good," Vsevolod said, which only proved he didn't know Ortalis well. "And I know King Grus is hunting man. Maybe here is not so bad. Maybe."

"I hope you will be happy here," Lanius said again. "Now, can you tell me a little more about the gods your people worshiped before you learned of King Olor and Queen Quelea and the rest of the true dwellers in the heavens?"

Vsevolod's broad shoulders went up and down in a shrug. "I do not know. I do not care." He heaved himself to his feet. "I have had too much of questions. I go look for hunt." He lumbered away.

Lanius knew he'd angered the Prince of Nishevatz, but didn't understand why. Vsevolod had said he would answer questions. The king went off to console himself with his monkeys. If they could have answered questions, he would have asked even more than he'd put to Vsevolod. As things were, he could only watch them cavort through their chamber. A fire always burned there, keeping the room at a temperature uncomfortably warm for him. The monkeys seemed to like it fine. The Chernagor who'd given them to Lanius had warned they couldn't stand cold.

They stared at the king from the branches and poles that reached almost to the ceiling. Both male and female had white eyebrows and long white mustaches on otherwise black faces. They looked like plump little old men. Lanius eyed the female. He nodded to himself. She'd looked particularly plump these past couple of weeks. That Chernagor had said they would never breed in captivity, but maybe he was wrong.

Behind Lanius, the door opened. He turned in annoyance. But it wasn't Bubulcus or any other servant he could blister with impunity. King Grus stood there. He made a point of closing the door quickly, giving Lanius no excuse to grumble even about that. "Hello, Your Majesty," he said. "How are your creatures here?"

"I think the female's pregnant," Lanius answered.

Grus eyed her, then nodded. "Wouldn't be surprised if you're right. You'd have fun with the babies, wouldn't you?"

"Oh, yes, but it's not just that," Lanius said. "If an animal will breed for you, you know you're treating it the way you should. From what the fellow who gave it to me said, the Chernagors can't get monkeys to breed. I'd like to do something they can't."

With a judicious nod, Grus said, "Mm, yes, I can see that." His right hand folded into a fist. "It's not what *I'd* like to do to the Chernagors right now, but I can see it." He chuckled. "I was pretty sure you'd question Vsevolod to pieces, you know. He just tried to talk me into going hunting. I sent him off to Anser. He has more time for it than I do."

"I *told* Vsevolod I wanted to ask him things," Lanius said. "Didn't he believe me?"

"Nobody who's never met you believes how many questions you can ask," Grus said. "But that isn't what I wanted to talk to you about. I've got some questions of my own."

"Go ahead." Lanius realized Grus wouldn't have come here to talk about monkeys. The other king did show some interest in Lanius' beasts, but not enough for that. "What do you want to know?"

Grus let out a long sigh. "What about my son?"

Lanius had known this was coming. He hadn't expected it so soon. "What about him?"

"Don't play games with me." Grus seldom showed Lanius how dangerous he could be. The impatient snap to that handful of words, though, warned of trouble ahead if he didn't get a straight answer.

"Have you spoken with a serving girl named Cristata yet?" Lanius asked.

"Cristata? No." Again, Grus sounded thoroughly grim. "What does she say? How bad is it this time?"

Lanius reached around to pat himself on the back of the shoulder. "I don't think those scars will go away. I don't know what other marks she has—this was what she showed me."

"Oh," Grus said, and then nothing more.

He was silent long enough, in fact, to make Lanius ask, "Is that all?"

"That's all I'm going to say to *you*," King Grus answered. But then he shook his head. "No. I have a question I think you can answer. Is this Cristata the same girl I heard about when I was up in the land of the Chernagors?"

"I . . . don't know," Lanius said carefully.

His father-in-law heard him speaking carefully, which he hadn't intended. Frowning, Grus asked, "What do you think?"

"I think that, since I don't know, I wouldn't be doing anyone any good by guessing."

By the way Grus cocked his head to one side, Lanius feared his real opinion was only too evident. But the older man didn't press him on it. "Fair enough, Your Majesty. I daresay you're right. The world would be a better place if people didn't guess and gossip so much. It might be a duller place, but it would be better." Again, he paused for so long, Lanius thought he'd finished. Again, Lanius proved wrong. Grus went on, "Never mind. One way or the other, I'll find out."

Lanius didn't like the sound of that. He suspected he would have liked it even less if he were Ortalis.

King Grus turned to go. Over his shoulder, he said, "Have fun with your creatures. Believe me, they don't cause nearly as much trouble as people do." Before Lanius could answer that, Grus left the room.

With no one else there, Lanius naturally turned toward the monkeys, saying, "Do you think he's right?" The monkeys didn't answer. They certainly made less trouble than a human audience, which might have given Lanius some reply he didn't want to hear. Laughing, the king went on, "I bet you wish you could make more trouble. You make plenty when you get the chance."

Still no answer from the monkeys. Lanius took from his belt a small, slim knife. *That* got the animals' attention. They chattered excitedly and swarmed down from the branches. One of them tugged at Lanius' robe. They both held out beseeching little hands, as a human beggar might have.

He laughed. "Think I've got something, do you? Well . . . you're right." He had a couple of peeled hard-boiled eggs he'd brought from the kitchens. The monkeys loved eggs, and healers assured Lanius they were good for them. Healers assured Lanius of all sorts of things he found unlikely. He believed some and ignored others. Here, because the monkeys not only enjoyed the eggs but flourished on them, he chose to believe.

He cut a slice from an egg and gave it to the male, who stuffed it into his mouth. One ancient archival record spoke of teaching monkeys table manners. Lanius had trouble believing that, too. He gave the female some egg. She ate it even faster than the male—if she hesitated, he was liable to steal it from her. Lanius had tried withholding egg from him when he did that, but he didn't understand. It just infuriated him.

Today, the monkeys seemed in the mood for affection. One of them wrapped its little hand around Lanius' thumb as he scratched it behind the ears with his other hand. The expression on the monkey's face looked very much like the one Lanius would have worn had someone done a nice job of scratching his back. He knew he shouldn't read too much into a monkey's grin. Sometimes, though, he couldn't help it.

Prince Ortalis shuffled his feet. He stared down at the floor mosaic. He might have been a schoolboy who'd gotten caught pulling the wings off flies. Back when he was younger, he *had* been a schoolboy who'd gotten caught pulling the wings off flies. "Well?" Grus growled in disgust. "What have you got to say for yourself?"

"*I* don't know," Ortalis answered sullenly. "I don't really *want* to do things like that. Sometimes I just can't help it."

Grus believed him. If he could have helped it, he wouldn't have done—Grus hoped he wouldn't have done—a lot of the things he undoubtedly had. But, while that explained, it didn't justify. "I warned you what would happen if you ever did anything like this again," Grus said heavily.

Ortalis only sneered at him. Grus feared he understood that all too well. He'd warned his legitimate son about a lot of things. He'd warned him, and then failed to follow through on the warnings. No wonder Ortalis didn't believe he ever would.

"How am I supposed to get it through your thick, nasty head that I mean what I tell you?" Grus demanded. "I know one way, by the gods."

"What's that?" Ortalis was still sneering. He might as well have said, *You can't make me do anything.*

He looked almost comically surprised when his father slapped him in the face. "This—and I should have done it a long time ago," Grus said, breathing hard.

"You can't do that," Ortalis blurted in disbelief.

"Oh, yes, I can." Grus slapped him again. "It's not a hundredth part of what you did to those girls. How do you like getting it instead of giving it?"

Ortalis' eyes went so wide, Grus could see white all around his irises. Then, cursing as foully as any river-galley sailor, Ortalis hurled himself at Grus. His churning fists thudded against his father's ribs. "I'll murder you, you stinking son of a whore!" he screamed.

"Go ahead and try." Grus ducked a punch that would have flattened his nose. Ortalis' fist connected with the top of his head. That hurt his son more than it did him. Ortalis howled. Grus hit him in the pit of the stomach. The howl cut off as Ortalis battled to breathe.

He kept fighting even after that. He had courage, of a sort. What he lacked was skill. Grus had learned to fight in a hard school. Ortalis, who'd had things much easier in his life, had never really learned at all. His father gave him a thorough, professional beating.

At last, Ortalis threw up his hands and wailed. "Enough, Father! In the names of the gods, enough! Please!"

Grus stood over him, breathing hard. The king's fists stayed clenched. He willed them open. *If you don't stop now, you'll beat him to death,* he told himself. Part of him wanted to. Realizing that was what made him back away from his son.

"All right," he said, his voice boulders in his throat. "All right. Get up."

"I—I don't think I can."

"You can," Grus ground out. "I know what I did to you. I know what I should have done to you, too—what you really deserved. And so do you."

Ortalis didn't try to argue with him. Keeping quiet was one of the smarter things his son had ever done. Had he denied what Grus said, Grus might have started hitting him again, and might not have been able to stop. Tears and blood and snot smeared across his face, Ortalis struggled upright.

"They—" The prince stopped. He might have started to say something like, *They were just serving girls.* Again, he was smart to keep quiet. That might have fired Grus' fury, too. After a moment, Ortalis said, "I'm sorry."

That was better. It wasn't enough, not even the bare beginnings of enough, but it was better. Grus said, "If you ever do anything like that again, you'll get twice what I just gave you. Do you understand me, Ortalis? I'm not joking. You'd better not think I am."

"I understand you." Ortalis' voice was mushy. His lip was swollen and cut and bleeding. He glared at Grus as well as he could; one eye was swollen shut, the other merely blacked. Grus stared stonily back. His hands ached. So did his ribs, on which Ortalis had connected several times. And so did the heart thudding under those ribs. His heart ached worst of all.

If he'd shown that, everything he'd done to Ortalis would have been wasted. Making his voice stay hard, he said, "Get out of my sight. And go wash yourself. You'll want to stay out of everyone's sight for a few days, believe me."

Ortalis inhaled and opened his mouth. Once more, though, nothing came out. He might have started to say, *I'll tell people my father beats me.* Again, that would have been the wrong thing to throw at the king. Again, he realized it and kept quiet. Left hand clutched to *his* sore ribs, Grus' son and heir turned away from him and made his slow, painful way out the door.

Servants chattered among themselves. Their gossip, though, took a while to drift up through clerks and scribes and noblemen and finally to King Lanius' ears. By the time Lanius heard Grus and Ortalis had had a falling-out, most of the evidence was gone from Ortalis' person. A black eye fades slowly, but a black eye could also have happened in any number of ways. Lanius asked no questions. Ortalis volunteered nothing.

Lanius thought about asking Grus what had happened. His father-in-law, though, did not seem approachable—which was, if anything, an understatement. Lanius resigned himself to never knowing what had gone on.

Then one day he got word that Cristata wanted to see him. He didn't mind seeing her at all, though he carefully didn't wonder about what Sosia would have thought of that sentiment. After curtsying before him, Cristata said, "The gods have blessed Avornis with two fine kings."

"I'm glad you think so," Lanius answered. *Would I be happier if the gods had blessed Avornis with only one fine king? For the life of me, I don't know.* He made himself stop woolgathering. "Do you care to tell me why?"

"Because you told King Grus about what happened to me, and he went and made his own son sorry he did what he did—and then he gave me gold, too," the maidservant answered.

"Did he?" Lanius said. Grus hadn't said a word about doing any such thing.

But Cristata nodded. "He sure did. It's more money than I ever had before. It's almost enough to make me a taxp—" She broke off.

Almost enough to make me a taxpayer. She hadn't wanted to say anything like that to someone who was interested in collecting taxes and making sure other people paid them. Most of the time, she would have been smart not to say anything like that. Today, though, Lanius smiled and answered, "I'll never tell."

Did he feel so friendly to her just because she was a pretty girl? Or was he also trying to show her not everyone in the royal family would behave the way Ortalis had, even if he chanced to get her alone? *What I'd like to do if I chanced to get her alone . . .* He shook his head. *Stop that.*

"King Grus even said he was sorry." Cristata's eyes got big and round. "Can you imagine? A king saying he was sorry? To *me*? And he was so friendly all the time we were talking."

What would Queen Estrilda say if she heard that? Would she wonder whether Grus had shown his . . . friendliness in ways that had nothing to do with talking? Lanius knew he did.

Oblivious to the questions she'd spawned, Cristata went on, "He's going to see if he can send me to the kitchens. There's room to move up there; it's not like laundry or sweeping."

"No, I don't suppose it would be." Lanius' voice was vague. He couldn't have said which branches of palace service offered the chance to get ahead and which were dead ends. Grus knew. He knew—and he acted.

Why don't I know things like that? Lanius wondered after Cristata curtsied again and left the little audience chamber where they'd been talking. Not even the sight of her pertly swinging backside as she left was enough to make him stop worrying at the question. Up until now, knowing things like that had never seemed important the way the reign of, say, King Alcedo—who'd sat on the throne when the Scepter of Mercy was lost—had.

Cristata knew the kitchens, and laundry and sweeping. Lanius would have fainted to learn she'd ever heard of King Alcedo. But Lanius was as ignorant of the world of service as Cristata was of history. Grus knew some of both—less history than Lanius, but also more of service. Lanius wished he had a manual to learn more of that other world.

There was no such manual. He knew that perfectly well. He knew of every book written in Avornis since long before Alcedo's day. He hadn't read them all, or even most of them, but he knew of them.

"I could write it myself," he said thoughtfully. It wouldn't be useful just for him; Crex and all the Kings of Avornis who came after him might find it interesting. First, though, he'd have to learn quite a bit he didn't know yet. And if he needed to summon Cristata now and again to answer questions—well, it was all in the cause of advancing knowledge. Even Sosia would—might—have a hard time complaining.

CHAPTER SEVEN

Grus and Pterocles took turns looking through a peephole in the ceiling of the palace room where the remaining thralls the king had brought back from the south were confined. The winter before, two thralls had gotten out. One of them had almost killed Lanius. The other had almost killed Estrilda, though Grus had no doubt the thrall wanted him dead and not his queen.

The thralls paid no attention to the peephole. They might not have paid any attention even if he'd stood in the room with them. What made them thralls made them less than fully human. Their wits were dulled down to the point where they barely had the use of language. They were more than domestic animals that happened to walk on two legs and not four, but they weren't much more than animals.

They could, after a fashion, manage farms. Down south of the Stura River, in the lands the Menteshe ruled, they raised the crops that helped feed the nomads. The Menteshe didn't have to worry about uprisings from them, any more than they had to worry about uprisings from their cattle.

And yet, the thralls' ancestors had been Avornans who were unlucky enough to dwell in the south when the Menteshe conquered the land. The magic that made them thralls came from the Banished One. Human wizards had had little luck reversing it. Avornan armies had tried to reconquer the lost southern provinces a couple of times—tried and failed, with most of the defeated soldiers made into thralls. After the last such disaster, more than two hundred years before (Lanius knew the exact date), Avornis had given up trying.

Without some way to make thralls back into men and women of the ordinary sort, any reconquest was doomed to fail. Grus realized that, however much he wished he could have gotten around it. And so, leaning toward Pterocles, he asked, "What do you see down there?"

Even if the Chernagor wizard in Nishevatz—or was it the Banished One himself?—had not laid Pterocles low, Grus would have had no enormous confidence that he had the answer. Avornan wizards had wrestled with curing thralls for centuries—wrestled with it and gotten thrown, again and again and again. Alca seemed to have had the beginnings of some good new ideas . . . but Alca was gone, and she wouldn't be coming back. Pterocles was what the king had to work with.

"What do I see?" the wizard echoed. Grus hadn't bothered holding his voice down. Pterocles spoke in a hoarse, worried whisper. "I see emptiness. I see emptiness everywhere."

That didn't surprise Grus. He asked, "How do we go about filling the emptiness with everything people have and thralls don't?"

"Fill the emptiness?" Pterocles laughed. That wasn't mirth coming out, or no sort of mirth with which Grus wanted to be acquainted. Pterocles went on, "If I knew how to fill emptiness, Your Majesty, don't you think I would fill my own? I wish I could. I wonder if I ever will."

"Have you learned anything by watching the thralls?" Grus asked. "Would you like to go in among them and study them at close quarters?"

"Empty. So empty," Pterocles said, and then, "If I went in, how would you tell me apart from them?"

"It wouldn't be hard," Grus answered. "You would be the one acting like an idiot. They wouldn't be acting. They really are idiots."

Again, the laugh that came from Pterocles only raised Grus' hackles. The wizard bent, backside in the air, and peered down at the thralls again. His face bore an expression of horrified fascination. He might have been asking himself whether he was or was not one with them.

After a little while, Grus elbowed him out of the way and looked down at the thralls again on his own behalf. He expected them to be doing what they usually did, which was not very much. Like cats, they spent a lot of time sleeping. Several of them stretched out on couches, snoring or simply lying motionless. One, though, stared up at the peephole with as much interest as Grus showed looking in the other direction.

Alarm ran through Grus. This wasn't the way thralls were supposed to behave. Thralls that acted like thralls were harmless, pitiable things. Thralls that didn't were deadly dangerous, not least because no one expected them to strike.

This one turned away after meeting his eye. It was as though the thrall cared nothing for him. It had been interested when Pterocles was looking down at it, though. What did that mean? Grus hoped it didn't mean the Banished One looked out through the thrall's eyes.

When he asked Pterocles about it, the wizard gave back a vague shrug and answered, "We understand each other, he and I."

"What's that supposed to mean?" Grus demanded. Pterocles only shrugged again.

Grus asked more questions, but Pterocles' answers only got vaguer. At last, the king threw his hands in the air. He went off to his desk to get some work done. If he didn't keep a thumb on Avornis' pulse, who would? Lanius? Grus didn't want his son-in-law getting experience at running the kingdom. He also didn't want Pterocles staying close to the thralls if he wasn't there. He made sure the wizard came away with him. Pterocles looked unhappy, but didn't argue.

When Grus sat down behind the great marble-topped desk from which Kings of Avornis had administered their realm for years uncounted, he found a leather courier's sack on top of it. A note on a scrap of parchment was tied to it. *Brought back from the land of the Chernagors,* it said. *Letters inside with seals still intact.*

"What the . . . ?" Grus muttered. Then he snapped his fingers. This had to be the bundle he'd gotten just before learning the Chernagors from the eastern city-states were marching on his army. What with everything that had happened since, he'd forgotten all about it. Some diligent clerk hadn't.

He thought about chucking the sack. What were the odds any of the letters would matter? In the end, though, sighing, he poured the parchments out onto the broad desktop. *I can go through them in a hurry,* he told himself, and popped the wax seal off the first one with his thumbnail.

A moment later, that letter lay in the trash bin by the desk. It touched on something Lanius had long since dealt with. The second letter followed the first. So did the third. The fourth had to do with a land-tenure case down in the south that had dragged on for years. Grus set it aside to add to the stack he already had on that case.

The fifth letter was from Pelagonia, a medium-sized city down in the middle of the southern plains. From a king's point of view, Pelagonia's chief virtue was that not much ever happened there. Rulers needed places like that, places they didn't have to worry about. Grus couldn't remember the last time he'd gotten a petition from Pelagonia. And yet the script on the outside of the parchment, the script that addressed the letter to him, looked somehow familiar.

"No," he said as he broke the seal. "It can't be." But it was. Estrilda had insisted that he send Alca away from the city of Avornis when she discovered his affair with the witch. He'd picked Pelagonia for her, not least because it was such a quiet, sedate town.

Your Majesty, Alca wrote, *I send this as from a worried subject to her king, not because of anything else that may have happened between us.* Grus grunted at that. As soon as Alca mentioned it, even to disclaim it—maybe especially to disclaim it—she also claimed it. He sighed. He couldn't do anything about that. And if he'd known how big a disappointment Pterocles would prove, he would have thought twice about sending Alca away at all.

She continued, *I am afraid the investigation of the thralls may not be going as well as it should. I should have left more behind in writing, to guide those who would come after me. I would have, if I had known I was leaving the capital so suddenly.* Grus mumbled something under his breath. If that wasn't a dig, he'd never run into one.

I hope that all is well for you and for yours (the last three words were inserted above the line, with a caret to show where they should go) *in the city of Avornis. I hope also that wizards are still studying the thralls. I have heard how two thralls turned on you and Lanius. I rejoice that you are both safe. The thralls still in the palace, I think, can be as dangerous as the ones who already attacked. Unless I am altogether mistaken, the Banished One reaches them in this way.*

The sorcerous charms and calculations that followed meant nothing to Grus. He hadn't expected them to. He knew nothing of magic. Alca went on, *I hope you will show this to a wizard you trust. He will be able to judge whether I am right.*

"I can do that," Grus said, as though she stood there before him. He wondered what Pterocles would make of those scribbled symbols. He also wondered if Pterocles was in any condition to make anything of them.

What I have shown here may also give new hope to returning thralls to true humanity, Alca finished. *The spells will not be easy to shape. Here is a new road, though, and Avornis has long needed that. What I need . . . is something I may not have. I knew that when we began. I cannot imagine why, all this time later, it comes as such of a surprise. With—* A scratched-out word, and then a scrawled signature.

He stared at it for a long time. Because of the calculations, he couldn't even throw the letter away. He made a fist and brought it down hard on the marble desktop, over and over again.

"What did you do to yourself?" Lanius asked Grus; his father-in-law's right hand was puffy and bruised.

"Banged it," Grus said uninformatively.

"Well, yes, but how?" Lanius asked.

"Oh, I managed," Grus answered.

Lanius sent him an exasperated look. Why couldn't Grus just say he'd dropped something on it or caught it in a door or whatever he'd really done to himself? How could you be embarrassed about hurting your hand? Grus evidently was.

Too bad he didn't hurt it knocking some sense into Ortalis, Lanius thought. But then he remembered Grus *had* done his best to knock sense into Ortalis. He probably would have done better if he'd started years earlier. He had tried this time, though. And Ortalis had done his best to stay invisible ever since. That suited Lanius fine.

He tried another question, asking, "What are you going to do when spring comes around again?"

Grus didn't evade there. "Go back to the country of the Chernagors with a bigger army," he answered. "I'm not going to let Vasilko keep Nishevatz any longer than I can help it. That would be like letting someone carrying a plague set up shop across the street from the palace. Life hands you enough troubles without your asking for more."

"Can you take enough soldiers north to beat all the Chernagors?" Lanius inquired.

"You're full of questions today, aren't you?" Grus gave him a quizzical look. "While you're at it, why don't you ask me about my love life, too?"

"How's your love life?" Lanius said, deadpan.

"Certainly nice weather we're having, isn't it?" Grus answered, just as deadpan.

They eyed each other. Then they both started to laugh. "All right,"

Lanius said. "I asked for that, and I think you enjoyed giving it to me. I assume you have something in mind against Prince Vasilko and the rest of the Chernagors and the Banished One?"

"Certainly nice weather we're having, isn't it?" Grus repeated.

That annoyed Lanius. Maybe Grus didn't have anything in mind but didn't want to admit it. Maybe he did, but didn't want to tell his fellow king for fear that Lanius might use it against him or for some other reason, darker still. "What is it?" Lanius snapped. "Do you think I'll take whatever you've got in mind straight to . . . to the Banished One?" He almost said *Milvago,* but decided he didn't want to voice that particular name.

This time, Grus paid him the courtesy of a serious answer. "No, Your Majesty, I don't think that," he said. "What I do think is, the Chernagors and the Banished One are bound to have plenty of spies and plenty of wizards trying to find out what I've got in mind. The more I talk, the more help I give them. I don't want to do that, thanks."

"Oh." Lanius considered. Reluctantly, he nodded. "Yes, all right." It wasn't altogether; he still suspected Grus feared he would use the knowledge himself, and didn't want to give it to him for that reason. That being so, he went on, "But we're the ones who worry the Banished One, aren't we? The ones he comes to in dreams. The two of us, and Alca the witch."

Grus slammed his bruised hand against the wall. He hissed in pain, and then cursed. "Sorry," he said in a gray voice. "You caught me by surprise there. I don't want to remember those dreams."

"Or Alca?" Lanius asked.

Instead of replying, Grus turned away. Did that mean he didn't want to remember Alca or that he didn't want to forget her? Lanius could guess, but a lot of his guesses about Grus had turned out to be wrong. Maybe this one would, too.

Lanius also guessed Grus would storm out of the chamber. That turned out to be a mistake. In fact, the other king turned back. He said, "For whatever it may be worth to you, you have my sympathy on Queen Certhia's passing."

Now Lanius was the one who got angry. "You say that? You're sorry my mother's dead?" he said, his voice rising with every word. "You're the one who sent her to the Maze!"

"I'm sorry she's dead anyhow," Grus answered. "She might have died if she'd stayed in the city of Avornis, you know. She wasn't an ancient granny, but she wasn't a young woman, either." That was true, and hadn't occurred to Lanius. Even so, it did very little to quell his fury. But Grus went on, "I know you don't care to be reminded of it, but she tried to slay me by sorcery—nasty sorcery, too. If it weren't for a strong amulet and Alca's magic, I wouldn't be here now."

Again, Lanius imitated Grus, this time by turning his back. Remembering Alca had probably made Grus remember Queen Certhia. He hadn't said anything about her death up until now. Lanius started to blame him for that, but then checked himself. His mother *had* tried to kill Grus, and Grus hadn't killed her in return. Didn't that count for anything?

With a long, wary sigh, Grus said, "Politics only make families more complicated. You've seen that since you were a baby."

"Politics, yes." If not for politics, Lanius wouldn't have wed Sosia, wouldn't have had Ortalis as brother-in-law or Grus as father-in-law, wouldn't have seen Grus' bastard as Arch-Hallow of Avornis . . . wouldn't have had the Banished One for an enemy.

Grus is the Banished One's enemy, too, Lanius reminded himself. However much he sometimes detested Grus, that was worth remembering. Nobody the Banished One wanted horribly dead could be all bad. One way to know people was by the friends they made. Another was by their foes. Lanius often thought the latter gave the clearer picture.

Then Grus said, "And speaking of politics, how did you like sending soldiers out against that noble last summer?" His voice was oddly constrained.

He's as nervous with me as I am with him, Lanius realized. That was something new. Up until now, Grus had effortlessly dominated him. *I'm growing. The balance between us is shifting.* Lanius answered, "It needed doing." He didn't want Grus too nervous about him. That could prove hazardous.

"I never said it didn't," Grus told him. "I asked how you liked it."

How much do you want power? How much do you enjoy using it? Lanius gave back a shrug. "I wish the nobles didn't cause trouble in the first place."

That drew a laugh from Grus. "Wish for the sun to rise in the west while you're at it. They wish we weren't on the throne, so they could do as they please."

"Yes, no doubt," Lanius said. "They can't always get what they want, though."

"You're right." Now Grus spoke with complete assurance, and addressed Lanius as one equal to another. "What we have to do is give them what they need. And do you know what else?" He waited for Lanius to shake his head, then finished, "When we do, they'll hate us for it." Lanius wanted to tell him he was wrong. His experience and reading, though, suggested Grus was only too likely to be right.

When the first snows of winter fell, Grus wondered whether the Banished One would send blizzard after blizzard against Avornis, as he'd done more than once in the past. Had the king had it in his power, he knew he would have used the weather against his enemies.

But winter was only . . . winter—nothing pleasant, but nothing out of the ordinary, either. Changing the weather couldn't have been easy, even for a being who'd once been a god. The couple of times the Banished One tried it, Avornis had come through better than he'd expected. Grus knew that was largely Lanius' doing; thanks to the other king, the capital and the rest of the cities had laid in supplies well ahead of time. The smaller towns and the countryside didn't need to worry so much.

Because the winter stayed on the mild side, Grus used it to gather soldiers and horses and supplies around the city of Avornis. This time, when he went up into the land of the Chernagors, he would lack nothing a general could possibly bring with him. An afterthought also made him summon wizards from the provinces to the capital. He didn't know how much good they would do him—from what he'd seen, most wizards from small towns and the countryside knew a lot less than those who succeeded in the city of Avornis—but he didn't see how they could hurt.

If anything, the tent cities that sprang up around the walls of the capital were healthier in winter than they would have been in summer. Sicknesses that would have flourished in the heat lay dormant with snow on the ground. Latrines didn't stink the way they would have when the sun shone high and bright and warm in the sky. Flies were nowhere to be seen.

When spring came, Grus was ready to move. He hoped he would catch Prince Vasilko by surprise. Even if he didn't, he thought he could beat Prince Vsevolod's ungrateful son. *If I can't beat him with what I've got here, I can't beat him at all,* he thought. He knew what Vasilko and the other Chernagor princes could throw at him. He thought his chances were good.

"Gods keep you safe," Estrilda said in the quiet of their bedchamber the night before he left for the north.

"Thanks." Grus set a hand on her hip. They lay bare in the royal bed. They'd just made love, which had left both of them almost satisfied. Something had broken after Estrilda found out about his affair with Alca. It was repaired these days, but the broken place and the rough spots where the glue held things together still showed, were still easy to feel. Grus wondered if they would ever smooth down to where he couldn't feel them. After more than a year, he was beginning to doubt it.

She said, "Be careful. The kingdom needs you."

Grus grunted. Estrilda didn't say anything about what *she* needed. There were bound to be good reasons for that. Almost too late, he realized ignoring her words except for that grunt wouldn't be good. He said, "The one thing that worries me is, I won't be able to lay proper siege to their cities, the way I could to Avornan towns."

"Why not?" Estrilda asked. Talking about cities and sieges was impersonal, and so safe enough.

"Because I can't take a fleet north with me," Grus answered. Here, at least, he could talk. Estrilda wouldn't blab, and the royal bedchamber was as well warded against wizardry as any place in Avornis. "The Chernagors can fill their big seagoing ships with more than trade trinkets, curse them. When my army stood in front of Nishevatz last summer, Prince Vasilko brought grain in by sea, and I couldn't do a thing about it. I don't see how I'll be able to stop it this year, either. I'll have to take their cities by storm. I won't be able to starve them out."

"That will cost more men, won't it?" Estrilda said. "That's . . . unfortunate."

"Yes it will, and yes it is," Grus agreed. "I don't see any way around it, though. Most of our galleys sail the Nine Rivers. Some of them scuttle along the coast, but I don't see how I could bring them up to the Chernagor country. One storm along the way and . . ." He shook his head.

"Wouldn't storms wreck the Chernagor ships, too? Then you wouldn't have to worry about them."

Moodily, Grus shook his head. "It's not that simple. Their ships are made to sail on the open sea. Ours mostly aren't. Ours are fine for what they do, but sailing on the Northern Sea isn't it. For the Chernagors, it is. They build stronger than we do. They need to, traveling from one little island to the next the way they do."

"You'll find something." When it came to ships, Estrilda had confidence in the onetime river-galley captain she'd married. When it came to women—she had confidence there, but confidence of the wrong sort.

When Grus thought about it, he had to admit he'd given her reason.

Lanius came out of the city to see him and the army off. "Gods go with you," the other king told him. "We both know how important this is, and why." Again, he didn't say the name Milvago, or even suggest it. Even so, it was there.

Prince Ortalis came out, too. He said not a word to Grus. Grus said nothing to him, either. Each of them looked at the other as though he hoped never to see him again. That was likely to be true.

"Gods bless this army and lead it to victory." Arch-Hallow Anser sounded more cheerful than either Grus or Lanius. If he noticed the way Grus and Ortalis eyed each other, it didn't show on his smiling face.

With a resigned sigh, Grus swung up into the saddle of his horse. *Another summer of riding lessons,* he thought. *I'm turning into a tolerable horseman in spite of myself.*

The only ones who looked eager to return to the land of the Chernagors were Prince Vsevolod and his countrymen who'd gone into exile in Avornis with him. "I will see my son again," Vsevolod said, in tones of fierce anticipation. Grus realized that, as badly as he got along with Ortalis, the two of them were perfect comrades next to Vsevolod and Vasilko.

"Are we ready?" Grus asked General Hirundo.

"If we're not, by Olor's beard, we've certainly wasted a lot of time and money," Hirundo answered.

"Thank you so much. You've made everything clear," Grus said. Hirundo bowed in the saddle. Grus laughed. Prince Vsevolod scowled. Vsevolod, as Grus had seen, spent a lot of time scowling. Grus waved to the trumpeters. The sun flashed golden from the bells of their horns as they raised them to their lips. Martial music filled the air. The Avornans began moving north.

King Lanius wore shabby clothes when he went exploring in the archives. That kept the palace washerwomen happy. It also let him feel easier about putting on hunting togs to go hunting with Arch-Hallow Anser. Was he in perfect style? He neither knew nor cared. If anyone but Anser had invited him out on a hunt, he not only would have said no but probably laughed in the other man's face. But he really liked Anser, and so he'd decided to see just what it was the arch-hallow so enjoyed.

Grus joked about being uncertain on a horse. Lanius really was. He felt too high off the ground, and too likely to arrive there too suddenly. He also felt sure he would be saddlesore come morning. If Olor had meant men to splay their legs apart like that, he would have made them bowlegged to begin with.

Anser took his bow from the case that held both it and a sheaf of arrows. He skillfully strung it, then set an arrow to the string, drew, and let fly. The arrow quivered in the trunk of a tree, a palm's breadth above a prominent knot. "A little high," he said with a rueful shrug. "You try."

Clumsily, Lanius strung his own bow. He couldn't remember the last time he'd held a weapon in his hand. Even more clumsily, he fitted an arrow to the string. Drawing the bow made him grunt with effort. The shaft he loosed came nowhere near the tree, let alone the knot.

Some of the beaters and bodyguards riding along with the king and the arch-hallow snickered. "Oh, dear," Anser said. It wasn't scornful, just sympathetic. There were reasons why everyone liked him.

"I'm in more danger from the beasts than they are from me," Lanius said. If he laughed at himself, maybe the rest of the hunting party wouldn't, or at least not so much.

"You will not be in any danger, Your Majesty," one of the bodyguards declared. "That's why we're along." He had a thoroughly literal mind. No doubt that helped make him a good guard. No doubt it also helped make him a bore.

Bird chirped in the oaks and elms and chestnuts. Lanius heard several different songs. He wondered which one went with which bird. "Look!" He pointed. "That one has something in its beak."

"Building a nest," Anser said. "It's that time of year."

Sunlight came through the leaves in dapples. The horses wanted to stop every few steps and nibble at the ferns that sprang up at the bases of gnarled tree trunks. Lanius would have let them, but Anser pressed on, deeper into the woods. The city of Avornis was only a few miles away, but might have lain beyond the Northern Sea. City air stank of smoke and people and dung. The air here smelled as green as the bright new leaves on the trees.

Wildflowers blazed in a meadow. Butterflies, flitting jewels, darted from one to another. A rabbit nibbled clover. "Shoot it!" Anser said.

"What?" Lanius wondered if he'd heard straight. "Why?"

"Because you're hunting," Anser replied with such patience as he could muster. "Because we want the meat. Rabbit stew, rabbit pie, rabbit with pepper, rabbit . . . Rabbit's run off now."

Lanius almost said, *Good.* If he'd been out with anyone but Anser, he would have. He was more interested in watching the rabbit than in shooting it or eating it. Alive and hopping about, it was fascinating. Dead? No.

Anser made the best of things. "Not easy to shoot a rabbit anyhow. They're best caught with dogs and nets."

"You chase them with *dogs*?" Lanius knew he should have kept quiet, but that got past him. Weakly, he added, "It doesn't seem sporting."

"The idea *is* to catch them, you know," Anser said.

"Well, yes, but . . ." Lanius gave up. "Let's ride some more. It's a nice day."

"So it is," Anser said agreeably. On they rode. If they were going to hunt something, Lanius had imagined bear or lion—something dangerous, where killing it would do the countryside good. When he said as much to the arch-hallow, Anser gave him an odd look. "Aren't deer and boar enough to satisfy you? A boar can be as dangerous as any beast around."

They saw no bears. They saw no lions. They saw no boar, which left Lanius not at all disappointed. They saw a couple of deer. Anser courteously offered Lanius the first shot at the first stag. He thought about shooting wide on purpose, but then decided he was more likely to miss if he aimed straight at it. Miss he did. The stag bounded away, spoiling any chance Anser might have had of hitting it.

Anser didn't say anything. If he thought Lanius had intended to miss, he was too polite and good-natured to start a quarrel by accusing him of it. The next time they saw a deer, though, Anser shot first. "Ha! That's a hit!" he shouted.

"Is it?" Lanius had his doubts. "It ran away, too."

"Now we track it down. I hit it right behind the shoulder. It won't go far." Anser rode after the wounded animal. Wounded it was, too—he used the trail of blood it left to pursue it. The blood came close to making Lanius sick. When he thought of shooting an animal, he thought of it falling over dead the instant the arrow struck home. He'd seen one battle. He knew people didn't do that. But, no matter what Anser said, the trail of blood was much too long to suit Lanius. He tried to imagine what the deer was feeling, then gulped and wished he hadn't.

When they caught up with it, the deer was down but not dead. Blood ran from its mouth and bubbled from its nose. It blinked and tried to rise and run some more, but couldn't. Anser knelt beside it and cut its throat. Then he slit its belly and reached inside to pull out the offal. How Lanius held down his breakfast, he never knew.

"Not such a bad day," Anser said as they rode back toward the city of Avornis. Lanius didn't reply.

But he also didn't refuse the slab of meat the arch-hallow sent to the palace. Once the cooks were done with it, it proved very tasty. And he didn't have to think of where it came from at all.

As they had the year before, the farmers along the path Grus' army took toward the north fled when it came near. The army was bigger this year, which only meant more people ran away from it. They took their livestock, abandoned their fields, and ran off to the hills and higher ground away from the road.

Prince Vsevolod seemed surprised that bothered Grus. "Is an army," he said, waving to the tents sprouting like mushrooms by the side of the road.

"Well, yes," Grus agreed. "We're not here to churn butter."

General Hirundo snickered. He took himself even less seriously than Grus did. "Churning butter?" Vsevolod said with another of his fearsome frowns—his big-nosed, strong-boned, wrinkled face was made for disapproval. "What you talk about? Is an army, like I say. Army steals. Army always steals."

"An army shouldn't steal from its own people," Grus said.

Vsevolod stared at him in even more confusion than when he'd talked about butter. "Why not?" the Chernagor demanded. "What difference it make? No army, no people. So army steal. So what?"

"You may be right." Grus used that phrase to get rid of persistent nuisances. Vsevolod went off looking pleased with himself. Like most nuisances, he didn't realize it wasn't even close to the agreement it sounded like.

The breeze brought the odors of sizzling flatbread, porridge in pots, and roasting beef to Grus' nostrils. It also brought another savory odor, one that sent spit flooding into his mouth. "Tell me what that is," he said to Hirundo.

Hirundo obligingly sniffed. "Roast pork," he answered without hesitation.

"That's what I thought, too," Grus said. "Now, did we bring any pigs up from the city of Avornis?"

They both knew better. Pigs, short-legged and with minds of their own, would have been a nightmare to herd. Grus couldn't imagine an army using them for meat animals, not unless it was staying someplace for months on end. The only place soldiers could have gotten hold of a pig was from farmers who hadn't fled fast enough.

"Shall I try to track down the men cooking pork?" Hirundo asked.

"No, don't bother," Grus answered wearily. "They'll all say they got it from someone else. They always do." Vsevolod hadn't been wrong. Armies *did* plunder their own folk. The difference between the Prince of Nishevatz and the King of Avornis was that Grus wished they didn't. Vsevolod didn't care.

When morning came, the army started for the Chernagor country again. Day by day, the mountains separating the coastal lowlands from Avornis climbed higher into the sky, notching the northern horizon. Riding along in the van, Grus had no trouble seeing that. Soldiers back toward the rear of the army probably hadn't seen the mountains yet, because of all the dust the men and their horses and wagons kicked up. When the king looked back in the direction of the city of Avornis, he couldn't see more than half the army. The rest disappeared into a haze of its own making.

The army had come within two or three days' march of the mountains when a courier rode up from the south. "Your Majesty! Your Majesty!" he shouted, and then coughed several times from the dust hanging in the air.

"I'm here," Grus called, and waved to show where he was. "What is it?" Whatever it was, he didn't think it would be good. Good news had its own speed—not leisurely, but sedate. Bad news was what had to get where it was going as fast as it could.

"Here, Your Majesty." The courier came up alongside him. His horse was caked with dusty foam. It was blowing hard, its dilated nostrils fire-red. The rider thrust a rolled parchment at Grus.

He broke the seal and slid off the ribbon that helped hold the parchment closed. Unrolling it was awkward, but he managed. He held it out at arm's length to read; his sight had begun to lengthen. Before he got even halfway through it, he was cursing as foully as he knew how.

"What's gone wrong, Your Majesty?" General Hirundo asked.

"It's the Chernagors, that's what," Grus answered bitterly. "A whole great fleet of them, descending on the towns along our east coast. Some are sacked, some besieged—they've caught us by surprise. Some of the bastards are sailing up the Nine Rivers, too, and attacking inland towns by the riverside. They haven't done anything like this in I don't know how long." *Lanius could tell me,* he thought. But Lanius wasn't here.

Hirundo cursed, too. "What do we do, then?" he asked.

Grus looked ahead. Yes, he could cross into the land of the Chernagors in two or three days. How much good would that do him? Nishevatz was ready, more than ready, to stand siege. While he reduced it—if he could reduce it—what would the Chernagor pirates be doing to Avornis? What did he have to put into river galleys and defend his own cities but this army here? Not much, and he knew it. Tasting gall, he answered, "We turn around. We go back."

CHAPTER EIGHT

King Lanius had hoped to welcome King Grus back to the city of Avornis as a conquering hero. Grus was back in the capital, all right, but as a haggard, harried visitor, ready to rush toward the south and east to fight the Chernagors. "You got this news before I did," Grus said in his brief sojourn in the palace. "What did you do?"

"Sent it on to you," Lanius answered.

Grus exhaled through his nose. "Anything else?"

Hesitantly, Lanius nodded. "I sent an order to river-galley skippers along the Nine Rivers to head for the coast and fight the invaders. That doesn't count the ships here by the capital. I told them to stay put because I thought your army would need them." He waited. If he'd made a botch of things, Grus would come down on him like a rockslide.

His father-in-law exhaled again, but on a different note—relief, not exasperation. "Gods be praised. You did it right. You did it just right. I couldn't have done better if I'd been here myself."

"You mean that?" Lanius asked. Praise had always been slow heading his way. He had trouble believing it even when he got it.

But Grus nodded solemnly. "We can't do anything without men and ships. The faster they get to the coast, the better." His laugh held little mirth. "A year ago, I was wondering how the Chernagors' ocean-going ships would measure up against our river galleys. This isn't how I wanted to find out."

"Yes, it should be interesting, shouldn't it?" To Lanius, the confrontation was abstract, not quite real.

"You don't understand, do you?" Grus was testy now, not handing out praise. "If we lose, they'll ravage our coast all year long. They'll go up the rivers as far as they like, and they'll keep on plundering the riverside cities, too. This isn't a game, Your Majesty." He turned the royal title into one of reproach. "The kingdom hasn't seen anything like this since the Chernagors first settled down in this part of the world, however many years ago that was."

Lanius knew, but it didn't matter right this minute. He nodded. "All right. I do take your point."

"Good." Grus, to his relief, stopped growling. "You must, really, or you wouldn't have done such a nice job setting things up so we'll be able to get at the Chernagors in a hurry."

For a moment, that praise warmed Lanius, too. Then he looked at it with the critical eye he used when deciding how much truth a chronicle or a letter held. Wasn't Grus just buttering him up to make him feel better? Lanius almost called him on it, but held his peace. What was even worse than Grus trying to keep him happy? The answer came to mind at once—Grus not bothering to keep him happy.

Three days later, Lanius was able to stop worrying about whether Grus kept him happy. The other king had loaded his men aboard river galleys and as much other shipping around the capital as Lanius had commandeered. The army's horses stood nervously on barges and rafts. Lanius watched from the wall as the force departed with as little ceremony as it had arrived.

One vessel after another, the fleet slid around a bend in the river. A grove of walnuts hid the ships from sight from the capital. Lanius didn't wait for the last one to disappear. As soon as the river galley that held Grus glided around that bend, he turned away. Bodyguards came to stiff attention. They formed a hollow square around him to escort him back to the palace.

He was about halfway there, passing through a marketplace full of honking geese and pungent porkers, when he suddenly started to laugh. "What's so funny, Your Majesty?" a guardsman asked.

"Nothing, really," Lanius answered. He wasn't about to tell the soldier that he'd suddenly realized the city of Avornis was *his* again. Grus had taken it back in his brief, tumultuous stay. He would reclaim it again after this campaigning season ended. But for now, as it had the past summer, the royal capital belonged to Lanius.

If the king said that to the guard, it might reach the other king. Unpleasant things might happen if it did. Lanius had learned a courtier's rules of survival ever since he'd stopped making messes on the floor. One of the most basic was saying nothing that would land you in trouble if you could avoid it. He still remembered, and used, it.

The doors to the palace were thrown wide to let in light and air. That almost let Lanius ignore how massive they were, how strong and heavy their hinges, how immense the iron bar that could help hold them closed. They weren't saying anything they didn't have to, either. For now, they seemed innocent and innocuous and not especially strong.

But they really are, he thought. *Am I?*

Hirundo looked faintly—maybe more than faintly—green. To Grus, the deck of a river galley was the most natural thing in the world. "Now you know how I feel on horseback," the king said.

His general managed a faint smile. "Your Majesty, if you fall off a horse, you're not likely to drown," he observed, and then gulped. Yes, he was more than faintly green.

"Horses don't come with rails," Grus said. "And if you need to give back breakfast there, kindly lean out over the one the galley has. The sailors won't love you if you get it on the deck."

"If I need to heave it up, I won't much care what the sailors think," Hirundo replied with dignity. Grus gave him a severe look. Puking on the deck proved a man a lubber as surely as trying to mount from the right side of the horse proved a man no rider. Under the force of that look, Hirundo grudged a nod. "All right, Your Majesty. I'll try."

Grus knew he would have to be content with that. A weak stomach could prove stronger than good intentions. That thought made the king wonder how Pterocles was taking the journey. As far as Grus knew, the wizard hadn't traveled far on the Nine Rivers.

Pterocles stood near the port rail. He wasn't hanging on to it, and he didn't seem especially uncomfortable. As he looked out at the fields and apple and pear orchards sliding by, the expression on his face was more . . . distant than anything else. King Grus nodded to himself. That was the word, all right. Pterocles had never quite been himself after the Chernagor wizard—or *had* it been the Banished One himself?—struck him down outside of Nishevatz. Something was missing . . . from his spirit? From his will? Grus had a hard time pinpointing where the trouble lay, but he feared it was serious.

Prince Vsevolod had stayed behind in the city of Avornis. Nothing he could say would be likely to make the Chernagor pirates change their minds. Grus didn't miss him. *Lanius likes being king,* he thought. *Let him put up with Vsevolod. That'll teach him.*

Before long, groves of olives and almonds would replace the fruit trees that grew here. The fleet wasn't very far south or east of the capital; they'd just emerged from the confusing tangle of streams in the Maze the day before. Down farther south, farmers would grow only wheat and barley; rye and oats would disappear. Before long, though, vineyards would take the place of some of the grainfields.

The Granicus ran down toward the Azanian Sea through the middle of a wide, broad valley. The hills to the north and south were low and weathered, so low they hardly deserved the name. But smaller streams flowed into the Granicus from those hills to either side. Beyond the watersheds, the streams ran into neighbors from among the Nine Rivers.

I sent Alca to a riverside town, Grus thought, and hoped none of the pirates had come to Pelagonia. This was the first time he'd come to the south himself since sending her away from the capital. But Pelagonia did not lie along the Granicus, and the king had other things on his mind besides the witch he'd once loved—still loved, though he hadn't let himself think that while he was anywhere near Estrilda.

As day followed day and Grus' fleet sped down the Granicus, he spent more and more time peering ahead, looking for smoke to warn him he was drawing near the Chernagors. Once he saw some rising into the air, but it proved only a grass fire in a field. It might have been a catastrophe for the farmer the field belonged to. To Grus, it was just a distraction.

And then, a day later, lookouts—and, very soon, Grus himself—spied another black column of smoke. Grus had a good idea of where they were along the Granicus, though he hadn't traveled the river for several years. To make sure, he asked the steersman, "That's Araxus up ahead, isn't it?"

"Yes, Your Majesty." The man at the steering oar nodded. "When we round this next bend in the river, we'll be able to see the place."

He proved not quite right. When they rounded the bend, all they could see was the smoke spilling out from the gutted town. Of Araxus itself there was no sign. But Grus pointed to the ships tied up at the quays. "No one in Avornis ever built those."

"How can you tell, Your Majesty?" Hirundo asked.

Grus gaped. His general *was* a lubber, and no more a judge of ships than Grus was of horseflesh. "By looking," the king answered. "They're bigger and beamier than anything we build, and see those masts?"

"They're ships," Hirundo said.

"Yes, and we're going to sink them." Grus turned to the oarmaster. "Step up the stroke. Let's hurry." As the man nodded and got the rowers working harder, Grus told the trumpeter, "Signal the rest of the fleet to up the stroke, too. We don't want to waste any time."

"Yes, Your Majesty." The man raised the trumpet to his lips and sent the signal to the other ships close by. Their trumpets passed it along to the rest of the fleet.

The Chernagors ravaging Araxus were alert. They spotted the Avornan fleet as soon as it rounded the bend in the river. Grus couldn't see the pirates in the town itself, but he saw them when they came out and ran for their ships. He wondered what they would do once they had them manned. The wind blew out of the east, from the direction of the sea. That had let them sail up the Granicus to Araxus. But the only way they could flee down the river, away from the galleys, was by drifting with the current. If they tried that, the oar-powered Avornan ships would catch them in short order.

Grus wondered what he would have done if caught in a like predicament. No sooner had the thought, *Make the best fight I could,* crossed his mind than the Chernagor ships put on their full spread of sail—a stunning spread, by Avornan standards—and started *up* the Granicus toward the river galleys.

"Now I see it. They *are* bigger than we are." Hirundo sounded nervous. "Can we beat them?"

"If we can't, we'd have done better to stay back in the city of Avornis, don't you think?" Grus asked. Hirundo grinned. Grus knew he had to seem confident. In truth, he had no idea what would happen next. How long had it been since the Chernagors and Avornans squared off against each other on the water? He had no idea. Lanius had tried to tell him, but he hadn't let the other king finish.

He wished things happened quicker aboard ship, but no help for that. The Chernagor pirates had to claw their way upstream against the current. More than a quarter of an hour passed between their weighing anchor and the first arrows splashing into the Granicus. The pirates had only half a dozen ships, but they were all jammed full of men. And with their high freeboard, getting Avornan warriors into them from the lower galleys wouldn't have been easy even if they hadn't been.

"Ram the bastards!" Grus shouted. Without his giving the order to the trumpeter, the man sent it on—cleansed of the curse by his mellow notes—to the rest of the fleet. To his own crew, Grus called, "'Ware boarders! If we stick fast when we ram, they'll swarm down onto us."

More and more arrows flew from the pirate ships. Grus had never had to worry about so many in a river battle; he might almost have been fighting on land. A couple of rowers were hit. That fouled the stroke. The oarmaster screamed curses until the wounded men were dragged from their benches and replaced. Archers at the bows of the river galleys were shooting along with the Chernagors, emptying their quivers as fast as they could. A pirate threw up his hands and splashed into the Granicus, an arrow through his throat.

The oarmaster upped the stroke again, this time without waiting for a command from Grus. The steersman aimed the bronze-tipped ram at the planking just to port of the bow of a pirate ship. Where everything had seemed to move slowly before, all at once the pirate ship swelled enormously.

"Brace yourselves!" Grus shouted just before the collision.

Crunch! The ram bit. Grus staggered but kept his feet. "Back oars!" the oarmaster screamed. The rowers did, with all the strength they had in them. If the ram did stick fast in the pirate's timbers, the Chernagors would board and slaughter them.

"Olor be praised!" Grus gasped when the river galley pulled free. The pointed ram had torn a hole two feet wide in the pirate ship, just below the waterline. The Granicus flooded in. The extra weight, growing every moment, slowed the ship to a crawl.

"Ram 'em again, sir?" the steersman asked.

Grus shook his head. "No. We got enough of what we needed." He would have done far more damage striking another river galley. The Chernagor ships, built to withstand long voyages and pounding ocean waves, were even more strongly made than he'd expected.

He looked around to see how the rest of the fight was going. One pirate ship had ridden up and over the luckless river galley that tried to ram it. Avornans, some clutching oars, splashed in the Granicus. Another Chernagor ship traded archery with three river galleys. Two more pirate ships besides the one Grus had struck had been rammed, and were taking on water. One pirate ship was afire. A river galley burned, too—the Chernagors had flung jars of oil lit with wicks down onto its deck. More Avornans went into the river. So did Chernagors from the northerners' burning ship. Grus wondered whether they'd set themselves ablaze. Savagely, he hoped so.

He pointed to the ship that had defeated one ramming attempt. "Turn about!" he called to the steersman. "We'll get 'em in the rear."

"Right!" The steersman threw back his head and laughed. "Just what they deserve, too, Your Majesty."

How the Chernagors on the pirate ship howled as the sharp-beaked river galley sped toward its stern! They sent a blizzard of arrows at Grus, who wished he wore something less conspicuous. He wanted to go below, but that would have made him look like a coward in front of his men. *The things we do for pride,* he thought as an arrow stood thrilling in the river galley's deck a few inches in front of his boot.

Crunch! Again, the river galley shuddered as the ram struck home. Again, the oarmaster bellowed, "Back oars!" Again, the rowers pulled like men possessed. Again, Grus breathed a sigh of relief when the ram *did* pull free.

This time, though, the Chernagor ship didn't sink. The skipper ran her aground in the shallows before she filled too much and became altogether unmanageable. Pirates leaped off her and splashed ashore. Grus knew he would have to land men, too. The galleys had outpaced other forces following on the river and by land. If all the pirates had taken to their heels through the fields, they would have been very troublesome. The survivors from one ship? Probably not.

Hirundo seemed to think along the same lines. "Not *too* bad, Your Majesty," he said.

"No, not too," Grus agreed. "Not yet. But we've only just started cleaning them out. This is the first bunch we've run into, and maybe the smallest."

Hirundo made a horrible face. Then, very reluctantly, he nodded.

King Lanius sat in the royal archives, delightfully encased in quiet. More dust motes than usual danced in the sunbeams that pushed through the dirty skylights overhead. Lanius had been shoving boxes around again, looking for interesting things he hadn't seen before. He often did that. He didn't often get rewarded as handsomely as he had this time.

He had to stop and think how long ago King Cathartes had reigned. Seven hundred years ago? Eight hundred? Something like that. Cathartes hadn't spent an especially long time on the Diamond Throne, nor had his reign been distinguished. But, like all Kings of Avornis until the Menteshe stole it, he'd wielded the Scepter of Mercy. Unlike most of them, he'd worked hard to describe what that was like.

Without both patience and luck, Lanius never would have come across the time-yellowed scrap of parchment. Patience encompassed the labor of digging out new boxes of documents and the different but even more wearing labor of going through them one by one to see what each was. Luck came in when King Cathartes' letter got stuck by fragments of wax from its seal to a much less interesting report on sheep farming in the Granicus valley that was only a quarter as old. If Lanius hadn't been paying attention, he would have put the report on wool and mutton aside without noticing it had another document riding on its back.

King Cathartes' script looked strange, but Lanius could puzzle it out. The language was old-fashioned, but not impossibly so. And Cathartes was talking about something that fascinated Lanius, so the present king worked especially hard. *Oft have men of me inquired, What feel you? What think you? on laying hold of the most excellent Scepter. Hath it the massiness of some great burthen in your hand, as seemingly it needs must, being of size not inconsiderable? Let all know, as others have said aforetimes, a man seizing the Scepter of Mercy in the cause of righteousness is in sooth likewise seized by the same.*

Lanius wondered what the cause of righteousness was, and how any man, let alone a King of Avornis holding the Scepter of Mercy, could know he was following it. Did Cathartes mean the Scepter gave some sign of what was right and what wasn't? Perhaps he did, for he went on, *Know that, when rightly wielded, the Scepter weigheth in the hand, not naught—for that were, methinks, a thing impossible e'en 'mongst the gods— but very little, such that a puling babe, purposing to lift it for the said righteous cause, would find neither hindrance nor impediment.*

But if a man depart from that which is good, if he purpose the use of the aforesaid Scepter of Mercy in a cause unjust, then will he find he may not lift it at all, but is prevented from all his ends, Cathartes wrote.

"Well, well," Lanius murmured. "Isn't that interesting?" It wasn't just interesting. It was new, and he'd almost despaired of finding anything new about the Scepter of Mercy. Most Kings of Avornis who'd written about it at all had been maddeningly vague, insisting the wielding of the Scepter was a matter of touch without ever explaining how. Cathartes had been far more forthcoming.

It also explained far more than Cathartes could have dreamed. For four hundred years, the Scepter of Mercy had lain in Yozgat. In all that time, so far as Lanius knew, the Banished One had never picked it up and used its powers against his foes. Like all Avornan kings over those four centuries, Lanius was glad the Banished One hadn't, but he'd never understood why not. Now, perhaps, he did. After the Menteshe brought it back to him, had he tried to lift it, tried and failed? No proof, of course. But it seemed more reasonable to Lanius than any other idea he'd ever had along those lines.

Maybe it meant even more than that. Maybe it meant the gods had been justified in casting Milvago down from the heavens, making him into the Banished One. Didn't it argue that his goal of forcing his way back into the heavens was anything but righteous? Or did it just say their magic rejected him even as they had themselves?

Lanius laughed. *How am I, one mortal man sitting by himself in these dusty archives, supposed to figure out all the workings of the gods?* If that wasn't unmitigated gall, he couldn't imagine what would be.

He wished he could talk with Grus about it. That failing, he wished Avornis had an arch-hallow whose passion was learning about and seeking to understand the gods, not tracking down a deer after he'd put an arrow in its side. Lanius might have trusted such an arch-hallow with the terrifying secret of Milvago. Anser? No. However much Lanius liked Grus' bastard, he knew he was a lightweight.

He even understood why Grus had chosen to invest Anser with the red robe. Anser was unshakably loyal to his father. (*And how many people are unshakably loyal to me?* Lanius wondered. *Is anyone?*) That had enormous advantages for the other king. But sometimes an arch-hallow who did more than fill space would have been useful. Lanius almost wished Bucco still led services in the cathedral, and Bucco would have married him off to King Dagipert of Thervingia's daughter if he'd had his way.

Now, Lanius asked himself, *what to do with Cathartes' letter?* At first, he wanted to put it in some prominent place. Instead, he ended up using its bits of sealing wax to reattach it to the report on sheep in the Granicus valley to which it had clung for so long. Sometimes obscurity was best.

Only after Lanius had left the archives did he wonder whether that applied to him as well as to what King Cathartes had written all those years ago. Little by little, he'd realized he didn't much want to challenge Grus for the sole rule of Avornis, so maybe it did. And if he didn't, he might get along with—and work with—his father-in-law better than he ever had before.

Down the Granicus toward the Azanian Sea sailed the fleet of river galleys Grus commanded. Other flotillas and contingents of soldiers were, he hoped, clearing more of the Nine Rivers and their valleys of the Chernagor pirates.

He'd had to fight again, at Calydon. The Chernagors there weren't plundering the town. They were holding it, and hadn't intended to give it back to any mere Avornans. Grus used the same ploy he'd succeeded with against Baron Lev at the fortress of Varazdin. He made an ostentatious attack against the waterfront from the river. When he judged most of the pirates had rushed to that part of Calydon, he sent soldiers against the land wall. They got inside the city before the Chernagors realized they were in trouble. After that, Calydon fell in short order. His biggest trouble then was keeping the inhabitants from massacring the Chernagors he'd taken prisoner.

When he heard some of the stories about what the Chernagors did while holding Calydon, he was more than halfway sorry he hadn't let the people do what they wanted. By then, he'd sent the captured pirates back into the countryside under guard. He didn't know just what he would do with them—put them to work in the mines, maybe, or exchange them for Avornans their countrymen had taken. *And if I don't do either of those,* he thought, *I can always give them back to the people of Calydon.*

As his river galleys and soldiers headed east again, he asked Hirundo, "Did you expect anything like what we saw there?"

"Not me, your Majesty." Hirundo shook his head, then looked as though he wished he hadn't; any motion might be enough to make him queasy while he paced the deck of a river galley. After a gulp, he went on, "They fought us clean enough in their own country last year. Hard, yes, but clean enough. Not like . . . that."

"No, not like that," Grus agreed. "They might as well have been Menteshe, slaughtering the wounded and killing men who tried to yield. And what they did to the people in Calydon was ten times worse." Over by the rail, Pterocles stirred. The king waved to the wizard. "You have something to say?"

"I'm . . . not sure, Your Majesty," Pterocles replied. Grus hoped he hid his frown. Pterocles wasn't sure of much of anything these days. To be fair, he also wasn't the best of sailors, though he was better than Hirundo. Like the general, he paused to gather himself before continuing, "I'm not as surprised as you are, I don't think."

"Oh? Why not?" Grus asked.

The wizard looked not north, not east, but to the south. In the hollow tones that had become usual since his double overthrow in the land of the Chernagors, he said, "Why not? Because they've had a year longer now to listen to the Banished One, to let him into their hearts."

"Oh," Grus said again, this time on a falling note. Pterocles made more sense than the king wished he did. The wizard didn't seem to care whether he made sense or not. Somehow, that made him seem more convincing, not less.

Grus hoped the fleet was still outrunning the news of its coming. If he could get to the sea before the Chernagors along the coast heard he was there, he would have a better chance against them. On the Granicus and, he believed, the rest of the Nine Rivers, his galleys had the advantage over the Chernagors' sailing ships. They were both faster and more agile. Whether that would hold true on the wide waters of the sea was liable to be a different question.

The Granicus, a clear, swift-flowing stream, carried little silt and had no delta to speak of. One moment, or so it seemed to Grus, the river flowed along as it always had. The next, the horizon ahead widened out to infinity. The Azanian Sea awed him even more than the Northern Sea had. That probably had nothing to do with the sea itself. In the Chernagor country, the weather had been cloudy and hazy, which limited the seascape. Here, he really felt as though he could see forever.

But seeing forever didn't really matter. On the north bank of the Granicus, the town of Dodona sat by the edge of the sea. It lay in Chernagor hands. The fresh smoke stains darkening the wall around the town said the corsairs had burned it when they took it.

Several Chernagor ships were tied up at the wharves. The pirates didn't seem to expect trouble. Grus could tell exactly when they spied his fleet. Suddenly, Dodona began stirring like an aroused anthill. *Too late,* he thought, and gave his orders. "We'll hit 'em hard and fast," he declared. "It doesn't look like it'll be even as tough as Calydon. If it is, we'll try the same trick we used there—feint at the harbor and then go in on the land side. But whatever we do, we have to keep those ships from getting away and warning the rest of the Chernagors."

Almost everything went the way he'd hoped. Some of the pirates fought bravely as individuals. He'd seen in the north and here in Avornis that they were no cowards. But in Dodona they had no time to mount a coordinated defense. Like ice when warm water hits it, they broke up into fragments and were swept away.

Several of their ships burned by the piers. Avornan marines and soldiers swarmed onto others. But the Chernagors got a crew into one, hoisted sail, and fled northward propelled by a strong breeze from out of the south. That was when Grus really saw what the great spread of canvas they used could do. He sent two river galleys after the Chernagor ship. The men rowed their hearts out, but the pirate ship still pulled away. Grus cursed when it escaped. The Granicus might be cleared of Chernagors, but now all the men from the north would know he was hunting them.

"No, thank you," Lanius said. "I don't feel like hunting today."

Arch-Hallow Anser looked surprised and disappointed. "But didn't you enjoy yourself the last time we went out?" he asked plaintively.

"I enjoyed the company—I always enjoy your company," Lanius said. "And I liked the venison. The hunt itself? I'm very sorry, but . . ." He shook his head. "Not to my taste."

"We should have flushed a boar, or a bear," Anser said. "Then you'd have seen some real excitement."

"I don't much care for excitement." Lanius marveled at how the arch-hallow had so completely misunderstood him. "I just don't see the fun of tramping through the woods looking for animals to slaughter. If you do, go right ahead."

"I do. I will. I'm sorry you don't, Your Majesty." Hurt still on his face, Anser strode down the palace hallway.

Oh, dear, Lanius thought. He almost called after Anser, telling him he'd come along after all. He was willing to pay nearly any price to keep Anser happy with him. But the key word there was *nearly.* Going hunting again flew over the limit.

Instead, he went to the moncats' room, where he had an easel set up. He'd discovered a certain small talent for painting the last few years, and he knew more about moncats than anyone else in Avornis. *Than anyone who doesn't live on the islands they come from,* he thought, and wondered how many people lived on those islands out in the Northern Sea. That was something he'd never know.

What he did know was that Petrosus, Grus' treasury minister, was slow and stingy with the silver he doled out. No doubt that was partly at Grus' order, to help keep Lanius from accumulating power to threaten the other king. But Petrosus, whatever his reasons, enjoyed what he did. Lanius had sold several of the pictures of moncats he'd painted. As far as he knew, no King of Avornis had ever done anything like that before. He felt a modest pride at being the first.

He watched the moncats scramble and climb, looking for a moment he could sketch in charcoal and then work up into a real painting. When he'd first started painting the animals, he'd tried to get them to pose. He'd even succeeded once or twice, by making them take a particular position to get bits of food. But, as with any cats, getting moncats to do what he wanted usually proved more trouble than it was worth. These days, he let the moncats do what they wanted and tried to capture that on canvas.

A moncat leaped. His hand leaped, too. There was the moment. He'd known it without conscious thought. His hand was often smarter than his brain in this business. He sketched rapidly, letting that hand do what it would. His stick of charcoal scratched over the canvas.

When he finished the sketch, he stepped back from it, took a good look—and shook his head. This wasn't worth working up. Every so often, his leaping hand betrayed him. *If I'd really been taught this sketching business, I'd do better.*

He laughed. Several moncats sent him wide-eyed, curious stares. If the sketch had looked as though it was pretty good, Bubulcus or some other servant would have knocked on the door in the middle of it, and it never would have been the same afterwards. That had happened, too.

Before long, he tried another sketch. This one turned out better— not great, but better. He concentrated hard, working to make the drawing show some tiny fraction of a climbing moncat's fluidity. He was never happier than when he concentrated hard. Maybe that was why he enjoyed both the painting and his sorties into the archives.

Both painting and archive-crawling would have made Anser yawn until the top of his head fell off. Put him in the woods stalking a deer, though, and he concentrated as hard as anyone—and he was happy then (unless he missed his shot, of course).

For a moment, Lanius thought he'd stumbled onto something important. But then he realized he'd just rephrased the question. Why did old parchments make him concentrate, while the arch-hallow needed to try not to crunch a dry leaf under his foot? Lanius still didn't know.

He worked hard turning the sketch into a finished painting, too. He always put extra effort into getting the texture of the moncats' fur right. He'd had some special brushes made, only a few bristles wide. They let him suggest the countless number of fine hairs of slightly different colors that went into the pelts. The real difficulty, though, didn't lie in the brushes. The real difficulty lay in his own right hand, and he knew it. If he'd had more skill and more training, he could have come closer to portraying the moncats as they really were.

Every so often, one of the animals would come over and sit close by him while he painted. The moncats never paid any attention to the work on his easel; they did sometimes try to steal his brushes or his little pots of paint. Maybe the linseed oil that held the pigments smelled intriguing. Or maybe it was the odor of the bristles. Then again, maybe the moncats were just nuisances. When one of them made a getaway to the very top of the room with a brush, Lanius was inclined to believe it. After gnawing at the handle of the brush, the moncat got bored with it and let it drop. Lanius scooped it up before another animal could steal it.

He was carrying the finished painting down the hall when a maidservant coming the other way stopped to admire it. "So that's what your pets look like, Your Majesty," she said.

"Yes, that's right, Cristata," he answered.

"That's very good work," she went on, looking closer. "You can see every little thing about them. Are their back feet really like that, with the funny big toes that look like they can grab things?"

"They *can* grab things," he said. "Moncats are born climbers—and born thieves." After a moment, he added, "How are you these days?"

"Fair," she answered. "*He* doesn't bother me anymore, so that's something." She didn't want to name Ortalis, for which Lanius couldn't blame her. She went on, "The money you and King Grus gave me, that's nice. I've never had money before, except to get by on from day to day. But . . ." Her pretty face clouded.

"What's the matter?" Lanius asked. "Don't tell me you're running short already."

"Oh, no. It isn't that. I try hard to be careful," she said. "It's just that . . ." She turned red; Lanius watched—watched with considerable interest—as the flush rose from her neck to her hairline. "I shouldn't tell you this."

"Then don't," Lanius said at once.

"No. If I can't tell you, who can I tell? You saw . . . what happened . . . with my shoulder and my back." Cristata waited for him to nod before continuing, "Well, there was a fellow, a—oh, never mind what he does here. I liked him, and I thought he liked me. But when he got a look at some of that . . . he didn't anymore." She stared down at the floor.

"Oh." Lanius thought, then said. "If that bothered him, you're probably well rid of him. And besides—"

Now he was the one who stopped, much more abruptly than Cristata had. He feared he was also the one who turned red. "You're sweet, Your Majesty," the serving girl murmured, which meant she knew exactly what he hadn't said. She went up the hall. He went down it, trying to convince himself nothing had happened, nothing at all.

CHAPTER NINE

The ocean was an unfamiliar world for Grus. Up until now, he'd been out upon it only a handful of times. If his river galley and the rest of the fleet sailed much farther, they would go out of sight of land. Avornan coastal traders never did anything like that. Even now, with the horizon still reassuringly jagged off to the west, he worried about making his way back to the mainland.

He worried about it, yes, but he went on, even though he increasingly had the feeling of being a bug on a plate, just waiting for someone to squash him. He didn't see that he had much choice. To the Chernagors, the open ocean wasn't a wasteland, a danger. It was a highway. They'd come all this way from their own country to Avornis to prey on his kingdom. He couldn't sail back to theirs, not from here. His ships couldn't carry enough supplies for their rowers or spread enough sail to do without those rowers. He didn't want to think about how they would handle in a bad storm, either.

But he could—he hoped he could—convince the pirates that they couldn't harry his coasts without paying a higher price than they wanted. As far as he knew, his men had cleared them out of all the river valleys where they'd landed. But their ships weren't like his. They could linger offshore for a long time—exactly how long he wasn't sure—and strike as they pleased. They could . . . if he didn't persuade them that was a bad idea.

Tall and proud, the Chernagors' ships bobbed in line ahead, not far out of bowshot. The wind had died to a light breeze, which made the river galleys more agile than the vessels from out of the north. The Chernagors wouldn't be easy meat, though, not when their ships were crammed with fighting men. If a ramming attempt went wrong, the pirates could swarm aboard a galley and make it pay. They'd proved that in earlier fights.

Hirundo checked his sword's edge with his thumb. He nodded to Grus. "Well, Your Majesty," he said, "This ought to be interesting." The river galley slid down into a trough. He jerked his hand away from the blade. He'd already cut himself once in a sudden lurch.

At the bow, the chief of the catapult crew looked back to Grus. "I think we can hit them now, Your Majesty, if we shoot on the uproll."

"Go ahead," Grus told him.

The crew winched back the dart and let fly. The catapult clacked as it flung the four-foot-long arrow, shaft thick as a man's finger, toward the closest pirate ship. The dart splashed into the sea just short of its target. The Chernagors jeered.

"Give them another shot," Grus told the sailors, who were already loading a fresh dart into the catapult.

This one thudded into the planking of the Chernagors' ship. It did no harm, and the Chernagors went right on mocking. One or two of them tried to shoot at Grus' ship, but their arrows didn't come close. The catapult could outreach any mere man, no matter how strong.

Grimly, its crew reloaded once more. This time, when they shot, the great arrow skewered not one but two pirates. One splashed into the sea. The other let out a shriek Grus could hear across a quarter of a mile of water. The catapult crew raised a cheer. The Chernagors stopped laughing.

"Form line abreast and advance on the foe," Grus told the officer in charge of signals. The pennants that gave that message fluttered along both sides of the galley. The ships to either side waved green flags to show they understood. The system had sprung to life on the Nine Rivers, and was less than perfect on the ocean. But it worked well enough. Grus saw no signals from the Chernagor ships. When had the pirates last faced anyone able to fight back?

Catapult darts flew. Every now and then, one would transfix a pirate, or two, or three. Marines at the bows of the river galleys started shooting as soon as they came close enough to the Chernagor ships.

By then, of course, the Chernagors were close enough to shoot back. Carpenters had rigged shields to give the river galleys' rowers some protection—that was a lesson the first encounters with the big ships full of archers had driven home. Every so often, though, an arrow struck a rower. Replacements pulled the wounded men from the oars and took their places. The centipede strokes of the galleys' advance didn't falter badly.

Clouds covered the sun. Grus hardly noticed. He was intent on the Chernagor ship at which his ram was aimed like an arrow's point. The wind also began to rise, and the chop on the sea. Those he did notice, and cursed them both. The wind made the Chernagor ships more mobile, and with their greater freeboard they could deal with worse waves than his galleys.

"Your Majesty—" Pterocles began.

Grus waved the wizard to silence. "Not now! Brace yourself, by the—"

Crunch! The ram bit before he could finish the warning. He staggered. Pterocles fell in a heap. The Chernagor ship had tried to turn away at the last instant, to take a glancing blow or make the river galley miss, but Grus' steersman, anticipating the move, countered it and made the hit count. "Back oars!" the oarmaster roared. The river galley pulled free. Green seawater flooded into the stricken pirate ship.

A couple of other Chernagor vessels were rammed as neatly as the one Grus' galley gored. Not all the encounters went the Avornans' way, though. Some of the Chernagor captains did manage to evade the river galleys' rams. The kilted pirates, shooting down into the galleys while they were close, made the Avornans pay for their attacks.

And one river galley had rammed, but then could not pull free—every skipper's nightmare. Shouting Chernagors dropped down onto the galley and battled with the marines and the poorly armed rowers. Grus ordered his own ship toward the locked pair. His marines shot volley after volley at the swarming Chernagors. Pirates and Avornans both went over the side, sometimes in an embrace as deadly as their vessels'.

Pterocles struggled to his feet. He plucked at Grus' sleeve. "Your Majesty, this storm—"

"Storm?" Grus hadn't realized it was one. But even as he spoke, a raindrop hit him in the face, and then another and another. "What about it? Blew up all of a sudden, that's for sure."

"That's what I'm trying to tell you, Your Majesty," the wizard said. "It's got magic behind it, magic or . . . something."

"Something?" Grus asked. Pterocles' expression told him what the wizard meant—something that had to do with the Banished One. The king said, "What can you do about it? Can you hold it off until we've finished giving the Chernagors what they deserve?" As he spoke, another river galley rammed a pirate ship, rammed and pulled free. The Chernagor ship began to sink.

At the same time, though, a wave crashed up over the bow of Grus' river galley, splashing water into the hull. The steersman called, "Your Majesty, we can't take a lot of that, you know."

"Yes," Grus said, and turned back to Pterocles. "What can you do?" he asked again.

"Not much," the wizard answered. "No mortal can, not with the weather. That's why I think it's . . . something."

"Should we break off, then?" Grus asked doubtfully. "We're beating them." First one, then another, Chernagor ship hoisted all sail and sped off to the north at a speed the river galleys, fish in the wrong kind of water, couldn't hope to match.

"I can't tell you what to do, Your Majesty. You're the king. I'm just a wizard. I can taste the storm, though. I don't like it," Pterocles said.

Grus didn't like it, either. He didn't like letting the Chernagors get away, but their ships could take far more weather than his. "Signal *Break off the fight*," he shouted to the man in charge of the pennants. Another waved smashed over the bow. That convinced him he was doing the right thing. He added, "Signal *Make for shore*, too." In the thickening rain, the pennants drooped. He hoped the other captains would be able to make them out.

The last Chernagor ships that could escaped. The others, mortally wounded, wallowed in the waves. One had turned turtle. So had a wrecked river galley. Here and there, men splashed by the ruined warships. Some paddled; others clung to whatever they could. The river galleys fished out as many sailors—Avornans and Chernagors—as they could.

Make for shore. It had seemed an easy enough command. But now, with the storm getting worse, with rain and mist filling the air, Grus was out of sight of land. He and the steersman had to rely on wind and wave to tell them what their eyes couldn't.

"We beat them," Hirundo said. "Now, the next question is, will we get to celebrate beating them, or do they have the last laugh?"

"They may be better sailors on the open sea than I am," Grus said, "but, by the gods, I still know a little something about getting home in a storm."

As though to answer that, the freshening sea sent a wave that almost swamped and almost capsized the river galley. Grus seized a line and clung for his life. When the ship at last righted herself—slowly, so slowly!—the first thing he did was look around for Pterocles. The wizard, no sailor, was all too likely to go overboard.

But Pterocles was there, dripping and sputtering as he hung on to the rail. And the fleet made shore safe—much battered and abused, but safe. The storm blew higher and harder and wilder yet after that, but after that it didn't matter.

Prince Vsevolod took a long pull at the cup of wine in front of him. "Ask your questions," he said, like a wounded man telling the healer to go ahead and draw the arrow.

Getting the exiled Prince of Nishevatz to show even that much cooperation was a victory of sorts. He thought everyone else should cooperate with *him,* not the other way around. Lanius said, "Which city-states in the Chernagor country are likely to oppose Prince Vasilko and the Banished One?"

Vasilko sent him a scornful stare. "This you should answer for yourself. King Grus takes prisoners from Nishevatz, from Hisardzik, from Jobuka, from Hrvace. This means no prisoners from Durdevatz, from Ravno, from Zavala, from Mojkovatz. These four, they no sail with pirate ships. They no love Vasilko, eh?"

That made good logical sense, but Lanius had seen that good logical sense often had little to do with the way the Chernagors behaved. He said, "Would they ally with Avornis if we send our army into the land of the Chernagors?"

"No. Of course not." Yes, while Lanius thought Vsevolod strange, Vsevolod thought him dull. The Prince of Nishevatz continued, "You want to drive Durdevatz and other three into Banished One's hands, you march in."

"But you were the one who invited us up to the Chernagor country in the first place!" Lanius exclaimed in considerable exasperation.

Prince Vsevolod shrugged broad, if somewhat stooped, shoulders. "Is different now. Then I was prince. Now I am exile." A tear gleamed in his eye. Regret or self-pity? By the way Vsevolod refilled the wine cup and gulped it down, Lanius would have bet on self-pity.

"Why do the city-states line up the way they do?" he asked.

Holding up the battered fingers of one hand, Vsevolod said, "Nishevatz, Hisardzik, Jobuka, Hrvace." Holding up those of the other, he said, "Durdevatz, Ravno, Zavala, Mojkovatz." He fitted his fingertips together, alternating those from one hand with those from the other. "You see?"

"I see," King Lanius breathed. Immediate neighbors were hostile to one another. Pro- and anti-Nishevatz city-states alternated along the coast. After some thought, the king observed, "Vasilko would be stronger if all the Chernagor towns leaned his way. Can he get them to do that?"

"Vasilko?" The rebel prince's father made as though to spit, but at the last moment—the *very* last moment—thought better of it. "Vasilko cannot get cat to shit in box." That Vasilko had succeeded in ousting him seemed not to have crossed his mind.

"Let me ask it a different way," Lanius said. "Working through Vasilko, can the Banished One bring them together?"

Now Vsevolod started to shake his head, but checked himself. "These city-states, they are for long time enemies. You understand?" he said. Lanius nodded. Vsevolod went on, "Not easy to go from enemy to friend. But not easy to stand up to Banished One, either. So . . . I do not know."

"All right. Thank you," Lanius said. But it wasn't all right. If Vsevolod wasn't sure the Banished One couldn't bring all the Chernagor towns under his sway, he probably could. And if he could . . .

"If he can," Grus said when Lanius raised the question, "the fleet that raids our west coast next year or the year after is liable to be twice as big as the one we beat back."

"I was afraid you'd say that," Lanius said.

"Believe me, Your Majesty, I would rather lie to you," Grus said. "But that happens to be the truth."

"Did I ever tell you I found out what King Cathartes had to say about the Scepter of Mercy?" Lanius asked suddenly.

"Why, no. You never did." King Grus smiled a crooked smile. "Up until this minute, as a matter of fact, I wouldn't have bet anything I worried about losing that I'd ever even heard of King, uh, Cathartes."

"I would have said the same thing, until I found a letter of his in the archives while you were on campaign," Lanius said. Grus smiled that crooked smile again; like Lanius' fondness for strange pets, his archives-crawling amused his fellow king. But Grus' expression grew more serious as he heard Lanius out. Lanius finished, "Now maybe we have some idea why the Banished One hasn't tried to turn the Scepter against us."

"Maybe we do," Grus agreed. "That's . . . some very pretty thinking, Your Majesty, and you earned what you got. How many crates full of worthless old parchments did you go through before you came on that one?"

"Seventeen," Lanius answered promptly.

Grus laughed. "I might have known you'd have the number on the tip of your tongue. You usually do." He spoke with a curious blend of scorn and admiration.

Lanius said, "One of the parchments turned out not to be worthless, though, so it was worth doing. And who knows whether another will mean a lot a hundred years from now, and who knows which one it might be? That's why we save them."

"Hmm." Grus stopped laughing. Instead of arguing or teasing Lanius some more, he changed the subject. "Did that monkey of yours ever have babies?"

"She did—twins, just like the moncats," Lanius answered. "They seem to be doing well."

"Good for her," Grus said. "Good for you, too. I've been thinking about what you said, about how breeding animals shows you're really doing a good job of caring for them. It makes sense to me."

"Well, thank you," Lanius said. "Would you like to see the little monkeys?"

Grus started to shake his head. He checked the gesture, but not quite soon enough. But when he said, "Yes, show them to me," he managed to sound more eager than Lanius had thought he could.

And the smile that spread over his face when he saw the young monkeys couldn't have been anything but genuine. Lanius also smiled when he saw them, though for him, of course, it was far from the first time. Nobody could look at them without smiling. He was convinced of that. They were all eyes and curiosity, staring at him and Grus and then scurrying across the six inches they'd ventured away from their mother to cling to her fur with both hands, both feet, and their tails.

"They act a lot like children. They look a lot like children, too," Grus said. "Anybody would think, looking at them, that there was some kind of a connection between monkeys and people."

"Maybe the gods made them about the same time as they made us, and used some of the same ideas," Lanius said. "Or maybe it's just happenstance. How can we ever hope to know?"

"The gods . . ." Grus' voice trailed off in a peculiar way. For a moment, Lanius didn't understand. Then he did, and wished he hadn't. What if it wasn't *the gods,* but only Milvago—only the Banished One?

He forced that thought out of his mind, not because he didn't believe it but because he didn't want to think about it. This was another of the times when at least half of him wished he'd never stumbled upon that ancient piece of parchment under the great cathedral. Had finding it been worth doing?

"Anyhow," Grus said, "I'm very glad for your sake that your monkeys have bred. I know you've done a lot of hard work keeping them healthy, and it seems only fair that you've gotten your reward."

"Thank you very much." At first, Grus' thoughtfulness touched Lanius. Then he realized the other king might be doing nothing more than leading both of them away from thoughts of Milvago. He couldn't blame Grus for thinking along with him, and for not wanting to think about what a daunting foe they had. He didn't care to do that himself, either.

Rain pattered down outside the palace. In one hallway, rain pattered down *inside* the palace. A bucket caught the drips. When the rain stopped, the roofers would repair the leak—if they could find it when the rain wasn't there. Grus had seen that sort of thing before. Odds were, the roofers would need at least four tries—and the roof would go right on leaking until they got it right.

Turning to Pterocles, Grus asked, "I don't suppose there's any way to find leaks by magic, is there?"

"Leaks, Your Majesty?" Pterocles looked puzzled. Grus pointed to the bucket. The wizard's face cleared, but he shook his head. "I don't think anyone ever worried about it up until now."

"No? Too bad." They turned a corner. Grus got around to what he really wanted to talk about. "You've never said anything about the letter I gave you—the one from Alca the witch. What do you think of her notions for new ways to shape spells to cure thralls?"

"I don't think she's as smart as she thinks she is," Pterocles answered at once. He went on, "She doesn't understand what being a thrall is like."

"And you do?"

Grus had intended that for sarcasm, but Pterocles nodded. "Oh, yes, Your Majesty. I may not understand much, but I do understand that." The conviction in his voice commanded respect. Maybe he was wrong. He certainly thought he was right. Considering what had happened to him, maybe he was entitled to think so, too.

Backtracking, Grus asked, "Can you use anything in the letter?"

"A bit of this, a dash of that." Pterocles shrugged. "She's clever, but she doesn't understand. And I have some ideas of my own."

"Do you?" Grus wished he didn't sound so surprised. "You haven't talked much about them." That was an understatement of formidable proportions. Pterocles had shown no signs of having ideas of any sort since being felled outside of Nishevatz.

He shrugged again. "Sometimes things go better if you don't talk about them too soon or too much," he said vaguely.

"I . . . see," said Grus, who wasn't at all sure he did. "When will you be ready to test some of your ideas? Soon, I hope?"

"I don't know," the wizard said. "I'll be ready when I'm ready—that's all I can tell you."

Grus felt himself getting angry. "Well, let me tell *you* something. If you're not ready with your own ideas, why don't you go ahead and try the ones the witch sent me?"

"Why? Because they won't work, that's why," Pterocles answered.

"How can you say that without trying them?"

"If I walk out into the sea, I'll drown. I don't need to try it to be sure of that. I know beforehand," Pterocles said. "I may not be quite what I was, but I'm not the worst wizard around, either. And I know some things I didn't used to know, too."

"What's that supposed to mean?" Grus demanded.

"I've already told you." Pterocles sounded impatient. "I know what it's like to be emptied out. I ought to. It's happened to me. Your Alca's a good enough witch, but she doesn't *know.*" Again, he spoke with absolute conviction.

If only he spoke that way when he really has to do *something,* Grus thought unhappily. But he was the one who turned away. Pterocles at least thought he knew what he was doing. Grus had a pretty good idea of how far he could push a man. If he pushed Pterocles any further here, he'd put the wizard's back up, but he wouldn't get him to change his mind.

At his impatient gesture, Pterocles ambled back down the hall. Grus wondered whether the wizard would bump into the bucket that caught the drips from the roof, but he didn't. Grus also wondered whether he ought to pension Pterocles off, or just send him away. If he did, though, would whomever he picked as a replacement prove any better?

Alca would. How many times had he had that thought? But, for one thing, no matter how true it was, Estrilda would make his life not worth living if he tried it. And was it as true as he thought it was? Pterocles had a different opinion. What if he was right? Grus muttered under his breath. He wasn't sure he could rely on Pterocles to remember his name twice running, let alone anything more.

And yet Pterocles had warned of the storm the Banished One raised, out there on the Azanian Sea. Grus had listened to him then, and the fleet had come back to shore without taking much harm.

Yes, and the Chernagor ships got away, the king thought. But that wasn't Pterocles' fault. Was it? Surely blame there belonged to the Banished One? Grus didn't know what to believe. He ended up doing nothing, and wondering every day whether he was making a mistake and how big a mistake it was.

If only I hadn't taken Alca to bed. If only her husband hadn't found out. If only my wife hadn't found out. If only, if only, if only . . .

Lanius threw a snowball at Crex. He didn't come close to hitting his son. Crex scooped up snow in his little mittened hands. He launched a snowball at Lanius, whose vision suddenly turned white. "*Got* you!" Crex squealed, laughing gleefully.

"Yes, you did." Lanius wiped snow off his face. "Bet you can't do it again." A moment later, Crex proved him wrong.

After taking three more snowballs in the face—and managing to hit his son once—Lanius had had enough. He himself had never been accused of grace. There were good reasons why not, too. Grus, on the other hand, made a perfectly respectable soldier—perhaps not among the very best, but more than able to hold his own. Through Sosia, Crex looked to have inherited that blood.

The boy didn't want the sport to end; he was having fun pelting his father with snow. But Lanius couldn't stand being beaten at a game by a boy who barely came up to his navel. "Not fair!" Crex squalled, and burst into tears.

That tempted Lanius to leave him out in the snow. But no, it wouldn't do. Losing a game wasn't excuse enough for freezing his son. *If I were a great and terrible tyrant, I could get away with it,* Lanius thought. But he wasn't, and he never would be, and so Crex, quite unfrozen even if still loudly discontented, went back into the palace with him.

A handful of apricots preserved in honey made Crex forget about the game. Lanius paid the bribe for the sake of peace and quiet. Sosia probably wouldn't have approved, but Sosia probably had too much sense to get into a snowball fight with their son. If she didn't, she probably could throw well enough to give as good as she got. Lanius couldn't.

I'm no good with the bow, either, he thought glumly. The only time he'd ever thrown something when it really counted, though, he'd managed to pitch a moncat into the face of the knife-wielding thrall who intended to murder him. Remembering that made the king feel a little better—not much, but a little.

Feeling better must not have shown on his face, for several servants asked him what was wrong when he walked through the palace corridors. "Nothing," he said, over and over, hoping he would start to believe it before long. He didn't, but kept saying it anyhow.

Most of the servants nodded and went on their way. They weren't about to contradict the king. When he said, "Nothing," to Cristata, though, she shook her head and said, "I don't believe you, Your Majesty. You look too gloomy for it to be nothing."

Lanius needed serious thought to realize Cristata spoke to him as a worried friend might. He couldn't remember the last time anyone had spoken to him like that. Kings didn't have friends, as far as he could see. They had cronies. Or maybe they had lovers.

That thought had crossed his mind before. Of course, Cristata had had Prince Ortalis for a lover. If that wasn't enough to put her off royalty for life, what would be? But she still sounded . . . friendly as she asked, "What *is* wrong, Your Majesty?"

Because she sounded as though she really cared, Lanius found himself telling her the truth. When he was done, he waited for her to laugh at him.

Only later did he realize how foolish that was. A maidservant didn't laugh at a King of Avornis, even at one without much power. But friendship left him oddly vulnerable to her. If she had laughed, he wouldn't have punished her and he would have been wounded.

But she didn't. All she said was, "Oh, dear. That must seem very strange to you." She sounded sympathetic. Lanius needed longer than he might have to recognize that, too. He wasn't used to sympathy from anybody except, sometimes, Sosia.

He didn't want to think about Sosia right this minute, not while he savored Cristata's sympathy. *Grus probably didn't want to think about Sosia's mother while he was with Alca, either,* Lanius thought. Looking at the way Cristata's eyes sparkled, at how very inviting her lips were, Lanius understood what had happened to his fellow king much better than he ever had before.

When he leaned forward and kissed her, he waited for her to scream or to run away or to bite him. After Ortalis, why wouldn't she? But she didn't. Her eyes widened in surprise, then slid shut. Her arms tightened around him as his did around her. "I wondered if you'd do that," she murmured.

"Did you?" Now Lanius was the one who wondered if he ought to run away.

But Cristata nodded seriously. "You don't think I'm ugly."

"Ugly? By the gods, no!" Lanius exclaimed.

"Well, then," Cristata said. She looked up and down the corridor. Lanius did the same thing. No one in sight. He didn't think anyone had seen them kiss. But someone might come down the hallway at any time. His heart pounded with nerves—and with excitement.

Now, for once, he didn't want to think. He opened the closest door. It was one of the dozens of nearly identical storerooms in the palace, this one half full of rolled carpets. He went inside, still wondering if Cristata would flee. She didn't. She stepped in beside him. He closed the door.

It was gloomy in the storeroom; the air smelled of wool and dust. Lanius kissed the serving girl again. She clung to him. "I knew you were sweet, Your Majesty," she whispered.

Were those footsteps on the other side of the door? Yes. But they didn't hesitate; they just went on. And so did Lanius. He tugged Cristata's tunic up and off over her head, then bent to kiss her breasts and their darker, firmer tips. Her breath sighed out.

But when he put his arms around her again, he hesitated and almost recoiled. He'd expected to stroke smooth, soft skin. Her back was anything but smooth and soft.

She noticed his hands falter, and knew what that had to mean. "Do you want to stop?" she asked. "Do you want me to go?"

"Hush," he answered roughly. "I'll show you what I want." He set her hand where she could have no possible doubt. She rubbed gently.

Before long, he laid her down on the floor and poised himself above her. "Oh," she whispered. She might have been louder after that, but his lips came down on hers and muffled whatever noises she would have made . . . and, presently, whatever noises he would have.

Afterwards, they both dressed quickly. "That's—what it's supposed to be like, I think," Cristata said.

It had certainly seemed that way to Lanius. Now, of course, he was screaming at himself because of the way he'd just complicated his life. But, with the afterglow still on him, he couldn't make himself believe it hadn't been worth it. They kissed again, just for a heartbeat. Cristata slipped out of the storeroom. When Lanius heard nothing in the hallway, he did, too. He grinned, a mix of pleasure and relief. He'd gotten away with it.

Grus turned to Estrilda. "The cooks did a really good job with that boar, don't you think?" he said, licking his mustache to get all the flavorful grease.

His wife nodded. Then she said, "If you think it was good, shouldn't you tell Ortalis and not me?"

"Should I?" The king frowned. "You're usually harder on him than I am. Why should I say anything to him that I don't have to?"

"Fair is fair," Estrilda answered. "You . . . did what you did when he . . . made a mistake. When he goes hunting, he's probably not making that particular mistake. And shouldn't you notice him when he does something well?"

"If he did things well more often, I would notice him more." Grus sighed, then nodded reluctantly. "You're right. I wish I could tell you you weren't, but you are. The meat is good, and he made the kill. I'll thank him for it."

On the way to Ortalis' room, he asked several servants if the prince was there. None of them knew. He got the idea none of them cared. He didn't suppose he could blame the women. The men? Ortalis seemed to have a gift for antagonizing everyone. *That's not good in a man who'll be king one day,* Grus thought. *Not good at all.*

He knocked on Ortalis' door. When no one answered, he tried the latch. The door opened. The sweet smell of wine filled the room, and under it a gamier odor that said Ortalis hadn't bathed recently enough. Grus' son cradled a wine cup in his lap like the son he'd never had. An empty jar of wine lay on its side at his feet. One with a dipper in it stood beside the stool on which he perched.

Ortalis looked up blearily. "What d'you want?" he slurred.

"I came to thank you for the fine boar you brought home," Grus answered. "How long have you been drinking?"

"Not long enough," his son said. "You going to pound on me for it?" He raised the cup and took another swig.

"No. I have no reason to," Grus said. "Drinking by yourself is stupid, but it's not vicious. And if you do enough of it, it turns into its own punishment when you finally stop. Once you sober up, you'll wish your head would fall off."

Ortalis shrugged. That he could shrug without hurting himself only proved he wasn't close to sobering up yet. "Why don't you go away?" he said. "Haven't you done enough to make my life miserable?"

"I said you shouldn't hurt women for the fun of it. I showed you some of what getting hurt was like. You didn't much care for that," Grus said. "If you're miserable on account of what I did . . . too bad." He'd started to say *I'm sorry,* but caught himself, for he wasn't.

His son glared at him. "And didn't you have fun, giving me my lesson?"

"No, by Olor's beard!" Grus burst out. "I wanted to be sick afterwards."

By the way Ortalis laughed, he didn't believe a word of it. Grus turned away from his son and strode out of the room. Behind him, Ortalis went on laughing. Grus closed the door, dampening the sound. Praising Ortalis' hunting wouldn't heal the rift between them. Would anything? He had his doubts.

Not for the first time, he wondered about making Anser legitimate. That would solve some of his problems. Regretfully, he shook his head. It would hatch more than it solved, not just with Ortalis but also with Estrilda and Lanius. No, he was stuck with the legitimate son he had, and with the son-in-law, too. He wondered if Crex, his grandson, would live to be king, and what kind of king he would make.

Wonder was all Grus would ever do. He was sure of that. By the time Crex put the royal crown on his head and ascended to the Diamond Throne, Grus knew he would be gone from the scene.

I haven't done enough, he thought. Bringing the unruly Avornan nobles back under the control of the government was important. He'd taken some strong steps in that direction. He'd fought the Thervings to a standstill, until King Dagipert gave up the war. King Berto, gods be praised, really was more interested in praying than fighting. But letting the Banished One keep and extend his foothold in the land of the Chernagors would be a disaster.

And, ever since Grus' days as a river-galley captain down in the south, he'd wanted a reckoning with the Menteshe, a reckoning on their side of the Stura River and not on his. He hadn't gotten that yet. He didn't know if he ever would. If his wizards couldn't protect his men from being made into thralls after crossing the Stura, if they couldn't cure the thralls laboring for the Menteshe, how could he hope to cross the border?

If he couldn't cross the Stura, how could he even dream about recovering the Scepter of Mercy? He couldn't, and he knew it. If he got it back, Avornis would remember him forever. If he failed . . . If he failed, Avornis would still remember him—as a doomed fool.

CHAPTER TEN

Outside the royal palace, snow swirled through the air. The wind howled. When people had to move about, they put on fur-lined boots, heavy cloaks, fur hats with earflaps, and sometimes wool mufflers to protect their mouths and noses. King Lanius didn't think the Banished One was giving the city of Avornis a particularly hard winter, but this was a nasty blizzard.

It was chilly inside the palace, too. Braziers and fires could do only so much. The cold slipped in through windows and around doors. Lanius worried about the baby monkeys. Even the grown ones were vulnerable in the wintertime. But all the little animals seemed healthy, and the babies got bigger by the day.

Lanius didn't worry about them as much as he might have. He had other things on his mind—not least, how to go on with his affair with Cristata without letting Sosia find out about it. Cristata, he discovered, worried about that much less than he did. "She'll learn sooner or later, Your Majesty," she said. "It can't help but happen."

Knowing she was right, Lanius shook his head anyhow. They lay side by side in that same little storeroom—this time on one of the carpets, which they'd unrolled; the floor was cold. "What would happen then?" the king said.

"You'd have to send me away, I suppose." Cristata had few illusions. "I hope you'd pick somewhere nice, a place where I could get by easy enough. Maybe you could even help me find a husband."

He didn't want to think of her in some other man's arms. He wanted her in his. Holding her, he said, "I *will* take care of you."

She studied him before slowly nodding. "Yes, I think you will. That's good."

"If I don't find you a husband, I'll be your husband," Lanius said.

Cristata's eyes opened enormously wide. "You would do that?" she whispered.

"Why not?" he said. "First wives are for legitimate heirs, and I have one. I may get more. It's not that Sosia and I turn our backs on each other when we go to bed. We don't. I wouldn't lie to you. But second wives, and later ones, can be for fun."

"Would I be . . . a queen?" Cristata asked. Not long before, she'd been impressed at having almost enough to count as a taxpayer. She seemed to need a moment to realize how far above even that previously unimaginable status she might rise.

"Yes, you would." Lanius nodded. "But you wouldn't have the rank Sosia does." *Any more than I have the rank Grus does,* he thought unhappily.

Up until this moment, he'd never imagined taking a second wife. The King of Avornis was allowed six, as King Olor in the heavens had six wives. But, just as Queen Quelea was Olor's principal spouse, so most Kings of Avornis contented themselves with a single wife. King Mergus, Lanius' father, hadn't, but King Mergus had been desperate to find a woman who would give him a son and heir. He'd been so desperate, he'd made Lanius' mother, a concubine, his seventh wife to make the boy she bore legitimate. He'd also made himself a heretic and Lanius a bastard in the eyes of a large part of the ecclesiastical hierarchy.

Mergus' troubles had gone a long way toward souring his son on the idea of having more than one wife . . . until now. *It wouldn't be adultery then,* he thought. *But if it's not, would it still be as much fun?*

Grus could have wed Alca. He'd sent her away, instead. That, without a doubt, was Queen Estrilda's doing. Would Queen Sosia's views be any more accommodating than her mother's? Lanius dared hope. They could hardly be less.

Cristata asked, "What will Her Majesty say if you do that?" She'd thought along with him, then.

"She has a right to complain if I take a mistress," Lanius answered. "If I take another wife, though, how can she be upset?" He could, in fact, think of several ways. But he wanted to keep things as simple as possible for Cristata.

She, however, seemed able to see complications without him pointing them out. "She's King Grus' daughter," she said. "What will the other king do?"

"He may grumble, but how could he do more?" Lanius said. "How can he fuss much about what I do after the way he carried on winter before this?"

"People *always* manage to forget what they did and to fuss about what other people do," Cristata said, words that held an unpleasant ring of truth.

To stop thinking about that, Lanius kissed her. The medicine worked so well, he gave himself a second dose, and then a third. One thing led to another, and he and Cristata didn't leave the storeroom for quite a while.

"Tell me I'm not hearing this." Grus' head ached as though he'd had too much wine, but he hadn't had any. "A second wife? A serving girl my own son abused? Why, in the name of the gods?"

"I said, if I can't find her a husband that suits her," Lanius answered.

"You told *her* that?" Grus asked. Lanius nodded. Grus groaned. "What makes you think she'll find anyone else 'suitable' if she has the chance to be a queen?"

Lanius frowned. Grus recognized the frown—it was thoughtful. Hadn't that occurred to him? Maybe it hadn't. At last, he said, "Have you paid any attention to Cristata? Say what you will about her, she's honest."

"She's certainly made you think she is, anyhow," Grus said. "Whether that's the same thing is a different question. And here's one more for you—why are you doing this to my daughter?"

"Who knows just why a man and a woman do what they do?" Lanius answered. "Why did you do *this* to your wife, for instance?"

Grus gritted his teeth. He might have known Lanius would find that particular question. As a matter of fact, he had known it, even if he hadn't wanted to admit it to himself. Now he had to find an answer for it. His first try was an evasion. "That's different," he said.

"Yes, it is," Lanius agreed. "You exiled your other woman. I want to marry mine. Which of us has the advantage there?"

"You're not being fair," Grus said, flicked on a sore spot. He wasn't happy about what he'd done about—with—to—Alca, and wasn't proud of it, either. It had been the only way he saw to keep peace with Estrilda. That might have made it necessary, but he had the bad feeling it didn't make it right.

The other king shrugged. "I never said anything—not a word—about what you did with your women up until now. You might have the courtesy to stay out of my business, too."

"It's also my business, you know," Grus said. "You're married to my daughter. I know Sosia's not happy about this. She's told me so."

"She's told me so, too," Lanius admitted. "But *I'd* be happier with Cristata than without her. I'm King of Avornis . . . I think. Don't I get to decide anything at all about how I live—Your Majesty?"

When Grus used the royal title with Lanius, he was usually being polite. When Lanius used it with Grus—which he seldom did—he was usually being reproachful. Grus felt his face heat. He held his hands a few inches apart. "Only about this much of you is 'happier' with this girl. You're thinking with your crotch, not with your head. That isn't like you."

Lanius turned red, but he didn't change his mind. "Well, what if I am?" he said. "I'm not the only one who ever has." He looked straight at Grus.

He's going to do this, Grus realized. *He's not going to pay attention to me telling him no. What can I do about it?* He saw one thing he might try, and said, "Go talk to Anser about this. He's closer to your age, but I think he'd also tell you it's not a good idea."

"I like Anser. Don't get me wrong—I do," Lanius said. "I like him, but I know he'd tell me whatever you tell him to tell me. And we both know he's arch-hallow on account of that, not because he's holy."

"Yes." Grus admitted in private what he never would in public. "Even so, I swear to you, Lanius, I have not spoken with him about this. Whatever he says, he will say, and that's all there is to it. Talk to him. He has good sense—and you, right now, don't."

"When you say I don't have good sense, you mean I'm not doing what you want me to," Lanius said, but then he shrugged. "All right. I'll talk to him. But he won't change my mind."

Back stiff with defiance, Lanius went off to the cathedral. Grus waited until he was sure the other king had left the palace, then pointed to three or four servants. "Fetch me the serving woman named Cristata," he told them. His voice held the snap of command. They hurried away.

Before long, one of them led her into the little audience chamber. "Oh!" she said in surprise when she saw Grus. "When he told me the king wanted to see me, I thought he meant—"

"Lanius," Grus said, and Cristata nodded. He went on, "Well, I do." He could see why Lanius wanted her, too, and why Ortalis had. But that had nothing to do with anything. He went on, "Are you really bound and determined to become Queen of Avornis, or would being quietly set up for life in a provincial town be enough to satisfy you?"

If she said she *was* bound and determined to be Lanius' queen, Grus knew his own life would get more difficult. She paused to consider before she answered. *She's not stupid, either,* Grus thought. *Is she smart enough to see when she's well off? Or is she as head-over-heels for Lanius as he is for her?*

She said, "I'll go, Your Majesty. If I stay, I'll have you for an enemy, won't I? I don't want that. Anyone in Avornis would be a fool to want you for an enemy, and I hope I'm not a fool."

"You're not," Grus assured her. " 'Enemy,' I think, goes too far. But I am going to protect my own family as best I can. Wouldn't you do the same?"

"Probably," Cristata answered. "I have to trust you, don't I, about what 'quietly set for life' means? You were generous paying for what Ortalis did."

Grus found himself liking her. She had nerve, to bargain with someone with so much more power—and to make him feel guilty for using it. He said, "By the gods, Cristata, I won't cheat you. Believe me or not, as you please." When she nodded, he went on, "We have a bargain, then?" She nodded again. So did he. "Gather up whatever you need to take with you. If we're going to do this, I want you gone before Lanius can call you again."

"Yes, I can see how you might." Cristata sighed. "I *will* miss him. He's . . . sweet. But you could have done a lot worse to me, couldn't you?"

Only after she was gone did Grus realize that last wasn't necessarily praise.

"You . . . You . . ." Lanius' fury rose up and choked him. What he could do about it, however, knew some very sharp bounds. Grus was the one with the power, and he'd just used it.

"Think whatever you like," he said now. "Call me whatever you like. If you're going to take serving girls to bed now and again, I won't fuss, though Sosia might. You're a man. It happens. I ought to know."

His calm words gave Lanius' rage nowhere to light. Absurdly, Lanius realized he never had taken Cristata to *bed*. Coupling on the floor, even on a carpet, wasn't the same. "I love her!" he exclaimed.

"She's nice-looking. She's clever. She's got spirit," Grus said. "And you picked her out yourself. You didn't have her forced on you. No wonder you had a good time with her. But love? Don't be too sure."

"What do you know about it, you—?" Lanius called him the vilest names he knew.

"I think you're sweet, too," Grus answered calmly. Lanius gaped. Grus went on, "What do I know about it? Oh, a little something, maybe. Cristata reminds me more than a little of Anser's mother."

"Oh," Lanius said. Try as he would to stay outraged, he had trouble. Maybe Grus did know what he was talking about after all. Lanius went on, "You still had no business—none, do you hear me?—interfering in my affairs . . . and you can take that last however you want."

"Don't be silly," Grus answered, still calm. "Of course I did. You're married to my daughter. You're my grandchildren's father. If you do something that's liable to hurt them, of course I'll try to stop you."

Lanius hadn't expected him to be quite so frank. He wondered whether that frankness made things better or worse. "You have no shame at all, do you?" he said.

"Where my family is concerned? Very little, though I've probably been too soft on Ortalis over the years," Grus said. "He's embarrassed me more times than I wish he had, but that isn't what you meant, and I know it isn't. I'll do whatever I think I have to do. If you want to be angry at me, go ahead. You're entitled to."

And no matter how angry you are, you can't do anything about it. That was the other thing Grus meant. He was right, too, as Lanius knew only too well. His impotence was at times more galling than at others. This . . . He couldn't even protect a woman he still insisted to himself he loved. What could be more humiliating than that? Nothing he could think of.

"Where did you send her?" he asked after a long silence.

Some of the tension went out of Grus' shoulders. He must have realized he'd won. He said, "You know I won't tell you that. You'll find out sooner or later, but you won't be up in arms about it by the time you do."

His obvious assumption that he knew exactly how Lanius worked only irked the younger man more. So did the alarming suspicion that he might be right. Lanius said, "At least tell me how much you're giving her. Is she really taken care of?"

"You don't need to worry about that." Grus named a sum. Lanius blinked; he might not have been so generous himself. Grus set a hand on his shoulder. He shook it off. Grus shrugged. "I told you, I'm not going to get angry at you, and you can go right ahead and be angry at me. We'll sort it out later."

"Will we?" Lanius said tonelessly, but Grus had turned away. He wasn't even listening anymore.

Lanius slept by himself that night. Sosia hadn't wanted to sleep beside him since finding out about Cristata. He didn't care to sleep by her now, either. He knew he would have to make peace sooner or later, but sooner or later wasn't yet.

He thought he woke in the middle of the night. Then he realized it was a dream, but not the sort of dream he would have wanted. The Banished One's inhumanly cold, inhumanly beautiful features stared at him.

"You see what your friends are worth?" the Banished One asked with a mocking laugh. "Who has hurt you worse—Grus, or I?"

"You hurt the whole kingdom," Lanius answered.

"Who cares about the kingdom? Who has hurt *you*?"

"Go away," Lanius said uselessly.

"You can have your revenge," the Banished One went on, as though the king hadn't said a word. "You can make Grus pay, you can make Grus weep, for what he has done to you. Think on it. You can make him suffer, as he has made you suffer. The chance for vengeance is given to few men. Reach out with both hands and take it."

Lanius would have liked nothing better than revenge. He'd already had flights of fantasy filled with nothing else. But, even dreaming, he understood that anything the Banished One wanted was something to be wary of. And so, not without a certain regret, he said "No."

"Fool! Ass! Knave! Jackanapes! Wretch who lives only for a day, and will not make himself happy for some puny part of his puny little life!" the Banished One cried. "Die weeping, then, and have what you deserve!"

The next thing Lanius knew, he was awake again, and drenched in sweat despite the winter chill. He wished the Banished One would choose to afflict someone else. He himself was getting to know the one who had been Milvago much too well.

Land travel in winter was sometimes easier than it was in spring or fall. In winter, rain didn't turn roads to mud. Land travel was sometimes also the only choice in winter, for the rivers near the city of Avornis could freeze. After Grus' troubles with Lanius, he was glad to get away from the capital any way he could. If the other king tried to get out of line, he would hear about it and deal with it before anything too drastic could happen. He had no doubt of that.

Once Grus reached the unfrozen portion of the Granicus, he went faster still—by river galley downstream to the seaside port of Dodona. The man who met him at the quays was neither bureaucrat nor politician, neither general nor commodore. Plegadis was a shipwright and carpenter, the best Avornis had.

"So she's ready for me to see, is she?" Grus said.

Plegadis nodded. He was a sun-darkened, broad-shouldered man with engagingly ugly features, a nose that had once been straighter than it was now, and a dark brown bushy beard liberally streaked with gray. "Do you really need to ask, Your Majesty?" he said, pointing. "Stands out from everything else we make, doesn't she?"

"Oh, just a bit," Grus answered. "Yes, just a bit."

Plegadis laughed out loud. Grus stared at the Avornan copy of a Chernagor pirate ship. Sure enough, it towered over everything else tied up at the quays of Dodona. To someone used to the low, sleek lines of river galleys, it looked blocky, even ugly, but Grus had seen what ships like this were worth.

"Is she as sturdy as she looks?" the king asked.

"I should hope so." The shipwright sounded offended. "I didn't just copy her shape, Your Majesty. I matched lines and timber and canvas, too, as best I could. She's ready to take to the open sea, and to do as well as a Chernagor ship would."

Grus nodded. "That's what I wanted. How soon can I have more just like her—a proper fleet?"

"Give me the timber and the carpenters and it won't be too long— middle of summer, maybe," Plegadis answered. "Getting sailors who know what they're doing in a ship like this . . . That'll take a little while, too."

"I understand." Grus eyed the tall, tall masts. "Handling all that canvas will take a lot of practice by itself."

"We do have some Chernagor prisoners to teach us the ropes," Plegadis said. When a shipwright used that phrase, he wasn't joking or spitting out a cliché. He meant exactly what the words implied.

He wasn't joking, but was he being careful enough? "Have you had a wizard check these Chernagors?" Grus asked. "We may have some of the same worries with them that we do with the Menteshe, and even with the thralls. I'm not saying we will, but we may."

Plegadis' grimace showed a broken front tooth. "I didn't even think of that, Your Majesty, but I'll see to it, I promise you. What I was going to tell you is, some of the fishermen here make better crew for this Chernagor ship than a lot of river-galley men. They know what to do with a good-sized sail, where on a galley it's row, row, row all the time."

"Yes, I can see how that might be so." Grus looked east, out to the Azanian Sea. It seemed to go on and on forever. He'd felt that even more strongly when he went out on it in a river galley. He'd also felt badly out of his element. He'd gotten away with fighting on the sea, but he wasn't eager to try it again in ships not made for it. *Would I be more ready to try it in a monster like that?* he wondered. *Once I had a good crew, I think I might be.* Out loud, he went on, "I don't care where the men come from, as long as you get them."

"Good. That's the right attitude." Plegadis nodded. "We have to lick those Chernagor bastards. I'm not fussy about how. They did us a lot of harm, and they'd better find out they can't get away with nonsense like that. I'll tell you something else, too. Along this coast, plenty of fishermen'll think an ordinary sailor's wages look pretty good, poor miserable devils."

"I believe it," Grus answered. The eastern coast was Avornis' forgotten land. If a king wanted to make a man disappear, he sent him to the Maze. If a man wanted to disappear on his own, he came to the coast. Even tax collectors often overlooked this part of the kingdom. Grus knew he had until the Chernagors descended on it. He added, "If all this makes us tie the coast to the rest of Avornis, some good will have come from it."

To his surprise, Plegadis hesitated before nodding again. "Well, I think so, too, Your Majesty, or I suppose I do. But you'll find people up and down the coast who won't. They *like* being . . . on their own, you might say."

"How did they like it when the pirates burned their towns and stole their silver and raped their women?" Grus asked. "They were glad enough to see us after that."

"Oh, yes." The shipwright's smile was as crooked as that tooth of his. "But they got over it pretty quick." Grus started to smile. He started to, but he didn't. Once again, Plegadis hadn't been joking.

When all else failed, King Lanius took refuge in the archives. No one bothered him there, and when he concentrated on old documents he didn't have to dwell on whatever else was bothering him. Over the years, going there had served him well. But it didn't come close to easing the pain of losing Cristata.

And it wasn't just the pain of losing her. He recognized that. Part of it was also the humiliation of being unable to do anything for someone he loved. If Grus had ravished her in front of his eyes, it could hardly have been worse. Grus hadn't, of course. He'd been humane, especially compared to what he might have done. He'd even made Lanius see his point of view, but so what? Cristata was still gone, she still wouldn't be back, and Lanius still bitterly missed her.

Next to that ache in his heart, even finding another letter as interesting and important as King Cathartes' probably wouldn't have meant much to him. As things turned out, most of what Lanius did find was dull. There were days when he could plow through tax receipts and stay interested, but those were days when he was in a better mood than he was now. He found himself alternately yawning and scowling.

He fought his way through a few sets of receipts, as much from duty as anything else. But then he shook his head, gave up, and buried his face in his hands. If he gave in to self-pity here, at least he could do it without anyone else seeing.

When he raised his head again, sharp curiosity—and the beginnings of alarm—replaced the self-pity. Any noise he heard in the archives was out of the ordinary. And any noise he heard here could be a warning of something dangerous. If one of the thralls had escaped . . .

He turned his head this way and that, trying to pinpoint the noise. It wasn't very loud, and it didn't seem to come from very high off the ground. "Mouse," Lanius muttered, and tried to make himself believe it.

He'd nearly succeeded when a sharp clatter drove such thoughts from his mind. Mice didn't carry metal objects—knives?—or knock them against wood. Today, Lanius had a knife at his own belt. But he was neither warrior nor assassin, as he knew all too well.

"Who's there?" he called, slipping the knife from its sheath and sliding forward as quietly as he could. Only silence answered him. He peered ahead. Almost anything smaller than an elephant could have hidden in the archives. He'd never fully understood what *higgledy-piggledy* meant until he started coming in here. He often wondered whether anyone ever read half the parchments various officials wrote. Sometimes it seemed as though the parchments just ended up here, on shelves and in boxes and barrels and leather sacks and sometimes even wide-mouthed pottery jugs all stacked one atop another with scant regard for sanity or safety.

Elephants Lanius didn't much worry about. An elephant would have had to go through a winepress before it could squeeze between the stacks of documents and receptacles. Assassins, unfortunately, weren't likely to be so handicapped.

"Who's there?" the king called again, his voice breaking nervously.

Again, no answer, not with words. But he did hear another metallic clatter, down close to the ground.

That made him wonder. There were assassins, and then there were . . . He made the noise he used when he was about to feed the moncats. Sure enough, out came one of the beasts, this time carrying not a wooden spoon but a long-handled silver dipper for lifting soup from a pot or wine from a barrel.

"You idiot animal!" Lanius exclaimed. Unless he was wildly mistaken, this was the same moncat that had frightened him in here before. He pointed an accusing finger at it. "How did you get out this time, Pouncer? And how did you get into the kitchens and then out of them again?"

"Rowr," Pouncer said, which didn't explain enough.

Lanius made the feeding noise again. Still clutching the dipper, the moncat came over to him. He grabbed it. It hung on to its prize, but didn't seem otherwise upset. That noise meant food most of the time. If, this once, it didn't, the animal wasn't going to worry about it.

"What shall I do with you?" Lanius demanded.

Again, Pouncer said, "Rowr." Again, that told the king less than he wanted to know.

He carried the moncat back to its room. After putting it inside and going out into the hallway once more, he waved down the first servant he saw. "Yes, Your Majesty?" the man said. "Is something wrong?"

"Something or someone," Lanius answered grimly. "Tell Bubulcus to get himself over here right away. Tell everybody you see to tell Bubulcus to get over here right away. Tell him he'd better hurry if he knows what's good for him."

He hardly ever sounded so fierce, so determined. The servant's eyes widened. "Yes, Your Majesty," he said, and hurried away. Lanius composed himself to wait, not in patience but in impatience.

Bubulcus came trotting up about a quarter of an hour later, a worried expression on his long, thin, pointy-nosed face. "What's the trouble now, Your Majesty?" he asked, as though he and trouble had never met before.

Knowing better, the king pointed to the barred door that kept the moncats from escaping. "Have you gone looking for me in there again?"

"Which I haven't." Bubulcus shook his head so vigorously, a lock of greasy black hair flopped down in front of one eye. He brushed it back with the palm of his hand. "Which I haven't," he repeated, his voice oozing righteousness. "No, sir. I've learned my lesson, I have. Once was plenty, thank you very much."

Once hadn't been plenty, of course. He'd let moncats get loose twice—at least twice. He might forget. Lanius never would. "Are you sure, Bubulcus? Are you very sure?" he asked. "If you're lying to me, I *will* send you to the Maze, and I won't blink before I do it. I promise you that."

"Me? Lie? Would I do such a thing?" Bubulcus acted astonished, insulted, at the mere possibility. He went on, "Put me on the rack, if you care to. I'll tell you the same. Give me to a Menteshe torturer. Give me to the Banished One, if you care to."

The king's fingers twisted in a gesture that might—or might not—ward off evil omens. "You don't know what you're talking about," he said. "Thank the true gods for your ignorance, too."

"Which I do for everything, Your Majesty," Bubulcus said. "But I'm not ignorant about this. I know I didn't go in there. Do what you want with me, but I can't tell you any different."

Sending him to the rack had more than a little appeal. With a certain amount of regret, Lanius said, "Go find a mage, Bubulcus. Tell him to question you about this. Bring him back here with you. Hurry. I'll be waiting. If you don't come back soon, you'll wish some of the foolish things you just said did come true."

Bubulcus disappeared faster than if a mage had conjured him into nothingness. Lanius leaned against the wall. Would the servant come back so fast?

He did, or nearly. And he had with him no less a wizard than Pterocles himself. After bowing to Lanius, the wizard said, "As best I can tell, Your Majesty, this man is speaking the truth. He was not in those rooms, and he did not let your pet get out."

"How *did* the moncat get loose, then?" Lanius asked.

Pterocles shrugged. "I can't tell you that. Maybe another servant let it out. Maybe there's a hole in the wall no one has noticed."

Bubulcus looked not only relieved but triumphant. "Which I told you, Your Majesty. Which I didn't have anything to do with."

"This time, no," Lanius admitted. "But your record up until now somehow didn't fill me with confidence." Bubulcus looked indignant. Pterocles let out a small snort of laughter. Lanius gestured. "Go on, Bubulcus. Count yourself lucky and try to stay out of trouble."

"Which I've already done, except for some people who keep trying to put me into it," Bubulcus said. But then he seemed to remember he was talking to a King of Avornis, not to another servant. He bobbed his head in an awkward bow and scurried away.

"Thank you," Lanius told Pterocles.

"You're welcome, Your Majesty." The wizard tried a smile on for size. "Dealing with something easy every once in a while is a pleasure." He too nodded to Lanius and ambled down the corridor.

Something easy? Lanius wondered. Then he decided Pterocles had a point. Finding out if a servant lied was bound to be easier—and safer— than, say, facing a Chernagor sorcerer. But how *had* Pouncer escaped? That didn't look as though it would be so easy for Lanius to figure out.

Grus listened to Pterocles with more than a little amusement. "A moncat, you say?" he inquired, and the wizard nodded. Grus went on, "Well, that's got to be simpler than working out how to cure thralls."

Pterocles nodded. "It was this time, anyhow."

"Good. Not everything should be hard all the time," Grus said, and Pterocles nodded again. Grus asked, "And how *are* you coming on curing thralls?"

Pterocles' face fell. He'd plainly hoped Grus wouldn't ask him that.

But, once asked, he had to answer. "Not as well as I would like, Your Majesty," he said reluctantly, adding, "No one else in Avornis has figured out how to do it, either, you know, not reliably, not since the Menteshe wizards first started making our men into thralls however many hundred years ago that was."

"Well, yes," Grus admitted with a certain reluctance of his own. He didn't want to think about that; he would sooner have forgotten all those other failures. That way, he could have believed Pterocles was starting with a clean slate. As things were, he could only ask, "Do you think you've found any promising approaches?"

"Promising? No. Hopeful? Maybe," Pterocles replied. "After all, as I've said, I've been . . . emptied myself. So have thralls. I know more about that than any other Avornan wizard ever born." His laugh had a distinctly hollow note. "I wish I didn't, but I do."

"What about the suggestions Alca the witch sent me?" Grus asked once more.

With a sigh, the wizard answered, "We've been over this ground before, Your Majesty. I don't deny the witch is clever, but what she says is not to the point. She doesn't understand what being a thrall means."

"And you do?" Grus asked with heavy sarcasm.

"As well as any man who isn't a thrall can, yes," Pterocles replied. "I've told you that before. Will you please listen?"

"No matter how well you say you understand, you haven't come up with anything that looks like a cure," Grus said. "If you do, I'll believe you. If you don't, if you don't show me you have ideas of your own, I am going to order you to use Alca's for the sake of doing *something*."

"Even if it's wrong," Pterocles jeered.

"Even if it is," Grus said stubbornly. "From all I've seen, doing something is better than doing nothing. Something *may* work. Nothing never will."

"If you think I'm doing nothing, Your Majesty, you had better find yourself another wizard," Pterocles said. "Then I *will* go off and do nothing with a clear conscience, and you can see what happens after that."

If he'd spoken threateningly, Grus might have sacked him on the spot. Instead, he sounded more like a man delivering a prophecy. That gave the king pause. Too many strange things had happened for him to ignore that tone of voice. And Pterocles, like Alca, had dreamed of the Banished One—the only sign Grus had that the Banished One took a mortal opponent seriously. Where would he find another wizard who had seen that coldly magnificent countenance?

"If you think you're smarter than Alca, you'd better be right," he said heavily.

"I don't think anything of the sort," Pterocles said. "I told you she was clever. I meant it. But I've been through things she hasn't. A fool who's dropped a brick on his toe knows better why he'd better not do that again than a clever fellow who hasn't."

That made sense. It would have made more sense if the wizard had done anything much with what he knew. "All right, then. I know you're pregnant," Grus said. "I still want to see the baby one of these days before too long."

"If the baby lives, you'll see it," Pterocles said. "You don't want it to come too soon, though, do you? They're never healthy if they do."

Grus began to wish he hadn't used that particular figure of speech. Even so, he said, "If you miscarry with your notions in spite of what you think now, I want you to try Alca's."

He waited. Pterocles frowned. Obviously, he was looking for one more comment along the lines he'd been using. When the wizard's eyes lit up, Grus knew he'd found one. Pterocles said, "Very well, Your Majesty, though that would be the first time a woman ever got a man pregnant."

After a—pregnant—pause, Grus groaned and said, "Are you wizard enough to make yourself disappear?"

"Yes, Your Majesty," Pterocles said, and did.

His mulishness still annoyed Grus. But he had a twinkle in his eye again, and he was getting back the ability to joke. Grus thought—Grus hoped—that meant he was recovering from the sorcerous pounding he'd taken outside of Nishevatz. Maybe the baby—if it ever came—would be worth seeing after all.

CHAPTER ELEVEN

Lanius had just finished telling Sosia the story of the moncat and the stolen silver dipper. It was an amusing story, and he knew he'd told it well. His wife listened politely enough, but when he was through she just sat in their bedchamber. She didn't even smile. "Why did you tell me that?" she asked.

"Because I thought it was funny," Lanius answered. "I hoped you would think it was funny, too. Evidently I was wrong."

"Evidently you were," Sosia said in a brittle voice. "You can tell me funny stories, but you can't even tell me you're sorry. Men!" She turned her back on him. "You're worse than my father. At least my mother wasn't around when he took up with somebody else."

"Oh." More slowly than it should have, a light went on in Lanius' head. "You're still angry about Cristata." He was angry about Cristata, too—angry that Grus had paid her off and sent her away. Sosia had other reasons.

"Yes, I'm still angry about Cristata!" his wife blazed. Lanius blinked; he hadn't realized *how* angry she was. "I loved you. I thought you loved me. And then you went and did that. How? Why?"

"I never stopped loving you. I still love you," Lanius said, which was true—and which he would have been wiser to say sooner and more often. "It's just . . . she was there, and then . . ." His voice trailed away, which it should have done sooner.

"She was there, and then you were *there*." Sosia made a gesture boys used in the streets of the city of Avornis, one that left nothing to the imagination. "Is there anything else to say about that?"

"I suppose not," Lanius answered. From Sosia's point of view, what he'd done with Cristata didn't seem so good. From his own . . . He sighed. He still missed the serving girl. "Kings of Avornis are allowed to have more than one wife," he added sulkily.

"Yes—if they can talk their first one into it," Sosia said. "You didn't. You didn't even try. You were having a good time screwing her, so you decided you'd marry her."

"Well, what else but fun are wives after the first one for?" Lanius asked, he thought reasonably. "Oh, once in a while a king will be trying to find a woman who can bear him a son, the way my father was. But most of the time, those extra wives are just for amusement."

"Maybe you were amused, but I wasn't," Sosia snapped. "And I thought I amused you. Was I wrong?"

Even Lanius, who didn't always hear the subtleties in what other people said, got the point there. "No," he said hastily. "Oh, no indeed."

Sosia glared at him. "That's what you say. Why am I supposed to believe you?"

He started to explain why he saw little point in lying to her, especially now that Cristata was gone. He didn't get very far. That wasn't the answer she was looking for. He needed another heartbeat or two to figure out the sort of answer she did want.

Some time later, he said, "There. Do you see now?" They were, by then, both naked and sweaty, though snow coated the windowsills. Sometimes answers didn't need words.

"Maybe," Sosia said grudgingly.

"Well, I'll just have to show you again," Lanius said, and he did.

After that second demonstration, he fell asleep very quickly. When he woke up, it was light. What woke him was Sosia getting out of bed. He yawned and stretched. She nodded without saying anything.

"Good morning," he told her.

"Is it?" she asked.

"Well, I thought so."

"Of course you did," she said. "You got what you wanted last night." In some annoyance, Lanius said, "I wasn't the only one."

"No?" But Sosia saw that wouldn't do. She shrugged. "One night's not enough to set everything right between us."

Lanius sighed. "What am I going to have to do now?"

"You're not going to *have* to do anything," Sosia said. "You need to show me there are things you *want* to do, the kinds of things people who care about each other do without thinking."

Since Lanius hardly ever did anything without thinking, he almost asked her what she was talking about. He quickly decided not to. *Show me you love me,* was what she meant. *Keep on showing me until I believe you.*

Some of what he did would be an act. He knew that. Sosia undoubtedly knew it, too. She wanted a convincing act—an act good enough to convince him as well as her. If he kept doing those things, maybe he *would* convince himself. *Maybe I won't, too,* he thought mulishly. But he would have to make the effort.

He did his best. He went out into the hall and spoke to a serving woman, who hurried off to the kitchens. She came back with a tray of poached eggs and pickled lamb's tongue, Sosia's favorite breakfast. Lanius preferred something simpler—bread and honey and a cup of wine suited him very well.

As Sosia sprinkled salt over the eggs, she smiled at Lanius. She'd noticed what he'd done. That was something, anyhow.

A snowstorm filled the air around the palace with soft, white silence. In the middle of that silence, King Grus and Hirundo tried to figure out what to do when sunshine and green leaves replaced snow and cold. "How many men do you want to leave behind to make sure the Chernagors don't ravage the coast again?" Hirundo asked. "And if you leave that many behind, will we have enough left to go up into the land of the Chernagors and do something useful ourselves?"

Those were both good questions. Grus wished they weren't quite so good. He said, "Part of that depends on how many ships Plegadis can build, and on whether we can fight off the pirates before they ever come ashore."

"You'd know more about that than I do," Hirundo answered. "All I know about ships is getting to the rail in a hurry." He grinned and then stuck out his tongue. "Give me a horse any day."

"You're welcome to mine," Grus said. The general laughed. More seriously, Grus went on, "I don't know as much about these ships as I wish I did. No Avornan does. I don't even know if they'll be able to find the pirates on the sea and keep them from landing. We'll find out, though."

Hirundo nodded. "Oh, yes. The next question, of course, is *when* we'll find out. Are the pirates going to keep us from getting up into the Chernagor country again?"

"No," Grus declared. "No, by Olor's beard. I'll let the garrisons and the ships deal with the Chernagors in the south. It's not just a question of throwing Prince Vasilko out on his ear. If it were, I wouldn't worry so much. We have to drive the Banished One out of the land of the Chernagors."

"When we started out in this fight, I wondered whether Vasilko or Vsevolod was the Banished One's cat's-paw," Hirundo said.

"I spent a lot of time worrying about that, even though Vsevolod would probably want to strangle me with his big nobbly hands if he ever found out," Grus said. "But there's not much doubt anymore."

Hirundo considered that. "Well," he said, "no."

Grus sent out orders for cavalrymen and foot soldiers to gather by the city of Avornis. He also sent out other orders this winter, strengthening the garrisons in the river towns near the Azanian Sea and moving the river-galley fleets toward the mouths of the Nine. That meant he would take a smaller force north with him this coming spring when he moved against Nishevatz. But it also meant—he hoped it meant—the Chernagors wouldn't be able to pull off such a nasty surprise in the new campaigning season.

No sooner had his couriers ridden away from the capital than a blizzard rolled out of the north and dumped a foot and a half of snow on the city and the countryside. Grus tried to tell himself it was only a coincidence. The Banished One didn't really have anything to do with it . . . did he?

The king thought about asking Pterocles, thought about it and then thought better of it. He'd asked that question of Alca once before, in an earlier harsh winter. He'd found out the Banished One *had* used the weather as a weapon against Avornis, but the deposed god had almost slain Alca and him and Lanius in the aftermath of the witch's magic. Some knowledge came at too high a price.

Mild weather returned after this snowstorm finally blew itself out. That made Grus doubt the Banished One lay behind it. When he struck at Avornis, he sent blizzard after blizzard after blizzard. He was very strong, and reveled in his strength. Being so strong, he'd never had to worry much about subtlety. He left his foes in no doubt about what he was doing, and also in no doubt that they couldn't hope to stop him.

Milvago. Had the Banished One been as overwhelmingly mighty in the heavens as he was here on earth? Perhaps not quite, or the gods he'd fathered would never have been able to cast him out, to cast him down to the material world. But Grus would have been astonished if they hadn't used their sire's strength against him. Maybe he'd been arrogant, thinking they couldn't possibly challenge him.

He knew better than that now—one more thought Grus wished he hadn't had.

Soldiers started coming up out of the south to gather for this year's invasion of the land of the Chernagors. A new blizzard howled down on the capital once their encampment began to swell. By then, though, winter was dying. Even the Banished One had limits to what he could do to the weather . . . if he was doing anything. Grus still hoped he wasn't.

He couldn't stop the sun from climbing higher in the sky every day, couldn't stop the days from getting longer and warmer, couldn't stop the snow from melting. Even after it vanished from the ground, Grus had to wait a little longer, to let the roads dry out and keep his army from bogging down. As soon as he thought he could, he climbed aboard a horse—mounting with the same reluctance Hirundo showed at boarding a river galley—and set off for the north.

Every so often, he looked back over his shoulder, wondering if a messenger was galloping up behind the army with word of some new disaster elsewhere in Avornis that would make him turn around. Every time he saw no such messenger, he felt as though he'd won a victory. On went the army, too, toward the Chernagor country.

Each time Grus set out on campaign, Lanius waved farewell and wished him good fortune. And each time Grus set out on campaign, Lanius' smile of farewell grew wider. With Grus off to or beyond the frontiers, power in the city of Avornis increasingly rested in Lanius' hands.

Lanius thought he could rise against Grus with some hope of success. Thinking he could do it didn't make him anxious to try, though. For one thing, he wasn't a man to take many chances. For another, even success could only mean winning a civil war. He doubted there was any such thing as *winning* a civil war. If he and Grus fought—if they wasted Avornis' men and wealth, who gained besides the Banished One? Nobody Lanius could see. And, though he didn't like to admit it even to himself, having someone in place to handle those parts of kingship he didn't care for wasn't always the worst thing in the world. He was no campaigner, and never would be. Having authority in the palace was a different story.

As usual, Queen Sosia, Crex, Pitta, Queen Estrilda, and Arch-Hallow Anser came out beyond the walls of the capital to send Grus off and wish him well. Also as usual, Prince Ortalis stayed away.

That worried Lanius. The more he thought about it, the more it worried him. If Ortalis had to choose between Grus and the Banished One, which would he pick? Remembering what had happened in Nishevatz, remembering how Prince Vasilko had risen against his father and helped the Banished One enter his city-state, did nothing to give Lanius peace of mind.

Normally, he would have talked things over with Sosia and found out how worried she was. Ortalis was her brother, after all; she knew him better than Lanius did. But she was still touchy—which put it mildly—about Cristata, and so Lanius didn't want to provoke her in any way.

He thought about hashing it out with Anser, too. But Anser wasn't the right man to deal with such concerns. With his sunny nature, he had a hard time seeing the bad in anyone else. And he didn't know enough about the true nature of the Banished One, nor did Lanius feel like instructing him.

With nobody to talk to about Ortalis, Lanius did his brooding in privacy on the way back to the royal palace. He was used to that. Once upon a time, he'd resented being so much alone. Now he took it for granted.

When he and the rest of the royal family returned to the palace, they found the servants in a commotion. "He's done it! He's gone and done it!" they exclaimed in ragged chorus.

That sounded inflammatory. It didn't sound very informative. "Who's gone and done what?" Lanius asked.

The servants looked at him as though he were an idiot for not knowing. "Why, Prince Ortalis, of course," several of them answered, again all at once.

Lanius, Sosia, Estrilda, and Anser all looked at one another. Crex and Pitta were too small to worry about what their uncle did, and ran off to play. Lanius said, "All right, now we know who. What has Ortalis done?" He braced himself for almost any atrocity. Had Ortalis hurt *an-*

other serving girl? Had he decided to have a couple of moncats served up in a stew? The king wouldn't have put anything past him.

But the servants replied, "He's gotten married."

"He *has?*" Now the king, two queens, and the arch-hallow all cried out in astonishment. That wasn't just news; that was an earthquake. Grus had been trying to find Ortalis a bride on and off for years. He hadn't had any luck, either. Ortalis' reputation was too ripe. Grus had sent Lepturus, the head of the royal bodyguards, to the Maze for refusing to let his granddaughter marry the prince. And now Ortalis had found himself a wife?

"To whom?" Lanius asked. "And how did this happen?"

"How did it happen without us hearing about it?" Sosia added.

Bubulcus knew all the details. Lanius might have guessed he would. "He's married to Limosa, Your Majesty. You know, the daughter of Petrosus, the treasury minister." He seemed to sneer at the king for being in the dark.

They deserve each other, was the first uncharitable thought that went through Lanius' mind. But that wasn't fair to Limosa, whom he'd met only a couple of times. He disliked her father, who was stingy and bad-tempered even for a man of his profession.

"How did it happen?" Sosia asked again. She might have been speaking of a flood or a fire or some other disaster, not a wedding.

"In the usual way, I'm sure," Bubulcus replied. "They stood before a priest, and he said the proper words over them, and then they . . ." He leered.

"Don't be a bigger fool than you can help," Lanius snapped, and Bubulcus, knowing he'd gone too far, turned pale. Lanius added, "You know what Her Majesty meant."

"And which priest who wed them?" Anser added, sounding very much like the man in charge of ecclesiastical affairs. "He did it without the king's leave, and without mine. He'll have more than a few questions to answer—you may be sure of that."

Perdix, who'd wed King Mergus and Queen Certhia after Lanius was born, had had more than a few questions to answer, too. He'd prospered while Lanius' father lived . . . and gone to the Maze not long after Mergus died. He was years dead now.

"Well, I don't know the name of the priest, though I'm sure you can find out," Bubulcus said, implying that, if he didn't know it, it couldn't possibly be important. "But I do know they were wed in some little temple at the edge of town, not in the cathedral."

"I should hope not!" Lanius said. "Wouldn't *that* be a scandal? A worse scandal, I mean. He shouldn't have wed at all, not on his own. It's not done in the royal family." A dozen generations of kings spoke through him.

"It is now," Queen Estrilda said. "And it's not the worst match he could have made, even if he shouldn't have made it himself."

"What do you want to bet Petrosus proposed it?" said Sosia, who liked the treasury minister no better than Lanius did. "He's likely eager to make any kind of connection with our family."

"Does he . . . know about Ortalis?" Anser asked.

"How could he not know?" Lanius replied.

"If he does, how could he do that to the girl?" the arch-hallow wondered. "I hope she won't be too unhappy."

Hoping Limosa wouldn't be too unhappy was the kindest thing anyone found to say about the marriage. Lanius had seen omens he liked better.

Grus had just gotten off his horse when a messenger from the south galloped into the Avornan army's encampment shouting his name. "Here!" he called, and waved to show the rider where he was.

General Hirundo had just dismounted, too. "Can't we get a couple of days out of the city of Avornis without having one of these excitable fellows come after us, riding like he's got a fire under his backside?"

"No, that's me." Grus made as though to rub the afflicted parts. Up came the messenger, and thrust a rolled-up sheet of parchment at him. "Thanks—I suppose," the king said, taking it. "What's this?"

"Uh, Your Majesty, it speaks for itself," the messenger replied. "I think it had better talk and I'd better keep quiet."

"Don't like the sound of *that*," Hirundo remarked.

"Neither do I." King Grus broke the seal, slid off the ribbon holding the parchment closed, unrolled the sheet, and read the letter, which was from King Lanius. When he was done, he muttered a curse that didn't come close to satisfying him.

"What is it, Your Majesty?" Hirundo asked.

"My son," Grus answered. "It seems Prince Ortalis has taken it into his head to marry Petrosus' daughter, Limosa. He hasn't just taken it into his head, in fact—he's gone and done it."

"Oh," Hirundo said. Seldom had a man managed to pack more meaning into a single syllable.

"My thoughts exactly." Grus wanted to doubt Lanius, but the other king, no matter how clever, would never have had the imagination to make that up.

"What will you do about it?" Hirundo asked.

The more Grus thought about that, the less he liked the answers that occurred to him. "I don't see what I *can* do about it, except tell Anser to land on the priest who married them like a landslide," he answered reluctantly. "The wedding's legal, no doubt about it. I can't break off this campaign to go back to the capital and try to set things right. But oh, I wish I could." The only reason Petrosus could have dangled Limosa in front of Ortalis was to gain himself more influence. No one else around the palace had been willing to use a daughter in a gambit like that. If Petrosus thought it would work, he would have to think again before too long.

"Yes." Hirundo didn't say any of the things he might have, which proved him an unexpected master of diplomacy. But the expression on his face was eloquent. "Maybe it will turn out all right." He didn't sound as though he believed it.

"Yes, maybe it will." Grus sounded even less convinced than Hirundo, which wasn't easy. *And I'm talking about my own son.* That was a bitter pill. If he'd sounded any other way, though, he would have been hiding what he really felt. He sighed. "I have to go on. We have to go on. Whatever happens back at the capital is less important than what we do against the Chernagors."

Hirundo inclined his head. "Yes, Your Majesty." If the king said it, they would go on. Grus was sure the news of Ortalis' wedding was spreading through the army with the usual speed of rumor. No one but Hirundo seemed to have the nerve to beard him about it. That suited him fine.

I almost wish a Chernagor fleet would strike our western coast hard enough to make *me turn around,* he thought, and then quick, in case gods or the Banished One somehow overheard that, *I did say "almost."*

Except for the hunger for something nasty often smoldering in Ortalis' eyes, there had never been anything wrong with his looks. And now even those low fires seemed banked, as they had when he was hunting regularly. The smile he gave King Lanius was just about everything a smile ought to be. The bow that followed was more in the way of formal politeness than Lanius had had from him in years. "Your Majesty," Ortalis said, "let me present to you my wife, Princess Limosa."

"Thank you, Your Highness," Lanius said, as formally. He nodded to the treasury minister's daughter. "We *have* met before. Let me welcome you to the royal family." *What else can I do?* "I hope you will be very happy." *I don't really believe you will, but anyone can hope.* He also hoped none of what he was thinking showed on his face.

Evidently it didn't, for Limosa smiled as she dropped him a curtsy and said, "Thank you very much, Your Majesty. I'm sure I will." She gazed at Ortalis with stars in her dark eyes. She was a little on the plump side, with a round, pink face, curly brown hair with reddish glints in it, and a crooked front tooth. No one would have called her beautiful, but she was pleasant enough.

Sosia came into the dining room. Ortalis introduced Limosa again. As Lanius had, Sosia said all the right things. If she was insincere, as he was, he couldn't hear it in her voice. He hoped that meant Ortalis and Limosa couldn't, either.

To her brother, Sosia did say, "This was very sudden."

"Well . . ." Was Ortalis blushing? Lanius wouldn't have believed such a thing possible. The prince went on, "We found we suited each other, and so we did what we did." Limosa turned even pinker, but she nodded.

Suited each other? What did that mean? *Do I really want to know?* Lanius wondered. Before he could find any way to ask, servants came in with bread and butter and honey and apples for breakfast. He and Sosia and Ortalis and his new bride settled down to eat. Lanius also wondered if Petrosus would wander in. But Limosa's father did not put in an appearance. Being polite to Limosa was easy enough. Lanius would have had to work harder to stay polite to Petrosus.

Ortalis raised his cup of wine to Limosa's lips. It was a pretty, romantic gesture—about the last thing Lanius would have expected from his brother-in-law. *Cristata was happy with Ortalis at first, too,* he reminded himself. *She said so. Then look what happened.*

Limosa said, "I hope the war against the Chernagors goes well."

No one could argue with that. No one tried. Lanius said, "*I* hope your father keeps our allowance at something close to a reasonable level."

She blushed again. "You mean he doesn't always?" Lanius solemnly shook his head. Limosa said, "That's terrible!"

"Yes, Sosia and I think so, too," Lanius agreed, his voice dry. He wondered how much influence Limosa had on Petrosus. If she really thought it was terrible, and if she really had some influence . . .

But she said, "I'm sorry, but it's not like he listens to me very much." She'd understood Lanius' hint, then. That didn't surprise him. Petrosus had been a courtier for many years; why wouldn't his daughter see that what seemed a comment was in fact a request for her to do something about it? Then Limosa added, "He didn't even know we were going to get married until after the priest conducted the ceremony."

"No?" Lanius said in surprise and disbelief.

Now she shook her head. So did Ortalis. Lanius glanced at Sosia. She looked as astonished as he was. If Limosa had asked her father whether he wanted her to wed Ortalis, what would he have said? What every other father and grandfather said when approached about it? That *wouldn't* have surprised Lanius . . . too much. Petrosus might have been willing to sacrifice happiness for the sake of his own advancement. *Or is that just my dislike for Petrosus coming out?* Lanius wondered. Hard to be sure.

Sosia asked, "What does your father think about it now?"

"He'd better like it," Ortalis growled before Limosa could answer. She seemed willing to let him speak for her. That was interesting. *Someone new I'm going to have to try to learn to figure out,* Lanius thought. Archives were much more tractable than living, breathing people. Even inscrutable moncats were easier to make sense of than people.

He lifted his cup of wine in salute. "I hope you'll be . . . very happy together," he said. He'd started to say, *I hope you'll be as happy as Sosia and I have been.* Considering the jolt his affair with Cristata had given their happiness, those weren't such favorable words as they would have been a little while before.

Ortalis and Limosa beamed. They must not have noticed the hesitation. Sosia had. Did she know what he'd almost said? He wouldn't have been surprised. She knew him better than anyone else did—save perhaps her father. Lanius didn't like admitting, even to himself, that Grus had a knack for getting inside his mind. But he didn't like denying the truth, either.

He eyed Ortalis and Limosa again. How were they at facing up to the truth? Did the thought so much as cross their minds? He doubted it. *Too bad for them,* he thought.

"Come on," Grus said. His horse trudged up toward the top of the pass that linked Avornis to the land of the Chernagors. He leaned forward in the saddle and squeezed the beast's barrel with his knees. "*Get* up, there." The horse went a little faster—not much, but a little.

Beside the king, Hirundo beamed. "You're becoming a horseman after all, Your Majesty."

"Go ahead—insult me," Grus said. "If things had gone the way I wish they would have, I'd hardly ever need to get onto one of these miserable beasts."

Hirundo didn't seem to know what to make of that. Grus had hoped he wouldn't. The king rode on. The army followed. Every so often, Grus looked back over his shoulder to see if a messenger was coming out of the south. He'd already had one. He spied no more this time. That either meant the Chernagors weren't raiding the Avornan coast or that the Avornan garrisons and river galleys and new oceangoing ships were beating them back. Grus hoped it meant one of those two things, anyhow.

At the top of the pass, he looked back toward his own kingdom once more. He hadn't thought he'd climbed all that high, but he could see a long way. The bright green of newly planted fields of wheat and barley and rye and oats contrasted with the darker tones of orchards and forests. Here and there, smoke plumes rose from towns and obscured the farmland beyond. Only very gradually did natural mist and haze blur the rest of the landscape.

When he looked ahead, the story was different. Fog rolling off the Northern Sea left the land of the Chernagors shrouded in mystery. But Grus didn't need to see the Chernagor country to know what lay ahead—trouble. If the Chernagors weren't going to cause trouble, he wouldn't have had to come here and look out across their land.

He also looked around. There was Prince Vsevolod, hard-faced and grim, riding along at the head of a handful of retainers. Did he believe Grus could restore him as Prince of Nishevatz after two years in exile? Grus hoped he did; he might yet prove valuable to the Avornan cause.

And there rode Pterocles. In one sense, he wasn't far from Prince Vsevolod. In another, he might have belonged to a different world. The wizard didn't even seem to see Vsevolod and his kilted retainers. All his attention focused on the view ahead. He looked like a man riding into a battle he expected to lose—brave enough, but far from hopeful. Remembering what had happened to Pterocles in the Chernagor country a couple of years before, Grus didn't suppose he could blame him.

Pterocles also stood out because of his bad riding. Next to the seasoned cavalry troopers, Grus wasn't much of a rider. Next to Pterocles, he might have been a centaur. The wizard rode as though he'd never heard of riding before climbing aboard his mule. He was all knees and elbows and apprehension. Every slightest jounce took him by surprise, and threatened to pitch him out of the saddle and under the horse's hoofs. Watching him made Grus nervous and sympathetic at the same time.

"You're doing fine," the king called to the wizard. "Relax a little, and everything will be all right."

Pterocles eyed him as though he'd taken leave of his senses. "Relax a little, and I'll be dead . . . Your Majesty," he answered.

Grus wondered whether he was talking about the mule or about the sorcerous challenges ahead. After some thought, he decided he didn't want to ask.

To Grus' surprise, the Chernagors didn't try to defend the fortress of Varazdin. They evacuated it instead, fleeing ahead of the advancing Avornans. Grus left a small garrison in it—enough men to make sure the Chernagors didn't seize it again as soon as he'd gone on toward Nishevatz.

"This is a funny business," Hirundo said as they headed for the coastal lowlands. "When the fellow commanding that fort was loyal to Prince Vsevolod, he fought us teeth and toenails. Now the man in charge of it gets his orders from Vasilko, and he runs off. Go figure."

"Everything about the war with the Chernagors has been backward," Grus said. "Why should this be any different?"

He hadn't come very far into the Chernagor country before realizing he'd left Avornis behind. The look of the sky and the quality of the sunlight weren't the same as they had been down in his own kingdom. A perpetual haze hung over the lowlands here. It turned the sunlight watery and the sky a color halfway between blue and gray. Drifting clouds had no sharp edges; they blurred into the sky behind them in a way they never would have in a land of bright sun and a sky of a respectable, genuine blue.

The landscape had a strange look, too. Roofs of thatch replaced those of red tiles. In this damp, dripping country, fire wasn't the worry it would have been farther south. Even the haystacks were different here; they wore canvas covers on top to keep off the rain. Gliding gulls mewed and squawked overhead.

And the Northern Sea was nothing like the Azanian Sea. Gray and chilly-looking, it struck Grus as far from inviting. He knew the Chernagors thought otherwise. To them, it was the high road to trading—and raiding—riches. As far as he was concerned, they were welcome to it.

He and his army reached the sea sooner than he'd expected. Instead of offering battle away from Nishevatz, Prince Vasilko seemed intent on defending the city with everything he had. A few archers harassed the advancing Avornans, but only a few. They would shoot from ambush, then either rely on concealment or try to get away on fast horses. They would not stand and fight.

That mortified Prince Vsevolod. "Not enough my son should give self to Banished One," he rumbled in disgust. "No, not enough. Also he show self coward. Better he should die."

"Better he should surrender, so you can have your throne back and we can go home to Avornis." Grus didn't believe that would happen. Vasilko had something in mind. The king hoped discovering what it was wouldn't prove too painful.

In any case, Vsevolod wasn't listening to him. "Disgrace," he muttered. "My son is disgrace."

There was a feeling Grus knew all too well. He set a hand on Vsevolod's shoulder. "Try not to blame yourself, Your Highness. I'm sure you did everything you could." *I did with Ortalis.*

Vsevolod shrugged off the hand and shook his massive head. Grus didn't like to think about his own quarrels with his son, either. And what would come of Ortalis' marriage to Limosa? What besides trouble, anyhow?

A grandson who might be an heir, Grus thought. Of course, Crex was already a grandson who might be an heir. If having two grandsons who might be heirs wasn't trouble, Grus had no idea what would fit the definition. How *would* things play out once he wasn't there to make sure they went the way he wanted?

"Your Majesty!" A cavalry captain rode up to Grus. "Ask you a question, Your Majesty?"

"Go ahead," Grus told him. Whatever questions a cavalry captain could come up with were bound to be less worrisome than thoughts of two grandsons going to war with each other over which one got to wear the crown.

"Well, Your Majesty, these fields are full—full to bursting, you might say—of cows and sheep, and I'd banquet off my boots if the sties aren't full of pigs, too," the officer said. "Now, I know we're here to help His Highness the prince, but it would make things a lot easier if we could do some foraging, too."

Grus didn't have to think about that. He didn't have to ask Prince Vsevolod, either. He said, "As far as we're concerned, Captain, this is enemy country. Go ahead and forage to your heart's content, and I hope you stuff yourself full of beefsteaks and mutton chops and roast pork. Right now, we worry about hurting Vasilko. Once we've cast him down, then we start worrying about helping Vsevolod. Or do you think I'm wrong?"

"Oh, no, sir!" the officer said quickly. Grus laughed at the naked hunger on his face. He went on, "We'll forage, all right. We'll take the war right to the Chernagors. Let 'em go hungry." They wouldn't go hungry enough, not when the other Chernagor city-states helped supply them by sea. Grus knew as much. But his own side would eat well. That counted, too.

CHAPTER TWELVE

King Lanius looked at the moncat, and the moncat looked at Lanius. "How did you get out?" the king demanded. Bubulcus
wasn't the only servant who denied having anything to do with
Pouncer's latest escape. Had it found some way out of the chamber all
by itself? If it had, none of the other animals in here had proved smart
enough to use it.

What did that mean? Did it mean anything? Could one moncat be
so much smarter and sneakier than the rest that it kept an escape route
a secret? Lanius didn't know. He would have liked to ask Pouncer with
some hope of getting back an answer he could understand. That failing,
he would have liked to catch the beast in the act of escaping.

Neither seemed likely. Moncats were sneaky enough—and enough
like ordinary cats—not to do something while a lowly human being
was watching. And, to a moncat, even a King of Avornis counted as a
lowly human being.

"Mrowr," Pouncer said, staring at Grus out of large amber eyes.
Then it scampered up the scaffolding of branches and poles that did
duty for a forest canopy. Its retractile claws, always sharp, bit into the
wood. Moncats climbed even better than monkeys.

He still wondered which were smarter, moncats or monkeys. Moncats were more self-centered and perverse; of that he had no doubt.
Monkeys thought more along the lines of human intelligence. That
made them *seem* smarter, at least at first glance. But Lanius remained
unconvinced they really were.

Try as he would, he couldn't think of any way to test the animals that would prove anything. If the moncats didn't feel like playing along, they simply wouldn't. What did that prove? Were they stupid, or just willful? Or would he be the stupid one for trying to get them to do things they weren't inclined to do?

As things stood now, he certainly felt like the stupid one. He eyed the moncat he'd twice encountered in the archives. Maybe the servants were lying, and someone had opened a door that second time, as Bubulcus had the first time. If they weren't, though, Pouncer did have a secret it wasn't telling.

"If you come to the archives again, I'll . . ." Lanius' voice trailed away. What *would* he do to Pouncer if it escaped again? Punish it? Congratulate it? Both at once? If the moncat didn't already think so, that would convince it human beings were crazy.

Reluctantly, he left the moncats' chamber. He wasn't going to find out what he wanted to know there. He wondered if a wizard could figure out what Pouncer was doing. But plenty of more important things needed wizards. What a moncat was up to didn't. Odds were it wouldn't—couldn't—do it again anyway.

So Lanius told himself. All the same, the first few times he went back to the archives, he kept looking around at every small noise he imagined he heard. He waited for the moncat to meow and to emerge from concealment brandishing something it had stolen from the kitchens.

He waited, but nothing out of the ordinary happened. He decided those small noises really were figments of his imagination. When he stopped worrying about them, he got more work done than he had for weeks. He turned up several parchments touching on how Avornis had ruled the provinces south of the Stura River before the Menteshe—and the Banished One—took them from the kingdom.

Would those ever really matter again? Every time Avornis tried to reclaim the lost provinces, disaster had followed. No King of Avornis for the past two centuries and more had dared do any serious campaigning south of the Stura. And yet Grus talked about going after the Scepter of Mercy in a way that suggested he *was* serious and *would* do it if he got the chance. Lanius would have been more likely to take that as bluster if the Banished One hadn't stirred up so much trouble for Avornis far from the Stura. Didn't that suggest he was worried about what might happen if the Avornans did try once more to reclaim the Scepter and their lost lands?

Didn't it? Or did it? How could a mere mortal know? Maybe the outcast god was stirring up trouble elsewhere for its own sake. Or maybe he was laying an uncommonly deep trap, building up belief in their chances so he could do a better job of cutting them down.

That troubled Lanius enough to drive him out of the royal archives—and over to the great cathedral and the ecclesiastical archives. He'd seen they held more about the Banished One than the royal archives did. The expelled deity had been a theological problem even before he became a political problem.

Lanius paid his respects to Arch-Hallow Anser. Then he called on Ixoreus. The green-robed priest held no high rank. But what he didn't know of the archives under the cathedral, no man living did.

After a moment's thought, the king wondered about that. As he and the white-bearded archivist went downstairs, Lanius asked, as casually as he could, "Have you ever run across the name Milvago in all these parchments?"

Ixoreus stopped. His eyes widened slightly—no, more than slightly. "Oh, yes, Your Majesty," he said in a low voice. "I have run across that name. I didn't know you had."

"I often wish I hadn't," Lanius said. "Do you know what that name means?"

"Oh, yes," the archivist repeated. "But I have never told a living soul of it. Have you?"

"One," Lanius answered. "I told Grus. He had to know."

Ixoreus considered. At last, with some reluctance, he nodded. "Yes, I suppose he did. But can he keep his mouth shut?" He spoke of the other king with a casual lack of respect. Lanius was suddenly sure the old man spoke about him the same way when he was out of earshot.

"Yes," he said. "Grus and I don't always get along, but he can hold a secret."

"I suppose so," Ixoreus said. "He hasn't told the arch-hallow. I'm sure of that—and Anser is his own flesh and blood. *I* never told anybody—not Arch-Hallow Bucco, not King Mergus, not King Scolopax—gods, no!—not anybody. And I wouldn't have told you, either, if you hadn't found out for yourself."

Considering what this secret was . . . "Good," Lanius told the priest.

The gray stone walls of Nishevatz frowned down on the Avornan army encamped in front of them. Grus studied the formidable stonework.

"Here we are again," he said to Hirundo. "How do we do better this time than we did two years ago?"

"Yes, here we are again," the general agreed lightly. "How do we do better? Taking the city would be good, don't you think?"

"Now that you mention it, yes." King Grus matched him dry for dry. "And how do we go about that, if you'd be so kind?"

They stood not far from the outer opening of the tunnel Prince Vsevolod had used to escape from Nishevatz, the tunnel Avornan and Chernagor soldiers had entered to sneak into the town . . . and from which, by all appearances, they'd never emerged. Hirundo's eyes flicked in the direction of that opening. "One thing we'd better *not* do," he said, "and that's try going underground again."

"True," Grus said. "That means we have to go over the wall—or through it."

He and Hirundo both looked toward Nishevatz's works. From behind battlements, Chernagor fighting men in iron helmets and mailshirts looked back. Two years earlier, Grus had seen how well they could fight defending one of their towns. He had no reason to believe they'd gone soft in those two years. That meant breaking into Nishevatz wouldn't be easy.

"Do you think the wizard can do us any good?" Hirundo asked.

"I don't know," Grus answered. "We'd better find out, though, eh?"

Pterocles looked his usual haggard self. Grus could hardly blame him. The last time he'd looked at these walls, he'd almost died. Now, though, he managed a nod. "I'll do what I can, Your Majesty."

"How much do you think that will be?" Grus asked. "If you *can't* help us, tell me now so I can try to make other plans."

"I think I can," the wizard said. "I don't feel anything of the presence that beat me the last time. That makes me think it *was* the Banished One, and that now he's busy somewhere else."

Was that good news? Grus wasn't altogether sure. "Do you know where? Can you sense what he's doing?"

"No, Your Majesty," Pterocles replied. "I don't feel him at all. That's all I can tell you." He paused. "No. It's not. I'm not sorry not to feel him, either."

Grus pointed north, toward the sea. "Without a sorcerous foe here, can you do anything about the supply ships that are keeping Nishevatz fed? If the grain doesn't come in, this turns into a real siege, one we can win without trying to storm the walls."

"I don't know." Pterocles looked dubious. "I can try, but magic doesn't usually travel well over water—not unless you're the Banished One, of course. He can do things ordinary wizards only dream of."

There are reasons for that, too, Grus thought; he knew more of them than even Pterocles did. Since he couldn't tell the wizard what he knew, he said, "It's not the water we want to aim the magic at. It's those ships."

"Yes, I understand that," Pterocles said impatiently. "I'm not altogether an idiot, you know."

"Well, good," Grus murmured. "I do like to have that reassurance." As he'd hoped, Pterocles sent him a dirty look. An angry wizard, he thought, would do a better job than one just going through the motions. He hoped so, anyhow.

Ships full of grain kept getting into Nishevatz for the next few days. Grus could watch them put in at quays beyond the reach of his catapults. He could watch men haul sacks of grain into the Chernagor town on their backs and load more sacks into carts and wagons that donkeys and horses took inside the walls. As far as he could tell, Prince Vasilko's soldiers were eating better than his own men. And he couldn't do anything about it.

He couldn't—but maybe Pterocles could. The wizard didn't show his face for some time. Grus checked on him once, and found him sitting with his chin in his hands staring down at a grimoire on a folding table in front of him. Pterocles didn't look up. He didn't seem to notice the king was there. Grus silently withdrew. If Pterocles was getting ready to do something large and important, Grus didn't want to interfere. If, on the other hand, the wizard was just sitting there . . .

If that's all he's doing, he'll be very sorry, Grus thought. *I'll make sure he's very sorry.*

In due course, Pterocles emerged. He looked pale but determined. He always looked pale. Determination often seemed harder to come by. Nodding to Grus, the wizard said, "I'm ready, Your Majesty."

Grus nodded. "Good. So are we. Gods grant you good fortune."

"Thank you, Your Majesty. What I can do, I will." Pterocles brought out a basin filled with water. On it floated toy ships made of chips of wood, with stick masts and scraps of cloth for sails. Pointing to the basin, he told Grus, "It's filled with seawater from the Northern Sea."

To him, the point of that seemed clear. To Grus, it was opaque. The king asked, "Why?"

"To make it more closely resemble that which is real," the wizard replied. "The more closely the magical and the real correspond, the better the result of the spell is likely to be."

"You know your business," Grus said. *I hope you know your business.*

Pterocles got down to it as though he knew his business. He began to chant in a dialect of Avornan even older than the one priests used to celebrate the sacred liturgies in temples and cathedrals. When a cloud drifted close to the sun, he pointed a finger at it and spoke in threatening tones, though the dialect was so old-fashioned, Grus couldn't make out exactly what he said. The cloud slid past without covering the sun. Maybe the wind would have taken it that way anyhow. Grus didn't think so, not with the direction in which it was blowing, but maybe. Still, mortal wizards had trouble manipulating the weather, so maybe not, too.

The king wondered why Pterocles wanted to preserve the sunshine, which was about as bright as it ever got in the misty Chernagor country. He soon found out. The wizard drew from his leather belt pouch what Grus first took to be a crystal ball. Then he saw it was considerably wider than it was thick, though still curved on top and bottom.

Chanting still, Pterocles held the crystal a few inches above one of the miniature ships floating in the basin. A brilliant point of light appeared on the toy ship's deck. To Grus' amazement, smoke began to rise. A moment later, the toy ship burst into flame. Pterocles shouted out what was plainly a command.

And then Grus shouted, too, in triumph. He pointed out to sea. One of the real ships there had also caught fire. A thick plume of black smoke rose high into the sky. Pterocles never turned his head to look. He went right on with his spell, poising the crystal over another ship.

Before long, that second toy also burned. When it did, another Chernagor ship bound for Nishevatz also caught fire. "Well done!" Grus cried. "By Olor's beard, Pterocles, well done!"

Pterocles, for once, refused to be distracted. For all the difference the king's shout made to his magic, Grus might as well have kept quiet. A third miniature ship caught fire. A third real ship out on the Northern Sea burst into flame.

That was enough for the rest of the Chernagor skippers. They put about and fled from Nishevatz as fast as the wind would take them. That wasn't fast enough to keep another tall-masted ship from catching fire and burning. The survivors fled faster yet.

Pterocles might have burned even more ships, but the strain of what he was doing caught up with him. He swayed like a tall tree in a high wind. Then his eyes rolled up in his head and he toppled over in a faint. Grus caught him before he hit his head on the ground, easing him down.

Once Pterocles wasn't working magic anymore, he soon recovered. His eyes opened. "Did I do it, Your Majesty?" he asked.

"See for yourself." Grus pointed out toward the Northern Sea, and toward the smoke rising from the burning ships upon it.

The wizard made a fist and smacked it softly into the open palm of his other hand. "Yes!" he said, one quiet word with more triumph in it than most of the shouts the king had heard.

"Well done. More than well done, by the gods." Grus gave Pterocles all the praise he could. "You had a hard time when you were in the Chernagor country a couple of years ago, but now you're making our foes pay."

"This was . . . much easier than what I did year before last," Pterocles replied. "Then . . ." He shook his head, plainly not wanting to remember. "Well, you saw what happened to me then. Now . . . Now I feel as though I'm not fighting somebody three times as tall as I am, and ten times as strong."

Grus wondered what that meant. Probably that, as he'd thought, the Banished One wasn't watching Nishevatz as closely as he had then, and didn't land on Pterocles like a landslide when the wizard threatened to do something inconvenient. When that first occurred to him, Grus knew nothing but relief. But it quickly spawned another obvious question. If the Banished One wasn't concentrating on the land of the Chernagors these days, where *was* he concentrating, and why?

When Grus asked the worrisome question out loud, Pterocles said, "I'm sorry, Your Majesty, but I have no way of learning that."

"I know you don't—not until the Banished One shows all of us," the king said. "Meanwhile, though, all we can do is keep on here. If we can turn this into a real siege, we'll starve Vasilko into yielding up Nishevatz."

Pterocles nodded. "Yes," he repeated, even more low-voiced than before. It wasn't triumphant this time—he'd seen how uncertain war could be. But it held as much anticipation as Grus felt himself.

Little by little, Lanius had resigned himself to Cristata's being gone. He wouldn't see her again. He wouldn't hold her again. He'd made peace with Sosia. He'd never stopped caring for his wife. Maybe she finally believed that. Or maybe she'd decided showing she didn't believe it wasn't a good idea.

But Lanius also began to notice that the serving women in the palace looked on him with new eyes these days. Before he slept with Cristata, they'd seemed to think he wouldn't do anything like that. Now they knew he might. And they knew how much they might gain if he did—with them. They straightened up whenever he came by. They batted their eyes. They swung their hips. Their voices got lower and throatier. They leaped to obey his every request. It was all very enjoyable, and all very distracting.

Sosia also noticed. She didn't find it enjoyable. "They're a pack of sluts," she told Lanius. "I hope you can see that, too."

"Oh, yes. I see it," he said. That seemed to satisfy Sosia. He'd hoped it would. He'd even meant it. That didn't mean he didn't go on enjoying. Few men fail to enjoy pretty women finding them attractive, regardless of whether they intend to do anything about it.

Lanius hadn't particularly intended to do anything about it. He understood that some—a lot—of the serving women's new interest was mercenary. As things worked out, though, his eyes didn't ruin his good intentions. His nose did.

He was going down the corridor that led to the royal archives when he suddenly stopped and sniffed. The scent was sweet and thick and spicy. He'd never smelled it before, or at least never noticed it before. He noticed it now. He couldn't have noticed it much more if he'd been hit over the head.

"What *is* that perfume?" he said.

"It's called sandalwood, Your Majesty." The maidservant's name, Lanius recalled, was Zenaida. She was from the south, with wavy midnight hair, black eyes, and a delicately arched nose. When she smiled at the king, her lips seemed redder and fuller and softer than ever before. "Do you like it?"

"Very much," Lanius answered. "It . . . suits you."

"Thank you." Zenaida smiled again, without any coyness about what she had in mind. "And what would suit *you*, Your Majesty?"

Not even Lanius, who often failed to notice hints, could misunderstand that. He coughed once or twice. If not for the perfume, he might have passed it off with a joke or pretended not to hear. But the fragrance unlocked gates in his defenses before he even realized the citadel was under attack. Up until now, he'd hardly noticed Zenaida. He wondered why not.

"What *would* suit me?" he murmured. The answer came without hesitation. "Come along," he told Zenaida. Smiling once more—a woman's secret smile of victory—she stepped up by his side.

The palace was full of little rooms—storerooms, small reception halls, rooms with no particular purpose. Finding an empty one was as easy as walking down the hallway and opening a door. Lanius and Zenaida went in together. The king closed the door and barred it. When he turned back to Zenaida, the maidservant was already pulling her dress off over her head.

Half an hour later, they came out of the chamber—Zenaida first, then Lanius, who was still setting his clothes to rights. He blew the maidservant a kiss as she went off on whatever business he'd interrupted when he smelled the sandalwood perfume. Laughing a happy little laugh, she fluttered her fingers at him and disappeared around a corner.

"Oh. The archives." Lanius had to remind himself where he'd been going when he smelled Zenaida's perfume. He suspected he wore a silly grin as he opened the doors that let him in and closed them behind him.

He sat down and started poking through old tax registers. After a moment, he realized he was paying no attention to them. Now he laughed. Thinking about Zenaida's smooth, creamy skin, about the way she arched her back and moaned when pleasure took her, was more fun than finding out how many sheep villagers two hundred years dead had claimed they owned.

Thinking about that also made him realize he'd enjoyed lying with her as much as he ever had with Cristata. He wondered what that meant. Actually, he had a pretty good idea. It meant what he'd thought was love for the other serving woman had probably been nothing but satisfaction.

Grus had told him as much not long after sending Cristata off to a provincial town. Lanius hadn't wanted to listen. Now . . . Now he had to admit to himself (he never would have admitted it to Grus) that his father-in-law had been right. Making love with Zenaida had taught him more than he'd imagined when he first sniffed sandalwood.

And not only had he learned something about himself, he'd also learned something about Grus. The other king got high marks for cleverness. Lanius also had a better idea why Grus sometimes bedded other women. Sosia wouldn't care for that bit of insight, or how he'd gotten it. Neither would Estrilda. Lanius shrugged. He had it, come what might.

Another tall-masted, high-pooped ship burned in the waters off Nishevatz. It lit up the night. The Chernagors had quit trying to resupply the city during the day; Pterocles' magic made that impossibly expensive. They'd tried to sneak the merchantman past the wizard under cover of darkness. They'd tried, they'd failed, and now they were paying the price—he'd found that setting ships alight with sorcerously projected ordinary fire worked at night as well as using sunlight did in the daytime.

Standing beside King Grus, Prince Vsevolod folded his big, bony hands into fists. "Cook!" he shouted out to the sailors aboard the burning ship. "You help my son, the scum, you get what you deserve. Cook!"

"I think we're getting somewhere, Your Highness," Grus said.

"I know where I want to get." Vsevolod turned to the gray stone walls of Nishevatz, now bathed in flickering red and gold. "And I know what I want to do. I want to get hands on son."

"What would you do with Vasilko if you had him?" Grus asked.

"Make him remember who is rightful Prince of Nishevatz," Vsevolod answered, which didn't go into detail but did sound more than a little menacing.

"I wonder how much food they've got in there," Grus said in musing tones. "Maybe not so much, if they thought they could bring in fresh supplies whenever they needed them. They're going to get hungry by and by, if they aren't hungry already."

Vsevolod shook his fist at the city-state he'd ruled for so many years. "Starve!" he shouted angrily. "Let them all starve. I take bodies out, bury in fields, raise cabbages from them. Then I bring in new people, honest people—not thieves who take away crown from honest man."

Grus didn't argue with him. He'd long since seen there was no point to arguing with Vsevolod. The exiled prince knew what he knew, or thought he knew what he knew, and didn't care to change his mind.

Sure enough, Vsevolod demanded, "How soon we attack Nishevatz?"

"When we're sure the defenders are too hungry and too weak to put up much of a fight," Grus answered. "We fought too soon and too hard year before last, if you'll remember. We want to win when we go in."

Vsevolod made a noise down deep in his chest. It wasn't agreement, or anything even close to agreement. The prince sounded like a lion balked of its prey. He didn't want to wait. He wanted to spring and leap and kill.

Grus also wanted Nishevatz. What he didn't want was to pay a crippling price for the Chernagor city-state. He'd done worse than that on his earlier campaign against it—he'd paid a high price and failed to take the place. Another embarrassment of that sort would be the last thing he—or Avornis—needed.

Vsevolod's thinking ran along different lines. "When do you attack?" he asked again. "When is Nishevatz mine once more?"

"I told you, I'll attack when I think I can win without bankrupting myself."

"This is coward's counsel," Vsevolod complained.

"Oh?" King Grus sent him a cold stare. "How many men are *you* contributing to this attack, Your Highness?"

The deposed Prince of Nishevatz returned a glance full of fury—full of something not far from hate. "Traitors. My people are traitors," he mumbled, and slowly and deliberately turned his back on Grus.

An Avornan who did something like that to his sovereign would find himself in trouble in short order. But Grus wasn't Vsevolod's sovereign. Vsevolod was, or had been, a sovereign in his own right. The way he acted in exile made Grus understand why the people of Nishevatz had been inclined to give Vasilko a chance to rule them. Since Vasilko relied on the Banished One for backing, that choice hadn't been a good one. But Vsevolod hadn't been the best of rulers, either.

Sighing, Grus wished *he* had some other choice besides Vsevolod or Vasilko to offer the Chernagors inside Nishevatz. But, as he knew all too well, he didn't. If only Vsevolod had a long-lost brother or cousin, or Vasilko had a brother or even a bastard half brother. But they didn't. Grus was stuck with one or the other—was, in effect, stuck with Vsevolod, since Vasilko had chosen the Banished One. The King of Avornis sighed again. In a poem, some other candidate for Prince of Nishevatz would turn up just when he was needed most. In real life, this bitter old man, no bargain himself, was the only tool that fit Grus' hand.

"Traitors," Vsevolod muttered again. He swung back toward Grus. "Your wizard can find way over wall, yes?"

"Maybe." Grus wasn't sure himself. "I'd better see, though."

He sent a messenger to find Pterocles and bring the wizard to him. Pterocles came promptly enough. The wizard seemed more cheerful than he had since being felled in front of Nishevatz during the last siege. Succeeding with his spells had buoyed him, the same way a string of victories would have buoyed a general.

"What can I do for you, Your Majesty?" he asked.

"I don't know yet," Grus answered. "Prince Vsevolod has asked what you can do to help take Nishevatz away from Vasilko. It strikes me as a reasonable question."

"Set walls afire, like you set ships afire," Vsevolod said eagerly. "Roast Vasilko like saddle of mutton in oven."

Pterocles shook his head. "I'm sorry, Your Highness, but I can't manage that. The ships are wooden, and burn easily. I'm not wizard enough to set stone afire. I'm not sure any mortal could do that." *Maybe the Banished One could* hung in the air, unspoken but almost palpable.

"Burn gates, in that case," Vsevolod said, which was actually a good suggestion.

Grus looked at Pterocles. Pterocles looked toward the gates, which were of timbers heavily plated with iron. "Maybe," the wizard said. "I could try, anyhow, when the sun comes out again. For that, I'd want the strongest, purest sorcery I can work, and sunlight is stronger and purer than earthly fire." The day, like many around Nishevatz, was dim and overcast, with fog rolling in off the Northern Sea.

"Get ready to try, then," Grus told Pterocles. "We'll see what happens." He didn't say anything suggesting he would blame the wizard if the magic failed. He wanted to build up the other man's confidence, not tear it down.

Vsevolod cared nothing for such concerns. Glowering at Pterocles, he demanded, "Why you have to wait for sun?"

"As I said, it gives the best fire to power my spells," Pterocles replied.

"You want fire?" Vsevolod pointed toward the rows of cookfires throughout the Avornan encampment. "We have plenty fires for you."

"You may think so, but the magic is stronger with the sun," Pterocles said. "For a ship that's very easy to burn, the other fire, I've found, will do. For the gates, which will be much harder, I have to have the strongest fire I can get. Do I tell you how to run your business, Your Majesty?"

Vsevolod muttered something in the Chernagor language. Grus

didn't understand a word of it. All things considered, that was probably just as well. Before the Prince of Nishevatz could return to Avornan, Grus spoke up, saying, "We have to trust Pterocles' judgment here. When he's ready, he can cast the spell. Until then, he would do better to wait."

More mutters from Vsevolod. "Thank you, Your Majesty," Pterocles said.

"You're welcome," Grus answered, but he couldn't help adding, "I hope you don't have to wait too long."

Later, he wished he hadn't said that. He couldn't help wondering whether he'd jinxed the wizard and his magic. Day after day of gloom and fog followed, with never more than a halfhearted glimpse of the sun. Such stretches of bad weather could happen here, sure enough. Was this one natural, though?

At last, Grus grew impatient and frustrated enough to ask the question aloud. Pterocles only shrugged. "Hard to know for certain, Your Majesty. I will say this once more, though—weatherworking's not easy, not for mortals."

"Not for mortals." The king chewed on that. "Is the Banished One turning his eye this way again, then?"

"I haven't noticed any sign of it." Pterocles' sigh sent more fog into the cool, moist air. "I think I would. A man who's known the lion's claw recognizes it when he feels it again."

Four days later, the weather finally changed, but not for the better. Rain began dripping from the heavens. It went on and on, never too hard but never letting up, either. Avornan soldiers squelched glumly through their camp, pulling each boot out of the mud in turn.

The rain frustrated Pterocles in more ways than one. "I hope the Chernagors don't try to sneak ships into Nishevatz while the weather stays bad," he said. "Bad for us, I mean—good for them. They might manage it without our even noticing. For that matter, using ordinary fire in the spells against their ships wouldn't be easy now."

"How likely are they to do that?" Grus asked. "*I* wouldn't want to try sailing through rain and fog." He shuddered, imagining rocks or other ships unseen until too late. Pterocles only gave him another shrug. That did nothing to reassure him. With a shrug of his own, Grus said, "Be ready to do what needs doing when the weather finally clears. Sooner or later, it has to."

"I'll be ready, Your Majesty," the wizard declared. Grus could only accept that. If he nagged Pterocles after such a promise, he would likely do the Avornan cause more harm than good.

After another week of fog and drizzle and rain, the king felt about ready to burst. So did Vsevolod, who muttered darkly into his white beard. Pterocles paced back and forth like a caged bear. Even General Hirundo, among the most cheerful men ever born, began snapping at people.

Grus felt like cheering when he finally saw a sunny dawn. Thanks to the rain that had gone before, it was a beautiful day. All the weeds and shrubs around Nishevatz glowed like emeralds. Sunbeams sparkled off drops of water in the greenery, spawning countless tiny rainbows. The bushes might have been full of diamonds. The air still tasted sweet and damp; the rain had washed it clean of the stinks that clung to an en-camped army.

"Let's go, Pterocles," Grus called. He didn't ask if the wizard was ready to work his magic against the gate. He assumed Pterocles was. If that assumption proved wrong, the king would have something to say. Until it proved so, he would go forward.

Pterocles said, "Your Majesty, I can try the spell now if you order me to. It may work, but it may not. If you let me wait until the sun stands higher in the sky and its light is stronger, the spell is almost sure to work then. I will do as you require either way. What would you like?"

However much Grus wished it weren't, that was a legitimate ques-tion. "Wait," he said after thinking a little while. "Your magic is the most important part of the attack. It needs to work to give us a chance of taking Nishevatz. Do it when you think the odds are best."

"Thank you." Pterocles sketched a salute.

Grus watched the skies, looking for clouds to roll across the sun and steal the wizard's chance. He thought he would tell Pterocles to try with ordinary fire then—if it started the gate burning, well and good; if not, they could wait for sun again. But the day only got brighter, and about as warm as it ever seemed to around Nishevatz. Steam rose from the walls of the city-state, and from the ground around it. The king was about to ask Pterocles if he was ready to begin when a rider pounded up from the south. Mud flew from his horse's hooves as it trotted forward. "Your Majesty!" the messenger called. "I have important news, your Majesty!"

"Give it to me," Grus said, as calmly as he could. News like that, news important enough to rush up from the south, was unlikely to be good.

And, sure enough, the messenger said, "I'm sorry, Your Majesty, but Prince Ulash's Menteshe have come north over the Stura. They're hitting the provinces on our side of the river hard."

"*Ulash's* Menteshe?" Grus said, and the rider nodded. Grus cursed. That was the worst news he could have gotten. Ulash had stayed quiet when Prince Evren raided the southern provinces a few years before. If he was running wild now . . . He was at least as strong as all the other Menteshe princes put together. *No wonder the Banished One stopped worrying about the land of the Chernagors,* Grus thought.

"Shall I go ahead and cast the spell, Your Majesty?" Pterocles asked.

"No," Grus said, hating the word. "We have to break off the siege again. We have to go back."

CHAPTER THIRTEEN

Lanius wished he weren't once more briefly seeing Grus in the city
of Avornis as the other king hurried from one trouble spot to
another. Grus looked harried. Lanius couldn't blame him. Grus
said, "Is it really as bad as it's sounded from all the reports I've had?"

"All I have are the same reports," Lanius answered. "It doesn't sound
good, does it?"

"This isn't just a raid, sure enough," Grus said. "They're throwing
everything they've got into it."

"In a way, it's a compliment," Lanius said. Grus eyed him as though
he'd lost his mind. "It is," Lanius insisted. "You were doing too well up
in the Chernagor country. The Banished One couldn't find any way to
stop you up there, so he got Ulash moving down in the south."

The other king frowned as he thought things over. "Something to
that," he said at last. His frown got deeper, pulling the lines of his face
into harsh relief. *He's not a young man anymore,* Lanius thought. But
even if Grus wasn't as young as he had been, he remained vigorous. He
also hadn't lost his wry wit. "It's a compliment I could do without, you
know."

"I believe it." Lanius waited for Grus to warn him not to get too enthusiastic about running the kingdom from the capital while his fellow
king took the field. Grus didn't do it. Instead, he threw back his head—
and yawned. Lanius asked him, "How long do you aim to stay in the
city of Avornis?"

"Today, maybe tomorrow," Grus answered. "No longer than that. A couple of things I need to take care of here, and then I'll be on my way down toward the Stura. It's not like I haven't fought in those parts before."

"What are you going to do here?" Lanius asked.

Grus' smile was all sharp teeth. "I know Petrosus isn't your favorite minister," he said. Lanius nodded. The other king went on, "You'll be dealing with someone else from now on. Petrosus will spend the rest of his days in the Maze."

"Even though he's Ortalis' father-in-law?" Lanius said in surprise.

"*Because* he's Ortalis' father-in-law," Grus answered grimly.

"But Ortalis and Limosa ran off and got married by themselves," Lanius said. "That's how they both tell it."

"I don't care how they tell it," Grus said. "Ortalis wouldn't have chosen her if her father hadn't pulled wires. And any which way, you can't tell me Petrosus wouldn't try to pull more now that he's wedged his way into my family."

In a way, that was funny. Grus had wedged *his* way into Lanius' family the same way. And Grus didn't just pull wires. He had the whole web of the kingdom in his hands. Pointing that out would not have endeared Lanius to him. The only thing Lanius found to say was, "You would know best."

Even that earned him a sharp look from Grus. The other king was far from a fool, even if Lanius had to remind himself of that every so often. Grus said, "There are times when I wonder whether I know anything about anything."

You know enough to hold on to things for yourself, Lanius thought. He said, "Will you use river galleys against the Menteshe?"

"If I can," Grus answered. "Past that, I'll just have to see."

Lanius nodded. "All right. Until you see how things are down in the south, I don't suppose you can say anything more." He hesitated, then added, "Are you sure you want to send Petrosus to the Maze? He hasn't done anything out of line that I've been able to see—and you're right, I don't like him a bit, so I wouldn't be shy about telling you if he had."

"I'm sure." The older king sounded altogether determined.

"By all the signs, Ortalis and Limosa are happy newlyweds," Lanius said.

Grus snorted. "Ortalis is getting laid regularly. Of course he's happy. But what happens when that isn't enough to keep him happy?" He made a particularly sour face. So did Lanius, who knew what his father-in-law meant, and wished he didn't. He wondered what Limosa would think when she found out about her new husband's . . . peculiar tastes.

Changing the subject seemed a good idea. Lanius said, "Gods go with you on your trip to the south."

"Yes," Grus said. They sat alone in a small audience chamber. A low table with a jug of wine and a couple of cups stood between them. Grus emptied his cup, then looked around to make sure no one lurked outside a window or in the hallway by the door. Only after he'd satisfied himself did he continue, "They'd better, don't you think? Considering who's behind Ulash, I mean."

"Oh, yes. That's what I had in mind, too." Lanius also took another sip of wine.

Grus got up, came around the table, and set a hand on his shoulder. "You take care of things here. I'll do what I can with the Menteshe—*to* the Menteshe."

"Good." Lanius beamed. Grus was starting to accept him as a real partner, not just as one in name only. No doubt Grus did so only because he had no choice. Lanius knew as much. He was no less pleased on account of that.

The fastest way south was by ship through the Maze. That made Hirundo unhappy. Even on the placid waters of the marsh, Grus' general was less than a good sailor. He wagged a finger at the king. "Don't you laugh at me now, Your Majesty, or I'll pay you back when you get on a horse."

"Me? I didn't say a thing." Grus contrived to look innocent.

Hirundo laughed, which made him suspect his contrivance could have been better. "I saw what you were thinking. The only thing I can say for this is, it's better than going out on the open sea." He shuddered at the memory.

"It's better than horseback, too," Grus said.

"*Some* people might think so," Hirundo answered pointedly. "I don't happen to be one of them." He glanced around at the water, the weeds and branches floating in it, the muddy, grassy tussocks rising just out of it, and shook his head. "I think the only real reason you came through here was so you could see for yourself the monastery you picked out for Petrosus."

Grus had seen the monastery. It sat in the middle of a tussock big enough to be called an island. The only way off was by boat, and even boats had trouble getting through the mud surrounding it. All the same, the place was built like a fortress. Monks who came there would assuredly spend the rest of their lives in prayer.

Something landed on Grus' arm. It bit him. He swatted. He didn't know whether he smashed it or not. A moment later, something else bit him on the back of the neck. He swatted there, too. The bug squashed under his fingers. He wiped his hand on a trouser leg. Monks at Petrosus' new monastery might spend every spring and summer praying to be plagued by fewer bugs.

Hirundo was swatting, too. "Miserable things. This place is good for nothing—not a single cursed thing."

"Oh, I don't know about *that,*" Grus said. "I can't think of any place much better for getting rid of troublemakers." He sent Hirundo a speculative stare.

"Don't look at me that way!" the general exclaimed. "Don't you dare, Your Majesty! You tell anybody—me, for instance—he's liable to have to stay here for the rest of his days, and he'll be good forever. I know I would."

"Don't give me that. I've known you too long, and I know you too well," Grus said. "Nothing could make you stay good forever, or even very long."

"The threat of staying here for the rest of my life would do it," Hirundo insisted. "Offhand, I can't think of anything else."

When the sun set, the flies and gnats went away and the mosquitoes came out. Their high, thin whine was enough to drive anyone mad. Some of the sailors, more used to traveling through the Maze than Grus was, draped fine mesh nets over themselves and slept without being badly bothered. Grus got some of the netting for himself, too. One of the things nobody told him, though, was how to pull it over himself without letting mosquitoes get in under it. The king passed an uncomfortable night and woke with several new bites from the company he hadn't wanted.

Noticing Pterocles scratching as the wizard ate bread and ale for breakfast, he asked, "Don't you have any magic against mosquitoes?"

Mournfully, the wizard shook his head. "I wish I did, Your Majesty. Maybe I've spent too much time worrying about big things and not enough about small ones," he answered, and scratched some more.

Oarmasters on the river galleys got their rowers working as soon as they could. They worked them hard, too, harder than Grus would have in their place. When he remarked on that to the oarmaster of his own ship, the man replied, "Sooner we get out of this miserable place, sooner we stop getting eaten alive." Grus had a hard time disagreeing with that.

But getting through the Maze in a hurry wasn't easy, either. Galleys and barges went aground on mud banks and had to back oars or, when badly stuck, to be towed off by other ships. Rowers and officers shouted curses.

Hirundo said, "There ought to be clearly marked channels, so people know where they're going."

"Part of me says yes to that," Grus answered. "The other part wonders whether it's a good idea to show enemies how to get through the Maze—or, for that matter, to show people shut up inside the Maze how to get out of it. I had to dredge one place out so river galleys could get through the whole length of the Maze. They didn't used to be able to, you know."

"Maybe we should have gone around," Hirundo said.

"Going through it is still the fastest way to get south," Grus said. "We're not crawling now. We're just not going as fast as we would if everything were perfect."

"Oh, hurrah," Hirundo said sourly.

His general's sarcasm didn't faze Grus. He peered south, waiting for the steersman to find the channel of the Nedon, which ran south for some little distance after escaping the flat swampland of the Maze. As soon as the ships were in a place where they could easily tell the difference between the river and the countryside through which it flowed, they made much better time.

This left Hirundo no happier. As the river galleys sped up, their motion grew rougher. Every mile the fleet traveled south, Hirundo got greener.

Grus, by contrast, enjoyed the journey on the Nedon. Eventually, the river would turn east, toward the Azanian Sea. Since the Menteshe were fighting farther south, his men and horses would have to leave the galleys and barges then. He would have to get on one of those horses. That prospect left him as delighted as river travel left Hirundo.

When Lanius heard clanks and then a meow in the royal archives, he wasn't very surprised, not anymore. He didn't jump. He didn't wish he were a soldier, or even that he had weapons more deadly than pen, parchment, and ink. He just got to his feet and went over to see if he could find the moncat responsible for the racket.

After some searching, he did. Pouncer was carrying a stout silver serving spoon. Lanius wondered how it had gotten the spoon from the kitchens here to the archives; they weren't particularly close. For that matter, the chamber where the moncat lived wasn't all that close to the kitchens, either. There had to be passages in the walls a moncat could go through, regardless of whether a man could.

The king scooped up Pouncer—and the spoon. The moncat twisted and tried to bite. He tapped it on the nose, hard enough to get its attention. "Stop that!" he told it, not that it understood Avornan. But it did understand the tap and the tone of voice. Both told it biting was something it wasn't supposed to do. Little by little—about as fast as an ordinary cat would—it was learning.

Servants exclaimed as Lanius carried Pouncer down the corridor. "How did it get out this time?" a man asked.

"I don't know," the king replied. "I wish I did, but I've never seen it leave its room. I don't think any cooks have ever seen it sneak into the kitchens, either."

"Maybe it's a ghost." The servant sounded serious. The workers in the royal palace were a superstitious lot.

"Feels too solid to be a ghost—and I've never heard of a ghost that steals spoons," Lanius said. The moncat twisted again, lashing out with its free front foot. It got Lanius on the forearm. "Ow! I've never heard of a ghost that scratches, either."

"You never can tell," the servant said darkly. He went down the corridor shaking his head. Lanius went up the corridor to the moncats' chamber.

When he got there, he set Pouncer down. Then he had another small struggle getting the silver spoon away from the moncat. He watched for a while, hoping the beast would disappear down whatever hole it had used while he was there. But, perverse as any cat, it didn't.

At last, Lanius gave up. He took the spoon off to the kitchens. As he walked through the palace, he wondered if Pouncer would get there ahead of him, steal something else, and then disappear again. But he saw no sign of it when he went through the big swinging doors.

One after another, the cooks denied seeing the moncat. "Has that miserable beast been in here again?" a fat man asked, pointing to the spoon in Lanius' hand.

He held it up. "I didn't steal this myself."

He got a laugh. "I don't suppose you did, Your Majesty," the fat cook said, and took it from him. "But how does the moncat keep sneaking in?"

"That's what I want to find out," Lanius answered. "I was hoping you could tell me."

"Sorry, Your Majesty," the cook said. The other men and women who worked in the kitchens shook their heads. A lot of them sported big bellies and several chins. That was, Lanius supposed, hardly surprising, not when they worked with and around food all the time.

A woman said, "What do you suppose the animal's been eating with that spoon?" She got a louder laugh than Lanius had, and added, "I suppose we'd better wash it." The fat man who was holding it tossed it into a tub of water ten or fifteen feet away. He had perfect aim. The spoon splashed into the tub and clattered off whatever crockery already sat in there.

Lanius wondered whether they would have washed it if the cook hadn't asked if the moncat had eaten from it. Some things, perhaps, were better left unknown. He walked out of the kitchen without asking.

He was walking back to his own chambers when he almost bumped into Limosa, who was coming up the corridor. She dropped him a curtsy, murmuring, "Good morning, Your Majesty."

"Good morning, Your Highness," the king answered. "How are you today?"

"I am well, thank you," she answered. "May I please ask you a question, Your Majesty?"

Lanius thought he knew what the question would be. Since he didn't see how he could avoid it, he nodded. "Go ahead."

"Thank you." Limosa visibly gathered her courage. "Is there any way you can release my father from the Maze?"

He'd been right. "I'm sorry," he said, and did his best to sound as though he really *were* sorry. He knew he had to work at it, considering what he really thought of Petrosus.

Unfortunately, he wasn't the only one who knew what he thought of the former treasury minister. Flushing, Limosa said, "I know you aren't fond of my father, Your Majesty. But could you please free him for my sake?"

"If I could, I would," Lanius answered, thinking, *If I could, I . . . might. I did ask Grus not to send him to the Maze, so maybe I would.* He wasn't brokenhearted at having a good excuse not to, though. "But King Grus sent him away, and King Grus is the only one who can bring him back to the palace."

"And King Grus won't," Limosa said. Lanius didn't contradict her. Biting her lip, she went on, "He thinks my father tricked Ortalis into marrying me. By the gods, Your Majesty, I tell you again it isn't true."

"I see," Lanius said—as neutral a phrase as he could find.

"It *isn't* true," Limosa insisted. "I wanted to marry Ortalis. I love him." Lanius wanted to say, *Are you out of your mind?* Before either did more than cross his mind, Limosa went on, "He's the most wonderful man I ever met—uh, meaning no disrespect to you, Your Majesty, of course." She blushed.

"Of course," Lanius echoed. He was too bewildered, too astonished, to find anything else to say. Ortalis? The Ortalis who hunted because he was fond of blood? The Ortalis who hurt women because it excited him? *That* Ortalis was the most wonderful man Limosa had ever met? Something, somewhere, didn't add up. Lanius had no idea what. He did know the only individual to whom he less wanted to be married than he did to Ortalis was the Banished One.

Limosa sighed. "He's so sweet. And he does such marvelous things." She blushed again, this time a bright, bright red. Lanius only scratched his head. He really did wonder if they were talking about the same Ortalis. If he hadn't seen Grus' son with Limosa, he wouldn't have believed it.

Horse-drawn wagons full of grain rattled along with Grus' army. They didn't slow it down badly, but they did help tie it to the roads. Grus wasn't happy about that, but knew he gained as well as lost from having them along. The Menteshe made a habit of burning farms and fields and anything else they came across. Carrying supplies with him was the only way he could be sure of having them when he needed them most.

The horizon to the south should have been smooth, or gently rolling with the low hills between the valleys of the Nine Rivers. Instead, an ugly brown-black smudge obscured part of it. Pointing that way, Grus said, "We'll find the nomads there."

Hirundo nodded. "That's how it looks to me, too." He sent the king a sly smile. "Are you ready to ride into battle, Your Majesty?"

Did *ride* have a little extra stress, or was Grus imagining things? Knowing Hirundo, he probably wasn't. He answered, "I'm as ready as I'm going to be," and set a hand on his horse's neck. The beast was a placid gelding. It did what Grus wanted it to do, and didn't put up much in the way of argument. That suited him fine. Hirundo rode a stallion. It had more flash, more fire. Grus cared very little about that. To him, a horse with fire was a horse that was all too likely to pitch him out of the saddle and onto the ground headfirst.

He nodded to a trumpeter who rode close by. The man blew *Trot*. The king used his knees and the reins to urge his horse up from a walk. The sooner his men closed with the Menteshe, the better, as far as he was concerned. Prince Ulash's men had already come too far north to suit him.

"Scouts out in the van! Scouts out to the flanks!" Hirundo called. Riders peeled off from the main body of the army and hurried out to take those positions. Grus nodded again. He would have given that command in a moment if Hirundo hadn't. Generations of painful experience fighting the southern nomads had taught Avornis that attacks could come from any direction at any time.

Lanceheads glittered in the sun. His army was split fairly evenly between lancers and archers. If they could come to close quarters with the Menteshe, they would have the edge. More painful experience had taught that closing with the hard-riding nomads wasn't always easy, or even possible.

Grus glanced toward Pterocles. "What of their wizards?" the king asked.

"I don't feel anything . . . out of the ordinary, Your Majesty," the wizard said after a pause for thought. After another pause, he added, "Not everything is the way it ought to be, though."

"What do you mean?" Grus asked. Pterocles only shrugged. Grus tried again, asking, "Why do you say that?" Pterocles gave back another shrug. The king said, "Could it be because you feel the Banished One paying attention to what happens here, where you didn't up by Nishevatz?"

Pterocles jerked, as though someone had stuck him with a pin when he wasn't looking. He nodded. "Yes. It could be. In fact, I think it is. There's . . . something watching, sure enough."

"What can you do?"

"What can I do?" Pterocles laughed, more than a little wildly. "I can hope he doesn't notice me, that's what. And a forlorn hope it is, too." He pulled on the reins and steered his horse away from the king's.

Grus hadn't intended to ask him any more questions anyhow.

Late that afternoon, a scout came galloping back to the king. "Your Majesty! Your Majesty!" he called, his voice cracking with excitement. "We just saw our first Menteshe, Your Majesty!"

"Did you?" Grus said, and the young man nodded, his head jerking up and down, his eyes shining. "Did you catch him? Did you kill him?"

Some of that fervid excitement faded. "No, Your Majesty. I'm sorry. He rode off to the southwest. We sent a few men after him, but he got away."

"Don't worry about it," Grus told him. "Plenty more where he came from. And maybe he showed us where some of his friends are." *If I find them, will the Banished One be brooding over the battlefield?* Grus wondered. *If I don't, though, what am I doing here? Why aren't I just yielding my southern provinces to Prince Ulash?* He couldn't do that, not if he wanted to stay King of Avornis, not if he wanted to be able to stand the sight of his own face whenever he chanced to see a reflection. But he didn't relish going forward, either.

The Avornan army didn't go much farther forward that day. When the army encamped for the night, Grus ringed it with sentries a long way out. "That's very good," Hirundo said. "That's very good. I remember how much trouble Evren's men gave us at night."

"So do I," Grus answered. "That's why I'm doing this." The Menteshe would sneak close if they could, and pepper a camp with arrows. They didn't do much harm, but they stole sleep soldiers needed.

Despite all the sentries, a handful of nomads did manage to sneak close enough to the main camp to shoot a few arrows at it. They wounded two or three men before shouts roused soldiers who came after them. Then they disappeared into the night. They'd done what they'd come to do.

The disturbance roused Grus. He lost a couple of hours of sleep himself, and was yawning and sandy-eyed when the Avornans set out not long after sunrise. They went past fields the raiders had torched perhaps only the day before. Sour smoke still hung in the air, rasping the lungs and stinging the eyes.

He actually saw his first Menteshe on Avornan soil the next morning. A band of Ulash's riders had slipped past the Avornan sentries, leaving them none the wiser. By the surprise with which the Menteshe reacted to the sight of the whole Avornan army heading their way, they hadn't so much eluded the scouts as bypassed them without either side's noticing.

Despite the way the Menteshe threw up their hands and shouted in their guttural language, they didn't wheel their horses and gallop off as fast as they could go. Instead, they rode toward the Avornans, and started shooting at a range Avornan bows couldn't match.

Grus had seen that before, too, most recently in his fight with Prince Evren's nomads. "Forward!" he shouted to the trumpeters, who blew the appropriate horn call. The Avornans pushed their horses up to a gallop as fast as they could. Grus' own mount thundered forward with the rest. He hoped he could stay aboard the jouncing beast. A fall now wouldn't be embarrassing. It would be fatal.

The Menteshe, vastly outnumbered, were not ashamed to flee. Grus had expected nothing else. They kept shooting over their shoulders, too, and shooting very well. But the Avornans were also shooting now, and some of them had faster horses than the nomads did. Whether the Menteshe liked it or not, their pursuers came into range.

And the Avornans could shoot well, too, even if they didn't carry double-curved bows reinforced with horn and sinew the way Ulash's men did. One nomad after another threw up his hands and crumpled to the ground. A horse went down, too, and the beast just behind fell over it and crashed down. Grus hoped both riders got killed.

The surviving nomads scattered then, galloping wildly in all directions. A few of them might have gotten away, but most didn't. Grus waved to the trumpeters. They blew the signal to rein in. Little by little, the Avornans slowed. Sides heaving, Grus' horse bent its head to crop a wisp of grass.

"Very neat, Your Majesty," Hirundo called, a grin on his face.

"Do you mean this little skirmish, or do you mean that I managed to stay on the horse?" Grus inquired.

Hirundo's grin got wider. "Whichever you'd rather, of course."

"I'm prouder of staying on and even keeping up," the king said. "This little band of Menteshe was nothing special—beating them was like cracking an egg with a sledgehammer. They're scattered over the countryside, raiding and looting. Until they come together again, we'll win some easy victories like this."

"We want to win as many of them as we can, too, before they *do* come together," his general said. "The more of them we can get rid of that way, the fewer we'll have to worry about then."

"I know. Believe me, I know," Grus said. "And even if we do hit them hard, they spatter like quicksilver. We won't always be able to pursue the way we did here, either. If we split up to go after them, they're liable to jump us instead of the other way around."

"Well, Your Majesty, you certainly do understand the problem," Hirundo said. "Now if you can figure out a way to solve it . . ."

Grus grunted and leaned forward to pat the side of his horse's neck. Avornans had understood the problem ever since the Menteshe boiled up from the south centuries before. The nomads, trained since childhood to ride and to tend their flocks, were simply better horsemen than the Avornans. Not only did they carry more powerful bows, but they could also cover more ground. If Avornis hadn't had the advantage of numbers . . . Grus didn't care to think about what might have happened then.

Forcing himself to look on the bright side instead, Grus said, "Well, we solved it here, anyhow."

"So we did." Hirundo nodded. "How many more times will we have to solve it, though, before we finally drive the Menteshe back over the Stura?"

"I don't know," Grus answered with a sigh. He didn't even know yet whether the Avornans *could* drive Prince Ulash's men back over the river this year. That was something else he preferred not to think about. With another sigh, he went on, "The other question is, how much damage will they do before we can throw them out? They haven't mounted an invasion like this for years."

"Yes, and we both know why, or think we do," Hirundo said. The response made the king no happier. Up until recently, Ulash had seemed both reasonable and peaceable, qualities Grus wasn't in the habit of associating with the Menteshe. But he and his folk reverenced the Banished One—the Fallen Star, they called him. If he told Ulash to cause trouble for Avornis, Ulash would—Ulash had—no matter how reasonable and peaceable he'd seemed for many years.

"I wonder . . ." Grus said slowly.

"What's that, Your Majesty?" Hirundo asked.

"I wonder if we can do anything to persuade Ulash he'd be better off worshiping the gods in the heavens than the Banished One."

"I doubt it." Hirundo, a practical man, sounded like one. "If the Menteshe haven't figured out who the true gods are yet, we can't teach 'em."

He was probably right, no matter how much Grus wished he were wrong. But things were more complicated than Hirundo realized. King Olor and Queen Quelea and the rest were undoubtedly the gods in the heavens. That made them stronger than the Banished One, yes. Whether it made him any less a true god . . . was yet another thing Grus would sooner not have contemplated.

That evening, drums boomed in the distance. Grus knew what that meant—the Menteshe were signaling back and forth across the miles. The drumbeats carried far better than horn calls could have. The king wondered what the nomads were saying with those kettledrums. He kicked at the dirt inside his tent. He'd served down in the south for years, but he hadn't learned to make sense of the drums. He knew no Avornans who had. *Too bad,* he thought.

The drums went on all through the night. Grus woke several times, and each time heard them thudding and muttering, depending on how far off they were. Every time he woke, he had more trouble falling back to sleep.

"A letter from King Grus, Your Majesty," a courier said, and handed King Lanius a rolled and sealed parchment.

"Thank you," Lanius said in some surprise; he hadn't expected anything from Grus. He broke the wax seal and opened the letter. *King Grus to King Lanius—greetings,* he read, and then, *I wonder if you would be kind enough to do me a favor. Does anyone in the royal archives talk about the drum signals the Menteshe use? Does anyone know what the different signals mean? If you can find out, please let me know as quickly as possible. Many thanks for your help.* A scrawled signature completed the letter.

"Is there an answer, Your Majesty?" the courier asked.

"Yes." Lanius called for parchment, pen, and ink. *King Lanius to Grus—greetings,* he wrote; he still hesitated to admit that Grus deserved the royal title. But that reluctance didn't keep him from continuing, *I do not know of any records such as you request, but I have never looked for them, either. I will now, and as soon as I can I will let you know if I find what you want—and, for that matter, if I don't.* He signed the letter, sealed it with candle wax and his signet ring, and gave it to the courier. "Take this to Grus in the south. I want him to know I will give it my full attention."

"Yes, Your Majesty. Thank you, Your Majesty." The courier bowed and hurried away.

Lanius, bemused, headed straight for the archives. Grus had never asked him for information before. He wondered if he could come up with it. He hoped he could. No Avornan could think of the southern provinces being ravaged without cringing. Lanius might still wish Grus didn't wear the crown. That had nothing to do with whether he wanted Grus to drive the Menteshe out of the kingdom.

"Drum signals," Lanius muttered. He knew where a lot of old parchments that had to do with the Menteshe in one way or another were stored. Maybe he could find what Grus wanted in among them.

He spent the rest of the day trying, but had no luck. He did discover there were even more documents in those crates than he'd thought. He vanished back into the archives after breakfast, and didn't come out again until suppertime.

When he disappeared early the following morning, too, Sosia called after him, "I hope I'll see you again before too long."

"That's right," answered Lanius, who'd only half heard her. Sosia laughed and shook her head; she'd seen such fits take her husband before.

He found the best light he could in the archives. No one ever did a proper job of cleaning the skylights far above, which left the dusty daylight in there all the more wan and shifting. Lanius had complained about that before. He wondered whether complaining again would do any good. He had his doubts.

Then he started going through the parchments once more, and forgot about skylights and everything else but the work at hand. He had no trouble finding parchments mentioning the Menteshe drums. The Avornans hadn't needed long to realize the nomads didn't pound them for amusement alone. But what they meant? That was a different question.

The more Lanius read, the more annoyed he got. *Why* hadn't his countrymen paid more attention to the drums? More than a few of them, traders and soldiers, had learned the spoken and written language of the Menteshe. Why hadn't anyone bothered to learn their drum signals? Or, if someone had, why hadn't he bothered to write them down?

Lanius kept plugging away. He learned all sorts of interesting things about the Menteshe, things he'd never known or things he'd seen once before and then forgotten. He learned the commands a Menteshe used with a draft horse. Those fascinated him, but they had nothing to do with what Grus wanted.

I can't come up empty, Lanius told himself. *I just can't.* If he failed here, Grus would never ask him for anything again. As though that weren't bad enough, the other king would despise the archives. Lanius took that as personally as though Grus were to despise his children.

And then, half an hour later, the king let out a whoop that echoed through the big archives chamber. He held a report by a soldier who'd served along the Stura in the reign of his own great-great-great-grandfather. The man had carefully described each drum signal the Menteshe used and what it meant.

After making a copy of the report, Lanius left the chamber. He scribbled a note to go with the copy, sealed them both, and gave them to a courier for the long journey south.

"You look pleased with yourself," Sosia answered when he went back to the royal chambers in triumph.

"I am," Lanius answered, and then looked down at the dusty finery he wore. "But the servants won't be pleased with me. I forgot to change before I went into the archives."

CHAPTER FOURTEEN

"Well, well." Grus eyed the parchment he'd just unrolled. "King Lanius came through for us."

Hirundo looked over his shoulder. "He sure did," the general agreed. "This was in the archives?"

"That's what the note with it says," Grus answered.

"If we knew this once upon a time, I wonder why we forgot," Hirundo said.

"A spell of peace probably lasted longer than any one man's career," Grus said. "The people who knew wouldn't have passed it on to the younger officers who needed to know, and so the chain got broken."

"That makes sense," Hirundo said.

"Which doesn't mean it's true, of course," Grus said. "How many things that seem to make perfect sense turn out not to have anything to do with what looks sensible?"

"Oh, a few," his general replied. "Yes, just a few."

"We don't have to worry about tracking down the whys and where-fores here," Grus said with a certain relief. "If what Lanius says in that note is true, it happened a long time ago."

"Now that we have what we need, though, let's see what we can do about giving the Menteshe a surprise," Hirundo said.

"Oh, yes." Grus nodded. "That's the idea."

The drums started thumping at sunset that day. In the evening twilight, Grus peered down at the list of calls Lanius had sent him. Three beats, pause, two beats . . . That meant *west*. Five quick beats was *assem-*

ble. Having found those meanings, the king started laughing. Knowing what the drums meant helped him less than he'd hoped it would. Yes, Ulash's men were to assemble somewhere off to the west. But *where?*

Grus snapped his fingers. *He* didn't know; this wasn't a part of Avornis with which he was intimately familiar. But the army had soldiers from all parts of Avornis in it. He called for runners, gave them quick orders, and sent them on their way through the encampment.

Inside half an hour, they came back with four soldiers, all of them from farms and towns within a few miles of where the army had camped. They bowed low before the king. "Never mind that nonsense," Grus said impatiently, which made their eyes widen in surprise. "If you were going to gather a large force of horsemen somewhere within a day's ride west of here, where would you do it?"

They looked surprised again, but put their heads together even so. After a few minutes of talk, they all nodded. One of them pointed southwest. "Your Majesty, there's a meadow just this side of the Aternus, before it runs into the Cephisus." The latter was one of the Nine. The soldier went on, "It's got good grazing—Olor's beard, sir, it's got wonderful grazing—the whole year around. It's about half a day's ride that way."

"Can you guide us to it?" Grus asked. The man nodded. So did his comrades. And so did the king. "All right, then. Every one of you will do that come morning. You'll all have a reward, too. Keep quiet about this until then, though."

The men loudly promised they would. Grus hoped so, though he wasn't overoptimistic. His father had always said two men could keep a secret if one of them was dead, and that, if three men tried, one was likely a fool and the other two spies. After leaving a farm not impossibly far from here, his father had come to the city of Avornis and served as a royal guard, so he'd seen enough intrigue to know what he was talking about.

After sending away the soldiers, Grus summoned Hirundo and Pterocles. He explained what he had in mind. "Can we do this?" he asked.

"A little risky," Hirundo said. "More than a little, maybe. We'll look like idiots if the Menteshe catch on. We may look like *dead* idiots if they catch on."

Grus nodded. He'd already figured that out for himself. He turned to Pterocles. "Can you mask us, or mask some of us?"

"Some of us," the wizard answered. "It would have to be some of us.

All?" He rolled his eyes. "That would be an impossibly large job for any human wizard."

"Do the best you can," Grus told him. "I don't expect you to do more than a human wizard's capable of."

"All right, Your Majesty," Pterocles said.

"You're going ahead with this scheme, Your Majesty?" Hirundo asked.

"Yes," Grus said. "If it works, we'll give Ulash's men a nasty surprise." *And if it doesn't, they'll give us one.* He refused to worry—too much—about that. By its nature, war involved risk. The gamble here seemed good to the king. If they won, they would win a lot.

They rode out before sunrise the next morning, the men from close by leading the two divisions into which Grus had split the army. Out of a certain sense of fairness, Grus sent Pterocles off with the division Hirundo led. The king hadn't ridden far before regretting his generosity. If Pterocles had come with him, he would have had a better chance of staying alive.

No help for it now, though. As Grus had told his guides to do, they led him and his men on a looping track that would take them around to strike the Menteshe from the west—if the Menteshe were there. Whether they struck them at the same time as Hirundo's men did was going to be largely a matter of luck.

One of the guards pointed. "There, Your Majesty! Look!"

They'd guessed right. Prince Ulash's nomads were gathering on the meadow. Grus knew exactly the moment when they realized the large force approaching wasn't theirs but Avornan. So ants boiled after their hill was kicked.

"Forward!" Grus shouted to the trumpeters. As the fierce horn calls clove the air, he set spurs to his gelding. The horse whinnied in pained protest. Grus roweled it again. It bounded ahead. He drew his sword. The sun flashed fire from the blade. "Forward!" he yelled once more.

Some of the Menteshe started shooting. Others fled. King Grus doubted the nomads were under any sort of unified command. Each chieftain—maybe even each horseman—decided for himself what he would do. That made the Menteshe hard for Avornis to control. It also made them hard for their own warlords to control.

The Avornans shot back as soon as they came within range. A few of them had already pitched from the saddle. But Ulash's warriors began falling, too. Soon the Menteshe still hale started fleeing. They had never seen any shame in running away when the odds seemed against them.

Grus brandished the sword, though he had yet to come within fifty feet of a foe. Where were Hirundo and Pterocles and the other division? Had the wizard masked them so well, they'd disappeared altogether? Had the Banished One swept them off the field, as a man might have removed them from a gaming board? Or had their guides simply gotten lost?

No sooner had Grus begun to worry than the other Avornan force appeared, as suddenly as though a fog in front of them had blown away. His own men burst into cheers. The Menteshe, suddenly caught between hammer and anvil, cried out in dismay. They all tried to flee now, shooting over their shoulders as they desperately galloped off.

A lot of the nomads did escape. Grus never had to use his sword. Somehow, none of that mattered much. Many Menteshe lay dead. Looking around, the king could see that his own force hadn't suffered badly.

Hirundo saw the same thing. "We hurt 'em this time, your Majesty," the general said, riding up to Grus.

"That's what we set out to do," Grus replied, though he knew the Avornans didn't always do what they set out to do against the Menteshe. "Where's Pterocles? He kept you hidden, all right."

"He sure did," Hirundo said enthusiastically. "Even I didn't know where we were until just before we got here." He looked around, then scratched his head. "I don't know where he's gotten to now, though." His shrug might have been apology.

Grus also eyed the field. His men, swords drawn, were moving over it. They plundered the dead Menteshe and cut the throats of the wounded nomads they found. Had the fight gone against them, the invaders would have done the same, though they would have reserved some Avornans for torment before death's mercy came. Here a trooper held up a fine sword with a glittering edge, there another displayed a purse nicely heavy with coins, in another place a man threw on a fur-edged cape not badly bloodstained.

Several Avornans picked up recurved Menteshe bows. One fitted an arrow to the string, then tried to draw the shaft back to his ear. At the first pull, he didn't use enough strength. His friends jeered. Gritting his teeth, he tried again. This time, the bow bent. He turned it away from his fellows and let fly. They all exclaimed in surprise at how far the arrow flew.

"There's the wizard!" Hirundo pointed as Pterocles emerged from a clump of bushes. "I thought the rascal had gone and disappeared himself this time."

When Grus waved, Pterocles nodded back and made his way toward the king. Grus clasped his hand and slapped him on the back. Pterocles, none too steady on his feet, almost fell over. Holding him up, Grus said, "Well done!"

"Er—thank you, Your Majesty." Pterocles did not sound like a man who'd just helped win a good-sized victory. He sounded more like one who'd had too much to drink and was about to sick up much of what he'd poured down. His greenish color suggested the same.

"Are you all right?" Grus asked.

Pterocles shrugged. "If you love me, Your Majesty—or even if you hate me, but not too much—do me the courtesy of never asking me to use that masking spell against the Menteshe again." He gulped, and then ran back into the bushes from which he'd just emerged. When he came out again, his face was deathly pale, but he looked better. He might have gotten rid of some of what ailed him.

"Your spell here helped us win," Grus said, surprised and puzzled. "Why not use it again?"

"Why not?" The wizard took a deep breath—almost a sob. "I'll tell you why not, Your Majesty. I was holding the spell against the Menteshe horsemen. Thus far, well and good. Then I was holding it against Ulash's wizards, which was not such an easy thing, but I managed well enough. But soon I was also holding it against the Banished One—and gods spare me from ever having to do that again." He sat down on the ground; his legs didn't seem to want to hold him up anymore.

"But you did it." The king squatted beside him.

"Oh, yes. I did it." Pterocles' voice was hollow, not proud. "He didn't take the spell seriously, you might say, until too late. By the time he grew fully aware of it and realized it might hurt his followers, it already had. He doesn't make mistakes twice. He doesn't make many mistakes once."

And what would you expect from a foe who was a god? Grus wondered. But Pterocles already knew about that—not all about it, but enough.

"It will be as you say," Grus promised, and the wizard's shoulders sagged with relief.

The forest smelled clean and green. When King Lanius was in the city of Avornis, he didn't notice the mingled stinks of dung and smoke and unwashed people crowded too close together. When he left, which wasn't often enough, the air seemed perfumed in his nostrils. He relished each inhalation and regretted every breath he had to let out. He also regretted having to go back to the capital when this day ended. He knew he would smell the stench he usually ignored.

And part of him regretted letting Arch-Hallow Anser talk him into coming along on another hunt. After the first one the year before, he'd vowed never to go hunting again. But this excursion had promised to be too interesting for him to refuse. For Prince Ortalis also rode with Anser—and the prince and the arch-hallow had quarreled years before Lanius disappointed Anser by being immune to the thrills of the chase.

King Grus, of course, was down in the southern provinces fighting the Menteshe. And yet, though he'd gone hundreds of miles, his influence still lingered over the city of Avornis—and, indeed, over the hunting party. Here were his legitimate son, his bastard, and his son-in-law. Had he not taken the crown, would any of the three younger men even have met the other two? Lanius doubted it. He would have been just as well pleased never to have made Ortalis' acquaintance, but it was years too late to worry about that.

Some of their beaters were men Anser regularly used in his sport—lean, silent fellows in leather jerkins and caps who slipped through the trees with the silent skill of practiced poachers. The rest were Lanius' royal bodyguards. The men who served Anser sneered at their jingling mailshirts. The bodyguards pretended not to hear. They were along to protect King Lanius first. If they happened to flush out a stag or a wildcat, so much the better.

Lanius suspected that Anser's beaters might end up beaten after the hunting party went back to the city of Avornis. The bodyguards, sensitive to the royal mood, didn't want to spoil the day. But they weren't used to being mocked, and they had long memories for slights. The men who put Lanius in mind of poachers seemed strong and tough enough, but the royal guardsmen were the best Avornis had.

A sharp, staccato drumming high up in an oak made Lanius' head whip around. Laughing, Anser said, "It's nothing—only a wood-pecker."

"What kind?" the king asked. "One of the big black ones with the red crest, or the small ones that are all black and white stripes, or a flicker with a black mustache?"

Anser blinked. Ortalis laughed. "Trust Lanius to know about wood-peckers," he said. Lanius listened for the malice that usually informed Ortalis' words. He didn't hear it. Maybe not hearing it was wishful thinking on his part. Or maybe being married to Limosa agreed with Grus' son—at least so far. And Lanius didn't know as much about woodpeckers, or birds in general, as he would have liked to, but he was learning.

The drumming rang through the woods again. One of the soft-moving men in a jerkin said, "Your Majesty, that's the noise those small, stripy woodpeckers make. The others, the bigger birds, drum more slowly."

"Thank you," Lanius said.

"Yes, thank you," Anser agreed. "I've found something out, too. Who would have wondered about woodpeckers?"

"Let's push on," Ortalis said. "We've still got a lot of hunting ahead of us, woodpeckers or no woodpeckers."

Anser's beater vanished among the trees, to drive game back toward the men with rank enough to kill it. Some of Lanius' guardsmen went with them. More, though, stayed behind with the king. "They take no chances, do they?" Anser said.

"We don't get paid to take chances, Your Arch-Reverence." A guard spoke up before the king could.

A stag bounded past. Ortalis had his bow drawn and an arrow hiss-ing through the air before Lanius even began to raise his bow. *I am a hopeless dub at this,* Lanius thought. *I will always be a hopeless dub at this.* Ortalis, meanwhile, whooped. "That's a hit!" he called, and loped after the deer.

In the palace, Grus' legitimate son seemed as useless a mortal as any Lanius had ever seen. Here in the field, he proved to know what he was doing. Following in his wake, Lanius saw blood splashed on leaves and bushes. He did not care for the pursuit of wounded animals. Killing beasts cleanly was one thing. Inflicting such suffering as this on them struck him as something else again.

It was something else for Ortalis, too—something he relished, as his excited chatter showed. Lanius would have sneered at his bloodlust—Lanius had sneered at his bloodlust in the past—but he'd also seen Anser get excited in the chase. The arch-hallow was mild as milk when he wasn't hunting. The king didn't understand the transformation. Understand it or not, though, he couldn't deny it was real.

"Nice shot, Your Highness," one of the beaters told Ortalis. "He went down right quick there." It hadn't seemed quick to Lanius, who brushed a twig from his hair as he came up. He didn't think it had seemed quick to the stag, either.

Ortalis' eyes glowed. He knelt beside the fallen deer. Its sides still heaved feebly as it fought to suck in air. Bloody froth showed at each nostril; Ortalis' arrow must have punctured a lung. Drawing a belt knife, Ortalis cut the stag's throat. More blood yet poured out onto his hands and the ground. "Ah," he said softly, as he might have after a woman. Lanius' stomach lurched. He turned away, hoping breakfast would stay down.

It did. When he looked back, Ortalis was plunging the knife into the deer's belly to butcher it. The animal's eyes were opaque and lusterless now. That obvious proof of death helped ease the king's conscience along with his nausea. Ortalis went right on with the butchering. He seemed to enjoy it as much as the killing.

Looking up from the work, he remarked, "It's a bloody job, but somebody's got to do it."

Lanius managed to nod. It wasn't that Ortalis was wrong. But did a butcher have to do his work with such fiendish gusto? Lanius doubted that. He'd doubted it for years.

Getting back on the trail was a relief for him, if not for Ortalis. Anser had the first shot at the next stag they saw, had it and missed. He cursed good-naturedly, but with enough pointed comments to startle anyone who, after hearing him, might suddenly learn he was Arch-Hallow of Avornis.

Nodding to Lanius, Anser said, "Next one we see, Your Majesty, you can let fly first."

"That's all right," Lanius said; the honor was one he would gladly have done without. But both the arch-hallow and Prince Ortalis sent him looks full of horror. Even his own guardsmen clucked disapprovingly. Without even knowing it, he'd broken some hunt custom. He did his best to repair things, adding, "I just don't want a deer to get away—I'm not much of a shot." The last part of that was true, the first part one of the bigger lies he'd ever told.

But, because he had a reputation for sticking to the truth no matter what, both Anser and Ortalis accepted his words. "Don't worry, Your Majesty," Anser said. "I missed, and the world won't end if you do, too, as long as you try your best."

"Of course," said the king, who still couldn't stomach the idea of shooting at an animal for the sport of it.

But, before long, he had to try. A magnificent stag stood at the edge of a clearing twenty or thirty yards away. The wind blew from the stag to the hunters; the beast, which depended so much on its sensitive nose, had not the slightest notion they were there. Reluctantly, Lanius drew his bow and let fly. The arrow flew alarmingly straight. For a bad heartbeat, he feared he'd actually hit what he aimed at. The shaft zipped over the deer's back and thudded into the pale, parchment-barked trunk of a birch behind it.

The stag bounded away. But Anser and Ortalis' bowstrings twanged in the same instant. One of those shafts struck home. The stag crashed to the ground in the middle of a leap. The arch-hallow and the prince both cried out in triumph.

And they both turned to Lanius. "Well shot!" Ortalis told him. "You spooked it perfectly. Now Anser and I have to see who got the kill."

By the time they reached the carcass, the deer, mercifully, was already dead. It had two arrows in it—one in the throat, the other through the ribs. Ortalis had loosed the first, Anser the second. They began arguing over who deserved credit for bringing down the stag. "Perhaps," Lanius said diffidently, "you should share the—" He broke off. He'd almost said *blame*. That was what he thought of the whole business, but he knew it wouldn't do.

Even though he'd stopped, prince and arch-hallow both stared at him as though he'd started spouting the Chernagors' throaty language. Then they went back to their argument. He wondered if he'd violated some other unwritten rule of the hunt.

Thinking of unwritten rules made him wonder if there were written ones. Poking through the archives trying to find out would be more fun than looking at flies beginning to settle in the blood that had spilled from the stag, and to walk across the eyeballs that could no longer blink them away.

Again, Ortalis got the privilege—if that was what it was—of butchering the deer. He made the gory job as neat as he could. Even so, Lanius saw, or thought he saw, a gleam of satisfaction in his brother-in-law's eyes. *It could be worse,* the king thought. *If he were hunting women, the way he'd wanted to, he'd butcher them after he made the kill.*

He shivered. No, he didn't think Ortalis had been joking about that, not at all. And he was anything but reassured when Grus' legitimate son, after wiping his gory hands on the grass, licked the last of the stag's blood from his fingers. Ortalis smacked his lips, too, as though at fine wine.

Anser and the beaters seemed to find nothing wrong with that. Lanius told himself he was worrying too much. He also told himself he would be glad to eat the venison the hunt was bringing home. He believed that. Try as he would, though, he couldn't make himself believe the other.

Sestus lay by the Arzus River. When Grus' army reached the city, the Menteshe had had it under siege for some little while. Their idea of besieging a town was different from Grus' at Nishevatz. They didn't aim to storm the walls. They had no catapults or battering rams to knock down its towers. But that didn't mean they'd had no chance of forcing the place to yield. If the royal army hadn't come when it did, they probably would have done just that.

They'd ravaged the farms around Sestus. Not a cow, not a sheep, not a pig survived. Not many farmers did, either. The Menteshe had trampled or burned most of the wheatfields within a day's ride of the town. Vineyards and olive groves and almond orchards also went under the ax or the torch. The Arzus was not a wide stream. Menteshe on the banks had peppered with arrows the ships that tried to bring grain into Sestus. They hadn't stopped all of them, but they had made skippers most reluctant to run their gauntlet. Little by little, Sestus had started starving.

Prince Ulash's men didn't put up much of a fight when the Avornan army thundered down on them. The nomads simply rode away. Why not? They could afflict some other city, and the devastation they'd left behind remained. Sestus would have a hard and hungry time of it now, regardless of whether it had opened its gates to the Menteshe.

Riding through fields black with soot or prematurely yellow and dead, Grus saw that at once. It was, understandably, less obvious to the local governor, a bald baron named Butastur. He rode out from the city to welcome the king. "By the gods, Your Majesty, it's good to see you here!" he said, beaming. "Another couple of weeks of those demons prowling around out there and we'd've been eating the grass that grows between the ruts in the street and boiling shoeleather for soup."

"I'm glad it won't come to that." Grus wasn't beaming; he was grim. His wave encompassed the ravaged fields. "Only Queen Quelea can judge how much you'll be able to salvage from this."

Butastur nodded. "Oh, yes. We'll be a while getting over this, no doubt about it. But now you'll be able to bring supplies in to us from places where the cursed Menteshe haven't reached."

He sounded as confident as a little boy who was sure his father could reach out, pluck the moon from the sky, and hand it to him on a string. Grus hated to disillusion him, but felt he had no choice. "We'll be able to do something for you, Baron," he said, "but I'm not sure how much. Sestus isn't the only hungry city, and yours aren't the only fields the nomads have ruined. This is a big invasion—look how far north you are, and we're only now reaching you."

By Butastur's expression, he cared not a pin for any other part of Avornis unless it could send him food. "Surely you can't mean you're going to let us famish here!" he cried. "What have we done to deserve such a fate?"

"You haven't done anything to deserve it," Grus answered. "I hope it doesn't happen. But I don't know if I can do all I'd like to help you, because this isn't the only town in the kingdom that's suffering."

He might as well have saved his breath, for all the effect his words had on Butastur. "Ruined!" the baron said, and tugged at his bushy beard as though he wanted to get credit for pulling chunks out by the roots. "Ruined by the cursed barbarians, and even my sovereign will do nothing to relieve my city's suffering!"

"You seem to misunderstand me on purpose," Grus said.

Butastur, by now, wasn't even listening to him, let alone under-standing. "Ruined!" he cried once again, more piteously than ever. "How shall we ever recover from the ravages of the Menteshe?"

Grus lost his temper. He'd just paid in blood to drive the nomads away from Sestus, and the local governor seemed not to have noticed. "How will you recover?" he growled. "Shutting up and buckling down to repair the damage makes a good start. I told you I'd do what I could for you. I just don't know how much that's going to be. Am I plain enough, Your Excellency?"

Butastur flinched away from him as though he were one of Prince Ulash's torturers. "Yes, yes, Your Majesty," he said. But he didn't speak from conviction. He just didn't dare argue. Grus had seen plenty of palace servants who yielded to authority like that—not because it was right, but because it *was* authority, and something worse would happen to them if they didn't.

Crossing the Arzus in pursuit of the Menteshe came as nothing but a relief. When the army camped that evening, the king turned to Hirundo and said, "I can fight the nomads. But what am I supposed to do when someone on my own side makes me want to hang him from the tallest tower in his town?"

"You could go ahead and hang him," the general answered. "You'd have a lot fewer idiots bothering you afterwards."

"Don't tempt me," Grus said. "But if I start hanging all the fools in Avornis, how many people will be left alive in six months' time? And who hangs me, for being fool enough to start hanging fools in the first place?"

"A nice question," Hirundo said. "If you start hanging fools, who would dare rebel against you and confess that he's one of those fools?" He grinned.

"Stop that!" Grus said. "You're making my head ache, and I couldn't even enjoy getting drunk first."

The next morning, the Avornans rode on. The bands of Menteshe had melted away during the night. But for burned-out fields and farmhouses, no one would have known Ulash's men had come so far. Ahead, though, more plumes of black smoke rising into the sky said they were still busy at their work of destruction. Grus tasted smoke every time he breathed. He felt it in his lungs, and in his stinging eyes.

He sent scouts out by squadrons, fearing the Menteshe weren't far away. As the main force of Avornans advanced, he waited for one scout or another to come pelting back, bringing word the nomads had attacked his squadrons. He was ready to strike and strike hard.

But, to his surprise and more than a little to his disappointment, nothing like that happened. His army pushed on through the ravaged countryside, hardly seeing any Menteshe at all. Maybe Ulash's men were fleeing back toward the Stura. Grus wanted to believe they were. He wanted to, but he couldn't.

It was midafternoon before he realized he hadn't heard anything at all from one scout squadron since the early morning. He pointed west, where they'd ridden when the army broke camp. "Are things going so very well over that way, do you suppose?" he asked Hirundo.

"They could be," the general answered. "We've had a pretty quiet day." But he fidgeted when Grus eyed him. "All right, Your Majesty. It doesn't seem likely."

"Send out another squadron," Grus said. "If the first one's all right, you can call me a fussy old woman. But if it's not . . ." *If it's not, it's liable to be too late to do the men any good. Why didn't I start worrying sooner?*

Off trotted the horsemen. Grus' unease grew. It reminded him of the feeling he got when someone was staring at him from behind. He wished he hadn't had that thought. It made him suddenly look back over his shoulder, again and again. Naturally, no one was looking his way—until his antics drew other people's attention.

After a while, impatient and nervous, the king summoned Pterocles. "Can you tell me anything about those scouts?" he demanded.

"I don't know, Your Majesty. Let me see what I can divine." Pterocles set to work, murmuring a charm. Grus recognized the chant; it was the sort of spell wizards used to find lost coins or strayed sheep. He'd thought Pterocles would use something fancier, but if a simple charm would serve. . . .

Pterocles hadn't finished the spell when he broke off with a gasp of horror. His long, lean face went white as bone, leaving him looking like nothing so much as an appalled skull. Before Grus could even ask him what was wrong, he doubled over and was noisily and violently ill.

Grus wondered if he'd eaten something bad, or perhaps been poisoned. Before he could do more than stare, galloping hoofbeats distracted him. "Your Majesty!" shouted the leader of the party Hirundo had ordered out after the missing scouts. "Oh, Your Majesty! By the gods, Your Majesty!"

"I'm here," Grus called, now torn. "What is it? Did you find them?"

The captain nodded. He was as pale as Pterocles, and looked not far from sickness himself. "Yes, Your Majesty." He gulped and went even paler. "We found them."

"And?" Grus said.

"I will not speak of this," the captain said. "I *will* not. If you order me to, I will take you to them. If you do not order me, I will never go near that spot again. Never!" The last word was almost a scream. He shuddered.

"Whatever this is, I had better see it," Grus said. "Take me there at once, Captain. At once, do you hear me?"

"I hear you, Your Majesty." The officer shuddered again. "I do not thank you for the order, but I will obey it. Come, then."

"Guards," Pterocles croaked. "Take guards."

That hadn't crossed Grus' mind. It was plainly a good idea, though. A squadron of bodyguards surrounded him as he rode with the officer toward . . . what?

Coming up over the swell of a low rise, he first saw, from perhaps a quarter of a mile, that the first squadron of scouts and their horses were down, with some of the would-be rescuers still by them. He was braced for that much of a disaster. He hadn't thought he'd lose a whole squadron of scouts, but it seemed to have happened. "The Menteshe caught them?" he asked.

"Yes." The captain managed a ghastly nod. "The Menteshe caught them, Your Majesty."

As Grus rode closer, he began to get a better look at how the scouts—and their horses—had died, and how their bodies had been used after they were dead . . . or while they were dying. "No," he said, as though someone had told him about it and he didn't believe the fellow. "No one would do that." But his eyes, his treacherous, truth-telling eyes, insisted someone had. That they'd been mutilated was bad enough. That the dead men had also been violated . . .

"You see, Your Majesty," the Avornan officer said heavily. "I've seen, and I wish I hadn't."

Grus didn't answer. He rode through that scene of horror and torture. He felt he needed to see it all. He learned more about cruel ingenuity in those few minutes than he'd ever known, or ever wanted to know. At last, he said, "I didn't think even the Menteshe did things like this."

"They usually don't," the officer replied. "I've served in the south for years. This . . ." He turned his head away. "There are no words for this."

"The Banished One," Grus said in a voice like iron. "This is his doing. He's trying to put us in fear."

With a laugh on the ragged edge of hysteria, the Avornan captain said, "He knows how to get what he wants, doesn't he?"

But Grus shook his head. "No. This—shakes me, but it doesn't make me afraid. It makes me angry. I want revenge." He paused. Did that mean paying back the Menteshe in their own coin? Could he stomach ordering his men to do something like this to their foes? If he did that, didn't he invite the Banished One to take up residence in Avornis? "The best revenge I know is whipping them out of the kingdom."

"What do we do about . . . this, Your Majesty?"

"We make pyres. We burn the dead. We're all equal in the flames." Grus paused again, then added, "This time, we burn the horses, too. They deserved what the Menteshe did even less than our troopers. They weren't enemies, just animals."

As he ordered, so it was done. The smoke of the great pyre mingled with the smoke from burning fields. To his relief, the men who made the pyres and laid the dead on them seemed to feel as he did. The bodies inspired horror and rage, but not fear. "We've got to whip the sons of whores who did this," a soldier said. "We owe it to the dead."

"We'll give the Menteshe everything we owe," Grus promised. "Everything."

CHAPTER FIFTEEN

To Lanius' surprise, he found himself missing King Grus. Yes, he'd chafed when Grus spent his time in the city of Avornis and held the kingdom in his own hands. With Grus down in the south fighting the Menteshe, Lanius pulled a lot of strings himself—but they were mostly the uninteresting strings. He'd wanted to administer Avornis . . . until he did it for a while. That made him decide Grus was welcome to the day-to-day drudgery.

But Grus was at war, which meant Lanius was stuck with it. He knew he was less diligent about it than Grus. It embarrassed him, even shamed him, to get a reminder from the provinces about something he should have dealt with the first time, weeks earlier. But he didn't seem able to do anything about such mishaps.

He knew why, too. If he'd given administering Avornis all the time it needed, he wouldn't have been able to dive into the archives or watch his monkeys or try to figure out how Pouncer kept getting out of its room and into the kitchens. Those were more enjoyable pastimes, and he had trouble thinking of them as less important.

He also would have had less time for amusing himself with maidservants. Keeping track of the kingdom was more important than that, but it wasn't nearly as much fun. So far, Sosia hadn't found out about his sport—or rather, hadn't found out that he'd kept on with it after Grus sent Cristata away. That his wife hadn't found out helped keep the sport pleasurable.

And he would have had less time for talks with Prince Vsevolod.

Having less time to talk with the Prince of Nishevatz, however, wouldn't have broken his heart. He'd learned less about the Chernagors than he wanted to, and more about the way Vsevolod thought.

"When will war in south be over?" the Prince asked in his blunt, throaty Avornan. He cared nothing about fighting in the war in the south himself, only about how it affected things in the north—things that mattered to him.

"I don't know, Your Highness," Lanius answered. "I wish I did. I wish someone did."

Vsevolod scowled. To Lanius, he looked more than ever like a scrawny old vulture. "He will win war?"

"By the gods, I hope so!" Lanius exclaimed.

"He will win war by wintertime?"

"I told you, Your Highness—I don't know that. I don't think anyone can. If the gods in the heavens let him do it, he will." As usual, Lanius said nothing about the Banished One, who had been Milvago. As usual, the not-quite-god who no longer dwelt in the heavens wasn't far from his mind.

"If Grus does not win war this winter, he fights again in south when spring comes?" Vsevolod persisted.

"I don't know," Lanius replied, his patience beginning to unravel. "I wouldn't be surprised, though. Would you?"

"No. Not surprised," the prince said darkly. "He cares nothing for Nishevatz, not really. All lies." He turned away.

Lanius was tempted to kick him in the rear. The king didn't, but the temptation lingered. If Vsevolod wasn't the most self-centered man in the world, who was? All he cared about was Nishevatz, regardless of what Avornis needed. More testily than Lanius had expected to, he said, "We've been invaded, you know."

"Yes, you are invaded. Yes, I know. And what of me? I am robbed. I am exiled," Vsevolod said. "I live in strange place, eat strange food, talk strange, ugly language, with no one to care if I live or die."

"We do care," Lanius insisted, though he would have had trouble saying he cared very much himself. "But we have to drive the invaders from our own realm before we can worry about anyone else's."

Prince Vsevolod might not even have heard him. "I will die in exile," he said gloomily. "My city-state will go down to ruin under accursed Vasilko, my own son. I cannot save it. Life is bitter. Life is hard."

He's powerless, Lanius realized. *He's powerless, and he hates it, the way*

I hated it for so long under Grus. And he's old. He's used to power, and can't change his ways now that he doesn't have it anymore. I'd never had it. I kept wondering what it was like, the way a boy will before his first woman.

"We'll do all we can for you, Your Highness." Lanius' voice was as gentle as he could make it. "Don't worry. We'll get Nishevatz back for you. By the gods in the heavens, I swear it."

"The gods in the heavens are—" Vsevolod violently shook his head. "No. If I say that, if I think that, I am Vasilko. This I never do." He got to his feet and stomped away, as though angry at Lanius for making him think things he didn't want to think.

But I didn't. I couldn't, Lanius thought. *Only he can turn his mind one way or another.* Did Vsevolod wonder if the Banished One were more powerful than the gods in the heavens? The king wouldn't have been surprised. He would have had trouble blaming the exiled Prince of Nishevatz. It still worried him.

Grus relaxed in a roadside tavern. The barmaid, who was a young cousin of the fellow who ran the place, set a fresh mug of wine in front of him. He'd had several already. His men had driven the Menteshe off just as they were riding up with torches in their hands, ready to burn the tavern and everyone inside it.

"Thank you, sweetheart," Grus told the barmaid.

"You're welcome, Your Majesty," she answered. "Plenty more where that came from. Don't be shy." She wasn't shy herself. Her name, he'd learned, was Alauda. She was a widow; her husband had laid his leg open threshing grain, and died when the wound went bad. She wouldn't take any silver for the wine, though Grus had offered. "No," she'd said, shaking her head. "You saved us. This is the least we can do."

Hirundo sat on another three-legged stool at the rickety table with Grus. "She's not bad, is she?" the general said, eyeing her as she went to get more wine.

"No, not bad at all," Grus agreed. Alauda had a barmaid's brassy prettiness, wider through the hips and fuller in the bosom than would have been fashionable back in the city of Avornis. Her hair was light brown and very straight. Her saucy blue eyes were probably her best feature; they sparkled with life.

Hirundo was also drinking wine he didn't have to pay for. "Just how grateful do you suppose she'd be?" he murmured.

"What an interesting question." Grus glanced toward Hirundo.

"You seem to have noticed her first. Do you want to be the one who finds out?"

"And deprive you, Your Majesty? Gods forbid!" By the dramatic pose the general struck, he might have been a soldier in a besieged city offering his sovereign his last bit of bread. But the generous gesture turned out to be not quite as noble as all that, for he went on, "I've already found a lady friend or two down here. I don't think you've had the chance yet."

"Well, no," Grus admitted. The trouble he'd gotten into over Alca the witch left him leery of angering Estrilda again. On the other hand, Estrilda was far to the north, unlikely to learn he'd tumbled a barmaid.

"Then go on, if you feel like it—and if she feels like it." Hirundo sounded as predatory here as he did on the battlefield. He might have sounded different if he'd had a wife back in the capital. But he didn't; he was single. And, knowing him, he might not have, too.

He drank up and strolled out of the tavern, clapping Grus on the back as he went. The king ostentatiously finished his mug of wine, too. When Alauda brought him the fresh one she'd poured, he said, "Drink with me, if you care to."

"Sure," she said, smiling. Her mouth was wide and generous. "When will I ever get another chance like this? I can bore people with the story until I'm an old granny." She bent her back and hobbled as she went to get wine for herself. Grus laughed. So did she. He knew then taking her to bed wouldn't be hard.

When she came back with her mug, he sat her on his lap. She slipped an arm around his shoulder as though she'd expected nothing else. One thing did worry him. Pointing to the tavern keeper, he asked, "Will your cousin there be angry?" He didn't want an outraged male relative lurking and brooding and maybe trying to stick a knife in him. Sometimes such people tried to kill without caring whether they lived or died, which made them hard to stop.

But Alauda only stared in surprise. "No, Morus won't mind. It's not like I'm a maiden. And it's not like you're a goatherd, either. You're the *king*."

To make sure Morus didn't mind, she spoke with him after she'd emptied her cup. He looked from her to Grus and back again. Then he walked out of the tavern and closed the door behind him.

"You see?" Alauda said.

"I see." Grus got to his feet. The room swayed when he did. He suddenly wished he hadn't had quite so much to drink. Wine could inflame desire and ruin performance at the same time—and he wasn't as young as he had been.

He took Alauda in his arms. She tilted her face up to him—not very far up, for she was a tall woman. Her mouth was sweet with wine. His arms tightened around her. She molded herself against him. The kiss went on and on.

When it finally ended, Grus had a new reason for feeling dizzy. "Where?" he asked.

"Here, this way. Morus has given me a little room in back."

The room couldn't have been much smaller. It barely held a bed. Grus was sure it had been a closet or storeroom before Alauda came to the tavern. Alauda threw off her tunic and long skirt. Naked, she was as round and ripe as Grus had thought she would be. He bent his mouth to the tips of her breasts. She murmured something wordless. He got out of his own clothes as quickly as he could. They lay down together.

Her legs opened. When he stroked her there, he found her wet and ready. He poised himself above her. "Oh," she said softly when he thrust home. Her thighs gripped his flanks. Her arms squeezed tight. Their mouths clung.

It seemed more like a frenzy than any sort of lovemaking Grus had done lately. Alauda yowled like a cat. Her nails scored the flesh of his back. She threshed and flailed beneath him. He pounded away until pleasure almost blinded him.

When he returned to himself, he noticed the taste of blood in his mouth along with the wine they'd both drunk. Alauda stared up at him past half-lowered eyelids. "*So* nice to meet you, Your Majesty," she purred.

He laughed. When he did, he flopped out of her. Regret flitted across her face, just for a moment. Grus certainly felt regret, too—regret that he wasn't twenty years younger, so they could have started over again right away. He kissed the smooth, white skin in the hollow of her shoulder. She giggled. He said, "You can bring me my wine—or anything else—any time you please."

Alauda smiled. But then her expression darkened. She said, "Tomorrow or sometime soon, you'll be gone, won't you?"

"I can't stay here," Grus answered, as gently as he could. "You know that, dear. I've got to drive back the Menteshe." *If I can.*

Everything else moved sweetly when Alauda nodded. "Oh, yes.

Gods only know what they would have done if your soldiers hadn't chased them away from this place. That wasn't what I meant. I hope I'm not that silly. But . . . couldn't you take me with you? I wouldn't be any trouble, and if I did make trouble you could just leave me somewhere. I'd land on my feet. I always have. And in the meantime—" She wriggled to show what they might do in the meantime.

Grus started to say no. Then he hesitated. Like anyone who hesitated, he was lost. Trying not to admit it even to himself, he warned Alauda, "You know I have a queen. You won't come back to the city of Avornis with me, no matter what."

"Yes, of course I know that," Alauda said impatiently. "I told you, I hope I'm not silly. And by the gods, Your Majesty, I'm not out for what I can get, except maybe this." She took hold of him, then sighed. "It's been a bit since my husband died. I'd almost forgotten how much I missed it."

"You say that now," Grus told her. "Some people say things like that, and then later on they forget what they've said. I wouldn't be very happy—and neither would you—if that happened."

"You've got a bargain," Alauda said at once. "Does that mean the rest of it's a bargain, too?" Before he could answer, she went on, "I'll keep up my end." She laughed again. "And I'll keep up your end. That's part of the bargain, isn't it?"

"I hope so," Grus answered. "I was just thinking I'm not so young anymore—but yes, I do hope so."

Summer heat beat down on the city of Avornis. People who'd spent time in the south said it wasn't all that bad, but it was plenty bad enough to suit Lanius. Plants began to wilt and turn yellow. Flies and other bugs multiplied as though by magic. Little lizards came out of what seemed to be nowhere but were probably crevices in boards and holes in the ground to eat the bugs, or at least some of them.

King Lanius and everyone else in the royal palace did what they could to beat the heat. He doffed the royal robes and plunged into the river naked as the day he was born. That brought relief, but only for a little while. However much he wanted to, though, he couldn't stay in the water all the time.

Arch-Hallow Anser and Prince Ortalis disappeared into the woods to hunt for days at a time. Anser tried to talk Lanius into coming along, but the king remained unconvinced that that was a good bargain. Yes,

the woods were probably cooler than the city, but weren't they also going to be buggier? Lanius thought so, and stayed in the royal palace.

The monkeys flourished in the heat. Even their mustaches seemed to
stick out farther from their faces than before. They ate better than they
ever had, and bounced through the branches and sticks in their rooms
with fresh energy. As far as they were concerned, it could stay hot forever.

Not so the moncats. The Chernagor merchant who'd brought the first
pair to the palace had told Lanius they came from islands in the Northern Sea—islands with, the king supposed, a cooler climate than that of
the city of Avornis. They drooped in the heat the same way flowers did.
Lanius made sure they had plenty of water and that it was changed often
so it stayed fresh. Past that, he didn't know what he could do.

One thing could jolt the moncats out of their lethargy. Whenever a
lizard was foolish enough to show itself in their rooms, they would go
after it with an enthusiasm Lanius had hardly ever seen from them.
They got the same thrill from chasing lizards as Anser did from chasing
deer (Lanius resolutely refused to think about what sort of thrill Ortalis
got from chasing deer). And, like Anser, they got to devour their quarry
at the end of a successful hunt.

Lanius suddenly imagined the arch-hallow, in full ecclesiastical regalia,
with a still-twitching lizard tail hanging from the corner of his mouth. He
started laughing so hard, he frightened the moncats and made servants out
in the hallway pound on the door and ask what was wrong.

"Nothing," he called back, feeling like a little boy whose parents demanded out of the blue what he was doing when it was something
naughty.

"Then what's that racket, Your Majesty?" The voice on the other
side of the door sounded suspicious, even accusing. Was that Bubulcus
out there in the hallway? Lanius thought so, but couldn't be sure.

Whether it was Bubulcus or not, the king knew he had to say,
"Nothing," again, and he did. He couldn't expect the servants to find
that blasphemous image funny. He was more than a little scandalized
that he found it funny himself, but he did, and he couldn't do anything
about it.

"Are you *sure*, Your Majesty?" the servant asked dubiously.

"I'm positive," Lanius answered. "One of the moncats did something foolish, and I was laughing, that's all." That wasn't quite what had
happened, but it came close enough.

"Huh," came from the corridor. That made Lanius more nearly certain it was Bubulcus out there. Whoever it was, he went away; the king listened with no small relief to receding footsteps. When Lanius came out of the moncats' room, no one asked him any more questions. That suited him fine.

Two days later, the hot spell broke. Clouds rolled down from the north. When morning came, the city of Avornis found itself wrapped in chilly mist. Lanius hurried down to the monkeys' room and lit the fire that he'd allowed to die over the past few days. They needed defense against the cold once more, and he made sure they got it.

It started to rain that afternoon. To his horror, Lanius discovered a leak in the roof of the royal archives. He sent men up there to fix it, or at least to cover it, in spite of the rain. There were certain advantages to being the King of Avornis. A luckless homeowner would have had to wait for good weather. But Lanius couldn't stand the notion of water dripping down onto the precious and irreplaceable parchments in the archives. Being who he was, he didn't have to stand for it, either.

Grus looked down from the hills on a riverside town. Like a lot of riverside towns, it had had its croplands ravaged. He'd seen far worse devastation elsewhere, though. The landscape wasn't what kept him staring and staring.

"Pelagonia," he murmured.

Hirundo nodded. "That's what it is, all right," he said. "Looks like a provincial town to me."

"And so it is," Grus agreed. But that wasn't all it was, not to him. Just seeing it made his heart beat faster.

Pterocles understood, but then Pterocles had a wizard's memory for detail. "This is the place where you sent the witch," he said. "Will you ship me back to the city of Avornis and turn her loose on the Menteshe?"

It had crossed Grus' mind. Shipping Alauda back to her cousin's tavern had also crossed his mind. He hadn't seen Alca for three years, not since his wife made him send her away. *Life gets more complicated all the time,* he thought, and laughed, even though it wasn't funny.

"Well, Your Majesty?" Pterocles spoke with unwonted sharpness. "*Will* you?"

He'd had trouble standing up against the Banished One. Of course, so had Alca. Any mortal wizard had trouble standing up against the Banished One. Grus found his answer. "No, I won't," he said. "We're all on the same side in this fight, or we'd better be."

He waited to see what Pterocles would say to that. To his relief, the wizard only nodded. "Can't say you're wrong. She acts like she's pretty snooty, but her heart's in the right place."

Grus bristled at any criticism of his former lover. Fighting to hold on to his temper, he asked Hirundo, "Can we reach the town tonight?"

"I doubt it," the general replied. "Tomorrow, yes. Tonight? We're farther away than you think."

Grus stared south. Only the keep and the spires of the cathedral showed above Pelagonia's gray stone walls. In the nearer distance, a handful of Menteshe rode through the burnt fields in front of the town. They would flee when the Avornan army advanced. Grus knew a lot about fighting the nomads. Unless they had everything their own way, they didn't care for stand-up fights. Why should they? Starvation and raids unceasing worked well for them.

"Tomorrow, then," the King of Avornis said, reluctance and eagerness warring in his voice—reluctance at the delay, eagerness at what might come afterwards. *Alca.* His lips silently shaped the name.

As he'd thought they would, Prince Ulash's men withdrew at the Avornan host's advance. He and Hirundo picked a good campground, one by a stream so the Menteshe couldn't cut them off from water—a favorite trick of theirs. He also made certain he scattered sentries widely about the camp.

"Is something wrong?" Alauda asked in his tent that night.

"No," Grus answered, quicker than he should have. Then, hearing that too-quick word, he had to try to explain himself. "I just want to make sure the town is safe."

The explanation sounded false, too. Alauda didn't challenge him about it. Who was she—a barmaid, a whim, a toy—to challenge a king? No one, and she had sense enough to know it. But she also had the sense to hear that Grus wasn't telling her the truth, or all of the truth. No, she said not a thing, but her eyes showed her hurt.

When they made love that night, she rode Grus with a fierce desperation she'd never shown before. Maybe she sensed he worried more about someone inside Pelagonia than about the city itself. Was she trying to show him he needed to worry about her, too? After the day's travel and after that ferocious coupling, Grus worried about nothing and nobody, but plunged headlong into sleep, one arm still around Alauda.

He almost died before dawn, with no chance to worry about Alauda or Alca or, for that matter, Estrilda. The Menteshe often shied away from stand-up fights, yes. But a night attack, an assault that caught their enemies by surprise, was a different story.

Their wizards must have found some way to fuddle the sentries, for the Avornans knew nothing of their onslaught until moments before it broke upon them. They would have been caught altogether unaware if Pterocles hadn't started up from his pallet, shouting, "Danger! Danger!" By the confused shock in his voice, he didn't even know what sort of danger it was, only that it was real and it was close.

His cry woke Grus. The king's dreams had been of anything but danger. When he woke, one of Alauda's breasts filled his hand. He'd known that even in his sleep, and it had colored and heated his imaginings.

Now . . . now, along with the wizard's shouts of alarm, he heard the oncoming thunder of hoofbeats and harsh war cries in a language not Avornan. Cursing, he realized at least some of what must have happened. He threw on drawers, jammed a helmet down on his head, seized sword and shield, and ran, otherwise naked, from the tent.

"Out!" Grus shouted at the top of his lungs. "Out and fight! Quick, before they kill you all!"

Soldiers started spilling from their tents. In the crimson light of the dying campfires, they might have been dipped in blood. Many of them were as erratically armed and armored as the king himself—this one had a sword, that one a mailshirt, the other a shield, another a bow.

They were a poor lot to try to stop the rampaging Menteshe. And yet the nomads seemed to have looked for no opposition whatever. They cried out in surprise and alarm when Avornans rushed forward to slash at them, to pull them from their horses, and to shoot arrows at them. They'd been looking to murder Grus' soldiers in their tents, to take them altogether unawares. Whatever happened, that wouldn't. More and more Avornans streamed into the fight, these more fully armed than the first few.

One of Prince Ulash's men reined in right in front of Grus. The nomad stared around, looking for foes on horseback. He found none— and had no idea Grus was there until the king yanked him out of the saddle. He had time for one startled squawk before landing in a campfire. He didn't squawk after that. He shrieked. The fire was dying, but not yet dead. And the coals flared to new life when he crashed down on them.

As for Grus, he sprang into the saddle without even thinking about how little he cared for horses and horsemanship. The pony under him bucked at the sudden change of riders. He cuffed it into submission, yelling, "Avornis! Avornis! To me, men! We can beat these cursed raiders!"

"King Grus!" shouted a soldier who recognized his voice. An instant later, a hundred, a thousand throats had taken up the cry. "King Grus! Hurrah for King Grus!"

That proved a mixed blessing. His own men did rally to him. But the Menteshe cried out, too, and pressed him as hard as they could in the crimson-shot darkness. Arrow after arrow hissed past his head. If the archers had been able to see clearly what they were shooting at, he doubted he could have lasted long. At night, though, they kept missing. Even as he slashed with his sword, he breathed prayers of thanks to the gods.

In the screaming, cursing chaos, he took longer to realize something than he should have. When he did, he bawled it out as loud as he could. "There aren't very many of them. Hit them hard! We *can* beat them!"

Maybe the magic—Grus presumed it was magic—that had let the Menteshe slip past his sentries couldn't have hidden more of them; Pterocles had also had trouble masking too many men. Whatever the reason, this wasn't an assault by their whole army, as he'd feared when Pterocles' cry of alarm first woke him. It was a raid. It could have been a costly raid, but now it wouldn't be.

Prince Ulash's men didn't need much more time to figure that out for themselves. When they did, they weren't ashamed to flee. The Avornans spent some small, panicky stretch of time striking at one another before they realized the enemy had gone.

More fuel went on the fires. As they flared up, Hirundo waved to Grus. "Well, that's one way to settle your supper," the general said cheerfully.

Grus noticed three or four cuts, luckily all small, that he'd ignored in the heat of battle. "For a little while there, I wondered if we'd get settled along with supper," he remarked. Hirundo laughed, as though the Menteshe had done no more than play a clever joke on the Avornan army. Grus was in no mood for laughter. He raised his voice, shouting, "Pterocles!"

He had to call the wizard's name several times before he got an answer. He'd begun to fear the nomads had slain Pterocles. No sorcerer was immune to an arrow through the throat or a sword cut that tore out his vitals. But, at length, Pterocles limped into the firelight. He had an arrow through him, all right, but through one calf. He'd wrapped a rag around the wound. Not even the ruddy light of the flames could make his face anything but pallid.

"Are you all right?" Grus exclaimed.

"That depends, Your Majesty," the wizard said, biting his lip against the pain. "Is the wound likely to kill me? No. Do I wish I didn't have it? Yes."

Hirundo said, "I've never known a wound I was glad I had."

"Nor I," Grus agreed. "Have a healer draw the shaft and give you opium for the pain. You're lucky the arrowhead went through—the healer won't have to cut it out of you."

"Lucky." Pterocles savored the word. After a moment, he shook his head. "If I were lucky, it would have missed me."

Grus nodded, yielding the point. He said, "We're all lucky you sensed the nomads coming. What sort of spell did they use to get past the sentries, and can we make sure it won't work if they try it again?"

"A masking spell on the sentries," Pterocles answered. "A masking spell on them, and a sleep spell on me—maybe on this whole camp, but I think just on me—so we wouldn't know the Menteshe were here until too late. It might have done everything the nomads wanted if I hadn't had an extra cup of wine last night."

"What's that?" Hirundo said. "Wine makes me sleepy."

The wizard managed a bloodless smile, though blood was darkening the cloth he'd put around his wounded leg. He said, "Wine makes me sleepy, too. But it also makes me wake up in the middle of the night— which I did, for I had to piss or burst. And when I woke . . ."

Hirundo clapped his hands. Grus was sure that was the first time he'd ever heard anyone's bladder applauded. "Stay where you are. Don't move on it anymore," the king told Pterocles, and turned to a soldier standing not far away. "Fetch a healer to treat the wizard's wound."

"Yes, Your Majesty." The man hurried off.

"You didn't answer the second half of my question," Grus said to Pterocles. "*Can* we make sure Ulash's men don't get away with this again?"

Pterocles said, "The sleep spell isn't easy. It caught me by surprise this time. It won't the next."

"What about other wizards?" Grus asked.

"I can let them know what to be wary of," Pterocles told him. "That will give them a good chance to steer clear of the spell, anyhow."

"Better than nothing," Grus said. It wasn't enough to suit him, but he judged it would have to do. His army had come through here. And tomorrow . . . *Tomorrow, Pelagonia,* he thought.

Sosia hurried up to Lanius. Some strong emotion was on her face. Had she found out he'd been dallying with serving women again? He didn't want to go through another row.

But instead of screaming at him or trying to slap his face, Sosia burst out, "He does! Oh, Lanius, he does!"

Lanius knew he was gaping foolishly. He couldn't help himself. "Who does?" he inquired. "And, for that matter, who does what?"

She stared at him as though he should have understood at once what she was talking about. "My brother," she answered with a grimace. "And he does . . . what you'd expect."

"Are you sure?" Lanius grimaced, too. That was very unwelcome news. "Ortalis is hurting serving girls again, even though he's hunting? Even though he's got a wife?"

"No, no, no!" Sosia's expression said she'd been right the first time— he *was* an idiot. "He's hurting *Limosa.*"

"You're crazy." The words were out of Lanius' mouth before he had the chance to regret them. Even then, only part of him *did* regret them, for he went on, "I saw her yesterday. She looked as happy as a moncat with a lizard to chase. She's looked—and sounded—that way ever since they got married. I don't know why, but she has. She loves your brother, Sosia. She's not pretending. Nobody's that good an actress. And he *does* go out hunting. If he were hurting her, she could come to you or to me or to Anser and scream her head off. She hasn't. She doesn't need to do it, yes?"

"I don't know." Now his wife looked confused.

"What exactly *do* you know? And how do you know it?"

"I know Limosa's got scars on her back, the same sort of scars . . . the same sort of scars Ortalis has put on other girls," Sosia answered. Lanius grimaced again, remembering Cristata's ravaged back. Sosia's eyes said she noticed him remembering, and knew he was remembering the rest of Cristata, too. But she visibly pushed that aside for the time being and continued, "And I know because a serving woman happened to walk in on Limosa while she was bathing. She doesn't usually let any servants attend her then, and that's strange all by itself."

The king nodded; it *was* unusual. Did it mean Limosa had scars she didn't want anyone to see? Try as he would, he couldn't think of anything else.

"But Limosa hasn't said anything about this?" he asked.

"No." Sosia shook her head. "She chased the maidservant away, and she's been going on as though nothing happened ever since."

"I wonder if the maid was wrong, or if she was making it up," Lanius said.

"No," Sosia repeated. "I know Zenaida. She wouldn't. She's reliable."

"Well, so she is," Lanius agreed, his voice as expressionless as he could make it. He wondered what Sosia would have called the serving woman had she known he was sleeping with her. Something other than reliable, he was sure.

He went through the palace the next morning looking for Limosa, and naturally didn't find her. Then, after he'd given up, he came around a corner and almost bumped into her. She dropped him a curtsy, saying, "Hello, Your Majesty."

"Hello, Your Highness." Lanius had almost gotten used to calling Limosa by the title. He'd also paid her a bigger compliment than that—he'd almost forgotten she was Petrosus' daughter. "How are you today?"

Her smile lit up her face. She wasn't a beautiful woman, but when she smiled it was easy to forget she wasn't. "I'm very well, Your Majesty, very well indeed. I hope you are, too."

"Pretty well, anyhow," Lanius said.

"Good. I'm so glad to hear it." That wasn't, or didn't sound like, simple courtesy alone; it sounded as though Limosa meant it. "If you'll excuse me . . ."

"Of course," Lanius said. She smiled again, even more brightly than before. Fluttering her fingers at him, she hurried down the hall, her skirt rustling at each step.

She was radiant. That was the only word Lanius could find. *And she's supposed to bear the mark of the lash on her back?* The king shook his head. He couldn't believe it. He didn't believe it. He didn't know what Zenaida thought she'd seen. Whatever it was, he was convinced she'd gotten it wrong.

CHAPTER SIXTEEN

Pelagonia's iron-shod gates swung open. The Avornan defenders on the wall—soldiers of the garrison in helmets and mailshirts, armed with swords and spears and heavy bows, plus a good many militiamen in leather jerkins, armed with daggers and with hunting bows good for knocking over rabbits and squirrels but with no range or punch to speak of—cheered Grus and his army as he led it into the town.

He waved back to the men who'd held Pelagonia against the Menteshe. He pasted a smile on his face. His heart pounded as though he were storming Yozgat and driving Prince Ulash from his throne. That had nothing to do with Pelagonia itself, so he didn't want the people here noticing anything amiss. It had everything to do with one woman who'd come—been sent—to live here.

He wanted to see Alca as soon as he got the chance. And yet, he would be quietly setting up housekeeping with Alauda while he stayed here. He recognized the inconsistency. Recognizing it and doing anything about it were two different beasts.

A baron named Spizastur commanded in Pelagonia. He was a big, bluff fellow with gray eyes and a red face—an even redder nose, one that suggested he put down a lot of wine. "Greetings, Your Majesty!" he boomed. "Mighty good to see you, and that's the truth!" Was he drunk? Not in any large, showy way, anyhow, though he did talk too loud.

"Good to be here," the king replied.

"I'm not sorry to see the last of those thieving devils," Spizastur declared, again louder than he needed to. "Been a long time since they came this far north. Won't be sorry if I never see 'em again, either."

Grus knew it was far from certain Pelagonia *had* seen the last of the Menteshe. He didn't say that to Spizastur. It would only have disheartened the noble and the soldiers who'd held Prince Ulash's men out of the city. He did say, "I hope you have billets for my men—and a place for me to stay."

"Billets for some, anyhow," Spizastur replied. "This isn't the big city, where you can fit in a great host and never notice. For you yourself, Your Majesty, I've got rooms in the keep."

"I thank you." Grus would sooner have stayed with some rich merchant—odds were that would have been more comfortable. But he couldn't tell Spizastur no. "I have a . . . lady friend with me," he murmured.

"Do you?" The local commander didn't seem surprised. "I'll see to it."

Grus didn't pay much attention to Alauda until that evening. He was busy with Spizastur and Hirundo, planning where the army would go next and what it would try to do. And he kept hoping Alca would come to the keep.

Alauda yawned as the two of them got ready for bed. She said, "I need to tell you something."

"What is it?" Grus, his mind partly on the campaign and partly on Alca, paid little attention to the widowed barmaid he'd brought along on a whim.

But she found half a dozen words to make him pay attention. "I'm going to have a baby," she said. Any man who hears those words, especially from a woman not his wife, *will* pay attention to them.

"Are you sure?" Grus asked—the timeworn, and foolish, common response to such news.

She nodded, unsurprised. "Yes, I'm positive. My courses should have come, and they haven't. My breasts are tender"—Grus had noticed that—"and I'm sleepy all the time. I had a baby girl, but she died young, poor thing. I know the signs."

Are you sure it's mine? But no, he couldn't ask that. He didn't think she'd played him false since they'd become lovers, and they'd been together long enough so the father couldn't be anyone from before even if she hadn't made it plain she'd slept alone since her husband died. Grus said, "Well, well. I'll take care of you, and I'll take care of the baby. You don't need to worry about that."

"Thank you, Your Majesty," Alauda breathed. By the way she said it, she *had* worried. In her place, Grus supposed he would have, too.

He shook his head. He might have been trying to clear it after a punch in the jaw. "I hope you'll forgive me, but I still don't intend to bring you back to the capital with me. I don't think my wife would understand." Actually, Estrilda would understand altogether too well. That was what Grus was afraid of.

"I'm not worried about that," Alauda said quickly. "You told me you wouldn't once before."

"All right. Good." He realized he needed to do something more, and went over and gave her a kiss. She clung to him, making her relief obvious without a word. He kissed her again, and patted her, and lay down beside her. She fell asleep almost at once. She'd said being pregnant left her sleepy. Lying awake beside her as she softly snored, Grus sighed and shook his head. He'd been thinking about saying good-bye to her. He couldn't very well do that now.

And he was drifting off to sleep himself when a new thought woke him up again. What would Alca think when she found out? After that, sleep took even longer to find Grus.

Lanius studied Grus' letters from the south with the obsessive attention of a priest trying to find truth in an obscure bit of dogma. Naturally, Grus put the best face he could on the news he sent up to the city of Avornis—what he said quickly spread from the palace out to the capital as a whole. Piecing together what lay behind his always optimistic words was a fascinating game, one made more interesting when played with a map.

Just now, Lanius suspected his fellow king of cheating. Grus wrote of a night attack his army had beaten back, and then said, *We have entered a town on the north bank of the Thyamis River, from which, as opportunity arises, we will proceed against the Menteshe.*

"*Which* town on the north bank of the Thyamis?" Lanius muttered, more than a little annoyed. It could have been Naucratis, it could have been Chalcis, or it could have been Pelagonia. Grus didn't make himself clear. Depending on where he was, he could strike at the nomads several different ways.

From the context, the Avornan army seemed most likely to be in Pelagonia. But why hadn't Grus come out and said so? Up until now, he'd at least told people in the capital where he was, if not always why he'd gone there. Figuring out why was part of the game, too.

And then, after one more glance from the letter to the map, Lanius said, "Oh," and decided he knew where the army was after all. If Estrilda saw the name Pelagonia, she wouldn't need to look at a map to know where it was. She already knew that, in the only way likely to matter to her—it was where Grus had sent his mistress. What was he doing there now? That was what she would want to know. Did it have anything to do with fighting Prince Ulash's men, or was the king seeing the witch again?

If Grus failed to send a dispatch up to the capital, everyone there would wonder what disaster he was trying to hide. But if he sent a dispatch that said, *We have entered a town on the north bank of the Thyamis River*—well, so what? If Estrilda saw the dispatch, would she realize *a town on the north bank of the Thyamis River* meant *Pelagonia*? Not likely.

From being annoyed at Grus, Lanius went to admiring him. The other king had had a problem, had seen it, and had solved it in a way that caused him no more problems. If that wasn't what being a good king was all about, Lanius didn't know what would be.

Back in the palace, Lanius had problems of his own. He might have known rumors about Limosa would race through it like a fire through brush in a drought. He *had* known it, in fact. And now it had. Servants gossiped and joked, careless of who heard them. He didn't want the royal family mocked. He was touchy about his own dignity—after people had called him a bastard through much of his childhood, who could blame him for that? And he was touchy about the dignity of the family.

"What can we do?" he asked Sosia. "I don't believe it, but people still spread it."

"I don't know," she answered. "I don't really think we *can* do anything about it. And I'm not so sure I don't believe it. Why would Zenaida lie about something like that?"

"How could Limosa seem so happy if it's true?" Lanius retorted. "We've seen what happens when Ortalis starts abusing serving girls. You can't tell me that's happening now."

His wife shrugged. "Maybe not. Whether the stories are true or not, though, all we can do is ignore them. If we say they're lies, people will think we have reasons for hiding the truth. If we pretend we don't hear, though, what can they do about it?"

"Laugh at us." To Lanius, that was as gruesome as any other form of torture.

But Sosia only shrugged again. "The world won't end. Before long, some new scandal will come along. Some new scandal always does. By this time next month, or month after at the latest, people will have forgotten all about Limosa."

Things weren't quite that simple, and Lanius knew it. Limosa was part of the royal family now. People would always wonder what she was doing and gossip about what they thought she was doing. Yet Sosia had a point, too. When new rumors came along, old ones would be forgotten. People didn't shout, "Bastard!" at him anymore when he went out into the streets of the city of Avornis. His parentage had been a scandal, but it wasn't now. People had found other things to talk about. They would with Limosa, too.

"Maybe you're right," Lanius said with a sigh. "But I don't think it will be much fun until the rumors do die down."

Grus looked south across the Thyamis River from the walls of Pelagonia. Clouds of smoke rising in the distance showed the Menteshe had no intention of leaving Avornis until he threw them out. As he'd known, this wasn't a raid; this was a war. The king had been eager to come into Pelagonia for reasons of his own. Now, for different reasons, he was just as eager to leave the town.

His bodyguards stirred and stepped aside. Pterocles was one of the men who could come—limp, these days—right up to him without a challenge. At Grus' gesture, the guardsmen moved back so Pterocles and he could talk in privacy.

"I owe you an apology, Your Majesty," the wizard said.

"You do?" That wasn't something Grus heard every day. "Why?"

"Because I thought Alca the witch was a sly little snip who was clever without really knowing what she was doing," Pterocles answered. "I was wrong. I admit it. She's really very sharp."

"Oh? How do you know that?"

The look Pterocles gave him said the wizard wondered whether *he* was very sharp. "Because I've been working with her ever since we got here, of course. Do you think I'd say that about somebody I didn't know?"

"No, I don't suppose you would," Grus admitted. "But I wondered, because I haven't seen her since we got here."

"Do you want to?" Pterocles sounded surprised. "Uh, meaning no disrespect, Your Majesty, but you've got another woman with you, and Alca knows it."

"Oh," Grus said. "Does she?" Pterocles nodded. The king wondered whether Alca knew Alauda was pregnant. She wouldn't be very happy about that if she did. Even so, Grus went on, "I would like to see her, yes. Not because . . . because of what we used to be, but because she's a powerful witch."

Pterocles nodded again, enthusiastically this time. "She really is. You know how you've been nagging me about spells to cure thralls?"

"I know I've been interested in that, yes." Grus' voice was dry. "I also know you made a point of telling me Alca's ideas were worthless."

"Well, they were. She didn't understand. But now she does," the wizard said. "When I get back to the capital, I'll have all sorts of good ideas—hers and mine—to try out."

"Good. We can use all the good ideas we can find," Grus said. "And if you'd be so kind, tell her I can see her this afternoon."

"I'll do that." Pterocles went on his way.

Grus wondered if he'd just been clever or very foolish. Alca *was* a powerful witch—and he'd sent her away from the city of Avornis. Now he came to Pelagonia not with his wife, which would have been bad enough, but with a new mistress, and one who would have his child. Would it be surprising if Alca felt like turning him into a dung beetle?

The real irony was that he didn't love Alauda. He never had and never would. He enjoyed her in bed, and that was about as far as it went. She had the outlook of a peasant girl who'd become a barmaid, which was exactly what she was. Alca, on the other hand, he'd liked and admired long before they slept together. That wasn't a guaranteed recipe for falling in love, but it was a good start.

He waited more than a little nervously in a small, bare room in the quarters in the keep Spizastur had given Alauda and him. He didn't know what Alauda was doing. He hoped she was napping.

A guardsman stuck his head into the room. "Your Majesty, the witch is here." He had tact. He'd served Grus back in the palace. He had to know all the lurid gossip about the king and Alca. What he knew didn't show in his voice.

Gratefully, Grus answered, "Send her in."

Alca came into the chamber slowly and cautiously. Until Grus saw how she moved, how her pale, fine-boned face was set to show as little as it could, he hadn't realized she was at least as nervous as he was. She brushed a lock of black hair back from her forehead. "Your Majesty," she said, her voice not much above a whisper.

"Hello, Alca," Grus replied, and he wasn't much louder. "It's good to see you."

"It's good to see you, too," Alca said. "I wasn't sure it would be, but it is, in spite of everything."

"How have you been?" he asked.

"This place is an even bigger hole than I thought it would be, and most of the men here ought to be horsewhipped," she answered. "I didn't much care for watching the Menteshe burn our fields, either."

"Oh." Grus winced. "I'm sorry. Curse it, I *am* sorry—about everything. When we started, I didn't think it would end up like . . . this."

"I did," Alca said bleakly. "I did, but I went ahead anyhow—and so it's partly my own fault that this happened to me. Partly." She cocked her head to one side and eyed him in a way he remembered painfully well. "Will you tell this latest woman of yours that you're sorry about everything, too?"

Pterocles had said she knew about Alauda. Grus wondered if the wizard had told her, or if she'd found out by magic, or maybe just by market gossip. Any which way, a king had a demon of a time keeping secrets, especially about himself. However Alca knew, her scorn burned. Gruffly, Grus answered, "I hope not."

Alca nodded. "Yes, I believe that. You always hope not. And when things go wrong—and they *do* go wrong—you're always surprised. You're always disappointed. And that doesn't do anybody any good, does it?"

"Is that why you came here? To rail at me?"

"What will you do if I say yes? Exile me to some no-account town in the middle of nowhere? I take it back, Your Majesty"—the way Alca used the royal title flayed Grus—"I'm not so glad to see you after all."

They glared at each other. After a long, furious silence, Grus asked, "Have you been glad to see Pterocles?"

Alca's face changed. "Yes," she breathed. "Oh, yes, indeed. That is a clever young man. He needs to be kicked every so often—or more than every so often—but he'll do great things if—" She broke off.

"If the Banished One doesn't kill him first," Grus finished for her.

"Yes. If." The witch nodded again. "He's dreamed of the Banished One. Did you know that?"

"It's one of the reasons I made him my chief wizard aft—" Now Grus stopped short. *After I sent you away* was what he'd started to say, but he decided not to say it. "One of the reasons I made him my chief wizard," he repeated. "It's a sign the Banished One takes you seriously, I think."

"An honor I could do without," Alca said, and shivered in the warm little room.

Grus agreed with her there, no matter how much the two of them quarreled about their personal affairs. The king asked, "Have you made any progress on spells to cure the thralls? Pterocles seemed to think you had."

Her eyes lit up. "Yes. I really think we have. He knows some things I never could have imagined. But then, he found out about them the hard way, too. To be struck down by the Banished One . . . I'd sooner have the dreams, and that's the truth."

"I believe it. I think you're right." Grus hesitated. "It's dead, isn't it? When I came to Pelagonia, I thought . . ." He shook his head. "But no. It really is dead."

"You thought that, when you came here with another woman?" Alca shook her head, too—in disbelief. "You can still surprise me, Your Majesty, even when I ought to know better. But yes, it's as dead as that table there." She pointed. "And it would be even if you hadn't brought her along. I know how big a fool I am—not big enough to let you hurt me twice, and I thank the gods I'm not."

Suddenly Grus was much more eager to escape this provincial town than he ever had been to come here. "I won't trouble you anymore," he mumbled.

"I'll work with your wizard," Alca said. "I'll do whatever I can to help Avornis. I told you that when I wrote to you. But I don't think I ever want to see you again."

"All right," Grus said. Just then, it was more than all right. It came as an enormous relief.

Whenever a courier came into the city of Avornis from the south, King Lanius worried. His chief fear was that Grus might have met disaster at the hands of the Menteshe. That would have put him back on the Diamond Throne as full-fledged ruler of the kingdom, but only by ruining the kingdom. Some prices were too high to pay.

He had another worry, small only in comparison to that one. So far this fighting season, the Chernagor pirates had stayed away from the Avornan coast. If they descended on it while Grus was busy against the

Menteshe . . . Lanius didn't know what would happen then, but he knew it wouldn't be good.

Reports from Grus came in regularly. He seemed to be making as much progress against the nomads as anyone could reasonably expect. And the coast stayed quiet. No tall-masted ships put in there. No kilted buccaneers swarmed out to loot and burn and kill—and to distract the Avornans from their campaign against Prince Ulash's Menteshe.

Lanius wondered why not. If the Banished One's hand propelled both the Menteshe and the Chernagors against Avornis, couldn't he set both foes in motion against her at the same time? Failing there struck Lanius as inept, and, while he might wish the god cast down from the heavens made many such mistakes, he'd seen that the Banished One seldom did.

He asked Prince Vsevolod why the Chernagors were holding back. "Why?" Vsevolod echoed. "I tell you why." Maybe the sour gleam in his eye said he thought Lanius should have figured it out for himself. Maybe it just said he didn't care for the King of Avornis. In that case, the feeling was mutual.

"Go ahead," Lanius urged.

"Are two reasons," Vsevolod said. "First reason is, Avornan ships fight hard two years ago. Not all Chernagor ships get home. Many losses. They not want many losses again."

"Yes, I follow that," Lanius said. "What's the other reason?"

"Magic." The exiled Prince of Nishevatz spoke the word with somber relish. "This spring, they send supply ships to my city-state, send food to my cursed son. And they watch ships burn up. They see food burn, see sailors burn. Not want to see that off coast of Avornis. So they stay home." Vsevolod jabbed a thumb at his own broad chest. "Me, I like to watch ships burn. Oh, yes. I like very much. Let me watch Vasilko burn—I like that better yet."

Lanius believed him. All the same, the king wondered whether the Banished One could have set the Chernagors in motion against Avornis despite their hesitation. Evidently not. The Chernagors, or some of them, were his allies, yes, but not—or not yet—his puppets, as the Menteshe were.

We can still win, Lanius thought. Avornis wasn't the only one with troubles. He tried to imagine how the world looked from the Banished One's perspective. Avornis' great foe was already doing all he could with the Menteshe. Up in the north, he'd managed to keep Grus from driving Vasilko out of Nishevatz and putting Vsevolod back on the throne there. But if he couldn't get the Chernagors to work with the Menteshe, they had to make very unsatisfactory tools for him.

What could he do about that? Lanius wondered if thralls would start showing up in the land of the Chernagors. In an odd way, he hoped so. If anything could frighten the Chernagors who followed the Banished One into changing their allegiance, that might do the trick. Down in the south, the Menteshe wizards had made Avornan peasants into thralls. That bothered the nomads not at all. They would have abused those peasants any which way. But in the north, thralls would have to be Chernagors, not members of an alien folk, and that could work against the Banished One. Despising his mortal opponents, he did sometimes overreach himself. Why not in the north, where things weren't going just as he wished?

Vsevolod said, "When you end this silly war in south? When you go back to what is important? When you drive Vasilko from Nishevatz? Two times now, you lay siege, then you quit and go home. Another time, you go home before you lay siege. For me, is like being woman with man who is bad lover. You tease, you tease, you tease—but I never go where I want to go."

Perspective. Point of view, Lanius thought again. Vsevolod's was invincibly self-centered—not that Lanius hadn't already known that. With some asperity, he said, "I don't think driving invaders out of our southern provinces is a silly war. What would you do if someone invaded Nishevatz?"

"No one invades Nishevatz," Vsevolod said complacently. "Chernagors rule seas. Even Avornis does not dare without me at your side." He struck a pose.

Lanius felt like hitting him. Plainly, the King of Avornis had no chance of making things clear to the Prince of Nishevatz. "Your turn will come," Lanius said. Only after the words were gone did he wonder how he'd meant them. Better not to know, maybe.

"Not come soon enough," Vsevolod grumbled, proving he hadn't taken it the way Lanius feared he might. He gave Lanius a creaky bow. "Not soon enough," he repeated, and lumbered out of the room.

As a matter of fact, Lanius agreed with him. The sooner the king got the prince out of the city of Avornis and back to Nishevatz—or anywhere else far, far, away—the happier he would be. Lanius wondered if he could send Vsevolod to the Maze until Grus was ready to campaign in the Chernagor country again. He wouldn't tell Vsevolod it was exile; he would tell him it was a holiday—a prolonged holiday. Maybe he could bring it off without letting Vsevolod know what was really going on.

With a sigh of regret, Lanius shook his head. Vsevolod *would* figure out he'd been insulted. His beaky nose smelled out insults whether they were there or not. And Grus would be furious if Vsevolod thought he was insulted. The other king needed Vsevolod as a figurehead when he fought in the north. Otherwise, he would seem an invader pure and simple.

Or would he? Vsevolod had henchmen, several of high blood, in the city of Avornis. If anything happened to him, one of them might make a good enough cat's-paw. Slowly, thoughtfully, Lanius nodded. Yes, that might work. And if it did prove enough, if the king found a cooperative Chernagor, couldn't he do without the obnoxious Vsevolod? He didn't know, not for certain, but he did know one thing—he was tempted to find out.

King Grus looked down into the valley of the Anapus, the river just north of the Stura. He let out a long sigh of relief. He'd spent a lot of time and he'd spent a lot of men coming this far, clearing the Menteshe from several valleys farther north. They'd left devastation behind them, but it was—he hoped—devastation that could be repaired if the no-mads didn't come back and make it worse.

Hirundo looked down into the valley, too. "Wasn't too far from here that we first met, if I remember right," the general remarked.

"I thought it was down in the valley of the Stura, myself," Grus answered.

"Was it?" Hirundo shrugged. "Well, even if it was, it wasn't *too* far from here, not if you're looking from the city of Avornis. I know one thing for certain—we were both a lot younger than we are now."

"Well . . . yes." Grus nodded. "I think time is what happens to you when you're not looking. Except for a few things, I don't feel any older now than I did then—but how did the gray get into my beard if I'm not?" He plucked a hair from the middle of the chin. It wasn't gray. It was white. Muttering, he opened his fingers and let the wind sweep it away. And if the wind could have taken the rest of the white hairs with it, he would have been the happiest man in the world.

Time, Grus thought, and muttered under his breath. Time worked evils the Banished One couldn't come close to matching. If Lanius and Grus himself alarmed the Banished One, all the exiled god really had to do was wait. Soon enough, they would be gone, and he could return to whatever schemes he'd had before they came to power. But he who had been Milvago was caught up in time, too, since he'd been cast down from the heavens to the material world. He might not be mortal in any ordinary sense of the word, but he too knew impatience, the sense that he couldn't wait for things to happen, that he had to *make* them happen.

Because of that impatience, he sometimes struck too soon. Sometimes. Grus dared hope this was one of those times.

"Forward!" he called, and waved to the trumpeters. Their notes blared out the command. Forward the Avornan army went.

River galleys glided along the Anapus. As Grus and Hirundo had done when they first met, they could use soldiers on land and the galleys as hammer and anvil to smash the Menteshe. The nomads were vulnerable trying to cross rivers. There, the advantage of mobility they had over the Avornans broke down.

"Let's push them," Grus said. Hirundo nodded.

But the Menteshe didn't feel like being pushed. Instead of riding south toward the river, they galloped off to east and west, parallel to the stream. And everywhere they went, new fires, new pyres, rose behind them. The Avornans slogged along behind them. The nomads lived off the country even as they ravaged it. Grus' army remained partly tied to supply wagons.

And the Menteshe had plans of their own. Grus listened to drums talking back and forth through the night. He'd done that before, but now he understood some of what the drums were saying. If he understood them rightly, the nomads intended to smash his army between two of theirs.

When he said as much to Hirundo, the general nodded. "We're trying to do the same to them, Your Majesty," he said. "All depends on who manages to bring it off."

"I know," Grus said. "Let's see if we can't give them a little surprise, though, shall we? I don't think they know yet that we can follow what the drums say."

"We'd better make this win important, then," Hirundo said. "Otherwise, we'll have given away a secret without getting a good price for it."

Grus hadn't thought of that. He slowly nodded. Hirundo, as usual, made good sense. The king and the general put their heads together, trying to figure out how to turn what they knew into a real triumph. Grus liked the plan they hammered out.

Even so, it almost came to pieces at first light the next morning, because the Menteshe attacked sooner than Grus had thought they would. Arrows started arcing toward the Avornan army from east and west even before the sun cleared the eastern horizon. If the Avornans hadn't pieced together what the drums were saying, his soldiers might have been caught still in their tents. As things were, not all of them had reached the positions he wanted by the time the fighting started.

But they'd done enough, especially in the east, where he wanted to hold the Menteshe. He had to delay his attack in the west until he had some confidence the east *would* hold. That meant the nomads peppered his men with arrows for an extra hour or so. But they didn't push their attack as hard as they might have. Their main assault was supposed to be in the east. So the drums had said, and so it proved.

"Forward!" Grus shouted when everything was at least close to his liking. The Avornans' horns wailed. The Menteshe probably understood horn calls the same way he understood their drum signals, but it didn't matter here. The Avornans rode bigger horses and wore sturdier armor than the Menteshe. At close quarters, they had the edge on the nomads. And, because Prince Ulash's men were so intent on their own plan, they'd come to close quarters.

They shouted in dismay when the iron-armored wedge of the Avornan army thundered at them, smashed their line, and hurled it aside. Grus struck out to right and left with his sword. A couple of times, it bit into flesh. More often, it kept one Menteshe or another from getting a good swipe at him.

When things went wrong, the nomads thought nothing of running away to try again some other time. Grus had expected that. This time, he tried to use it to his own purposes. He'd deployed outriders who shot at the nomads trying to escape to the north. The Menteshe, still surprised at the vigor of his response, recoiled from that direction and galloped south instead.

That was where he wanted them to go. Only when they drew close to the Anapus did they realize as much. They cried out in dismay again, for the river galleys waited there. Not only that, but the ships also landed marines who shot volley after volley of arrows into the Menteshe. And the catapults on the galleys kept the nomads from closing with the marines and riding them down. After darts from those catapults pinned two or three Menteshe to their horses and knocked several more off their mounts, Ulash's riders didn't want to go anywhere near the river.

Their other choice was charging at Grus and the men he led. That wasn't the sort of fight they wanted, but desperation served where nothing else would. Shouting fiercely in their own language, the nomads swarmed toward the Avornan army.

A volley from the Menteshe made several Avornan horsemen pitch from the saddle and crumple to the ground. Wounded horses squealed and screamed. But soon the attacking Menteshe got close enough for Grus' men to shoot back. And they did, with well-disciplined flights of arrows that tore into the invaders' front ranks. "Grus! Grus! King Grus!" the Avornans cried.

Then it wasn't just arrows anymore. It was swords and javelins and lances. It was men shouting and cursing and shrieking at the top of their lungs. It was iron belling off iron, iron striking sparks from iron, the hot iron stink of blood in the air. It was cut and hack and slash and thrust—and, for Grus, it was hoping he could stay alive.

He cut at a Menteshe. Along with a shirt of boiled leather that turned arrows almost as well as a mailcoat, the fellow wore a close-fitting iron cap. Grus' blow jammed it down onto his forehead; the cut from the rim made blood run down into his eyes. He yammered in pain and yanked the iron cap back up with his left hand. But Grus struck again a heartbeat later. His sword crunched into the nomad's cheek. He felt the blow all the way up into his shoulder. Face a gory mask, the Menteshe slid off over his horse's tail.

Another nomad hacked at Grus. He managed to block the blow with his shield. He felt that one all the way to the shoulder, too, and knew his shield arm would be bruised and sore come morning. But if he hadn't turned the blade aside, it would have bitten into his ribs. He hoped his mailshirt and the padding beneath would have kept it out of his vitals, but that wasn't the sort of thing anybody wanted to find out the hard way.

An Avornan to Grus' left engaged the Menteshe before he could slash at the king again. An arrow hissed past Grus' head, the sound of its passage as malignant as a wasp's buzz—and its sting, if it had struck home, far more deadly.

For a little while, he worried that the nomads' fear and desperation would fire them to break through his battle line. But the Avornans held, and then began pushing Ulash's riders back toward the Anapus regardless of whether they wanted to go that way. When the marines from the river galleys and the catapults on the ships began galling them again, they broke, riding off wildly in all directions.

"After them!" Grus croaked. He took a swig from his water bottle to lay the dust in his throat, then shouted out the command. Still crying out his name, the Avornans thundered after their foes. Some of the Menteshe got away, but many fell.

Hirundo was bleeding from a cut on the back of his sword hand. He didn't even seem to know he had the wound. "Not bad, Your Majesty," he said. "Not bad at all, by the gods. We hurt 'em bad this time."

"Yes," Grus said. "It's only fair—they've done the same to us."

CHAPTER SEVENTEEN

King Lanius sat on the Diamond Throne. The weight of the royal crown was heavy on his head. His most splendid royal robes, shot through with gold threads and encrusted with jewels and pearls, were as heavy as a mailshirt. Down below his high seat, royal bodyguards clutched swords and spears. The men were as nervous as big, tough farm dogs when wolves came near. And Lanius was nervous, too. He hadn't expected an embassy from the Chernagor city-state of Durdevatz. Men from Durdevatz had brought him his monkeys. In those days, though, peace had reigned between the Chernagors and Avornis. Things were different now.

But how different were they? Lanius himself didn't know. From what he did know, Durdevatz wasn't one of the city-states that had helped resupply Nishevatz when Grus besieged it. Who could say for certain what had happened since then, though? No one could—which explained why the guards clung so tightly to their weapons.

And along with the guards stood a pair of wizards tricked out in helmets and mailshirts, shields and swords. They wouldn't be worth much in a fight, but the disguise might help them cast their spells if any of the Chernagors in the embassy tried to loose magic against the king.

Would the men from Durdevatz do such a thing? Lanius didn't know that, either. All he knew was, he didn't want to find out the hard way that he should have had sorcerers there.

A stir at the far end of the throne room. Courtiers' heads swung that way. The envoys from Durdevatz came toward the throne. They were large, burly men with proud hooked noses, thick dark curly beards, and black hair worn in neat buns at the napes of their necks. They wore linen shirts enlivened by fancy embroidery at the chest and shoulders, wool knee-length kilts with checks on dark backgrounds, and boots that reached halfway up their calves. They all had very hairy legs, judging by the bits that showed between boot tops and kilts.

Their leader wore the fanciest shirt of all. He bowed low to Lanius, low enough to show the bald spot on top of his head. "Greetings, Your Majesty," he said in fluent but gutturally accented Avornan.

"Greetings to you." As he went through the formula of introduction with the ambassador, Lanius kept his voice as noncommittal as he could. "You are . . . ?"

"My name is Kolovrat, Your Majesty," the ambassador from Durdevatz replied. "I bring you not only my own greetings but also those of my overlord, Prince Ratibor, and also the greetings of all the other princes of the Chernagors."

A brief murmur ran through the throne room. Lanius would have murmured, too, if he hadn't been sitting on the Diamond Throne before everyone's eye. "Prince . . . Ratibor?" he said. "What, ah, happened to Prince Bolush?" Asking a question like that broke protocol, but no one in Avornis had heard that Bolush had lost his throne.

Kolovrat didn't seem put out at the question. "A hunting accident, Your Majesty," he replied. "Very sad."

Lanius wondered how accidental the accident had been. He also wondered where Ratibor and Kolovrat stood on any number of interesting and important questions. For now, though, formula prevailed. He said, "I am pleased to accept Prince Ratibor's greetings along with your own." *Am I? Well, I'll find out.* He didn't mention the other Chernagor princes. For one thing, Kolovrat had no real authority to speak for them. For another, at least half of them were at war with Avornis at the moment.

"In my prince's name, I thank you, Your Majesty." Kolovrat bowed.

"I am pleased to have gifts for you and your comrades," Lanius said. A courtier handed leather sacks to the ambassador and the other Chernagors.

"I thank you again," Kolovrat said with another bow. "And I am pleased to have gifts for you as well, Your Majesty."

Now all the courtiers leaned forward expectantly. Lanius had gotten not only his first monkeys but also his first pair of moncats from Chernagor envoys. Those earlier ambassadors had been at least as much merchants as they were diplomats. Lanius thought Kolovrat really did come straight from Prince Ratibor.

The king's guardsmen and the wizards masquerading as guardsmen also leaned forward, ready to protect Lanius if this embassy turned out to be an elaborate disguise for an assassination attempt. That had occurred to the king, too. For once, he wished the Diamond Throne didn't elevate him to quite such a magnificent height. Sitting on it, he made a good target.

But when one of the Chernagors standing behind Kolovrat opened a box, no arrows or sheets of flame or spiny, possibly poisonous monsters burst from it. Instead, it held . . . Were those, could those be . . . parchments?

Kolovrat said, "Prince Ratibor discovered these old writings in the cathedral after the High Hallow of Durdevatz set the princely crown upon his head. He has heard of your fondness for such things, and sends them to you with his warmest esteem and compliments."

The guardsmen relaxed. So did the wizards. Whatever Ratibor thought about Lanius, he didn't seem inclined to murder him. The Avornan courtiers drew back with dismay bordering on disgust. Old parchments? Not a lot interesting about *them*!

Lanius? Lanius beamed. "Thank you very much!" he exclaimed. "Please give my most sincere thanks to His Highness as well. I look forward to finding out what these old parchments say. They're from the cathedral, you tell me?"

"Yes, Your Majesty." Kolovrat nodded.

"How . . . interesting." Now the king could hardly wait to get his hands on the documents. Parchments from the cathedral at Durdevatz could be very old indeed. Lanius wondered if they went back to the days before the Chernagors swooped down on the coast of the Northern Sea and took the towns there away from Avornis. That didn't seem likely, but it wasn't impossible, either.

"I am sure your pleasure will delight Prince Ratibor." Kolovrat said all the right things. He still sounded more than a little amazed, though, that Lanius was pleased with the present.

That amazement made Lanius curious. "How did Prince Ratibor know I would like this gift so well?" he asked.

"How, Your Majesty? Prince Ratibor is a clever man. That is how,"

Kolovrat answered. "And he knows you too are a clever man. He knows you will aid Durdevatz in her hour of need."

Aha. Now we come down to it, Lanius thought. He hadn't supposed Ratibor had sent an embassy just for the sake of sending one—and Ratibor evidently hadn't. "What does your prince want from Avornis?" the king asked cautiously.

"Nishevatz and the city-states allied with Nishevatz harry us," Kolovrat said. "Without help, we do not know how long we can stay free. We fear what will come if we lose our struggle. Vasilko is the Prince of Nishevatz, but everyone knows who Vasilko's prince is."

He means the Banished One, Lanius thought unhappily. He wished the new Prince of Durdevatz had come to him with some foolish, trivial request, something he could either grant or refuse with no twinge of conscience. Whatever he did now, he would have more than twinges. "Tell me what Prince Ratibor wants from us," he said. "I do not know how much I can give. We are at war in the south, you know. Avornis itself is invaded."

"Yes. I know this," Kolovrat said. "But what you can do, with soldiers or ships, Prince Ratibor hopes you will. Durdevatz is hard pressed. If you can send us any aid at all, we will be ever grateful to the rich and splendid Kingdom of Avornis. So my prince swears, by all the gods in the heavens."

Not too long before, in the archives, Lanius had come across a copy of a letter from his father to some baron or another. That happened every so often; it never failed to give him an odd feeling. He'd been a little boy when King Mergus died, and didn't remember him well. Surviving documents helped him understand the cynical but sometimes oddly charming man who'd sired him.

The Avornan noble had apparently promised King Mergus eternal gratitude if he would do something for him. And Mergus had written back, *Gratitude, Your Excellency, is worth its weight in gold.*

That came back to Lanius now, though he rather wished it wouldn't have. But sometimes things needed doing regardless of whether the people for whom you did them could ever properly repay you. The king feared this would be one of those times. He said, "When you go back to Durdevatz, tell him Avornis will do what it can for him. I don't know what that will be, not yet, but we'll do it."

Kolovrat bowed very low. "May the gods bless you, Your Majesty."

"Yes," Lanius said, wondering how he would meet the promise he'd just made. "May they bless me indeed."

Grus was questioning prisoners when a courier came down from the north. Quite a few Menteshe spoke at least a little Avornan, and the nomads were often breathtakingly candid about what they wanted to do to Avornis. "We will pasture our flocks and our herds in your meadows," a chieftain declared. "We will kill your peasants—kill them or make them into thralls, whichever suits us better. Your cities will be our cities. We will worship the Fallen Star, the true light of the world, in your cathedrals."

"Really? Then how did we happen to capture you?" Grus asked in mild tones.

With a blithe shrug—surprisingly blithe, considering that he was a captive—the fellow answered, "I made a mistake. It happens to all of us. You, for instance"—he pointed at Grus—"do not bow before the Fallen Star. You will pay for your mistake, and worse than I have paid for mine."

"Oh?" Grus said. "Suppose I kill you now?"

Another shrug. "Even then." As far as Grus could tell, that wasn't bravado. The Menteshe meant it. Scowling, the king gestured to the guards who surrounded the prisoner. They took him away. But his confidence lingered. It worried Grus. As far as he could tell, all the nomads felt that way. It made them more dangerous than they would have been if they'd had the same sort of doubts he did.

And yet, no matter how confident they were, he'd driven them back a long way and inflicted some stinging defeats on them. As soon as he cleared them from the valley of the Anapus, he could move down to the Stura and drive them off Avornan soil altogether. He hoped he would be able to do that before winter ended campaigning. He didn't want the Menteshe lingering in Avornis until spring. That would be a disaster, nothing less.

What they'd already done was disastrous enough. Because of their devastation, crops here in the south were going to be only a fraction of normal. Pelagonia wasn't the only city liable to see hunger this winter— far from it. And how were farmers supposed to pay their taxes when they had no crops to sell for cash? The government of Avornis would see hunger this winter, too.

And all that said nothing about men killed, women violated, children orphaned, livestock slaughtered. Every time he thought about it, he seethed. What he wanted to do was go after the Menteshe south of the Stura, take the fighting to them, and let them see how they liked it.

What he wanted to do and what he could do were two different things. Until he had—until Avornis had—some reliable way to cure thralls and to keep men from being made into thralls, he didn't dare cross the river. Defeat would turn into catastrophe if he did. And then his son and his son-in-law would fight over who succeeded him. That would be another catastrophe, no matter who won. Grus had his own opinion about who would, had it and refused to dwell on it.

The guards brought up another prisoner. This one blustered, saying, "I do not care how you torture me. I am Prince Ulash's man, and the Fallen Star's."

"Who said anything about torturing you?" Grus asked.

"Avornans do that," the Menteshe said. "Everyone knows it."

"Oh? How many prisoners whom we've tortured have you met?" King Grus knew Avornans sometimes *did* torture prisoners, when they were trying to pull out something the captive didn't want to say. But his folk didn't do it regularly, as the Menteshe did.

"Everyone knows you do it," the nomad repeated.

"How do you know?" Grus said again. "Who told you? Did you meet prisoners who told you what we did to them?" If the man had, he was out of luck.

But the Menteshe shook his head. "There is no need. Our chieftains have said it. If they say it, it must be true."

Grus sent him away. It was either that or go to work on him with ropes and knives and heated iron. Nothing short of torture would persuade him what his chieftains said was untrue—and torture, here, would only prove it was true. The king muttered to himself, most discontented. The nomad had won that round.

He muttered more when his army crossed the Anapus. Devastation on the southern side of the river was even worse than it had been in the north. The Menteshe might have had trouble crossing the Anapus. They'd spent more time below it, and found more ways to amuse themselves while they were there. Grus began to wonder what things would be like in the valley of the Stura. Could they be worse than what he was seeing here? He didn't know how, but did know the Menteshe were liable to instruct him.

Before he could worry too much about the valley of the Stura, he had to finish clearing Prince Ulash's men from the valley of the Anapus. The Menteshe on the southern side of the river didn't try to make a stand. Instead, after shooting arrows at his army as it landed, they scattered. That left him with a familiar dilemma—how small were the chunks into which he could break up his army as he pursued? If he divided it up into many small ones, he ran the risk of having the Menteshe ambush and destroy some of them. Remembering what had happened to the troop farther north, he wasn't eager to risk that.

Eager or not, he did. Getting rid of the Menteshe came first. This time, things went the way he wanted them to. The nomads didn't linger and fight. They fled over the hills to the south, toward the valley of the Stura.

As Grus reassembled his army to go after them, he said, "I wonder if they'll fight hard down there, or if they'll see they're beaten and go back to their own side of the river."

"That's why we're going down there, Your Majesty," Hirundo answered. "To find out what they'll do, I mean."

"No." The king shook his head. "That's not why. We're going down there to make sure they do what we want."

The general thought it over. He nodded. "Well, I can't tell you you're wrong. Of course, if I tried you'd probably send me to the Maze."

"No, I wouldn't." Grus shook his head again. "I have a worse punishment than that in mind." Hirundo raised a questioning eyebrow. Grus went on, "I'll leave you right here, in command against the cursed Menteshe."

"No wonder people say you're a cruel, hard king!" Hirundo quailed in artfully simulated terror.

Even though he was joking, what he said touched a nerve. "Do people say that?" Grus asked. "It's not what I try to be." He sounded wistful, even a little—maybe more than a little—plaintive.

"I know, Your Majesty," Hirundo said quickly.

Grus stayed thoughtful and not very happy the rest of the day. He knew he'd given people reason to curse his name. He'd sent more than a few men to the Maze. He reckoned that merciful; he could have killed them instead. But they and their families would still find him cruel and hard, as Hirundo had said. And he hadn't given towns ravaged by the Menteshe as much help as they would have liked. He didn't think he could afford to. Still . . . He wished he could do all the things the people of Avornis wanted him to do. He also wished none of those people spent any time plotting against him. That would have made his life easier. It would have, yes, but he feared he couldn't hold his breath waiting for it to happen.

What *could* he do? "Go on," he muttered to himself. Seeing nothing else, he turned back to Hirundo. "Let's finish cleaning the Menteshe out of this valley, and then we'll go on to the next."

"Yes, Your Majesty. Ahh . . ." The general paused, then said, "If you want to push on to the Stura, and to leave garrisons in the passes to keep Ulash's men from getting through, our second-line soldiers could probably finish hunting down the nomads left behind. Or don't you think so?"

Grus paused, too. Then he nodded. "Yes. That's good, Hirundo. Thank you. We'll do it. Farther north, I wouldn't have, but here? You bet I will. It lets me get down to the border faster, and we may be able to give the Menteshe a surprise when we show up there sooner than they expect us to."

He set things in motion the next day. Some of the armed peasants and townsmen and the river-galley marines he ordered out against the Menteshe would probably get mauled. But he would be getting the best use out of his soldiers, and that mattered more. Hirundo had done what a good general was supposed to do when he made his suggestions.

From the top of the pass the army took down into the valley of the Stura, Grus eyed the pillars of black smoke rising into the sky here and there. They spoke of the destruction Ulash's men were working, but they also told him where the Menteshe were busy. He pointed to the closest one. "Let's go hunting."

Hunt they did. They didn't have the bag Grus would have wanted, for Prince Ulash's riders fled before them. Here, though, the ground through which the Menteshe could flee was narrow—unless, of course, they crossed the Stura and left Avornis altogether. Grus would sooner have wiped them off the face of the earth than seen them get away, but he would sooner have seen them get away than go on ravaging his kingdom.

Not all of the men who tried to get away succeeded. Avornan river galleys slid along the Stura. As Grus had, their skippers enjoyed nothing more than ramming and sinking the small boats the Menteshe used to cross the river. But here the Avornans didn't have everything their own way, as they had farther north. Ulash had river galleys in the Stura, too. When Grus first saw them come forth and assail his ships, he cursed and grinned at the same time. Yes, the Menteshe could cause trouble on the river. But they could also *find* trouble there, and he hoped they would.

Before long, they did. The Menteshe had galleys in the Stura, true, but their crews weren't and never had been a match for the Avornans. After Grus' countrymen sank several galleys full of nomads and lost none themselves, the Menteshe stopped challenging them.

"Too bad," Grus said. "They're trouble on land. On the water?" He shook his head, then waved toward Hirundo. "They make you look like a good sailor."

"Then they *must* be hopeless," Hirundo declared.

"Maybe they are," Grus said. "Now if only they were horsemen like me, too."

That the Menteshe weren't. They shot up a squadron of Avornan cavalry who pursued them too enthusiastically, then delivered a charge with the scimitar that sent Grus' men, or those who survived, reeling off in headlong retreat. It was a bold exploit, especially since the Menteshe had spent so long falling back before the Avornans. Grus would have admired it more if the nomads hadn't hacked up the corpses of the men they'd slain.

"We think, when we die, we die dead," a captured Menteshe told him. "Only when the Fallen Star regains his place do we live on after death. But you foolish Avornans, you think you last forever. We treat bodies so to show you what is true—for now, you are nothing but flesh, the same as us."

He spoke excellent Avornan, with conviction chilling enough to make Grus shiver. If this life was all a man had, why *not* do whatever pleased at the moment? What would stop you, except brute force here on earth? How could a man sure he was trapped in one brief life show any signs of conscience? By all the evidence from the Menteshe, he couldn't. And no wonder the nomads clung so strongly to the Banished One. If they thought his triumph was their only hope for life after death . . .

If they thought that, Grus was convinced they were wrong. "The gods in the heavens are stronger," he told the nomad. "They cast the Banished One out, and he will never return."

"Yes, he will," the Menteshe answered. "Once he rules the world, he will take back the heavens, too. The ones you call gods were jealous of the Fallen Star. They tricked him, and so they cast him down."

Grus wondered how much truth that held. Only the gods in the heavens and the Banished One, the one who had been Milvago, knew for sure. Grus feared the Banished One would send him a dream where the exiled god set forth his side of the story, as he must have for the Menteshe. But no dream came. At first, that relieved the king. Then he wondered what else the Banished One was doing, what left him too busy to strike fear into the heart of a foe. Imagining some of the possibilities, he felt plenty of fear even without a dream.

Limosa bowed low before King Lanius. "Your Majesty, may I ask a favor of you?" she said.

"You may always ask, Your Highness," Lanius said. "But until I hear what the favor is, I make no promises."

Ortalis' wife nodded. "I understand. No doubt you are wise. The favor I ask is simple enough, though. Could you please bring my father out of the Maze?"

"You asked that before. I told you no then. Why do you think anything is different now? King Grus sent Petrosus to the Maze. He is the one who would have to bring him out."

"Why do I think things are different? Because you have more power than I thought you did," Princess Limosa answered. "Because King Grus is far away. You *can* do this, if you care to."

She might well have been right. Grus would fume, but would he do anything more than fume? Lanius wondered, especially when Ortalis and Limosa did seem happy together. And yet . . . Lanius knew one of the reasons he was allowed power was that he used it alongside the power Grus wielded. Up until now, he'd never tried going dead against Grus' wishes.

What would happen if he did? Grus was distracted by the war against the Menteshe, yes. Even so, he would surely hear from someone in the capital that Petrosus had come back. If he didn't like the idea, Lanius would have thrown away years of patient effort—and all on account of a man he didn't like.

Caution prevailed. "Here's what I'll do," the king said. "I'll write a letter to Grus, urging that he think again in the light of everything that's happened since you married Prince Ortalis. I'm sorry, but that's about as far as I can go."

"As far as you dare go, you mean," Limosa said.

No doubt she meant it for an insult. But it was simple truth. "You're right—that is as far as I dare to go," Lanius answered. "If Ortalis writes at the same time as I do, it might help change Grus' mind."

Limosa went off with her nose in the air. The day was hot and sticky, one of those late summer days made bearable only by thinking fall would come soon. Even so, she wore a high-necked, long-sleeved tunic. *What do she and Ortalis do together?* Lanius wondered. *Do I really want to know?* He shook his head. No, he didn't think so.

He did write the letter. He had trouble sounding enthusiastic, but felt he could honestly say, *I do not believe Petrosus will prove a danger to you, especially if you leave him without a position on his return to the city of Avornis.*

He also wrote to Grus of an order he'd given the day before, an order sending four of Avornis' new tall-masted ships from the west coast north to Durdevatz. He hadn't stripped the coast of all the new ships, but he had done what he thought he could for Kolovrat and Prince Ratibor.

When he gave the letter to a southbound courier, he asked the man if Ortalis had also given him one to send to Grus. The fellow shook his head. "No, Your Majesty."

"Thank you," Lanius said. Did Ortalis want nothing to do with his father, even for his father-in-law's sake? Was Ortalis one of those people who never got around to writing, no matter what? Or did he dislike Petrosus, no matter what he felt about Limosa?

Here, for once, was a topic that failed to rouse Lanius' curiosity. *None of my business,* the king thought, *and a good thing, too.* He'd gone as far as he intended to go for Petrosus.

He didn't have long to wait for Grus' reply. It came back to the capital amazingly fast, especially considering how far south the other king had traveled. It was also very much to the point. *Petrosus will stay a monk,* Grus wrote. *Petrosus will also stay in the Maze.* Then he added two more sentences. *As for the other, I approve. In those circumstances, what else could you do?*

Relieved Grus was not angry at him for his move with the ships, Lanius read the other part of the note to Limosa. "I'm sorry, Your Highness," he lied. "I don't think I'd better go against King Grus' will when he makes it so clear." That last was true.

Petrosus' daughter scowled. "You haven't got the nerve."

That was also true. Lanius shrugged. "I'm sorry," he said again. "Maybe you and Ortalis can persuade him with letters. For your sake, I hope you do."

"For *my* sake," Limosa said bitterly. "As far as *you're* concerned, my father can stay in the Maze until he rots."

And *that* was true, no matter how little Lanius felt like coming out and saying so. He shrugged again. "If Grus wants to let your father out, he will. I won't say a word about it. But he has to be the one to do it."

Limosa turned her back on him. She stalked away without a word. Lanius sighed. As soon as he heard what she had in mind, he'd been sure he was going to lose no matter what happened. He'd been sure, and he'd been right, and being right had done him no good at all.

"Well, well," King Grus said when a courier handed him three sealed letters from the city of Avornis. "What have we here?"

"Letters, Your Majesty," the courier said unhelpfully. "One from His Majesty, one from Prince Ortalis, and one from Princess Limosa." He was just a soldier, with a provincial accent. Odds were he neither knew nor cared how Limosa had become Ortalis' wife. Grus wished he could say the same.

He opened Lanius' letter first. The other king wrote, *King Lanius to Grus—greetings. Your son and his wife will be petitioning you to let Petrosus out of the Maze. They expect me to write you yet another letter to the same effect, which is why I am sending this to you. In point of fact, I am profoundly indifferent to whatever you choose to do with or to Petrosus. But now I have written, and they will suppose I am once more urging you to release him. You will, I am sure, also have written letters intended to keep the peace. I hope all goes well in the south, for that is truly important business.* He'd scrawled his name below the carefully written words.

Grus couldn't help smiling as he read the letter. He could almost hear Lanius' voice in the words—intelligent, candid, detached, more than a little ironic. When he got letters from son, daughter-in-law, and son-in-law all at once, he'd had a pretty good idea of what they were about. Now that he knew he was right, he broke the seal on Ortalis' letter, and then on Limosa's. From what they (especially Limosa—Ortalis' letter was brief, and less enthusiastic than his wife's) said about Petrosus, Grus might have installed him as Arch-Hallow of Avornis after recalling him from the Maze. He was good, he was pure, he was honest, he was reliable, he was saintly . . . and he was nothing like the Petrosus Grus had known for so long before sending him away from the capital.

If he didn't let Petrosus come out of the Maze, he would anger Ortalis and Limosa. They made that plain. But if he did let Petrosus come out, he would endanger himself. He could see that, even if Ortalis and Limosa couldn't. Petrosus would want revenge. Even if he didn't get his position back (Lanius' suggestion in his earlier letter)—and he wouldn't— he still had connections. An angry man with connections . . . *I'd need eyes in the back of my head for the rest of my life,* the king thought.

He called for parchment and ink. Grus wrote, *I am sorry*—a polite lie—*but, as I have written before, it is necessary for Petrosus to remain in the monastery to which he has retired. No further petitions on this subject will be entertained.* He signed his name.

Limosa would pout. Lanius would shrug. Ortalis . . . Grus gritted his teeth. Who could guess what Ortalis would do? Grus sometimes wondered if his son knew from one minute to the next. Maybe he would shrug, too. But maybe he would throw a tantrum instead. That could prove . . . unpleasant.

The king had just finished sealing his letter when a guard stuck his head into the tent and said, "Your Majesty, Pterocles would like to speak to you if you have a moment to spare."

"Of course," Grus answered. The guard disappeared. A moment later, the wizard came in. Grus nodded to him. "Good evening. What can I do for you? How is your leg?"

Pterocles looked down at the wounded member. "It's healed well. I still feel it now and again—well, a little more than now and again—but I can get around on it. I came to tell you I've been doing some thinking."

"I doubt you'll take any lasting harm from it," Grus said. Pterocles started to reply, then closed his mouth and sent Grus a sharp look. The king looked back blandly. He asked, "And what have you been thinking about?"

"Thralls."

No one word could have been better calculated to seize and hold Grus' interest. "Have you, now?" he murmured. Pterocles nodded. Grus asked, "What have you been thinking about them?"

"That I wish I were back in the city of Avornis to try some spells on the ones you brought back from the south," Pterocles answered. "I think . . ." He paused and took a deep breath. "I think, Your Majesty, that I know how to cure them."

"*Do* you?" Grus said. The wizard nodded again. "By Olor's beard, you have my attention," Grus told him. "Why do you think you know this now, when you didn't before we left the city?" He sent Pterocles a wry smile. "When you were where the thralls are, you didn't know. Now that you're hundreds of miles from them, you say you do. Will you forget again when we get back to the capital?"

"I hope not, Your Majesty." The wizard gave back a wry smile of his own. "Part of this has to do with my own thinking, thinking that's been stewing for a long time. Part of it has to do with the masking spell the Menteshe threw at us the night before we went into Pelagonia. And part of it has to do with some of the things your witch said when we were in Pelagonia."

Grus remembered some of the things Alca had said to *him* while the army was in Pelagonia. He wished he could forget a lot of them, but those weren't things she'd said in connection with the thralls. "Go on," he told Pterocles. "Believe me, I'm listening."

"For a few days there, I couldn't do much but lie around and listen to her," Pterocles said. "She made herself a lot clearer, a lot plainer, than she ever had before. And I told her some things she hadn't known before, things I know because of . . . because of what happened to me outside of Nishevatz."

Because I almost got killed outside of Nishevatz, he meant. "Go on," Grus said. "What does the masking spell have to do with all this?"

"Well, Your Majesty, part of what makes a thrall is emptying out his soul," Pterocles answered. Grus nodded; that much he knew. The wizard went on, "It finally occurred to me, though, that that's not all that's going on. The Menteshe sorcerers have to leave something behind. They can't empty out the *whole* soul, or a thrall would be nothing but a corpse or a beast. And we all know there's a little more to them than that."

"Yes, a little. Sometimes more than a little," Grus said, remembering the thralls who'd tried to kill Lanius and, in lieu of himself, Estrilda.

"Sometimes more than a little," Pterocles agreed. "But now it seems to me—and to Alca—that the emptying spell isn't the only one the Menteshe wizards use. It seems to us that they also use a masking spell. Some of the true soul that makes a man remains in a thrall, but it's hidden away even from him."

Grus considered. Slowly, he nodded again. "Yes, that makes sense," he said. "Which doesn't mean it's true, of course. A lot of the time, we've found that the things that seem to make the most sense about thralls turn out not to be true at all. But you're right. It may be worth looking into. You and Alca figured all of this out, you say?"

He could name the witch without flinching now. He could also name her without longing for her, which he wouldn't have believed possible. People said absence made the heart grow fonder. And if the person you cared about suddenly *wasn't* absent, and the two of you found you *didn't* care for each other anymore? There was a gloomy picture of human nature, but one Grus couldn't deny. It had happened to him.

Pterocles said, "We started working on it in Pelagonia, yes. I've added some new touches since. That's why I'm so eager to get back to the city of Avornis and try them out on the thralls there."

"I understand," Grus said. "But the other thing I understand is, I need you here as long as we're campaigning. We'll head back in the fall, I expect. They won't go anywhere in the meantime." Reluctantly, Pterocles spread his hands, admitting that was so.

CHAPTER EIGHTEEN

For a long time, thralls had fascinated King Lanius. They were men robbed of much of their humanity, forced down to the dusky, shadow-filled borderland between mankind and the animal world. The existence of thralls made whole men think about what being human really meant.

Then a thrall tried to kill Lanius.

It wasn't just a fit of bestial passion, of course. It was the Banished One reaching out through the thrall, controlling him as a merely human puppeteer controlled a marionette. From that moment on, thralls hadn't seemed the same to Lanius. They didn't strike him as just being half man and half animal. Instead, he also saw them as the Banished One's tools, as so many hammers and saws and knives (oh yes, knives!) to be picked up whenever the exiled god needed them.

And tools weren't so fascinating.

Since the thralls tried to murder Lanius and Estrilda, the king had paid much less attention to them, except for making sure the ones still in the palace couldn't get out and try anything like that again. He didn't know what sudden spasm of curiosity had brought him to the room above the one in which they were imprisoned. Whatever it was, though, he peered down at them through the peephole in their ceiling.

He started to, anyhow. As soon as he drew back the tile that covered the peephole, he drew back himself, in dismay. A thick, heavy stench wafted up through the opening. The thralls cared not a bit about keeping clean.

By all appearances, they didn't care much about anything else, either. Two sprawled on mattresses on the floor. A third tore a chunk off a loaf of bread and stuffed it into his mouth with filthy hands. He filled a cup with water and drank it to go with the snack. Then he walked over to a corner of the room and eased himself. The thralls were in the habit of doing that. They had chamber pots in the room, but seldom used them. That added to the stench.

The thrall started to lie down with his comrades, but checked himself. Instead, he stared up at the peephole. Lanius didn't think he'd made any noise uncovering it, but that didn't always matter. The thralls seemed able to sense when someone was looking at them. Or maybe it wasn't the thralls themselves. Maybe it was the Banished One looking out through them.

That suspicion always filled Lanius whenever he had to endure a thrall's gaze. This thrall's face showed nothing but idiocy. Who could guess what lay behind it? Maybe nothing did. Maybe the man (no, the not-quite-man) was as empty, as *emptied,* as any other thrall laboring on a little plot of land down south of the Stura. Maybe. Lanius had trouble believing it.

Did something glint in the thrall's eyes? His face didn't change. His expression stayed as vacant as ever. But that didn't feel like a beast's stare to Lanius. Nervously, the king shook his head. It might have been the stare of a beast of sorts—a beast of prey eyeing an intended victim.

Nonsense, Lanius told himself. *That's only a thrall, with no working wits in his head.* He tried to make himself believe it. He couldn't.

The thrall kept staring and staring. Sometimes, during one of these episodes, a thrall would mouth something up at him, or even say something—a sure sign something more than the poor, damaged thrall was looking out through those eyes. Not this time. After a couple of minutes, the thrall turned away.

Lanius turned away, too, with nothing but relief. He covered the peephole. His knees clicked as he got to his feet. He rubbed his nose, as though that could get rid of the stink from the thralls' room. Still, he kept coming back to look at them. He was no wizard. He couldn't learn anything about them that would help anyone find out how to cure them—if, indeed, anyone *could* cure them. But he stayed intrigued. He couldn't help wondering what went on in the thralls' minds. Logic and observation said nothing much went on there, but he wasn't sure how far to trust them. Where sorcery was involved, were logic and observation the right tools to use?

If they weren't, what was? What could be? More good questions. La-nius could come up with any number of good questions. Finding good answers for them was harder. Maybe the hope of good answers was what kept him coming back to the peephole.

Not long after that thought crossed his mind, he walked past Limosa in the hallway. She nodded politely as she went by—she thought he'd tried harder than he really had to get her father out of the Maze. He nodded back, though it took an effort. He had plenty of good questions about her and Ortalis, too, but no good answers, however much he would have liked to have them.

What you need is a peephole into their bedchamber, he thought. *That would tell you what you want to know.*

He violently shook his head. What he wanted to know was none of his business. Knowing it was none of his business didn't keep him from wanting to find out. Sosia would be angry at him if she learned he wanted to peep into other people's bedrooms—except she was even more curious about this than he was.

No, he told himself firmly. *Some curiosity doesn't need to be satisfied.* That went dead against everything he'd ever believed. He tried to convince himself of it anyway.

Here was the Stura. Grus had spent a lot of years traveling up and down the river in a war galley. Now he approached it on horseback. The sour smell of old smoke filled his nostrils. This was the valley the Menteshe had overrun most thoroughly. That meant it was the valley where Prince Ulash's men had done the most damage.

Seeing that damage both infuriated and depressed the king. "How am I supposed to set this to rights?" he demanded of Hirundo.

"Driving the Menteshe back over the river would be a good start," the general answered.

Hirundo smiled. He joked. But that was kidding on the square. Unless the Avornans could drive the Menteshe south of the Stura once more, Grus had exactly no chance of setting any of this to rights. And here, where their countrymen could slip north over the river in small boats by night, where the Menteshe could also bring river galleys—some of them rowed by brainless thralls—into the fight, driving them out of Avornis was liable to prove doubly hard.

"We can do it," Hirundo said. "They don't want to fight a stand-up battle. Whenever they try that, they lose, and they know it."

"They don't *need* to make a stand-up fight," Grus said darkly. "All they need to do is keep riding around and burning things. What kind of harvest will anyone here in this valley have? None to speak of, and we both know it. The Menteshe know it, too. Wrecking things works as well for them as winning battles." He waved toward what had been a vineyard. "No one will grow grapes here for years. No grapes, no wine, no raisins. It's the same with olive groves. Cut the trees down and burn them and it's years before you have olives and olive oil again. What do people do in the meantime?"

"I'll tell you what they do," Hirundo answered. "They do *without.*"

Another joke that held entirely too much truth. The trouble was that people *couldn't* very well do without wine and raisins and grapes and olive oil. Here in the south, those things were almost as important as wheat and barley—not that the grainfields hadn't been ravaged, too. A good harvest next year would go a long way toward putting that worry behind people . . . provided they didn't starve in the meantime. But the other crops would take longer to recover.

"And what happens if the Menteshe swarm over the Stura again next spring?" Grus demanded.

"We try to hit them before they can cause anywhere near this much mischief," Hirundo answered reasonably.

"But can we really do it? Wouldn't you rather go up into the Chernagor country and finish what we've been trying to do there for years now? And what about the Chernagor pirates? What if they hit our east coast again next spring while the Menteshe cross the Stura?"

"You're full of cheerful ideas," Hirundo said.

"It could have happened this year," Grus said. "We're lucky it didn't."

Hirundo shook his head. "That isn't just luck, Your Majesty. True, you didn't take Nishevatz, but you came close, and you would have done it, odds are, if the war down here hadn't drawn you away. And our ships gave the Chernagor pirates all they wanted, and more besides. It's no wonder they didn't move along with the cursed Menteshe. You put the fear of the gods in them."

"The fear of the gods," Grus murmured. He hoped some of the Chernagors still felt it, as opposed to the fear of the Banished One. But what he hoped and what was true were liable to be two different things, as he knew too well. Confusing the one with the other could only lead to disappointment.

As he was getting ready to lie down on his cot that evening, Alauda said, "Ask you something, Your Majesty?"

Grus looked at her in surprise. She didn't ask a lot of questions. "Go ahead," the king said after a moment. "You can always ask. I don't know that I'll answer."

The peasant girl's smile was wry. "I understand. You don't have to, not for the likes of me. But when we were up in Pelagonia . . . You had another woman up there, didn't you?"

"Not another woman I slept with," Grus said carefully. He'd had enough rows with women (that a lot of those rows were his own fault never crossed his mind). He didn't want another one now. If he had to send Alauda somewhere far away to keep from having another one, he was ruthlessly ready to do that.

But she only shrugged. "Another woman you care about, I mean. I don't know if you slept with her or not." She waited. Grus gave her a cautious nod. She went on, "And you'd cared about her for a while now," and waited again. Again, the king nodded. Now he waited. Alauda licked her lips and then asked, "Why didn't you just throw me over for her, then?" That was what she'd really wanted to know all along.

I intended to. But Grus didn't say that. He got in trouble over women because he took them to bed whenever he got the chance, not because he was wantonly cruel. What he did say was, "We aren't lovers anymore. We used to be, but we aren't."

Alauda surprised him again, this time by laughing. "When we got there, you thought you were going to be, though, didn't you?"

"Well . . . yes," he said in dull embarrassment. He hadn't thought she'd noticed that. Now he asked a question of his own. "Why didn't you bring up any of this when we were there?"

She laughed once more, on a self-deprecating note. "What good would it have done me? None I could see. Safer now, when I'm here and she's not."

She did have her share of shrewdness. Grus had seen that before. "Now you know," he said, although he'd told her as little as he could. He changed the subject, asking, "How are you feeling?"

"I'm all right," she answered. "I'm supposed to have babies. I'm made for it. It's not always comfortable—about half the time, breakfast doesn't want to stay down—but I'm all right. Is the war going as well as it looks?"

"Almost," Grus said. "We're still going forward, anyhow. I hope we'll keep on doing it."

"Once we chase all the Menteshe out of Avornis, how do we keep them out for good?" Alauda asked.

"I don't know," Grus said, which made her blink. He went on, "Avornans have been trying to find the answer to that for a long time, but we haven't done it yet. If we had, they wouldn't be in Avornis now, would they?" He waited for Alauda to shake her head, then added, "One thing I can do—one thing I will do—is put more river galleys on the Stura. That will make it harder for them to cross, anyhow."

She nodded. "That makes good sense. Why weren't there more river galleys on the Stura before?"

"They're expensive," he answered. "Expensive to build, even more expensive to man." The tall-masted ships that aped the ones the Chernagor pirates made cost more to build. River galleys, with their large crews of rowers, cost more to maintain. And every man who became a sailor was one more man who couldn't till the soil. After the disasters of this war, Avornis was liable to need farmers even more desperately than she needed soldiers or sailors. The king hoped she could find enough. If not, lean times were coming, in the most literal sense of the words.

Lanius liked coming into the kitchens. He nodded to the head cook, a rotund man named Cucullatus. "Tomorrow is Queen Sosia's birthday, you know," he said. "Do up something special for her."

Cucullatus' smile was almost as wide as he was, which said a good deal. "How about a kidney pie, Your Majesty? That's one of her favorites."

"Fine." Lanius hoped his own smile was also wide and seemed sincere. Sosia did love kidney pie, or any other dish with kidneys in it. Lanius didn't. To him, cooked kidneys smelled nasty. But he did want to make his wife happy. He worked harder to keep Sosia happy since he'd started taking lovers among the serving women than he had before. He thought himself unique in that regard, which only proved he didn't know everything there was to know about straying husbands.

"We'll take care of it, Your Majesty," Cucullatus promised. "And whatever kidneys don't go into the pie, we'll save for the moncats."

"Fine," Lanius said again, this time with real enthusiasm. The moncats loved kidneys, which didn't stink nearly as much raw.

The king started to leave the kitchens. A startled noise from one of the sweepers made him turn back. There was Pouncer, clinging to a beam with one clawed hand. The moncat's other hand clutched a big wooden spoon. Reading moncats' expressions was a risky game, but Lanius thought Pouncer looked almost indecently pleased with itself.

"Come back here! Come down here!" the king called in stern tones. But Pouncer was no better at doing what it was told than any other moncat—or any other cat of any sort.

Cucullatus said, "Here, don't worry, Your Majesty. We can lure it down with a bit of meat."

"Good idea," Lanius said. But the sweeper who'd first spotted Pouncer wasn't paying any attention to either Cucullatus or the king. He tried to knock the moncat from the beam with his broom. He missed. Pouncer yowled and swung up onto the beam, with only its tail hanging down. The sweeper sprang, trying to grab the tail. He jumped just high enough to pull out a few of the hairs at the very end. Pouncer yowled again, louder this time, and took off like a dart hurled from a catapult.

"You stupid, manure-brained idiot!" Cucullatus bawled at the poor sweeper. Then he turned on the rest of the men and women in the kitchens. "Well? Don't just stand there, you fools! Catch the miserable little beast!"

If that wasn't a recipe for chaos, Lanius couldn't have come up with one. People bumped into one another, tripped one another, and cursed one another with more passion than Lanius had ever heard from them. Several of them carried knives, and more knives, long-tined forks, and other instruments of mayhem lay right at hand. Why they didn't start stabbing one another was beyond the king.

After a couple of minutes of screaming anarchy, somebody asked, "Where did the stinking creature go?"

Lanius looked around. So did the kitchen staff, pausing in their efforts to tear the place down. "Where *did* the stinking creature go?" somebody else said.

Pouncer had disappeared. A wizard couldn't have done a neater job of making the moncat disappear.

However he got in here, that's the way he must have gone, Lanius thought. Unlike the kitchen staff, he had, or believed he had, a pretty good idea of where the moncat would go next. He pointed to Cucullatus. "Give me two or three strips of raw meat."

"But the moncat is gone, Your Majesty," Cucullatus said reasonably.

"I know that. I'll eat them myself," Lanius said. Cucullatus stared. "Never mind what I want with them," the king told him. "Just give them to me."

He got them. Servants gaped to see him hurrying through the palace corridors with strips of raw, dripping beef in his hand. A couple of them even worked up the nerve to ask him what he was doing. He didn't answer. He just kept on, not quite trotting, until he got to the archives.

When he closed the heavy doors behind him, he let out a sigh of relief. No more bellowing cooks, no more nosy servants. Only peace, quiet, dust motes dancing in sunbeams, and the soothing smell of old parchment. This was where he belonged, where no one would come and bother him.

Even as he pulled some documents—tax registers, he saw they were—from the shelf of a cabinet that had known better centuries, he was shaking his head. Today, he hoped he would be bothered. If he wasn't . . . If he wasn't, Pouncer had decided to go back to the moncats' chamber instead. Or maybe the perverse beast would simply wander through whatever secret ways it had found until it decided to come out in the kitchens again.

Lanius looked at the registers with one eye while looking all around the archives chamber with the other. He didn't know where Pouncer would appear. Actually, he didn't know whether Pouncer would appear at all, but he did his best to forget about that. He did know this was the best bet he could make.

And it paid off. Just when he'd gotten engrossed in one of the registers in spite of himself, a faint, rusty, "Mrowr?" came from behind a crate that probably hadn't been opened in at least two hundred years.

"Come here, Pouncer!" Lanius called, and then he made the special little chirping noise that meant he had a treat for the moncat.

Out Pouncer came. The moncat still clutched the spoon it had stolen. Even the spoon paled in importance, though, before the lure of raw meat. "Mrowr," Pouncer said again, this time on a more insistent note.

"Come on," Lanius coaxed, holding a strip of beef where the moncat could see—and smell—it. "Come on, you fuzzy moron. You know you want this."

Want it Pouncer did. Sidling forward, the moncat reached out with a clawed hand. Lanius gave it the first piece of meat. The moncat ate quickly, fearful of being robbed even though none of its fellows were near. In some ways it was very much like a man. Once the meat had disappeared, Pouncer held out that little hand and said, "Mrowr," yet again.

Give me some more, or you'll be sorry. Lanius had no trouble translating that particular meow into Avornan. The king gave the moncat another piece of meat. This one vanished more slowly. As it did, Pouncer began to purr. Lanius had been waiting for that. It was a sign he could pick up the moncat without getting his hand shredded. He did. Pouncer kept on purring.

Feeling more than a little triumphant, Lanius carried the moncat—and the serving spoon it had stolen—out of the royal archives. The tax registers he left where they were. They dated from the early years of his father's reign. No one had looked at them since; Lanius was sure of that. They weren't going anywhere for the time being. And one of these days he would have to have a peek inside that crate Pouncer had been hiding behind.

Pouncer started twisting in the king's arms and trying to get free before Lanius reached the moncats' chamber. Lanius still had one strip of meat left. He offered it to the moncat, and bought just enough contentment to keep from getting clawed the rest of the way there. Pouncer even let him take away the wooden spoon.

Cucullatus clapped his hands when Lanius brought the spoon back to the kitchens. "Well done, Your Majesty!" he said, as though Lanius had just captured Yozgat and reclaimed the Scepter of Mercy.

"Thank you so much," Lanius said.

"Kidney pie," Cucullatus went on, ignoring or more likely not noticing the king's irony. Lanius frowned; the commotion with the moncat had almost made him forget why he'd come to the kitchens in the first place. The chief cook went on, "Her Majesty will enjoy it. You wait and see."

"Ah." Lanius nodded. "Yes, I hope she does."

Sosia did. When she sat down to supper on her birthday, she smiled and wagged a finger at Lanius. "Somebody's been talking to the kitchens," she said as a servant gave her a big helping of the pungent dish.

"Why would anyone talk to a kitchen?" Lanius asked. "Ovens and pots and skewers don't listen very well."

His wife gave him a severe look. "You know what I mean," she said. "You've been talking to the people who work in the kitchens. There. Are you happier?"

"I couldn't be happier, not while I've got you," Lanius answered.

Sosia smiled. "That's sweet," she said. But then the smile slipped. "In that case, why—?" She stopped and shook her head. "No, never mind. Not tonight."

Lanius had no trouble figuring out what she'd started to say. *In that case, why did you take Cristata to bed? Why did you want to make her your second wife?* To Lanius, it made good enough sense. He hadn't been unhappy with Sosia. He'd just wanted to be happy with Cristata, too. He still didn't see anything wrong with that. Grus' daughter, however, had a decidedly different opinion.

And what about Zenaida? Lanius asked himself. He knew what Sosia's opinion of her would be. He didn't think he was in love with her, the way he had with Cristata. Maybe seeing that he didn't would keep Sosia from getting so furious this time. On the other hand, maybe it wouldn't do him any good at all. *She'd better not find out about Zenaida,* the king thought.

He smiled at Sosia. "Happy birthday," he told her.

"You're even eating the kidney pie yourself," she said in some surprise.

And so Lanius was. His thoughts full of maidservants, he'd hardly noticed he was doing it. Now that he did notice, he was reminded again that this was not his favorite dish—too strong for his taste. Still, he shrugged and answered, "I don't hate it," which was true. As though to prove it, he took another bite. What he did prove, to himself, was that he didn't love it, either.

"I'm glad," Sosia said.

Later that evening, Lanius made love with his wife. He didn't hate that, either. If Zenaida was a little more exciting . . . well, maybe that was because she wasn't as familiar as Sosia—and maybe, also, because the thrill of the illicit added spice to what they did. Nothing illicit about Sosia, but nothing wrong with her, nothing that made him want to sleep apart. He did his best to please her when they joined.

By the way she responded, his best proved good enough. "You *are* sweet," she said, as though reminding herself.

"I think the same thing—about you," he added hastily, before she could tease him about thinking himself sweet. That was what he got for being precise most of the time.

He waited there in the darkness, wondering if Sosia would ask why he'd gone after Cristata if he thought she was sweet. But she didn't. She just murmured, "Well, good," rolled over on her side, and fell asleep. Lanius rolled over, too, in the opposite direction. His backside bumped hers. She stirred a little, but kept on breathing slowly and deeply. A few minutes later, Lanius also drifted off, a smile on his face.

A lieutenant from one of the river galleys on the Stura stood before King Grus. "Your Majesty, an awful lot of the Menteshe are sneaking south across the river. More and more every day, and especially every night. We've sunk half a dozen boats full of the stinking buggers, and more have gotten by us."

This wasn't the first such report Grus had heard. He scratched his head. Up until a few days before, Prince Ulash's men hadn't been doing anything of the sort. Sudden changes in what the Menteshe were up to made the King of Avornis deeply suspicious. "What have they got in mind?" he asked, though the lieutenant wasn't going to know.

As he'd expected, the young officer shrugged and answered, "No idea, sir. We don't get the chance to ask them a whole lot of questions. When we ram 'em, we sink 'em." By the pride in his voice, he wanted to do nothing *but* sink them.

That suited Grus fine. He wanted his river-galley officers aggressive. He said, "Thank you, Lieutenant. I'll see what I can do to get to the bottom of this."

The officer bowed and left. Grus scratched his head again. He didn't shake any answers loose. He hadn't really thought he would. Being without answers, he summoned Pterocles. The wizard heard him out, then said, "That *is* interesting, Your Majesty. Why would they start going over the river now when they had seemed to want to stay on this side and fight?"

"I was hoping you could tell me," Grus said. "Has there been a magical summons? Has the Banished One taken a hand in things?"

"I haven't noticed anything out of the ordinary." Pterocles spoke cautiously. Grus approved of that caution. Pterocles recognized the possibility that something might have slipped past him. He said, "I have spells that would tell me if something *has* gone on under my nose. A summons like that lingers on the ether. If it was there, I'll find out about it."

"Good," Grus said. "Let me know."

When Pterocles came back that afternoon, he looked puzzled and troubled. "Your Majesty, if any sort of sorcerous summons came north, I can't find it," he said. "I don't quite know what that means."

"Neither do I," Grus said. Had the Banished One deceived his wizard? Or was Pterocles searching for something that wasn't there to find? "If you know any other spells, you ought to use them," Grus told him.

Pterocles nodded. "I will, though I've already tried the ones I think likeliest to work. You ought to try to take some Menteshe prisoners, too. They may know something I don't."

"I'll do that," Grus said at once. "I should have sent men out to do it when I first called you. A lot of the time, the Menteshe like to sing."

He gave the orders. His men rode out. But Menteshe were starting to get scarce on the ground. Even a week earlier, discovering so few of them on the Avornan side of the Stura would have made Grus rejoice. He would have rejoiced now, if his men were the ones responsible for making the nomads want to get back to the lands they usually roamed. But his men hadn't driven the Menteshe over the Stura, and he knew it. That left him suspicious. Why were the Menteshe leaving—fleeing— Avornis when they didn't have to?

"I know what it is," Hirundo said when a day's search resulted in no prisoners.

"Tell me," Grus urged. "I haven't got any idea why they're going."

"It's simple," the general answered. "They must have heard you were going to put a tax on nomads in Avornis, so of course they ran away from it." He grinned at his own cleverness. "By Olor's beard, I would, too."

"Funny." Grus tried to sound severe, but a smile couldn't help creeping out from behind the edges of his beard—it *was* funny, even if he wished it weren't. He wagged a finger at Hirundo, who kept right on grinning, completely unabashed. Grus said, "Do you have any *real* idea why they're doing it?"

"No," Hirundo admitted. "All I can say is, good riddance."

"Certainly, good riddance." But Grus remained dissatisfied, like a man who'd just enjoyed a feast but had an annoying piece of gristle stuck between two back teeth. "They *shouldn't* be running away, though, not when we haven't finished beating them. They've never done that before."

"Maybe they know we're going to win this time, and so they want to save themselves for fights next year or the year after," Hirundo suggested.

"Maybe." Grus still didn't sound happy—still wasn't happy. He explained why, repeating, "They've never done that before." The Menteshe usually did the same sort of things over and over again. If they changed their ways, they had to have a reason . . . didn't they?

"Maybe the Banished One is telling them what to do," Hirundo said.

"Of course the Banished One is telling them what to do," Grus answered. He hated the idea, which didn't mean he disbelieved it. "They're his creatures. They're proud to be his creatures. But why is he telling them to do that? And how is he telling them? Pterocles can't find any of his magic."

Hirundo considered, then brightened. "Maybe he's trying to drive you mad, to make you find reasons for things that haven't got any."

"Thank you so much," Grus said. Hirundo bowed back, as he might have after any extraordinarily meritorious service. The worst of it was, Grus couldn't be sure the general was wrong. The king knew he would go right on wasting time and losing sleep until he found an answer he could believe. He sighed. "The more we go on like this, the plainer it gets that we need prisoners. Until we know more, we'll just keep coming out with one stupid guess after another."

"I don't think my guesses were stupid." Mock anger filled Hirundo's voice. "I think they were clever, perceptive, even brilliant."

"You would," the king muttered. "When your men finally do bring back a captive or two, we'll see how brilliant and perceptive you were."

"They're doing their best, the same as I am," Hirundo said.

"I hope theirs is better than yours." Grus made sure he smiled so Hirundo knew he was joking. The horrible face the general made said he got the message but didn't much care for it.

Along with the cavalry, the men aboard the river galleys got orders to capture Menteshe if they could. If they could . . . Suddenly, the lands on this side of the Stura began to seem like a country where the birds had just flown south for the winter. They had been here. The memory of them lingered. They would come back. But for now, when you wanted them most, they were gone.

Grus had never imagined that winning a war could leave him so unhappy. He had questions he wanted to ask, questions he needed to ask, and nobody to whom to ask them. He'd snarled at Hirundo in play. He started snarling at people in earnest.

"They're gone," Alauda said. "Thank the gods for it. Praise the gods for it. But, by Queen Quelea's mercy, don't complain about it."

"I want to know why," Grus said stubbornly. "They aren't acting the way they're supposed to, and that bothers me." He'd been down this same road with Hirundo.

His new mistress had less patience for it. "Who cares?" she said with a toss of the head. "As long as they're out of the kingdom, nothing else matters." That held enough truth to be annoying, but not enough to make Grus quit trying to lay his hands on some of the nomads.

When at last he did, it was much easier than he'd thought it would be. Like a flock of birds that had fallen behind the rest because of a storm, a band of about twenty Menteshe rode down to the Stura and then along it, looking for boats to steal so they could cross. Three river galleys and a regiment of Hirundo's horsemen converged on them. When Grus heard the news, he feared the nomads would fight to the death just to thwart him. But they didn't. Overmatched, they threw up their hands and surrendered.

Their chieftain, a bushy-eyebrowed, big-nosed fellow named Yavlak, proved to speak good Avornan. "Here he is, Your Majesty," Hirundo said, as though he were making Grus a present of the man.

And Grus felt as though Yavlak were a present, too. "Why are you Menteshe leaving Avornis?" he demanded.

Yavlak looked at him as he would have looked at any idiot. "Because we have to," he answered.

"You have to? Who told you you have to? Was it the Banished One?" The king knew he sounded nervous, but couldn't help it.

"The Fallen Star?" Now Yavlak looked puzzled. With those eyebrows, he did it very well. "No, the Fallen Star has nothing to do with it. Can it be you have not heard?" He didn't seem to want to believe that; he acted like a man who had no choice. "By some mischance, we found out late. I thought even you miserable Avornans would surely know by now."

"Found out what? Know what?" Grus wanted to strangle him. The only thing that held him back was the certain knowledge that he would have to go through this again with another nomad, one who might not be so fluent in Avornan, if he did.

Yavlak finally—and rudely—obliged him. "You stupid fool," he said. "Found out that Prince Ulash is dead, of course."

CHAPTER NINETEEN

"Prince Ulash is dead."

King Lanius stared at the messenger who brought the word north to the city of Avornis. "Are you sure?" he blurted. He realized the question was foolish as soon as it came out of his mouth. He couldn't help asking, though. Ulash had been the strongest and canniest prince among the Menteshe for longer than Lanius had been alive. Imagining how things would go without him was nothing but a leap in the dark.

The messenger took the question seriously. That was one of the privileges of being a sovereign. "Yes, Your Majesty. There's no doubt," he answered. "The nomads went south of the Stura when they didn't have to, and prisoners have told King Grus why."

"All right. Thank you," Lanius said, and then, as an afterthought, "Do you know who succeeds him? Is it Prince Sanjar or Prince Korkut?"

"That I can't tell you. The nomads King Grus caught didn't know," the messenger said. "Grus is on his way back here now, with part of the army. The rest will stay in the south, in case whichever one of Ulash's sons does take over decides to start the war up again."

"Sensible," Lanius said, hoping neither the messenger nor his own courtiers noticed his small sigh. With Grus back in the capital, Lanius would become a figurehead again. Part of Lanius insisted that didn't matter—Grus was better at the day-to-day business of running Avornis than he was, and was welcome to it. But Lanius remembered how often he'd had power taken away from him. He resented it. He couldn't help resenting it.

He dismissed the messenger, who bowed his way out of the throne room. As the king descended from the Diamond Throne, the news beat in his brain, pulsing like his own blood, pounding like a drum. *Prince Ulash is dead.*

What *would* come next? Lanius didn't know. He was no prophet, to play the risky game of foreseeing the future. But things wouldn't be the same. Neither Sanjar nor Korkut could hope to match Ulash for experience or cleverness.

Will whichever one of them comes to power in Yozgat make an apter tool for the Banished One's hand? Lanius wondered. Again, he could only shrug. He had believed Ulash's cleverness and power and success had won him more freedom of action than most Menteshe owned. But then the prince had hurled his nomads northward to help hold Grus away from Nishevatz. When the Banished One told him to move, he'd moved. So much for freedom of action.

By the time Lanius got back to his living quarters, news of Ulash's death had spread all over the palace. Not everyone seemed sure who Ulash was. The king went past a couple of servants arguing over whether he was King of Thervingia or prince of a Chernagor city-state.

"Well, whoever he is, he *isn't* anymore," said the man who thought he'd ruled Thervingia.

"That's true," the other servant said. "It's the first true thing you've said all day, too."

They could afford to quarrel, and to be ignorant. Lanius, who couldn't, almost envied them. Almost—he valued education and knowledge too highly to be comfortable with ignorance.

Rounding a corner, the king almost bumped into Prince Ortalis. They both gave back a pace. Grus' son said, "Is it true?"

"Is what true?" Lanius thought he knew what Ortalis meant, but he might have been wrong.

He wasn't. "Is the old bugger south of the Stura dead at last?" Ortalis asked, adding, "That's what everybody's saying."

"That's what your father says, or rather his messenger," Lanius answered, and watched his brother-in-law scowl. Ortalis and Grus still didn't get along. They probably never would. Lanius went on, "Now that the Menteshe have gone back to their own side of the border, your father will be coming home."

"Will he?" Ortalis didn't bother trying to hide his displeasure at the news. "I hoped he'd stay down there and chase them all the way to what's-its-name, the place where they've stashed the what-do-you-call-it."

"Yozgat. The Scepter of Mercy." Yes, Lanius did prefer knowledge to ignorance. He brought out the names Ortalis needed but didn't bother remembering as automatically as he breathed. He judged that his brother-in-law wanted Grus to go on campaigning in the south not so much because he hoped Avornan arms would triumph as because Grus would stay far away from the city of Avornis. Lanius couldn't do anything but try to stay out of the way when Grus and Ortalis clashed. Doing his best to stay on safer ground, the king said, "I hope Princess Limosa is well?"

"Oh, yes," Ortalis said with a smile. "She's fine. She's just fine."

In a different tone of voice, with a different curve of the lips, the answer would have been fine, just fine, too. As things were, Lanius pushed past his brother-in-law as fast as he could. He tried telling himself he hadn't seen what he thought he had. Ortalis had looked and sounded that very same way, had had that very same gleam in his eye, when he was butchering a deer and up to his elbows in blood. He'd never seemed happier.

Lanius shook his head again and again. But no, he couldn't make that certainty fall out. And he couldn't make himself believe anymore that Zenaida hadn't known exactly what she was talking about.

He also couldn't help remembering how serene, how radiant, how *joyful* Limosa looked. That couldn't be an act. But he didn't see how it could be real, either.

"Well, well," Grus said when he saw the towers of the palace, the cathedral's heaven-reaching spire, and the other tall buildings of the city of Avornis above the walls that protected the capital from invaders. "I'm really coming home. I'm not just stopping for a little while before I have to rush north or south as fast as I can."

"You hope you're not, anyhow," Hirundo said.

Grus glared at him, but finally gave back a reluctant nod. "Yes. I hope I'm not."

Guards on the wall had seen the approaching army, too. A postern gate opened. A rider came out to make sure it really was an Avornan force. When he waved, the main gates swung open.

Not all the army that had accompanied Grus up from the south went into the city of Avornis. Much of the part that wasn't on garrison duty down by the Stura had gone into barracks in towns on the way north, to spread the problem of feeding the soldiers over as much of the kingdom as possible. If a dreadful winter—say, a dreadful winter inspired by the Banished One—overwhelmed Avornis, extra mouths to feed in the capital, which was already much the largest city in the kingdom, would only make matters worse.

Instead of waiting at the royal palace, Lanius met Grus halfway there. "You must tell me at once—did Sanjar or Korkut succeed Prince Ulash?" Lanius said. By his expression, he was ready to do something drastic if Grus didn't take that *at once* seriously.

"I'll tell you everything I know," Grus promised. "And everything I know is—I don't know."

"Oh . . . *drat!*" Lanius got more use out of what wasn't even really a curse than Grus could have from a couple of minutes of blasphemy and obscenity. His son-in-law went on, "I think which of them takes over in Yozgat really is important for Avornis. Korkut will cause us more trouble than Sanjar, though neither one of them is half the man their father was."

"How do you know even that much about them?" Grus asked. "They're both just names to me."

"I've been going through the archives—how else?" Lanius answered. "Things our traders who went south of the Stura in peacetime heard about them, things Ulash's ambassadors who came up here had to say. Korkut is older, but Sanjar is the son of the woman who became Ulash's favorite."

"Isn't that interesting?" Grus said. "You'll have to tell me more."

Now the other king looked faintly abashed. "I've already told you almost everything I know."

"Oh." Grus shrugged. "Well, you're right—it is important. And it's already more than I knew before." After that, Lanius brightened. Grus went on, "How are things here? How's Prince Vsevolod?"

The other king's lip curled. "About the way you'd expect. He's still annoyed that we had the nerve to defend our own borders instead of going on with the fight to put him back on the throne of Nishevatz, which would actually be important."

"Oh," Grus said again, his tone falling. "Well, you're right. I can't say I'm surprised. How are other things?"

"They seem all right," Lanius answered. "Most of them, anyhow."

What was that supposed to mean? One obvious answer occurred to Grus. "Is my son all right?" he asked.

"Prince Ortalis is fine. He and Princess Limosa seem very happy together, no matter how they happened to meet and wed," Lanius said.

He spoke with caution he didn't try to hide. Grus knew he didn't like Ortalis. Maybe that explained the caution. Or maybe there were things he could have said if they weren't out in the street. Finding out which would have to wait. Grus said, "Let's get back to the palace. I'm glad the Chernagors didn't raid our coast this year."

"Yes, so am I," Lanius said. "How would you have handled it if they did?"

"Badly, I suspect," Grus answered. Lanius blinked, then laughed; maybe he hadn't expected such blunt honesty. Grus asked, "How are your moncats doing?"

"Very well," Lanius said enthusiastically, and told Grus more than he wanted to hear about the antics and thievery of the beast called Pouncer.

Not least because Lanius had bored him, Grus put a sardonic edge in his voice when he asked, "And have you found any other pets while I was away?" He made it plain he didn't mean any that walked on four legs.

Just as plainly, Lanius understood him, for he turned red. "Well, yes," he confessed with no great eagerness. "You were right about that." He did have integrity; not many men would have admitted as much. But then, with a certain edge of his own, he inquired, "And how was Pelagonia?"

Grus remembered that he hadn't named the town in his letters north. He hadn't wanted to remind Estrilda he was anywhere near it— or near Alca. He supposed he shouldn't have been surprised that Lanius had seen through his ploy; Lanius saw through all sorts of things. For a moment, he thought of talking about the town and not about the witch. But Lanius had given him a straight answer, and he supposed he owed his son-in-law one in return. With a shrug, he said, "It's dead. I didn't know if it would be, but it is."

He said nothing about Alauda. He most especially said nothing about the baby Alauda would have. Word that he'd been carrying on with a new woman down in the south might eventually reach his wife. Since he hadn't brought Alauda back to the city of Avornis, Estrilda might not—he hoped she wouldn't—get too upset about that. He'd been in the field and away from her for a long time, after all. But she wouldn't be happy if she found out he'd sired another bastard.

Suddenly worried, he wondered whether Lanius knew about Alauda. The other king gave no sign of it. Lanius wasn't usually very good at keeping secrets off his face. That eased Grus' mind—a little.

And there was the palace, and there, standing in the doorway waving to him, was Estrilda. That eased Grus' mind, too. His wife kept her own counsel about some things, but not about his other women. She didn't know about Alauda, either, then, or not yet. Only when Grus was already hurrying up the steps toward her did he wish those last three words hadn't occurred to him.

Lanius studied the harvest reports that came into the capital with even more attention than he usually gave them. Ever since that one dreadful winter, he'd worried that the Banished One would wield the weather weapon once again, and wanted to be as ready as he could in case the exiled god did. This year, though, he also eyed the news from the south with unusual attention.

It was every bit as bad as Grus had warned him it would be. Half the dismal harvest reports from the regions the Menteshe had ravaged asked for grain and fodder to be sent to towns whose governors insisted their populace would go hungry and animals would starve if they didn't get that kind of help.

Grus examined the reports from the south, too. He'd seen what was going on down there with his own eyes, and was grim about it. "We'll have hunger," he said bluntly. "I'll thank Queen Quelea for her kindness if we don't have famine. And if the nomads keep coming up over the Stura year after year, I don't know what we'll do. They hurt us badly."

"Didn't we hurt them, too?" Lanius asked.

"I hope so," Grus said. "I hope so, but how can I be sure? They're so cursed hard to get a grip on."

"We drove them back over the Stura," Lanius said.

"No." Grus shook his head, as relentlessly precise as Lanius was himself most of the time. "We drove them back to the valley of the Stura. They went over by themselves. If Ulash hadn't chosen that moment to drop dead, we would have had another big fight on our hands."

"I do wonder what's happening on the far side of the river," Lanius said. "Sanjar or Korkut? Korkut or Sanjar? How will the Menteshe choose? How long will it take them?"

"How much trouble will we be in once they do?" Grus was also relentlessly practical.

Since Lanius preferred not to dwell on trouble, he asked, "How did Pterocles fare against the nomads' wizards?"

"Fair," Grus said, and then shook his head, correcting himself. "No—better than fair. If he hadn't woken up during that one night attack the Menteshe tried to bring off, it would have done us much more harm. Oh!" He shook his head again. "He also says he's full of new ideas about how to cure thralls."

"Does he?" Lanius wished he could have sounded more excited. As he'd seen in the archives, Avornan wizards had been full of new ideas about how to cure thralls ever since the Menteshe sorcerers started creating them. The only trouble was, very few of the new ideas did any good. "And what are they?"

"I couldn't begin to tell you," Grus answered. "I never even asked, not in any detail. I don't care how he does what he does, though I wouldn't mind watching him try. All I care about is whether he can do it."

How fascinated Lanius almost as much as *why*. He almost asked the older man how he could be so indifferent to it, and why. After a moment's hesitation, though, he decided not to. A straightforward insistence on results also had its advantages.

Lanius did say, "You wouldn't mind watching him? You really think he has a chance to bring this off?"

"I think he thinks he had a chance to bring it off," Grus said, and Lanius smiled at the convolution. His father-in-law went on, "And I think he's earned the chance to try. How are we worse off if he fails?"

He'd intended that for a rhetorical question, but Lanius had no trouble finding a literal answer for it. "How are we worse off? Suppose the Banished One kills him and the thralls try murdering us again. That would be worse, wouldn't it?"

"Maybe a little," Grus allowed. Lanius yelped indignantly. Grus said, "We'll be as careful as we can. You made your point there, believe me."

"When will the wizard try?" Lanius asked.

"When he's ready," Grus answered with a shrug. "He has to have all his spells ready before he begins. If he doesn't, he shouldn't even try.

You're right about that—this could be one of those things where trying and failing is worse than not trying at all. Or do you look at it differently?"

"No, I think you've got it straight," Lanius said at once. "Throwing rocks at the Banished One isn't enough. We have to make sure we hit him. We have to make sure we hurt him."

He listened to himself. He sounded bold enough. Did he sound like a fool? He wouldn't have been surprised. Could he and Grus and Pterocles really hurt Milvago's plans? *We'd better be able to,* Lanius thought. *If we can't, we're going to lose. Avornis is going to lose.*

It was more than a week later that Grus hauled Lanius off to the chamber where the thralls were kept. "Where were you?" Grus asked irritably while they were on the way. "I looked for you for quite a while, and it was only luck we ran into each other in the hall here."

Lanius had been sporting with Zenaida. He didn't feel like admitting that to Grus. He just shrugged and answered, "Well, you've found me. Pterocles is ready?"

"He says he is," Grus told him. "We'll find out, won't we?"

"So we will," Lanius said. "One way or the other . . ."

Half a dozen armed guards brought a thrall from the room where the not-quite-men were kept to the chamber next door. The guards looked scornful, plainly wondering why Grus had ordered out so many of them to deal with one unarmed fellow who hadn't much more in the way of brains than a goat. The thrall glanced around with the usual dull lack of curiosity of his kind.

No matter how dull the thrall seemed, Lanius eyed him suspiciously. The Banished One could be peering out through those almost unblinking eyes. Pterocles was giving the thrall that same sharp scrutiny. The haggard expression the wizard wore said he knew the risk he was taking. Lanius nodded to him. He wouldn't have wanted Pterocles to try to free the man from thralldom without bearing in mind the danger of failure.

"Are you sure you're ready?" Grus asked.

"I'm sure. We're here to find out whether I'm right, which is not the same thing," Pterocles answered. "I think I am, Your Majesty. I aim to—" He broke off. "No, I won't say what I aim to do, not while this fellow's ears may pass it on to the Banished One. I'll just go ahead and try the sorcery."

At first, whatever he was doing didn't seem much like magic at all. He stepped over to a window and took a small crystal on a silver chain from a pouch on his belt. Idly, he began to swing the crystal back and forth. It sparkled in the sunlight streaming in through the window. The glitter and flash drew Lanius' eyes to the crystal. He needed an effort of will to pull them away.

Looking at the thrall helped keep Lanius from looking at the crystal. The thrall didn't look at the king. His eyes went back and forth, back and forth, following the swinging, flashing chunk of clear rock.

"You are an empty one," Pterocles said quietly. "Your will is not your own. You have always been empty, your will never your own."

"I am an empty one," the thrall repeated. His voice sounded empty—eerily inhuman, all emotion and feeling washed from it. "My will is not my own. I have always been empty, my will never my own."

"Queen Quelea's mercy," Grus whispered to Lanius. "Just listen to what the wizard's done."

"What do you mean?" Lanius whispered back.

"I've heard plenty of thralls down in the south," Grus answered. "They can talk, a little, but they don't talk as well as that, not usually they don't. Pterocles has managed something special to get even that much out of this fellow."

"I don't know," Lanius said dubiously. "I think the thrall was just echoing the wizard."

Pterocles waved impatiently at the two kings. Lanius nodded and fell silent. Grus looked as though he wanted to say something more, but he too subsided when Pterocles waved again. The sorcerer kept on swinging his shining bit of crystal. The thrall's eyes kept following it. It might have been the only thing in all the world with meaning for the filthy, scruffily bearded man.

Softly, Pterocles asked, "Do you want to find your own will? Do you want to be filled with your own self?"

"I want to find my own will," the thrall droned. "I want to be filled with my own self." Did he understand what he was saying? Or was he only parroting Pterocles' words? Lanius still thought he was, but the king had to admit to himself that he wasn't so sure anymore.

"I can lift the shadow from your spirit and give you light." Pterocles sounded confident. How many Avornan wizards over the years, though, had sounded confident trying to cure thralls? Many. How many had

had reason to sound confident? Few. No—none. None yet, anyhow. Pterocles went on, "Do you *want* me to lift the shadow from your spirit and give you light?"

"I want you to lift the shadow from my spirit and give me light." By what was in his voice, the thrall still wanted nothing, regardless of the words he mouthed. Or was that so? Buried under the indifference, was there a terrible longing struggling to burst free? For an instant, Lanius heard it, or thought he did. Though he doubted himself again in the very next heartbeat, a sudden surge of hope warmed him.

"I will do what I can for you, then," Pterocles said.

"Do what you can for me, then," the thrall said. Pterocles blinked, then grinned enormously. Lanius realized the wizard hadn't expected the thrall to respond there. If the man did, even if the response was just another near-echo, wasn't that a sign he was trying to escape the shadow on his own? Lanius dared hope it was, anyhow.

Pterocles began to chant, very softly, in a very old dialect of Avornan. Lanius fancied himself a scholar, but even he had trouble following what the wizard said. Beside him, Grus looked altogether bewildered.

Pterocles also kept swinging the crystal in the sunbeam. It cast rainbows on the walls of the chamber—more and more rainbows by the moment. The chant went on and on. It got more insistent, though no louder. Ever more rainbows sprang into being—far more than a single bit of crystal had any business extracting from an ordinary sunbeam.

Suddenly, the wizard said, "Let them be assembled." Lanius understood that very clearly. Pterocles made a pass, and all the rainbows, still glowing, came off the walls and began to spin around the thrall's head. Lanius exclaimed in wonder—no, in awe. Those same two qualities also filled Grus' voice. They were watching both the beautiful and the impossible. Lanius couldn't have said which side of that coin impressed him more.

Even the thrall, who was supposed to be hardly more than a beast, took notice of what was going on around him. He reached up with his right hand, as though to pluck one of the spinning rainbows out of the air. Was that awe on *his* dull face? Lanius would have had a hard time claiming it wasn't.

The king couldn't see whether the swirling bands of color went around the thrall's hand, whether they slipped between his fingers, or whether they simply passed through his flesh. In the end, what did it matter? His hand did them no harm, which was all that counted.

"Let them come together!" Pterocles called out in that archaic dialect of Avornan. And come together the rainbows did. Instead of swirling around the thrall's head, they began passing *into* it. For a moment, even after they entered his flesh, they kept their brilliance, or so it seemed to Lanius' dazzled eye.

"Ahhh!" the thrall said—a long, involuntary exclamation of wonder. His eyes opened very wide. By then, Lanius had thought himself as full of awe as he could be. He found out he was wrong. Unless his imagination had altogether run away with him, the thrall's eyes held something that had never been in them before. They held reason.

Grus said it in a slightly different way—he whispered, "By Olor's strong right hand, that's a *man* there"—but it meant the same thing. If this wasn't a cured thrall, maybe there never would be one.

Little by little, the rainbows faded. No—the rainbows became invisible from the outside. Lanius was convinced that, in some way he could not fully fathom, they went on swirling and spinning inside the thrall's mind, lighting up all the corners over which darkness had lain for so long.

Chief proof of that was the way the thrall himself reacted. Tears ran down his grimy cheeks. He seized Pterocles' hand and brought it up to his mouth and kissed it again and again. "Good," he said, and, "Thank you," over and over. He didn't yet have all the words a man might have, but he had the feelings behind the words. The feelings, up until this moment, might as well have floated a mile beyond the moon.

Pterocles turned to Grus. "Your Majesty, what I have said I would do, I have done." He bowed, then seemed to remember Lanius was there and bowed to him, too. "Your Majesties, I should say."

"You *have* done it." Grus still took it for granted that he was the one to speak for Avornis. "But the next question is, how hard is the spell? Can other wizards learn it and use it in the field?"

"I don't see why not, Your Majesty," Pterocles answered. "Putting the spell together, seeing what had to go into it—that was hard. Using it?" He shook his head. "Any halfway decent wizard ought to be able to do that. I'd like to experiment with the rest of the thralls here in the palace to be sure, but we've seen what can happen." He pointed to the man he'd just cured.

"Yes," Grus said.

"Yes," Lanius echoed. The two kings looked at each other and nodded. With any luck at all, they had a weapon they could use against the

Menteshe if Avornan armies ever went south of the Stura. Avornis had been looking for a weapon like that for a very long time. Lanius asked, "Do you want to cure those other thralls now? How wearing is the spell?"

"It's not bad at all, Your Majesty," Pterocles replied. "I could do more now, if you like. But if you don't mind, I'd like to wait a day or two instead, so I can incorporate what I've learned just now into the spell. I think I can make it better and simpler yet."

"Good. Do that, then." Lanius spoke with the voice of royal command. Grus didn't contradict him. Even though he knew Grus could have, for a little while he felt every inch the King of Avornis.

"Your Majesty! Your Majesty!" Someone pounded on the door to Grus' bedchamber. He opened his eyes. It was still dark. Beside him, Estrilda stirred and murmured. The pounding went on. "Come quick, Your Majesty!"

"What's going on?" Estrilda asked sleepily.

"I don't know, but I'd better find out." Grus sat up in bed. "If it won't wait for daylight, it usually isn't good news." He raised his voice and called, "Quit that racket, by Olor's teeth! I'm coming." The pounding stopped.

When Grus went to the door, he went sword in hand, in case whoever waited there wasn't an ordinary servant. But, when he opened the door a crack, he recognized the man. The servant said, "Come with me, Your Majesty. It's the thralls!"

That got Grus' attention, as no doubt it was calculated to do. "Take me to them," he said at once. "What's happened?"

"You'd better see for yourself, Your Majesty," the servant answered. Grus swore under his breath. He might have known the man would say something like that.

They hurried through silent corridors lit only by guttering torches set in every third sconce. From that, and from the feel of the air, Grus guessed it was a couple of hours before dawn. He yawned as he half trotted after the servant, the sword still in his hand. The mosaic tiles of the floor were cold against his bare feet.

Around the chamber where the thralls were kept, all the sconces held torches, and all the torches blazed brightly. The door to the chamber stood open. Grus stopped in his tracks when he saw that. "Oh, by the gods!" he said. "Have they gotten loose?" That could be a deadly dangerous disaster.

But one of the guards standing in the hallway outside the open door shook his head. "No, Your Majesty. They're in there, all right."

"Then what's happened?" Grus demanded.

The guard didn't answer. Neither did any of his comrades or the servant who'd fetched the king. Muttering, Grus strode forward. The stink of the thralls' room hit him like a slap in the face. Doing his best to ignore it, he walked in . . . and found the last two thralls brought north from the Stura lying dead on the floor.

They had strangled each other. Each still had his hands clenched on the other's throat. The chamber was no more disarrayed than usual. By all the signs, the thralls had both decided to die and taken care of the job as quickly and neatly as they could. But, unless Grus was very wrong, the thralls hadn't decided any such thing. The Banished One had.

"By the gods," the king said softly. He hoped the magic that made men into thralls hadn't so stunted their souls as to keep them from winning free of this world. He hoped so, but had no way of knowing if that was true.

"You see, Your Majesty," a guard said.

"I see, all right," Grus agreed grimly. He nodded to the guard, who no longer had anything to do here. "Go fetch me Pterocles." The man hurried away. Almost as an afterthought, Grus turned to the servant who'd brought him to the thralls' room and added, "Fetch King Lanius here, too."

"Yes, Your Majesty." The servant went off even faster than the guard had.

Even so, Pterocles got to the thralls' chamber before the other king. The wizard was yawning and rubbing his eyes, but he stared at the dead thralls without astonishment; the guard must have told him what had happened. "Well, so much for that," he said.

"Eh?" Grus scratched his head. "I don't follow you."

"I was going to do what I could to improve the spell I used to free the first thrall," the wizard replied. "I was, but I can't very well do it now, not when I don't have any more thralls to work with—to work on."

"Oh." The king thumped his forehead with the heel of his hand. "I should have seen that for myself."

"Should have seen what?" King Lanius asked around a yawn of his own. Then he got a good look at the thralls who'd killed each other. He also said, "Oh," and then turned to Pterocles. "We'll have to get you more thralls, won't we, if you're going to do all the experiments you need to?"

"Afraid so," Pterocles said.

Grus grunted, obscurely annoyed with himself. The other king and the wizard had both seen at once what he'd missed—why the Banished One had decided to end the lives of the captive thralls. How was he supposed to run Avornis when other people in the kingdom were smarter than he was?

Then Lanius asked him, "What do we do now?" Pterocles leaned forward expectantly, also waiting for his answer.

They think I can lead them, Grus realized. *Well, they'd better be right, hadn't they?* He said, "The only way we can get more thralls is to go over the river and take them out of the lands the Menteshe rule. I don't know that we want to do that until we see how things go with Sanjar and Korkut. If they want to quarrel with each other instead of us, why give them an excuse to change their minds?"

Pterocles looked disappointed. Pterocles, in fact, looked mutinous. He wanted more thralls, and wanted them badly. But Lanius nodded and said, "That makes good sense."

To Pterocles, Grus said, "I know you want to make your spell better. But isn't it good enough now?" Reluctantly—ever so reluctantly— the wizard nodded. "All right, then," Grus told him. "For now, good enough will have to do."

"How do you decide so quickly?" Lanius sounded more than abstractly curious. He sounded as though he wanted to learn the trick so he could do it himself.

"Being on the battlefield helps," Grus said after a momentary pause. "Sometimes it's better to try something—to try anything—of your own than to let the enemy decide what you're going to do next. If it turns out that what you tried isn't working, you try something else instead. The trick is to impose your will on whatever's going on, and not to let the other fellow impose his on you."

"But there is no other fellow here," Lanius said.

"No?" Slowly and deliberately, Grus turned toward the south, toward the lands the Banished One ruled. He waited. Lanius bit his lip.

A guard asked, "Your Majesty, shall we get rid of the bodies here?"

"Yes, do that," Grus answered. "Put them on a proper pyre. Don't just throw them into a hole in the ground or chuck them in the river. In a strange sort of way, they're soldiers in the war against the Menteshe."

The guard shook his head, plainly not believing that. But he didn't argue with Grus. Neither did his comrades. They got the dead thralls apart—not so easy, for the corpses had begun to stiffen—and carried them away. Not having people argue was one of the advantages of being king.

Wherever we're going, we're going because I *want us to get there,* Grus thought. *Now . . . I'd better not be wrong.*

CHAPTER TWENTY

Outside the royal palace, the wind screamed. Snow blew by almost horizontally. Braziers and hearth fires blazed everywhere inside, battling the blizzard. Despite them, the palace was still cold. From the lowliest sweeper on up, people wore robes of wool or furs over their everyday trousers and tunics. The noise of chattering teeth was never far away, even so.

Lanius' teeth chattered more than most. The king sat in the archives. He had a brazier by him, but it did less than he would have wished to hold the chill at bay. No hearth fire here. Even the one brazier made him nervous. With so many parchments lying around, a single spark escaping could mean catastrophe.

But he wanted—he needed—to do research, and the archives were simply too cold to tolerate without some fire by him. Now that Pterocles had—or thought he had—brought one thrall out from under the shadow the Banished One's spell had cast over him, Lanius was wild to learn more about all the earlier efforts Avornan wizards had made to lead thralls out of darkness.

He found even more than he'd expected. The archives held dozens, maybe hundreds, of spells intended to cure thralls. They held just as many descriptions of what had happened once the spells were tried. The spells themselves were a monument to ingenuity. The descriptions were a monument of a different sort, a monument to discouragement. Lanius read of failure after failure after failure. He marveled that Avornan wizards had kept on trying after failing so often.

Before long, he realized why they'd kept on trying. Kings of Avornis could see perfectly well that they had no hope of defeating the Menteshe in any permanent way if they couldn't cure thralls. They kept the wizards at it.

What the present king found gave him pause. Every so often, a wizard would claim to have beaten the spells that made thralls what they were. Reports would come into the capital of thralls being completely cured and made into ordinary men. Every once in a while, the cured thralls themselves would come into the capital.

That was all very well. But none of the wizards had won enduring fame, for most of the thralls proved not to be cured after all. Some gradually drifted back into their previous idiocy. Others—and these were the heartbreakers—turned out to be the eyes and ears of the Banished One.

The more Lanius thought about that, the more he worried. After a while, he couldn't stand the worry anymore, and summoned Pterocles not to the archives but to a small audience chamber heated by a couple of braziers. He asked, "Are you sure this thrall is cured, or could the Banished One still control him?"

"Ah," the wizard said. "You wonder about the same thing as I do, Your Majesty."

"I have reason to." Lanius spoke of all the reports he'd found of thralls thought to be cured who proved anything but.

Pterocles nodded. "I know of some of those cases, too. I think you've found more than I knew of, but that doesn't matter so much." Lanius had to fight not to pout; *he* thought his thoroughness mattered. The wizard went on, "What matters is, by every sorcerous test I know how to make, the thrall is a thrall no more. He's a man."

"By every sorcerous test you know how to make," King Lanius repeated. The wizard nodded again. Lanius said, "You're not the first to make that claim, either, you know."

"Yes, I do," Pterocles replied. "But I am the first to make that claim who knows from the inside what being emptied by the Banished One is like. I know the shape and size of the hole inside a man. I know how to fill it. By the gods, Your Majesty, I *have* filled it, at least this once."

He sounded very sure of himself. Lanius would have been more sure of him if he hadn't read reports by wizards years, sometimes centuries, dead who'd been just as sure of themselves and ended up disappointed. Still, Pterocles had a point—what he'd gone through in front of Nishevatz gave him a unique perspective on how the Banished One's wizardry worked.

"We'll see," the king said at last. "But I'm afraid that thrall will need to be watched to the end of his days."

"I understand why you're saying that," Pterocles answered. "If we can cure enough other thralls, though, maybe you'll change your mind."

The only way to cure other thralls was to cross the Stura and take them away from the Menteshe; as far as Lanius knew, the thrall Pterocles had cured (or believed he had cured?) was the only one left on Avornan soil. "I think the war against the Chernagors will come first," Lanius said.

"I think you're probably right," Pterocles replied. "That does seem to be what His Majesty—uh, His other Majesty—has in mind."

"His other Majesty. Yes," Lanius said sourly. Pterocles hadn't intended to insult him, to remind him he was King of Avornis more in name than in fact. Intended or not, the wizard had done it. If anything, the slight hurt worse because it was unintentional.

"Er . . . I meant no offense, Your Majesty," Pterocles said quickly, realizing where he'd gone wrong.

"I know you didn't." Lanius still sounded sour. Just because the offense hadn't been meant didn't mean it wasn't there.

Two messengers came north, each from a different town on the north bank of the Stura. They had left for the city of Avornis on different days. They'd both struggled through bad roads and blizzards and drifted snow. And, as luck would have it, they both came before King Grus within the space of an hour and a half.

The first messenger said, "Your Majesty, Prince Sanjar is sending you an ambassador to announce his succession to the throne Prince Ulash held for so long. The ambassador is trailing behind me, and should get to the city of Avornis before too long."

"All right. Good, in fact," Grus said. "I'm glad to know who came out on top there. When Sanjar's ambassador gets here, I'll be as polite as I can, considering that we've just fought a war with the prince's father." He dared hope Sanjar wanted peace. That the new Menteshe prince was sending an envoy struck him as a good sign.

Grus had just sat down to lunch when the second messenger arrived. The king asked the servant who announced the fellow's presence if his news was urgent. The man said it was. With a sigh, Grus got up from his bread and cheese and wine. "I'll see him, then."

After bowing, the second messenger said, "Your Majesty, Prince Korkut is sending you an ambassador to announce his succession to the throne Prince Ulash held for so long. The envoy is on his way to the capital, and should get here in a few days."

"Wait a minute. Prince Korkut, you say?" Grus wanted to make sure he'd heard straight. "Not Prince Sanjar?"

"No, Your Majesty." The courier shook his head. "From what Prince Korkut's ambassador said, Sanjar is nothing but a rebel."

"Did he say that? How . . . interesting." Grus dismissed the second messenger and summoned the first one again. He asked, "Did Prince Sanjar's envoy say anything about Prince Korkut?"

"Why, yes, Your Majesty. How did you know that?" the first messenger replied. "He said Korkut was nothing but a filthy traitor, and he'd be hunted down soon."

"Did he? Well, well, well." King Grus looked up at the ceiling. "We may have some sparks flying when the embassies get here."

"Embass*ies,* Your Majesty?" The courier, who didn't know he wasn't the only man to come to the capital with news from the south, stressed the last syllable.

"That's right." Grus nodded. "Korkut's sending one, too. If you listen to *his* ambassador, he's Ulash's rightful heir and Sanjar's nothing but a rebel."

"Oh," the courier said, and then, "Oh, my."

"Well, yes." King Grus grinned like a mischievous little boy. "And do you know what else? It ought to be a lot of fun."

He did his best to make sure it would be fun, too. Korkut's ambassador got to the city of Avornis first. Grus put the man—his name was Er-Tash—up in a hostel and made excuses not to see him right away. Sanjar's representative, a Menteshe called Duqaq, reached the capital three days later. Grus invited both envoys to confer with him on the same day at the same time. He made sure neither saw the other until they both reached the throne room.

Er-Tash glared at Duqaq. Duqaq scowled at Er-Tash. Both of them reached for their swords. Since they were in the throne room, they'd been relieved of those swords and other assorted cutlery beforehand. They snarled and shouted at each other in their own language. Their retainers—each had a small handful—also growled and made threatening noises.

At Grus' gesture, Avornan soldiers got between the two rival embassies, to make sure they didn't start going at each other with fists—and to make sure nobody had managed to sneak anything with a point or an edge past the guards.

"Your Majesty!" Duqaq shouted in good Avornan. "This is an outrage, Your Majesty!"

"*He* is an outrage, Your Majesty!" Er-Tash cried, pointing at Duqaq. "How dare he come before you?"

Before Duqaq could let loose with more indignation, Grus held up a hand. "Enough, both of you," he said. Several guards pounded the butts of their spears down on the marble floor of the throne room. The solid thumps probably did more to convince the Menteshe envoys to keep quiet than any of the king's words. When Grus saw they *would* keep quiet, he went on, "Both of you came to me on your own. Don't you think I ought to hear you both? If I do send one of you away, which one should it be?"

"Him!" Er-Tash and Duqaq exclaimed at the same time. Each pointed at the other. Both looked daggers at each other.

"One of you represents Prince Ulash's legitimate successor," Grus said. "One represents a rebel. How do I figure out which is which?"

"Because Prince Ulash left my master—" Duqaq began.

"Liar!" Er-Tash shouted. "The land is Korkut's!"

"Liar yourself!" Duqaq yelled. Grus reflected that they both could end up right, if Ulash's sons split the territory their father had ruled. By the signs, they were more interested in splitting each other's heads. That didn't break the King of Avornis' heart. Just the opposite, in fact.

None of what Grus thought showed on his face. Up there on the Diamond Throne, he remained calm, collected, above it all—metaphorically as well as literally. "Why should I recognize one of your principals and not the other?" he inquired, as though the question might be interesting in theory but had no bearing on the real world.

"Because he is the rightful Prince of Yozgat!" Er-Tash said.

Duqaq shouted, "Liar!" again. He went on, "Sanjar was Ulash's favorite, Ulash's chosen heir, not this—this thefter of a throne." His Avornan wasn't quite perfect.

Again, as though the question were only theoretical, Grus asked, "Which man does the Banished One prefer?" If the ambassadors knew—

and if they would admit they knew—that would tell Grus which contender Avornis ought to support.

But Er-Tash answered, "The Fallen Star has not yet made his choice clear." Duqaq, for once, did not contradict him.

How interesting, Grus thought. Did that mean the Banished One didn't care, or that he was having trouble making up his mind, or something else altogether? No way to be sure, not for a mere man.

Then Er-Tash said, "If you recognize Korkut, he will promise peace with Avornis."

"Will he?" Grus said. "Now you begin to interest me. How do I know he will keep his promises? What guarantees will he give me?"

"*I* will give you a guarantee," Duqaq broke in. "I will give you a guarantee Er-Tash is lying, and Korkut is lying, too."

"Oh?" Again, Grus carefully didn't smile, though he felt like it. "Does Sanjar want peace with Avornis? If he does, what guarantees will *he* give? We need guarantees. We have seen we cannot always trust the Menteshe." He went no further than that. What he wanted to say about the Banished One would only anger both ambassadors.

"Sanjar wants peace," Duqaq said. "Sanjar will pay tribute to have peace."

"And try to steal it back again!" Er-Tash burst out. Duqaq snarled at him, no doubt because he'd told nothing but the truth.

"What will Korkut give?" Grus asked Duqaq.

"He too will pay tribute," Korkut's ambassador replied, at which Er-Tash laughed loud and long. Flushing under his swarthy skin, Duqaq went on, "And he will also give hostages, so you may be sure his intentions are good."

"You may be sure he will cheat, giving men of no account who—whom—who he says are important," Er-Tash said.

"Will Sanjar give hostages?" Grus asked. If he had hostages from the Menteshe, they might think twice about attacking Avornis. Money, he was sure, would not give him nearly as big an advantage.

Reluctantly, Er-Tash nodded. Now Duqaq was the one who laughed a raucous laugh. Er-Tash said, "Shut your fool's mouth, you son of a backscuttling sheep." The insult had to be translated literally from his own tongue; Grus had never heard it in Avornan. Duqaq answered in the Menteshe language. The rival envoys snapped at each other for a minute or two.

At last, Duqaq turned away from the quarrel and toward King Grus.

"You see, Your Majesty," he said. "You will get no more from the rebel and traitor than you will from Prince Korkut, so you should recognize him."

"You will get no more from the robber and usurper than you will from Prince Sanjar, so you should recognize *him,*" Er-Tash said.

They both waited to hear what Grus would say. He thought for a little while, then spoke. "As long as two sons of Ulash claim to be Prince of Yozgat, I will not recognize either of them—unless one attacks Avornis. Then I will recognize the other, and do all I can to help him. When you have settled your own problems, I will recognize the prince you have chosen, however you do that. Until then, I am neutral—unless one of your principals attacks my kingdom, as I said."

Duqaq said, "Sanjar's rogues will attack you and make it look as though my master's followers did the wicked deed."

"You blame Sanjar for what Korkut plans himself," Er-Tash said.

Again, they started shouting at each other in their own language. "Enough!" Grus said. "Too much, in fact. I dismiss you both, and order you to keep the peace as long as you stay in Avornis."

"When we cross the Stura, this is a dead dog." Er-Tash pointed to Duqaq.

"A mouse dreams of being a lion," Duqaq jeered.

"Dismissed, I said!" Grus was suddenly sick of both of them. They left the throne room. Avornan guards had to rush in to keep the men from their retinues from going at one another as they were leaving.

But no matter how severe Grus' expression while the rival Menteshe embassies were there to see it, the king smiled a broad and cheerful smile as soon as they were gone. Nothing pleased him more than strife among his foes.

Zenaida pouted prettily at King Lanius. "You don't love me anymore," the serving girl complained.

I never loved you, Lanius thought. *I had a good time with you, and either you had a good time with me or you're a better actress than I think you are. But that isn't love, even if it can be a start.* He hadn't known as much when he fell for Cristata. Grus had been right, even if Lanius hated to admit it.

He had to answer Zenaida. "I've been busy," he said—the same weak reply men have given lovers for as long as men have taken lovers.

This time, Zenaida's pout wasn't as pretty. "Busy with who?"

"Nobody," he answered, which was true, as long as he didn't count his wife.

The maidservant tossed her head. "Ha!" she said. "A likely story! You've found somebody else. You took advantage of me, and now you throw me aside?" She'd been at least as much seducer as seduced—so Lanius remembered it, anyhow. He didn't suppose he should have been surprised to find she recalled it differently. She went on, "If Queen Sosia ever found out about what was going on . . ."

"If Queen Sosia ever finds out, my life will be very unpleasant," Lanius said, and Zenaida smirked. He added, "But if she finds out from you, you will go straight to the Maze, and you won't come out again. Not ever. Is that plain enough?"

"Uh . . ." Zenaida's smirk vanished. Lanius could all but read her mind. Did he have the power to do what he threatened? Would he be angry enough to do it if he could? He could see her deciding he did and he would. "Yes, Your Majesty," she said in a very small voice.

"All right, then," Lanius said. "Was there anything else?"

"No, Your Majesty," she whispered.

"Good," Lanius said.

Zenaida wasn't pouting as she walked away from him. She was scowling, black as midnight. He sighed. An affair with love had complications. Now he discovered an affair without love had them, too. She thought he'd taken advantage of her, or said she did.

I'll give her a present, Lanius thought. With luck, that would sweeten her. He'd have to do it in such a way that he didn't look to be paying her for whoring. He nodded to himself. He could manage that.

Another problem solved, or so it seemed. He walked through the corridors of the palace suite smiling to himself. He liked solving problems. He liked few things better, in fact.

Guards came to stiff attention as he approached. He waved for them to stand at ease and asked, "How is Otus?"

"He's fine, Your Majesty," one of the guardsmen answered. "Couldn't be better, as far as I can see. You wouldn't know he was ever a thrall, not hardly you wouldn't."

"Bring him out," Lanius said. "I'd like to talk to him."

The guardsmen saluted. One of them unbarred the door, which could only be done from the outside. The guards kept their weapons ready. No matter how normal Otus acted, they didn't completely trust him. Lanius could hardly quarrel with them on that score, not with what he knew about "cured" thralls from years gone by.

But things had changed for the man on whom Pterocles had worked his magic. When the door to Otus' room opened, no thick barnyard reek poured out. Nor was Otus himself encrusted with ground-in filth. He looked like an ordinary Avornan, and was as clean as any of the guards. He'd been bathed and barbered and had his shaggy beard trimmed. His clothes were of the same sort as palace servants wore.

He'd learned enough to bow to the king without being told. "Your Majesty," he murmured.

"Hello, Otus," Lanius said. The thrall hadn't even had a name before they gave him one. "How are you today?"

"Just fine, thanks," replied the man brought up from the south. His accent didn't just sound southern. It sounded old-fashioned, and was the one thing that could have placed Otus to the far side of the Stura. Thralls didn't speak much, and their way of speaking had changed little since the Menteshe overran their lands. Over the past centuries, the currents of Avornan had run on without them. Though born a thrall, Otus had learned hundreds, maybe thousands, of new words since the shadow was lifted from his mind, but he spoke them all with his old accent.

"Glad to hear it," Lanius told him. "What was it like, being a thrall?"

"What was it . . . like?" Otus echoed, frowning. "It was . . . dark. I was . . . stupid. I still feel stupid. So much I don't know. So much I ought to know. You say—all you people say—someone did this to me?"

"The Banished One," Lanius said. "The Menteshe call him the Fallen Star."

"Oh." Otus' frown remained, but now showed awe rather than puzzlement or annoyance. "The Fallen Star. Yes. I would see him in . . . in dreams they were. All thralls would. He was bright. Nothing in our lives was bright. But the Fallen Star . . . The Fallen Star made everything shine inside our heads."

Did he mean that literally? Or was he trying to express something that didn't lend itself to words? Lanius tried to get him to say more, but he wouldn't. Maybe he couldn't. The king asked, "How do you feel about the Banished One now?"

Yet another sort of frown from Otus, this one the kind a thoughtful man might use before speaking. "I feel . . . free of him," the—former?—thrall said at last. "He has nothing to do with me anymore."

"And how does that make you feel?" Lanius asked.

"Glad," Otus said simply. "I am not an ox. I am not a donkey. I am a man. Here, I can be a man. Before, I never knew what it meant to be a man."

"Would you fight against the Banished One if you had the chance?"

"Give me a sword. Give me a spear." Otus frowned thoughtfully again. "I stand here. I talk to you. I say what I think. When I do that, I fight the Fallen Star. Is it not so, Your Majesty?"

"I think it is," Lanius answered. The thrall spoke against the Banished One. By all appearances, Otus was indeed cured of the exiled god's baneful influence. But how much were those appearances worth? Below them, was the Banished One still watching and listening and laughing? Lanius didn't know. He couldn't tell. He wasn't altogether sure whether Pterocles, for all his skill, could tell, either. That being so, he knew he wouldn't trust Otus' cure any time soon.

Grus read the letter from the south with a satisfaction he could hardly disguise. "You know what this says?" he asked the courier.

"Yes, Your Majesty," the man answered. "I had to read it, in case it came to grief while I traveled."

"Good." Grus nodded. "Now—do you know anything more than what's written here?"

"I'm sorry, Your Majesty, but I don't," the courier said. "I've never been down near the Stura. I only brought this the last thirty miles."

"All right." Grus did his best to hide his disappointment. "The news in here"—he tapped the parchment—"is plain enough, anyhow."

He dismissed the courier and summoned General Hirundo. When Hirundo walked into the audience chamber, he looked grumpy. "Did it have to be right now, Your Majesty?" He sounded grumpy, too. "You spoiled what might have been a tender moment with a maidservant. *She* was certainly tender, and I didn't have to do much more to get her to say yes."

"This is more important than fooling around with a woman," Grus declared.

"Yes, Your Majesty." Hirundo's words were perfectly obedient. Only a raised eyebrow reminded Grus of Alauda and all the other women the general might not happen to know about.

Grus felt himself redden. He passed Hirundo the letter that had just come up from the south. "Here," he said. "See for yourself."

Hirundo started the letter with the same perfect but sarcastic obedience he'd used to answer the king. He didn't get very far, though, before the sarcasm disappeared. "Well, well," he said when he was through. "You were right. Every once in a while, the gods do answer a prayer, don't they?"

"I was thinking something along those very same lines, as a matter of fact," Grus replied. "We couldn't have asked King Olor for anything much nicer than a real civil war between Sanjar and Korkut."

The general tapped the letter with his index finger. "Sounds like they're going at it hammer and tongs, too."

"Who do you suppose will win?" Grus asked.

"Beats me," Hirundo said cheerfully. "Let's sit back and drink some wine and watch and find out."

"I don't intend to do anything else," Grus said. "I hope they spend the next five years smashing away at each other, and that all the other Menteshe jump into the fight and jump on each other, too. That way, with a little luck, they'll stay too busy to bother Avornis. And after what they did to us this past year, we can use the time to heal."

"If I could tell you you were wrong, that would mean we were stronger than we really are," Hirundo said.

"We'll have to strengthen the river-galley fleet on the Stura," Grus said. "I was going to do that anyway, but now it's especially important. I don't want the Menteshe getting distracted from their own fight to go after us."

Hirundo gave him a brisk nod. "Makes sense. You do most of the time, Your Majesty." He paused, then added, "So does Lanius, as a matter of fact."

"Well, so he does," Grus admitted, a little uncomfortably. The more sense Lanius showed, the more worrisome he became. He also became more valuable to the kingdom; Grus consoled himself with that.

"With the Menteshe busy playing games among themselves, what do you aim to do about the Chernagors?" Hirundo asked.

"You're thinking along with me. Either that means you make sense, too, or else we're both crazy the same way," the king said. Hirundo laughed. So did Grus, although he hadn't been kidding, or at least not very much. He went on, "If Korkut and Sanjar are still bashing each other over the head come spring, I do aim to go north. We'll never have a better chance to take Nishevatz without distractions from the south—or from the Banished One."

"You'll make Prince Vsevolod happy," the general observed.

"I know." Grus heaved a sigh. "I suppose I'll have to do it anyhow." Again, Hirundo laughed. Again, so did Grus. Again, though, he hadn't been kidding, or at least not very much.

Lanius was pleased with himself as he walked back toward the royal bedchamber. He'd had a good day in the archives, coming up with a map of Nishevatz as it had been when it was the Avornan city of Medeon. Vsevolod, no doubt, would laugh at the map and go on about how much things had changed. But no one had been able to get Vsevolod to sit down and draw his own map of Nishevatz. Even old clues were better than no clues at all.

He opened the door. Sosia was standing by the bed, about fifteen feet away. "Hello, sweetheart," he said, smiling.

Instead of smiling back, she picked up a cup and flung it at him. "Sweetheart!" she screeched. The cup smashed against the wall, six inches to the left of his head. A sharp shard scored his cheek.

"What the—?" Lanius yelped.

Sosia grabbed another cup. She let fly again. This one smacked against the door, about six inches to the right of Lanius' head. "Zenaida!" Sosia shouted. She had one more cup handy. She threw it without a moment's hesitation.

This one was aimed dead center. But Lanius ducked.

Now he knew what the trouble was. "Stop that!" he said, straightening up. He hoped Sosia would. She was, after all, out of cups. But the brass tray on which they'd stood remained handy. A moment later, it clanged off the wall. She didn't aim well. "*Stop* that!" Lanius said again.

"I told you to stop that after Cristata, and see how you listened to me," Sosia retorted. Now the closest available thing to throw was a table. Sosia looked tempted, but she didn't try it. She said, "Why did I ever let you touch me?"

"Because we're married?" Lanius suggested.

"That hasn't made any difference to you. Why should it make any to me?" Sosia said. "I thought you weren't going to wander around like a dog in heat anymore, and—"

"This was different," Lanius said. "It wasn't like what it was with Cristata."

"Oh? How was it different?" his wife inquired acidly. "Did you find a posture you hadn't used before?"

Lanius' ears heated. "No," he said, which happened to be the truth, but which wasn't the part of the truth he wanted to get across. "I meant, I didn't fall in love with Zenaida, or anything like that."

Sosia stared at him across the gulf separating men and women. "Queen Quelea's mercy!" she exclaimed. "Then why did you bother?"

"Why did I bother?" Lanius stared back; the gulf was as wide from his side as from hers. "Because . . ." *Because it's fun,* came to mind. So did, *Because I could.* Even from across the gulf, he could see neither of those would strike her as a good enough explanation. "Just because," he said.

His wife rolled her eyes. "Men," she said in tones that wished half the human race would tumble into the chasm separating the sexes and never be seen again. "And my own father is the same way."

"Yes, he is a man," Lanius said, although he knew that wasn't what Sosia had meant. He also knew, or at least had strong suspicions, that Grus had found company for himself while campaigning in the south. He didn't say anything about that. If Sosia or Estrilda found out about it, he didn't want them finding out from him. He had to get along with his father-in-law, and didn't want the other king to think he'd told tales out of school.

But Sosia only snapped, "Don't you play the fool with me. You're a lot of different things, and I'm not happy with any of them, but you're not stupid, and you don't do a good job of acting stupid. You know what I meant. You both lie down with sluts whenever you find the chance."

Lanius stirred at that. He didn't think of Cristata as a slut, or Zenaida. He also didn't think of Alca the witch as one, and he was sure Grus didn't, either. If you lay down with a woman who would lie down with anyone, what made you special? The other side of that coin was, if you lay down with any woman yourself, what would make you special and worth lying down with to some other woman? To that side of the coin, Lanius remained blind.

"I'm sorry," he said, later than he should have.

It might not have done him any good even if he'd said it right away. "You've told me that before," Sosia answered. "You're sorry I found out. You're not sorry you did it. And I thought I could count on Zenaida!" She didn't say anything about counting on Lanius. That stung.

"I *am* sorry," the king said, and more or less meant it. "I didn't want to hurt you." He did mean that.

"You didn't want to get caught," Sosia said. "But how did you think you wouldn't? Everybody knows everything that happens in the palace, and everybody usually knows it in a hurry, too."

"I'm sorry," Lanius said for the third time. If he kept saying it, maybe she'd believe him sooner or later.

Or, then again, maybe she wouldn't. She said, "Are you sorry enough to promise me you'll never do it again?"

"With Zenaida? Yes, by the gods, I promise you that," Lanius said at once. He'd begun to tire of the serving girl anyhow.

"Oh, I've taken care of Zenaida. She's not in the palace anymore," Sosia said. Lanius wondered if she'd sent Zenaida to the Maze, as he'd threatened to. He didn't think she meant the maidservant was no longer among the living anymore. He hoped it didn't; his quarrel with her hadn't been anywhere near bad enough for him to want her dead. Meanwhile, though, his wife went on, "That wasn't what I meant. I meant, you'll never run around again with *anyone* else. Promise me that."

Had he been Grus, he would have promised right away, knowing that his promise didn't mean anything if he saw another pretty face. Lanius almost made the same sort of promise himself. He almost did, but a sort of stubborn honesty made him hesitate. He said, "How can anyone know the future?"

Sosia looked at him as though she'd found him smeared on the bottom of her shoe. "Do you know what your future will be like if you fool around with another slutty little maidservant?" she asked.

"Nasty," Lanius answered. He had no doubt Sosia could make that kind of future very nasty indeed. Of course, if life with the queen turned nasty, didn't the king have all the more reason to look for consolation with someone else? So it seemed to Lanius. Somehow, he didn't think Sosia would agree.

She said, "It's not as though I haven't given you whatever you've wanted from me. When we *are* together, you've tried to please me. I know that. And you can't say I haven't done the same for you."

"You're trying to shame me," Lanius muttered, for she was telling the truth. She wasn't the lover he would have picked for himself, but the King of Avornis didn't always have the luxury of such choices. She did everything she knew how to do, everything he'd taught her to do.

And he still looked at, still looked for, other women every now and again. He didn't know why, except for variety's sake. He did know he was far from the only man who did. He also knew some women acted the same way.

He knew one more thing, too—he was glad Sosia wasn't one of those women (or, if she was, that no one had caught her at it). If she were, he would have been even more upset with her than she was with him now. He was sure he would have.

With a sigh, he said, "I'll try, Sosia."

How would she take that? She didn't seem to know how to take it for a little while. Then, slowly, her face cleared. "That's as much as I'm going to get from you, isn't it?" she said. "Maybe you even mean it."

"I do," he said, wondering if he did.

"You'll try," she said bitterly. "You'll try, and every so often you'll do what you please anyway. And you'll be sorry afterwards. You're always sorry afterwards, when it doesn't do anybody any good. What should I do the next time you're sorry afterwards? Practice my aim so I hit you with the first cup?"

Lanius' ears burned. He looked at the broken crockery by his feet. Whether or not Sosia had hit him with a cup, her words had struck dead center. She saw what lay ahead the same way as he did. If he admitted as much, he delivered himself into her hands.

Instead of admitting it, he said, "I am sorry. I will try." His wife nodded, as though she believed him.

CHAPTER TWENTY-ONE

In the years since Grus first met Prince Vsevolod, the exiled lord of Nishevatz's beard had grown whiter. His craggy features, always wrinkled, were now gullied like steep, bare country after hard rain. And his hands put the King of Avornis more in mind of tree roots than ever.

The one thing about Vsevolod that had not changed was the fire in his eyes. As winter reluctantly gave way to spring, the Prince of Nishevatz came up to Grus and said, "You get rid of Vasilko, yes?"

Grus had his problems with Ortalis. Set against Vsevolod's problems with *his* son, they hardly seemed worth noticing. Ortalis, after all, had never tried to usurp the Avornan throne. Vasilko had not only tried to steal Nishevatz from Vsevolod, he'd succeeded. Grus replied, "We will go north this spring, Your Highness, yes."

"This is good. This is very good. I go back to my own city. I rule in my own city. I do not have to live on charity of strangers, on charity of foreigners," Vsevolod said.

"We have not kept you here out of charity, Your Highness," Grus said.

"No. This is true. Charity is to help someone out of goodness of your heart," Vsevolod said. "You do not do this. You help me because of what I can do for you." He strode away, his back still straight—if stiff—despite his years. Grus stared after him, feeling obscurely punctured.

Regardless of his reasons for harboring Vsevolod in the city of Avornis, Grus did want to return him to the throne of Nishevatz. He assembled men and horses and supplies outside the city of Avornis, ready to move as soon as the weather turned mild and the roads dried out.

With extra men in the south in case the Menteshe decided to fight Avornis instead of among themselves, with sailors filling the growing fleet of Chernagor-style seagoing ships protecting the kingdom's east coast, Grus' army was smaller than it had been on either of his two earlier moves up into the Chernagor country. That didn't unduly worry him, for he thought it would be big enough.

Lanius and Sosia came out from the city to wish him good fortune. His son-in-law and daughter were wary around each other. He understood why. Their quarrels through the winter had hardly stayed secret. Grus wished he were in a position to give Lanius good advice. With one of his own partners waiting in a provincial town to bear his bastard, he wasn't, and he knew it.

To his surprise, Ortalis and Limosa also came out to wish the army luck. Grus couldn't remember the last time his legitimate son had cared enough to bid him farewell. Maybe it had been Limosa's idea. In spite of her irregular marriage to Ortalis, she seemed to be making him a good wife.

Or maybe Ortalis was just interested in looking at men who hunted other men for a living. Grus had sometimes wondered if his son would try to turn into a soldier. That would have given Ortalis a way to let out his thirst for blood without having other people give him strange looks. But Ortalis had never shown any interest in going to war. Of course, in war the people you hunted also hunted you. That might have dampened his enthusiasm for soldiering.

Now he said, "Good fortune go with you, Father."

"My thanks." Not even Grus could find anything wrong with that.

"Good fortune go with you indeed," Lanius said. "May you return Vsevolod to his throne." He looked around to make sure the Chernagor was nowhere nearby, then quietly added, "May you get Vsevolod out of our hair for good."

"May it be so." Grus and Lanius shared a smile. No denying the Prince of Nishevatz had made a difficult guest in the city of Avornis.

Lanius said, "I will also pray for peace inside the kingdom."

"Good. You do that," Grus said. He glanced toward the other King of Avornis. Lanius wasn't looking south toward the Stura. He wasn't looking east toward the coast. He was looking straight at Sosia. Grus nodded to himself. He'd thought Lanius meant that kind of peace, not the sort that came with armies staying home.

"I know you'll win, Your Majesty," Limosa said. "Time is on your side, after all."

Was it? Grus had his doubts. She might as well have said, *Third time's the charm*—not that it had been. Vasilko had had plenty of time to consolidate himself in Nishevatz. How many people there still longed for Vsevolod's return? How many people who had longed for Vsevolod's return had Vasilko disposed of? A lot of them—Grus was sure of that. It wouldn't make reconquering the Chernagor town any easier.

He shrugged. Nothing he could do about it. He said, "If the gods are kind, we'll come back with victory—and without Vsevolod."

"That would be perfect," Lanius said. Ortalis didn't seem so concerned—but then, he'd paid as little attention to Vsevolod as he had to anything else connected to actually ruling Avornis.

Grus turned away from his family and back toward the army. "Let's move!" he called. A trumpeter echoed his command. The horsemen who'd go out ahead of the rest of the force as scouts urged their mounts into motion. One piece at a time, the remainder of the army followed.

"I'm off," Grus said when he had to ride or fall out of place. As he used knees and the reins to get his horse moving, Lanius and Sosia and Ortalis and Limosa all waved. He waved back. Then, for the fourth time, he set out for the land of the Chernagors.

Twice, he'd failed to take Nishevatz. Once, he hadn't even gotten up into the Chernagor country before bad news forced him to turn away. Oddly, those disasters heartened him instead of leaving him discouraged. He'd seen every sort of misfortune when he went north. Didn't that mean he was due for good luck sometime soon?

He hoped it did. Maybe it meant he'd see no good luck against the Chernagors no matter what happened. He refused to believe that. If he did believe it, he wouldn't have sent forth this army. He didn't think he would have, anyhow.

Not far away, Prince Vsevolod rode toward his homeland. Like the rest of the beasts in the army, the Prince of Nishevatz's horse went at a walk. Vsevolod had to know he couldn't take back Nishevatz all by himself. Even so, he gave the impression of heading north at a headlong gallop. That impression might have been—was—false, but seemed real all the same.

Hirundo, by contrast, might have been sauntering along. It wasn't that he didn't want to get to Nishevatz. Grus knew he did. But he knew he wouldn't get there right away, and showed he knew it, too. Grus preferred his attitude. It struck him as being more sensible than Vsevolod's.

And what about me? the king asked himself. He answered with a shrug. With the Menteshe distracted down in the south, he thought he had a better chance on this campaign than on the ones of years gone by—if the nomads were distracted, the Banished One should be distracted, too. Grus hoped to bridge the gap between *should be* and *is*. If he did, he might win. If not, he'd come home disappointed again—if he came home at all.

Lanius wondered how long he would have to wait this time for Sosia to let him back into her bed. He was curious and interested for more than one reason. First and . . . most urgent was the interest any man would have shown about that particular question.

A more abstract curiosity, though, accompanied that . . . urgent interest. Sosia had to make some careful calculations of her own. If she showed she warmed to him too soon, what would he think? Why, that he could enjoy himself with a serving girl whenever he felt like it. He'd make Sosia angry for a little while, but she'd soon forgive and forget.

But if she really was furious—or wanted him to believe she was—and kept herself to herself for a long time, what would spring from that? He *was* a man, after all, with a man's desires. Wouldn't he go looking for another serving girl and slake those desires with her? She wouldn't want him doing that.

Yes, a nice calculation.

Lanius tried to think along with his wife. She'd known him for a long time now. She would know how much he heated through each day of denial. He had a pretty good notion of when he would get fed up and start smiling at the prettier maidservants if Sosia hadn't softened by then.

Two days before the time when he figured his impatience would get the better of his good sense, Sosia sighed and said, "I can't make you change very much, can I?"

"I wouldn't think so," Lanius answered seriously. "One person usually can't change another. By the gods, not many people can change themselves."

His wife studied him. "You know what I'm talking about, don't you?"

"I have some idea." His voice was dry.

"Good." The queen sounded relieved. "I wasn't sure. Sometimes you see only the questions, not what's behind them."

That was true enough. Lanius said, "I'm glad you're not angry at me anymore," then quickly amended that to, "Not *too* angry at me, I mean."

"Not *too* angry is right," Sosia said, "and even that's just barely right. Still, you're what I've got. I can either make the best of it or else find we're in even more trouble."

Her thinking did mirror his. He said, "I'll do my best to make you happy."

"I know," Sosia answered. "You always do when you're with me. It's one of the reasons I can stand having you touch me again after—after everything you've done." She looked at him with more defiance than desire on her face. "Shall we?"

"All right." Lanius was more worried than he wanted her to know. If she didn't want him to please her, then he wouldn't, no matter what he did. He'd seen that with her and with other women. Men were simpler there. If it felt good, they didn't worry about much else. *We're lucky,* Lanius thought; he didn't wonder if it was good luck or bad.

Physical acts counted, too. He worked especially hard to give Sosia pleasure when they lay down together. And, to his relief, he succeeded. She murmured something wordless, then stroked the back of his head. "You," she said, and her voice sounded as much accusing as anything else.

"At your service," he said. "And now—" He poised himself above her. He'd wondered if she would just lie there when they joined, to punish him for making love with Zenaida. But she didn't. Even as his own pleasure built, he nodded in respect. Sosia didn't stint. She deserved credit for that.

Afterward, he kissed the side of her neck. She wiggled; that was a ticklish spot for her. "You," she said again, even more accusingly than before.

"Yes, me," Lanius said. "You . . . had better believe it." He'd almost said, *You were expecting someone else?* Considering that he'd enjoyed himself with someone else, she might have answered, *What if I was?* Better not to travel some roads than to see where they led.

"When we started," Sosia said, "I wasn't sure I really wanted you touching me, kissing me, kissing me *there,* at all. But you know what you're doing." In the dark stillness of the bedchamber, her eyes were enormous. "Do you study that along with everything else?"

"Not much in the archives about it," Lanius said. A man studied such things whenever he made love with a woman, but that wasn't what Sosia had meant. He didn't think many men realized that was what they were doing. *The more fools they,* he thought.

"Archives," Sosia muttered, so maybe she had something else in mind for the source of his research. But she didn't snipe at him. Instead, she asked, "What *am* I going to do with you?"

"Put up with me, I hope," Lanius answered. "I'll try to do the same for you."

"For me? Why do I need putting up with?" But then Sosia shook her head. "Never mind. Don't tell me. I'll try to put up with you, you try to put up with me, and we'll both try to get along. Bargain?"

"Bargain," Lanius said. They clasped hands.

Up ahead of the Avornan army, Chernagor cavalry skirmished with King Grus' scouts. More Chernagor horsemen galloped off toward the north. Grus cursed, more in resignation than anything else. "So much for surprise," he said.

"Did you really think we'd keep it?" Hirundo asked. "We can't just appear out of nowhere, like ghosts in a story to frighten children."

"Maybe not, but we'd win a lot of battles if we could," Grus said.

He wondered whether the men of Nishevatz would try to hold Varazdin against him, but his men found the fortress not only abandoned but destroyed, the keep wrecked and one of the outer walls pulled down. Maybe they thought he could quickly overcome whatever garrison they put into the place, or maybe they were saving everything they had to defend the walls of their city-state.

Either way, Grus thought they were making a mistake. Had he been in charge of Nishevatz, he would have defended the place as far forward as he could. If Vasilko was willing to let him get close, he would say thank you and do his best to take advantage of that. He pressed on into the land of the Chernagors.

Three days later, one of his scouts came riding back to the main body of the army, calling, "The sea! The sea!" The man pointed north.

Grus soon rode up over a low rise and spied the sea for himself. As always, he was struck by how different it was from the Azanian Sea on the east coast of Avornis. The waters there were blue and warm and inviting, the beaches made from golden sand. The beaches here were mud flats. The sea was greenish gray, a color that didn't seem quite healthy to him. The sky was gray, too, the gray of newly sheared wool before it was washed. Wisps of mist kept the king from getting as good a view of either sea or sky as he would have wanted.

"No wonder the Chernagors like to turn pirate," Hirundo said, gazing out at the bleak landscape. "If I lived in country like this, I'd do my best to get away from it, too."

Sandpipers scurried along at the border between sea and land, poking their beaks into the mud to look for whatever little creatures they hunted. Gulls mewed overhead, soaring along on narrow pointed wings. The air smelled of moisture and salt and seaweed and faintly nasty things Grus couldn't quite name.

Prince Vsevolod rode up to him. The Chernagor's eyes shone, though his breath smoked each time he exhaled. "Is wonderful country, yes?" he boomed.

"I'm glad it pleases you, Your Highness," Grus answered, as diplomatically as he could.

"Wonderful country," Vsevolod repeated. "Not too hot like Avornis, with sweat all time in summer. Not cold all through winter, either. Just right."

"To each his own," Grus said.

"To each his own, yes." Vsevolod seemed to cherish the cliché. "And Nishevatz—Nishevatz is my own."

"May we soon set you back on the throne there, then," Grus said, thinking, *And if I never see you again, that will not disappoint you, and it will not disappoint me, either.*

They'd come to the sea east of the town, and moved toward it until they made camp for the night. Grus took care to post sentries well out from the camp, to bring back warning if the Chernagors tried to strike. And, remembering the disaster that had almost befallen his army while fighting the Menteshe, he summoned Pterocles. "Be sure you drink your fill of wine this evening," he told the wizard. "If you have to ease yourself, you'll beat any sleep spell the enemy sends your way."

Pterocles smiled. "I will set up sorcerous wards, too, Your Majesty," he replied. "They will not take me by surprise twice the same way."

"Good." Grus nodded. "Do you have any idea what new surprises they'll try to use?"

"If I did, they wouldn't be surprises, would they?" Pterocles held the cheerful expression.

"Do you sense the Banished One?" Grus asked.

Now the wizard's smile blew out like a candle flame. "So far, I have not, except in a general way. This is a land where he has an interest, but it is not a land where he is concentrating all his attention, the way he did when he laid me low."

"He has other things on his mind right now," Grus said, and Pterocles nodded. The king went on, "As long as Sanjar and Korkut keep whacking away at each other, the Banished One ought to worry most about the south." Pterocles nodded again. Grus finished, "In that case, I hope they fight each other for the next ten years."

"That would be nice," Pterocles agreed, and some of his smile came back.

The army went on toward Nishevatz the next morning. Offshore, far out of bowshot or even catapult range, tall-masted Chernagor ships sailed along, keeping an eye on the Avornans. Grus wished he had tall ships of his own in these waters; the little flotilla Lanius sent out had come back to Avornis during the winter, having lost one ship, sunk several, and earned what the Chernagors of Durdevatz said would be their undying gratitude. Every so often here, one of these ships would sail off to Nishevatz, presumably to report on whatever its crew had seen. The rest kept on shadowing Grus' army.

After a while, he got fed up with that and called for Pterocles again. "You made a magic against the Chernagor transports," he said. "Can you use the same spell against these snoops?"

The wizard eyed the clouds and swirling mist overhead. He spread his hands in apology—or started to. His mule chose that moment to misstep, and he had to make a hasty grab for the reins. *Some people really do ride worse than I do,* Grus thought, amused. Pterocles said, "Your Majesty, I can try that spell. But it works best with real sunshine to power it. It may well fail." He rode on for half a minute or so before something else occurred to him. "The Chernagors may have worked out a counterspell by now, too. These things do happen. Spells are often best the first time you use them, because then you catch the other fellow by surprise."

"I see." Trouble was, Grus did; what Pterocles said made altogether too much sense. Now the king rode thoughtfully for a little while before saying, "Well, when you see the chance, take it."

"I will, Your Majesty," Pterocles said.

As though to mock Grus' hopes, a fine drizzle began sifting down out of the sky. Grumpily, he put on a broad-brimmed felt hat to keep the water off his face and to keep it from trickling down the back of his neck. "Remind the men to grease their mail well tonight," he called to Hirundo. "Otherwise, it will rust."

"I'll take care of it," Hirundo promised.

But the drizzle also made it harder for the Chernagors aboard ship to watch the Avornan army. They had to come closer and closer to the shore, until finally they were almost within bowshot. Curses wafted across the water when one of them ran aground. Grus cursed, too, for he couldn't do anything about it. There was no point to assembling his catapults to pound the ships when they would be as useless with wet skeins of hair as a bow with a wet string.

Hirundo shared his frustration, but said, "They're still in trouble out there, whether we put them in trouble or not."

"I suppose so," Grus said. "I wish we could take better advantage of it, though." He shrugged ruefully. "I wish for all sorts of things I won't get. Who doesn't?"

"Best way to take advantage is to take Nishevatz," Vsevolod said. "When we take Nishevatz, we punish all traitors. Oh, yes." He rubbed his hands together in anticipation of doing just that.

Grus wondered how much like Vsevolod his son Vasilko was. He wouldn't have been surprised if Vasilko took after his father a great deal indeed. And if Vsevolod had followed the Banished One, would Vasilko have fled to the city of Avornis and bowed down to Olor and Quelea and the rest of the gods in the heavens? Grus wouldn't have been surprised there, either. Whatever one of them chose, the other seemed to want the opposite.

That didn't mean Vsevolod was wrong here. "We'll do our best, Your Highness," Grus said. "Then you should do your best."

"Oh, I will," Vsevolod said. "I will." His tone suggested that what he meant by *best* was likely to be different from what Grus meant by the word. Whether what he thought best for him would also prove best for Nishevatz was liable to be an . . . interesting question.

I'll worry about that later, Grus told himself. *One thing at a time. Getting Vasilko out of Nishevatz, getting the Banished One's influence out of Nishevatz—that comes first. Everything else can wait. If Vsevolod turns out to be intolerable, maybe I'll be able to do something about it.*

He rode on toward Nishevatz for a while. Then something else occurred to him. If a lot of people in Nishevatz hadn't already decided Vsevolod was intolerable, would they have banded together behind

Vasilko and helped him oust his father? Grus sighed. He looked over to the white-bearded Prince of Nishevatz. The longer he looked, the more he wished he hadn't thought of that.

"Excuse me," Limosa said. Ortalis' wife got up and left the supper table faster than was seemly. When she came back a few minutes later, she looked more than a little green.

"Are you all right?" Lanius asked.

Sosia found a different question. She asked, "Are you going to have a baby?"

Limosa turned from one of them to the other. "Yes, Your Majesty," she told the king. A moment later, she said the same thing to the queen, adding, "Until this"—she gulped—"I managed to keep it a secret. I wanted to see how long I could."

"Well, you did," Lanius said. "Congratulations!" Sosia echoed him. Lanius turned to Ortalis and congratulated him, too. He hoped he didn't sound grudging. Ortalis had behaved . . . pretty well lately.

"I thank you." Grus' legitimate son raised his wine cup. "Here's hoping it's a boy."

For the sake of politeness, Lanius drank to that. So did Sosia. But their eyes met with complete understanding and agreement. They both hoped Limosa had a little girl—had lots of little girls, if she conceived again. Boys would make the succession more complicated. Grus and his family had managed to graft themselves on to the ancient ruling dynasty. That was one thing. Uprooting it altogether—having the crown descend through Ortalis and his line—would be something else again.

Ortalis had never shown any great interest in ruling Avornis. If he had a son, he might change his mind. That would make court intrigue all the more intriguing. Lanius hoped he didn't, but how much was such hope worth?

That evening, Sosia seemed not just willing but actually eager to make love for the first time since she found out about Zenaida. While she and Lanius caressed each other and then joined, he accepted that as good luck. Afterwards, she rolled over and went straight to sleep. The king smiled a little. She was doing what men were supposed to do, and he wasn't.

He lay on his back, looking up at the ceiling. With no lamp burning, it was just part of the darkness. As he hadn't before, he wondered what made Sosia act the way she had. He didn't need to wonder long. What was likelier to drive her into his arms than a threat from outside?

He would rather have believed his own charms had more to do with it. But, since she'd had no trouble resisting those charms before Limosa's news, he couldn't very well do that. Every so often, he wished he were better at fooling himself. This was one of those times.

In the morning, he went to see Otus. Every time he did, the man from south of the Stura seemed more like an ordinary Avornan and less like a thrall. More and more, Lanius believed the guards who surrounded Otus' chamber were unnecessary. He didn't order them away, though. He might have been wrong, and being wrong here could have unfortunate consequences.

"Good morning, Your Majesty," Otus said, and bowed politely. His eyes went to the guards who came in with the king, too. He didn't complain about them. As far as Lanius knew, he never complained. That did set him apart from ordinary Avornans.

"Good morning to you," the king replied. "You speak very well these days. You've learned a lot."

"I like to learn things," Otus said. "I never had the chance before." He paused and shook his head. "I never could before."

That let Lanius ask a question he'd wanted to ask for a long time. "What was it like, being a thrall? Now you have the words to talk about it, which you didn't before."

Otus looked startled, another mark of how far he'd come. "Why, so I do," he said. "It was hard. It was boring. If you had a cow that could talk, it would tell you the same thing, I think. As far as the Menteshe cared, I *was* a cow. Oh, I could do more than a cow. I was smarter than a cow. But they treated me like a beast. I *was* a beast, near enough."

"What made you decide to cross over the Stura, to come into Avornis?" Lanius asked.

"I didn't decide," Otus said at once. He repeated that. "I *didn't* decide. I just did it. It came into my head that I had to, and I went. I left my woman. I left my children. I went." He stopped, biting his lip.

Gently, Lanius asked, "Do you miss your wife?"

"Woman," Otus said again. "We weren't—like people are. I couldn't be with her now. She hasn't . . . changed. It would be like . . . screwing a cow, almost. But if the wizard cured her, then—oh, then!" His face lit up. Plainly, the thought was crossing his mind for the first time. He was becoming a man, beginning to think beyond himself as men could—and did, though not often enough.

Lanius wondered if the female thrall would care for him once she was fully herself. The king didn't say anything about that. Even a man who had been a thrall was entitled to his dreams.

Suddenly, Otus pointed at him. "One of these days, you go south of the river. Avornis goes south of the river."

"Maybe," Lanius answered, embarrassed at being unable to say more. "That's more for King Grus to decide than it is for me. I know he wants to go south of the Stura. I don't know whether he thinks he can."

Otus paid no attention to him. The cured thrall—Lanius had an ever harder time thinking of him as *the possibly cured thrall*—went on, "You *will* go south of the river. You have the wonderful magic that set me free. You can use that magic on the other thralls, on the rest of the thralls. So many men, so many women, made into beasts." He took Lanius' hands in his. "Save them, Your Majesty! You can save them!"

Lanius didn't know what to say to that. What he did finally say was, "I'll try." Otus' face lit up. That only made Lanius turn away so the other man wouldn't see him blush. His words might have sounded like a promise—Otus had taken them for one—but he knew they were anything but. He still lacked the power to make a promise like that. Only Grus had it, and Grus was far off in the north.

Watery sunshine—the only kind the Chernagor country seemed to know—did little to make the walls of Nishevatz seem anything but unlovely. The sunshine did help King Grus spot the town's defenders; it sparkled off swords and spearheads and the tips of arrows and shone from helms and mailshirts. The men who followed Prince Vasilko looked ready to fight, and to fight hard.

Whether they were ready might prove a different question. They hadn't tried to keep the Avornans from shutting them up inside Nishevatz, preferring to stand siege rather than to come forth and challenge their foes. But how much in the way of supplies did they have? Grus dared hope it wasn't so much.

He also dared hope the other Chernagor city-states allied with Nishevatz had no luck shipping grain into the town. So far, they hadn't had the nerve to try. If that wasn't a compliment to Pterocles' sorcery—and a sign they had no counterspell for it—Grus didn't know what would be. The Chernagors presumed the wizard had come north with the Avornan army. That also made them presume he would burn their ships if they tried to feed their allies. Grus hoped they were right. (In fact, he hoped he didn't have to find out. If the other Chernagors didn't try to feed Nishevatz, he wouldn't have to.)

"Do you aim to assault the town?" Hirundo asked after the siege lines on land were as tight as the Avornans could make them.

"Not right away," Grus answered. "They've made us pay every time we did. Or do you think I'm wrong?"

"Not me, Your Majesty," the general said. "I'd rather be at the top of a wall pushing a scaling ladder over than at the bottom trying to get up the ladder before it tips and smashes."

"Yes. If it will." Grus looked out to the farmland that had fed Nishevatz. Now it would have to feed his men instead. Could it? He wouldn't be taking grain from it, not this early in the year—and not much later, either, if it wasn't cultivated in the meanwhile. Livestock was a different story, though. Cows and pigs and sheep—if need be, horses and donkeys—would feed Avornan soldiers well.

After a little thought, Grus nodded to Hirundo. "Fetch me one of Vsevolod's pals," he said.

"I'll get you one," Hirundo said. "I take it you don't want Vsevolod to notice me doing this?"

"How right you are," the king said fervently, and his general chuckled.

Hirundo brought Grus a nobleman named Beloyuz. He was one of the younger men who clung to Vsevolod's cause, which meant his bushy beard was gray rather than white. "What do you wish of me, Your Majesty?" he asked in Avornan better than Prince Vsevolod's.

"I would like you to go up to the walls of Nishevatz, Your Excellency," Grus replied. "I want you to tell the Chernagors in the city that they won't have to go through this siege if they cast out Vasilko and give the throne back to Vsevolod."

Beloyuz plucked at that bushy gray beard. "His Highness should do this," he said, his voice troubled.

"Maybe," Grus said, "but he has enough enemies inside the walls, it would not be safe to have him go up to them." He didn't mention that most of the Chernagors inside Nishevatz had made it plain they preferred Vasilko to Vsevolod.

Beloyuz's eyes said he knew what Grus was thinking. They also said

he was grateful Grus had found a way not to come right out and say it.
He bowed stiffly to the king. "All right, Your Majesty. Let it be as you
say."

With Avornan shieldmen accompanying him forward, Beloyuz approached the walls the next morning. One of the shieldmen carried a
flag of truce, but they all remained very alert. They could not be sure
the Chernagors would honor that flag. Beloyuz began to speak in the
throaty, guttural, consonant-filled Chernagor language. Grus did not
understand it, but he had a good idea of what the noble would be saying.

The defenders did not need to hear much before they made up their
minds. They roared abuse at Beloyuz. Some of them shot arrows despite the flag of truce, but Grus didn't think they were trying to hit the
nobleman or his protectors. Beloyuz took no chances, but hastily re-
treated out of range. Grus didn't see how he could blame him for that.

Vsevolod came over to Grus in high dudgeon, demanding, "Why I
not go to wall?"

"I did not want the folk of Nishevatz to insult you, your Highness,"
Grus replied, which was perhaps a tenth part of the truth.

"I do not worry over insults," Vsevolod said. "I can tell folk of Nishevatz better than Beloyuz can."

That's what I was afraid of, Grus thought. He reminded himself he
had to be tactful when speaking to Vsevolod. He needed to remind
himself, because the temptation to tell the unvarnished truth was very
strong. Choosing his words with care, then, he said, "The people of Nishevatz had heard you before, Your Highness, and did not decide to cast
Vasilko out and bring you back into the city. I thought Beloyuz could
give them a different slant on your virtues." *Such as they are, Your Highness.* The only one Grus could think of offhand was Vsevolod's genuine
and sincere opposition to the Banished One.

With a sniff, Vsevolod drew himself up very straight. "I know my
virtues better than any of my followers."

"Yes, Your Highness." Grus hoped his resignation wasn't too obvious—but if it was, he intended to lose no sleep over it. He said, "No
harm done. Beloyuz didn't persuade them, either, but he got away safe.
Now we'll go on with what we were going to do anyhow. We're going
to take Nishevatz away from Vasilko. That's what we came here for, and
that's what we'll do."

Prince Vsevolod didn't want to let him off the hook. "You say this before," the Chernagor grumbled. "You say before, and then something else happen, and then you change mind."

"I am allowed to defend my own homeland," Grus said mildly. "But, with a better fleet on our east coast to guard against Chernagor pirates and with the Menteshe caught in their own civil war, I don't think we'll have to break things off this time."

"Better not," Vsevolod rumbled in ominous tones. "By gods, better not."

CHAPTER TWENTY-TWO

Standing in his robe of crimson silk behind the magnificent altar of the great cathedral, Arch-Hallow Anser cut a splendid ecclesiastical figure. By his bearing and appearance, Lanius would readily have believed him the holiest man in all of Avornis. And then King Grus' bastard waved and called, "Hang on for a minute, Your Majesty, and I'll change into hunting togs."

"No hurry," Lanius answered. He wished Anser hadn't bounded away from the altar with such obvious eagerness. The arch-hallow might seem like a very holy man, but he didn't like playing the part.

When he returned, he looked more like a poacher than a prelate. He wore a disreputable hat, a leather jerkin over a linen tunic, and baggy wool trousers tucked into suede boots that rose almost to his knees. He also wore an enormous smile. He put on the crimson robe because his father told him to. Hunting togs were different. Lanius, on the other hand, felt as though he were in costume for a foolish show, although he looked much less raffish than Anser.

"Let's see what we can bag, eh?" he said. "Pity Prince Ortalis couldn't come with us today."

"Why? Did you—?" Lanius broke off, shaking his head. "Never mind. Forget I said that. Forget I even started to say that."

"I'd probably better." Anser made a face. He said, "You'll have a horse outside?"

"Oh, yes." The king nodded. "I'm not going to walk to the woods— I'll tell you that."

"Let's go, then."

A couple of hours later, Lanius and the arch-hallow dismounted under the trees. Grooms took charge of the horses. The king, the arch-hallow, and their beaters and guards walked into the woods. "Maybe you'll hit something this time, Your Majesty," Anser said. "You never can tell."

"No, you never can," Lanius agreed in a hollow voice. Hitting a stag with an arrow remained about the last thing he wanted to do.

Birds chirped overhead. Looking up, the king wondered what kind they were. Being able to tell one bird from another when neither was a pigeon or a sparrow would be interesting, but he hadn't gotten good at it yet. Learning to recognize them by their looks and by their songs necessarily involved staying out in the woods until he could. That made it more trouble than it was worth to him.

"Are you sure you want me to take the first shot, Your Majesty?" Anser said. "It's very kind, but you don't need to give me the honor."

"My pleasure," Lanius said, which was absolutely true. He went on, "Besides, you're the one who's *liable* to hit something. If I do, it'll just be by accident, and we both know it."

The beaters fanned out into the woods. Anser's men vanished silently among the trees. Lanius' guards were noisy enough to make the arch-hallow's followers smile. But they did no more than smile. The two groups had tangled after earlier hunts. Lanius' guards came out on top in tavern brawls.

Anser chose a spot on the edge of a clearing. Before long, a stag bounded out into the open space. The arch-hallow let fly. He cursed more or less good-naturedly when his arrow hissed past the deer's head. The stag sprang away.

"Well, you won't do worse than I did, anyhow," Anser said to Lanius.

"No," the king agreed. He'd never had the nerve to tell Anser he always shot to miss. He enjoyed eating venison, but not enough to enjoy killing animals himself so he could have it. He wouldn't have wanted to be a butcher, either. He recognized the inconsistency without worrying about reconciling it.

Half an hour passed with no new game in the clearing. Lanius, who didn't mind, said nothing. Anser, who did, grumbled. Then another stag, smaller and less splendid than the first, trotted out into the open space. It stopped not fifteen yards in front of Lanius and Anser.

"Your shot, Your Majesty," Anser whispered.

Awkwardly, with unpracticed fingers, Lanius fit an arrow to the bowstring. Here was his dilemma, big as life, for he knew he could hit the stag if he but shot straight. Wouldn't it have an easier death if he shot it than if it died under the ripping fangs of wolves or from some slow, cruel disease?

He drew the bow, let fly . . . and the arrow zoomed high, well over the stag's back. The animal fled.

"Oh . . . too bad, Your Majesty," Anser said, doing his good-natured best not to show how annoyed he was.

"I told you before—I'm hopeless," Lanius answered. As a matter of fact, he was rather proud of himself.

Out on the Northern Sea, a ship made for Nishevatz, its great spread of sail shining white in the spring sun. On the shore, a tiny ship made from a scrap of wood, a twig, and a rag bobbed in a bowl of seawater. The spring sun shone on it, too. Hundreds of defenders on the walls of Nishevatz anxiously eyed the real ship. King Grus and Pterocles paid more attention to the toy in the bowl.

"Whenever you're ready," the king said.

"Now is as good a time as any," Pterocles replied. He held his curved bit of crystal above the toy ship. A brilliant spot of light appeared on the toy. Grus wondered how the crystal did that. He had ever since he first saw this sorcery. Now was *not* the time, though, to ask for an explanation.

Pterocles began a spell—a chant mixed with passes that pointed from the little ship in the bowl to the big one on the sea. On and on he went, until smoke began to rise from the toy ship. More and more smoke came from it, and then it burst into flame. Pterocles cried out commandingly and pointed once more to the tall-masted ship on the Northern Sea.

Grus' eye went that way, too. The ship still lay some distance offshore, but Grus could spot the smoke rising from it. Before long, that smoke turned to flickering red-yellow flame, too. "Well done!" he exclaimed.

A loud groan rose from the walls of Nishevatz. The defenders must have hoped the supply ship would be able to get through, even though they had found no counterspell against Pterocles' charm. If it had, the siege would have become much more difficult. As things were, the Avornans held on to the advantage.

A longtime sailor himself, Grus knew a certain amount of sympathy for the Chernagors aboard that burning ship. Nothing afloat could be a worse horror than fire. That had to be doubly true on the long seagoing voyages the northern men, formidable traders and formidable pirates, often undertook. And these flames, springing from magic as they did, would be all the harder to fight.

The sailors soon gave up trying to fight them. Instead, they went over the side and made for Nishevatz in boats while the ship burned. The boats could not hold all the men. Maybe more clung to lines trailing behind them. Grus hoped so. He wanted to stop the grain the ship carried, but had nothing special against the sailors.

Another Chernagor ship had come up over the horizon while Pterocles was casting his spell. When smoke and flame burst from the vessel nearing Nishevatz, the other ship hastily put about and sailed away from the besieged city-state. Pointing to it, Pterocles asked, "Do you want me to see if I can set that one afire, too, Your Majesty?"

"No," Grus said. The wizard looked surprised. The king explained, "Let that crew go. They'll spread the word that our magic still works. That will make the rest of the Chernagors not want to come to Nishevatz. I hope it will, anyhow."

"Ah." Pterocles nodded. "Yes, now that you point it out to me, I can see how that might be so. If the other ship had kept coming . . ."

Grus nodded, too. "That's right. If it had kept coming, I would have told you to do your best to sink it. This way, though, better not. Bad news isn't bad news unless someone's left to bring it."

"I'll be ready in case the Chernagors try again," the wizard said. "If they come at night, I can use real fire to kindle my symbolic ships. The spell isn't as elegant that way, but it should still work. It did the last time."

"Working is all I worry about," Grus said. "I know you sorcerers sweat for elegance, but it doesn't matter a bit to me."

"It should," Pterocles said. "The more elegant a spell is, the harder the time wizards on the other side have of picking it to pieces."

"Really? I didn't know that," Grus admitted. "Still, though, the Chernagor wizards haven't had any luck trying to cope with this spell. Doesn't that mean they won't be able to no matter what?"

"I wish it did." Pterocles' smile was distinctly weary. "All it really means, though, is that they haven't figured out how yet. They may work out a counterspell tomorrow. If they do"—he shrugged—"then that means I have to come up with something new. And it means Nishevatz gets fed."

He was frank. He was, perhaps, more frank than Grus would have liked. After a moment's thought, the king shook his head. Pterocles had told him what he needed to know. "Thank you," Grus said. "If they do find a counterspell, I know you'll do your best to get around it." *You'd better do your best. Otherwise, we'll have to try storming the place, and I don't know if we can. I don't want to have to find out, either.*

That evening, Prince Vsevolod came up to him and asked him to do exactly that. "Sooner we are in Nishevatz, sooner we punish Vasilko," Vsevolod boomed.

"Well, yes, Your Highness, if we *get* into Nishevatz," Grus said. "If the men on the walls throw us back, I don't know if we'll be able to go on with the siege afterwards. That would depend on how bad they hurt us."

"You do not want to fight," Vsevolod said in accusing tones.

"I want to win," Grus said. "If I can win without throwing away a lot of my men, I want that most of all."

For all Prince Vsevolod followed that, the king might as well have spoken in the language of the Menteshe. Vsevolod said, "You do not want to fight," again. Then he turned his back and stalked away without giving Grus a chance to reply.

Grus was tempted—sorely tempted—to fling Vsevolod into chains for the insult. With a mournful sigh, he decided he couldn't. It was too likely to cause trouble not only with the Chernagors who'd accompanied the prince to Nishevatz but also with those inside the city. Grus let out a grunt also redolent of regret. No matter what his good sense said, the temptation lingered.

Grus would never have made a poet or a historian, but he did get the essential facts where they belonged. Lanius had come to rely on that. So far, everything seemed to be going as the other king hoped. Experience had taught Lanius not to get too excited about such things. The end of the campaign—if it didn't have to break off in the middle—would be the place to judge.

Other reports came up from the south—reports of the fighting between Sanjar and Korkut. Lanius enjoyed every word of those. Each account of another bloody battle between Prince Ulash's unloving sons made his smile wider. The more the Menteshe hurt one another, the harder the time they would have hurting Avornis.

Before the spring was very old, other news came up from the south, news that the Menteshe to the east and west of what had been Ulash's realm were sweeping in to seize what they could from it. In the same way, ravens and vultures that would never harm a live bear snatched fragments from its carcass once the beast was dead. Again, the more those Menteshe stole, the happier Lanius got.

And what made him more cheerful yet was hearing no news at all from the east. News from that direction, news from the shore of the Azanian Sea, was unlikely to be good. If the Chernagors sent a fleet to harry the coast, cries for help would fly back to the city of Avornis. So far . . . none.

That left Lanius in an unusually good mood. Even if Sosia had had nothing to do with causing it, she responded to it, and seemed to forgive him for amusing himself with Zenaida. He gratefully accepted that.

But the king's exuberance also made the serving women pay more attention to him than they did when he was his usual sobersided self. "You're so—bouncy, Your Majesty!" exclaimed a plump but pretty maidservant named Flammea.

No one in all of Lanius' life up until that moment had ever called him bouncy—or anything like bouncy. He managed a smile that, if not bouncy, might at least be taken as friendly. Flammea smiled back. Lanius patted her in an experimental way. If she'd ignored him and gone about her business, he would have shrugged and forgotten about her. Instead, she giggled. He took that as a promising sign.

One thing led to another—led quite quickly to another, as a matter of fact. "Oh, Your Majesty!" Flammea gasped, an oddly formal salute at that particular moment. Lanius was too busy to be much inclined to literary criticism.

Afterwards, the maidservant looked smug. Did that mean she was going to brag to all her friends? If she did, she would be sorry. Of course, if she did, Sosia would find out, and then Lanius would be sorry, too.

"Don't worry, Your Majesty," she said as she got back into her clothes. "I don't blab."

"Well, good." Lanius hoped she meant it. If she didn't, he—and Sosia, too—would make her regret it.

Flammea slipped out of the little storeroom where they'd gone. A minute or so later, so did Lanius. Another serving woman—a gray-haired, severely plain serving woman—was coming up the hallway when he did. She gave him a curious look, or possibly a dubious look. He nodded back, as imperturbably as he could, and went on his way. Behind him, the serving woman opened the door to the storeroom. Lanius smiled to himself. She wouldn't learn anything that way.

The king's smile slipped when he wondered what would happen if Flammea found herself pregnant. Grus had coped well enough, but Anser was born long before Grus became king. Lanius laughed at himself. He might be thinking about making a child with Flammea now, but he hadn't worried about it one bit before lying down with her. What man ever did?

Day followed day. Sosia didn't throw any more crockery at his head. From that, he concluded Flammea could indeed keep her mouth shut. She also didn't make a nuisance of herself when they saw each other. They did contrive to go off by themselves again not too long after the first time. Lanius enjoyed that as much as he had earlier on. If Flammea didn't, she pretended well.

"You *are* in a good humor," Sosia said that evening. "The Menteshe should have civil wars more often. They agree with you."

Lanius didn't choke on his soup. If that didn't prove something about his powers of restraint, he couldn't imagine what would. "The Menteshe should have civil wars more often," he agreed gravely. "Avornis would be better off if they did."

His wife was a queen, the wife of one king and the daughter of another (even if Lanius thought Grus as illegitimate a king as a lot of Avornis had once reckoned him). She said, "How do we *make* the Menteshe fight among themselves?"

"If I knew the answer to that, I'd do it," Lanius said. "The way things are, I'm happy enough to try to take advantage of it when it happens." He was also happy Sosia thought his good cheer came from policy. Raising his wine cup, he said, "Here's to more civil war among the Menteshe."

Sosia drank with him.

Beloyuz came up to Grus as the King of Avornis eyed the walls of Nishevatz early one misty morning. "May I speak to you, Your Majesty?" the Chernagor noble asked.

"If I say no now, you're a man in trouble, for you just did," Grus answered. Beloyuz stared at him in puzzlement. Grus swallowed a sigh. None of the nobles who followed Prince Vsevolod had much in the way of humor. The king went on, "Say what you will."

"I thank you, Your Majesty. "Last night, a peasant came to me." He paused portentously. Grus nodded and waved for him to continue. The exiles would have been of small use if they didn't have connections with folk of their own land. Beloyuz said, "An army is coming—so this man hears from a man of Durdevatz."

A man of Durdevatz? Grus thought. Maybe the city-state really was showing its gratitude. That would be a pleasant novelty. "From which direction is it coming?" he asked.

The Chernagor noble pointed to the east. "So he said."

Durdevatz lay to the east, so the Chernagors there would be in a position to know what their neighbors were doing. Grus said, "All right. Thank you. I'll send scouts out that way." He also intended to send scouts to the west, in case the peasant had lied to Beloyuz or the man from Durdevatz had lied to the peasant. He didn't say a word about that, not wanting to insult the noble by making him think he wasn't believed. That wasn't how Grus thought about it, though. To him, it was more on the order of not taking chances.

Out went the scouts, in both directions. Grus cursed the fog, being unable to do anything else about it. His riders were liable to find the Chernagor army by tripping over it instead of seeing it at some distance.

He summoned Hirundo, told him what was likely to happen next, and asked, "Can we keep the men of Nishevatz from sallying while we beat back whatever comes at us from the east?" *If it is the east,* he added silently to himself.

"We managed it a few years ago, if you'll recall," Hirundo answered. "Well, they did sally, but we beat 'em back. I think we can do it again. We have a tighter, stronger line around Nishevatz now than we did then. We can hold it with fewer men, and that will leave more to fight the relieving force."

"Good. Make ready to hold it with as few as you can, then," Grus told him. "Free up the others and have them ready to defend our position against the Chernagors whenever they get the word."

"Right you are." The general nodded and started to turn away, but then checked himself. "Ah . . . what happens if the Chernagors don't come?"

"In that case, someone's been lying to Beloyuz, or lying to someone who's gone to Beloyuz," Grus said. "It's possible. But we have to be ready just the same." Hirundo thought that over, nodded, saluted, and briskly went off to do what needed doing.

Grus made sure his own horse was ready to mount. His place, of course, was at the van. He'd finally become a tolerable rider—just about at the time when his years were starting to make him something less than a tolerable warrior. He would have appreciated the irony more if it weren't of the sort that might get him killed.

Little by little, the mist burned off. The sky went from watery gray to watery blue. Grus peered this way and that, but spied no telltale cloud of dust to east or west to warn of the Chernagor army. He wasn't sure how much that meant, or whether it meant anything. There had been enough mist and drizzle lately to lay a lot of dust.

The day dragged on. Grus began to believe the Chernagor peasant had come to Beloyuz for no better reason than to make him jump. But in that case, how had he known of Durdevatz? About halfway through the afternoon, two Avornan horsemen came galloping back to the camp—sure enough, from the east. "Your Majesty! Your Majesty!" they called.

"I'm here." Grus waved to let them see him, though they were already making for the royal pavilion. "What news?"

"Chernagors, Your Majesty, a lot of Chernagors," they answered in ragged chorus. The man in the lead went on, "They're about an hour away. Most of them are foot soldiers—only a few riders."

"Well, well. Isn't that interesting?" The peasant—or the emissary from Durdevatz who'd talked to the peasant (or posed as a peasant?)—had gotten it straight after all. And the scouts had smelled out the attack before it could turn into a nasty surprise. "Thank you, friends," the king said. "I think we'll be able to deal with them." He shouted for Hirundo.

"Yes, Your Majesty?" the general said. "So they really are coming after all?" Grus nodded. Hirundo clucked mournfully. "Well, better late than never. I expect we'll make a good many of them later still." His smile held a certain sharp-toothed anticipation.

"Good. That's what I hoped you'd tell me." Grus pointed toward the walls of Nishevatz. "And if Vasilko's men make their sally?"

"They're welcome to try," Hirundo said. "I hope they do, in fact.

Maybe we can take the city away from them when they have to retreat back into it."

He didn't lack for confidence. Grus clapped him on the back. "Good enough. Make sure we're ready to receive whatever attack the Chernagors can deliver. I'm not charging out against them. If they want me, they can attack on ground of my choosing, by the gods."

Hirundo nodded and hurried away. Grus knew he might have to move out against the Chernagors whether he wanted to or not. If they started ravaging the countryside so his army couldn't feed itself, he'd have to try to stop them. But if they'd had something like that in mind, wouldn't they have brought fewer foot soldiers and more horsemen? *He* would have; he knew that.

He donned his gilded mailshirt and helm. Even in the cool, damp air of the Chernagor country, the quilted padding he wore under the chainmail and helmet made sweat spring out on his forehead. He swung up onto his horse. Cavalrymen hurrying to take their places in line gave him a cheer. He waved to them. The mailshirt clinked musically as he raised his arm.

The Avornans had already taken a good defensive position on a ridgeline when the Chernagor army came over the last low rise to the east. The Chernagors roared like bears when they saw Grus' men drawn up before them. They were big and blocky and hairy like bears, too. Most of them wore iron helmets, but a good many had no coats of mail, only tunics and knee-length kilts. They carried axes and swords— Grus didn't see many bows, not in proportion to their numbers.

His eyes kept flicking toward Nishevatz. If he could see the oncoming Chernagors, so could the men besieged in the city. Were they hoping the relieving army could do the job without them having to sally? Grus thought they were wildly optimistic if they did. But that was their business, not his.

Roaring still, the Chernagors from the east swarmed toward Grus' men, whose line held steady. But pipes skirled as the foes came near, and they drew up out of bowshot. "Come fight us, heroes!" yelled men who spoke Avornan.

"You come fight us!" Grus' men shouted back. A few of them had picked up some words of the Chernagor language. They used those words, which were less than complimentary. The Chernagors cursed back.

They did more than curse, too. They surged forward toward the Avornan line. Grus had all he could do not to cheer. He hadn't thought they would be so foolish. His men held the high ground, and they had lots of arrows. They started shooting at the Chernagors as soon as the kilted attackers came into range. In fact, a lot of them started shooting before the Chernagors came into range, but that happened in every battle.

Of course, the Chernagors started shooting back at the same time. But they had fewer archers to begin with, and they were moving into position, while the Avornans were already where they wanted to be. Also, the Chernagors were shooting uphill, the Avornans downhill, which gave Grus' men another advantage.

Onrushing Chernagors crumpled, some of them clutching at their wounds and howling while others lay very still. Here and there, an Avornan fell, too, but more Avornans wore armor than their foes. King Grus would not have wanted to be one of those squat, blocky, pigtailed foot soldiers trying to close with opponents who could hurt him while he couldn't hit back.

Grus hoped the withering blast of archery would stop the Chernagors before they closed with his men, but no such luck. They had courage, no doubt of that. And, no matter how fast the Avornans shot, they could not put enough arrows in the air to knock down all the enemies between the time when the Chernagors first came into range and when they got close enough to strike with spears and axes.

Just as the Avornan foot soldiers were stronger in archery, the Chernagors had the edge on them when the fighting came to close quarters. The men of the north had their cavalry on the wings to protect their foot from the Avornans on horseback. Grus didn't think the Chernagors had nearly enough in the way of cavalry to bring that off. He turned to Hirundo and asked, "Now?"

"Yes, I think so," his general answered. "Right about now."

Hirundo and Grus both waved to the trumpeters, who blared out the signal for the Avornan cavalry to advance. Grus urged his horse forward. He drew his sword. All those young Chernagors would be hoping to bring down the King of Avornis. They would get their chance.

The Chernagor horsemen spurred toward the Avornans. The Chernagors rode big, strong, heavy beasts. The Avornans outmaneuvered them as readily as the Menteshe outrode Avornans down in the south. The results were about the same as they often were down in the south, too. Beset from several directions at once, the Chernagor riders could not make the most of what they had. Before long, it was either flee or stay and be cut to pieces. They *were* brave. Most of them held their ground as long as they could. And most of them went down holding it.

"Keep moving forward!" Grus shouted to his men. "We need to help our foot soldiers."

The Avornan cavalry crashed into the flank of the Chernagor force. Grus slashed at a Chernagor axman. His blade bit into the fellow's shoulder. The Chernagor shrieked. Grus never found out what happened to him. Battles were like that. As often as not, you had no idea how badly you'd hurt your foe. Sometimes, you didn't know if you'd hurt him at all.

Grus cut again. A shield turned his stroke. A Chernagor chopped at him with an ax. He got his own shield in front of the blow. He felt it all the way up to his shoulder, and knew his left arm would have a bruise. He counted himself lucky the ax hadn't split the shield. He counted himself even luckier that the Chernagor swinging the ax had time for only one stroke before the battle swept the two of them apart.

He didn't get to do too much more fighting after that encounter. For one thing, his own horsemen got between him and the Chernagors. They hadn't done things like that when his beard had less gray in it. Try as he would, he had a tough time getting angry at them on account of it. And the Chernagors, who had failed to break the Avornan line, who had taken a lot of punishment from the Avornan archers before they ever reached it, and who were taken in the flank by Avornan cavalry, did not fight hard for long. They began streaming back toward the east as soon as they became convinced they could not hope to win, which they soon did.

"After them!" Grus shouted. "Don't let them get away thinking they almost beat us. Make sure they know we're stronger than they are."

"We don't want to go too far," Hirundo said. "If Vasilko does sally . . ."

"He hasn't done it yet," Grus said. "If he wouldn't do it before he knew we'd win, why should he try it now?" Hirundo had no answer for him. The Avornan cavalry pushed the retreating Chernagors hard until sunset, killing many and capturing more. Vasilko kept his men on the walls of Nishevatz, and did not dare to venture beyond them. Seeing what he'd done to the Chernagors from the east, Grus nodded in sober satisfaction and said, "Now we can get on with our business here."

Pouncer prowled through a small room. Carpenters and masons had assured King Lanius the moncat couldn't escape. Of course, those same carpenters and masons hadn't been able to figure out how Pouncer was escaping from the chamber where he spent most of his time, so Lanius didn't fully trust them. Still, Pouncer had shown no signs of disappearing over the past hour.

Lanius lay down on his back on the floor in the bare little room. Had any of his subjects seen him, they would have been sure he'd lost his mind. With the door closed and barred behind him, nobody could see him but Pouncer. That suited him fine.

He thumped on his chest with the palm of his right hand, as though he were playing himself like a drum. Pouncer stopped prowling, came over to him, and climbed up onto his belly.

"What a good boy!" Lanius praised the moncat and scratched and stroked it and gave it a piece of meat as a reward. Pouncer held the meat in one clawed hand before devouring it. The moncat scrambled down from Lanius a minute or two later.

The king got to his feet. He watched Pouncer for a little while, then lay down again. He thumped his chest once more. Pouncer hurried over, climbed up onto his belly, and waited expectantly. He gave the moncat another tasty reward.

He wondered if he could have taught an ordinary cat the same trick. He supposed so, though it might have taken longer. Moncats were clever beasts, especially where their self-interest was concerned.

Training moncats, he thought. *Is that a job for a King of Avornis?* He'd trained them. He'd painted their pictures. He'd learned to paw through the royal archives and those under the great cathedral. Had he been an ordinary man instead of King of Avornis, none of that would have kept him from starving to death. As king, he had a lot of worries. Starving, fortunately, wasn't one of them.

He picked Pouncer up and carried the moncat back to the room where it spent most of its time, the room with most of the other moncats. Pouncer kept wiggling, maybe trying to get away, maybe hoping to see if he had any more treats it might steal. When he hung on to it, it snapped at him.

"Don't you bite me!" He tapped it on the nose with a forefinger. The moncat subsided. It knew it wasn't supposed to bite. It forgot every once in a while, and needed to be reminded.

When he opened the door to the moncats' chamber, Lanius had to be careful none of them got out. They knew the open door meant they had a chance, so they crowded toward it. He had to drive them back, flapping his robe and making loud, horrible noises, before they would retreat.

On leaving the chamber, he made sure he barred the door from the outside. No matter how clever the moncats were, that had defeated them. It defeated human prisoners all over Avornis, and no doubt in Thervingia and the Chernagor country and the lands the Menteshe ruled, too. He just had to make sure he did it every single time.

The king was pleased with himself. Teaching any cat a trick felt like a triumph. As tricks went, this one was pretty simple. Anyone who trained dogs wouldn't have thought much of it. Still, it made Lanius wonder what else Pouncer could learn. A moncat that could manage more complicated tricks might be entertaining.

Nodding to himself, Lanius walked on down the corridor. After he got the idea, he shoved it down to the back of his mind. He didn't forget about it, but it wasn't anything he had to worry about right away. Pouncer wouldn't learn a new trick tomorrow.

That night, the Banished One visited him in a dream. The exiled god's perfectly handsome, perfectly chilly visage stared at—stared through—Lanius with what seemed to be even more contempt than usual. "So," the Banished One said, "you seek to trifle with me again."

Lanius kept quiet. If the Banished One had only just now learned Otus was truly cured, the king did not intend to tell him anything more.

Silence helped less than it would against a human opponent, for the Banished One's words cut like whips even in a dream. "You will fail," he said. "You will fail, and you will die."

"All men die," Lanius said with such courage as he could muster.

"All men die, yes, and all beasts, too," the Banished One snarled. "Some, though, sooner than others."

At that, Lanius woke up, his heart pounding. He didn't forget the dream; he never forgot a dream where the Banished One came calling. He did not forget, but he did not understand, either.

CHAPTER TWENTY-THREE

S omewhere in the world, there was probably something that seemed more progress-free than a long siege. Grus supposed snail races might fill the bill. Other than a field of mollusks languidly gliding along eyestalk to eyestalk, nothing even came close. So the king felt outside of Nishevatz, anyhow.

Day followed day. Vasilko's men on the walls hurled insults at the Avornans who surrounded the city. When the Avornans came too close to the wall, the Chernagors would shoot at them. Every once in a while, somebody got hurt. Despite the occasional casualties, though, it hardly seemed like war.

When Grus grumbled about that, Hirundo laughed at him. "It could be a lot worse," the general said. "They could be sallying every day, trying to break out. They could have ships trying to bring in more supplies. We could have a pestilence start. They could have hit us from east and west at the same time, and the army that did hit us from the east could have shown more in the way of staying power. Are those the sorts of things you'd rather see, Your Majesty?"

Laughing, Grus shook his head. "Now that you mention it, no. All at once, I'm happy enough to be bored."

"Good for you," Hirundo said. "They're not bored inside Nishevatz—I promise you that. They've got plenty to think about. How to break our ring around the place tops their list, if I'm any judge."

Whatever Vasilko and his henchmen were thinking, they gave no sign of it. Spring waned. Summer came on. Here in the north, summer days were noticeably longer than at the city of Avornis—a good deal longer than they were down by the Stura, where Grus had spent so much time before becoming king. The weather grew mild, sometimes even fairly warm. For the Chernagor country, it doubtless counted as a savage heat wave.

Couriers from the capital brought news of the civil war among the Menteshe. Grus avidly read those. The more the nomads squabbled, the happier he was. King Lanius wrote that he'd taught a moncat to do tricks. That amused Grus, anyhow, and livened up what would have been a dull day. Besides, if Lanius stayed busy with his moncats, he probably wasn't planning anything too nefarious.

One day, a letter came up to Nishevatz that hadn't started or gone through the city of Avornis. That in itself was interesting enough to make Grus open it right away. When he'd read it, he smiled to himself and then put it aside.

One of the advantages of being King of Avornis was that nobody presumed to ask him what he was smiling about. He didn't go around bragging, either, even if part of him felt like it. But if he advertised having a new bastard boy, word would get to Estrilda sooner than if he kept quiet. He wanted to put off that evil day as long as possible—forever, if he could.

Alauda had named the baby Nivalis. It wasn't a name Grus would have chosen, but he'd been up here in the north, and hadn't had any say in it. "Nivalis." He tasted the sound of it. It wasn't so bad, not after he thought about it. From what the letter said, both the baby and Alauda were doing well. That mattered more than the name. New mothers and infants died too easily.

Pterocles answered the king's smiles with smiles of his own. Did the wizard use his sorcerous powers to divine why Grus was so pleased with himself? Or did he just remember that Alauda had been pregnant and would be having her baby about now? Grus didn't ask him. How much difference did it make, one way or the other?

Hirundo kept his usually smiling face serious. He had to remember Alauda, too. But he, unlike Pterocles, had affairs of his own wherever he found willing women. He understood discretion. Whatever questions or congratulations he might have had, he kept them to himself.

Grateful for that, Grus asked, "How hungry do you think they're getting in there?"

"They're not at the end of their tether," Hirundo replied at once. "If they were, they'd be slipping down over the wall just to get fed. But they can't be in the best of shape, either."

That marched well with what Grus thought himself. He'd hoped Hirundo would tell him something more optimistic. But Hirundo, however discreet, would not say something was so when he thought otherwise. That would get men who might otherwise live killed, and he was too good a soldier to do any such thing.

"Fair enough," Grus said, eyeing the battlements of Nishevatz. Chernagors on the walls looked out at the army hemming them in. The king pointed their way. "They aren't going anywhere. We've made sure of that."

The pyre that rose on the burning grounds was relatively modest. The white-bearded priest lying atop it wore only a green robe; he had never advanced to the yellow of the upper clergy. And yet, not only had the Arch-Hallow of Avornis come to say farewell to him, so had King Lanius.

After the usual prayers, the priest in charge of the service touched a torch to the oil-soaked wood. It caught at once and burned strongly, swallowing Ixoreus' mortal remains. "May his spirit rise with the smoke to the heavens," the priest intoned.

"May it be so," the mourners murmured. The small crowd began to break up. Most of the people there were priests who'd served with Ixoreus in the great cathedral. By all appearances, he'd had few real friends.

That saddened Lanius, but did not surprise him. Arch-Hallow Anser came up to him and clasped his hand, saying, "It was good of you to come."

"A lot of knowledge died with him." Lanius wondered if Anser had any idea how much. The king doubted it. Anser knew more—and cared more—about the hunt than about matters ecclesiastical. To his credit, he'd never pretended otherwise. Lanius went on, "You will never find another archivist who comes close to matching him."

To his surprise, Anser smiled, shook his head, and replied, "Oh, I don't know about that, Your Majesty."

Lanius had some notion of the abilities of Ixoreus' assistants, and a low opinion of them. "Who?" he demanded.

"Why, you, of course," the arch-hallow said.

"Me?" The king blinked. "You do me too much credit, I think. I know the royal archives tolerably well, but Ixoreus was always my guide to the ones under the cathedral." *And now one person fewer knows the name Milvago. That may be just as well.*

"You could do the job," Anser said. "If you had no other, I mean."

Not so long before, Lanius had wondered how he might have earned his bread if he weren't king. Now he bowed. "If I had no other, maybe I could." Anser meant well. Anser never meant less than well. But the job Lanius had, that of King of Avornis, was less, much less, than it might have been, which was the fault of one man and one man only—Anser's father, King Grus. Lanius brooded on that less than he had in years gone by, but he knew it was true. Still, he made himself smile and said, "As I told you before, you flatter me."

"I don't think so," Anser said. "It's in your blood, the way it was in Ixoreus', and you can't tell me any different. These other fellows, they'll do it, but they'll do it because someone tells them to. If it fell to you, you'd do it *right.*"

Given a choice, Lanius might well have preferred being an archivist to wearing the crown. His blood did not give him that choice. He nodded to the arch-hallow. "You may be right. But you at least had one good archivist. At the palace, I've spent years sifting through chaos."

"Before long, you may have to do that with our records, too," Anser said.

"I hope not," Lanius said. And yet, if the ancient document that named Milvago and told what he was were to be lost for a few more generations, would he be unhappy? He knew perfectly well he would be anything but.

His guardsmen fell in around him as he made his way back to the royal palace. The priests who'd come to Ixoreus' cremation stared at him as he left. They had to be wondering why he'd chosen to pay his personal respects to an old man good for nothing but shuffling through parchments. He always found what he was looking for? So what?

Lanius sighed and shook his head. Who but another archivist could possibly appreciate what an archivist did? Not even Anser really understood it. He'd come because he liked Ixoreus. But then, he liked everybody, just as much as everybody liked him, so how much did that prove?

On the way back to the palace, one of the guardsmen asked, "Your Majesty, what's the point of even keeping old parchments, let alone going through them?"

By the way he said it, he plainly expected the king to have no good answer for him. Several of the other guards craned their necks toward

Lanius to hear what he would say. The last thing he wanted was to seem a fool in front of them. He thought for several paces before asking a question of his own. "Do you read and write, Carbo?"

"Me, Your Majesty?" Carbo laughed. "Not likely!"

"All right. Have you ever gotten into an argument with the paymaster about what he gives you every fortnight?" Lanius asked. To his relief, Carbo nodded at that. Lanius said, "You know how he settled things, then. He went through the parchments that said how much pay you get and when you got it last. That's what the archives are—they're like the pay records for the whole kingdom, as far back as anybody can remember. No matter what kind of question you ask about how things were a long time ago, the answer's in there—if the mice haven't chewed up the parchment where it was hiding."

"But why would you care about what happened before anybody who's alive now was born?" Carbo asked.

"So in case the kingdom gets into a kind of trouble it's seen before, I'll know how it fixed things a long time ago," Lanius answered. Carbo could see that that made sense. But no matter how much sense it made, it was only part of the truth. The main reasons Lanius liked to go exploring in the archives were that he was interested in the past for its own sake and that people hardly ever bothered him while he was poking through old parchments.

And Carbo didn't bother him the rest of the way back to the palace. *Another triumph for the archives,* he thought.

Three Chernagors stood nervously before King Grus. They'd escaped from Nishevatz with a rope they'd let down from the wall. All three were hollow-cheeked and scrawny. Through Beloyuz, Grus asked them, "How bad off for food is Nishevatz?"

They all tried to talk at once. Beloyuz pointed to the man in the middle, the tallest of the three. He spewed forth a mouthful of gutturals. "He says the city is hungry," Beloyuz told Grus. "He says to look at him, to look at these fellows with him. He says they were strapping men when this siege started. They might as well be ghosts now, he says."

They were, to Grus' eye, rather substantial ghosts even now. The king asked, "How hard will the Chernagors fight if we attack them?"

Again, all three talked at once. This time, they began to argue. Beloyuz said, "One of them says Vasilko's men will strike a blow or two for appearance's sake and then give up. The others say they will fight hard."

"I heard Prince Vsevolod's name in there," Grus said. "What did they say about him?"

Vsevolod's name in Grus' mouth was plenty to start the Chernagors talking. Whatever they said, it sounded impassioned. Beloyuz let them go on for a while before observing, "They do not think well of His Highness, Your Majesty."

"I would have guessed that," Grus said—an understatement, if anything. "But what do they think of fighting on the same side as the Banished One?"

When Beloyuz translated that into the Chernagor tongue, the three escapees began arguing again. Without a word of the language, Grus had no trouble figuring that out. One of them said something that touched a nerve, too, for Beloyuz shouted angrily at him. He shouted back. Before long, all four Chernagors were yelling at the top of their lungs.

"What do they say?" Grus asked. Beloyuz paid him no attention. "What do they say?" he asked again. Still no response. "*What do they say?*" he roared in a voice that might have carried across a battlefield.

For a heartbeat, he didn't think even that would remind Beloyuz he was there. Then, reluctantly, the noble broke away from the other Chernagors. "They say vile things, insulting things, Your Majesty," he said, his voice full of indignation. "One of them, the vile dog, says better the Banished One than Vsevolod. You ought to burn a man who says things like that."

"No, the Banished One burns men who don't agree with him, burns them or makes them into thralls," Grus said. "They will be free of a bad master once he is gone from Nishevatz. Tell them that, Beloyuz."

The nobleman spoke. The Chernagors who'd escaped from the besieged city spoke, too. Beloyuz scowled. Reluctantly, he turned back to the king and returned to Avornan. "They say Nishevatz will be free of one bad master, but it will have another one if Vsevolod takes it."

Grus muttered to himself. He'd known the people of Nishevatz disliked Prince Vsevolod. He could hardly have helped knowing it. But somehow he had managed to avoid realizing how much they despised Vsevolod. If they thought him no different from the Banished One . . . If they thought that, no wonder they put up with Vasilko even if he followed the exiled god.

"Send them away," Grus told Beloyuz, pointing to the men who had come out of Nishevatz. "Feed them. Keep them under guard. Then come back to me."

"Just as you say, Your Majesty, so shall it be." Beloyuz went off with the other three Chernagors. When he returned a few minutes later, curiosity filled his features. "What do you want, Your Majesty?"

"How would you like to be Prince of Nishevatz once we take the place?" Grus came straight out with what he had in mind.

Beloyuz stared. "You ask me to . . . to betray my prince?"

"No," Grus said. *Yes*, he thought. Aloud, he went on, "How can Vsevolod be Prince of Nishevatz if everybody in the place hates him? If we have to kill everyone in the city to set him back on the throne, what kind of city-state will he rule? And if we have to kill everyone in Nishevatz to set him back on the throne, and decide to do it, how are we different from the Banished One? Whose will do we really work?"

"I think you use this for an excuse to do what you want to do anyhow because you do not like Prince Vsevolod," Beloyuz said. "You ask me to betray my prince, when I went into exile for him."

That set Grus to muttering again. Beloyuz was right—he didn't like Vsevolod. By all appearances, next to nobody could stand Vsevolod. The three Chernagors who'd gotten out of Nishevatz had had no use for him. From what they'd said, the rest of the people on the walls and behind them felt the same way. It was just Grus' luck to want to replace the unpleasant exiled Prince of Nishevatz with one of the few men who actually thought well of him.

With a sigh, the king said, "Well, Your Excellency, I won't ask you to do anything that goes against your conscience. Still, you ought to think about what's best for you and what's best for Nishevatz."

"What is best for Nishevatz is Prince Vsevolod. What is best for me is Prince Vsevolod." Beloyuz bowed and strode off.

What Grus muttered this time made two or three of his guardsmen gape. He'd said worse while a river-galley captain, but not since taking the crown. He knew what would happen next, too. Beloyuz would tell Vsevolod about the usurpation he'd tried to arrange, and Vsevolod would throw a fit. Grus' head started to ache just thinking about that.

But Vsevolod didn't come to bother him. Day followed day, and the King of Avornis didn't meet the Prince of Nishevatz. He didn't ask where Vsevolod was or what he was doing, either. He didn't care.

Then one of the Avornans who guarded Vsevolod and his followers came to Grus and said, "Your Majesty, I think you'd better go see the prince."

"Why?" Even to himself, Grus sounded like a boy told to take a bath he didn't want.

"He's . . . not well," the guard answered.

"Oh." Grus made a sour face. "All right, in that case."

When he went to Vsevolod's tent, he went with two squads of his own guardsmen. He assumed Beloyuz would have told the other Chernagors who'd left Nishevatz with Vsevolod about his proposal. He also assumed they wouldn't like the idea, and wouldn't like him on account of it.

Beloyuz saw him coming, and walked up to greet him with three or four other refugee Chernagor noblemen. "So you have heard, then," Beloyuz said.

"Yes, Your Excellency, I've heard," Grus said, though he hadn't heard very much. He asked, "How is His Highness this morning?" With a little luck, that would tell him more than he already knew.

But Beloyuz only shrugged and answered, "About the same. He has been about the same since it happened." Grus nodded as though he understood what the Chernagor meant. Beloyuz went on, "I suppose you want to see him."

"That is why I'm here, yes." The king nodded.

Beloyuz didn't argue. He and the other exiles simply stood aside. Surrounded by his bodyguards, Grus went on to Vsevolod's tent. He felt like scratching his head. The Chernagors seemed more resigned than furious. Were they finally fed up with Vsevolod, too? If they were, why had Beloyuz refused to supplant the prince? Things didn't add up.

And then, as soon as Grus got a glimpse of Vsevolod, they did. The Prince of Nishevatz lay on a cot much like the one in which Grus slept. He recognized Grus. The king could see it in his eyes—or rather, in his right eye. His left eye was half closed. The whole left side of his face was slack. The left corner of his mouth hung down in an altogether involuntary frown. He raised his right hand to wag a finger at Grus. The left side of his body seemed not to be under the control of his will anymore.

He tried to speak. Only gibberish came out of his mouth. Grus couldn't even tell if it was meant for the Chernagor language or Avornan. One of his guardsmen muttered, "Gods spare me from such a fate."

The guard was young and vigorous. Grus remained vigorous, but he was no longer young. Every now and then, his body reminded him it wouldn't last forever. But this . . . He shivered. This was like looking at living death. He completely agreed with the guard. Next to this, simply falling over dead was a mercy. "Gods spare me indeed," he said, and left the tent in a hurry.

"You see," Beloyuz said when Grus came out into the sunshine again.

"I see," Grus said heavily. "When did it happen?"

"After I told him what you wanted from me," Beloyuz replied. "He was angry, as you would guess. He was furious, in fact. But then, in the middle of his cursing, he said his head ached fit to burst. And he fell down, and he has been like—that—ever since."

"Has a healer seen him?" Grus asked.

"Yes." Beloyuz nodded. "He said he could do nothing. He also said the prince was not a young man, and it could have happened at any time. It could have."

He did not sound as though he believed it. But he also did not come right out and blame Grus to his face, as he easily might have. The king was grateful for his forbearance; he hadn't expected even that much. "I will send for my chief wizard," Grus said. "I don't know how much help he can give, but we ought to find out, eh?"

"Thank you." Now Beloyuz was the one who sounded surprised. "If I had thought you would do this, I would have come to you sooner. I thought you would say, 'Let him suffer. Let him die.'"

"That's what the Banished One does," Grus replied. "By the gods in the heavens, Beloyuz, I would not wish this on Vsevolod. I woud not wish this on anyone. It's the people of Nishevatz who don't want him as their prince, but that's a different story. You should not be angry with me for trying to get around it."

The Chernagor noble didn't answer. Grus sent one of his guardsmen to find Pterocles. The wizard came to Prince Vsevolod's tent a few minutes later. Grus told him what had happened to the prince. "You want me to cure him?" Pterocles asked. "I don't know if I can do anything like that."

"Do your best, whatever it turns out to be," Grus said. "Whatever it is, I don't think you'll hurt Vsevolod." He turned to Beloyuz. "If you want to say anything different, go ahead."

"No, not I," Beloyuz answered. "I say, thank you. I say, gods be with you."

Pterocles ducked his way into Vsevolod's tent. Grus heard the stricken prince yammering wordlessly. He also heard Pterocles begin a soft, low-voiced incantation. Vsevolod fell silent. After a little while, the rhythm of Pterocles' spell changed. When the wizard came out of the tent, his face was grave.

"What did you do?" Grus asked.

"Not as much as I would have liked," Pterocles answered. "Something is . . . broken inside his head. I don't know how to put it any better than that. I can't fix it any more than the healer could. The spell I used will make him more comfortable, but that's all. I'm sorry."

"Even this is better than nothing," Beloyuz said, and bowed to the wizard. "Thank you."

"I didn't do enough to make it worth your while to thank me," Pterocles said. "I only wish I could have." He bowed, too, and walked away kicking at the dirt.

Grus and Beloyuz looked at each other. After a moment, the king said, "You know what I'm going to ask, don't you?"

"Yes." Beloyuz looked even less happy than Pterocles had. "It makes me feel like a carrion crow, like a vulture."

"I understand that," Grus said. "But can you tell me it isn't needful? Nishevatz will need a prince who isn't Vasilko. Who better than you?"

"Vsevolod," the nobleman said at once.

"I told you no to that before," Grus answered. "You thought I was wrong then. You can't very well say I'm wrong now."

Beloyuz's face twisted. "I need to think this over," he said.

"Don't take too long," Grus warned.

Three days later, Vsevolod died. After that, Beloyuz had no excuses left.

Most of the time, Lanius was content being who and what he was. He had seen a battlefield when he was still a boy, and he never wanted to see another one. He never wanted to hear another one, either, nor to smell one. Every so often, that particular stink showed up in his nightmares.

But he sometimes had moments when he wished he could be, if not in the action, then closer to it than he was while staying in the royal palace and the city of Avornis. Those moments came most often when the latest dispatch from Grus in the Chernagor country or from the officers in the south reached the capital.

He didn't want to go into the field. But he wanted to know more about what went on there than he could find out from reading reports in the comfortable shelter of the palace. He would sometimes question the couriers who brought them. Some of the men who came down from the north had actually seen the things Grus was talking about. They helped make them seem real for Lanius.

The king had less luck with the dispatch riders who brought word of the civil war among the Menteshe up from the south. One of them said, "I'm sorry, Your Majesty, but we have to piece this together ourselves. We don't have our own people down by Yozgat watching the battles. We wait until word comes up to our side of the river, and then we try to figure out who's lying and who isn't."

"How do you go about doing that?" Lanius asked.

"Carefully," the courier answered, which made the king laugh. The other man went on, "I wasn't joking, Your Majesty. All sorts of rumors bubble up about what's going on between Sanjar and Korkut. We try to pop the bubbles and see which ones leave nothing but a bad smell behind."

"Shame Avornis can't do more," Lanius remarked.

Very seriously, the courier shook his head. "We're ordered *not* to favor either one of the Menteshe princes. If we did, the fellow we showed we didn't like would use that to rally the rest of the nomads to his side. We don't want to give either one of them that edge. Let them smash away at each other for as long as they please."

That gray wisdom sounded like Grus. "All right," Lanius said. "Just my impatience talking, I suppose."

His brother-in-law had a different sort of impatience driving him. "I can't wait for Limosa to have her baby," Ortalis said one hot summer afternoon.

"Ah?" Lanius said. If Ortalis started going on about how much he wanted a son, Lanius intended to find an excuse to disappear. He didn't want to hear about a baby that might prove a threat to his own son's position.

But that wasn't what was on his brother-in-law's mind. Ortalis nodded like a hungry wolf thinking about meat. "That's right," he said. "There are things you can't do when a woman's carrying a child."

"Ah?" Lanius said again. "Such as what?" Certain postures had been awkward after Sosia's belly bulged, but they'd gone on making love until not long before she bore Crex and Pitta.

"Things," Ortalis repeated, and declined to elaborate.

This time, Lanius didn't say, "Ah." He said, "Oh." He recalled the kinds of things his brother-in-law enjoyed. Cristata's scarred back, and the way the ruined skin had felt under his fingers, leaped vividly to mind. What *would* happen if you did that sort of thing with—to—a pregnant woman? After a moment's thought, he shook his head. Maybe it was squeamish of him, but he didn't really want to know.

What he was thinking must have shown on his face. Prince Ortalis turned red. "Don't get all high and mighty with me," he said. "I'm not the only one who does things like that."

"I didn't say you were." Lanius didn't want another quarrel with Ortalis; they'd had too many already. But he didn't want Grus' legitimate son to think he liked Ortalis' ideas of fun, either. Picking his words with care, he said, "There's enough pain in the world as is. I don't much see the point of adding more on purpose." He nearly added, *It seems like something the Banished One would do.* At the last instant, he swallowed that. If Ortalis didn't have ideas about the Banished One, why give them to him?

All Ortalis did now was make an exasperated noise. "You don't understand," he said.

"You're right." Lanius nodded emphatic agreement. "I don't."

He hadn't asked Ortalis to explain. He hadn't wanted Ortalis to explain. But explain his brother-in-law did. "Curse it," Ortalis said angrily, "it's not adding pain the way a Menteshe torturer would. It's different."

"How?" Now Lanius did ask. The word escaped him before he could call it back.

"How? I'll tell you how. Because while it's going on, both people are enjoying it, that's how." Ortalis sent Lanius a defiant stare.

The king remembered Cristata again. Not naming her, he said, "That isn't what . . . one of the other people told me."

Ortalis knew who he was talking about without a name. The prince laughed harshly. "That may be what she said afterwards. It isn't what she said while it was going on. By the gods, it's not. You should have heard her. 'Oh, Ortalis!'"

He was an excellent, even an alarming, mimic. And he believed what he was saying. The unmistakable anger in his voice convinced Lanius of that. Was he right? Lanius doubted it. Right or not, though, he was sincere.

How could he be so wrong about that, sincere or not? Well, even Cristata admitted she'd enjoyed some of it at first. And then, when it had gone too far for her, maybe Ortalis had taken real fear for the artificial fear that was part of the game. Maybe. Lanius could hope that was how it had been.

But he wanted to hunt girls for sport. How can I forget that? What would he have done once he caught them? Part of him, again, didn't want to know. Part feared he already knew.

When Lanius didn't say anything, Ortalis got angrier. "Curse it, I'm telling you the truth," he said.

"All right. I believe you." Lanius didn't, but he couldn't help believing Ortalis believed what he said. And he believed—no, he knew—arguing with Ortalis was more trouble than it was worth.

Limosa's labor began a few days later. Netta, the briskly competent midwife who'd attended Sosia, went in with Ortalis' wife. Lanius didn't linger outside Limosa's bedchamber, as he had outside the birthing chamber where Sosia had borne their son and daughter. That was Ortalis' job now. The king did get news from women who attended the midwife. From what they said, everything was going the way it should. Lanius hoped so. No matter what he thought of Petrosus, he didn't dislike the exiled treasury minister's daughter.

The sun had just set when the high, thin, furious wail of a newborn baby burst from the bedchamber. Lanius waited expectantly. Netta came out of the room and spoke to Ortalis in a voice that could be heard all over the palace. "Congratulations, Your Highness," she said. "You have a fine, healthy new daughter, and the lady your wife is doing well."

"A daughter?" Ortalis didn't bother keeping his voice down, either, or keeping the disappointment out of it. But then he managed a laugh of sorts. "Well, we'll just have to try again, that's all."

"Not for six weeks," the midwife said firmly. "You can do her a real injury if you go to her too soon. I'm not joking about this, Your Highness. Stay out of her bed until then."

How long had it been since anyone but Grus had spoken to Ortalis like that? Too long, probably. The prince took it from Netta, saying nothing more than, "All right, I'll do that."

"Princess Limosa said you were going to name a girl Capella. Is that right?" Netta asked.

"Yes. It's her mother's name," Ortalis answered.

"It's a good name," the midwife said. "I have a cousin named Capella. She's a lovely woman, and I'm sure your little princess will be, too."

What Ortalis said in response to that, Lanius didn't hear. He went into his bedchamber and told Sosia, "It's a girl!"

"Yes, I heard," the queen said. "I don't think there's anyone for half a mile around who didn't hear."

"Well, yes," Lanius said. "It's still good news."

"So it is," Sosia said. "I do worry about the succession."

Lanius worried about it, too. What *would* happen when Grus died? He wasn't a young man anymore. Lanius himself thought he ought to be sole king after that, but how likely was Ortalis to agree with him? Not very, he feared. At the moment, he had a son and Ortalis didn't. Ortalis wasn't happy about that, either; he'd just proved as much. If he had one, or more than one, too . . .

"It could be complicated," Lanius said.

"It's already complicated," Sosia replied. "It could be a disaster."

He started to smile and laugh and to say it couldn't be as bad as all that. He started to, yes, but he didn't. For months now, he'd been reading all the news about the civil war between Prince Sanjar and Prince Korkut. Would some Menteshe prince one day read letters about the civil war raging among the contenders and pretenders to the throne of Avornis? It could happen, and he knew it.

Sosia read his face. "You see," she said. "We dodged an arrow this time. We may not be so lucky a year from now, or two, or three."

"You're not wrong," Lanius said with a sigh. "By Olor's beard, I wish you were. Oh!" He stopped, then went on, "And there's something else you weren't wrong about."

"What's that?" Sosia asked.

"Ortalis and Limosa." Lanius told her what Ortalis had said, and what he thought it meant, finishing, "The other thing is, Limosa's head over heels in love with your brother in spite of—maybe even because of—this."

"You mean you think she *does* like the horrible things he does?" Sosia made a face. "That's disgusting!" But her pause was thoughtful. "Of course, you're right—somebody may like what somebody else thinks is disgusting." Lanius nodded at that. A moment later, he wished he hadn't, for her look said she had his sporting with the serving girls in mind. He turned away so he could pretend he didn't know what she was thinking. She laughed. She knew he knew, all right.

CHAPTER TWENTY-FOUR

Avornan soldiers scoured the countryside for timber and oil to make Prince Vsevolod the most magnificent funeral pyre anyone had ever seen. They built the pyre just out of bowshot of Nishevatz, and laid the body of the white-bearded Prince of Nishevatz atop it.

Beloyuz advanced toward the grim gray walls of the city-state behind a flag of truce. He shouted in his own language. Prince Vasilko's men stared down at him from the battlements. They said not a word until he finished, and let him go back to the Avornan lines without shooting at him in spite of that flag of truce.

To King Grus, that was progress of a sort. Beloyuz seemed to think the same. Well, Your Majesty, I told them His Highness has passed from among men," the Chernagor noble said. "I told them I would rule Nishevatz in his place once Vasilko was driven from the city. I told them—and they heard me! They did not hate me!"

"Good." Grus meant it. A small fire burned not far from the pyre. "Light a torch, then. Send Vsevolod's spirit up toward the heavens with the smoke, and then we'll get on with business here on earth."

"Yes." Beloyuz took a torch and thrust it into the flames. The tallow-soaked head caught at once. The Chernagor raised the torch high—once, twice, three times. Grus almost asked him what he was doing, but held back. It had to be some local custom Avornis didn't share. Then Beloyuz touched the torch to one corner of the pyre.

The blast of flame that followed sent him and Grus staggering back.

"Ahh!" said the watching Avornan soldiers, who, like their king, had seen a great many pyres in their day and eyed them with the appreciation of so many connoisseurs. When Grus watched an old man's body go up in smoke, he always thought back to the day when he'd had to burn his father. Crex, who'd come off a farm in the south to the city of Avornis and found a position as a royal guardsman, was gone forever. But in the blood of that Crex's great-grandson, another Crex, also flowed the blood of the ancient royal dynasty of Avornis. And that younger Crex would likely wear the crown himself one day.

Grus wondered what his father would have to say about that. Some bad joke or other, probably; the old man had no more been able to do without them than he'd been able to do without bread. He'd died before Grus won the crown, died quickly and quietly and peacefully. Days went by now when Grus hardly thought of him. And yet, every so often, just how much he missed him stabbed like a sword.

He blinked rapidly and turned away from Vsevolod's pyre. The heat and smoke and fire were enough to account for his streaming eyes. He wiped them on the sleeve of his tunic and looked toward Nishevatz. The burly, bearded warriors on the wall were watching Vsevolod's departure from this world as intently as the soldiers Grus commanded. He saw several of them pointing at the pyre, and wondered what they would be saying.

"Tell me," he said to Beloyuz, "do your people have the custom of reckoning one pyre against another?"

"Oh, yes," the Chernagor answered. "I think it must be so among every folk who burn their dead. Things may be different among those who throw them in a hole in the ground, I suppose. But a pyre, now, a pyre is a great thing. How could you *not* compare one to the next?"

"Prince Vsevolod will be remembered for a long time, then." Grus had to raise his voice to make himself understood above the crackling of the flames.

"Yes. It is so." Beloyuz nodded. "You have served him better in death, perhaps, than you did in life."

Grus sent him a sour stare. "Do you think so, Your Excellency? Excuse me—I mean, 'Your Highness.' Do you truly think so? If I did not care what became of Vsevolod, why did I spend so many of my men and so much of my treasure to try to restore him to the throne of Nishevatz?"

"Why? For your own purposes, of course," Beloyuz replied, with a shrug that could have made any world-weary Avornan courtier jealous.

"To try to keep the Banished One from gaining a foothold here in the Chernagor country. I do not say these are bad reasons, Your Majesty. I say they are reasons that have nothing to do with Vsevolod the man—may the gods guard his spirit now. He could have been a green goat, and you would have done the same. We are both men who have seen this and that. Will you tell me I lie?"

However much Grus would have liked to, he couldn't. He eyed Beloyuz with a certain reluctant respect. Vsevolod had never shown much in the way of brains. Here, plainly, was a man of a different sort. And would different mean difficult? It often did.

A difficult Prince of Nishevatz, though, would be a distinct improvement. Vasilko, Vsevolod's unloving son, wasn't just difficult. He was an out-and-out enemy, as much under the thumb of the Banished One as anybody this side of a thrall could be.

"Let the Chernagors in the city know where you stand about this and that," Grus told him. "Let them know you're not Vsevolod, and let them know you're not Vasilko, either. That's our best chance to get help from inside the walls, I think."

"Your best chance, you mean," Beloyuz said.

Grus exhaled in some annoyance. "When you're Prince of Nishevatz—when you're Prince *inside* Nishevatz—I want two things from you. I want you not to bow down to the Banished One, and I want you not to raid my coasts. Past that, Your Highness, I don't care what you do. You can turn your helmet upside down and hatch puffin eggs in it for all of me. Is that plain enough?"

Beloyuz sent him an odd look, and then the first smile he'd gotten from the Chernagor noble. "Yes, Your Majesty. That is very plain. The next question will be, do you mean it?"

Difficult, Grus thought. *Definitely difficult.* "You'll see," he told Beloyuz.

Lanius had almost gotten used to rustling noises and meows in the archives. He put away the diplomatic correspondence between his great-great-grandfather and a King of Thervingia and got to his feet. "All right, Pouncer," he said. "Where are you hiding this time, and what have you stolen from the kitchens?"

No answer from the moncat. *Difficult,* Lanius thought. *Definitely difficult.* He made his way toward the place from which he thought the noise had come. Pouncer was usually pretty easy to catch, not least because he didn't care to drop whatever he'd carried off. He would have been much more agile if he'd simply gotten rid of whatever it was this time when the king came after him. He hadn't figured that out; Lanius hoped he wouldn't.

"Come on, Pouncer," Lanius called. "Where are you?" How many hiding places the size of a moncat did the vast hall of the archives boast? *Too many,* the king thought. If Pouncer didn't make a noise or move when he was close enough for Lanius to see him, he could stay uncaught for a depressingly long time.

There! Was that a striped tail, sticking out from behind a chest of drawers stuffed full of rolled-up parchments? It was. It twitched in excitement. What had Pouncer spotted in there? A cockroach? A mouse? How many important documents had ended up chewed to pieces in mouse nests over the centuries? More than Lanius cared to think about—he was sure of that.

Pouncer . . . pounced. A small clunk said it hadn't put down its prize from the kitchens even to hunt. Half a minute later, it emerged from concealment with a spoon in one clawed hand and with the bloody body of a mouse dangling by the tail from its jaws. Seeming almost unbearably pleased with itself, it carried the mouse over to Lanius and dropped it at his feet.

"Thank you so much," Lanius said. Pouncer looked up at him, still proud as could be. Lanius picked up the mouse and then picked up the moncat. As soon as the mouse was in Lanius' hand, Pouncer wanted it back. Since the king was carrying the moncat, it had, essentially, three hands with which to try to take the dead mouse away from him. Lanius didn't try to stop it; he would have gotten clawed if he had.

Getting the mouse back, though, seemed much less important to Pouncer than trying for it. As soon as it belonged to the moncat and not to the king, Pouncer let it fall to the floor of the archives. Then the beast twisted in Lanius' arms, trying to get away and recover the mouse again. Moncats and ordinary cats were alike in perversity.

Lanius held on to Pouncer. "Oh, no, you don't," he said. The moncat bared its teeth. He tapped it on the nose. "And don't you try to bite me, either. You know better than that." Pouncer subsided. The king had managed to convince the beast that he meant what he said. If the moncat had decided to bite, it could have gotten away easily enough. But, having made its protest, it seemed content to let the king carry it back to the chamber where it lived.

It did show its teeth again when Lanius took away the serving spoon it had stolen. That was a prize, just like the murdered mouse. Lanius tapped the moncat on the nose once more. Pouncer started to snap at him, but then visibly thought better of it. He unbarred the door and put Pouncer inside.

"I'm going to take this back to the kitchens," he told the animal. "You'll probably get loose again and steal another spoon, but you can't keep this one." Then he closed the door in a hurry, before Pouncer or any of the other moncats could get out.

He was walking down the corridor to the kitchens when Bubulcus came around a corner and started bustling toward him. He wondered if the servant had been bustling before spying him. He had his doubts; Bubulcus, from what he'd seen, seldom moved any faster than he had to.

Bubulcus pointed to the spoon in Lanius' hand and asked, "Which the nasty moncat creature has stolen, Your Majesty?" When the king nodded, Bubulcus went on, "Which I had nothing to do with, not a thing." He struck a pose that practically radiated virtue.

"I didn't say you did," Lanius pointed out.

"Oh, no. Not this time." Now Bubulcus looked like virtue abused. "Which you have before, though, many a time and oft as the saying goes, and all when I had nothing to do with anything."

"Not all," said Lanius, precise as usual. "You've let moncats get loose at least twice, which is at least twice too often."

Bubulcus' long, mobile face—his whole scrawny frame, in fact—became the image of affronted dignity. He seemed insulted that the king should presume to bring up what were, after all, only facts. "Which wasn't my fault at all, hardly," he declared.

"No doubt," Lanius said. "Someone held a knife at your throat and made you do it."

"Hmp." Bubulcus looked more affronted still. Lanius hadn't thought he could. "Since you seem to have nothing better to do than insult me, Your Majesty, I had better be on my way, hadn't I?" And on his way he went, beaky nose in the air.

"You don't need to look for me in the moncats' chambers—I'm not there," Lanius said. Bubulcus stalked down the corridor like an offended cat. The king had all he could do to keep from laughing out loud. He'd won a round from his servant. Then the impulse to laugh faded. He wondered what sort of atrocity Bubulcus would commit to get even.

When Lanius walked into the kitchens, spoon in hand, the cooks and cleaners all exclaimed. "I saw it, Your Majesty!" a chubby woman named Quiscula exclaimed. She had a white smear of flour on the end of her nose, and another on one cheek. "That funny beast of yours came out right there. He grabbed the spoon from a counter, and then he disappeared again." She pointed.

Right there was what seemed like nothing more than a crack between wall and ceiling. Lanius tried to get up there for a closer look, but none of the stools or chairs in the kitchens raised him high enough. He sent a cleaner out to have a ladder fetched. He might not command everything in Avornis, but he could do that.

He could also wait close to half an hour for the ladder to get there. When it finally did, it proved old and rickety, anything but fit for a king. He went up it anyway, though not before saying, "Hang on tight down there. If this miserable thing slips, I'll land on my head."

He'd gone up several rungs before he thought to wonder whether his subjects *wanted* him to land on his head. That made him pause, but only for a moment. He couldn't very well ask them. That was liable to give them ideas they might not have had before. If he acted as though an accident weren't possible, that might at least make it less likely.

The ladder creaked, but the cooks and cleaners held it steady. And it was tall enough to let Lanius get a good look at the crack. It was wider than it had appeared from the ground—certainly wide enough for a moncat's head to go through it. And where the head would go, the rest of the moncat could follow.

Lanius stuck his hand into the crack and felt around. His palms and fingers scraped against rough stone and brickwork. The opening got wider farther back. A person couldn't have hoped to go through the passageway, but it wouldn't be any trouble for a moncat.

"This is how you get to the kitchens, all right," Lanius muttered. "Now—where do you sneak into the archives?" He'd never seen Pouncer come out there. The moncat usually appeared in about the same part of that large chamber, but cabinets and crates and barrels all packed with parchments made searching for an opening much harder than it was here.

He tried to reach in a little farther—and something tapped him on the back of the hand.

He jerked his hand away, and almost fell off the ladder. If he landed on his head and it wasn't the cooks' fault . . . He'd still end up with a smashed skull, or maybe a broken neck. A hasty grab made sure he wouldn't fall. But his heart still pounded wildly. What the demon had touched him in there?

Staring into the crack, he saw only blackness. "Let me have a lamp," he called to the people below. A skinny cook's helper who couldn't have been more than twelve came up the ladder to give him one. The rungs creaked again, but held.

Lanius held the clay lamp up to the crack. The little flame from the burning oil didn't reach very far. He poked his face toward the crack, trying to see farther into it. That only got in the way of the lamplight. He pulled back a little.

Suddenly, he saw light *inside* the crack—two lights, in fact. They appeared, vanished for a moment, and reappeared once more. That blink of a disappearance . . . As soon as he thought of it as a blink, he realized what he was seeing—the eyes of an animal, throwing back some of the lamplight that fell on them. And what sort of animal was most likely to lurk in this particular crack?

Again, Lanius realized the answer the moment he asked the right question. "Pouncer!" he exclaimed. "You come out of there this instant!"

"Mrowr," Pouncer said. The moncat, of course, did what it wanted to do, not what Lanius wanted it to do.

The king reached in after it. It batted at his hand once more. As far as it was concerned, it was playing a game. It kept its claws in their sheaths, and didn't try to hurt Lanius. He was enjoying himself a good deal less than the moncat. Pouncer was too far back in there for him to grab the beast and haul it out. If he tried, the game would quickly stop being one. The moncat had very sharp claws, and even sharper teeth. As long as it stayed in there, it could hurt him, and he couldn't get it out.

"Miserable, stupid creature," he grumbled.

That told the cooks and cleaners what was going on. "Is it the moncat again, Your Majesty?" a woman asked. Lanius nodded.

"What do you want to do?" asked a cook with a gray beard.

"I want to make the beast come out," the king replied. "If I try to haul it out by the scruff of the neck, it'll tear my hand to pieces."

"Give it some scraps," the cook suggested. Lanius hoped he would have thought of that himself in a few heartbeats. The cook called, "Bring a scrap of meat for His Majesty!"

Before long, the scrawny assistant who'd come up with the lamp did. Lanius held the bit of meat at the edge of the crack. Pouncer grabbed it and ate it without coming out. "Another scrap!" Lanius said. He could hear the moncat purring. It was having a fine time. He wished he could say the same.

He got the next scrap. He let Pouncer see this one, but held it far enough away to make the moncat come out after it.

Since he was still holding the lamp in his right hand, grabbing Pouncer was an awkward, clumsy business. He managed, though, and also managed to get down the ladder with lamp, moncat, and himself intact. The kitchen crew cheered. Pouncer finished the second scrap of meat and looked around for more.

The cook who'd thought of feeding scraps to the moncat saw that, too. "Now that thing won't want to steal spoons anymore," he said. "It'll want to steal meat instead."

That seemed depressingly probable to Lanius. "I'm going to take it back to its room for now," he said. "Maybe it will stay there for a while, anyhow." He looked down at Pouncer. The moncat stared back. Was that animal innocence or animal mischief in its eyes? Lanius couldn't tell. He suspected he'd find out.

One day followed another in the siege of Nishevatz. King Grus did his best to make sure the Avornan army had enough food, and to try to heal the soldiers who fell sick. Disease could devastate a force more thoroughly than battle. Healers and wizards did what they could against fluxes of the bowels and other ailments. None of the sicknesses raced through the camp like wildfire, as they so often did.

Grus wondered how things were on the other side of the wall. Every so often, one or two of Vasilko's warriors would slip down a rope and come out to the Avornan line. Like the first few men who'd given up the fight, they were hungry and weary, but they weren't starving. Vasilko's followers still fought back when Grus poked at them. They showed no signs of being ready to give up.

And then, one morning that had seemed no different from any other, a messenger came back from the siege line to the king's pavilion. "Your Majesty, Prince Vasilko is on the wall!" the young soldier said excitedly. "He says he wants to talk to you."

"Does he?" Grus said, and the young soldier nodded. Grus got off the stool he'd been sitting on. "Well, then, I'd better find out what he has to say for himself, hadn't I?"

In spite of his words, he didn't approach Nishevatz by himself. He brought a company of soldiers, enough men to protect himself if Vasilko turned treacherous, and he also brought Pterocles.

The wizard trembled a little—trembled more than a little—as he approached the walls of Nishevatz. "I hope I can protect you, Your Majesty," he said. "If the Banished One puts forth all his strength through Vasilko . . ."

"If I didn't think you could help me, I wouldn't have asked you to come along," Grus answered. "You're the best I've got, and by now you have the measure of what the Banished One can do."

"Oh, yes. I have his measure," Pterocles said in a hollow voice. "And he has mine. That's what I'm afraid of."

Grus clapped him on the back. Pterocles' answering smile was distinctly wan. Grus tried not to let it worry him. His own curiosity was getting the better of him as he drew near the walls of Nishevatz. He'd been at war against Vasilko for years, but had never set eyes on him up until now. He peered up, trying to pick Vsevolod's rebellious son out from the rest of the Chernagor defenders.

Nothing in Vasilko's dress gave him away. Grus wished he'd taken that same precaution. Vasilko and the other Chernagors would have no trouble figuring out who he was if they wanted to try something nasty instead of parleying. With a shrug, Grus cupped his hands in front of his mouth and called, "I'm here, Vasilko. What do you want to say to me?"

The Chernagor who stepped up to the very edge of the battlement was older than Grus had thought he would be. The King of Avornis had expected to face an angry youth, but Vasilko was on the edge of middle age. Grus realized he need not have been startled; Vsevolod had died full of years. Still, it was a surprise.

Vasilko looked down at him with as much curiosity as he felt himself. "Why do you persecute me?" the usurper asked in Avornan better than Vsevolod had spoken.

"Why did you overthrow your father when you were his heir?" Grus answered. "Why do you follow the Banished One and not the gods in the heavens?"

Some of the Chernagors up on the walls of Nishevatz stirred. Grus supposed they were the ones who could understand Avornan. In a town full of traders, that some men could came as no great wonder. A few of them sent Vasilko startled looks. Did they think he still worshiped King

Olor and Queen Quelea and the rest of the heavenly hierarchy? Maybe they were learning something new.

Vasilko said, "Avornis' throne was not yours by right, either, but you took it."

"I did not cast out King Lanius," Grus answered, wishing Vasilko hadn't chosen that particular comeback. Grus went on, "King Lanius is in the royal palace in the city of Avornis right now. And I never cast aside the gods in the heavens. They knew what they were doing when they exiled the Banished One." *I hope—I pray—they knew what they were doing.*

"And when did it become your business what god Nishevatz follows?" Vasilko plainly had a prince's pride.

"The Banished One has tried to kill me more than once," Grus said. "The nomads who follow him have worked all sorts of harm on Avornis. His friends are my foes, and if he is the sort of god usurpers follow, how safe are you on your stolen throne?"

That made Vasilko look around in sudden alarm, as though wondering which of his officers he might be better off not trusting. But then the Chernagor straightened once more. "We stand united," he said loudly.

"Is that what you called me here to tell me?" Grus asked. Beside him, Pterocles stirred. Grus knew what the wizard was thinking—that Vasilko had called him here to launch a sorcerous attack against him. Grus would have been happier if he hadn't found that fairly likely himself.

But some of Vasilko's pride leaked out of him as he stood there and looked out on land he could not rule because the Avornan army held him away from it. He spoke more quietly when he replied, "No. I want to learn what terms you may have in mind."

"Are you yielding? Is Nishevatz yielding?" Grus demanded, his voice taut with excitement.

"Not now. Not yet. Maybe not ever," Vasilko said. "I told you, I want to know your terms."

Grus hadn't thought hard about terms until this moment. He had always assumed the siege would have to drag on until the bitter end, until his men either stormed the walls or starved Nishevatz into surrender—or, with bad luck, failed. Slowly, he said, "The people of the city are to acknowledge Beloyuz as Prince of Nishevatz. They are to let my army into Nishevatz, and to give up all their weapons except for eating knives and one sword for every three men. You yourself are to come back to Avornis with me, to live out your days in exile in the Maze."

He waited to see how Vasilko would respond to that. He didn't have to wait long. "No," Vasilko said, and turned his back. "The fight goes on."

"So be it," Grus said. "You will not get a better bargain from me when we break into Nishevatz."

That made Vasilko turn back. "You talk about doing that. Go ahead and talk. But when you have done it, then you will have earned the right. Not now." He disappeared from Grus' view; the king supposed he had gone down from the wall.

"So much for that," Grus remarked as he returned to the siege line the Avornans had set up. "I'd hoped for better, but I hadn't really looked for it."

"You got more than I thought you would, Your Majesty," Pterocles said. Grus raised a questioning eyebrow. The wizard went on, "This was a real parley, even if it didn't work. I thought it would be nothing but a try at assassinating you."

"Oh." Grus thought that over. He set a hand on Pterocles' shoulder. "You have a pretty strange notion of what goes into progress, you know that?"

"I suppose I do," the sorcerer said.

"Any luck?" General Hirundo called when Grus came into the siege line.

The king shook his head. "Not a bit of it, except that Vasilko didn't try to murder me." Hirundo laughed. Grus would have meant it for a joke before Pterocles had spoken. Now he wasn't joking. The siege went on.

"Back when I was your age," King Lanius told his son, "the Thervings were a lot fiercer than they are now. They even laid siege to the city of Avornis a couple of times, though they couldn't take it."

Prince Crex listened solemnly. "How come they're different now?" he asked.

Lanius beamed. "Good question! King Berto, who rules them nowadays, is a peaceable fellow. He wants to be a holy man."

"Like Arch-Hallow Anser?" Crex asked.

"Well . . . in a way," Lanius said. Anser wasn't particularly holy; he just held a post that required the appearance of holiness from its occupant. From everything Lanius had seen, King Berto was sincere in his devotion to the gods. But how to explain that to a little boy? Not seeing how he could, Lanius continued, "Berto's father, King Dagipert, was more interested in fighting than in praying."

Crex frowned. "So if the next King of Thervingia would sooner fight than pray, will we have wars with the Thervings all the time again?"

That was an even better question. "I hope we won't," Lanius answered. "But both sides have to want peace for it to stick. Only one needs to want a war."

He waited to see what Crex would make of that. After another brief pause, Crex asked, "When is Grandpa coming home?"

"I don't know," Lanius said, blinking at the effortless ease with which children could change the subject. "When he's taken Nishevatz, I suppose."

"I miss him," Crex said. "If he were a king who liked to pray instead a king who likes to fight, would he be home now?"

Maybe he hadn't changed the subject after all. "I don't know, son," Lanius said again. "He might have to go fight anyhow, because up in the Chernagor country he's fighting against the Banished One."

"Oh," Crex said. "All right." And he went off to play without so much as a backward glance at his father.

He ought to know more about these things. He'll be king one day—I hope, Lanius thought. Crex needed to know about the different bands of Menteshe, about all the Chernagor city-states and how they fit together, about the Thervings, and about the barbarous folk who roamed beyond the Bantian Mountains but might swarm over them to trouble either Thervingia or Avornis itself. He needed to know about the Banished One, too, however much Lanius wished he didn't.

Right now, the only way for Crex to find out everything he needed to know was to ask someone who already knew. The trouble was, nobody, not even Lanius, knew offhand everything a King of Avornis might need to learn about his kingdom's neighbors.

"I ought to write it all down," Lanius said. He nodded, pleased with the idea. It would help Crex. He was sure of that. And it would give him the excuse to go pawing through the archives to find out whatever he didn't already know about the foreigners his kingdom had to deal with.

He laughed at himself. As though he needed excuses to go pawing through the archives! But now he would be doing it for a reason, not just for his own amusement. Didn't that count?

When he told Sosia what he had in mind, she didn't seem to think so. "Will I ever see you again?" she asked. "Or will you go into that nasty, dusty room and disappear forever?"

"It's not nasty," Lanius said. He couldn't deny the archives were dusty. On the other hand, he had a few very pleasant memories of things he'd done there, even if his wife didn't need to hear about them.

Sosia's shrug showed amused resignation. "Go on, then. At least when you're in there, I know what you're doing." Again, Lanius congratulated himself for not telling her it wasn't necessarily so.

He'd spent a lot of time going through the archives looking for what they had to say about the Banished One and the Scepter of Mercy. Now he was looking for some different things—for how his ancestors, and the kings who'd ruled Avornis before his ancestors came to the throne, had dealt with their neighbors.

He couldn't keep from laughing at himself. Arch-Hallow Anser hunted deer. So did Prince Ortalis, who would have hunted more tender game if he could have gotten away with it. *And me?* Lanius thought. *I hunt pieces of parchment the mice haven't nibbled too badly.* He knew Anser and Ortalis would both laugh at him if that thought occurred to them. Why not beat them to the punch?

Before the end of his first hunting trip in the archives—no serving girls along to act as beaters for the game he sought—he knew he would have no trouble coming up with all he needed and more besides. Then he found a new question. What would he do once he had everything he needed? He'd written countless letters. This was the first time he'd tried writing a book—he'd never begun the one on palace life.

What would he call it? The first thing that came to mind was *How to Be a King*. He wondered if that was too simple. Would any ambitious noble or officer think he could rule Avornis if he had the book? Of course, the kingdom had seen plenty of would-be usurpers without it, so how much would that matter? Would it matter at all?

How to Be a King, then. It said what he wanted to say, and it would do for now. If he got a better idea later, he could always change it. The next question was, how to go about writing it? What did he need to tell Crex, and how should he tell it? How could he make a book like that interesting enough to tempt a prince who could do anything he wanted to go on reading it?

He was, he realized, asking himself a lot of questions. As soon as the thought crossed his mind, he laughed and clapped his hands. He got pen and parchment. After inking the pen, he wrote, *What do you need to know, my son, to become the sort of king Avornis should have?* Having asked the question, he proceeded to answer it. He asked another, more specific, question, and answered that, too. The answer posed yet another question. He also answered that one.

The longer Lanius wrote, the more detailed the questions got, and the more poking through the archives he had to do to answer them. Not many days went by before he was trying to sort out the complicated history of Avornan dealings with the individual Chernagor city-states, and doing his best to give advice on how to play them off one against another.

He thought about having a scribe make a copy of that part of *How to Be a King* so he could send it up to Grus in the Chernagor country. He thought about it, but he didn't do it. Grus was liable to think he was interfering in the campaign—and Grus was also a pretty good horse-back diplomat, even if he didn't care to spend days at a time digging through the archives.

Lanius muttered. The older he got, the more complex his feelings toward his father-in-law became. Grus had stolen most of the royal power. He'd made Lanius marry his daughter. It hadn't turned out to be an altogether loveless marriage, but it wasn't the one Lanius would have made if he'd had a choice, either.

Set against that were all the things Grus might have done but hadn't. He might have taken Lanius' head or packed him off to the Maze. He hadn't. He might have become a fearsome tyrant, slaughtering anyone who presumed to disagree with him. Despite repeated revolts against his rule, he hadn't. And he might have lost big pieces of Avornis to the Thervings, to the Menteshe, or to the Chernagor pirates. He hadn't done that, either.

He *had* raised a worthless son, and he had fathered a bastard or two. He had also done his best to keep Lanius too poor to cause trouble for him. Set against that, he had gotten the Banished One's notice. If the Banished One took Grus seriously, Lanius didn't see how he couldn't.

Grus gets the job done, Lanius thought reluctantly. *Whatever he needs to do, he usually manages to do it.* The other king had even found a way to keep nobles from turning Avornan peasants into their personal retainers. That was a problem Lanius hadn't even noticed. Grus hadn't just noticed it. He'd solved it.

"He's still a usurper," Lanius murmured. That was true. It was also infuriating. But Grus could have been *so* much worse. Admitting it was even more infuriating for Lanius.

CHAPTER TWENTY-FIVE

R ain dripped from a sky the color of dirty wool. King Grus squelched through the mud, heading from his pavilion toward the Avornan line around Nishevatz. He could hardly see the walls of the city through the shifting curtain of raindrops. Rain in the summertime came every now and again to the city of Avornis; down in the south, it was rare, rare enough to be a prodigy. Here in the Chernagor country, the weather did whatever it pleased.

The mud tried to pull the boots right off Grus' feet. Each step took an effort. Every so often, he would pause to kick gobs of muck from his boots, or to scrape them against rocks. He tried to imagine Lanius picking his way through this dirt pudding of a landscape. The image refused to form. There was more to Lanius than he'd thought when he first took the throne; he was willing to admit that much. But the other king was irrevocably a man of the palace. Put him in charge of a siege and he wouldn't know what to do.

Each cat his own rat, Grus thought. He knew he would have as much trouble in the archives as Lanius would here in front of Nishevatz. In his own province, Lanius was perfectly capable. Grus remained convinced that what *he* did was more important for Avornis.

"Halt! Who comes!" A sentry who looked like a phantom called out the challenge.

"Grus," Grus answered.

That phantom came to attention. "Advance and be recognized, uh, Your Majesty." The king did. The sentry saluted. He wore a wool rain cape over a helmet and chainmail. He'd smeared the armor with grease and tallow, so that water beaded on it. Even so, when the weather finally dried—if it ever did—he and all the other Avornan soldiers would have plenty of polishing and scraping to do to keep rust from running rampant. With another salute, the sentry said, "Pass on, Your Majesty."

"I thank you." Grus' own helm and chainmail were gilded to mark his rank. That made the iron resist rust better, but he would have to do some polishing and scraping, too. He did not let servants tend to his armor, but cared for it himself. It protected him. How better to make sure it was as it should be than to tend it with his own eyes and hands?

Another sentry, alert as could be, challenged him. Again, Grus advanced and was recognized. The sentry said, "Forgive me, Your Majesty, but where are your bodyguards?"

"Back there somewhere," Grus answered vaguely. He felt a small-boy pride at escaping them.

The sentry clucked in disapproval. "You should let them keep an eye on you. How will you stay safe if they don't?"

"I can take care of myself," Grus said. The sentry, being only a sentry, didn't presume to argue. Grus went on. The farther he went, though, the more shame ate away at his pride. The man was right. He took good care of his armor and forgot his bodyguards, who might prove at least as important in keeping him alive.

Promising himself he wouldn't do that anymore, he pressed on now. He got away with it, too. When he found Hirundo, the general ordered half a dozen men to form up around him. Grus didn't quarrel. Hirundo wagged a finger. "You've been naughty."

"No doubt." The king's tone was dry—the only thing in the dripping landscape that was. "What do you propose to do about it?"

"Why, send you to bed without supper, Your Majesty," Hirundo answered with a grin. "Oh, and keep you safe, if I can, since you don't seem very interested in doing that for yourself." Unlike the guard, he had rank enough to point out Grus' folly.

"Believe me, you've made your point," Grus said. "I hope you're not going to turn into one of those tedious people who keep banging on tent pegs after they've driven them into the ground."

"Me? I wouldn't dream of such a thing." Hirundo was the picture of soggy innocence. "I hope you're not going to be one of those tedious tent pegs that keep coming loose no matter how you bang on them."

"Ha," Grus said, and then, for good measure, "Ha, ha." Hirundo bowed, unabashed as usual. The king pointed in the general direction of Nishevatz. "How would you like to try to attack the walls under cover of this rain?"

"I will if you give the order, Your Majesty." Hirundo turned serious on the instant. "If you give me a choice, though, I'd rather not. Archery is impossible in weather like this, and—"

"For us and for them," Grus broke in.

"Oh, yes." The general nodded. "But they don't need to shoot much. They can just drop things on our heads while we're coming up the ladders. We need archers more than they do, to keep their men on the walls busy ducking while we're coming up. And planting scaling ladders in gooey muck isn't really something I care to do, either."

"Oh," Grus said. "I see." To his disappointment, he *did* see. "You make more sense than I wish you did."

"Sorry, Your Majesty," Hirundo replied. "I'll try not to let it happen again."

"A likely story," Grus said. "All right, then. If you don't want to attack in a rainstorm, what about one of the fogs that come off the Northern Sea? Do you think that would be any better?"

Now Hirundo paused to think it over. "It might, yes, if you've given up on starving Vasilko out. Have you?"

"Summer's moving along," Grus said, which both did and did not answer the question. He continued, "It won't be easy for us to stay here through the winter, and who knows how long Vasilko can hold out?"

"Something to that." Hirundo sounded willing but not consumed by enthusiasm. "Well, I suppose we could get ready to try. No telling when another one of those fogs will roll in, you know. The more you want one, the longer you're likely to wait."

"You're probably right," Grus agreed. "But let's get ready. We'll see how hard they really want to fight for Vasilko." He hoped the answer was *not very.*

How do we keep the Chernagor pirates from descending on our coasts? Lanius' pen raced across the parchment. Since he'd started writing *How to Be a King* for Crex, he'd discovered he was good at posing broad, sweeping questions. Coming up with answers for them seemed much harder.

He did his best here, as he'd done his best with every one of the questions he'd asked himself. He wrote about keeping the Chernagor city-states divided among themselves, about keeping trade with them strong so they wouldn't want to send out raiders, and about the tall-masted ships Grus had ordered built to match those the men from the Chernagor country used. His pen faltered as he tried to describe those ships. He'd ordered them forth, but he'd never seen anything except river galleys and barges. *I'll have to ask Grus more when he comes back from the north,* he thought, and scribbled a note on the parchment to remind himself to do that.

Once the note was written, the king paused, nibbling on the end of the reed pen. Some scribes used goose quills, but Lanius was better at cutting reeds, and was also convinced they held more ink. Besides, nibbling the end of a goose quill gave you nothing but a mouthful of soggy fluff.

After a few minutes of thought, he came up with another good, broad, sweeping question, and wrote it down to make sure he didn't forget it before he could put it on parchment. *How do we deal with the thralls who may cross into Avornis from the lands of the Menteshe, and with those we may find in the lands the Menteshe rule?*

He almost scratched out the last half of the question. It struck him as optimism run wild. In the end, he left it there. He didn't suppose he would have if the nomads weren't fighting one another, but the civil war that had started among them after Prince Ulash died showed no signs of slowing down.

With or without the second half, the question was plenty to keep him thoughtful for some little while. What would Crex or some king who came after him need to know? Lanius warned that, while some escaped thralls came across the Stura seeking freedom, others remained under the Banished One's enchantments in spite of appearances to the contrary, and served as the exiled god's spies. *Or sometimes his assassins,* Lanius thought with a shiver of memory.

Lanius also warned Crex that spells for curing thralls were less reliable than everyone wished they were. *Although,* he wrote, *lately it does seem as though these charms are attended with more success than was hitherto the case.*

The king hoped that was true. He looked at what he'd written. He decided he'd qualified it well enough. By the time Crex was old enough to want to look at something like *How to Be a King,* everyone would have a better idea of how effective Pterocles' spells really were.

After getting up and stretching, Lanius decided not to sit down again and go back to the book just then. Instead, he stored the parchment and pen and jar of ink in the cabinet he'd brought into the archives for them. At first, he'd been nervous each time he turned away from the book, wondering if he would be stubborn enough to come back to it later. By now, he'd gotten far enough into it to have some confidence he would keep returning and would, one day, finish, even if that day seemed a long way off.

When he came out of the archives in his plain tunic and breeches, several palace servants walked past without paying him the least attention. That amused him. *Clothes make the man,* he thought. Without them, he seemed just another servant himself.

When Bubulcus hurried past, oblivious to the rank of the nondescript fellow in the even more nondescript clothes, Lanius almost called him back. Showing the toplofty servant he didn't know everything there was to know always tempted the king. But Lanius didn't feel like listening to Bubulcus' whined excuses—or to his claims that of course he'd known who Lanius was all along. Bubulcus, after all, had never made a mistake in his life, certainly not in his own mind.

Otus, now, Otus was a different story. The former thrall liberated by Pterocles' magic seemed glad to be alive, glad to know he *was* alive. If he made a mistake, he just laughed about it. And, when Lanius came to his guarded room, he knew who the king was. Bowing low, he murmured, "Your Majesty."

"Hello, Otus," Lanius said. "How are you today?"

The thrall straightened, a broad smile on his face. "I'm fine, thank you. Couldn't be better. Isn't it a *good* day?"

To Lanius, it seemed a day no different from any other. But then, Lanius hadn't lived almost his entire life under the shadow of thralldom. To Otus, today *was* different from most of the days he'd known, not least because he knew it so much more completely. Lanius said, "I've got a question for you."

"Go ahead," Otus said. If he noticed the guards who flanked King Lanius, he gave no sign. Lanius still didn't trust the magic that had lifted the dark veil of thralldom. Did something of the Banished One lurk beneath the freed thrall's sunny exterior? There had been no sign of it, but that didn't mean it wasn't there.

Besides Otus' behavior, there was other evidence against any lingering influence from the Banished One in him. The other thralls in the royal palace had calmly and quietly killed themselves before Pterocles could try his magic on them. Didn't that argue that the Banished One feared its power? Probably. But was he ruthless enough and far-seeing enough to sacrifice a pair of thralls to leave his opponents thinking they'd gained an advantage they didn't really have? Again, probably. And so . . . bodyguards.

Lanius asked, "Do you really think we could free a lot of thralls using the spells that freed you?" Otus was the only one here who knew from the inside out what being a thrall was like. If his answer couldn't be fully trusted, it had to be considered.

"I sure hope so, Your Majesty," Otus answered. Then he grinned sheepishly. "But that wasn't what you asked, was it?"

"Well, no," Lanius admitted.

Otus screwed up his face into a parody of deep thought. He finally shrugged and said, "I do think so. If it freed me, I expect it could free anybody. I'm nothing special."

"You are now," Lanius told him. Otus laughed. The king was right. But the former thrall also had a point. The longer he was free, the more ordinary he seemed. These days, he sounded like anyone else—anyone from the south, for he did keep his accent. When first coming out of the shadows, he'd had only a thrall's handful of words, and wouldn't have known what to do with more if he had owned them. *He truly must be cured,* Lanius thought, but then, doubtfully, *mustn't he?*

Beloyuz came up to King Grus. He pointed toward the walls of Nishevatz. Bowing, the Chernagor nobleman—the Chernagor whom Grus now styled Prince of Nishevatz—asked, "Your Majesty, how long is this army going to do nothing but sit in front of my city-state?"

Grus almost laughed in his face. He had to gnaw on the inside of his lower lip to keep from doing just that. Call Beloyuz the Prince of Nishevatz, and what did he do? Why, he started sounding just like Prince Vsevolod. After a few heartbeats, when Grus was sure he wouldn't say anything outrageous or scandalous, he answered, "Well, Your Highness, we are working on that. We're not ready to move yet, but we are working on it."

He waited to see if that would satisfy Beloyuz. The Chernagor frowned. He didn't look as glum or disgusted as Vsevolod would have, but he didn't miss by much, either. Suspicion clogging his voice, he said, "You are not just telling me this to make me go away and leave you alone?"

"By King Olor's beard, Your Highness, I am not," Grus said.

Now Beloyuz didn't answer for a little while. "All right," he said when he did speak. "I believe you. For now, I believe you." He bowed to Grus once more and strode away.

With a sigh, Grus walked down to the seashore. Guards flanked him. His shadow stretched out before him. It was longer than it would have been at high summer, and got longer still every day. He understood Beloyuz's worries, for the campaigning season was slipping away like grains of sand through an hourglass. If Nishevatz didn't fall on its own soon, he would have to move against it—either move, or try to press on with the siege through the winter, or give up and go back to Avornis. They were all unappetizing choices.

The weather was as fine as he'd ever seen it up here in the north. He muttered a curse at that, tasting the irony of it. He hadn't been lying to Beloyuz. He and Hirundo kept waiting for one of the famous fogs of the land of the Chernagors to come rolling in to conceal an attack on the walls. They waited and waited, while bright, clear day followed bright, clear day. The Chernagor country would have been a much more pleasant place if its summer days were like this all the time. Even so, Grus would gladly have traded this weather for the more usual murk.

Shorebirds skittered along the beach. Some of them, little balls of gray and white fluff, scooted on short legs right at the edge of the lapping sea. They would poke their beaks down into the sandy mud, every now and then coming away with a prize. Others, larger, waded on legs that made them look as though they were on stilts. Those had longer bills, too, some straight, some drooping down, and some, curiously, curving up.

Grus eyed those last birds and scratched his head, wondering what a bill like that could be good for. He saw no use for it, but supposed it had to have some, or the wading birds would have looked different.

Thanks to the clear weather, he could see a long way when he looked out to the Northern Sea. He spied none of the great ships the other Chernagor city-states had sent during the last siege of Nishevatz. They still feared Pterocles' sorcery.

That left Nishevatz to its own devices. Grus turned toward the gray stone walls that had defied his army for so long. They remained as sturdy as ever. Small in the distance, men moved along them. The Chernagors' armor glinted in the unusually bright sunshine. How hard *would* Vasilko's soldiers fight if he assailed those walls? He scowled. No sure way to know ahead of time. He would have to find out by experiment.

Not today, Grus thought. Today the Chernagors could see whatever he did, just as he could watch them. If one of the swaddling fogs this coast could breed ever came . . . then, maybe. But no, not today.

He and his guards weren't the only men walking up the beach. That lean, angular shape could only belong to Pterocles. The wizard waved as he approached. "Good day, Your Majesty," he called.

"Too good a day, maybe," Grus answered. "We could do with a spell of worse weather, if you want to know the truth."

Pterocles only shrugged. "Beware of any man who calls himself a weatherworker. He's lying. No man can do much with the weather. It's too big for a mere man to change. The Banished One . . . the Banished One is another story."

Grus suddenly saw the cloudless sky in a whole new light. "Are you saying the Banished One is to blame for this weather?" That gave him a different and more urgent reason for wanting fog.

And his question worried Pterocles. "No, I don't think so," the wizard answered after a long pause. "I believe I would feel it if he were meddling with the weather, and I don't. But he *could,* if he chose to. An ordinary sorcerer? No."

"All right. That eases my mind a bit." Grus turned and looked toward the south. His mind's eye leaped across the land of the Chernagors and across all of Avornis to the Menteshe country south of the Stura River. By all the dispatches that came up from Avornis, Sanjar and Korkut were still clawing away at each other. The princes to either side of what had been Ulash's realm were still tearing meat off its bones, too. By all the signs, the Banished One's attention remained focused on the strife among the people who had chosen him for their overlord.

They aren't thralls, though. They're men, Grus thought. They might be the Banished One's servants, but they weren't his mindless puppets, weren't his slaves. They worshiped him, but they had their own concerns, their own interests, as well. And, for the moment, those counted for more among them.

That had to infuriate the exiled god. So far, though, the Menteshe seemed to be doing as they pleased in their wars, not as the Banished One would have commanded. His eyes on them, he forgot about Nishevatz, about Vasilko.

"If the Menteshe make peace, or if one of them wins outright . . ." Grus began.

Pterocles nodded, following his thought perfectly. "If that happens, the Banished One could well look this way again."

"Frightening to think we depend on strife among our foes," Grus said.

"At least we have it," Pterocles replied. "And since we have it, we'd better make the most of it."

"We will," Grus said. "I don't think we're going to starve them out before we start running low on food ourselves. I hoped we would, but it doesn't look that way. If we want Nishevatz, we'll have to take it. I intend to try to take it. But I need fog, to let me move men forward without being seen."

"If I could give it to you, I would," Pterocles said. "Since I can't, I'll hope with you that it comes soon."

"When I didn't want them, we had plenty of fogs," Grus said. "Now that I do, what do we get? Weather the city of Avornis wouldn't be ashamed of. The best weather I've ever seen in the Chernagor country, by the gods—the best, and the worst."

"The gods can give you fog, if they will," Pterocles said.

"Yes. If they will." Grus said no more than that. If the Banished One had power over wind and weather, surely the gods in the heavens did, too. *Come on,* Grus thought in their direction. It wasn't a prayer—more like an annoyed nudge. *You can make things harder for the Banished One.*

Were they listening? Grus laughed at himself. How could he tell? If they didn't pay some attention to it, though, they could earn an eternity's worth of regrets. With the world in his hands, the Banished One might find a way back to the heavens. Grus tried to see beyond the sky. He couldn't—he was only a man. But the gods could do whatever they pleased. Olor could take six wives and still keep Quelea contented. If *that* wasn't a miracle, Grus didn't know what would be.

If he didn't believe in the power of the gods, what other power was there left to believe in? That of the Banished One. Nobody could deny his power. Yielding to it, worshiping it, was something else again.

"Fog," Grus said. "We need fog."

Fog filled the streets of the city of Avornis, rolling off the river, sliding silently over the walls, muffling life in the capital. The silence struck Lanius as almost eerie. Did the thick mist really swallow sound, or was it so quiet because people didn't care to go out and try to find their way around in the murk? The question seemed easier to ask than to answer.

When the king stepped out of the royal palace, it grew indistinct, ghostly, behind him. *If I walk back toward it,* he thought, *will it really be there? Or will it disappear or recede before me like a will-o'-the-wisp?*

Lanius exhaled. His own breath added to the fog swirling all around him. From what he had read, such smothering, obliterating fogs were far commoner in the land of the Chernagors than they were here. He hoped Grus kept his army alert through them, and didn't let Vasilko's men launch a surprise attack against the Avornan lines.

He walked a little farther from the palace. Even his footsteps seemed softer than they should have. Was that his imagination? He didn't think so, but he supposed it could have been.

"Your Majesty?" a guard called from behind him. The man sounded anxious. When Lanius looked back, he saw why. Or, better, he didn't see why, for the guardsman had disappeared altogether. "Your Majesty?" the fellow called again, something close to panic in his voice. "Where are you, Your Majesty?"

"I'm here," Lanius answered, and walked back toward the sound of the guardsman's voice. With each step, the royal palace became more decidedly real. The king nodded to the worried bodyguard. "Thick out there today, isn't it?"

"Thick as porridge," the guard said. "I'm glad you came back, Your Majesty. I would have gone after you in another moment, and the mist might have swallowed me whole. You never can tell."

"No, I suppose not." Lanius hid a smile. But it faded after a couple of heartbeats. The Banished One could do things with the weather no ordinary sorcerer could hope to match. If he had sent the fog, and if someone—or *something*—lurked in it . . . Lanius' shiver had nothing to do with the clammy weather. By way of apology, he said, "I was foolish to wander off in it myself."

The guardsman nodded. He would never have presumed to criticize the king. If the king criticized himself, the guard would not presume to disagree.

Lanius went back inside the palace. His cheeks and beard were beaded with moisture. He hadn't noticed it in the fog, where everything was damp, but he did once he came inside. He wiped his face with the sleeve of his royal robe. A servant coming up the hallway sent him a scandalized stare. His cheeks heated, as though he'd been caught picking his nose in public.

At least it wasn't Bubulcus, the king thought. Bubulcus would have made him feel guilty about it for the rest of his days.

"Your Majesty! Your Majesty!" That call echoing down the corridor came not from a guardsman but from a maidservant.

"I'm here," Lanius called back. "What's gone wrong now?" By the shrill note of hysteria in the woman's voice, something certainly had.

She came around the corner and saw him. "Come quick, Your Majesty!"

"I'm coming," Lanius said. "What is it?"

"It's the prince," she said. Terror gripped Lanius' heart—had something happened to Crex? Then the serving woman added, "He's done something truly dreadful this time," and Lanius' panic eased. Crex wasn't old enough to do anything dreadful enough to raise this kind of horror in a grown woman. Which meant . . .

"Ortalis?"

"Yes, Your Majesty," the woman said.

"Oh, by the gods!" Lanius said. "What has he done?" *Which serving girl has he outraged, and how badly?* was what he meant.

But this serving woman answered, "Why, he went and killed a man. Poor Bubulcus." She started to cry.

"Bubulcus!" Lanius exclaimed. "I was just thinking about him."

"That's all anybody will do from now on," the serving woman said. "He had a wife and children, too. Queen Quelea's mercy on them, for they'll need it."

"How did it happen?" Lanius asked in helpless astonishment. The woman only shrugged. Lanius spread his hands. "You were going to take me to him. You'd better do that."

She did. They had to push through a growing crowd of servants to get to Ortalis, who still stood over Bubulcus' body. A whip lay on the floor behind the prince. Blood soaked the servant's tunic. It pooled beneath him. His eyes stared up sightlessly. His mouth, Lanius was not surprised to find, was open. *In character to the last,* the king thought.

The bloody knife in Ortalis' right hand was a small one, such as he might have used for cutting up fruit. It had sufficed for nastier work as well.

"What happened here?" Lanius demanded as he shoved his way to the front of the crowd. "And put that cursed thing down, Ortalis," he added sharply. "You certainly don't need it now."

Grus' son let the knife fall. "He insulted me," he said in a distant— almost a dazed—voice. "He insulted me, and I hit him, and he jeered at me again—said his mother could hit harder than that. And the next thing I knew . . . The next thing I knew, there he was on the floor."

Lanius looked around. "Did anyone see this? Did anyone hear it?"

"I did, Your Majesty," said a sweeper with a grizzled beard. "You know how Bubulcus always likes—liked—to show how clever he was, to see how close to the edge he could come."

"Oh, yes," Lanius said. "I had noticed that."

"Well," the sweeper said, "he sees that there whip in His Highness' hand—"

"I'd just come in from a ride," Ortalis said quickly.

"In this horrible fog?" Lanius said. He wished he had the words back as soon as they were gone. He could guess what Ortalis had really been doing with the whip. *With whom, and did she like it?* he wondered, feeling a little sick.

"Anyways," the sweeper went on, "Bubulcus asks him if that's the whip he uses to hit little Princess Capella. And that's when His Highness smacked him."

"I . . . see," Lanius said slowly. Had he been in Ortalis' boots, he thought he would have hit Bubulcus for that, too. Using a whip on a willing woman was one thing. *Limosa thinks Ortalis is wonderful,* Lanius reminded himself, gulping. Using the same whip on a baby girl was something else again. Not even Ortalis would do such a thing— Lanius devoutly hoped.

If Ortalis had let it go there, Lanius didn't see how anyone could have said anything much. But Bubulcus had had to make one more crack, and then . . . "After that," the sweeper said, "His Highness punctured him right and proper, he did."

Chastising an offensive servant and killing him were also two different things. Lanius' sole relief was that Ortalis didn't seem to have done it for his own amusement. Again, killing in a fit of rage was different from killing for the sport of it.

A servant who killed in a fit of rage would be punished. He might lose his head. King Grus' son, Lanius knew, wouldn't lose his head for slaying Bubulcus. But Ortalis shouldn't get off scot-free, either. For all

Bubulcus' faults—which Lanius knew as well as anybody—he hadn't deserved to die for a crude joke or two.

"Hear me, Ortalis," Lanius said, his tone more for the benefit of the murmuring servants than for his brother-in-law. "When you killed Bubulcus, you went beyond what was proper."

"So did he," Ortalis muttered, but he didn't try to deny that he'd transgressed. That helped.

"Hear me," Lanius repeated. "Because you went beyond what was proper, I order you to settle on Bubulcus' widow enough silver to let her and her children live comfortably for the rest of their lives. That will repair some of what you have done."

He waited. Two things could go wrong with his judgment. Ortalis might prove arrogant enough to reject it out of hand, or the servants might decide it wasn't enough.

Ortalis did some more muttering, but he finally said, "Oh, all right. Fool should have known when to shut up, though." That struck Lanius as the most fitting epitaph Bubulcus would get.

The king's gaze swung to the servants. None of them said anything right away; they were gauging what he'd done. After a bit, one of the men said, "I expect most of us wanted to pop Bubulcus one time or another." Slowly, one after another, they began to nod.

Lanius let out a small sigh. He seemed to have gotten away with it on both counts. "Take the body away and clean up the mess," he said. The scarlet pool under Bubulcus' corpse unpleasantly reminded him how much blood a body held. "Let Bubulcus' wife—his widow—know what happened. And let her know Prince Ortalis will also pay for the funeral pyre."

Ortalis stirred, but again did not protest. Most of the servants drifted away. A few remained to carry out Lanius' orders. One of them said, "You took care of that pretty well, Your Majesty." A couple of other men nodded.

"My thanks," Lanius said. "Some of these things, you only wish they never would have happened in the first place."

Even Ortalis nodded. "That's true. If he'd just kept quiet . . ." He still didn't sound sorry Bubulcus was dead. Expecting him to was probably asking too much. And the servants had seemed satisfied that he would pay compensation. It could have turned out worse.

Then Lanius realized it wasn't over yet. *I have to write Grus and let him know what his son's done now.* He would almost rather have gone under a dentist's forceps than set pen to parchment for that. No help for it, though. Grus *would* surely hear. Better he should hear from someone who had the story straight.

Two men carried Bubulcus' body away. Women went to work on the pool of blood. Ortalis scowled at Lanius. "How much silver will you steal from me to pay for that wretch's worthless life?"

"However much it is, you can afford it better than he can afford what you took from him." Lanius sighed. "I know he could drive a man mad. More than once, I almost sent him to the Maze. Now I wish I would have. In the Maze, he'd still be breathing."

"If he made *you* angry, he was too big a fool to hope to live very long," Ortalis said. "You're too soft for your own good."

"Am I?" Lanius said.

His brother-in-law nodded. "You let the servants get away with murder."

No, you've just gotten away with murder, Lanius thought. No ordinary man would have come off so lightly. But Ortalis wasn't an ordinary man, not when it came to his family connections. That he'd paid any price at all probably surprised the palace servants.

Grus' son stooped and picked up the knife he'd used to stab Bubulcus. "What will you do with that thing?" Lanius asked. If Ortalis wanted to keep it for a souvenir, he would have to change his mind. The king made up his mind to be very firm about that.

But Ortalis answered, "I'm going to throw it away. I've got no more use for it now." He strode down the hallway. Lanius stared after him. Ortalis still didn't see that he'd done much out of the ordinary. Lanius sighed again. Bubulcus, could anyone have asked him, would have had a different opinion.

CHAPTER TWENTY-SIX

When Grus breathed in, he felt as though he'd fallen into a
vat of cold soup. The sky had gone from black to gray, but
he still couldn't see a hand in front of his face. The fog felt
as thick and smothering—though not nearly as warm—as wool bat-
ting.

"Hirundo!" he called softly. "Are you there?"

"Right here, Your Majesty," the general answered, almost at his el-
bow. Grus had to lean forward and peer to see him at all. Chuckling,
Hirundo said, "Our prayers are answered, aren't they?"

"*Too* well, maybe," Grus said. Hirundo laughed again, though the
king wasn't at all sure he'd been joking. Fog was fog, and this was excessive. It seemed like the boiled-down essence of every fog Grus had
ever seen in all his life. "By the gods, we'll be lucky to find the walls of
Nishevatz, let alone storm them."

"We may have fun finding them—true enough," Hirundo said,
though *fun* was the last word Grus would have used. "But just think
how much fun Vasilko and the Chernagors will have trying to keep us
out once we do get up on the battlements. We'll have a whole great
lodgement before they even realize we're anywhere close by."

"Gods grant it be so," Grus said. He and the Avornan army had
spent weeks waiting through what passed for a heat wave in the Chernagor country. Now the usual mists were back, with a vengeance. Grus
hoped the vengeance wouldn't be excessive.

"Your Majesty?"

That was Pterocles' voice. "I'm here," Grus said, and the wizard blundered forward until they bumped into each other. "Can you guide the men to Nishevatz?" Grus asked. "And can you keep the Chernagors from hearing them as they come?"

"Well, Your Majesty, if we all splash into the Northern Sea, you'll know something has gone wrong," the wizard replied.

"Heh," Grus said. "You *will* be able to do it?"

A glow that somehow pierced the fog where nothing else would illuminated Pterocles' hands. "I will."

"Good." Grus hesitated. "Uh—I hope the Chernagors on the walls won't be able to see your sorcery."

"So do I," Pterocles said cheerfully. "And yes, I just might be able to muffle things, too." Grus gave up. Either the wizard was teasing him or the whole campaign would unravel in the next few minutes. Grus chose to believe Pterocles was joking. *One way or the other, I'll find out soon,* the king thought.

"There's the light." At least a dozen Avornan officers, spying Pterocles' glowing hands, said the same thing at the same time. They all sounded relieved, too, no matter how the fog muffled their voices.

"Let's go," Pterocles said. "Nishevatz is . . . that way." He pointed with a gleaming forefinger. Grus wondered how he could have any idea of the direction in which Nishevatz lay. Looking down, the king couldn't even see his own feet. As far as he could tell, he disappeared from the knees down.

But Pterocles spoke with perfect confidence. And when he moved out in the direction he thought right, the Avornan soldiers followed him. They could see his hands through the fog. A party of men carrying a scaling ladder almost ran over Grus. He heard no cries from the walls of the city. Evidently, the Chernagors really couldn't see Pterocles.

Or maybe he's going the wrong way. Grus wished that hadn't occurred to him. He was committed now. He had to rely on Pterocles. If, for instance, the Banished One was fooling the wizard . . . Grus wished that hadn't occurred to him, too.

"Guards!" he called.

"Here, Your Majesty." The answer came in a chorus from all around him.

"Let's go forward," Grus said.

The guardsmen formed up in a tight knot, completely surrounding the king. They seemed under the impression that if they didn't, he would yank out his sword and swarm up a scaling ladder ahead of every ordinary Avornan soldier. He was glad they were under that impression. He'd done a lot of fighting in his time. By now, though, he was coming up against soldiers who weren't just half his age but a third his age. He knew more than a little pride that he could still hold his own when he had to, but he wasn't such an eager warrior anymore.

Not only the guards but Grus himself stumbled more than once on the way to the walls of Nishevatz. They might see Pterocles' sorcerously glowing hands, but they couldn't see rocks and holes in the ground under their own feet. Low-voiced curses and occasional thumps from all around said they weren't the only ones with that trouble.

Grus craned his neck to one side, trying to listen for shouts of alarm from Vasilko's men. He still heard none. His hopes began to rise. Maybe this would work after all. Maybe . . .

Then he did hear the unmistakable thud of a scaling ladder going up against a wall. Soldiers rushed toward the top of the ladder. Someone up on the wall called out in the Chernagor language—a challenge, Grus supposed. Pterocles hadn't managed to hide that noise. The answer came back in the Chernagor tongue, for Hirundo had thought to put some of the men who'd stayed loyal to Prince Vsevolod at the head of the storming party.

Whatever the response meant, it quieted the defender who'd challenged. That meant the Avornans got onto the wall without any trouble. Then more shouts rang out, and the clash of blade on blade. But Grus knew Vasilko's men were in trouble. If the attackers managed to seize a portion of the wall, they had an enormous advantage on the men trying to hold them off.

"Up!" shouted officers at the base of the wall. "Up, up, up! Quick! Quick!" They sounded like parents trying to keep unruly three-year-olds in line. No child took seriously something said only once. Repeat it and it might possibly sink in. Soldiers were often the same way.

Men cursed and grunted as they swarmed up toward the battlements of Nishevatz. More curses and screams rang out up above on those battlements. So did the sound of running feet as the Chernagors rushed to the threatened part of the wall. Then frightened shouts came from another part of the works around Nishevatz. Grus whooped. He knew what that had to mean—the Avornans had gotten up there, too.

A body thudded to earth at the king's feet. It was a Chernagor; the black-bearded officer had gear too fine for a common soldier. He writhed feebly and moaned in pain. One of Grus' guardsmen raised a spear to finish the man off. "Wait," Grus said. "Maybe the healers can save him. He's no danger to us, and we may learn something from him."

The guard said, "Whatever you want, Your Majesty, but I don't think you're doing him any favor by keeping him alive."

Blood ran from the Chernagor's mouth. One of his arms and both legs splayed out at unnatural angles. Grus decided the guardsman was right. "Go ahead," he said. The Avornan drove the spear into the injured man's throat. It was over quickly after that.

Up on the wall, the Chernagors began to sound desperate, while the Avornans' shouts grew ever more excited. "We're going into the city!" someone yelled in Avornan. That was even better than a foothold on the wall. If the Avornans could cut Vasilko's men off from their last citadels inside Nishevatz . . .

Grus felt his way to a scaling ladder. "I'm going up," he told his guards. "Some of you can go up before me if you like, but I'm going up now." He'd known the guards would protest, and they did. But the king managed to have his way. Half a dozen guardsmen did precede him up the wall, but he went.

Two Chernagors and an Avornan lay dead in a great pool of blood in front of the top of the ladder. More bodies came into view through the fog as Grus walked along the wall. All the Chernagors he saw were dead. Some Avornans were only wounded. One or two of them gave him feeble cheers.

His guards were as nervous as a mother watching a child take its first steps. "Be careful, Your Majesty!" they said, and, "Look out, Your Majesty!" and any number of things intended to keep the king away from the fighting.

"I do want to see what's going on, as best I can with the fog," he said.

They didn't want to listen to him. He hadn't really thought they would. Somewhere not far away, iron beat on iron—the Chernagors were still trying to hold off the Avornans and even to drive them back. Grus' bodyguards got between him and the sound of fighting, as though the ring of sword against sword were as deadly as point or edge.

In spite of the guardsmen, Grus saw a good deal. By now, long stretches of the walls were in Avornan hands. The only Chernagors left in these parts were dead, wounded, or disarmed and taken prisoner. The captives had the stunned look of men for whom disaster had come from out of the blue—or, here, out of the gray. One moment, they'd felt secure enough on the works that had held out for so long. The next, they saw their comrades bleeding while they themselves faced an uncertain fate. No wonder they looked as though they'd just, and just barely, survived an earthquake.

And, as the day advanced toward midmorning, the sun finally began to thin the fog—not to burn it off, but at least to thin it to the point where Grus could see farther than his own knees. He got his first real look inside Nishevatz. Most of the buildings had plastered fronts painted in various bright colors and steeply pitched slate roofs to shed the winter snow.

Parties of Avornans and Chernagors ran through the narrow, muddy streets, pausing every so often to exchange sword strokes or shoot arrows. Grus watched a shrieking Chernagor go down, beset by two Avornans who thrust their blades into him again and again until at last he stopped moving. It took a sickeningly long time.

One of the guardsmen pointed deeper into the city than Grus had been looking. "See, Your Majesty?" the guard said in pleased tones. "There's the first fire. Now they'll have to worry about putting that out along with fighting us."

"So they will," Grus agreed. This was what he'd been trying to accomplish for years. Now that he'd finally done it, he was reminded of the cost. His soldiers and Vasilko's weren't the only actors in the drama. Old men hobbled on sticks, trying to escape both foes and flames. Women and children ran screaming through the streets, fearing what fate had in store for them—and well they might.

A Chernagor archer saw Grus peering down from the wall. The man set an arrow to his bowstring and let fly. The shaft hissed past the king's face. Before the Chernagor could shoot again, Grus' guards pulled him back from the edge of the wall. "You see, Your Majesty?" one of them said. "It's not safe up here."

"Not safe anywhere," Grus answered. He shook off the guards and peered into Nishevatz again. "I wonder where Vasilko is and what he's doing."

"Quaking in his boots, most likely," a guardsman said. "This place is going to fall now, and he's got to know it." As though to prove his point, what had to be a regiment's worth of Avornans surged out from the wall, driving the Chernagor who'd shot at Grus and his comrades back toward the center of Nishevatz.

Another guard said, "They're shouting your name, Your Majesty."

"I hear them," Grus said. When he first wore the crown, hearing soldiers use his name as a battle cry had been thrilling. Now it was just something that happened. *I'm getting old—or older, anyhow,* he thought.

He also heard shouts of "Vasilko!" He wondered whether Vsevolod's son still enjoyed hearing soldiers shouting his name. With a little luck, that wouldn't matter much longer.

"Where can we get into the city from the wall?" Grus asked his guardsmen. That made them look unhappy all over again, but they couldn't very well pretend they hadn't heard him, however much they might have wanted to. Instead, they fussed all the way to a staircase and all the way down. Even after Grus came down inside Nishevatz, his bodyguards still grumbled and fumed.

Avornan soldiers with spears led out long columns of Chernagor prisoners—grim-faced men who tramped along with empty hands raised high over their heads or tied behind their backs. Somewhere not far away, women wailed. Grus winced, knowing they were all too likely to have reason to wail. His own men were only . . . men, a lot of them no better than they had to be.

"Where is the prince's palace?" he asked. "Chances are, that's where Vasilko will make his stand." He stopped and snapped his fingers. "Wait—I have a map of the town as it was, anyhow." Maybe Lanius' gift would do him some good after all.

A captain said, "I don't know if we can get anywhere in Nishevatz very easily. Do you see? The fire is starting to take hold."

So it was. Grus wondered if anyone in Nishevatz would ever see clearly again. Even as the fog thinned and the sun struggled to break through, thick clouds of black smoke began filling the streets of the city. A building fell down with a rending crash. New flames leaped up from the ruins. How long before most of Nishevatz was gutted? If it was, would Beloyuz thank him? He doubted that. If Beloyuz proved like most princes, he would stay grateful until Vasilko was dead or captive, and not much longer.

Grus suddenly stared. Was that part of the fire coming his way through the smoke and fog all on its own? A moment later, he realized it was Pterocles, whose hands still glowed brightly. "You can take off your spell now," the king called.

The wizard looked down at himself. "Oh," he said sheepishly. "I forgot all about that." He muttered in a low voice. His hands once more became no more than ordinary flesh and blood.

"Can you lead me past the worst of the fires to Vasilko's stronghold?" Grus asked.

"If someone will tell me where Vasilko's stronghold is, I'll try to take you there," Pterocles answered.

That proved more complicated than Grus had expected. None of the Avornans nearby had been inside Nishevatz until that morning. None of the Chernagor captives seemed willing to understand Avornan. At last, the Avornans rounded up a noble named Pozvizd, who had escaped with Vsevolod and Beloyuz. He understood Avornan—after a fashion. "Yes, I take you," he said, and started off at a brisk pace. Grus, Pterocles, and a host of guardsmen followed in his wake.

If he'd known just where he was going, all would have been well. But he promptly got lost. Smoke and fire confused him. No doubt, so did being away from Nishevatz for several years. And when he did know the way for a brief stretch, he often couldn't use what he knew because of battling Chernagors and Avornans.

"We get there," he said over his shoulder. "Soon or late, we get there."

"Huzzah," Grus said. "If we can, I'd like to get there before everyone involved in the fighting dies of old age."

Several of his guards grinned. Pterocles giggled, which was most unprofessional of him. And Pozvizd either hadn't heard all of that or didn't understand all of it, for he just kept smiling back over his shoulder and saying, "We get there. Yes, we get there soon."

And after a while—not soon enough to suit Grus, but not quite slowly enough to drive him altogether mad—they did get there. Most of Nishevatz had its own look, different from anything Grus would have seen in Avornis. When he came to Vasilko's stronghold, though, he felt a distinct shock of recognition. This building, plainly, had begun life as an Avornan noble's home. The lines were unmistakable, undeniable—and it was right where the map Lanius had given him said the city governor's residence should be. But, just as plainly, it had been serving different needs for a long, long time.

Heavy iron grills covered all the windows. Thick ironbound gates warded the entranceways. Towers full of archers rose from the roofs. "We'll have to knock it down with catapults or burn it down," Grus said in dismay. "Just taking it won't be too easy."

From inside, someone was shouting furiously. Pozvizd pointed. "That Vasilko," he said. "He yell for more soldiers. He say, somebody pay, he not get more."

"I hope he'll be the one who pays," Grus said.

Another voice came from the residence-turned-citadel—one not as loud, but full of authority. Pterocles stiffened. "That is a wizard," he said. "I know the serpent by its fangs. That man has power—some of his own, and some he can call upon from . . . elsewhere."

The Banished One. He means the Banished One, even if he doesn't care to say the name, Grus thought. Quietly, he asked, "Can you meet him?"

Pterocles shrugged. "We'll find out, won't we? Right now, he hardly seems aware of me. He's worried about how to keep Nishevatz from falling."

"A little late for that, wouldn't you say?" Grus asked.

"I think so," Pterocles answered, "but I know more about what's going on inside the city than . . . he does." The wizard stiffened. He pointed to a second-story window. "There he is!"

He didn't mean the Banished One now. He meant the Chernagor wizard. Grus couldn't have told the sorcerer from any other Chernagor—a burly, bearded man in a mailshirt. He wasn't even sure he was looking in the right window. But Pterocles seemed very sure. He flung up an arm and gasped out a counterspell.

"Are you all right?" Grus asked.

"He's strong," the wizard answered. "He's very strong. And he's drawing on more power than he owns. It's . . . him, sure enough."

"Him? Oh," Grus said. Pterocles had confused him for a moment. The Banished One hadn't paid much attention to the siege of Nishevatz. The civil war between Korkut and Sanjar had kept him occupied closer to home. How much could he do, intervening at the last minute? *We're going to find out,* Grus thought.

Pterocles staggered, as though someone had hit him hard. He used another counterspell. This one sounded more potent—or more desperate—than the first. If he could do nothing but defend . . . How long until he couldn't defend anymore, until the Chernagor sorcerer, aided by power from the Banished One, emptied and crushed him yet again?

"Hang on," Grus said. "I'll find a way out of this for you."

"How do you propose to manage that?" Pterocles panted. "Will you call down the gods from the heavens to fight on my side?"

"No, but I'll come up with something else," Grus said. The wizard snorted, obviously not believing a word of that. For a moment, Grus didn't know what he could do to make good on his promise. Then he shouted for a squadron of archers. He pointed to the window where the Chernagor wizard looked out. "Kill me that man!" he said. "Second story, third window from the left."

The bowmen didn't ask questions. They just said, "Yes, Your Majesty," took arrows from their quivers, and let fly. Not content with one shot apiece, they kept at it, sending scores of shafts at the window. A man with even an ordinary sense of self-preservation would have moved away from his dangerous position as soon as the arrows started flying. Infused with force from the Banished One, Vasilko's sorcerer stayed where he was. To him, destroying Pterocles must have seemed more important than anything else, even life itself.

But then he staggered back not because he wanted to but because he had to. A pair of arrows had struck him in the chest, less than a hand's breadth apart. "Well done!" Grus shouted. "You'll all have a reward for that!"

Pterocles, who had been bending like a sapling in a gale, suddenly straightened. "He stopped, Your Majesty," the wizard said, more than a little amazement in his voice. "He just . . . stopped. How did you do that? You're no sorcerer."

"Maybe not, but I know one magic trick," Grus replied. "Shoot a man a couple of times, and he's a lot less interested in wizardry than he was before."

Pterocles took a moment to think that over and, very visibly, to gather strength. "I see," he said at last. "That's—a less elegant solution than I would have come up with, I think."

Lanius would have said the same thing, Grus thought. *Some people are perfectionists. As for me . . .* "I don't care whether it's elegant or not. All I care about is whether it works, and you can't very well argue about that."

"No, Your Majesty, that's true." Pterocles seemed to realize something more might be called for. "And thank you."

"You're welcome," the king answered. "I presume that was Vasilko's best wizard. Now we have to find out whether he has any others the Banished One wants to try to use."

"Yes." Pterocles looked as though he wished Grus hadn't thought of that.

Meanwhile, though, more and more Avornan soldiers flooded into the square around the building Vasilko was using for a citadel. Grus didn't think it could hold out too much longer. Even with the additions and improvements the Chernagors had made to it, it hadn't been built as a fortress. Sooner or later, the Avornans would find a way to break in or to set it afire—and that would be the end for Prince Vsevolod's unloving and unloved son.

But then the entrance to the stronghold flew open. Out burst a swarm of Chernagors. They were roaring like lions, some wordlessly, others bawling out Prince Vasilko's name. The Avornans rushed to meet them. Vasilko must have seen the same thing Grus had—his citadel would not hold. Since it would not, why not sally forth to conquer or die?

That made a certain amount of sense in the abstract. Grus had perhaps half a dozen heartbeats to think of it in the abstract. Then he realized that swarm of Chernagors, Prince Vasilko at their head, was rushing straight toward him. If he went down under their swords and spears, he wouldn't much care what happened in the rest of the fight for Nishevatz. No, that wasn't true—if he went down, he wouldn't care at all.

"Rally to me!" he shouted to the Avornans in the square. "Rally to me and throw them back. We can do it!" He pulled his sword from its scabbard.

So did Pterocles beside him. The wizard probably had only the vaguest idea what to do with an unsorcerous weapon. Eyeing the Chernagors and how young and fresh and fierce they looked, Grus remembered every one of his own years, too. *How long can I last against an onslaught like this?*

He didn't have to find out on the instant, for his guardsmen sprang out in front of him and took the brunt of the Chernagor onslaught. Several of them fell, but they also brought down even more of Vasilko's men. Yet still more Chernagors pushed forward. Yelling and cursing, the surviving bodyguards met them head-on. By then, Grus was in the fight, too, slashing at a Chernagor who had more ferocity than skill.

The king's blade bit. The Chernagor reeled back with a shriek, clutching a gashed forearm. Grus knew a certain somber pride. He could still hold his own against a younger foe. For a while he could, anyhow. But the younger men could keep on going long after he flagged.

"Vasilko!" roared the Chernagors.

"Grus!" the royal guardsmen shouted back. Pterocles took a round-house swipe at one of Vasilko's men. He missed. But then he tackled the Chernagor. Grus' sword came down on the man's neck. Blood fountained. The Chernagor's body convulsed, then went limp.

"Are you all right?" Grus asked Pterocles, hauling him to his feet.

"I—think so," the wizard answered shakily. Then they were both fighting for their lives, too busy and too desperate to talk.

More Avornan soldiers rushed up to reinforce the bodyguards. The archers who'd hit the Chernagor wizard poured volley after volley into Vasilko's henchmen. The Chernagors had few archers with whom to re-ply. Those whistling shafts tore the heart out of their charge. Their shouts changed to cries of despair as they realized they weren't going to be able to break free.

There was Vasilko himself, swinging a two-handed sword as though it were a willow wand. He spotted Grus and hacked his way toward him. "I may die," Vsevolod's son shouted in Avornan, "but I'll make the Fallen Star a present of your soul!"

"By the gods in the heavens, you won't!" Grus rushed toward Vasilko. Only later did he wonder whether that was a good idea. At the time, he didn't seem able to do anything else.

Vasilko's first cut almost knocked Grus' sword out of his hand. Vsevolod had been a big, strong man, and his son was no smaller, but the power Vasilko displayed hardly seemed natural. The Banished One had lent the Chernagor wizard one kind of strength. Could he give Vasilko a different sort? Grus had no idea whether that was possible, but he thought so by the way the usurping prince handled his big, heavy blade.

Grus managed to beat the slash aside, and answered with a cut of his own. Vasilko parried with contemptuous ease; by the way he handled it, that two-handed sword might have weighed nothing at all. His next attack again jolted Grus from both speed and power. *Am I getting old that fast?* the king wondered.

"Steal my throne, will you?" Vasilko shouted. Even his voice seemed louder and deeper than a man's voice had any business being.

"You stole it to begin with," Grus panted.

Vasilko showered him with what had to be curses in the Chernagor language. He swung his sword again with that same superhuman strength. Grus' blade went flying. Vasilko roared in triumph. He brought up the two-handed sword to finish the king. Grus leaped close and seized his right wrist with both hands. It was like grappling with a bronze statue that had come to ferocious, malevolent life. He knew he wouldn't be able to hold on long, and knew he would be sorry when he could hold on no more.

Then Pterocles pointed his index finger at Vasilko and shouted out a hasty spell. Vasilko shouted, too, in shock and fury. All of a sudden, his voice was no more than a man's. All of a sudden, the wrist Grus fought desperately to hold might have been made from flesh and blood, not animate metal.

Pterocles grabbed Vasilko around the knees. The usurping Prince of Nishevatz fell to the cobbles. Grus hadn't been sure Vasilko could fall. He kicked the Chernagor in the head. When Vasilko kept on wrestling with Pterocles after Grus kicked him the first time, he did it again. Pain shot through his foot. Bleeding from the temple and the nose, Vasilko groaned and went limp.

"Thanks again, Your Majesty," Pterocles said, scrambling to his feet.

"Thank *you*," Grus answered. "I thought I was gone there. What did you do?"

"Blocked the extra strength the Banished One was feeding Vasilko," the wizard said. "Let's get him tied up—or chained, better still. I don't know how long the spell will hold. I wasn't sure it would hold at all, but I thought I'd better try it." He looked down at Vasilko. "Scrambling his brains there will probably stretch it out a bit."

"Good!" Grus exclaimed. "He was going to do worse than that to me. Now let's see what the rest of these bastards feel like doing."

With their leader captive, most of the Chernagors who'd sallied from the citadel threw down their weapons and raised their hands in surrender. A stubborn handful fought to the end. They shouted something in their own language, over and over again.

Before long, Grus found a Chernagor who admitted to speaking Avornan. "What are they yelling about?" he asked.

"They cry for Fallen Star," the Chernagor answered. "You know who is Fallen Star?"

"Oh, yes. I know who the Fallen Star is," Grus said grimly. "The Menteshe give the Banished One that name, too. But the Menteshe have always followed him. You Chernagors know the worship of the gods in the heavens."

The prisoner shrugged. "Fallen Star is strong power. We stay with strong power."

"Not strong enough," Grus said. The Chernagor shrugged again. Grus pointed at him. "If the Banished One is so strong and the gods in the heavens are so weak, how did we take Nishevatz?"

"Luck," the Chernagor said with another shrug. Grus almost hit him. There were none so stubborn as those who would not see. But then the king saw how troubled the man who had followed Vasilko looked. Maybe the Chernagor wouldn't admit it, but Grus thought his question had struck home.

He jerked a thumb at the guards who'd brought the prisoner before him. "Take this fellow away and put him back with his friends." The Avornans led off the Chernagor, none too gently. Grus hoped the captive would infect his countrymen with doubt.

Hirundo came up to Grus and saluted. "Well, Your Majesty, we've got this town," he said, and paused to dab at a cut on his cheeks with a rag as grimy as the hand that held it. Looking around, he made a sour face. "Now that I'm actually inside, I'm not so sure why we ever wanted it in the first place."

"We wanted it because the Banished One had it, and because he could make a nuisance of himself if he hung on to it. Now we've got it, and we've got Vasilko"—the king pointed to the deposed usurper, who wore enough chains to hold down a horse—"and I may have a broken toe."

"A broken toe? I don't follow," Hirundo said. "And what's Vasilko's problem? He looks like he can't tell yesterday from turnips."

Vasilko had regained consciousness, but he did indeed look as though he didn't know what to do with it now that he had it. "Maybe I kicked him in the head too hard," Grus answered. "That's how I hurt my toe, too—kicking him in the head."

"Well, if you had to do it, you did it for a good reason," Hirundo observed.

"Easy for you to say," Grus snapped. "And do you know what the healers will do for me? Not a thing, that's what. I broke a toe once, years ago, trying to walk through a door instead of a doorway. They told me, 'If we put a splint on it, it will heal in six weeks. If we don't, it will take a month and a half.' And so they didn't—and they won't."

"Lucky you," Hirundo said, still with something less than perfect sympathy.

Aside from his toe, Grus did feel pretty lucky. The Avornans had taken Nishevatz, and hadn't suffered too badly doing it. The Banished One would be cast out here. And, looking at Vasilko, Grus thought his wits remained too scrambled to do him much good.

The king waved to Pterocles. "Any sign the Banished One is trying to feed strength into this fellow again?"

"Let me check," the wizard answered. What followed wasn't exactly a spell. It seemed more as though Pterocles were listening intently than anything else. After a bit, he shook his head. "No, Your Majesty. If the Banished One is doing that, I can't tell he's doing it, and believe me, I would be able to."

"I have to believe you," Grus said. He glanced toward Vasilko again. If Vsevolod's son had any more working brains than a thrall right now, Grus would have been amazed. "I have to believe you, and I do." He turned back to Hirundo. "Where's Beloyuz? Prince Beloyuz, I ought to say?"

"He's somewhere in Nishevatz," the general answered. "I know he came up a ladder. What happened to him afterwards, I couldn't tell you."

"We'd better find him. It's time for him to start *being* the prince, if you know what I mean," Grus said. "I hope nothing's happened to him. That would be bad for us—as far as the Chernagors who stayed with Vsevolod go, he's far and away the best of the lot. He's one of the younger ones, and he's one of the more sensible ones, too."

"I'll take care of it." Hirundo started shouting for soldiers. They came running. He ordered them to fan out through Nishevatz calling Beloyuz's name. The general also made sure they knew what the Chernagor nobleman looked like. Turning to Grus, he said, "For all we know, every fifth man in Nishevatz is named Beloyuz. We don't want a crowd of them; we want one in particular."

"True," Grus said. There weren't a whole flock of Avornans who bore his name, but he was sure there were some. The same could easily hold true for the Chernagor.

Escorted by one of Hirundo's soldiers, Beloyuz strode into the square by the citadel about half an hour later. The new Prince of Nishevatz's face was as soot-streaked as anyone else's. But the tracks of Beloyuz's tears cut cleanly through the filth. "My poor city!" he cried to Grus. "Did you have to do this to take it?"

"It's war, Your Highness," Grus said. "Haven't you ever seen a sack before? It could have been a lot worse, believe me."

Beloyuz didn't answer, not directly. Instead, he threw his arms wide and wailed, "But this is Nishevatz!"

Grus put an arm around his shoulder. "It's the way I'd feel if someone sacked the city of Avornis. But you can set this to rights. Believe me, you can. Most of the city is still standing, and most of the people are still breathing. In five years or so, no one who comes here a stranger will have any idea what Nishevatz went through."

"Easy enough for you to say," Beloyuz retorted, as Grus had to Hirundo. "You are not the one who will have to rebuild this city."

"No, not this city," Grus replied. "But what do you think I'll be doing down in southern Avornis? The Menteshe have sacked a lot of towns there, and what they've done to the farmlands makes the way we behaved here look like a kiss on the cheek. You're not the only one with worries like this, Your Highness."

Beloyuz grunted. He cared nothing for cities in southern Avornis. In that, he was much like the late, not particularly lamented (at least by Grus) Prince Vsevolod. He said, "And what of Durdevatz and Ravno? When they see how weak we are, they will want to steal our lands."

"Well, do you want me to leave an Avornan garrison behind?" Grus asked. Beloyuz quickly shook his head. "I didn't think so," Grus told him. "If I did leave one, people would say I wanted to steal your lands, and I don't."

"Why did I let you talk me into being prince?" Beloyuz said.

"Someone has to. Who would be better? Vsevolod's dead." Grus wasn't at all convinced Vsevolod had been better, but passed over that in silence. He pointed to Vasilko instead. "Him?" Beloyuz shook his head again. "Do you have anyone else in mind?" Grus asked. Another headshake from the Chernagor. Grus spread his hands. "Well, then, Your Highness—welcome to the job."

"I'll try." Beloyuz very visibly gathered himself. He might have been taking the weight of the world on his shoulders. "Yes, I'll try."

CHAPTER TWENTY-SEVEN

King Lanius was gnawing the meat off a goose drumstick when he almost choked. "Are you all right?" Sosia asked.

"I think so," he replied once he could speak again. He tried to snap his fingers in annoyance, but they were too greasy. Muttering, he wiped his hands on a napkin—he did remember not to use the tablecloth, which would have been the style in his grandfather's day, or his own clothes, which would have been the style in his grandfather's grandfather's day. He sipped from his wine cup—his voice needed more lubricating even if his fingers didn't. "The only problem is, I'm an idiot."

"Oh." Sosia eyed him. "Well, I could have told you that."

"Thank you, sweetheart." Lanius gave her a seated bow. He waited. Nothing more happened. He muttered again, then broke down and said, "Aren't you going to ask me why I'm an idiot?"

His wife shrugged. "I hadn't intended to. But all right—how were you an idiot this time?" Her tone said she knew how he'd been an idiot before, and with which serving girls.

"It's not like that." Lanius hid his own smile. Sosia still hadn't found out about Flammea.

"In that case, maybe I really am interested," Sosia said.

"Thank you," Lanius repeated. By the elegant way she inclined her head, her family might have been royal much longer than his. Now he did smile. That struck him funny. Sosia laughed at him. In a couple of heartbeats, he was laughing, too.

"Tell me," the queen said.

"Do you remember the old parchments the envoy from Durdevatz brought me as a gift when he came down here last summer?"

Sosia shrugged again. "I didn't, not until you reminded me. Playing around with those old things is your sport, not mine." Quickly, she added, "But it's a better sport than playing around with young things, by the gods." Lanius made a face at her; he would have guessed she'd say that. She made one right back at him. "What about these precious parchments, then?"

"They may *be* precious parchments, for all I know. I was so excited to get them, and then I put them away to go through them in a little while . . . and here it is more than a year later, and I haven't done it. That's why I'm an idiot."

"Oh." Sosia thought that over, then shrugged. "Well, you've had reasons for being one that I've liked less, I will say."

"Yes, I thought you would." Lanius made another face at her. She laughed again, so she wasn't too peeved. Sure enough, she hadn't found out about Flammea.

Lanius almost charged away from the supper table to look at the documents from Durdevatz. He was halfway out of his seat before he realized that would be rude. Besides, the light was beginning to fail, and trying to read faded ink by lamplight was a lot less enjoyable than, say, trying to seduce a maidservant. Tomorrow morning would do.

When the morning came, he found himself busy with moncats and monkeys and a squabble between two nobles down in the south. He forgot the parchments again, at least until noon. Then he went into the archives to look at them. He was sure he remembered where they were, and he was usually good about such things. Not this time. He confidently went to where he thought he'd put the gift from Durdevatz, only to find the parchments weren't there. Some of the things he said then would have made a guardsman blush, or more likely blanch.

Cursing didn't help in any real way, even if it did make him feel better. Once he stopped filling the air with sparks, he had to go poking around if he wanted to find the missing parchments. They were bound to be somewhere in the archives. No one would have stolen them. He was sure of that. He was the only person in the city of Avornis who thought they were worth anything.

If they weren't where he thought he'd put them, where were they likely to be? He looked around the hall, trying to think back more than a year. He'd come in, he'd had the parchments in his hand . . . and what had he done with them?

Good question. He wished he had a good answer for it.

After some more curses—these less spirited than the ones that had gone before—he started looking. If he hadn't put them where he thought, what was the next most likely place?

He was on his way over to it when something interrupted him. Ancient parchments—even ancient parchments from up in the Chernagor country—were unlikely to say, "Mrowr?"

"Oh, by the gods!" Lanius threw his hands in the air and fought down a strong urge to scream. "I haven't got time to deal with you right now, Pouncer!"

"Mrowr?" the moncat said again. It didn't care where the king had put the documents from Durdevatz. It had gotten out of its room again, and had probably also paid a call on the kitchens. The cooks had stopped up the one hole in the wall, but the moncat had found another. It *liked* visiting the kitchens—all sorts of interesting things were there. Who was going to deal with it if the king didn't? Nobody, and Lanius knew it only too well.

These days, though, he had a weapon he hadn't used before. Because he'd thought he knew where the parchments were, he was wearing a robe instead of the grubby clothes he often put on to dig through the archives, but he didn't care. He lay down on the dusty floor and started thumping his chest with his right hand.

"Mrowr!" Pouncer came running. Lanius had trained the moncat to know what that sound meant—*if I get up onto him, he'll give me something good to eat.* That was what Pouncer had to be thinking. The moncat was carrying a big, heavy silver spoon. Sure enough, the archives hadn't been its first stop on its latest jaunt through the spaces between the palace's walls.

"You've stolen something expensive this time. Congratulations," Lanius said, stroking Pouncer under the chin and by the whiskers. Pouncer closed its eyes and stretched out its neck and rewarded him with a feline smile and a deep, rumbling purr. The moncat didn't even seem offended that he hadn't fed it anything.

He stood up, carefully cradling the animal in his arms. Pouncer kept acting remarkably happy. Lanius carried the moncat out of the archives and down the hall to the chamber where it lived—until it felt like escaping, anyhow. Pouncer didn't fuss until he took the silver spoon away from it. Even then, it didn't fuss too much. By now, it was used to and probably resigned to his taking prizes away from it.

Once Pouncer was back with the other moncats, Lanius brought the spoon to the kitchens. "You didn't steal that yourself, Your Majesty!" Quiscula exclaimed when she saw what he carried. "That miserable creature's been here again, and nobody even knew it."

"Pouncer doesn't think it's a miserable creature," Lanius told the pudgy cook. "*Talented* would probably be a better word."

"Talented, foof!" Quiscula said. "Plenty of thieves on two legs are talented, too, and what happens to them when they get caught? Not half what they deserve, a lot of the time."

"Thieves who go on two legs know the difference between right and wrong," Lanius said. "The moncat doesn't." He paused. "I don't think it does, anyhow."

"A likely story," Quiscula said. "It's a wicked beast, and you can't tell me any different, so don't waste your breath trying."

"I wouldn't think of it." Lanius held out the spoon. "Here. Take charge of this until Pouncer decides to steal it again."

"Oh, you're too generous to me, Your Majesty!" Quiscula played the coquette so well, she and Lanius both started laughing. She accepted the spoon from the king.

Lanius started back toward the archives, wondering if he would ever get to look for those parchments. Everything seemed to be conspiring against him. And everything, today, included Princess Limosa, who was carrying her baby down the corridor. "Hello, Your Majesty," Limosa said. "Isn't Capella the sweetest little thing you ever saw?"

"Well . . ." Lanius wondered how to answer that and stay truthful and polite at the same time. Truth won. He said, "If you don't count Crex and Pitta, yes."

Limosa stared at him, then giggled. "All right, that's fair enough. Who doesn't think their children are the most wonderful ones in the world?"

"I can't think of anybody," Lanius said. "That's what keeps us from feeding our children to the hunting hounds, I suppose."

Limosa's eyes got even wider than they had been before. She hugged Capella a little tighter and hurried away as though she feared Lanius had some dreadful, contagious disease. He wondered why. He hadn't said he wanted to feed Capella—or any other children—to hunting hounds. He sighed. Some people just didn't listen.

He'd just started searching through the spots likeliest to hold the missing documents when somebody began banging on the door to the archives. The king said something pungent. The servants knew they weren't supposed to do things like that. Bubulcus, the one who'd been most likely to "forget" such warnings, was dead. Either someone was making a dreadful mistake or something dreadful, something he really needed to know about, had just happened. Adding a few more choice phrases under his breath, he went to see who was bothering him in his sanctum.

"Sosia!" he said in astonishment. "What are you doing here? What's going on?"

"I was going to ask you the same question," his wife answered. "What on earth did you say to Limosa? Queen Quelea's mercy, it's frightened the life out of her, whatever it was."

"Oh, by the gods!" Lanius clapped a hand to his forehead in exasperation altogether unfeigned. "She really *doesn't* listen." He spelled out exactly what he'd said to Limosa.

Even before he got halfway through, one of Sosia's eyebrows started climbing. Lanius had seen that expression more often on Grus than on his wife. He liked it no better on her. Once he'd finished, she said, "Well, I don't blame Limosa a bit. Poor thing! Hunting dogs, indeed! You should be ashamed of yourself."

"You weren't listening, either," Lanius complained. "I didn't say that was what we did with children. I didn't say it was what we should do. I said it was what we would do if the people who had them didn't think they were wonderful. Don't you see the difference?"

"What I see is that nobody's got any business talking about feeding babies to any hounds." Sosia spoke with impressive certainty. "And that goes double for talking about babies and hounds to somebody who's just had one. Had a baby, I mean." She wagged a finger at him. "You're not going to make me sound foolish. This is important."

"I wasn't. This is already nothing but foolishness," Lanius said.

"It certainly is—*your* foolishness. Next time you see Limosa, you apologize to her, do you hear me?" Sosia didn't wait for an answer. She stared past Lanius into the cavernous archives. "So this is where you spend all your time. I feel as though I'm looking at the other woman."

"Don't be silly," Lanius said, although that comparison made much more sense to him than the other one had. "And I still don't see why you want me to apologize to Limosa when I didn't say anything bad to begin with."

"Yes, you did. You're just too—too logical to know it." Sosia turned her back and stalked off. Over her shoulder, she added, "And if you think people run on logic all the time, you'd better think again."

"I don't think anything of the sort. People cured me of it a long time ago," Lanius said plaintively. Sosia didn't even slow down. She went around a corner and disappeared. The king almost chased after her to go on explaining. But he realized—logically—that it wouldn't do him any good, and so he stayed where he was.

When he could no longer hear Sosia's angry footsteps, he shut the door to the archives once more. For good measure, he barred it behind him. Then he went back to looking for the parchments from Durdevatz.

He searched on and off for four days, and finally found them by accident. If he had told Sosia about that, she would either have laughed at him or rolled her eyes in despair. He'd forgotten he'd put the parchments in a stout wooden box to keep them safe. How many times had he walked past it without paying it any mind? More than he wanted to think about—he was sure of that. If he hadn't barked his knuckles on a corner of the box, he might never have found the documents at all.

That moment of sudden, unexpected pain made him take a long, reproachful look at the box. When he recognized it, he still felt reproachful—self-reproachful. After all that searching—and after its ludicrous end—he was almost afraid to look at the parchments. If they turned out to be worthless or dull, how could he stand it?

Of course, if he didn't look at them, why had he gone to all the trouble of finding them? After rubbing his hand, he carried the box over to the table where he'd written most of *How to Be a King*. When he opened the box, he started to laugh. The Chernagors had made him happy with some of the cheapest presents ever given to a King of Avornis—a pair of moncats, a pair of monkeys, and a pile of documents dug out of a decrepit cathedral. For all he knew, merchants in the north country laughed whenever they heard his name.

He didn't care. Happiness and having enough money weren't the same thing. He'd been happy enough even at times when Grus squeezed him hardest. That money and happiness weren't the same thing didn't mean happiness had nothing to do with money. Lanius' intuition, though, didn't reach that far.

The first few parchments he unrolled and read had to do with the cathedral, not with anything that went on inside it. They included a letter from the yellow-robed high-hallow then presiding in the building asking a long-dead King of Avornis for funds to repair it and add to its mosaic decoration. The letter had come to the capital and gone back to what was then Argithea, not Durdevatz, with the king's scribbled comment and signature below it. *We are not made of silver,* the sovereign had written. *If the projects are worthy, surely your townsfolk will support them. If they are not, all the silver in the world will not make them so.*

Lanius studied that with considerable admiration. "I couldn't have put it better myself," he murmured. He studied the response until he'd memorized it. He could think of so many places to use it. . . .

Other documents told him more about the history of Argithea than he'd ever known before. Some of them talked about the Chernagors as sea raiders. Up until then, he'd seen only a couple of parchments like that. They proved Argithea hadn't been the first town along the coast of the Northern Sea to fall to the Chernagors. Lanius tried to remember whether he'd known that before. Try as he would, he couldn't be sure.

More appeals—for money and for aid—to the capital followed, from the city governor and from the high-ranking priest at the cathedral. Only one of them had any sort of reply. *A relieving force is on the way,* the answer said. *Hold out until it arrives.*

There were no more letters in Avornan after the date of that one. The messenger bringing the answer must have managed to slip through the besieging Chernagors; Lanius had read elsewhere that they hadn't been polished at the art of taking cities. Polished or not, though, they'd surely taken Argithea before the promised relieving force arrived. They must have kept the Avornans from recapturing the town, too. From then on, the history of Argithea ended and that of Durdevatz began.

One parchment still sat at the bottom of the box. Lanius pulled it out as much from a sense of duty as for any other reason. Since he was going through the documents, he thought he ought to go through all of them. He didn't expect anything more interesting or exciting than what he'd already found.

But the first sentence caught and held his eye. *I wonder why I have written this,* it said, *when no one is ever likely to read it, or to understand it if he does.* After that, he couldn't have stopped reading for anything. The author was a black-robed priest named Xenops. He had been consecrated the year before the Chernagors took Argithea out of the Kingdom of Avornis, and had stayed on at the cathedral under the town's new masters for the next fifty years and more.

"Olor's beard!" Lanius whispered. "This shows how Durdevatz passed from one world to the other." He'd never imagined seeing such a document. In their early years in these parts, the Chernagors hadn't written in Avornan or their own language or any other. And he had not thought any Avornans left behind in the north had set down what they'd seen and heard and felt. No such chronicles existed in the royal archives—he was sure of that. A moment later, he shook his head. One did now.

Xenops had caught moments in the transition from the old way of life to the new. He'd mocked the crude coins the Chernagors began to mint a generation after the fall of Argithea. *Next to those of Avornis, they are ugly and irregular,* he'd written. *But new coins of Avornis come seldom if at all, while so many old ones are hoarded against hard times. Even these ugly things may be better than none.*

Later, he'd noted the demise of Avornan in the market square. *Besides me, only a few old grannies use it as a birthspeech nowadays,* he said. *Some of the younger folk can speak it after a fashion, but they prefer the conquerors' barbarous jargon. Soon, only those who need Avornan in trade will know it at all.*

Once, earlier, some of the Avornans left in the city had plotted to rejoin it to the kingdom from which it had been torn. The Chernagors discovered the plot and bloodily put it down. *But none of them so much as looked toward me,* Xenops wrote. *Had they done so, they might have been surprised. I have been for so long invisible to the new lords of this town, though, that they cannot see me at all. Well, I know their deeds, regardless of whether they know mine.*

That was interesting, to say the least. How deep in the conspiracy had Xenops been? Had he quietly started it and managed to survive unnoticed when it fell to pieces? The only evidence Lanius had—the only evidence he would ever have—lay before him now, and the priest did not go into detail. If someone had found and read his chronicle while he still lived in Durdevatz, he had said enough to hang himself, so why not more? Lanius knew he would never find out.

A chilling passage began, *He calls himself a spark from the Fallen Star.* Xenops went on to record how an emissary from the Banished One had come to Durdevatz even that long ago. He'd made a mistake—he'd gotten angry when the Chernagors didn't fall down on their knees before him right away. *I advised the lords of the Chernagors that such a one was not to be trusted, as he had shown by his own speech and deeds,* Xenops wrote. *They were persuaded, and sent him away unsuccessful.*

How much did Avornis owe to this altogether unknown priest? If the Chernagors had fallen under the sway of the Banished One centuries earlier, how would the other city-states—how would Avornis—have fared? Not well, not when Avornis might have been trapped between the Banished One's backers to north and south.

"Thank you, Xenops," Lanius murmured. "You'll get your due centuries later than you should have, but you'll have it." He could think of several passages in *How to Be a King* he would need to revise.

At the end of the long roll of parchment, Xenops wrote, *Now, as I say, I am old. I have heard that the old always remember the time of their youth as the sweet summer of the world. I dare say it is true. But who could blame me for having that feeling myself? Before the barbarians came, Argithea was part of a wider world. Now it is alone, and I rarely hear what passes beyond its walls. The Chernagors do not even keep its name, but use some vile appellation of their own. Their speech drives out Avornan; even I have had to acquire it, however reluctantly I cough out its gutturals. The tongue I learned in my cradle gutters toward extinction. When I am gone—which will not be long—who here will know, much less care, what I have set down in this scroll? No one, I fear me—no one at all. If the gods be kind, let it pass through time until it comes into the hands of someone who will care for it in the reading as I have in the writing. King Olor, Queen Quelea, grant this your servant's final prayer.*

Tears stung Lanius' eyes. "The gods heard you," he whispered, though Xenops, of course, could not hear him. But how many centuries had Olor and Quelea taken to deliver the priest's manuscript into the hands of someone who could appreciate it as it deserved? If they were going to answer Xenops' last request, couldn't they have done it sooner? Evidently not.

Was a prayer answered centuries after it was made truly answered at all? In one sense, Lanius supposed so. But the way the gods had chosen to respond did poor Xenops no good at all.

Lanius looked again at the long-dead priest's closing words. No, Xenops hadn't expected anyone in his lifetime could make sense of what he'd written. He'd merely hoped someone would someday. On reflection, the gods *had* given him what he'd asked for. Even so, Lanius would have been surprised if Xenops had thought his chronicle would have to wait so very long to find an audience.

But then, for all Xenops knew, the scroll might have stayed unread until time had its way with it. The priest must have thought that likely, as a matter of fact, for Avornan was a dying language in the town that had become Durdevatz. And, except among traders who used it for dealing with the Avornans farther south but not among themselves, it had died there. Yes, its getting here *was* a miracle, even if a slow one.

"A slow miracle." Lanius spoke the words aloud, liking the way they felt in his mouth. But the Banished One could also work what men called miracles when he intervened in the world's affairs, and he didn't wait centuries to do it. There were times when he waited, and wasted, not a moment.

The gods had exiled him to the material world. In a way, that made it *his*. Could they really do much to counter his grip on things here? If they couldn't, who could? Ordinary people? He had far more power than they did, as Lanius knew all too well. Yet somehow the Banished One had failed to sweep everything before him. Maybe that was a portent. Maybe it just meant the Banished One hadn't triumphed *yet*. Time was on his side.

But he still feared Lanius and Grus and Pterocles—and Alca as well, the king remembered. Lanius only wished he knew what he could do to deserve even more of the Banished One's distrust.

For a while, nothing occurred to him. Having the exiled god notice him at all was something of a compliment, even if one that he could often do without. Then Lanius nodded to himself. If he—or rather, if Avornis' wizards—could begin liberating thralls in large numbers, the Banished One would surely pay heed.

What would he do then? Lanius didn't know. He couldn't begin to guess. One thing he did know, though, was that he would dearly love to find out.

Hisardzik sat at the end of a long spit of land jutting out into the Northern Sea. Besieging Nishevatz had been anything but easy. Besieging this Chernagor city-state would have been harder still, for the defenders had to hold only a short length of wall against their foes. King Grus, a longtime naval officer, knew he could have made the Chernagors' work more difficult with a fleet, but they had a fleet of their own. Their ships were tied up at quays beyond the reach of any cata-pult.

Fortunately, however, it did not look as though it would come to fighting. Prince Lazutin, the lord of Hisardzik, not only spoke to Grus from the wall of his city, he came forth from a postern gate to meet the King of Avornis. Lazutin was in his midthirties, slim by Chernagor standards, with a sharp nose and clever, foxy features. He denied speak-ing Avornan, and brought along an interpreter. Grus suspected he knew more than he let on, for he listened with alert attention whenever any Avornan spoke around him.

Grus did his best to sound severe, saying, "You fell into bad com-pany, Your Highness, when you chose Vasilko's side."

Lazutin spoke volubly in the Chernagor tongue after that was trans-lated for him. The interpreter, a pudgy man named Sverki, said, "He says, Your Majesty, it was one of those things. It was political. It was not personal."

"Men who get killed die just as dead either way," Grus said.

"You have shown you are stronger than Vasilko," Lazutin said. Sverki did such a good job of echoing his master's inflections, Grus soon forgot he was there. Through him, the Prince of Hisardzik went on, "You have shown the gods in the heavens are stronger than the Ban-ished One. This also is worth knowing."

Grus had an Avornan who understood the Chernagor speech listen-ing to the conversation to make sure Sverki did not twist what Lazutin said or what Grus himself said to Lazutin. The king glanced over to him now. The Avornan nodded, which meant Lazutin really had spoken of the Banished One, and not of the Fallen Star. Grus took that for a good sign.

He said, "You should have known that anyhow, Your Highness."

Prince Lazutin shrugged delicately. "Some things are more readily accepted with proof. A man may say this or that, but what he says and what is are often not the same. Or have you found otherwise?" He arched an eyebrow, as though daring Grus to tell him he had.

And Grus couldn't, and knew it. "We are not dealing with men here," he said. "We are dealing with those who are more than men."

"The same also applies," Lazutin answered. "It applies even more, I would say, for those who are more than men make claims that are more than claims, if you take my meaning. The only way to be sure who is believable is to see who prevails when one is measured against another."

Here's a cool customer, Grus thought. "And now you have seen?" he asked.

"Oh, yes. Now I have seen." Even speaking a language Grus didn't understand, Prince Lazutin fairly radiated sincerity.

In light of the games Lazutin had played, that made Grus less inclined to trust him, not more. "Since you've seen, what do you propose to do about it?" the king said.

"Ah . . . do about it?" If doing anything about it had occurred to the Prince of Hisardzik, he concealed it very well.

But Grus nodded. "Yes, do about it. Ships from Hisardzik raided the coast of Avornis. Hisardzik sided with Vasilko and against me. Do you think you can get away with that and not pay a price?"

By the look on Lazutin's face, he'd thought exactly that. He didn't much take to the idea of discovering he might be mistaken, either. "If you think you can take my city as you took Nishevatz, Your Majesty, you had better think again."

"Not this late in the year, certainly, Your Highness," Grus replied in silky tones, and Lazutin looked smug. But then Grus went on, "But if I turned my men loose and did a proper job of ravaging your fields, you would have a lean time of it this winter."

By the way Prince Lazutin bared his teeth, that had hit home. "You might tempt me to go back to the Banished One, you know," he observed.

Yes, he was a cool customer. "I'll take the chance," Grus said, "for you've seen the true gods are stronger. You would do better to show you are sorry because you made a mistake before than you would to go back to it."

"Would I?" Lazutin said bleakly. Grus nodded. The Prince of Hisardzik scowled at him. "How sorry would you expect me to show I am?"

"Fifty thousand pieces of silver, or the equivalent weight," Grus answered, "and another fifty thousand a year for the next ten years."

Lazutin turned purple. He said several things in the Chernagor language that Sverki didn't translate. The Avornan who spoke the northern tongue stirred, but Grus declined to look his way. Finally, through Sverki, Lazutin sputtered, "This is an outrage! A robbery!"

"I'd sooner think of it as paying for the damage your pirates did, with interest to remind you those games can be expensive," Grus said.

Lazutin promptly proved he was a prince of merchants and a merchant prince—he started haggling with Grus over how much he would have to pay and for how long. Grus let him dicker the settlement down to a first payment of forty thousand plus thirty-five thousand a year for eight years. He was willing not to take all of Lazutin's pride. This way, the prince could go back to his people and tell them he'd gotten something from the hard-hearted King of Avornis.

Grus did say, "We'll leave your lands as soon as we receive the first payment."

"Why am I not surprised?" Lazutin said. After a moment, he chuckled ruefully. "You're wasted on the Avornans, Your Majesty. Do you know that? You should have been born a Chernagor."

"A pleasant compliment," said Grus, who supposed Lazutin had meant it that way. "I am what I am, though." *And what I am right now is the fellow holding the whip hand.*

"So you are," Lazutin said sourly. "What you are now is a nuisance to Hisardzik."

"What you were before was a nuisance to Avornis," Grus replied. "Do you think the one has nothing to do with the other?"

Prince Lazutin plainly thought just that. Why shouldn't he have been able to do as he pleased without worrying about consequences? What pirate ever needed to have such worries? After he sailed away, what could the folk whose coasts he had raided do? Here, it turned out the Avornans could do more than he had dreamed.

"The sooner we have the payment, the sooner we'll leave your land," Grus said pointedly, "and the sooner you can start the harvest."

Fury filled Lazutin's face. But it was impotent fury, for his warriors were shut up inside Hisardzik. They could stand siege, yes, but they could not break out. If Grus felt like burning the countryside instead of trying to break into the city, what could they do about it? Nothing, as their prince knew.

"You'll have it," Lazutin said. Then he turned his back and stalked off to Hisardzik. Sverki the interpreter stalked after him, mimicking his walk as expertly as he had conveyed his tone.

"He doesn't love you. He's not going to, either," Hirundo said.

"I don't care if he loves me or not," Grus said. "I want him to take me seriously. By Olor's beard, he'll do that from now on."

"Oh, darling!" The general sounded like a breathless young girl. "Tell me you—you take me seriously!"

Grus couldn't take him seriously. Laughing, he made as though to throw something at him. Hirundo ducked. "Miserable troublemaker," Grus said. By the way Hirundo bowed, it might have been highest praise.

But Grus stopped laughing when he read the letter from King Lanius that had caught up with his army on the march between Nishevatz and Hisardzik. Lanius sounded as dispassionate as any man could about what had happened between Ortalis and Bubulcus. However dispassionate he sounded, that made the servant no less dead. The penalty Lanius had imposed on Ortalis struck Grus as adequate, but only barely.

After rereading Lanius' letter several times, Grus sighed. Yes, Ortalis had been provoked. But striking a man in a fit of fury and killing one were far different things. Ortalis had always had a temper. Every so often, it got away from him. This time, he'd done something irrevocable.

What am I going to do with him? Grus wondered. For a long time, he'd thought Ortalis would outgrow his vicious streak, and ignored it. That hadn't worked. Then he'd tried to punish his son harshly enough to drive it out of him, and that hadn't worked, either. What was left? The only thing he could see was accepting that Ortalis was as he was and trying to minimize the damage he did.

"A fine thing for my son," Grus muttered.

When Grus took the Avornan throne, he had assumed Ortalis would succeed him on it, with Lanius remaining in the background to give the new rulers a whiff of respectability. What else was a legitimate son for? But he'd begun to wonder some time before. His son-in-law seemed more capable than he had expected, and Ortalis . . . Ortalis kept doing things where damage needed minimizing.

He read Lanius' letter one more time. The king from the ancient dynasty really had done as much as he could. If his account was to be believed, the servants despised Ortalis now only a little more than they had before. Considering what might have been, that amounted to a triumph of sorts. Grus hadn't imagined he could feel a certain debt toward his son-in-law, but he did.

Prince Lazutin made the payment of forty thousand pieces of silver the day after he agreed to it with Grus. The prince did not accompany the men bringing out the sacks of silver coins. The interpreter, Sverki, did. "Tell His Highness I thank him for this," Grus said (after he'd had a few of the sacks opened to make sure they really did hold silver and not, say, scrap iron).

"You are most welcome, I am sure," Sverki said, sounding and acting like Lazutin even when the Prince of Hisardzik wasn't there.

"I look forward to receiving the rest of the payments, too," Grus said.

"I am sure you do," Sverki replied. Something in his tone made Grus look up sharply. He sounded and acted a little too much like Lazutin, perhaps. If the interpreter here was any guide to what the prince felt, Grus got the idea he would be wise not to hold his breath waiting for future payments to come down to the city of Avornis.

What could he do about that? He said, "If the payments do not come, Hisardzik will not trade with Avornis, and we may call on you up here again. Make sure your principal understands that."

Sverki looked as mutinous as Lazutin would have, too. "I will," he said sulkily. Grus hid a smile. He'd gotten his message across.

CHAPTER TWENTY-EIGHT

L anius stared at Otus' guardsman. "You're joking," he said.
"By the gods, Your Majesty, I'm not," the soldier replied.
"He's sweet on Calypte. Can't argue with his taste, either. Nice-looking girl."

"Yes." Lanius had noticed her once or twice himself. That the thrall's eye—the ex-thrall's eye—might fall on her had never crossed his mind. He said, "But Otus has a woman down south of the Stura."

The guardsman shrugged. "I don't know anything about that. But even if he does, it wouldn't be the first time a fellow far from home finds himself a new friend."

"True." Lanius had found himself a few new friends without going far from home. He asked, "Does Calypte realize this? If she does, what does she think?"

"She thinks he's sweet." By the way the guard said the word, he might have been giving an exact quote. "Most of the serving girls in the palace think Otus is sweet, I suppose on account of he looks but doesn't touch very much."

"Is that what it is?" Lanius said.

"Part of it, anyway, I expect," the guard answered. "Me, I feel 'em when I feel like it. Sometimes they hit me, sometimes they enjoy it. You roll the dice and you see what happens."

"Do you?" Lanius murmured. He'd never been that cavalier. He could have been. How many women would haul off and hit the King of Avornis? He shrugged. Most of the time, he hadn't tried to find out. "How serious is Otus?" he asked now. "Is he like a mooncalf youth? Does he just want to go to bed with her? Or is he after something more? If he is, could she be?"

With a laugh, the guard said, "By the gods, Your Majesty, you sure ask a lot of questions, don't you?"

"Why, of course," Lanius answered in some surprise. "How would I find out if I didn't?" That was another question. Before Otus' guard could realize as much, the king said, "Take me to him. I'll see what he has to say."

"Come along with me, then, Your Majesty," the guard said.

When Lanius walked into Otus' little room, the ex-thrall bowed low. "Hello, Your Majesty," he said. "How are you today?" He was scrupulously polite. Only that lingering old-fashioned southern accent spoke of his origins. "What can I do for you?"

"I'm fine, thanks," Lanius replied. "I came by because I wondered how you were getting along."

"Me? Well enough." Otus laughed. "I've got plenty to eat. No one has given me much work to do. I even get to be clean. I remember what things were like on the other side of the river. Most ways, I'm as happy as a cow in clover."

"Most ways?" There was the opening Lanius had been looking for. "How aren't you happy? How can we make you happy?"

"Well, there is a girl here I've set my eye on." Otus was very direct. Maybe that sprang from his years as a thrall, when he couldn't have hidden anything and didn't have anything worth hiding. Or maybe it was simply part of his nature. Lanius didn't care to guess. Otus went on, "I don't know if she wants anything to do with me." He sighed. "If I had my own woman here—if she was cured, I mean—I wouldn't look twice at anybody else, but I'm lonesome."

"I understand," Lanius said. "Have you tried finding out what this girl thinks of you?"

"Oh, yes." The ex-thrall nodded. "But it's hard to tell, if you know what I mean. She doesn't come right out and say what she wants. She makes me guess." He sent Lanius a wide-eyed, guileless smile. "Is this what it's like when everybody is awake inside all the time?"

"It can be," Lanius said. "Are things more complicated than you're used to?"

"Complicated! That's the word!" Otus nodded again, more emphatically this time. "I should say so! What can I do?"

"Keep trying to find out. That's about all I can tell you," Lanius answered. "No, one thing more—I hope you have good luck."

"Thank you, Your Majesty." Suddenly, Otus looked sly. "Can I tell her you hope I have good luck? If she hears that, maybe it will help me have the luck I want to have."

Lanius said, "You can if you want to. I hope it does." When he left the ex-thrall's chamber, he told the guards, "If he needs privacy, give him enough. Make sure he can't go wandering through the palace without being watched—that, yes. But you don't need to stay in the same room with him."

The guards smiled and nodded. One of them said, "Curse me if I'd want company then—except the girl, of course."

"Yes. Except the girl. That's what I meant," the king said.

"Are you sure it's safe, Your Majesty?" a guardsman asked.

"No, I'm not sure," Lanius answered. "But I think so. Pterocles likely *did* cure him of being a thrall. And if the wizard didn't, I expect the lot of you will be able to keep Otus from doing too much harm."

The soldiers nodded. By their confidence, they expected the same thing. The man who'd first spoken with the king grinned and said, "There's one thing more. We know Otus wants to be alone with Calypte, not if she wants to be alone with him."

"True enough. We don't," Lanius said. "But I'll tell you this much— I think Otus has earned the chance to find out. Don't you?" The guardsmen looked at one another as they considered. Then, in better unison than they'd shown a moment earlier, they nodded once more.

King Grus had overthrown Prince Vasilko and reverence for the Banished One in Nishevatz. He'd persuaded Prince Lazutin in Hisardzik that backing the Banished One and joining in attacks against Avornis wasn't the smartest thing Lazutin could have done—persuaded him expensively, a way a man who was a merchant when he couldn't get away with piracy would remember. Now Grus led the Avornan army east toward Jobuka, which had also joined in raids along the Avornan coast. He wanted all the Chernagors to learn they could not harry their southern neighbor with impunity.

As the army moved east, Grus kept a wary eye on the weather and on the crops ripening in the fields. When the harvest was done, the army wouldn't be able to live off the land anymore and he would have to go home, and he wanted to remind not only Jobuka but also Hrvace, which lay farther east still, of his existence.

Ravno, which ruled the land between Hisardzik and Jobuka, was unfriendly to both of them, and had not sent ships to join the raiders who'd ravaged the eastern coast of Avornis. Grus ordered his men not to plunder the countryside as they traveled through Ravno's territory. In gratitude, Prince Osen, who ruled the city-state, sent supply wagons to the Avornan army. Along with the wagons still coming up from Avornis itself, they kept Grus' men well supplied with grain.

"I know what we ought to do," Hirundo said as the army encamped one evening. The setting sun streaked his gilded helmet and mailshirt with blood. "We ought to set up as bakers."

"As bakers?" Grus echoed, eyeing the grizzled streaks in the general's beard. They'd both been young officers when they first met, Hirundo the younger. Hirundo was still younger than Grus, of course, but neither of them was a young man anymore. *Where did all the years go?* Grus wondered. Wherever they were, he wouldn't get them back.

Hirundo, meanwhile, bubbled with enthusiasm. "Yes, bakers, by Olor's beard. We've got all this wheat. We can bake bread and sell it cheaper than anybody in the Chernagor city-states. We'll outdicker all the merchants, leave 'em gnashing their teeth, and go home rich." He beamed at Grus.

Grus smiled back. You couldn't help smiling when Hirundo beamed. "Do you know what?" Grus said. Still beaming, Hirundo shook his head. "You're out of your mind," Grus told him.

With a bow, the general said, "Why, thank you very much, Your Majesty." Grus threw his hands in the air. Some days, you were going to lose if you argued with Hirundo.

Jobuka wasn't as strongly situated as either Nishevatz or Hisardzik. To make up for that, the Avornans who'd built the town and the Chernagors who'd held it for centuries had lavished endless ingenuity on its walls. A wide, fetid moat kept would-be attackers from even reaching those walls until they had drained it, and the defenders could punish them while they were working on that. Grus would not have wanted to try to storm the town.

But, as at Hisardzik, he didn't have to. He needed to appear, to scare the city-state's army inside the walls, and then to position himself to devastate the countryside if Prince Gleb paid him no attention. That all proved surprisingly easy. If the Chernagors didn't care to meet his men in the open field—and they made it very plain they didn't—what choice did they have but falling back into their fortress? None Grus could see. And once they did fall back, that left the countryside wide open.

Instead of starting to burn and plunder right away, Grus sent a man under a flag of truce up to the moat—the drawbridge over it that led to the main gate had been raised. The herald bawled out that Grus wanted to speak with Prince Gleb, who led Jobuka, and that he wouldn't stay patient forever if Gleb chose not to speak to him. That done, the Avornan tramped back to the army.

Gleb came out the next day, also under a flag of truce. He didn't lower the drawbridge, but emerged from a postern gate and crossed the moat in a small boat. One guard accompanied him. "He is a symbol only," the Prince of Jobuka said in good Avornan. "I know I could not bring enough men to keep me safe in your midst."

"He is welcome, as you are welcome," Grus replied, trying to size Gleb up. The prince was older than Lazutin, older than Vasilko—*not as old as I am,* Grus thought sadly. Gleb looked much more ordinary than the clever, saturnine Lazutin. His beard needing combing and his nose, though large, had no particular shape. His eyebrows were dark and luxuriant.

He brought them down into a frown now. "What are you doing on my land?" he demanded. "You have no business here, curse it."

"What were your ships doing raiding my coast a few years ago?" Grus asked in turn.

"That's different," Gleb said.

"Yes, it is, by the gods, and I know how," Grus said. "The difference is, you never thought I'd come here to pay you back."

Gleb scowled. He didn't try to deny it, from which Grus concluded that he couldn't. All he said was, "Well, now that you *are* here, what do I have to do to get rid of you?"

"Wait." Grus held up a hand. "Don't go so fast. We're not done with this bit yet. What were your men doing helping Vasilko against Prince Vsevolod? What were they doing helping the Banished One against the gods in the heavens? Do you still bend the knee to the Banished One, Your Highness?"

"I never did." Gleb sounded indignant.

"No? Then what were you doing helping Vasilko? I already asked you once, and you didn't answer."

"What was I doing? You Avornans invaded the land of the Chernagors. What was I supposed to do, let you have your way here? If I could hurt you, I would."

Now Grus was the one who scowled. He'd had Chernagors tell him that before. He could understand it, even believe it. But it also made such a handy excuse. "And you're telling me you had no idea Vasilko had abandoned the gods in the heavens, and that the Banished One backed him? Do you expect me to believe you?"

"I don't care what you believe," Gleb said.

"No?" Grus said. "Are you sure of that? Are you very sure? Because if you are, I *am* going to ravage your countryside. Being a friend to other Chernagors is one thing. Being a friend to the Banished One is something else again."

Prince Gleb opened his mouth. Then he closed it again without saying anything. After an obvious pause for thought, he tried again. "I told you once, I do not worship the Banished One. I give reverence to King Olor and Queen Quelea and the rest of the gods in the heavens. I always have. So have my people."

Maybe he was telling the truth. Maybe. Grus said, "Whether that's so or not, you are still going to pay for raiding our coasts. You don't care for Avornis in the Chernagor country. We don't like Chernagors plundering Avornis."

Again, Gleb started to speak. Grus could make a good guess about what he was going to say—something like, *Well, what makes you any better than we are?* But the answer to that was so obvious, Gleb again fell silent. An Avornan army camped outside of Jobuka gave Grus a potent argument. The Chernagor prince's sour stare said he knew as much. Sullenly, he asked, "How much are you going to squeeze out of me?"

Grus told him the same thing as he'd told Prince Lazutin. He wondered how Gleb would go about haggling. The only thing he was sure of was that Gleb would.

Sure enough, the Prince of Jobuka exclaimed, "Letting you loose on the countryside would be cheaper!"

"Well, that can be arranged, Your Highness," Grus said with a bow. He called for Hirundo. When the general arrived, the king said, "If you'd be kind enough to give the orders turning our soldiers loose . . ."

"Certainly, Your Majesty." Hirundo turned to leave once more. Where Prince Gleb could see him, he was all brisk business.

He'd taken only a couple of steps before Gleb said, "Wait!" Hirundo paused, looking back toward the king.

"Why should he wait?" Grus asked. "You told us what your choice was, Your Highness. We're willing to give you what you say you want. Carry on, Hirundo."

"Wait!" Gleb said again, more urgently—almost frantically—this time. Again, Hirundo paused. Grus waved him on. Prince Gleb threw his hands in the air. "Stop, curse you! I was wrong. I'd rather pay."

"The full sum?" Grus demanded. Now that he had Gleb over a barrel—one the Prince of Jobuka had brought out himself and then fallen over—he intended to take full advantage of it.

"Yes, the full sum," Gleb said. "Just leave the crops alone!"

What did that say? That his storehouses were almost empty? Grus wouldn't have been surprised. "Bring out the silver by this hour tomorrow," the king told Gleb. "Otherwise . . ."

"I understood you," Gleb said sourly. "You don't need to worry about that, Your Majesty. I understood you very well."

Having made the promise to pay, he kept it. Grus checked the silver even more closely than he had the money he'd gotten from Prince Lazutin. All of it proved good. He doubted any of the Chernagors would pay when he didn't have an army at their doorstep, but he didn't intend to lose a lot of sleep over it. He'd squeezed them plenty hard as things were. He left the encampment near the formidable walls of Jobuka and marched his army south.

"Are we heading for home, Your Majesty?" Hirundo asked in some surprise. "I thought we'd pay a call on Hrvace, too."

"We will," Grus said.

"But . . ." Hirundo pointed west. "It's that way."

"Thank you so very much," Grus said, and the general winced. The king went on, "Before I turn west, I want to get Jobuka under the horizon. If Gleb sees me going that way, he's liable to send a ship to Hrvace. It could get there before we do, and that could let Prince Tvorimir set up an ambush."

Hirundo bowed in the saddle. "Well, I can't very well tell you you're wrong, because you're right. The only thing I will say is, Gleb's liable to send that ship anyway. We ought to be ready for trouble."

"So we should," Grus said. "I trust you'll make sure we are?"

"You're a trusting soul, aren't you?" the general replied.

King Grus laughed out loud at that. Maybe some Kings of Avornis had been trusting souls. Lanius was a dedicated antiquarian. He might know of one or two. Grus couldn't think of any. If a trusting soul had somehow mounted the Avornan throne, he wouldn't have lasted long.

Lanius knew he went to the archives like a lover to his beloved—the figure of speech Sosia had used held some truth. He would never have used it around her himself. It was too likely to stir up her suspicions.

Working on *How to Be a King* gave him a perfect excuse for poking through ancient documents. He laughed at himself. *Oh, yes, I really need an excuse to get dusty.*

He was looking for documents dealing with Thervingia during his father's reign and the early years of his own—the days when King Dagipert had ruled the kingdom to the west, and when Dagipert had threatened to rule Avornis as well.

For the moment, Lanius wrote, *Avornans do not often think of Thervingia. It is a quiet, peaceful land, not one to cause trouble or alarm here. But this has not always been so, nor is there any guarantee that it shall always be so. Time may reveal Thervingia once more as a frightful danger. This being so, my beloved son, you should know as much as possible about the bygone days when Thervingia threatened our very dynasty.*

To Crex, those days would seem as distant as the time before the Menteshe seized the Scepter of Mercy. They were beyond his memory, and all times before one's own memory ran together. But Lanius remembered them well, and hoped to give his son some hints about how to deal with Thervingia if it turned troublesome again.

Knowing how to deal with the Thervings meant knowing how Avornis had dealt with them in days gone by. So Lanius told himself, anyhow. It gave him a splendid excuse for going through the archives and reading old parchments.

How *had* his father and Grus dealt with Dagipert? Carefully, it seemed. Reading the letters Mergus and Grus and Arch-Hallow Bucco had exchanged with the King of Thervingia, it struck Lanius that Dagipert had had the upper hand more often than not. That wasn't the way Lanius remembered things, but he'd been young and hadn't been encouraged to worry about affairs of state. He'd assumed everything was all right, and in the end he hadn't been wrong. But the road to the end had been rockier than he realized.

He started to write advice for how to deal with the Thervings when they had a strong king, then realized that was foolish. When Thervingia had a weak king, it wasn't dangerous to Avornis. He was glad he'd avoided making a fresh muddle in the text. One of these days, a secretary would make a fair copy of this manuscript so Crex—and maybe others who came after Crex—could read it. Even without a new muddle, Lanius pitied that secretary. His own script was spidery, and the manuscript marred by scratch-outs, arrows sending what was written here to be placed there, words and sometimes sentences squeezed in between lines, and every other flaw that annoyed him when someone else committed it.

After putting down on parchment what was, in his judgment, the best way to keep Thervingia from causing trouble, he read over what he had written. If someone who really faced trouble from the Thervings read this, would it do him any good? Lanius found himself shrugging. He really didn't know. He didn't suppose it would hurt. That would have to do.

When he left the archives, he went to the moncats' room. Several of the beasts came up to him in search of handouts. Like any cats, they liked him better when he had presents than when he didn't. "Sorry," he said. "I didn't stop in the kitchens."

They kept sending him slit-eyed, reproachful stares. He perched on a stool and watched them. After a little while, they seemed to forget he was there, and went back to scrambling on their framework of boards and branches, to eating from the bowls of meat that were always there for them, and to snuggling up not far from the braziers that kept their chamber warm. They were less sensitive to cold than his mustachioed monkeys, but they still enjoyed the heat from the braziers. He paid more attention to the moncats than to the monkeys these days, probably because the moncats got into more mischief.

He looked around for Pouncer. He at least half expected not to find the moncat. Would it be off in the kitchen stealing spoons, or had it gone off to the archives to hunt mice while he came here? But no, Pouncer lolled by a brazier, not quite asleep but not inclined to do much more than loll, either.

"You are a nuisance," Lanius told the moncat. "You're worse than a nuisance—you're a pest."

Praise of that sort seemed to be what Pouncer wanted most. The moncat rolled and stretched, all without going any farther from the warmth. Lanius laughed. Pouncer would be charming for as long as it cared to be, and not a heartbeat longer. Then it would go back to being a pest again.

He watched Pouncer. Pouncer watched him. After watching for a while, Pouncer decided it didn't want to stay by the brazier anymore. It scrambled up the framework of boards and branches Lanius had had made so the moncats could feel more as though they were living in the forest. Two other moncats higher up on the framework squared off against each other, snarling and hissing. As usually happened, one of them intimidated the other, which backed down. Sometimes, though, they would fight.

When Lanius looked back to see what Pouncer was up to, he frowned and scratched his head. Where was the moncat? He couldn't find it.

He looked up and down the frame. He looked back toward the brazier. He looked all around the moncats' chamber. Then, for good measure, he looked again. He rubbed his eyes and looked for a third time.

Pouncer had disappeared.

Lanius got up and examined the part of the frame where Pouncer had been the last time he paid any attention to the moncat. He also examined the wall behind the frame. It looked like the brickwork that made up much of the rest of the palace. As far as the king could tell, Pouncer might have dug a hole, jumped into it, and pulled the hole in after itself.

How long did I take my eye off Pouncer to watch the other beasts? Lanius wondered. Half a minute? A minute? Maybe even a minute and a half? No more than that, surely. How far could an unwatched moncat go in, at most, a minute and a half?

Far enough, evidently.

"Cursed thing," Lanius said. If he had been paying attention, he would finally have found out Pouncer's secret. Instead, the moncat had outsmarted him. He could almost hear Bubulcus' mocking voice. *Which is hardly a surprise to anyone who knows them both,* the servant would say.

But Bubulcus was dead. Remembering that brought Lanius up as sharply as seeing—or rather, not seeing—Pouncer vanish. The servant had mocked once too often, and paid too high a price.

Where was Pouncer now? Somewhere in the spaces between the walls, heading for—where? The kitchens? The archives? Someplace else, a spot known only to the moncat? How did the beast find its way in what had to be absolute darkness? Smell? Hearing? Touch?

Those were all wonderful questions. Lanius had less trouble coming up with them than he'd had finding questions to answer for *How to Be a King*. He'd replied to those questions. These? No.

Staying here until Pouncer reappeared might give him at least some of the answers he wanted so badly. Of course, the moncat, left to its own devices, might not come back for days—might not, in fact, come back at all. Put a servant in here to watch? Keep sending in servants in shifts until Pouncer returned? Lanius shook his head. Opening and closing the door so often would only give the rest of the moncats chances to escape. And how much attention would servants pay if they did come in and watch? Not enough, probably.

What to do, then? Lanius let out a few soft curses, just enough to make some of the moncats look his way again. This was one of the rare times when he wished he took the field. He was convinced the curses of fighting soldiers had an unmatched sonorous magnificence.

As things were, once he got done swearing the best thing he could think to do was leave the moncats' room. Sooner or later, Pouncer would turn up somewhere. Then the beast would go back in here . . . and then, sooner or later, it would escape again.

And maybe, with a little luck, I'll get to see it escaping next time, Lanius thought.

The road to Hrvace, the easternmost of the Chernagor city-states that had joined Nishevatz in harrying Avornis, would have been as good as any Grus had seen in the north country. He wouldn't have had to worry about ambushes or anything else while traveling it. It would have been, if a driving rainstorm from off the Northern Sea hadn't turned it into a bottomless ribbon of mud. As things were, horses sank to their bellies, wagons to their hubs or deeper. Moving forward at all became a desperate struggle. Moving forward in a hurry—the very idea was laughable.

But Grus knew he had to move forward in a hurry if he wanted to punish Hrvace for what it had done. That same rain was ruining the last of the harvest hereabouts. Living off the land wouldn't be easy. Living off the land would, in fact, be just as hard as moving forward in a hurry.

"We have to," Grus said.

"Your Majesty, I don't work miracles," Hirundo replied, more than a little testily. "And if my horse goes down into the mud all the way to its nose so it drowns, I won't go forward one bit, let alone fast."

"*You* don't work miracles," Grus said. He raised his voice and shouted for Pterocles. The rain drowned his voice as effectively as mud would have drowned Hirundo's horse. He shouted again, louder.

Eventually, Pterocles heard him. Even more eventually, the wizard fought his way to the king's side. "What do you need, Your Majesty?" Pterocles asked.

Grus looked up into the weeping heavens, and got a faceful of rain for doing it. "Can you make this stop?" he inquired.

Pterocles shook his head. Water dripped from the end of his nose and from his beard. "Not me, Your Majesty, and any other wizard who says he can is lying through his teeth. Wizards aren't weatherworkers. Men aren't strong enough to do anything about rain or wind or sun. The Banished One could, but I don't suppose you'd want to ask him."

"No," Grus said. "I don't suppose I would. Is he aiming this weather at us, or is it just a storm?"

"I think it's just a storm," Pterocles replied. "It doesn't feel like anything but natural weather."

"All right," Grus said, though it wasn't. He murmured a prayer to the gods in the heavens. They surely had some control over the weather—if they chose to do anything about it. But how interested in the material world were they? Natural or not, this rain helped nobody but the Banished One. Didn't Olor and Quelea and the rest see as much?

Regardless of what Olor and Quelea and the other gods in the heavens saw, the rain kept falling. It didn't get lighter. If anything, it got worse. Grus kept the army moving west for as long as he could. But movement was at best a crawl. What should have taken a quarter of an hour took a quarter of a day.

At last, Hirundo said, "Your Majesty, may I tell you something obvious?"

"Go ahead," Grus said.

"Your Majesty, this is more trouble than it's worth," the general said. "Gods only know how long we're going to need to get to Hrvace. Once we're there, how are we going to feed ourselves? We won't be able to live off the country, and supply wagons will have a demon of a time getting through. The Chernagors inside the walls will laugh their heads off when they see us."

He was right. King Grus knew that all too well. Even though he knew it, he resisted acting on what he knew. Angrily, he asked, "What do you want me to do? Turn around and go back to the city of Avornis?"

Grus hoped that would make Hirundo say something like, *No, of course not, Your Majesty.* Instead, the general nodded emphatically. "Yes, that's just what I want you to do," he said. "If you ask me, it's the only sensible thing we *can* do."

"But—" Grus still fought the idea. "If we do that, then the Banished One still has a toehold in the Chernagor country."

"Maybe," Hirundo said. "But maybe not, too. Lazutin and Gleb swore up and down they didn't have much to do with him—certainly not directly. We don't really *know* he had a toehold anywhere but Nishevatz."

"Tempting to believe that," Grus said. "I'm almost afraid to, though, just because it's so tempting."

"Well, look at it this way," Hirundo said. "Suppose we go on to Hrvace and sit outside it and get weaker and hungrier by the day. We can't threaten to ravage the countryside, because the storm's already done most of that. Suppose the Chernagors come out when they see how weak we are. Suppose they smash us. Don't you think *that* would do the Banished One some good?"

Grus tried not to think how much good that would do the Banished One. He tried . . . and he failed. He sighed. "All right. You've made your point," he said, and sighed again. "We'll go home."

"King Olor be praised!" Hirundo exclaimed. "You won't regret this."

"I already regret it," Grus answered. "But I'm liable to regret pushing ahead even more. And so . . . and so we'll go home." He spent the next few minutes cursing the weather as comprehensively as he knew how.

Hirundo had heard a good deal. He'd sometimes been known to say a good deal. His eyes grew wide even so. "That's . . . impressive, Your Majesty," he said when Grus finally ran down.

The king chuckled self-consciously. "Only goes to show you can take the old river rat away from the river, but you can't get the river out of the river rat."

"You'll have to teach me some of that one of these days, you old river rat," Hirundo said. "But meanwhile—"

"Yes. Meanwhile," Grus said. "Go ahead. Give the orders. Turn us south. You've won."

"It's not me. It's the stinking weather," Hirundo said. He did give the necessary orders. He gave them with great assurance and without the slightest pause for thought. He had been planning those orders for a long time, and he'd gotten them right.

The army obeyed them with alacrity, too. A lot of the soldiers must have been thinking about going home. As soon as they had a chance to put their desires into action, they made the most of it. They could go no faster traveling south than they had traveling west, but they were much happier stuck in the mud while homeward bound than they had been on their way to attack Hrvace.

Even the weather seemed to think turning south was a good idea. Two days after Grus reluctantly decided to abandon his campaign in the land of the Chernagors, the rain stopped and the sun came out again. It shone as brightly as it had in the middle of summer. Grus said several more things Hirundo hadn't heard before. He said them with great feeling, too. The road remained muddy, and would for several more days. Even so, there was mud, and then there was *mud*, soupy ooze without a trace of bottom anywhere.

There was one more thing, too. "You know what would happen if I tried to use this good weather and went east again, don't you?" Grus asked Hirundo.

The general nodded. "Sure, I do, Your Majesty. It would start raining again. And it wouldn't stop until we all grew fins."

"That's right. That's just exactly right." Grus waved his hands. All around him, the landscape gently steamed as the warm sun began drying up the rain that had already fallen. "But Pterocles tells me it's just an ordinary storm. The Banished One has nothing to do with it, he says. By Olor's beard, if he doesn't know, who's likely to?"

"Nobody," Hirundo said.

"Nobody," Grus agreed sadly. "No matter how hard a time I have believing it, it's only a what-do-you-call-it. A coincidence, that's what I'm trying to say."

"Pterocles usually knows what he's talking about, sure enough," Hirundo said. "When it comes to magic, I usually don't, any more than Pterocles knows how to drive home a cavalry charge."

"He was brave inside Nishevatz," Grus said.

"Oh, I wouldn't be afraid to try a spell—not afraid like that, anyway," Hirundo said. "That doesn't mean a spell I tried would work. I haven't got the training, and I haven't got the talent."

"Neither have I." The king looked warily up at the sun. It smiled back, for all the world—*for all the world, indeed,* Grus thought—as though it had never gone away and never would. But he knew better. He wouldn't be able to trust it until the coming spring—and not even then, if he had to campaign in the Chernagor country.

For now . . . for now, he was going home. If he hadn't done everything he'd wanted to, he had managed most of it. That wouldn't have impressed the gods in the heavens. In the world where mere mortals had to live, it wasn't bad at all. Plenty had tried more and accomplished less. So Grus told himself, anyway.

CHAPTER TWENTY-NINE

K ing Lanius waited outside the brown stone walls of the city of
Avornis as King Grus brought the army back to the capital.
The whole royal family had come out to see Grus off. Lanius
was there by himself to welcome the other king and the army back.
King Grus waved from horseback. Lanius solemnly waved back.

"Welcome home," he called.

"By Olor's beard, it's good to be back," Grus answered.

"Congratulations on driving the Banished One from Nishevatz, and
from the land of the Chernagors." Lanius did not mind praising Grus
for that.

"I thank you," the other king replied. "I'm not sure we drove him
out of the Chernagor country altogether, but we did weaken his hold
there." He had a strong streak of honesty in him—except, perhaps,
when he was talking to his wife about other women (but how many
men had that particular streak of honesty in them?).

Grus guided his horse away from the rest of the army and over beside Lanius. He always joked about what a bad rider he was, but he
handled the animal perfectly well. Lanius wished he were as smooth.
Grus reviewed the soldiers as they rode and marched past and into the
city. The men were hard and scrawny and scraggly-bearded. Some of
them limped; others showed fresh scars on faces or forearms.

One of the foot soldiers waved to Grus and called, "We earned our
pay this time, didn't we, Your Majesty?"

"I'd say you did, Buteo," Grus answered. The soldier's face stretched to hold a pleased smile. He waved again, and kept looking back over his shoulder until the gateway hid him.

"You know him?" Lanius asked. "Was he one of your guards up there?"

"Buteo? No, just a soldier," Grus said. "He's brave, but not too smart. He'll never even make sergeant, not if he lives to be a hundred. But he's a good man at your back in a scrap."

"Is he?" Lanius said. Grus nodded. Lanius asked, "How many soldiers do you know by name—and by what they can do, the way you did with him?"

"I never thought about it." Now Grus did. "I can't tell you exactly," he said at last. "But I've got some notion of who about every other man is. Something like that. I know more about some—a lot more about some—and not so much about others."

Lanius believed him. Lanius didn't see how he could do anything else; Grus radiated conviction. "How do you manage that?" Lanius asked. "I couldn't begin to, not to save my life."

"How do you remember all the things you find in the archives? How do you put them together in interesting patterns?" Grus returned. "*I* couldn't do that."

"But knowing people, knowing how they work—that's more important." Lanius was sure it was more important, not least because he couldn't do it himself. "I wish I were better at it."

"You've done all right, seems to me," Grus said. "If you hadn't, more people would have taken advantage of you by now."

"You did," Lanius said. It was the first thing that came into his mind, and he brought it out with less bitterness than he would have expected.

It still made Grus give him a sharp look. "I wouldn't be where I am if your mother hadn't tried to kill me by sorcery," the other king said. Grus barked laughter. "I wouldn't be where I am if she'd done it, either."

"Well, no," Lanius admitted. Over the years, Grus had done any number of things he didn't like. Lanius could hardly deny that Grus might have done far worse than he had. It was funny, if you looked at it the right way. He had to like Grus to a certain degree, because he couldn't dislike him as much as he might have.

"How's my daughter?" Grus asked—a question any father-in-law might ask of a son-in-law.

"She's fine," Lanius said. By and large, it was true. If Sosia sometimes had reason to throw things at him, that was none of Grus' business. And it wasn't as though Estrilda didn't sometimes have reason to throw things at Grus.

"And what about Ortalis?" Grus said. "That was some nasty news you sent me about him and the servant."

Carefully, Lanius said, "You will know that Ortalis and I don't always get along as well as we might." Grus nodded. Lanius went on, "Even I will say it wasn't altogether Ortalis' fault. Bubulcus provoked him—provoked him outrageously. Something should have happened to Bubulcus. What did happen, though, shouldn't have."

"That's about how it seemed to me from your letter," Grus agreed. "At least he didn't do it for sport. That was what I was afraid of."

"Oh, yes." Lanius didn't try to pretend he misunderstood. "That was what I was afraid of, too. I don't know what I would have done then." He gnawed on the inside of his lower lip. He was glad he hadn't had to find out.

To his relief, Grus let it go there. He said, "And I've got a new granddaughter?"

"That's right." Lanius felt guarded there, too. If Capella had been a boy, what *would* that have done to the succession in Grus' eyes? "Limosa thinks she's the most wonderful baby in the world. I'd make a couple of exceptions myself."

King Grus chuckled. "Yes, I can see how you might." But the older man's grin slipped. "Limosa." He said the name of Ortalis' wife as though it tasted bad. "He finally found somebody who likes the welts he gives her." Grus made as though to spit in disgust, then—barely—thought better of it.

"She loves him," Lanius said, which didn't contradict Grus.

"Does that make it better or worse?" the other king asked.

Lanius thought it over. "I don't know," he said at last. "Do you?"

"What I know is . . . more about Ortalis than I wish I did," Grus said—not a direct answer to what Lanius had said, but not an evasion, either.

The last soldiers passed into the city of Avornis. They were happy to be home, looking forward to beds in their barracks, to wine, and to women. What went on in the palace meant nothing to them. If they had to go fight, they would. Until then, they'd enjoy themselves.

Not for the first time, Lanius found himself jealous of men who could live for the moment. He sometimes wished he could do the same, without worrying about what would happen next. He laughed at himself. Given the nature he'd been born with, he might as well have wished for the moon while he was at it.

Even though Grus had lived softer in the field than his soldiers had, he was glad to return to the comforts of the palace. He was older than his soldiers, too, and needed to live softer. So he told himself, anyhow.

Estrilda greeted him cautiously, the way she did whenever he came back from campaign. Her look plainly said she wondered what he'd been up to in the land of the Chernagors. This time, he could look her straight in the eye, for he'd been up to very little. For one thing, the Chernagor women hadn't much appealed to him. For another, he'd reached the age where conquests of that sort were less urgent than they had been in earlier years. That didn't mean he didn't enjoy them when they happened—Estrilda evidently hadn't yet found out about his bastard boy by Alauda, for which he was duly grateful—but he didn't go after them as energetically as he might have when he was younger.

Still somewhat suspicious, Estrilda said, "You were away for a long time."

"So I was," Grus said. "There was a lot to do, and doing it wasn't easy. If you paid any attention to my dispatches, you'd know that."

"Not everything you do ends up in your dispatches," his wife answered. "I've seen that."

He wanted to tell her she was wrong, or at least foolish, but she would know he was lying if he did. All he did do was shrug and say, "Not this time." If Estrilda felt like quarreling, she would.

She didn't. "It's good to have you back," she said.

"It's good to be back," Grus said. "If I had to right now, I do believe I'd kill for a hot bath."

He soaked in a copper tub for more than an hour, scrubbing away the grime of the campaign and simply luxuriating in the water. Whenever it began to cool down, servants drained some and fetched in more jars of hot water from the kitchens. The king hated to get out. After scrubbing, he leaned his head back in the tub, wondering if he could fall asleep there. Not quite, he discovered, though he did come close.

After the bath, supper. He'd had his fill of seafood up in the Chernagor country. Roast goose stuffed with bread crumbs and dried apples stuck to the ribs. He'd drunk a lot of ale in the north—better that than water, which often brought disease—but sweet wine was better. And, after that, lying down in his own bed might have been best of all.

Estrilda lay down beside him. She had, he noticed, put on fresh perfume. He'd thought he would go straight to sleep. As things turned out, he didn't. But when his eyes did close, he slept very soundly.

He woke up in the morning feeling, if not younger than the day before, then at least oiled and repaired. Now that he was back, he had to get on top of things again. Otherwise, who was the real king? Was he? Or was Lanius?

Before any of that, though, he saw his grandchildren. Crex and Pitta both wondered why he hadn't brought them any presents from the Chernagor country. "Sorry, my dears," he said. "I was worried about bringing me back. I didn't worry much about presents." He had tribute from Hisardzik and Jobuka, but he didn't think silver coins with the faces of shaggy-bearded princes on them would fascinate children.

Capella didn't ask for presents. She waved her arms and legs in Limosa's arms and smiled up toothlessly at the king. "She's a pretty child, Your Highness," Grus said.

"Thank you, Your Majesty," Limosa answered politely. "I wish her other grandfather could see her, too."

"I'm sorry," Grus said. "I *am* sorry, but Petrosus isn't coming out of the Maze."

"Even if he isn't why your son and I got married?" Limosa said. "Even if we got married because—" She didn't go on. She turned red and looked down at her baby.

Grus had a pretty good idea of what she would have said. It made him want to blush, too, even if he hadn't actually heard it. He was afraid she would show him her back. To his relief, she didn't. He gathered himself. "Even then," he told her. "If your father wasn't plotting that, he was plotting something else. He'll stay where he is."

"Yes, Your Majesty," Limosa whispered. She took Capella away, as though that was the only way she could find to punish Grus. And so it probably was.

Ortalis didn't come to pay his respects. Grus sent a servant after him. When the king finally saw his son, he said, "Well, now that you've finally done it, how does it feel to kill a man?"

"I knew you were going to bother me about that," Ortalis said sullenly. "I knew it. And I didn't even enjoy sticking the knife in him. It just . . . happened, that's all. I wish it hadn't. But he got me angry, and then he said something really foul, and—" He shrugged.

Eyeing him, Grus decided it could easily have been worse. Ortalis wasn't consumed by remorse, but at least he had some idea of what it was. Grus said, "You should have just punched him."

"I suppose so," his son said. "His woman and her brats are taken care of. Lanius made sure of that. Can I go now, or do you want to yell at me some more? I don't kill servants for fun."

"All right," Grus said, and Ortalis left. Grus sighed. Considering what Ortalis did do for fun, was it any wonder that Grus had wondered? He didn't think so.

Business, the king thought. If he was going to pick business, he wanted to pick interesting business to start with. He went to the chamber where Otus the former thrall dwelt. "Sorry, Your Majesty," a guard said. "He's not here right now."

"Where is he?" Grus asked.

"He's got a lady friend. He's with her," the guard answered.

"At this hour of the morning?" Grus exclaimed. The guard smirked and nodded. Grus said, "If I were wearing a hat, I'd take it off to him. Shall I wait until he's, ah, finished?"

"I can fetch him, if you like," the guardsman said.

"No, never mind," Grus said. "I'll come back and visit him later. He wouldn't thank me for interrupting him, would he?"

"I don't know about that, Your Majesty, but *I* wouldn't," the guard replied, chuckling at his own cleverness.

"All right, then. I'll try again in an hour or so," Grus said, and left.

When he came back, the guard nodded to him. "He's here now, Your Majesty," the fellow said. "He's waiting for you."

"Your Majesty!" Otus said when Grus walked into his chamber. "It is good to see you again."

"Good to see you," Grus answered. "I'm more pleased than I can tell you at how well you're doing." That was the truth. Only Otus' southern accent and a certain slight hesitation in his speech said that he had been a thrall. He looked bright and alert and altogether like a normal man. He evidently acted like a normal man, too. "Who's your, ah, friend?" Grus asked.

"Her name is Calypte, Your Majesty." Otus seemed less happy than Grus had thought he might. "She is very sweet. And yet . . . You know I have a woman down in the south, a woman who is still a thrall?"

"Yes, I know that." The king nodded.

Otus sighed. "I do her wrong when I do this. I understand that. But I am here, and she is there—and she is hardly more than a brute beast. I loved her when I was a beast myself. I might love her if she were a beast no more. Your Majesty, so many thralls down there! Save them!"

Otus' appeal didn't surprise Grus. The power with which the ex-thrall phrased it did. "I'll do what I can," the king answered. "I don't know how much that will be. It will depend on the civil war among the Menteshe, and on how well wizards besides Pterocles can learn to cure thralls."

And if they truly can, he thought. He didn't say that to Otus, who seemed normal enough. If Otus hadn't seemed normal, Grus wouldn't have thought of campaigning south of the Stura at all.

"You could make beasts into men." If the former thrall wasn't cured, he sounded as though he was. "Who but the gods could ever do that until now? You would be remembered forever."

Grus laughed. "Are you sure you weren't born a courtier?"

"I'm sure, Your Majesty," Otus said. "Courtiers tell lies. I'm too stupid to do that. I tell you the truth."

"I'm going to tell you the truth, too," Grus said. "I want to fight south of the Stura. I don't know if I can. It's dangerous for Avornan kings to go over the frontier. There have been whole armies that never came back. I want to cure thralls. I don't want to see free men taken down into thralldom."

"You wouldn't!" Otus exclaimed. "Look at me. I'm free. I'm cured. Whatever the Banished One can do, he can't make me back into what I was."

From what Lanius wrote, Otus had always insisted on that. The trouble was, he would have insisted on it as vehemently if it were a lie as he would have if it were true. Grus didn't know how to judge which it was. He didn't know what to do, either.

"I already told you—I'll decide what to do come spring," he said after some thought. "If the Menteshe have a prince by then and they're solidly behind him, I may have to sit tight. If they don't . . . If they don't, well, I'll figure out what to do next then, that's all."

"You ought to be ready to move, whether you do or not," Otus remarked.

That held a good deal of truth. "I already have soldiers in the south," Grus said. "There's one other thing I need to check up on before I make up my mind."

"What's that?" Otus asked.

Grus didn't answer, not directly. Instead, he chatted for a little while longer and then took his leave. He went to a small audience chamber and told a servant, "Find the serving girl named Calypte and tell her I'd like to talk with her, please."

"Yes, Your Majesty." The servant dipped his head and hurried off.

Calypte came into the room less than a quarter of an hour later. Until then, Grus couldn't have matched her name with her face. She was in her late twenties, short, a little on the plump side, with a round face, very white teeth, and dark eyes that sparkled. She wore a leaf-green dress and had tied a red kerchief over her black hair and under her chin. Dropping Grus a curtsy, she said, "What is it, Your Majesty?" She sounded nervous. Grus didn't suppose he could blame her. She had to think she was either in trouble or that he was about to try to seduce her.

He said, "You're . . . friends with Otus, aren't you?"

"Yes, I am." Now that she knew where the ground lay, her nerves vanished. She stuck out her chin. "Why shouldn't I be?"

A feisty little thing, Grus thought, and hid a smile. "No reason at all," he answered. "I just wanted to ask you a couple of questions about him."

"Why?" Calypte demanded. "What business is it of anybody except him and me?"

"It's also the kingdom's business, I'm afraid," Grus said. "You haven't forgotten he used to be a thrall, have you?"

"Oh." The maidservant's face clouded. "If you really want to know, I *had* forgotten until you reminded me. He doesn't act like a thrall—or the way I suppose a thrall would act. He just acts like—a man." She looked down at the mosaics on the floor and turned pink. Grus got the idea Otus had acted very much like a man earlier in the morning.

This time, he didn't try to hide his smile. He said, "I don't want to know about any of that. It isn't any of my business—you're right. What I want to know is, have you ever seen any places where he doesn't act just like a man, where being a thrall left him different?"

Calypte thought that over. She didn't need long. When she was done, she shook her head. A black curl popped free. Tucking it back under the kerchief, she said, "No, I don't think so. He hasn't been in the palace for years, the way most people I know have, so there are things he doesn't understand right away, but anybody new here is like that."

"Are you sure?" Grus asked. "It could be more important than you know."

"I'm not a witch or anything, Your Majesty," Calypte answered. "I can't cast a spell or do things like that. But from what I know, he's as much of a man as a man could be."

She was right. Pterocles could make tests she couldn't even imagine. But the wizard would have admitted—*had* admitted—he couldn't be altogether sure of the answers he got, not when he was measuring himself against the strength and subtlety of the Banished One. But the tests Calypte applied (not that she would have called them such) were ones that, by the very nature of things, Pterocles was not equipped to administer.

Grus found himself smiling again. "Fair enough," he said. "You can go. And the next time you see Otus, you can tell him from me that I think he's a lucky fellow."

The serving girl smiled, too. "I'll do better than that. I'll show him." And, by the way her hips swayed when she left the audience chamber, she would do a good, careful, thorough job of showing him, too.

Leaves blazed gold and maroon and scarlet. When the wind blew through the trees, it swirled them off branches and sent them dancing like bits of flame. Lanius admired the autumn. "This is reason to come out to the woods all by itself," he said.

Arch-Hallow Anser and Prince Ortalis both laughed at the king. "This is pretty enough," Anser said, "but the reason to come out here is the hunting."

"That's right," Ortalis said, not that Lanius had expected him to say anything else. Anser came hunting because he enjoyed it. Ortalis came hunting because he enjoyed hunting, too, but in a different way. Lanius was glad to have Ortalis hunt, because he might do something worse if he didn't.

And you—why do you come hunting? the king wondered. He didn't take pleasure in it, the way Anser did. He didn't need it, crave it, the way Ortalis did. But every so often Anser looked as though he would curl up and die of disappointment if he heard "No" one more time, and Anser was too nice a fellow to disappoint.

Smiling, the arch-hallow said, "Maybe you'll kill something this time."

"Maybe I will," Lanius said. "Maybe a stag will die laughing at how badly I shoot." Anser laughed, whether a stag would or not. Lanius managed a wry smile at his own ineptitude. He wasn't much of a bowman. He knew that. But he also used his bad archery as an excuse not to have to kill anything. He didn't think either Anser or Ortalis had ever figured that out. He hoped not, anyway.

"Think of venison," Ortalis said lovingly. "Think of a roasted haunch, or of chunks of venison stewed for a nice long time in wine and herbs, until all the gamy taste goes away. Doesn't it make your mouth water?"

Lanius nodded, because it did. He loved eating meat. Killing it himself had always been a different story. He recognized the inconsistency, and had no idea what to do about it.

One of Anser's beaters nodded to the arch-hallow. "We're off," he said. He and his comrades disappeared into the woods.

"They're better hunters than any of us," Lanius said.

"I don't know about that," Ortalis said. Anser didn't look convinced, either. They both enjoyed hunting for its own sake, which Lanius didn't. Ortalis added, "The two of us could come out here without beaters, because we can find game on our own. Some people I could name, though . . ."

"If that's what's bothering you—" Lanius began.

"What? You think you could do your own stalking?" Ortalis broke in. "Don't make me laugh." That wasn't what Lanius had started to say. He'd been about to tell Grus' legitimate son and his bastard that he couldn't have cared less about finding game on his own, that he came hunting for the sake of their company (especially Anser's, though he wouldn't have said that) and to get out to the forest and away from the palace. Maybe it was just as well Ortalis had interrupted him.

Something up in a tree chirped. Peering through the branches, Lanius got a glimpse of a plump brown bird with a striped belly. "Thrush," Anser said without even looking toward it. "They fly south for the winter every year about this time."

"Do they?" Lanius said. The arch-hallow nodded. Lanius still knew less about birds than he wished he did. He knew less than he wished he did about a lot of things. Not enough hours in the day, not enough days in the year to learn as much as he could about all the things he wanted to know.

"They're tasty baked in a pie," Ortalis said. Anser nodded again. This time, so did Lanius. Pies and stews full of songbirds were some of his favorite dishes. Again, though, he didn't care to hunt thrushes himself.

A rabbit bounded by and disappeared into the undergrowth. Anser started to set an arrow to his bowstring, then checked the motion and laughed at himself. "Not much point to shooting at rabbits," he said. "You only waste your arrows that way. If you want rabbits in your stew instead of songbirds, you go after them with dogs and nets."

"Then you whack them over the head with a club," Ortalis said. "That way, you don't hurt the pelts."

"I see," Lanius said. He wondered what he really saw. What Ortalis said made perfect sense. Did the prince really sound as though he enjoyed the idea of whacking rabbits over the head with a club, or was Lanius only hearing what he expected to hear? The king couldn't be sure, and decided he had to give his brother-in-law the benefit of the doubt.

"Come on," Anser said. "There's a clearing not far from here. If we post ourselves at the edge of it, we'll get good shots."

He glided down a game track as smoothly and silently as any of the men who served him, the men who looked so much like poachers. Lanius was sure he could find his own game if he had to. Ortalis did his best to move the same way, but wasn't as good at it. Lanius tried not to trip over his own feet and not to step on too many twigs. Anser winced only once, so he supposed he wasn't doing too bad a job.

The three high-ranking hunters had their usual low-voiced argument about who would shoot first. Lanius resigned himself to looking foolish in front of Grus' sons. He'd done it before. *You could try to kill a deer,* he said to himself, and then shook his head. That wasn't why he came out here.

A frightened stag bounded into the clearing. "Good luck, Your Majesty," Anser whispered.

"Try to frighten it, anyhow, Your Majesty," Ortalis whispered—a reasonable estimate of Lanius' talents.

Since the shot was fairly long, the king didn't worry much about taking aim, good, bad, or otherwise. He pointed the bow in the general direction of the stag and let fly. Even as he did so, the stag bounded forward. Anser and Ortalis sighed together. So did Lanius, with something approaching relief. This time, at least, he had a good enough excuse for missing.

If the stag had stood still, the arrow would have flown past in front of it. As things were, the shaft caught the animal just behind the left shoulder. The deer took four or five staggering steps, then fell on its side, kicking feebly. As Lanius stared in dismay, the kicking stopped and the stag lay still.

"Well shot, by Olor's beard!" Anser cried. "Oh, well shot!" Ortalis whooped and pounded Lanius on the back. The king's guards whooped, too.

He'd missed again, but he was the only one who knew it. This time, he'd missed at missing. Lanius gulped. He didn't want to look at the animal he'd just killed.

But his ordeal, evidently, hadn't ended. "Now you get to learn how to butcher the beast," Ortalis said. "I wondered if you ever would."

"Butcher it?" Lanius gulped. "That . . . isn't what I had in mind." He turned toward Anser for support.

The arch-hallow let him down. "It's part of the job," Anser said. "You ought to know what to do and how to do it. You don't need to cut its throat; it's plainly dead. That was as clean a kill as the one Ortalis had a while ago."

"Huzzah," Lanius said in a hollow voice. Anser and Ortalis clucked in disapproval and dismay when they discovered he had no knife on his belt. They would have sounded the same way if he'd gotten up in the morning and forgotten to put on his breeches. Ortalis drew his own knife and handed it to the king hilt first. He moved slowly and carefully as he did it, mindful of Lanius' bodyguards. The edge of the blade, lovingly honed and polished, glittered in the sunlight.

"Here's what you do," Anser said. Following his instructions, Lanius did it. He kept his breakfast down, but had no idea how.

"If you want to start a little fire and roast the mountain oysters, they're mighty good eating," a guard said helpfully. "Same with a chunk of liver when it's all nice and fresh, though it won't keep more than a few hours."

Lanius knew no more about starting a fire than about butchery. Anser took care of that. The guard skewered the mountain oysters on a stick and roasted them over the flames. When they were done, he handed Lanius the stick. The king wanted to throw it away. But the guardsman waited expectantly, and both Anser and Ortalis seemed to think he'd done Lanius a favor. With a silent sigh, Lanius ate.

"Well?" the guard said. "You won't get anything like that back at the palace."

That was true. "Not bad," Lanius said. The men around him laughed, so he must have sounded surprised.

Ortalis stooped and cut a bloody slice from the stag's liver. He skewered it and toasted it over the fire. "Here," he said as he thrust the stick at Lanius. "Best eating in the world."

It wasn't—not to the king, anyhow. "Needs salt," Lanius declared. To his amazement, not only Anser but also two of the guards carried little vials of salt in their belt pouches. They all offered it to him. "Thank you," he said, and flavored the meat. It still wouldn't have been his first choice, but it was tasty. He nodded to the other men. "Anyone who wants a slice can help himself."

Several of them did. The speed with which the liver disappeared told him what a delicacy they thought it. One of them poked at the deer's heart with his knife and looked a question at Lanius. He nodded again. The guards sliced up the heart and roasted it, too.

"Mighty kind of you to share like this, Your Majesty," one of them said, his mouth full.

"My pleasure," Lanius answered. The kidneys also went. He said, "Venison in the palace tonight."

"Your turn next," Anser said to his half brother. "Think you can match the king's shot?"

"I don't know." Ortalis sent Lanius a sidelong glance. "But then, seeing the way he usually shoots, I don't know if he can match it, either."

Lanius was sure he couldn't. "Show some respect for your sovereign, there," he said haughtily. In a slightly different tone, the retort would have frozen Ortalis. As it was, Grus' legitimate son laughed out loud. So did Anser and the guards. Lanius found himself laughing, too. He still cared nothing for the hunt as a chance to stalk and kill animals. For the hunt as a chance to enjoy himself . . . that was another story.

Ortalis not only didn't make a clean kill when he got a shot at a deer, he missed as badly as Lanius usually did. The deer sprang away. "What happened there?" Anser asked.

"A black fly bit me in the back of the neck just as I loosed," Ortalis answered. "You try holding steady when somebody sticks a red-hot pin in you." He rubbed at the wounded area.

"Well, it's an excuse, anyhow," Anser drawled. Ortalis made a rude noise and an even ruder gesture. The Arch-Hallow of Avornis returned the gesture. It wasn't one Lanius would have looked for from a holy man, but Anser hardly even pretended to be any such thing.

And he shot a bow better than well enough. He hit a stag when his turn came to shoot first. The deer fled, but not too far; the trail of blood it left made it easy to track. It was down by the time the hunters caught up with it. Anser had a knife on *his* belt. He stooped beside the stag and cut its throat.

"Your turn for the, uh, oysters," Lanius said.

"Good." Anser beamed. "I like 'em. You won't see me turn green, the way you did before you tasted them."

"Oh." Lanius hadn't known it had shown.

Anser, meanwhile, was grubbing in the dirt by the dead stag. He proudly displayed some mushrooms. "I'll toast these with a piece of liver. Not with the mountain oysters—those are so good, I'll eat them by themselves." And, not much later, he did.

Lanius took better care to miss the next time he got a shot. He did, and the stag ran off into the woods. Anser and Ortalis teased him harder than they would have before he'd made a kill.

He teased back. That was the biggest part of the reason he came hunting at all. And yet, after he'd shot the stag, his conscience troubled him much less than he'd expected. One of these days, he might even try to hit something when he shot.

CHAPTER THIRTY

King Grus sat on the Diamond Throne, staring down at the ambassadors from Hrvace. The Chernagors looked up at him in
turn. "Well?" Grus said in a voice colder than the autumn wind
that howled outside the palace. "What have you got to say for yourselves? What have you got to say for your prince?"

The Chernagors eyed one another. Even the Avornan courtiers in
the throne room muttered back and forth. Grus knew why. He wasn't
following the formulas Kings of Avornis used with envoys from the
Chernagor city-states. He didn't care. Unlike Lanius, he cared nothing
for ceremony for its own sake. He wasn't sure the polite formulas applied to a city-state with which Avornis was practically at war, anyhow.

"Your Majesty, I am Bonyak, ambassador from Prince Tvorimir of
Hrvace," said one of the Chernagors—the one with the fanciest embroidery on his tunic. He did his best to stay close to the formula, continuing, "I bring you Tvorimir's greetings, as well as those of all the
other Chernagor princes."

"By the gods, I've already dealt with the other Chernagor princes,"
Grus growled. "I would have dealt with Tvorimir, too, if it hadn't decided to rain cats and dogs up there. Do you also bring me greetings
from the Banished One?"

"No, Your Majesty," Bonyak replied. "I bring you assurances from
Prince Tvorimir that he has nothing to do with the Banished One, and
that he has never had anything to do with him."

"Oh? And will Tvorimir tell me his ships weren't part of the fleet that raided my coast? How much nerve does he have?"

Bonyak's smile was an odd blend of wolf and sheep. "Prince Tvorimir does not deny that his ships raided your coast. But he told me to tell you—he told me to remind you—that a Chernagor does not need to go on his knees to the Banished One to smell the sweet scent of plunder."

"Sweet, is it?" Grus had to work not to laugh. When Bonyak solemnly nodded, the king had to work even harder. He said, "And you would know this from personal experience, would you?"

"Oh, yes," Prince Tvorimir's ambassador assured him. Hastily, the Chernagor added, "Though I have never plundered the coast of Avornis, of course."

"Of course." Grus' voice was dry, so very dry that it made Bonyak look more sheepish than ever. But Grus grudged him a nod. "It could be. And I suppose that what Prince Tvorimir says could be, too. Why has he sent you down here to the city of Avornis?"

"Why? To make amends for our raids, Your Majesty." Bonyak gestured to his henchmen. "We have gifts for the kingdom, and we also have gifts for you."

"Wait." Now Grus nodded to a courtier who'd been waiting down below the Diamond Throne. The man had remained discreetly out of sight behind a stout pillar, so Grus could have failed to call on him without embarrassing the Chernagors. But, since Bonyak seemed conciliatory . . . "First, Your Excellency, I have presents for you and your men."

The courtier doled out leather sacks from a tray. Bonyak hefted the one the Avornan gave him. He nodded, for it had the right weight. He also looked relieved—Grus was steering the ceremony back into the lines it should take.

"My thanks, Your Majesty," the ambassador said. "My very great thanks indeed. Now shall we give our gifts in return?"

"If you would be so kind," Grus answered.

Bonyak nudged the flunkies, who were busy feeling the weight of their own sacks. They set one heavy, metal-bound wooden chest after another in front of the Diamond Throne. "These are for Avornis, Your Majesty," Bonyak said. Courtiers leaned forward, waiting for him to open one of the boxes, their faces full of avid curiosity.

At Bonyak's nod, one of the men who followed him undid the hasp on the topmost chest and opened it. "Fifty thousand pieces of silver, from Prince Tvorimir to Avornis," Bonyak said. "His Highness will also make an agreement like the ones the princes of Hisardzik and Jobuka made with your kingdom not long ago."

"Will he?" Grus said. Bonyak nodded again. The Avornan courtiers murmured among themselves. The present wasn't very interesting—they'd seen plenty of silver themselves—but the news that came with it was good. Grus nodded back. "I am pleased to accept this silver for the kingdom," he declared in loud, formal tones. "Never let it be said that I did not seek peace between Avornis and the Chernagor city-states."

"Prince Tvorimir has this same thought," Bonyak said. *Of course he does—for the time being,* Grus thought. *I've made him afraid of me.* The Chernagor ambassador went on, "Prince Tvorimir also sends you a personal gift, a gift from him to you, not from Hrvace to Avornis."

As Bonyak had before, he gestured to the burly, bearded men who accompanied him. One of them came forward with an enormous earthenware jug, which he set beside the chests of silver pieces. Bonyak said, "This is a special kind of liquor, which we have in trade from an island far out in the Northern Sea. It is stronger than any ale or wine, strong enough so that it burns the gullet a little on the way down."

"Does it indeed?" Grus said, his voice as neutral as he could make it.

Bonyak understood what he wasn't saying. "I will gladly drink of this, Your Majesty. And let your wizards test it, if you think I have taken an antidote," the envoy said. "By the gods in the heavens, may my head answer if it is poison."

He did drink, and with every sign of enjoyment. "I will make a magical test anyhow," Grus replied, "and if it is poison, your head *will* answer. For now, you and your comrades are dismissed."

Bowing, the Chernagors departed from the throne room. Grus summoned Pterocles and explained what he wanted. The wizard looked intrigued. "Liquor that isn't wine or ale? How interesting! I suppose it isn't mead, either, for mead's no stronger than either of the others. Yes, I can test it against poisons." He dipped out a little of the liquid from the mug, then poured it over an amethyst. Neither the stone nor the liquor showed any change. Pterocles added a couple of sprigs of herbs to the dipper. "Cinquefoil and vervain," he explained to Grus. "They're sovereign against noxious things." He murmured a charm, waited, and then shrugged. "All seems as it should, Your

Majesty. There is one other test to make, of course." He fished the herbs out of the dipper.

"What's that?" the king asked.

"A very basic one." Pterocles grinned. He raised the dipper to his lips and drank what was in it. He coughed as he swallowed. "Whew! That's strong as a demon—your Chernagor wasn't joking." He paused, considering. "Can't complain about the way it warms me up inside, though. I wonder how the people the Chernagors got it from made it."

"Ask Bonyak—not that he'll tell you even if he knows," Grus said. "Well, if it hasn't turned you inside out and upside down, why don't you let me have a taste, too?"

"I don't know. Why don't I?" Pterocles filled the dipper again and handed it to him.

Grus took it. He sniffed. The stuff smelled more like wine than anything else, though less fruity. He sipped cautiously. When he swallowed, he could feel the heat sliding down to his stomach. It spread out from there. "Not bad," he said after the same sort of pause for thought as Pterocles had used. "A mug's worth would be plenty to get you drunk."

Pterocles eyed the jug. "I'd say a mug's worth would be enough to get you dead—but what a way to go."

"If you were going to make something like this, how would you do it?" Grus asked.

The wizard laughed. "If I knew the answer to that, I'd already be doing it. Some things you can concentrate by boiling. But when you boil wine, you make it weaker than it was before, not stronger. I don't know why. But it is so—I know that."

"Maybe you need to save what's boiling away instead of what's left in the pot, then," Grus said with a laugh of his own.

"Who knows? Maybe I do." Pterocles kept on smiling. "I don't know how I'd do that, though."

"I was only joking," Grus said. "Probably nothing to it."

Lanius' head felt as though some demented smith with a heavy hammer were using it for an anvil. Pterocles insisted the liquor Prince Tvorimir gave to King Grus wasn't poisoned. But Lanius had poisoned himself with it the night before. His father-in-law had warned him a little would get him drunk. Lanius hated to admit it, but his father-in-law had been right and more than right.

And because Grus had been so right, Lanius faced the moncats' room with a wince. The warmth and the smells—especially the smells—were not what he wanted with a tender head. But he had never trusted the servants to take care of the animals. If they didn't do the work, that meant he had to. Despite the wince, he opened the door, went in, and quickly closed it behind him.

It was as bad as he'd thought it would be. His stomach twisted. He almost had to leave very abruptly. After one gulp, though, he brought things under control again and got to work. Cleaning the moncats' sandbox was a job nasty enough as things were, and seemed even worse when he was nauseated himself. He was glad the animals used a sandbox like ordinary cats; if they'd done what they wanted wherever they wanted, they would have been much harder to keep.

After he took care of that, he went to the kitchens to get them some meat. The fat cook named Cucullatus grinned at him and said, "Haven't seen that funny animal of yours for a while now. Did you chain it up?"

"No, but I'm tempted to," he answered. "Pouncer makes me suspicious when it's being good—it's probably up to something." Cucullatus laughed a sour laugh.

Lanius went back to the moncats' room with the meat. The animals swarmed around his feet, rubbing and purring and acting for all the world as though they really were lovable creatures and not furry opportunists. He knew better. They were as heartless and self-centered as any of his courtiers.

Before dumping most of the food in their dishes, he doled out treats to one moncat or another. He was busy doing that when he noticed Pouncer wasn't begging there with the rest of the moncats. He looked around the room—and didn't see it.

"Oh, by the gods, where has the stupid creature gone now?" he exclaimed. But the problem wasn't that Pouncer was stupid—the problem was that the moncat was too smart for its own good.

The two places where Lanius knew the moncat went were the kitchens and the archives. Pouncer hadn't gone to the kitchens lately. Did that mean it was likely to make an appearance there now, or that it would keep on staying away? The king pondered. Trying to think like a Chernagor was hard enough. Trying to think like a moncat? He wanted to throw up his hands at the mere idea.

But he had to decide. Kitchens or archives? He took some scraps of meat and hurried off toward the room where he'd spent so much happy time. If Pouncer did show up there, he wanted to kick the moncat for disturbing his peace of mind.

He still didn't know how Pouncer got into the archives, any more than he knew how the miserable beast escaped from its room. Instead of contentedly pawing through parchments, he had to poke around in dark corners where Pouncer was likely to come forth. Wherever the moncat did emerge, it always looked enormously pleased with itself. Lanius couldn't decide whether that amused him or infuriated him.

"Pouncer?" he called. "Are you there, Pouncer, you stinking, mangy creature?" Pouncer was as fastidious as any other moncat, and didn't stink. The beast's luxuriant fur proved it wasn't mangy. Lanius slandered it anyhow. Why not? It was no more likely to pay attention to anything he said to or about it than any other moncat, either.

It did, however, pay attention to food. Lanius lay down on his back on the least dusty stretch of floor he could find. He thumped on his chest. If Pouncer was anywhere close by, that noise ought to attract the moncat. It would do its trick, climb up on his chest, and win its tasty reward. It would . . . if it was close enough to hear.

"Mrowr?" The meow, though muffled, made Lanius want to cheer. It also made him proud—in a peculiar way. Here he was, congratulating himself for . . . what? For beating the Menteshe? For finding something important about the Chernagors in the archives? No. What had he done to win those congratulations? He'd outthought a moncat.

Of course, what was the alternative? As far as he could see, it was *not* outthinking a moncat. And how proud would he have been of *that*?

"Mrowr?" Pouncer's meow definitely sounded strange, as though the moncat were behind something that deadened the noise . . . or as though it had something in its mouth.

And so it did, as Lanius discovered when the moncat came toward him. A rat's tail dangled from one side of Pouncer's jaws, the rat's snout from the other. As it had been trained to do, Pouncer climbed up onto the king's chest. The moncat dropped the rat right there.

"Thank you so much!" Lanius exclaimed. He didn't want to grab the rat even to throw it away. And Pouncer, naturally, was convinced it had done him not only a favor but an honor by presenting him with its kill. Pouncer was also convinced it deserved a treat from his hands—it had gotten up on his chest the way it was supposed to.

He gave the moncat a scrap of meat. Pouncer purred and ate it.

Then Pouncer picked up the rat again, walked farther up Lanius' chest with it, and, still purring all the while, almost dropped it on his face.

"If you think you're trying to train me to eat that, you'd better think again," the king told the moncat.

"Mrowr," Pouncer answered, in tones that could only mean, *Why aren't you picking this up now that I've given it to you?*

"Sorry," said Lanius, who was anything but. When he sat up, the rat rolled away from where Pouncer had put it and fell on the floor. With another meow, this one of dismay, the moncat dove after it. The king grabbed the animal. The moncat grabbed the rat. "Mutton's not good enough for you, eh?" Lanius demanded. This time, Pouncer didn't say anything. The moncat held the rat in both clawed hands and daintily nibbled at its tail.

Lanius didn't try to take away its prize. Pouncer was less likely to kick or scratch or bite as long as it had the rat. That remained true even after the chunk of meat the king had fed it.

And yet, even though Pouncer had caught the rat on its own, it hadn't declined to clamber up onto him for the little bit of mutton. He'd trained it to do that, and it had.

"Not much of a trick," Lanius told the moncat. Pouncer didn't even pretend to pay attention. The rat's tail was much more interesting, to say nothing of tasty. The king went on, "Of course, I'm not much of an animal trainer, either. I wonder what someone who really knows what he's doing could teach you."

"Mrowr," Pouncer said, as though doubting whether anybody—Lanius included—could teach it anything.

How much *could* a moncat learn? Suppose a skilled trainer really went to work with the beasts. What could he teach them? Would it be worth doing, or would Grus grumble that Lanius was wasting money? Grus often grumbled about money he wasn't spending himself. Still, it might be amusing.

Or, just possibly, it might be more than amusing. Lanius stopped short and stared at Pouncer. "Could you learn something like that?" he said. "Are you smart enough? Could you stay interested long enough?"

With the rat's tail, now gnawed down to the bone here and there, dangling from the corners of Pouncer's mouth, the moncat didn't look smart enough for anything. Even so, Lanius eyed it in a way he never had before.

He put it back in its room, knowing it probably wouldn't stay there long. Then he went looking for King Grus, which wasn't something he did very often. He found the other king closeted with General Hirundo. They were hashing out the campaign in the Chernagor country over mugs of wine. "Hello, Your Majesty," Grus said, courteous as usual. "Would you care to join me?"

"As a matter of fact, Your Majesty, I'd like to talk to you in private for a little while, if I could," Lanius answered.

Grus' gaze sharpened. Lanius didn't call him *Your Majesty* every day, or every month, either. The older man rose. "If you'll excuse us, Hirundo . . ." he said.

"Certainly, Your Majesty. I can tell when I'm not wanted." The general bowed and left. Had he spoken in a different tone of voice, he would have thought himself mortally insulted, and an uprising would have followed in short order. As things were, he just sounded amused.

After Hirundo closed the door behind him, Grus turned back to Lanius. "All right, Your Majesty. If you wanted my attention, you've got it. What can I do for you?"

Lanius shook his head. "No, it's what I can do for you." Honesty compelled him to add, "Or it may be what I can do for you, anyhow." He set out the idea he'd had a little while earlier.

The other king stared at him, then started to laugh. Lanius scowled. He hated to be laughed at. Grus held up a hand. "No, no, no. By the gods, Your Majesty, it's not you."

"What is it, then?" Lanius asked stiffly.

"It's the idea," Grus said. "It's not you."

It's my idea, Lanius thought, still offended. "What's wrong with it?"

"Why—" Grus started to be glib, but caught himself. He did some thinking, then admitted, "I don't know that anything's wrong with it. It's still funny, though."

When Lanius went to bed that night, the Banished One appeared to him in a dream. Before that cold, beautiful, inhuman gaze, the king felt less than a moncat himself. The Banished One always raised that feeling in him, but never more than tonight. Those eyes seemed to pierce the very center of his soul. "You are plotting against me," the Banished One said.

"We are enemies," Lanius said. "You have always plotted against Avornis."

"You deserve whatever happens to you," the Banished One replied. "You deserve worse than what has happened to you. You deserve it, and

I intend to give it to you. But if you plot and scheme against me, your days will be even shorter than they would otherwise, and even more full of pain and grief. Do you doubt me? You had better not doubt me, you puling little wretch of a man."

"I have never doubted you," Lanius told him. "You need not worry about that."

The Banished One laughed. His laughter flayed, even in a dream. "I, worry over what a sorry mortal does? Your life at best is no more than a sneeze. If you think you worry me, you exaggerate your importance in the grand scheme of things."

Even in a dream, Lanius' logical faculties still worked—after a fashion. "In that case," he asked, "why do you bother appearing to me?"

"You exaggerate your importance," the Banished One repeated. "A flea bite annoys a man without worrying him. But when the man crushes the flea, though he worries not a bit, the flea is but a smear. And so shall you be, and sooner than you think."

"Sometimes the flea hops away," Lanius said.

"That is because there is very little difference between a man and a flea," the Banished One retorted. "But between a man and me—you shall see what the difference is between a man and me. Oh, yes—you shall see." As he had once before, years earlier, he made as though to reach out for Lanius.

In the nick of time—in the very nick of time—the king fought himself awake. He sat bolt upright in his bed, his heart pounding. "Are you all right?" Sosia asked sleepily.

"Bad dream. Just a bad dream," Lanius answered, his voice shaking. A bad dream it was. *Just* a bad dream? Oh, no. He knew better than that.

In the nick of time—in the very nick of time—the king fought himself awake. Grus sat bolt upright in bed, his heart pounding. "Are you all right?" Estrilda asked sleepily.

"Bad dream. Just a bad dream," Grus answered, his voice shaking. A bad dream it was. *Just* a bad dream? Oh, no. He knew better than that. The Banished One had been on the very point of seizing him when he escaped back into the world of mundane reality. And if the Banished One's hands had touched him, as they'd been on the point of doing . . .

He didn't know what would have happened then. He didn't know, and he never, ever wanted to find out.

Little by little, his thudding heart and gasping breath slowed toward normal. The Banished One had come too close to scaring him to death without touching him. But Grus had also learned more from that horrid nighttime visitation than the Banished One might have intended.

Fortified by the thought the exiled god had never come to him more than once of a night, he lay down and tried to go back to sleep. Try as he would, though, he couldn't sleep anymore. He let out a small sigh of frustration. The dream the exiled god had sent remained burned on his memory, as those dreams always did. He wished he could forget them, the way he forgot dreams of the ordinary sort. But no. Whatever else the Banished One was, he was nothing of the ordinary sort.

Estrilda muttered to herself and went back to sleep. Grus wished again that he could do the same. Whatever he wished, more sleep eluded him. He waited until he was sure his wife was well under, then poked his feet into slippers, pulled a cloak on over his nightshirt, and left the royal bedchamber. The guardsmen in the corridor came to stiff attention. "As you were," Grus told them, and they relaxed.

Torches in sconces on the wall guttered and crackled. Quite a few had burned out. Why not? At this hour of the night, hardly anyone was stirring. No need for much light. Grus walked down the hall. He was and was not surprised when another guarded door opened. Out came Lanius, wearing the same sort of irregular outfit as Grus had on.

After telling his own guards to stand at ease, Lanius looked up and down the corridor. He seemed . . . surprised and not surprised to discover Grus also up and about. "Hello, Your Majesty," Grus said. "You, too?"

"Yes, me, too . . . Your Majesty," Lanius answered. Grus nodded to himself. Whenever Lanius deigned to use his title, the other king took things very seriously indeed. As though to prove the point, Lanius gestured courteously. "Shall we walk?"

"I think maybe we'd better," Grus said.

Behind them, guardsmen muttered among themselves. The soldiers no doubt wondered how both kings had happened to wake up at the same time. Grus wished he wondered, too. But he had no doubts whatsoever.

Neither did Lanius. The younger king said, "The Banished One knows we have something in mind."

"He certainly does," Grus agreed.

"Good," Lanius said. "Next spring—"

Grus held up a hand. "Maybe next spring. Maybe the spring after that, or the spring after *that*. As long as the Menteshe want to keep doing part of our job for us, I won't complain a bit."

"Well, no. Neither will I," Lanius said. "We ought to use however much time we have wisely. I wish we could lay our hands on some more ordinary thralls."

"So do I," Grus said. "But we'd have to cross the Stura to do it, and I don't want to do that while the Menteshe are still in the middle of their civil war."

"I suppose you're right." Lanius sounded regretful but not mutinous. "Pterocles should start teaching other wizards the spell he's worked out. When we do go south of the Stura, we'll need it."

"We'd better need it," Grus said, and Lanius nodded. Grus went on, "I *have* had work for Pterocles up in the Chernagor country, you know."

"Oh, yes." Lanius did not seem in a quarrelsome mood. After facing up to the Banished One, mere mortals seldom felt like fighting among themselves. The younger king continued, "But he's not up in the Chernagor country now. And he can teach more wizards here in the capital than anywhere else in Avornis."

"More of everything here in the capital than anywhere else in Avornis," Grus said.

Lanius nodded again. This time, he followed the nod with a yawn. "I think I can sleep again," he said.

"Do you?" Grus looked inside himself. After a moment, he gave Lanius a sad little shrug. "Well, Your Majesty, I'm jealous, because I don't. I'm afraid I'm up for the rest of the night."

"Sorry to hear that." Lanius yawned again. He turned around. "If you'll excuse me—"

"Good night," Grus told him. "Don't snore so loud, you wake up my daughter." Laughing, Lanius headed back to his bedchamber.

Grus wandered down the hallway. The soft leather soles of his slippers scuffed over the floor's mosaic tiles. How many times had he walked along here, not noticing the hunting scenes over which so many craftsmen had worked so hard and so long? Tonight, he noticed. Tonight, he had nothing to distract him.

Another man's footsteps came from around a corner. Grus realized he had not even an eating knife on his belt. Had the Banished One come to Otus as he'd come to the two kings? Was the thrall on the prowl? Would his guards let him go because they thought him cured?

Did he have murder on his mind? Did he have a mind, or was he but a reflection of the Banished One's will?

The other man came into sight. For a moment, in the dim torchlight, Grus thought it *was* Otus. Then he saw with his eyes, not his late-night fears. "Hello, Pterocles," he called. "What are you doing up at this ghastly hour?"

"Your Majesty?" Pterocles sounded as surprised and alarmed as Grus had felt. "I could ask you the same question, you know."

"Well, so you could," Grus said. "I couldn't sleep. I . . . had a bad dream."

He knew Pterocles had dreamed of the Banished One. That the Banished One took Pterocles seriously enough to send him a dream was one reason he was chief wizard in Avornis these days. As far as the king knew, though, the Banished One had visited Pterocles only once in the night.

Until tonight. The wizard jerked as though Grus had poked him with a pin. "Why, so did I, Your Majesty." Pterocles nodded jerkily. "So did I."

"One of—those dreams?" Grus asked.

Pterocles nodded again. "Oh, yes, Your Majesty. One of—those dreams." He mimicked Grus' tone very well. "I haven't had one of—those dreams for years now. I wouldn't have been sorry not to have this one, either."

"I believe you," Grus said. "Nobody wants a visit from the Banished One." There. He'd said it. The ceiling didn't fall in on him. The name didn't even raise any particular echoes—except in his own mind. Gathering himself, he went on, "It's an honor of sorts, though, if you look at it the right way."

"An honor?" Pterocles frowned. "I'm not sure I see . . . Oh. Wait. Maybe I do."

Now King Grus was the one who nodded. "That's what I meant, all right. Most people never have to worry about seeing the Banished One looking out of their dreams. He never needs to notice them. If he notices you, it's a sign you've done something, or you're going to do something, to worry him."

"He visited both of us tonight, then?" the wizard asked.

"That's right." Grus gave him another nod. "And he visited King Lanius, too."

"Did he?" Pterocles said. "Do you know why he visited the, uh, other king?"

Grus smiled a slightly sour smile. Even after he and Lanius had shared the throne for a good many years, people still found the arrangement awkward every now and again. He chuckled. He still found it awkward every now and again himself. But that was neither here nor there. He told Pterocles why he thought the Banished One had paid the nighttime call.

"Really?" Pterocles said when he was done. "You surprise me, Your Majesty. When was the last time the Banished One sent three people dreams at the same time?" Pterocles wondered.

"I don't know," Grus said. "I don't know if he's ever done anything like that before. Interesting, isn't it?"

"It could be." Pterocles cocked his head to one side as he considered. "Yes, it could be."

"That's what I thought," Grus said. "And so I don't mind wandering the hallways here in the wee small hours of the night quite as much as I would if I'd gotten out of bed with a headache or a sour stomach."

Pterocles grunted. Then he yawned. "It could be so, Your Majesty. But whether it's so or not, I'm still sleepy. If you don't mind, I think I'm going to try to go back to bed."

"King Lanius did the same thing. I envied him, and I envy you, too," Grus said. "Maybe I'll nap in the afternoon, but I can't sleep more tonight. I'm sure of that."

"I'm off, then." Pterocles sketched a salute to Grus, turned around, and went back the way he had come.

Grus wandered the hallways aimlessly—or maybe not so aimlessly, for he ended up at the entrance to the palace. The guards there needed a heartbeat or two to recognize him. When they did, they sprang to attention all the more rigid for being embarrassed. His wave told them they could relax. He walked out into the night.

It was cold on the palace steps, but not cold enough to drive him back inside. When he looked to the east, he saw a faint grayness that said sunrise was coming. He stood and waited, watching the gray spread up the dome of the sky, watching the stars fade and then disappear, watching pink and gold follow the gray. All around him, the bricks and stone and slate roof tiles of the city of Avornis took on solid shape and then, a little at a time, color as well.

Lanius had had an idea that worried the Banished One. The more Grus thought about that, the better he liked it.

A new day dawned.